THE GREAT BOOKS FOUNDATION

SCIENCE FICTION OMNIBUS

SELECTED AND EDITED BY

Daniel Born

Peter Ponzio

Lindsay Tigue

Donald H. Whitfield

CONTRIBUTORS

Molly Benningfield

Nancy Carr

Rachel Claff

Steven Craig

Patrick Hurley

Kaara Kallen

Lucas Kavanaugh

Abigail Mitchell

Kathy Swain

Casey Talbot

Mary Williams

THE GREAT BOOKS FOUNDATION

SCIENCE FICTION OMNIBUS

THE GREAT BOOKS FOUNDATION
A nonprofit educational organization

With generous support from Harrison Middleton University,
a Great Books distance-learning college

Published and distributed by

THE GREAT BOOKS FOUNDATION
A nonprofit educational organization

35 E. Wacker Drive, Suite 400
Chicago, IL 60601
www.greatbooks.org

With generous support from
Harrison Middleton University,
a Great Books distance-learning college
www.chumsci.edu

First printing
9 8 7 6 5 4 3 2 1

Library of Congress Cataloging-in-Publication Data
The Great Books Foundation science fiction omnibus / selected and edited by
Daniel Born.
    p. cm.
  ISBN 978-1-933147-43-7
  1. Science fiction, American. 2. Science fiction, English. I. Born, Daniel.
II. Title: Science fiction omnibus.
  PS648.S3G695 2010
  823'.0876208--dc22

                                                        2010032453

Cover illustration: Lisa Haney
Book design: THINK Book Works

About the
Great Books Foundation

The Great Books Foundation, established in 1947 by two University of Chicago educators, Robert Maynard Hutchins and Mortimer Adler, is an independent, nonprofit educational organization whose mission is to empower readers of all ages to become more reflective and responsible thinkers. The Foundation teaches the art of civil discourse through the practice of Shared Inquiry,™ a text-based Socratic model of learning, and it publishes enduring works across the disciplines.

*Spelling and punctuation have been modernized
and slightly altered for clarity.*

Contents

Introduction

Certain readers believe that an appetite for science fiction is good—just so long as it is eventually outgrown. In this view, science fiction is a developmental phase that kids, mostly boys but also the occasional (nerdy) girl, learn to leave behind if given a proper education. Like a young fan's attachment to Luke Skywalker's light saber, or a fixation on Princess Leia's cinnamon-bun hairdo, such enthusiasm in the course of time gets shelved for higher pursuits.

This is heresy, but like most heresies it contains an element of truth. Veteran science fiction editor David Hartwell describes devotees young and old carrying on the perennial debate about what constitutes the genre's "golden age." Was it 1939? 1953? 1970? he asks, rhetorically, and then informs us: "The real golden age of science fiction is twelve." He provides a collective portrait of hard-core science fiction fans intent on stoking reading passions that were first stirred in childhood or early puberty. Citing one survey done in the early 1980s, he notes that "the initial involvement in science fiction of almost every respondent happened between the ages of ten and fourteen."

Yes, the science fiction bug tends to bite mostly the young. But the genre itself grew up, along with its audience, during the course of the twentieth century. Hugo Gernsback launched his magazine *Amazing Stories* in 1926, and a little more than three decades later, in 1959, the first critical journal of science fiction studies, *Extrapolation*, was established. By 1960 British literary lion Kingsley Amis would give the upstart genre full-fledged attention in *New Maps of Hell: A Survey of Science Fiction.* "As is the way with addictions," Amis gently chided, "this one is mostly contracted in adolescence or not at all, like addiction to jazz." Still, he took science fiction seriously enough to define it as presenting "with verisimilitude the human effects of spectacular changes in our environment, changes either deliberately willed or involuntarily suffered." He treated at some length the genre's various progenitors, including Mary Shelley, Jules Verne, and H. G. Wells. Science fiction was developing complexity and variety. It had evolved beyond its primitive pulp roots in gee-whiz tales of technological wonder and invasion stories that featured slimy, bug-eyed aliens. Now readers of all kinds, not just the twelve-year-old fans, were paying attention.

Yet not everyone in the science fiction community was pleased by this newfound respect. Some feared assimilation by mainstream culture. Author and scholar James Gunn writes that at the organizational meeting in 1970 of the Science Fiction Research Association, *Locus* coeditor Dena Brown famously declared: "Let's take science fiction out of the classroom and put it back into the gutter where it belongs." Right or wrong, that sentiment was unable to reverse the flow of history. Only a few more decades and the place of science fiction in the literary canon was assured. Notably, in 2009 the Library of America made a monumental statement, publishing thirteen of Philip K. Dick's novels in a nearly three-thousand-page, three-volume slipcase edition. Such treatment, granted to the author of the alternate-history novel *The Man in the High Castle* (1962) and *Do Androids Dream of Electric Sheep?* (1968), the basis for the Hollywood film classic *Blade Runner* (1982), made it clear that science fiction had moved from the margins to the center, from lowbrow pulp notoriety to highbrow cachet.

During the 1960s, science fiction was also fragmenting into a rich array of subgenres. By the 1980s these variants included "hard" science fiction, fantasy, space opera (essentially Westerns in space), alternate history, and cyberpunk. Even more significant, by the 1960s and 1970s, a number of gifted women—among them Ursula K. Le Guin, James Tiptree Jr., and Octavia Butler—had begun to break into the old boys' network. Men had defined the genre under influential editors such as Gernsback in the 1920s and 1930s and John W. Campbell, editor of *Astounding,* in the 1940s and 1950s. Campbell especially had shaped the careers of major authors such as Robert Heinlein, Arthur C. Clarke, and A. E. Van Vogt. He had also put his stamp on a kind of story that, according to critic Algirdas Jonas Budrys, "wedded believable technological extrapolation with social speculation."

Le Guin did not depart from Campbell's formula so much as improve upon it. She wrote stories and novels that carried this kind of social speculation to dazzling and utterly convincing lengths. She also became a leading theorist of the science fiction genre. Two major novels in her Hainish cycle, *The Left Hand of Darkness* (1969) and *The Dispossessed: An Ambiguous Utopia* (1974), went far toward establishing just how good a science fiction narrative could be when it immersed a reader in the thick description of anthropological detail; both novels won Hugo and Nebula awards, and they also succeeded in bringing more traditional reading audiences to the science fiction enclave. Le Guin reacted to the tradition as she found it, refining it and raising the literary stakes for science fiction writers as a whole. Taking as her inspiration the famous quarrel between Virginia Woolf and Arnold Bennett about what constitutes good fiction, she writes in her essay "Science Fiction and Mrs. Brown" that "the writers' interest is no longer really in the gadget, or the size of the universe, or the laws of robotics, or the destiny of social classes, or anything describable in quantitative, or mechanical, or objective terms. They are not interested in what things do, but in how things are. Their subject is the subject, that which cannot be other than subject: ourselves. Human beings."

But before the writer gets too comfortable with Le Guin's apparently seamless continuity with the English literary tradition, she drives a sharp wedge between the work of her predecessors, the late Victorian writers, and the science fiction written by her and her peers: "The subject matter of the novel was the conscious, articulate portion of the minds of certain Europeans and North Americans, mostly white, mostly Christian, mostly middle class, mostly quite unaffected by science and, though affected by technology, totally uninterested in it. . . . They thought their nature was human nature; but we don't; we can't. They thought themselves a norm; we have no norm."

Slyly, Le Guin doesn't add "mostly male" to her list of cultural blinders. But she could have, and elsewhere in her nonfiction, including *Dancing at the Edge of the World* (1989), she has addressed the uncritical male perspective not just of science fiction but of literature generally. If in the late 1960s science fiction in popular culture was still typified by the unabashedly macho, swashbuckling action hero Captain James T. Kirk of the starship *Enterprise*—boldly going where no man has gone before, as the television series *Star Trek* announced in its familiar opening sequence—we can see, with the benefit of retrospective vision, that during the 1960s and 1970s women writers were doing some of the boldest intellectual exploration the genre had seen to date.

The ideas encountered in this collection range across the full landscape of standard science fiction concepts, including cross-cultural communication (and miscommunication) with other species, the question of human identity in an environment increasingly shaped by machines and technology, alternative reproduction and gender formations, and ways to survive in post-apocalyptic environments. And yet the best science fiction narratives, imaginative works of art that they are, rise above predictability and convention to provoke new ideas and new thinking.

In short, we believe this anthology of science fiction will stand the test of time. Like other literary works that merit the adjective "great," these short stories and novellas are likely to last because they generate a variety of responses. They don't exhaust interpretation; rather, they open up new areas of intellectual inquiry and provoke many interpretations. They elude easy summary or formulation. They are the kinds of fictional narratives that not only demand rereading, but reward it.

As a result, this collection is not a historical survey of the field of science fiction, and it does not even purport to represent all the marquee science fiction writers of the twentieth century. Nor should the reader turn to this anthology for an answer to the question, Who started science fiction? In arguing that Edgar Allan Poe should be credited as the original father of the genre, the late writer and critic Thomas M. Disch makes a good case that trying to round up the form's ancient antecedents is a rather pointless exercise. He writes in *The Dreams Our Stuff Is Made Of* (1998), "Many . . . have been claimed as SF's essential ancestor, beginning with the nameless author of the legend of Gilgamesh, the first Superman. As well make the claim for J, who wrote of Noah and the flood, of Nimrod and the Tower of Babel—themes that will appear in many SF updates. But if myths and legends are to be credited as SF, then half of world literature before the novel must be accounted ancestral to SF." Brian W. Aldiss favors Mary Shelley's *Frankenstein* (1818) as the point of origin, but he too dismisses the frequent attempts to claim classical antecedents for the genre. Claims have been made for writers as diverse as Lucian, Thomas More, Jonathan Swift, Dante, and Shakespeare. Aldiss writes: "Trawls for illustrious ancestors are understandable, in critics as in impoverished families. But they lead to error, the first error being the error of spurious continuity—of perceiving a connection or influence where none exists."

Finally, it should be clearly stated at the outset that this anthology makes a distinction between science fiction and fantasy. The science fiction we speak of is the kind in which an alternate or future world can be plausibly extrapolated on the basis of our own. Such a framework for fiction does not jettison the laws of science, but attempts to build on them. James Gunn's basic distinction between the two genres seems useful here. "Fantasy creates its own universe with its own laws; science fiction exists in our universe with its shared laws,"

Gunn writes in his introduction to *Speculations on Speculation: Theories of Science Fiction* (2005).

Our hope is that this anthology will unite communities of readers in dialogue with lasting texts in the science fiction tradition, both within and outside academe, perhaps both in the gutter and in the seminar room. To skeptics who would dismiss this collection as an indulgence of the inner twelve-year-old, we can reply with confidence that we have reached a point in literary history when science fiction can no longer be ignored. Reading the best science fiction might be the elixir for our best minds, or at least our most thoughtful selves.

The questions that follow each of the selections are intended to begin the process of comprehension and interpretation. And at the back of this book we include a description of Shared Inquiry for readers interested in engaging the text and each other in Socratic fashion. If there is delight to be taken in the solitude of the reading experience, teachers, students, and members of serious book groups also know that conversation about the text—in the context of the interpretive community—is essential to making meaning.

—*Daniel Born*

E. M. FORSTER (1879–1970), one of the twentieth century's preeminent English novelists and critics, was born in London and educated at Cambridge. After traveling widely as a young man, he spent most of his life in England, publishing a series of novels that include *Where Angels Fear to Tread* (1905), *The Longest Journey* (1907), and *Howards End* (1910). Fourteen years passed between *Howards End* and his most celebrated work, *A Passage to India* (1924), which explores the relationship between a young Englishman and his Indian friend and, indirectly, relations between England and its largest colonial possession. Although Forster's output of science fiction was small, "The Machine Stops" (1909) is his classic response to the buoyantly optimistic vision of technological progress typical of many writers in the years prior to World War I.

The Machine Stops

PART 1

The Airship

Imagine, if you can, a small room, hexagonal in shape, like the cell of a bee. It is lighted neither by window nor by lamp, yet it is filled with a soft radiance. There are no apertures for ventilation, yet the air is fresh. There are no musical instruments, and yet, at the moment that my meditation opens, this room is throbbing with melodious sounds. An armchair is in the centre, by its side a reading desk—that is all the furniture. And in the armchair there sits a swaddled lump of flesh—a woman, about five feet high, with a face as white as a fungus. It is to her that the little room belongs.

An electric bell rang.

The woman touched a switch and the music was silent.

"I suppose I must see who it is," she thought, and set her chair in motion. The chair, like the music, was worked by machinery and it rolled her to the other side of the room where the bell still rang importunately.

"Who is it?" she called. Her voice was irritable, for she had been interrupted often since the music began. She knew several thousand people; in certain directions human intercourse had advanced enormously.

But when she listened into the receiver, her white face wrinkled into smiles, and she said:

"Very well. Let us talk, I will isolate myself. I do not expect anything important will happen for the next five minutes—for I can give you fully five minutes, Kuno. Then I must deliver my lecture on 'Music during the Australian Period.'"

She touched the isolation knob, so that no one else could speak to her. Then she touched the lighting apparatus, and the little room was plunged into darkness.

"Be quick!" She called, her irritation returning. "Be quick, Kuno; here I am in the dark wasting my time."

But it was fully fifteen seconds before the round plate that she held in her hands began to glow. A faint blue light shot across it, darkening to purple, and presently she could see the image of her son, who lived on the other side of the earth, and he could see her.

"Kuno, how slow you are."

He smiled gravely.

"I really believe you enjoy dawdling."

"I have called you before, mother, but you were always busy or isolated. I have something particular to say."

"What is it, dearest boy? Be quick. Why could you not send it by pneumatic post?"

"Because I prefer saying such a thing. I want—"

"Well?"

"I want you to come and see me."

Vashti watched his face in the blue plate.

"But I can see you!" she exclaimed. "What more do you want?"

"I want to see you not through the Machine," said Kuno. "I want to speak to you not through the wearisome Machine."

"Oh, hush!" said his mother, vaguely shocked. "You mustn't say anything against the Machine."

"Why not?"

"One mustn't."

"You talk as if a god had made the Machine," cried the other. "I believe that you pray to it when you are unhappy. Men made it, do not forget that. Great men, but men. The Machine is much, but it is not everything. I see something like you in this plate, but I do not see you. I hear something like you through this telephone, but I do not hear you. That is why I want you to come. Come and stop with me. Pay me a visit, so that we can meet face to face, and talk about the hopes that are in my mind."

She replied that she could scarcely spare the time for a visit.

"The airship barely takes two days to fly between me and you."

"I dislike airships."

"Why?"

"I dislike seeing the horrible brown earth, and the sea, and the stars when it is dark. I get no ideas in an airship."

"I do not get them anywhere else."

"What kind of ideas can the air give you?"

He paused for an instant.

"Do you not know four big stars that form an oblong, and three stars close together in the middle of the oblong, and hanging from these stars, three other stars?"

"No, I do not. I dislike the stars. But did they give you an idea? How interesting; tell me."

"I had an idea that they were like a man."

"I do not understand."

"The four big stars are the man's shoulders and his knees. The three stars in the middle are like the belts that men wore once, and the three stars hanging are like a sword."

"A sword?"

"Men carried swords about with them, to kill animals and other men."

"It does not strike me as a very good idea, but it is certainly original. When did it come to you first?"

"In the airship—" He broke off, and she fancied that he looked sad. She could not be sure, for the Machine did not transmit *nuances* of expression. It only gave a general idea of people—an idea that was good enough for all practical purposes, Vashti thought. The imponderable bloom, declared by a discredited philosophy to be the actual essence of intercourse, was rightly ignored by the Machine, just as the imponderable bloom of the grape was ignored by the manufacturers of artificial fruit. Something "good enough" had long since been accepted by our race.

"The truth is," he continued, "that I want to see these stars again. They are curious stars. I want to see them not from the airship, but from the surface of the earth, as our ancestors did, thousands of years ago. I want to visit the surface of the earth."

She was shocked again.

"Mother, you must come, if only to explain to me what is the harm of visiting the surface of the earth."

"No harm," she replied, controlling herself. "But no advantage. The surface of the earth is only dust and mud, no life remains on it, and you would need a respirator, or the cold of the outer air would kill you. One dies immediately in the outer air."

"I know; of course I shall take all precautions."

"And besides—"

"Well?"

She considered, and chose her words with care. Her son had a queer temper, and she wished to dissuade him from the expedition.

"It is contrary to the spirit of the age," she asserted.

"Do you mean by that, contrary to the Machine?"

"In a sense, but—"

His image is the blue plate faded.

"Kuno!"

He had isolated himself.

For a moment Vashti felt lonely.

Then she generated the light, and the sight of her room, flooded with radiance and studded with electric buttons, revived her. There were buttons and switches everywhere—buttons to call for food, for music, for clothing. There was the hot-bath button, by pressure of which a basin of (imitation) marble rose out of the floor, filled to the brim with a warm deodorised liquid. There was the cold-bath button. There was the button that produced literature. And there were of course the buttons by which she communicated with her friends. The room, though it contained nothing, was in touch with all that she cared for in the world.

Vashti's next move was to turn off the isolation switch, and all the accumulations of the last three minutes burst upon her. The room was filled with the noise of bells, and speaking tubes. What was the new food like? Could she recommend it? Has she had any ideas lately? Might one tell her one's own ideas? Would she make an engagement to visit the public nurseries at an early date?—say this day month.

To most of these questions she replied with irritation—a growing quality in that accelerated age. She said that the new food was horrible. That she could not visit the public nurseries through press of engagements. That she had no ideas of her own but had just been told one—that four stars and three in the middle were like a man: she doubted there was much in it. Then she switched off her correspondents, for it was time to deliver her lecture on Australian music.

The clumsy system of public gatherings had been long since abandoned; neither Vashti nor her audience stirred from their rooms. Seated in her armchair she spoke, while they in their armchairs heard her, fairly well, and saw her, fairly well. She opened with a humorous account of music in the pre-Mongolian epoch, and went on to describe the great outburst of song that followed the Chinese conquest. Remote and primeval as were the methods of I-San-So and the Brisbane school, she yet felt (she said) that study of them might repay the musicians of today: they had freshness; they had, above all, ideas.

Her lecture, which lasted ten minutes, was well received, and at its conclusion she and many of her audience listened to a lecture on the sea; there were ideas to be got from the sea; the speaker had donned a respirator and visited it lately. Then she fed, talked to many friends, had a bath, talked again, and summoned her bed.

The bed was not to her liking. It was too large, and she had a feeling for a small bed. Complaint was useless, for beds were of the same dimension all over the world, and to have had an alternative size would have involved vast alterations in the Machine. Vashti isolated herself—it was necessary, for neither day nor night existed under the ground—and reviewed all that had happened since she had summoned the bed last. Ideas? Scarcely any. Events—was Kuno's invitation an event?

By her side, on the little reading desk, was a survival from the ages of litter—one book. This was the Book of the Machine. In it were instructions against every possible contingency. If she was hot or cold or dyspeptic or at a loss for a word, she went to the book, and it told her which button to press. The Central Committee published it. In accordance with a growing habit, it was richly bound.

Sitting up in the bed, she took it reverently in her hands. She glanced round the glowing room as if someone might be watching her. Then, half ashamed, half joyful, she murmured "O Machine! O Machine!" and raised the volume to her lips. Thrice she kissed it, thrice inclined her head, thrice she felt the delirium of acquiescence. Her ritual performed, she turned to page 1367, which gave the times of the departure of the airships from the island in the Southern Hemisphere, under whose soil she lived, to the island in the Northern Hemisphere, whereunder lived her son.

She thought, "I have not the time."

She made the room dark and slept; she awoke and made the room light; she ate and exchanged ideas with her friends, and listened to music and attended lectures; she make the room dark and slept. Above her, beneath her, and around her, the Machine hummed eternally; she did not notice the noise, for she had been born with it in her ears. The earth, carrying her, hummed as it sped through silence, turning her now to the invisible sun, now to the invisible stars. She awoke and made the room light.

"Kuno!"

"I will not talk to you." he answered, "until you come."

"Have you been on the surface of the earth since we spoke last?"

His image faded.

Again she consulted the book. She became very nervous and lay back in her chair palpitating. Think of her as without teeth or hair. Presently she directed the chair to the wall, and pressed an unfamiliar button. The wall swung apart slowly. Through the opening she saw a tunnel that curved slightly, so that its goal was not visible. Should she go to see her son, here was the beginning of the journey.

Of course she knew all about the communication system. There was nothing mysterious in it. She would summon a car and it would fly with her down the tunnel until it reached the lift that communicated with the airship station: the system had been in use for many, many years, long before the universal establishment of the Machine. And of course she had studied the civilisation that had immediately preceded her own—the civilisation that had mistaken the functions of the system, and had used it for bringing people to things, instead of for bringing things to people. Those funny old days, when men went for change of air instead of changing the air in their rooms! And yet—she was frightened of the tunnel: she had not seen it since her last child was born. It curved—but not quite as she remembered; it was brilliant—but not quite as brilliant as a lecturer had suggested. Vashti was seized with the terrors of direct experience. She shrank back into the room, and the wall closed up again. "Kuno," she said, "I cannot come to see you. I am not well."

Immediately an enormous apparatus fell onto her out of the ceiling, a thermometer was automatically inserted between her lips, a stethoscope was automatically laid upon her heart. She lay powerless. Cool pads soothed her forehead. Kuno had telegraphed to her doctor.

So the human passions still blundered up and down in the Machine. Vashti drank the medicine that the doctor projected into her mouth, and the machinery retired into the ceiling. The voice of Kuno was heard asking how she felt.

"Better." Then with irritation: "But why do you not come to me instead?"

"Because I cannot leave this place."

"Why?"

"Because, any moment, something tremendous many happen."

"Have you been on the surface of the earth yet?"

"Not yet."

"Then what is it?"

"I will not tell you through the Machine."

She resumed her life.

But she thought of Kuno as a baby, his birth, his removal to the public nurseries, her own visit to him there, his visits to her—visits which stopped when the Machine had assigned him a room on the other side of the earth. "Parents, duties of," said the book of the Machine, "cease at the moment of birth. P.422327483." True, but there was something special about Kuno—indeed there had been something special about all her children—and, after all, she must brave the journey if he desired it. And "something tremendous might happen." What did that mean? The nonsense of a youthful man, no doubt, but she must go. Again she pressed the unfamiliar button, again the wall swung back, and she saw the tunnel that curved out of sight. Clasping the Book, she rose, tottered onto the platform, and summoned the car. Her room closed behind her: the journey to the Northern Hemisphere had begun.

Of course it was perfectly easy. The car approached and in it she found armchairs exactly like her own. When she signaled, it stopped, and she tottered into the lift. One other passenger was in the lift, the first fellow creature she had seen face to face for months. Few travelled in these days, for, thanks to the advance of science, the earth was exactly alike all over. Rapid intercourse, from which the previous civilisation had hoped so much, had ended by defeating itself. What was the good of going to Peking when it was just like Shrewsbury? Why return to Shrewsbury when it would be just like Peking? Men seldom moved their bodies; all unrest was concentrated in the soul.

The airship service was a relic from the former age. It was kept up, because it was easier to keep it up than to stop it or to diminish it, but it now far exceeded the wants of the population. Vessel after vessel would rise from the vomitories of Rye or of Christchurch (I use the antique names), would sail into the crowded sky, and would draw up at the wharves of the south—empty. So nicely adjusted was the system, so independent of meteorology, that the sky, whether calm or cloudy, resembled a vast kaleidoscope whereon the same patterns periodically recurred. The ship on which Vashti sailed started now at sunset, now at dawn. But always, as it passed above Rheims, it would neighbour the ship that served between Helsingfors and the Brazils, and, every third time it surmounted the Alps, the fleet of Palermo would cross its track behind. Night and day, wind and storm, tide and earthquake, impeded man no longer. He had harnessed Leviathan. All the old literature, with its praise of Nature, and its fear of Nature, rang false as the prattle of a child.

Yet as Vashti saw the vast flank of the ship, stained with exposure to the outer air, her horror of direct experience returned. It was not quite like the airship in the cinematophote. For one thing it smelt—not strongly or unpleasantly, but it did smell, and with her eyes shut she should have known that a new thing was close to her. Then she had to walk to it from the lift, had to submit to glances from the other passengers. The man in front dropped his Book—no great matter, but it disquieted them all. In the rooms, if the Book was dropped, the floor raised it mechanically, but the gangway to the airship was not so prepared, and the sacred volume lay motionless. They stopped— the thing was unforeseen—and the man, instead of picking up his property, felt the muscles of his arm to see how they had failed him. Then someone actually said with direct utterance: "We shall be late"—and they trooped on board, Vashti treading on the pages as she did so.

Inside, her anxiety increased. The arrangements were old fashioned and rough. There was even a female attendant, to whom she would have to announce her wants during the voyage. Of course a revolving platform ran the length of the boat, but she was expected to walk from it to her cabin. Some cabins were better than others, and she did not get the best. She thought the attendant had been unfair, and spasms of rage shook her. The glass valves had closed, she could not go back. She saw, at the end of the vestibule, the lift in which she had ascended going quietly up and down, empty. Beneath those corridors of shining tiles were rooms, tier below tier, reaching far into the earth, and in each room there sat a human being, eating, or sleeping, or producing ideas. And buried deep in the hive was her own room. Vashti was afraid.

"O Machine! O Machine!" she murmured, and caressed her Book, and was comforted.

Then the sides of the vestibule seemed to melt together, as do the passages that we see in dreams, the lift vanished , the Book that had been dropped slid to the left and vanished, polished tiles rushed by like a stream of water, there was a slight jar, and the airship, issuing from its tunnel, soared above the waters of a tropical ocean.

It was night. For a moment she saw the coast of Sumatra edged by the phosphorescence of waves, and crowned by lighthouses, still sending forth their disregarded beams. These also vanished, and only the stars distracted her. They were not motionless, but swayed to and fro above her head, thronging out of one skylight into another, as if the universe and not the airship was careening. And, as often happens on clear nights, they seemed now to be in perspective, now on a plane; now piled tier beyond tier into the infinite heavens, now concealing infinity, a roof limiting forever the visions of men. In either case they seemed intolerable. "Are we to travel in the dark?" called the passengers angrily, and the attendant, who had been careless, generated the light, and pulled down the blinds of pliable metal. When the airships had been built, the desire to look direct at things still lingered in the world. Hence the extraordinary number of skylights and windows, and the proportionate discomfort to those who were civilised and refined. Even in Vashti's cabin one star peeped through a flaw in the blind, and after a few hours' uneasy slumber, she was disturbed by an unfamiliar glow, which was the dawn.

Quick as the ship had sped westward, the earth had rolled eastward quicker still, and had dragged back Vashti and her companions towards the sun. Science could prolong the night, but only for a little, and those high hopes of neutralising the earth's diurnal revolution had passed, together with hopes that were possibly higher. To "keep pace with the sun," or even to outstrip it, had been the aim of the civilisation preceding this. Racing aeroplanes had been built for the purpose, capable of enormous speed, and steered by the greatest intellects of the epoch. Round the globe they went, round and round, westward, westward, round and round, amidst humanity's applause. In vain. The globe went eastward quicker still, horrible accidents occurred, and the Committee of the Machine, at the time rising into prominence, declared the pursuit illegal, unmechanical, and punishable by Homelessness.

Of Homelessness more will be said later.

Doubtless the Committee was right. Yet the attempt to "defeat the sun" aroused the last common interest that our race experienced about the heavenly bodies, or indeed about anything. It was the last time that men were compacted by thinking of a power outside the world. The sun had conquered, yet it was the end of his spiritual dominion. Dawn, midday, twilight, the zodiacal path, touched neither men's lives not their hearts, and science retreated into the ground, to concentrate herself upon problems that she was certain of solving.

So when Vashti found her cabin invaded by a rosy finger of light, she was annoyed, and tried to adjust the blind. But the blind flew up altogether, and she saw through the skylight small pink clouds, swaying against a background of blue, and as the sun crept higher, its radiance entered direct, brimming down the wall, like a golden sea. It rose and fell with the airship's motion, just as waves rise and fall, but it advanced steadily, as a tide advances. Unless she was careful, it would strike her face. A spasm of horror shook her and she rang for the attendant. The attendant too was horrified, but she could do nothing; it was not her place to mend the blind. She could only suggest that the lady should change her cabin, which she accordingly prepared to do.

People were almost exactly alike all over the world, but the attendant of the airship, perhaps owing to her exceptional duties, had grown a little out of the common. She had often to address passengers with direct speech, and this had given her a certain roughness and originality of manner. When Vashti swerved away from the sunbeams with a cry, she behaved barbarically—she put out her hand to steady her.

"How dare you!" exclaimed the passenger. "You forget yourself!"

The woman was confused, and apologised for not having let her fall. People never touched one another. The custom had become obsolete, owing to the Machine.

"Where are we now?" asked Vashti haughtily.

"We are over Asia," said the attendant, anxious to be polite.

"Asia?"

"You must excuse my common way of speaking. I have got into the habit of calling places over which I pass by their unmechanical names."

"Oh, I remember Asia. The Mongols came from it."

"Beneath us, in the open air, stood a city that was once called Simla."

"Have you ever heard of the Mongols and of the Brisbane school?"

"No."

"Brisbane also stood in the open air."

"Those mountains to the right—let me show you them." She pushed back a metal blind. The main chain of the Himalayas was revealed. "They were once called the Roof of the World, those mountains."

"You must remember that, before the dawn of civilisation, they seemed to be an impenetrable wall that touched the stars. It was supposed that no one but the gods could exist above their summits. How we have advanced, thanks to the Machine!"

"How we have advanced, thanks to the Machine!" said Vashti.

"How we have advanced, thanks to the Machine!" echoed the passenger who had dropped his Book the night before, and who was standing in the passage.

"And that white stuff in the cracks?—what is it?"

"I have forgotten its name."

"Cover the window, please. These mountains give me no ideas."

The northern aspect of the Himalayas was in deep shadow: on the Indian slope the sun had just prevailed. The forests had been destroyed during the literature epoch for the purpose of making newspaper pulp, but the snows were awakening to their morning glory, and clouds still hung on the breasts of Kinchinjunga. In the plain were seen the ruins of cities, with diminished rivers creeping by their walls, and by the sides of these were sometimes the signs of vomitories, marking the cities of today. Over the whole prospect airships rushed, crossing and intercrossing with incredible *aplomb*, and rising nonchalantly when they desired to escape the perturbations of the lower atmosphere and to traverse the Roof of the World.

"We have indeed advanced, thanks to the Machine," repeated the attendant, and hid the Himalayas behind a metal blind.

The day dragged wearily forward. The passengers sat each in his cabin, avoiding one another with an almost physical repulsion and longing to be once more under the surface of the earth. There were eight or ten of them, mostly young males, sent out from the public nurseries to inhabit the rooms of those who had died in various parts of the earth. The man who had dropped his Book was on the homeward journey. He had been sent to Sumatra for the purpose of propagating the race. Vashti alone was travelling by her private will.

At midday she took a second glance at the earth. The airship was crossing another range of mountains, but she could see little, owing to clouds. Masses of black rock hovered below her, and merged indistinctly into grey. Their shapes were fantastic; one of them resembled a prostrate man.

"No ideas here," murmured Vashti, and hid the Caucasus behind a metal blind.

In the evening she looked again. They were crossing a golden sea, in which lay many small islands and one peninsula.

She repeated, "No ideas here," and hid Greece behind a metal blind.

PART 2

The Mending Apparatus

By a vestibule, by a lift, by a tubular railway, by a platform, by a sliding door—by reversing all the steps of her departure did Vashti arrive at her son's room, which exactly resembled her own. She might well declare that the visit was superfluous. The buttons, the knobs, the reading desk with the Book, the temperature, the atmosphere, the illumination—all were exactly the same. And if Kuno himself, flesh of her flesh, stood close beside her at last, what profit was there in that? She was too well bred to shake him by the hand.

Averting her eyes, she spoke as follows:

"Here I am. I have had the most terrible journey and greatly retarded the development of my soul. It is not worth it, Kuno, it is not worth it. My time is too precious. The sunlight almost touched me, and I have met with the rudest people. I can only stop a few minutes. Say what you want to say, and then I must return."

"I have been threatened with Homelessness," said Kuno.

She looked at him now.

"I have been threatened with Homelessness, and I could not tell you such a thing through the Machine."

Homelessness means death. The victim is exposed to the air, which kills him.

"I have been outside since I spoke to you last. The tremendous thing has happened, and they have discovered me."

"But why shouldn't you go outside?" she exclaimed, "It is perfectly legal, perfectly mechanical, to visit the surface of the earth. I have lately been to a lecture on the sea; there is no objection to that; one simply summons a respirator and gets an Egression permit. It is not the kind of thing that spiritually minded people do, and I begged you not to do it, but there is no legal objection to it."

"I did not get an Egression permit."

"Then how did you get out?"

"I found out a way of my own."

The phrase conveyed no meaning to her, and he had to repeat it.

"A way of your own?" she whispered. "But that would be wrong."

"Why?"

The question shocked her beyond measure.

"You are beginning to worship the Machine," he said coldly. "You think it irreligious of me to have found out a way of my own. It was just what the Committee thought, when they threatened me with Homelessness."

At this she grew angry. "I worship nothing!" she cried. "I am most advanced. I don't think you irreligious, for there is no such thing as religion left. All the fear and the superstition that existed once have been destroyed by the Machine. I only meant that to find out a way of your own was—Besides, there is no new way out."

"So it is always supposed."

"Except through the vomitories, for which one must have an Egression permit, it is impossible to get out. The Book says so."

"Well, the Book's wrong, for I have been out on my feet."

For Kuno was possessed of a certain physical strength.

By these days it was a demerit to be muscular. Each infant was examined at birth, and all who promised undue strength were destroyed. Humanitarians may protest, but it would have been no true kindness to let an athlete live; he would never have been happy in that state of life to which the Machine had called him; he would have yearned for trees to climb, rivers to bathe in, meadows and hills against which he might measure his body. Man must be adapted to his surroundings, must he not? In the dawn of the world our weakly must be exposed on Mount Taygetus, in its twilight our strong will suffer euthanasia, that the Machine may progress, that the Machine may progress, that the Machine may progress eternally.

"You know that we have lost the sense of space. We say 'space is annihilated,' but we have annihilated not space, but the sense thereof.

We have lost a part of ourselves. I determined to recover it, and I began by walking up and down the platform of the railway outside my room. Up and down, until I was tired, and so did recapture the meaning of 'Near' and 'Far.' 'Near' is a place to which I can get quickly *on my feet,* not a place to which the train or the airship will take me quickly. 'Far' is a place to which I cannot get quickly on my feet; the vomitory is 'far,' though I could be there in thirty-eight seconds by summoning the train. Man is the measure. That was my first lesson. Man's feet are the measure for distance, his hands are the measure for ownership, his body is the measure for all that is lovable and desirable and strong. Then I went further: it was then that I called to you for the first time, and you would not come.

"This city, as you know, is built deep beneath the surface of the earth, with only the vomitories protruding. Having paced the platform outside my own room, I took the lift to the next platform and paced that also, and so with each in turn, until I came to the topmost, above which begins the earth. All the platforms were exactly alike, and all that I gained by visiting them was to develop my sense of space and my muscles. I think I should have been content with this—it is not a little thing—but as I walked and brooded, it occurred to me that our cities had been built in the days when men still breathed the outer air, and that there had been ventilation shafts for the workmen. I could think of nothing but these ventilation shafts. Had they been destroyed by all the food tubes and medicine tubes and music tubes that the Machine has evolved lately? Or did traces of them remain? One thing was certain. If I came upon them anywhere, it would be in the railway tunnels of the topmost story. Everywhere else, all space was accounted for.

"I am telling my story quickly, but don't think that I was not a coward or that your answers never depressed me. It is not the proper thing, it is not mechanical, it is not decent to walk along a railway tunnel. I did not fear that I might tread upon a live rail and be killed. I feared something far more intangible—doing what was not contemplated by the Machine. Then I said to myself, 'Man is the measure,' and I went, and after many visits I found an opening.

"The tunnels, of course, were lighted. Everything is light, artificial light; darkness is the exception. So when I saw a black gap in the

THE MACHINE STOPS

tiles, I knew that it was an exception, and rejoiced. I put in my arm—I could put in no more at first—and waved it round and round in ecstasy. I loosened another tile, and put in my head, and shouted into the darkness: 'I am coming, I shall do it yet,' and my voice reverberated down endless passages. I seemed to hear the spirits of those dead workmen who had returned each evening to the starlight and to their wives, and all the generations who had lived in the open air called back to me, 'You will do it yet, you are coming,'"

He paused, and, absurd as he was, his last words moved her.

For Kuno had lately asked to be a father, and his request had been refused by the Committee. His was not a type that the Machine desired to hand on.

"Then a train passed. It brushed by me, but I thrust my head and arms into the hole. I had done enough for one day, so I crawled back to the platform, went down in the lift, and summoned my bed. Ah, what dreams! And again I called you, and again you refused."

She shook her head and said:

"Don't. Don't talk of these terrible things. You make me miserable. You are throwing civilisation away."

"But I had got back the sense of space and a man cannot rest then. I determined to get in at the hole and climb the shaft. And so I exercised my arms. Day after day I went through ridiculous movements, until my flesh ached, and I could hang by my hands and hold the pillow of my bed outstretched for many minutes. Then I summoned a respirator, and started.

"It was easy at first. The mortar had somehow rotted, and I soon pushed some more tiles in, and clambered after them into the darkness, and the spirits of the dead comforted me. I don't know what I mean by that. I just say what I felt. I felt, for the first time, that a protest had been lodged against corruption, and that even as the dead were comforting me, so I was comforting the unborn. I felt that humanity existed, and that it existed without clothes. How can I possibly explain this? It was naked, humanity seemed naked, and all these tubes and buttons and machineries neither came into the world with us, nor will they follow us out, nor do they matter supremely while we are here. Had I been strong, I would have torn off every garment I had, and gone out into the outer air unswaddled. But this is not for me, nor perhaps for my generation. I climbed with my respirator and my hygienic clothes and my dietetic tabloids! Better thus than not at all.

"There was a ladder, made of some primeval metal. The light from the railway fell upon its lowest rungs, and I saw that it led straight upwards out of the rubble at the bottom of the shaft. Perhaps our ancestors ran up and down it a dozen times daily, in their building. As I climbed, the rough edges cut through my gloves so that my hands bled. The light helped me for a little, and then came darkness and, worse still, silence which pierced my ears like a sword. The Machine hums! Did you know that? Its hum penetrates our blood, and may even guide our thoughts. Who knows! I was getting beyond its power. Then I thought: 'This silence means that I am doing wrong.' But I heard voices in the silence, and again they strengthened me." He laughed. "I had need of them. The next moment I cracked my head against something."

She sighed.

"I had reached one of those pneumatic stoppers that defend us from the outer air. You may have noticed them on the airship. Pitch dark, my feet on the rungs of an invisible ladder, my hands cut; I cannot explain how I lived through this part, but the voices still comforted me, and I felt for fastenings. The stopper, I suppose, was about eight feet across. I passed my hand over it as far as I could reach. It was perfectly smooth. I felt it almost to the centre. Not quite to the centre, for my arm was too short. Then the voice said: 'Jump. It is worth it. There may be a handle in the centre, and you may catch hold of it and so come to us your own way. And if there is no handle, so that you may fall and are dashed to pieces—it is still worth it: you will still come to us your own way.' So I jumped. There was a handle, and—"

He paused. Tears gathered in his mother's eyes. She knew that he was fated. If he did not die today he would die tomorrow. There was not room for such a person in the world. And with her pity disgust mingled. She was ashamed at having borne such a son, she who had always been so respectable and so full of ideas. Was he really the little boy to whom she had taught the use of his stops and buttons, and to whom she had given his first lessons in the Book? The very hair that disfigured his lip showed that he was reverting to some savage type. On atavism the Machine can have no mercy.

"There was a handle, and I did catch it. I hung tranced over the darkness and heard the hum of these workings as the last whisper in a dying dream. All the things I had cared about and all the people I had spoken to through tubes appeared infinitely little. Meanwhile the handle revolved. My weight had set something in motion and I span slowly, and then—

"I cannot describe it. I was lying with my face to the sunshine. Blood poured from my nose and ears and I heard a tremendous roaring. The stopper, with me clinging to it, had simply been blown out of the earth, and the air that we make down here was escaping through the vent into the air above. It burst up like a fountain. I crawled back to it—for the upper air hurts—and, as it were, I took great sips from the edge. My respirator had flown goodness knows where, my clothes were torn. I just lay with my lips close to the hole, and I sipped until the bleeding stopped. You can imagine nothing so curious. This hollow in the grass—I will speak of it in a minute—the sun shining into it, not brilliantly but through marbled clouds—the peace, the nonchalance, the sense of space, and, brushing my cheek, the roaring fountain of our artificial air! Soon I spied my respirator, bobbing up and down in the current high above my head, and higher still were many airships. But no one ever looks out of airships, and in any case they could not have picked me up. There I was, stranded. The sun shone a little way down the shaft, and revealed the topmost rung of the ladder, but it was hopeless trying to reach it. I should either have been tossed up again by the escape, or else have fallen in, and died. I could only lie on the grass, sipping and sipping, and from time to time glancing around me.

"I knew that I was in Wessex, for I had taken care to go to a lecture on the subject before starting. Wessex lies above the room in which we are talking now. It was once an important state. Its kings held all the southern coast from the Andredswald to Cornwall, while the Wansdyke protected them on the north, running over the high ground. The lecturer was only concerned with the rise of Wessex, so I do not know how long it remained an international power, nor would the knowledge have assisted me. To tell the truth I could do nothing but laugh, during this part. There was I, with a pneumatic stopper by my side and a respirator bobbing over my head, imprisoned, all three of us, in a grass-grown hollow that was edged with fern."

Then he grew grave again.

"Lucky for me that it was a hollow. For the air began to fall back into it and to fill it as water fills a bowl. I could crawl about. Presently I stood. I breathed a mixture, in which the air that hurts predominated whenever I tried to climb the sides. This was not so bad. I had not lost my tabloids and remained ridiculously cheerful, and as for the Machine, I forgot about it altogether. My one aim now was to get to the top, where the ferns were, and to view whatever objects lay beyond.

"I rushed the slope. The new air was still too bitter for me and I came rolling back, after a momentary vision of something grey. The sun grew very feeble, and I remembered that he was in Scorpio—I had been to a lecture on that too. If the sun is in Scorpio and you are in Wessex, it means that you must be as quick as you can, or it will get too dark. (This is the first bit of useful information I have ever got from a lecture, and I expect it will be the last.) It made me try frantically to breathe the new air, and to advance as far as I dared out of my pond. The hollow filled so slowly. At times I thought that the fountain played with less vigour. My respirator seemed to dance nearer the earth; the roar was decreasing."

He broke off.

"I don't think this is interesting you. The rest will interest you even less. There are no ideas in it, and I wish that I had not troubled you to come. We are too different, mother."

She told him to continue.

"It was evening before I climbed the bank. The sun had very nearly slipped out of the sky by this time, and I could not get a good view. You, who have just crossed the Roof of the World, will not want to hear an account of the little hills that I saw—low colourless hills. But to me they were living and the turf that covered them was a skin, under which their muscles rippled, and I felt that those hills had called with incalculable force to men in the past, and that men had loved them. Now they sleep—perhaps forever. They commune with humanity in dreams. Happy the man, happy the woman, who awakes the hills of Wessex. For though they sleep, they will never die."

His voice rose passionately.

"Cannot you see, cannot all your lecturers see, that it is we who are dying, and that down here the only thing that really lives in the

Machine? We created the Machine, to do our will, but we cannot make it do our will now. It has robbed us of the sense of space and of the sense of touch, it has blurred every human relation and narrowed down love to a carnal act, it has paralysed our bodies and our wills, and now it compels us to worship it. The Machine develops—but not on our lines. The Machine proceeds—but not to our goal. We only exist as the blood corpuscles that course through its arteries, and if it could work without us, it would let us die. Oh, I have no remedy—or, at least, only one—to tell men again and again that I have seen the hills of Wessex as Ælfrid saw them when he overthrew the Danes.

"So the sun set. I forgot to mention that a belt of mist lay between my hill and other hills, and that it was the colour of pearl."

He broke off for the second time.

"Go on," said his mother wearily.

He shook his head.

"Go on. Nothing that you say can distress me now. I am hardened."

"I had meant to tell you the rest, but I cannot; I know that I cannot: goodbye."

Vashti stood irresolute. All her nerves were tingling with his blasphemies. But she was also inquisitive.

"This is unfair," she complained. "You have called me across the world to hear your story, and hear it I will. Tell me—as briefly as possible, for this is a disastrous waste of time—tell me how you returned to civilisation."

"Oh—that!" he said, starting. "You would like to hear about civilisation. Certainly. Had I got to where my respirator fell down?"

"No—but I understand everything now. You put on your respirator, and managed to walk along the surface of the earth to a vomitory, and there your conduct was reported to the Central Committee."

"By no means."

He passed his hand over his forehead, as if dispelling some strong impression. Then, resuming his narrative, he warmed to it again.

"My respirator fell about sunset. I had mentioned that the fountain seemed feebler, had I not?"

"Yes."

"About sunset, it let the respirator fall. As I said, I had entirely forgotten about the Machine, and I paid no great attention at the time, being occupied with other things. I had my pool of air, into which I could dip when the outer keenness became intolerable, and which would possibly remain for days, provided that no wind sprang up to disperse it. Not until it was too late did I realize what the stoppage of the escape implied. You see—the gap in the tunnel had been mended; the Mending Apparatus; the Mending Apparatus, was after me.

"One other warning I had, but I neglected it. The sky at night was clearer than it had been in the day, and the moon, which was about half the sky behind the sun, shone into the dell at moments quite brightly. I was in my usual place—on the boundary between the two atmospheres—when I thought I saw something dark move across the bottom of the dell, and vanish into the shaft. In my folly, I ran down. I bent over and listened, and I thought I heard a faint scraping noise in the depths.

"At this—but it was too late—I took alarm. I determined to put on my respirator and to walk right out of the dell. But my respirator had gone. I knew exactly where it had fallen—between the stopper and the aperture—and I could even feel the mark that it had made in the turf. It had gone, and I realized that something evil was at work, and I had better escape to the other air, and, if I must die, die running towards the cloud that had been the colour of a pearl. I never started. Out of the shaft—it is too horrible. A worm, a long white worm, had crawled out of the shaft and was gliding over the moonlit grass.

"I screamed. I did everything that I should not have done, I stamped upon the creature instead of flying from it, and it at once curled round the ankle. Then we fought. The worm let me run all over the dell, but edged up my leg as I ran. 'Help!' I cried. (That part is too awful. It belongs to the part that you will never know.) 'Help!' I cried. (Why cannot we suffer in silence?) 'Help!' I cried. Then my feet were wound together, I fell, I was dragged away from the dear ferns and the living hills, and past the great metal stopper (I can tell you this part), and I thought it might save me again if I caught hold of the handle. It also was enwrapped, it also. Oh, the whole dell was full of the things. They were searching it in all directions, they were denuding it, and the white snouts of others peeped out of the hole, ready if needed. Everything that could be moved they brought—brushwood, bundles of fern, everything, and down we all went intertwined into hell. The last things that I saw, ere the stopper closed after us, were certain stars, and I felt that a man of my sort lived in the sky. For I did fight, I fought till the very end, and it was only my head hitting against the ladder that quieted me. I woke up in this room. The worms had vanished. I was surrounded by artificial air, artificial light, artificial peace, and my friends were calling to me down speaking tubes to know whether I had come across any new ideas lately."

Here his story ended. Discussion of it was impossible, and Vashti turned to go.

"It will end in Homelessness," she said quietly.

"I wish it would," retorted Kuno.

"The Machine has been most merciful."

"I prefer the mercy of God."

"By that superstitious phrase, do you mean that you could live in the outer air?"

"Yes."

"Have you ever seen, round the vomitories, the bones of those who were extruded after the Great Rebellion?"

"Yes."

"They were left where they perished for our edification. A few crawled away, but they perished, too—who can doubt it? And so with the Homeless of our own day. The surface of the earth supports life no longer."

"Indeed."

"Ferns and a little grass may survive, but all higher forms have perished. Has any airship detected them?"

"No."

"Has any lecturer dealt with them?"

"No."

"Then why this obstinacy?"

"Because I have seen them," he exploded.

"Seen *what?*"

"Because I have seen her in the twilight—because she came to my help when I called—because she, too, was entangled by the worms, and, luckier than I, was killed by one of them piercing her throat."

He was mad. Vashti departed, nor, in the troubles that followed, did she ever see his face again.

PART 3

The Homeless

During the years that followed Kuno's escapade, two important developments took place in the Machine. On the surface they were revolutionary, but in either case men's minds had been prepared beforehand, and they did but express tendencies that were latent already.

The first of these was the abolition of respirators.

Advanced thinkers, like Vashti, had always held it foolish to visit the surface of the earth. Airships might be necessary, but what was the good of going out for mere curiosity and crawling along for a mile or two in a terrestrial motor? The habit was vulgar and perhaps faintly improper: it was unproductive of ideas, and had no connection with the habits that really mattered. So respirators were abolished, and with them, of course, the terrestrial motors, and except for a few lecturers, who complained that they were debarred access to their subject matter, the development was accepted quietly. Those who still wanted to know what the earth was like had after all only to listen to some gramophone, or to look into some cinematophote. And even the lecturers acquiesced when they found that a lecture on the sea was nonetheless stimulating when compiled out of other lectures that had already been delivered on the same subject. "Beware of first-hand ideas!" exclaimed one of the most advanced of them. "First-hand ideas do not really exist. They are but the physical impressions produced by love and fear, and on this gross foundation who could erect a philosophy? Let your ideas be second-hand, and if possible tenth-hand, for then they will be far removed from that disturbing element—direct observation. Do not learn anything about this subject of mine—the French Revolution. Learn instead what I think that Enicharmon thought Urizen thought Gutch thought Ho-Yung thought Chi-Bo-Sing thought Lafcadio Hearn thought Carlyle thought Mirabeau said about the French Revolution. Through the medium of these eight great minds, the blood that was shed at Paris and the windows that were broken at Versailles will be clarified to an idea which you may employ most profitably in your daily lives. But be sure that the intermediates are many and varied, for in history one authority exists to counteract another. Urizen must counteract the scepticism of Ho-Yung and Enicharmon, I must myself counteract the impetuosity of Gutch. You who listen to me are in a better position to judge about the French Revolution than I am. Your descendants will be even in a better position than you, for they will learn what you think I think, and yet another intermediate will be added to the chain. And in time"—his voice rose—"there will come a generation that had got beyond facts, beyond impressions, a generation absolutely colourless, a generation

'seraphically free
From taint of personality,'

which will see the French Revolution not as it happened, nor as they would like it to have happened, but as it would have happened, had it taken place in the days of the Machine."

Tremendous applause greeted this lecture, which did but voice a feeling already latent in the minds of men—a feeling that terrestrial facts must be ignored, and that the abolition of respirators was a positive gain. It was even suggested that airships should be abolished too. This was not done, because airships had somehow worked themselves into the Machine's system. But year by year they were used less, and mentioned less by thoughtful men.

The second great development was the reestablishment of religion.

This, too, had been voiced in the celebrated lecture. No one could mistake the reverent tone in which the peroration had concluded, and it awakened a responsive echo in the heart of each. Those who had long worshipped silently, now began to talk. They described the strange feeling of peace that came over them when they handled the Book of the Machine, the pleasure that it was to repeat certain numerals out of it, however little meaning those numerals conveyed to the outward ear, the ecstasy of touching a button, however unimportant, or of ringing an electric bell, however superfluously.

"The Machine," they exclaimed, "feeds us and clothes us and houses us; through it we speak to one another, through it we see one another, in it we have our being. The Machine is the friend of ideas and the enemy of superstition: the Machine is omnipotent, eternal; blessed is the Machine." And before long this allocution was printed on the first page of the Book, and in subsequent editions the ritual swelled into a complicated system of praise and prayer. The word "religion" was sedulously avoided, and in theory the Machine was still the creation and the implement of man. But in practice all, save a few retrogrades, worshipped it as divine. Nor was it worshipped in unity. One believer would be chiefly impressed by the blue optic plates, through which he saw other believers; another by the Mending Apparatus, which sinful Kuno had compared to worms; another by the lifts, another by the Book. And each would pray to this or to that, and ask it to intercede for him with the Machine as a whole. Persecution—that also was present. It did not break out, for reasons that will be set forward shortly. But it was latent, and all who did not accept the minimum known as "undenominational Mechanism" lived in danger of Homelessness, which means death, as we know.

To attribute these two great developments to the Central Committee is to take a very narrow view of civilisation. The Central Committee announced the developments, it is true, but they were no more the cause of them than were the kings of the imperialistic period the cause of war. Rather did they yield to some invincible pressure, which came no one knew whither, and which, when gratified, was succeeded by some new pressure equally invincible. To such a state of affairs it is convenient to give the name of progress. No one confessed the Machine was out of hand. Year by year it was served with increased efficiency and decreased intelligence. The better a man knew his own duties upon it, the less he understood the duties of his neighbour, and in all the world there was not one who understood the monster as a whole. Those master brains had perished. They had left full directions, it is true, and their successors had each of them mastered a portion of those directions. But Humanity, in its desire for comfort, had overreached itself. It had exploited the riches of nature too far. Quietly and complacently, it was sinking into decadence, and progress had come to mean the progress of the Machine.

As for Vashti, her life went peacefully forward until the final disaster. She made her room dark and slept; she awoke and made the room light. She lectured and attended lectures. She exchanged ideas with her innumerable friends and believed she was growing more spiritual. At times a friend was granted Euthanasia, and left his or her room for the Homelessness that is beyond all human conception. Vashti did not much mind. After an unsuccessful lecture, she would sometimes ask for Euthanasia herself. But the death rate was not permitted to exceed the birth rate, and the Machine had hitherto refused it to her.

The troubles began quietly, long before she was conscious of them.

One day she was astonished at receiving a message from her son. They never communicated, having nothing in common, and she had only heard indirectly that he was still alive, and had been transferred from the Northern Hemisphere, where he had behaved so mischievously, to the Southern—indeed, to a room not far from her own.

"Does he want me to visit him?" she thought. "Never again, never. And I have not the time."

No, it was madness of another kind.

He refused to visualize his face upon the blue plate, and speaking out of the darkness with solemnity said:

"The Machine stops."

"What do you say?"

"The Machine is stopping, I know it, I know the signs."

She burst into a peal of laughter. He heard her and was angry, and they spoke no more.

"Can you imagine anything more absurd?" she cried to a friend. "A man who was my son believes that the Machine is stopping. It would be impious if it was not mad."

"The Machine is stopping?" her friend replied. "What does that mean? The phrase conveys nothing to me."

"Nor to me."

"He does not refer, I suppose, to the trouble there has been lately with the music?"

"Oh no, of course not. Let us talk about music."

"Have you complained to the authorities?"

"Yes, and they say it wants mending, and referred me to the Committee of the Mending Apparatus. I complained of those curious gasping sighs that disfigure the symphonies of the Brisbane school. They sound like someone in pain. The Committee of the Mending Apparatus say that it shall be remedied shortly."

Obscurely worried, she resumed her life. For one thing, the defect in the music irritated her. For another thing, she could not forget Kuno's speech. If he had known that the music was out of repair—he could not know it, for he detested music—if he had known that it was

E. M. FORSTER

26

wrong, "the Machine stops" was exactly the venomous sort of remark he would have made. Of course he had made it as a venture, but the coincidence annoyed her, and she spoke with some petulance to the Committee of the Mending Apparatus.

They replied, as before, that the defect would be set right shortly.

"Shortly! At once!" she retorted. "Why should I be worried by imperfect music? Things are always put right at once. If you do not mend it at once, I shall complain to the Central Committee."

"No personal complaints are received by the Central Committee," the Committee of the Mending Apparatus replied.

"Through whom am I to make my complaint, then?"

"Through us."

"I complain then."

"Your complaint shall be forwarded in its turn."

"Have others complained?"

This question was unmechanical, and the Committee of the Mending Apparatus refused to answer it.

"It is too bad!" she exclaimed to another of her friends. "There never was such an unfortunate woman as myself. I can never be sure of my music now. It gets worse and worse each time I summon it."

"I too have my troubles," the friend replied. "Sometimes my ideas are interrupted by a slight jarring noise."

"What is it?"

"I do not know whether it is inside my head, or inside the wall."

"Complain, in either case."

"I have complained, and my complaint will be forwarded in its turn to the Central Committee."

Time passed, and they resented the defects no longer. The defects had not been remedied, but the human tissues in that latter day had become so subservient, that they readily adapted themselves to every caprice of the Machine. The sigh at the crises of the Brisbane symphony no longer irritated Vashti; she accepted it as part of the melody. The jarring noise, whether in the head or in the wall, was no longer resented by her friend. And so with the mouldy artificial fruit, so with the bathwater that began to stink, so with the defective rhymes that the poetry machine had taken to emit. All were bitterly complained of at first, and then acquiesced in and forgotten. Things went from bad to worse unchallenged.

It was otherwise with the failure of the sleeping apparatus. That was a more serious stoppage. There came a day when over the whole world—in Sumatra, in Wessex, in the innumerable cities of Courland and Brazil—the beds, when summoned by their tired owners, failed to appear. It may seem a ludicrous matter, but from it we may date the collapse of humanity. The Committee responsible for the failure was assailed by complainants, whom it referred, as usual, to the Committee of the Mending Apparatus, who in its turn assured them that their complaints would be forwarded to the Central Committee. But the discontent grew, for mankind was not yet sufficiently adaptable to do without sleeping.

"Someone is meddling with the Machine—" they began.

"Someone is trying to make himself king, to reintroduce the personal element."

"Punish that man with Homelessness."

"To the rescue! Avenge the Machine! Avenge the Machine!"

"War! Kill the man!"

But the Committee of the Mending Apparatus now came forward, and allayed the panic with well-chosen words. It confessed that the Mending Apparatus was itself in need of repair.

The effect of this frank confession was admirable.

"Of course," said a famous lecturer—he of the French Revolution, who gilded each new decay with splendour—"of course we shall not press our complaints now. The Mending Apparatus has treated us so well in the past that we all sympathize with it, and will wait patiently for its recovery. In its own good time it will resume its duties. Meanwhile let us do without our beds, our tabloids, our other little wants. Such, I feel sure, would be the wish of the Machine."

Thousands of miles away his audience applauded. The Machine still linked them. Under the seas, beneath the roots of the mountains, ran the wires through which they saw and heard, the enormous eyes and ears that were their heritage, and the hum of many workings clothed their thoughts in one garment of subserviency. Only the old and the sick remained ungrateful, for it was rumoured that Euthanasia, too, was out of order, and that pain had reappeared among men.

It became difficult to read. A blight entered the atmosphere and dulled its luminosity. At times Vashti could scarcely see across her room. The air, too, was foul. Loud were the complaints, impotent the remedies, heroic the tone of the lecturer as he cried: "Courage! courage! What matter so long as the Machine goes on? To it the darkness and the light are one." And though things improved again after a time, the old brilliancy was never recaptured, and humanity never recovered from its entrance into twilight. There was an hysterical talk of "measures," of "provisional dictatorship," and the inhabitants of Sumatra were asked to familiarize themselves with the workings of the central power station, the said power station being situated in France. But for the most part panic reigned, and men spent their strength praying to their Books, tangible proofs of the Machine's omnipotence. There were gradations of terror—at times came rumours of hope—the Mending Apparatus was almost mended—the enemies of the Machine had been got under—new "nerve centres" were evolving which would do the work even more magnificently than before. But there came a day when, without the slightest warning, without any previous hint of feebleness, the entire communication system broke down, all over the world, and the world, as they understood it, ended.

Vashti was lecturing at the time and her earlier remarks had been punctuated with applause. As she proceeded the audience became silent, and at the conclusion there was no sound. Somewhat displeased, she called to a friend who was a specialist in sympathy. No sound: doubtless the friend was sleeping. And so with the next friend whom she tried to summon, and so with the next, until she remembered Kuno's cryptic remark, "The Machine stops".

The phrase still conveyed nothing. If Eternity was stopping it would of course be set going shortly.

For example, there was still a little light and air—the atmosphere had improved a few hours previously. There was still the Book, and while there was the Book there was security.

Then she broke down, for with the cessation of activity came an unexpected terror—silence.

She had never known silence, and the coming of it nearly killed her—it did kill many thousands of people outright. Ever since her birth she had been surrounded by the steady hum. It was to the ear what artificial air was to the lungs, and agonizing pains shot across her head. And scarcely knowing what she did, she stumbled forward and pressed the unfamiliar button, the one that opened the door of her cell.

Now the door of the cell worked on a simple hinge of its own. It was not connected with the central power station, dying far away in France. It opened, rousing immoderate hopes in Vashti, for she thought that the Machine had been mended. It opened, and she saw the dim tunnel that curved far away towards freedom. One look, and then she shrank back. For the tunnel was full of people—she was almost the last in that city to have taken alarm.

People at any time repelled her, and these were nightmares from her worst dreams. People were crawling about, people were screaming, whimpering, gasping for breath, touching each other, vanishing in the dark, and ever and anon being pushed off the platform onto the live rail. Some were fighting round the electric bells, trying to summon trains which could not be summoned. Others were yelling for Euthanasia or for respirators, or blaspheming the Machine. Others stood at the doors of their cells fearing, like herself, either to stop in them or to leave them. And behind all the uproar was silence—the silence which is the voice of the earth and of the generations who have gone.

No—it was worse than solitude. She closed the door again and sat down to wait for the end. The disintegration went on, accompanied by horrible cracks and rumbling. The valves that restrained the Medical Apparatus must have weakened, for it ruptured and hung hideously from the ceiling. The floor heaved and fell and flung her from the chair. A tube oozed towards her serpent fashion. And at last the final horror approached—light began to ebb, and she knew that civilisation's long day was closing.

She whirled around, praying to be saved from this, at any rate, kissing the Book, pressing button after button. The uproar outside was increasing, and even penetrated the wall. Slowly the brilliancy of her cell was dimmed, the reflections faded from her metal switches. Now she could not see the reading stand, now not the Book, though she held it in her hand. Light followed the flight of sound, air was following light, and the original void returned to the cavern from which it has so long been excluded. Vashti continued to whirl, like the devotees of an earlier religion, screaming, praying, striking at the buttons with bleeding hands.

It was thus that she opened her prison and escaped—escaped in the spirit: at least so it seems to me, ere my meditation closes. That she escapes in the body—I cannot perceive that. She struck, by chance, the switch that released the door, and the rush of foul air on her skin, the loud throbbing whispers in her ears, told her that she was facing the tunnel again, and that tremendous platform on which she had seen men fighting. They were not fighting now. Only the whispers remained, and the little whimpering groans. They were dying by hundreds out in the dark.

She burst into tears.

Tears answered her.

They wept for humanity, those two, not for themselves. They could not bear that this should be the end. Ere silence was completed their hearts were opened, and they knew what had been important on the earth. Man, the flower of all flesh, the noblest of all creatures visible, man who had once made god in his image, and had mirrored his strength on the constellations, beautiful naked man was dying, strangled in the garments that he had woven. Century after century had he toiled, and here was his reward. Truly the garment had seemed heavenly at first, shot with the colours of culture, sewn with the threads of self-denial. And heavenly it had been so long as it was a garment and no more, so long as man could shed it at will and live by the essence that is his soul, and the essence, equally divine, that is his body. The sin against the body—it was for that they wept in chief; the centuries of wrong against the muscles and the nerves, and those five portals by which we can alone apprehend—glozing it over with talk of evolution, until the body was white pap, the home of ideas as colour-less, last sloshy stirrings of a spirit that had grasped the stars.

"Where are you?" she sobbed.

His voice in the darkness said, "Here."

Is there any hope, Kuno?"

"None for us."

"Where are you?"

She crawled over the bodies of the dead. His blood spurted over her hands.

"Quicker," he gasped, "I am dying—but we touch, we talk, not through the Machine."

He kissed her.

"We have come back to our own. We die, but we have recaptured life, as it was in Wessex, when Ælfrid overthrew the Danes. We know what they know outside, they who dwelt in the cloud that is the colour of a pearl."

"But Kuno, is it true? Are there still men on the surface of the earth? Is this—tunnel, this poisoned darkness—really not the end?"

He replied:

"I have seen them, spoken to them, loved them. They are hiding in the mist and the ferns until our civilisation stops. Today they are the Homeless—tomorrow—"

"Oh, tomorrow—some fool will start the Machine again, tomorrow."

"Never," said Kuno, "never. Humanity has learnt its lesson."

As he spoke, the whole city was broken like a honeycomb. An airship had sailed in through the vomitory into a ruined wharf. It crashed downwards, exploding as it went, rending gallery after gallery with its wings of steel. For a moment they saw the nations of the dead, and, before they joined them, scraps of the untainted sky.

---

1. Why do most people believe that because of the Machine "human intercourse had advanced enormously"?

2. Why do the sights Vashti sees from the airship give her "no ideas"? What kind of ideas are valued in this society?

3. Why does Vashti go to visit Kuno despite her fear of "direct experience"?

4. Why would Kuno rather die than continue to live with the Machine?

RAY BRADBURY (1920–), author of more than five hundred short stories, novels, children's books, plays, and poems, was born in Waukegan, Illinois. In 1950 he published *The Martian Chronicles*, a story cycle about Earth's colonization of Mars, now widely considered a science fiction classic. It was followed by the story collections *The Illustrated Man* (1951), in which "The Veldt" first appeared, *The Golden Apples of the Sun* (1953), and *I Sing the Body Electric!* (1969). Bradbury is considered a gifted and poetic stylist, and his science fiction is marked by insightful explorations of the impact of technological advances on human life. He has turned several of his best-known novels, including *Fahrenheit 451* (1953) and *Dandelion Wine* (1957), into plays; he is also the author of a number of television scripts for *Alfred Hitchcock Presents* and *The Twilight Zone*. In 2007 Bradbury received a Pulitzer Prize special citation for his prolific and influential writing career.

The Veldt

"George, I wish you'd look at the nursery."

"What's wrong with it?"

"I don't know."

"Well, then."

"I just want you to look at it, is all, or call a psychologist in to look at it."

"What would a psychologist want with a nursery?"

"You know very well what he'd want." His wife paused in the middle of the kitchen and watched the stove busy humming to itself, making supper for four.

"It's just that the nursery is different now than it was."

"All right, let's have a look."

They walked down the hall of their soundproofed Happylife Home, which had cost them thirty thousand dollars installed, this house which clothed and fed and rocked them to sleep and played and sang and was good to them. Their approach sensitized a switch somewhere and the nursery light flicked on when they came within ten feet of it. Similarly, behind them, in the halls, lights went on and off as they left them behind, with a soft automaticity.

"Well," said George Hadley.

They stood on the thatched floor of the nursery. It was forty feet across by forty feet long and thirty feet high; it had cost half again as much as the rest of the house. "But nothing's too good for our children," George had said.

The nursery was silent. It was empty as a jungle glade at hot high noon. The walls were blank and two-dimensional. Now, as George and Lydia Hadley stood in the center of the room, the walls began to purr and recede into crystalline distance, it seemed, and presently an African veldt appeared, in three dimensions, on all sides, in color, reproduced to the final pebble and bit of straw. The ceiling above them became a deep sky with a hot yellow sun.

George Hadley felt the perspiration start on his brow.

"Let's get out of this sun," he said. "This is a little too real. But I don't see anything wrong."

"Wait a moment, you'll see," said his wife.

Now the hidden odorophonics were beginning to blow a wind of odor at the two people in the middle of the baked veldtland. The hot straw smell of lion grass, the cool green smell of the hidden water hole, the great rusty smell of animals, the smell of dust like a red paprika in the hot air. And now the sounds: the thump of distant antelope feet on grassy sod, the papery rustling of vultures. A shadow passed through the sky. The shadow flickered on George Hadley's upturned, sweating face.

"Filthy creatures," he heard his wife say.

"The vultures."

"You see, there are the lions, far over, that way. Now they're on their way to the water hole. They've just been eating," said Lydia. "I don't know what."

"Some animal." George Hadley put his hand up to shield off the burning light from his squinted eyes. "A zebra or a baby giraffe, maybe."

"Are you sure?" His wife sounded peculiarly tense.

"No, it's a little late to be *sure*," he said, amused. "Nothing over there I can see but cleaned bone, and the vultures dropping for what's left."

"Did you hear that scream?" she asked.

"No."

"About a minute ago?"

"Sorry, no."

The lions were coming. And again George Hadley was filled with admiration for the mechanical genius who had conceived this room. A miracle of efficiency selling for an absurdly low price. Every home should have one. Oh, occasionally they frightened you with their clinical accuracy, they startled you, gave you a twinge, but most of the time what fun for everyone, not only your own son and daughter, but for yourself when you felt like a quick jaunt to a foreign land, a quick change of scenery. Well, here it was!

And here were the lions now, fifteen feet away, so real, so feverishly and startlingly real that you could feel the prickling fur on your hand, and your mouth was stuffed with the dusty upholstery smell of their heated pelts, and the yellow of them was in your eyes like the yellow of an exquisite French tapestry, the yellows of lions and summer grass, and the sound of the matted lion lungs exhaling on the silent noontide, and the smell of meat from the panting, dripping mouths.

The lions stood looking at George and Lydia Hadley with terrible green-yellow eyes.

"Watch out!" screamed Lydia.

The lions came running at them.

Lydia bolted and ran. Instinctively, George sprang after her. Outside, in the hall, with the door slammed, he was laughing and she was crying, and they both stood appalled at the other's reaction.

"George!"

"Lydia! Oh, my dear poor sweet Lydia!"

"They almost got us!"

"Walls, Lydia, remember; crystal walls, that's all they are. Oh, they look real, I must admit—Africa in your parlor—but it's all dimensional, superreactionary, supersensitive color film and mental tape film behind glass screens. It's all odorophonics and sonics, Lydia. Here's my handkerchief."

"I'm afraid." She came to him and put her body against him and cried steadily. "Did you see? Did you *feel*? It's too real."

"Now, Lydia . . ."

"You've got to tell Wendy and Peter not to read any more on Africa."

"Of course—of course." He patted her.

"Promise?"

"Sure."

"And lock the nursery for a few days until I get my nerves settled."

"You know how difficult Peter is about that. When I punished him a month ago by locking the nursery for even a few hours—the tantrum he threw! And Wendy too. They *live* for the nursery."

"It's got to be locked, that's all there is to it."

"All right." Reluctantly he locked the huge door. "You've been working too hard. You need a rest."

"I don't know—I don't know," she said, blowing her nose, sitting down in a chair that immediately began to rock and comfort her. "Maybe I don't have enough to do. Maybe I have time to think too much. Why don't we shut the whole house off for a few days and take a vacation?"

"You mean you want to fry my eggs for me?"

"Yes." She nodded.

"And darn my socks?"

"Yes." A frantic, watery-eyed nodding.

"And sweep the house?"

"Yes, yes—oh, yes!"

"But I thought that's why we bought this house, so we wouldn't have to do anything?"

"That's just it. I feel like I don't belong here. The house is wife and mother now, and nursemaid. Can I compete with an African veldt? Can I give a bath and scrub the children as efficiently or quickly as the automatic scrub bath can? I cannot. And it isn't just me. It's you. You've been awfully nervous lately."

"I suppose I have been smoking too much."

"You look as if you don't know what to do with yourself in this house, either. You smoke a little more every morning and drink a little more every afternoon and need a little more sedative every night. You're beginning to feel unnecessary too."

"Am I?" He paused and tried to feel into himself to see what was really there.

"Oh, George!" She looked beyond him, at the nursery door. "Those lions can't get out of there, can they?"

He looked at the door and saw it tremble as if something had jumped against it from the other side.

"Of course not," he said.

At dinner they ate alone, for Wendy and Peter were at a special plastic carnival across town and had televised home to say they'd be late, to go ahead eating. So George Hadley, bemused, sat watching the dining room table produce warm dishes of food from its mechanical interior.

"We forgot the ketchup," he said.

"Sorry," said a small voice within the table, and ketchup appeared.

As for the nursery, thought George Hadley, it won't hurt for the children to be locked out of it awhile. Too much of anything isn't good for anyone. And it was clearly indicated that the children had been spending a little too much time on Africa. That *sun*. He could feel it on his neck, still, like a hot paw. And the *lions*. And the smell of blood. Remarkable how the nursery caught the telepathic emanations of the children's minds and created life to fill their every desire. The children thought lions, and there were lions. The children thought zebras, and there were zebras. Sun—sun. Giraffes—giraffes. Death and death.

That *last*. He chewed tastelessly on the meat that the table had cut for him. Death thoughts. They were awfully young, Wendy and Peter, for death thoughts. Or, no, you were never too young, really. Long before you knew what death was you were wishing it on someone else. When you were two years old you were shooting people with cap pistols.

But this—the long, hot African veldt—the awful death in the jaws of a lion. And repeated again and again.

"Where are you going?"

He didn't answer Lydia. Preoccupied, he let the lights glow softly on ahead of him, extinguish behind him as he padded to the nursery door. He listened against it. Far away, a lion roared.

He unlocked the door and opened it. Just before he stepped inside, he heard a faraway scream. And then another roar from the lions, which subsided quickly.

He stepped into Africa. How many times in the last year had he opened this door and found Wonderland, Alice, the Mock Turtle, or Aladdin and his Magical Lamp, or Jack Pumpkinhead of Oz, or Dr. Dolittle, or the cow jumping over a very real-appearing moon—all the delightful contraptions of a make-believe world. How often had he seen Pegasus flying in the sky ceiling, or seen fountains of red fireworks, or heard angel voices singing. But now, this yellow hot Africa, this bake oven with murder in the heat. Perhaps Lydia was right. Perhaps they needed a little vacation from the fantasy which was growing a bit too real for ten-year-old children. It was all right to exercise one's mind with gymnastic fantasies, but when the lively child mind settled on *one* pattern . . . ? It seemed that, at a distance, for the past month, he had heard lions roaring, and smelled their strong odor seeping as far away as his study door. But, being busy, he had paid it no attention.

George Hadley stood on the African grassland alone. The lions looked up from their feeding, watching him. The only flaw to the illusion was the open door through which he could see his wife, far down the dark hall, like a framed picture, eating her dinner abstractedly.

"Go away," he said to the lions.

They did not go.

He knew the principle of the room exactly. You sent out your thoughts. Whatever you thought would appear.

"Let's have Aladdin and his lamp," he snapped.

The veldtland remained; the lions remained.

"Come on, room! I demand Aladdin!" he said.

Nothing happened. The lions mumbled in their baked pelts.

"Aladdin!"

He went back to dinner. "The fool room's out of order," he said. "It won't respond."

"Or—"

"Or what?"

"Or it *can't* respond," said Lydia, "because the children have thought about Africa and lions and killing so many days that the room's in a rut."

"Could be."

"Or Peter's set it to remain that way."

"Set it?"

"He may have got into the machinery and fixed something."

"Peter doesn't know machinery."

"He's a wise one for ten. That IQ of his—"

"Nevertheless—"

"Hello, Mom. Hello, Dad."

The Hadleys turned. Wendy and Peter were coming in the front door, cheeks like peppermint candy, eyes like bright blue agate marbles, a smell of ozone on their jumpers from their trip in the helicopter.

"You're just in time for supper," said both parents.

"We're full of strawberry ice cream and hot dogs," said the children, holding hands. "But we'll sit and watch."

"Yes, come tell us about the nursery," said George Hadley.

The brother and sister blinked at him and then at each other. "Nursery?"

"All about Africa and everything," said the father with false joviality.

"I don't understand," said Peter.

"Your mother and I were just traveling through Africa with rod and reel; Tom Swift and his Electric Lion," said George Hadley.

"There's no Africa in the nursery," said Peter simply.

"Oh, come now, Peter. We know better."

"I don't remember any Africa," said Peter to Wendy. "Do you?"

"No."

"Run see and come tell."

She obeyed.

"Wendy, come back here!" said George Hadley, but she was gone. The house lights followed her like a flock of fireflies. Too late, he realized he had forgotten to lock the nursery door after his last inspection.

"Wendy'll look and come tell us," said Peter.

"She doesn't have to tell *me*. I've seen it."

"I'm sure you're mistaken, Father."

"I'm not, Peter. Come along now."

But Wendy was back. "It's not Africa," she said breathlessly.

"We'll see about this," said George Hadley, and they all walked down the hall together and opened the nursery door.

There was a green, lovely forest, a lovely river, a purple mountain, high voices singing, and Rima, lovely and mysterious, lurking in the trees with colorful flights of butterflies, like animated bouquets, lingering in her long hair. The African veldtland was gone. The lions were gone. Only Rima was here now, singing a song so beautiful that it brought tears to your eyes.

George Hadley looked in at the changed scene. "Go to bed," he said to the children.

They opened their mouths.

"You heard me," he said.

They went off to the air closet, where a wind sucked them like brown leaves up the flue to their slumber rooms.

George Hadley walked through the singing glade and picked up something that lay in the corner near where the lions had been. He walked slowly back to his wife.

"What is that?" she asked.

"An old wallet of mine," he said.

He showed it to her. The smell of hot grass was on it and the smell of a lion. There were drops of saliva on it, it had been chewed, and there were blood smears on both sides.

He closed the nursery door and locked it, tight.

In the middle of the night he was still awake and he knew his wife was awake. "Do you think Wendy changed it?" she said at last, in the dark room.

"Of course."

"Made it from a veldt into a forest and put Rima there instead of lions?"

"Yes."

"Why?"

"I don't know. But it's staying locked until I find out."

"How did your wallet get there?"

"I don't know anything," he said, "except that I'm beginning to be sorry we bought that room for the children. If children are neurotic at all, a room like that—"

"It's supposed to help them work off their neuroses in a healthful way."

"I'm starting to wonder." He stared at the ceiling.

"We've given the children everything they ever wanted. Is this our reward—secrecy, disobedience?"

"Who was it said, 'Children are carpets, they should be stepped on occasionally'? We've never lifted a hand. They're insufferable—let's admit it. They come and go when they like; they treat us as if *we* were offspring. They're spoiled and we're spoiled."

"They've been acting funny ever since you forbade them to take the rocket to New York a few months ago."

"They're not old enough to do that alone, I explained."

"Nevertheless, I've noticed they've been decidedly cool toward us since."

"I think I'll have David McClean come tomorrow morning to have a look at Africa."

"But it's not Africa now, it's *Green Mansions* country and Rima."

"I have a feeling it'll be Africa again before then."

A moment later they heard the screams.

Two screams. Two people screaming from downstairs. And then a roar of lions.

"Wendy and Peter aren't in their rooms," said his wife.

He lay in his bed with his beating heart. "No," he said. "They've broken into the nursery."

"Those screams—they sound familiar."

"Do they?"

"Yes, awfully."

And although their beds tried very hard, the two adults couldn't be rocked to sleep for another hour. A smell of cats was in the night air.

"Father?" said Peter.

"Yes."

Peter looked at his shoes. He never looked at his father anymore, nor at his mother. "You aren't going to lock up the nursery for good, are you?"

"That all depends."

"On what?" snapped Peter.

"On you and your sister. If you intersperse this Africa with a little variety—oh, Sweden perhaps, or Denmark or China—"

"I thought we were free to play as we wished."

"You are, within reasonable bounds."

"What's wrong with Africa, Father?"

"Oh, so now you admit you have been conjuring up Africa, do you?"

"I wouldn't want the nursery locked up," said Peter coldly. "Ever."

"Matter of fact, we're thinking of turning the whole house off for about a month. Live sort of a carefree one-for-all existence."

"That sounds dreadful! Would I have to tie my own shoes instead of letting the shoe tier do it? And brush my own teeth and comb my hair and give myself a bath?"

"It would be fun for a change, don't you think?"

"No, it would be horrid. I didn't like it when you took out the picture painter last month."

"That's because I wanted you to learn to paint all by yourself, son."

"I don't want to do anything but look and listen and smell; what else *is* there to do?"

"All right, go play in Africa."

"Will you shut off the house sometime soon?"

"We're considering it."

"I don't think you'd better consider it anymore, Father."

"I won't have any threats from my son!"

"Very well." And Peter strolled off to the nursery.

"Am I on time?" said David McClean.

"Breakfast?" asked George Hadley.

"Thanks, had some. What's the trouble?"

"David, you're a psychologist."

"I should hope so."

"Well, then, have a look at our nursery. You saw it a year ago when you dropped by; did you notice anything peculiar about it then?"

"Can't say I did; the usual violences, a tendency toward a slight paranoia here or there, usual in children because they feel persecuted by parents constantly, but, oh, really nothing."

They walked down the hall. "I locked the nursery up," explained the father, "and the children broke back into it during the night. I let them stay so they could form the patterns for you to see."

There was a terrible screaming from the nursery.

"There it is," said George Hadley. "See what you make of it."

They walked in on the children without rapping.

The screams had faded. The lions were feeding.

"Run outside a moment, children," said George Hadley. "No, don't change the mental combination. Leave the walls as they are. Get!"

With the children gone, the two men stood studying the lions clustered at a distance, eating with great relish whatever it was they had caught.

"I wish I knew what it was," said George Hadley. "Sometimes I can almost see. Do you think if I brought high-powered binoculars here and—"

David McClean laughed dryly. "Hardly." He turned to study all four walls. "How long has this been going on?"

"A little over a month."

"It certainly doesn't *feel* good."

"I want facts, not feelings."

"My dear George, a psychologist never saw a fact in his life. He only hears about feelings; vague things. This doesn't feel good, I tell you. Trust my hunches and my instincts. I have a nose for something bad. This is very bad. My advice to you is to have the whole damn room torn down and your children brought to me every day during the next year for treatment."

"Is it that bad?"

"I'm afraid so. One of the original uses of these nurseries was so that we could study the patterns left on the walls by the child's mind, study at our leisure, and help the child. In this case, however, the room has become a channel toward—destructive thoughts, instead of a release away from them."

"Didn't you sense this before?"

"I sensed only that you had spoiled your children more than most. And now you're letting them down in some way. What way?"

"I wouldn't let them go to New York."

"What else?"

"I've taken a few machines from the house and threatened them, a month ago, with closing up the nursery unless they did their home-work. I did close it for a few days to show I meant business."

"Ah, ha!"

"Does that mean anything?"

"Everything. Where before they had a Santa Claus now they have a Scrooge. Children prefer Santas. You've let this room and this house replace you and your wife in your children's affections. This room is their mother and father, far more important in their lives than their real parents. And now you come along and want to shut it off. No wonder there's hatred here. You can feel it coming out of the sky. Feel that sun. George, you'll have to change your life. Like too many others, you've built it around creature comforts. Why, you'd starve tomorrow if something went wrong in your kitchen. You wouldn't know how to tap an egg. Nevertheless, turn everything off. Start new. It'll take time. But we'll make good children out of bad in a year, wait and see."

"But won't the shock be too much for the children, shutting the room up abruptly, for good?"

"I don't want them going any deeper into this, that's all."

The lions were finished with their red feast.

The lions were standing on the edge of the clearing watching the two men.

"Now *I'm* feeling persecuted," said McClean. "Let's get out of here. I never have cared for these damned rooms. Make me nervous."

"The lions look real, don't they?" said George Hadley. "I don't suppose there's any way—"

"What?"

"—that they could *become* real?"

"Not that I know."

"Some flaw in the machinery, a tampering or something?"

"No."

They went to the door.

"I don't imagine the room will like being turned off," said the father.

"Nothing ever likes to die—even a room."

"I wonder if it hates me for wanting to switch it off?"

"Paranoia is thick around here today," said David McClean. "You can follow it like a spoor. Hello." He bent and picked up a bloody scarf. "This yours?"

"No." George Hadley's face was rigid. "It belongs to Lydia."

They went to the fuse box together and threw the switch that killed the nursery.

The two children were in hysterics. They screamed and pranced and threw things. They yelled and sobbed and swore and jumped at the furniture.

"You can't do that to the nursery, you can't!"

"Now, children."

The children flung themselves onto a couch, weeping.

"George," said Lydia Hadley, "turn on the nursery, just for a few moments. You can't be so abrupt."

"No."

"You can't be so cruel."

"Lydia, it's off, and it stays off. And the whole damn house dies as of here and now. The more I see of the mess we've put ourselves in, the more it sickens me. We've been contemplating our mechanical, electronic navels for too long. My God, how we need a breath of honest air!"

And he marched about the house turning off the voice clocks, the stoves, the heaters, the shoe shiners, the shoe lacers, the body scrubbers and swabbers and massagers, and every other machine he could put his hand to.

The house was full of dead bodies, it seemed. It felt like a mechanical cemetery. So silent. None of the humming hidden energy of machines waiting to function at the tap of a button.

"Don't let them do it!" wailed Peter at the ceiling, as if he was talking to the house, the nursery. "Don't let Father kill everything." He turned to his father. "Oh, I hate you!"

"Insults won't get you anywhere."

"I wish you were dead!"

"We were, for a long while. Now we're going to really start living. Instead of being handled and massaged, we're going to *live*."

Wendy was still crying and Peter joined her again. "Just a moment, just one moment, just another moment of nursery," they wailed.

"Oh, George," said the wife, "it can't hurt."

"All right—all right, if they'll only just shut up. One minute, mind you, and then off forever."

"Daddy, Daddy, Daddy!" sang the children, smiling with wet faces.

"And then we're going on a vacation. David McClean is coming back in half an hour to help us move out and get to the airport. I'm going to dress. You turn the nursery on for a minute, Lydia, just a minute, mind you."

And the three of them went babbling off while he let himself be vacuumed upstairs through the air flue and set about dressing himself. A minute later Lydia appeared.

"I'll be glad when we get away," she sighed.

"Did you leave them in the nursery?"

"I wanted to dress too. Oh, that horrid Africa. What can they see in it?"

"Well, in five minutes we'll be on our way to Iowa. Lord, how did we ever get in this house? What prompted us to buy a nightmare?"

"Pride, money, foolishness."

"I think we'd better get downstairs before those kids get engrossed with those damned beasts again."

Just then they heard the children calling, "Daddy, Mommy, come quick—quick!"

They went downstairs in the air flue and ran down the hall. The children were nowhere in sight. "Wendy? Peter!"

They ran into the nursery. The veldtland was empty save for the lions waiting, looking at them. "Peter, Wendy?"

The door slammed.

"Wendy, Peter!"

George Hadley and his wife whirled and ran back to the door.

"Open the door!" cried George Hadley, trying the knob. "Why, they've locked it from the outside! Peter!" He beat at the door. "Open up!"

He heard Peter's voice outside, against the door.

"Don't let them switch off the nursery and the house," he was saying.

Mr. and Mrs. George Hadley beat at the door. "Now, don't be ridiculous, children. It's time to go. Mr. McClean'll be here in a minute and . . ."

And then they heard the sounds.

The lions on three sides of them, in the yellow veldt grass, padding through the dry straw, rumbling and roaring in their throats.

The lions.

Mr. Hadley looked at his wife and they turned and looked back at the beasts edging slowly forward, crouching, tails stiff.

Mr. and Mrs. Hadley screamed.

And suddenly they realized why those other screams had sounded familiar.

"Well, here I am," said David McClean in the nursery doorway. "Oh, hello." He stared at the two children seated in the center of the open glade eating a little picnic lunch. Beyond them was the water hole and the yellow veldtland; above was the hot sun. He began to perspire. "Where are your father and mother?"

The children looked up and smiled. "Oh, they'll be here directly."

"Good, we must get going." At a distance Mr. McClean saw the lions fighting and clawing and then quieting down to feed in silence under the shady trees.

He squinted at the lions with his hand up to his eyes.

Now the lions were done feeding. They moved to the water hole to drink.

A shadow flickered over Mr. McClean's hot face. Many shadows flickered. The vultures were dropping down the blazing sky.

"A cup of tea?" asked Wendy in the silence.

1. According to the story, are George and Lydia to blame for what happens to them?

2. Why do Peter and Wendy choose the nursery over their parents?

3. At the end of the story, do the children know what they are doing to their parents, or is it just another fantasy for them?

4. Why does the story end with Peter and Wendy having a picnic and behaving politely toward David McClean?

ARTHUR C. CLARKE (1917–2008) was born in Somerset, England. He served as a radar instructor and flight lieutenant in the Royal Air Force during World War II, and he earned a bachelor of science degree in mathematics and physics at King's College in 1948. Clarke originated the idea of using satellites as telecommunication devices. For his scientific achievements Clarke earned various awards from aerospace agencies, including NASA's Distinguished Public Service Medal in 1995. Still, it is Clarke's science fiction that secured his fame. Among many other literary awards, he received the title of Grand Master from Science Fiction and Fantasy Writers of America in 1985. While many consider *Childhood's End* (1953) to be his greatest novel, Clarke is best known for his collaboration with legendary film director Stanley Kubrick on *2001: A Space Odyssey* (1968). Both works explore human-alien contact and evolution. They also display the technical and scientific proficiencies that led to the classification of Clarke's work as "hard" science fiction.

The Star

It is three thousand light-years to the Vatican. Once, I believed that space could have no power over faith, just as I believed that the heavens declared the glory of God's handiwork. Now I have seen that handiwork, and my faith is sorely troubled. I stare at the crucifix that hangs on the cabin wall above the Mark VI Computer, and for the first time in my life I wonder if it is no more than an empty symbol.

I have told no one yet, but the truth cannot be concealed. The facts are there for all to read, recorded on the countless miles of magnetic tape and the thousands of photographs we are carrying back to Earth. Other scientists can interpret them as easily as I can, and I am not one who would condone that tampering with the truth which often gave my order a bad name in the olden days.

The crew are already sufficiently depressed: I wonder how they will take this ultimate irony. Few of them have any religious faith, yet they will not relish using this final weapon in their campaign against me—that private, good-natured, but fundamentally serious war which lasted all the way from Earth. It amused them to have a Jesuit as chief astrophysicist: Dr. Chandler, for instance, could never get over it (why are medical men such notorious atheists?). Sometimes he would meet me on the observation deck, where the lights are always low so that the stars shine with undiminished glory. He would come up to me in the gloom and stand staring out of the great oval port, while the heavens crawled slowly around us as the ship turned end over end with the residual spin we had never bothered to correct.

"Well, Father," he would say at last, "it goes on forever and forever, and perhaps *Something* made it. But how you can believe that Something has a special interest in us and our miserable little world— that just beats me." Then the argument would start, while the stars and nebulae would swing around us in silent, endless arcs beyond the flawlessly clear plastic of the observation port.

It was, I think, the apparent incongruity of my position that caused most amusement to the crew. In vain I would point to my three papers in the *Astrophysical Journal,* my five in the *Monthly Notices of the Royal Astronomical Society.* I would remind them that my order has long been famous for its scientific works. We may be few now, but ever since the eighteenth century we have made contributions to astronomy and geophysics out of all proportion to our numbers. Will my report on the Phoenix Nebula end our thousand years of history? It will end, I fear, much more than that.

I do not know who gave the nebula its name, which seems to me a very bad one. If it contains a prophecy, it is one that cannot be verified for several billion years. Even the word "nebula" is misleading: this is a far smaller object than those stupendous clouds of mist—the stuff of unborn stars—that are scattered throughout the length of the Milky Way. On the cosmic scale, indeed, the Phoenix Nebula is a tiny thing—a tenuous shell of gas surrounding a single star.

Or what is left of a star . . .

The Rubens engraving of Loyola seems to mock me as it hangs there above the spectrophotometer tracings. What would *you*, Father,

ARTHUR C. CLARKE

50

have made of this knowledge that has come into my keeping, so far from the little world that was all the universe you knew? Would your faith have risen to the challenge, as mine has failed to do?

You gaze into the distance, Father, but I have traveled a distance beyond any that you could have imagined when you founded our order a thousand years ago. No other survey ship has been so far from Earth: we are at the very frontiers of the explored universe. We set out to reach the Phoenix Nebula, we succeeded, and we are homeward bound with our burden of knowledge. I wish I could lift that burden from my shoulders, but I call to you in vain across the centuries and the light-years that lie between us.

On the book you are holding the words are plain to read. AD MAJOREM DEI GLORIAM, the message runs, but it is a message I can no longer believe. Would you still believe it, if you could see what we have found?

We knew, of course, what the Phoenix Nebula was. Every year, in our galaxy alone, more than a hundred stars explode, blazing for a few hours or days with thousands of times their normal brilliance before they sink back into death and obscurity. Such are the ordinary novae—the commonplace disasters of the universe. I have recorded the spectrograms and light curves of dozens since I started working at the Lunar Observatory.

But three or four times in every thousand years occurs something beside which even a nova pales into total insignificance.

When a star becomes a *supernova*, it may for a little while outshine all the massed suns of the galaxy. The Chinese astronomers watched this happen in AD 1054, not knowing what it was they saw. Five centuries later, in 1572, a supernova blazed in Cassiopeia so brilliantly that it was visible in the daylight sky. There have been three more in the thousand years that have passed since then.

Our mission was to visit the remnants of such a catastrophe, to reconstruct the events that led up to it, and, if possible, to learn its cause. We came slowly in through the concentric shells of gas that had been blasted out six thousand years before, yet were expanding still. They were immensely hot, radiating even now with a fierce violet light, but were far too tenuous to do us any damage. When the star had exploded, its outer layers had been driven upward with such speed that they had escaped completely from its gravitational field. Now they formed a hollow shell large enough to engulf a thousand solar systems, and at its center burned the tiny, fantastic object which the star had now become—a white dwarf, smaller than the Earth, yet weighing a million times as much.

The glowing gas shells were all around us, banishing the normal night of interstellar space. We were flying into the center of a cosmic bomb that had detonated millennia ago and whose incandescent fragments were still hurtling apart. The immense scale of the explosion, and the fact that the debris already covered a volume of space many billions of miles across, robbed the scene of any visible movement. It would take decades before the unaided eye could detect any motion in these tortured wisps and eddies of gas, yet the sense of turbulent expansion was overwhelming.

We had checked our primary drive hours before, and were drifting slowly toward the fierce little star ahead. Once it had been a sun like our own, but it had squandered in a few hours the energy that should have kept it shining for a million years. Now it was a shrunken miser, hoarding its resources as if trying to make amends for its prodigal youth.

No one seriously expected to find planets. If there had been any before the explosion, they would have been boiled into puffs of vapor, and their substance lost in the greater wreckage of the star itself. But we made the automatic search, as we always do when approaching an unknown sun, and presently we found a single small world circling the star at an immense distance. It must have been the Pluto of this vanished solar system, orbiting on the frontiers of the night. Too far from the central sun ever to have known life, its remoteness had saved it from the fate of all its lost companions.

The passing fires had seared its rocks and burned away the mantle of frozen gas that must have covered it in the days before the disaster. We landed, and we found the Vault.

Its builders had made sure that we should. The monolithic marker that stood above the entrance was now a fused stump, but even the first long-range photographs told us that here was the work of intelligence. A little later we detected the continent-wide pattern of radioactivity that had been buried in the rock. Even if the pylon above the Vault had been destroyed, this would have remained, an immovable and all but eternal beacon calling to the stars. Our ship fell toward this gigantic bull's-eye like an arrow into its target.

The pylon must have been a mile high when it was built, but now it looked like a candle that had melted down into a puddle of wax. It took us a week to drill through the fused rock, since we did not have the proper tools for a task like this. We were astronomers, not archaeologists, but we could improvise. Our original purpose was forgotten: this lonely monument, reared with such labor at the greatest possible distance from the doomed sun, could have only one meaning. A civilization that knew it was about to die had made its last bid for immortality.

It will take us generations to examine all the treasures that were placed in the Vault. They had plenty of time to prepare, for their sun must have given its first warnings many years before the final detonation. Everything that they wished to preserve, all the fruit of their genius, they brought here to this distant world in the days before the end, hoping that some other race would find it and that they would not be utterly forgotten. Would we have done as well, or would we have been too lost in our own misery to give thought to a future we could never see or share?

If only they had had a little more time! They could travel freely enough between the planets of their own sun, but they had not yet learned to cross the interstellar gulfs, and the nearest solar system was a hundred light-years away. Yet even had they possessed the secret of the Transfinite Drive, no more than a few millions could have been saved. Perhaps it was better thus.

Even if they had not been so disturbingly human as their sculpture shows, we could not have helped admiring them and grieving for their fate. They left thousands of visual records and the machines for projecting them, together with elaborate pictorial instructions from which it will not be difficult to learn their written language. We have examined many of these records, and brought to life for the first time in six thousand years the warmth and beauty of a civilization that in many ways must have been superior to our own. Perhaps they only showed us the best, and one can hardly blame them. But their words were very lovely, and their cities were built with a grace that matches anything of man's. We have watched them at work and play, and listened to their musical speech sounding across the centuries. One scene is still before my eyes—a group of children on a beach of strange blue sand, playing in the waves as children play on Earth. Curious whiplike trees line the shore, and some very large animal is wading in the shallows yet attracting no attention at all.

And sinking into the sea, still warm and friendly and life-giving, is the sun that will soon turn traitor and obliterate all this innocent happiness.

Perhaps if we had not been so far from home and so vulnerable to loneliness, we should not have been so deeply moved. Many of us had seen the ruins of ancient civilizations on other worlds, but they had never affected us so profoundly. This tragedy was unique. It is one thing for a race to fail and die, as nations and cultures have done on Earth. But to be destroyed so completely in the full flower of its achievement, leaving no survivors—how could that be reconciled with the mercy of God?

My colleagues have asked me that, and I have given what answers I can. Perhaps you could have done better, Father Loyola, but I have found nothing in the *Exercitia Spiritualia* that helps me here. They were not an evil people: I do not know what gods they worshiped, if indeed they worshiped any. But I have looked back at them across the centuries, and have watched while the loveliness they used their last strength to preserve was brought forth again into the light of their shrunken sun. They could have taught us much: why were they destroyed?

I know the answers that my colleagues will give when they get back to Earth. They will say that the universe has no purpose and no plan, that since a hundred suns explode every year in our galaxy, at this very moment some race is dying in the depths of space. Whether that race has done good or evil during its lifetime will make no difference in the end: there is no divine justice, for there is no God.

Yet, of course, what we have seen proves nothing of the sort. Anyone who argues thus is being swayed by emotion, not logic. God has no need to justify His actions to man. He who built the universe can destroy it when He chooses. It is arrogance—it is perilously near blasphemy—for us to say what He may or may not do.

This I could have accepted, hard though it is to look upon whole worlds and peoples thrown into the furnace. But there comes a point when even the deepest faith must falter, and now, as I look at the calculations lying before me, I know I have reached that point at last.

We could not tell, before we reached the nebula, how long ago the explosion took place. Now, from the astronomical evidence and the record in the rocks of that one surviving planet, I have been able to date it very exactly. I know in what year the light of this colossal conflagration reached our Earth. I know how brilliantly the supernova whose corpse now dwindles behind our speeding ship once shone in terrestrial skies. I know how it must have blazed low in the east before sunrise, like a beacon in that oriental dawn.

There can be no reasonable doubt: the ancient mystery is solved at last. Yet, oh God, there were so many stars you could have used. What was the need to give these people to the fire, that the symbol of their passing might shine above Bethlehem?

---

1. Why does the narrator think that the crew "will not relish using this final weapon" in their campaign against him as a Jesuit astrophysicist?

2. What does the narrator mean when he says that "perhaps it was better thus" that the extinct race did not have the technology to save more than a few million people?

3. Why does the narrator's deepest faith falter when his scientific calculations make him realize that the supernova was the star shining above Bethlehem?

4. Is it possible to reconcile the findings of the story's scientific investigations with the belief that the world is governed by a just and merciful God?

J. G. BALLARD (1930–2009) was born in Shanghai and experienced
the turmoil of the Japanese invasion of China as a young boy, later
recounted in his highly acclaimed autobiographical novel, *Empire of the
Sun* (1984). These early experiences with desolation and destruction
are reflected in Ballard's work, which includes more than fifteen novels
and numerous short stories. In novels such as *The Wind from Nowhere*
(1962), *The Drowned World* (1962), *The Atrocity Exhibition* (1970),
Crash (1973), *Concrete Island* (1974), and *High-Rise* (1975), Ballard has
created characters and situations that reflect his vision of a modern,
technologically dominated world that is both the cause and effect of
mental disintegration and psychotic behavior. Ballard was a stylistic
innovator and a part of the New Wave of science fiction writers who
emerged in the 1960s.

The Voices of Time

1

Later Powers often thought of Whitby, and the strange grooves the
biologist had cut, apparently at random, all over the floor of the empty
swimming pool. An inch deep and twenty feet long, interlocking to
form an elaborate ideogram like a Chinese character, they had taken
him all summer to complete, and he had obviously thought about
little else, working away tirelessly through the long desert afternoons.
Powers had watched him from his office window at the far end of the
neurology wing, carefully marking out his pegs and string, carrying
away the cement chips in a small canvas bucket. After Witby's suicide
no one had bothered about the grooves, but Powers often borrowed
the supervisor's key and let himself into the disused pool, and
would look down at the labyrinth of mouldering gulleys, half filled

with water leaking in from the chlorinator, an enigma now past any solution.

Initially, however, Powers was too preoccupied with completing his work at the Clinic and planning his own final withdrawal. After the first frantic weeks of panic he had managed to accept an uneasy compromise that allowed him to view his predicament with the detached fatalism he had previously reserved for his patients. Fortunately he was moving down the physical and mental gradients simultaneously—lethargy and inertia blunted his anxieties, a slackening metabolism made it necessary to concentrate to produce a connected thought-train. In fact, the lengthening intervals of dreamless sleep were almost restful. He found himself beginning to look forward to them, and made no effort to wake earlier than was essential.

At first he had kept an alarm clock by his bed, tried to compress as much activity as he could into the narrowing hours of consciousness, sorting out his library, driving over to Whitby's laboratory every morning to examine the latest batch of X-ray plates, every minute and hour rationed like the last drops of water in a canteen.

Anderson, fortunately, had unwittingly made him realize the pointlessness of this course.

After Powers had resigned from the Clinic he still continued to drive in once a week for his checkup, now little more than a formality. On what turned out to be the last occasion Anderson had perfunctorily taken his blood count, noting Powers's slacker facial muscles, fading pupil reflexes, and unshaven cheeks.

He smiled sympathetically at Powers across the desk, wondering what to say to him. Once he had put on a show of encouragement with the more intelligent patients, even tried to provide some sort of explanation. But Powers was too difficult to reach—neurosurgeon extraordinary, a man always out on the periphery, only at ease working with unfamiliar materials. To himself he thought: *I'm sorry, Robert. What can I say—"Even the sun is growing cooler"*—? He watched Powers drum his fingers restlessly on the enamel desk top, his eyes glancing at the spinal level charts hung around the office. Despite his unkempt appearance—he had been wearing the same unironed shirt and dirty white plimsolls a week ago—Powers looked composed and self-possessed, like a Conradian beachcomber more or less reconciled to his own weaknesses.

"What are you doing with yourself, Robert?" he asked. "Are you still going over to Whitby's lab?"

"As much as I can. It takes me half an hour to cross the lake, and I keep on sleeping through the alarm clock. I may leave my place and move in there permanently."

Anderson frowned. "Is there much point? As far as I could make out Whitby's work was pretty speculative—" He broke off, realizing the implied criticism of Powers's own disastrous work at the Clinic, but Powers seemed to ignore this, was examining the pattern of shadows on the ceiling. "Anyway, wouldn't it be better to stay where you are, among your own things, read through Toynbee and Spengler again?"

Powers laughed shortly. "That's the last thing I want to do. I want to *forget* Toynbee and Spengler, not try to remember them. In fact, Paul, I'd like to forget everything. I don't know whether I've got enough time, though. How much can you forget in three months?"

"Everything, I suppose, if you want to. But don't try to race the clock."

Powers nodded quietly, repeating this last remark to himself. Racing the clock was exactly what he had been doing. As he stood up and said goodbye to Anderson he suddenly decided to throw away his alarm clock, escape from his futile obsession with time. To remind himself he unfastened his wristwatch and scrambled the setting, then slipped it into his pocket. Making his way out to the car park he reflected on the freedom this simple act gave him. He would explore the lateral byways now, the side doors, as it were, in the corridors of time. Three months could be an eternity.

He picked his car out of the line and strolled over to it, shielding his eyes from the heavy sunlight beating down across the parabolic sweep of the lecture theatre roof. He was about to climb in when he saw that someone had traced with a finger across the dust caked over the windshield:

96,688,365,498,721

Looking over his shoulder, he recognized the white Packard parked next to him, peered inside, and saw a lean-faced young man with blond sun-bleached hair and a high cerebrotonic forehead watching him behind dark glasses. Sitting beside him at the wheel was a raven-haired girl whom he had often seen around the psychology department. She had intelligent but somehow rather oblique eyes, and Powers remembered that the younger doctors called her "the girl from Mars."

"Hello, Kaldren," Powers said to the young man. "Still following me around?"

Kaldren nodded. "Most of the time, Doctor." He sized Powers up shrewdly. "We haven't seen very much of you recently, as a matter of fact. Anderson said you'd resigned, and we noticed your laboratory was closed."

Powers shrugged. "I felt I needed a rest. As you'll understand, there's a good deal that needs rethinking."

Kaldren frowned half mockingly. "Sorry to hear that, Doctor. But don't let these temporary setbacks depress you." He noticed the girl watching Powers with interest. "Coma's a fan of yours. I gave her your papers from *American Journal of Psychiatry*, and she's read through the whole file."

The girl smiled pleasantly at Powers, for a moment dispelling the hostility between the two men. When Powers nodded to her she leaned across Kaldren and said: "Actually I've just finished Noguchi's autobiography—the great Japanese doctor who discovered the spirochete. Somehow you remind me of him—there's so much of yourself in all the patients you worked on."

Powers smiled wanly at her, then his eyes turned and locked involuntarily on Kaldren's. They stared at each other sombrely for a moment, and a small tic in Kaldren's right cheek began to flicker irritatingly. He flexed his facial muscles, after a few seconds mastered it with an effort, obviously annoyed that Powers should have witnessed this brief embarrassment.

"How did the clinic go today?" Powers asked. "Have you had any more . . . headaches?"

Kaldren's mouth snapped shut, he looked suddenly irritable. "Whose care am I in, Doctor? Yours or Anderson's? Is that the sort of question you should be asking now?"

Powers gestured deprecatingly. "Perhaps not." He cleared his throat; the heat was ebbing the blood from his head and he felt tired and eager to get away from them. He turned towards his car, then realized that Kaldren would probably follow, either try to crowd him into the ditch or block the road and make Powers sit in his dust all the way back to the lake. Kaldren was capable of any madness.

"Well, I've got to go and collect something," he said, adding in a firmer voice: "Get in touch with me, though, if you can't reach Anderson."

He waved and walked off behind the line of cars. From the reflection in the windows he could see Kaldren looking back and watching him closely.

He entered the neurology wing, paused thankfully in the cool foyer, nodding to the two nurses and the armed guard at the reception desk. For some reason the terminals sleeping in the adjacent dormitory block attracted hordes of would-be sightseers, most of them cranks with some magical anti-narcoma remedy, or merely the idly curious, but a good number of quite normal people, many of whom had travelled thousands of miles, impelled towards the Clinic by some strange instinct, like animals migrating to a preview of their racial graveyards.

He walked along the corridor to the supervisor's office overlooking the recreation deck, borrowed the key, and made his way out through the tennis courts and callisthenics rigs to the enclosed swimming pool at the far end. It had been disused for months, and only Powers's visits kept the lock free. Stepping through, he closed it behind him and walked past the peeling wooden stands to the deep end.

Putting a foot up on the diving board, he looked down at Witby's ideogram. Damp leaves and bits of paper obscured it, but the outlines were just distinguishable. It covered almost the entire floor of the pool and at first glance appeared to represent a huge solar disc, with four radiating diamond-shaped arms, a crude Jungian mandala.

Wondering what had prompted Whitby to carve the device before his death, Powers noticed something moving through the debris in the centre of the disc. A black, horny-shelled animal about a foot long was nosing about in the slush, heaving itself on tired legs. Its shell was articulated, and vaguely resembled an armadillo's. Reaching the edge of the disc, it stopped and hesitated, then slowly backed away into the centre again, apparently unwilling or unable to cross the narrow groove.

Powers looked around, then stepped into one of the changing stalls and pulled a small wooden clothes locker off its rusty wall bracket. Carrying it under one arm, he climbed down the chromium ladder into the pool and walked carefully across the slithery floor towards the animal. As he approached it sidled away from him, but he trapped it easily, using the lid to lever it into the box.

The animal was heavy, at least the weight of a brick. Powers tapped its massive olive-black carapace with his knuckle, noting the triangular warty head jutting out below its rim like a turtle's, the thickened pads beneath the first digits of the pentadactyl forelimbs.

He watched the three-lidded eyes blinking at him anxiously from the bottom of the box.

"Expecting some really hot weather?" he murmured. "That lead umbrella you're carrying around should keep you cool."

He closed the lid, climbed out of the pool and made his way back to the supervisor's office, then carried the box out to his car.

> . . . Kaldren continues to reproach me (Powers wrote in his diary). For some reason he seems unwilling to accept his isolation, is elaborating a series of private rituals to replace the missing hours of sleep. Perhaps I should tell him of my own approaching zero, but he'd probably regard this as the final unbearable insult, that I should have in excess what he so desperately yearns for. God knows what might happen. Fortunately the nightmarish visions appear to have receded for the time being . . .

Pushing the diary away, Powers leaned forward across the desk and stared out through the window at the white floor of the lake bed stretching towards the hills along the horizon. Three miles away, on the far shore, he could see the circular bowl of the radio telescope revolving slowly in the clear afternoon air, as Kaldren tirelessly trapped the sky, sluicing in millions of cubic parsecs of sterile ether, like the nomads who trapped the sea along the shores of the Persian Gulf.

Behind him the air conditioner murmured quietly, cooling the pale blue walls half hidden in the dim light. Outside the air was bright and oppressive, the heat waves rippling up from the clumps of gold-tinted cacti below the Clinic blurring the sharp terraces of the twenty-storey neurology block. There, in the silent dormitories behind the sealed shutters, the terminals slept their long dreamless sleep. There were now over five hundred of them in the Clinic, the vanguard of a vast somnambulist army massing for its last march. Only five years had elapsed since the first narcoma syndrome had been recognized, but already huge government hospitals in the east were being readied for intakes in the thousands, as more and more cases came to light.

Powers felt suddenly tired, and glanced at his wrist, wondering how long he had to eight o'clock, his bedtime for the next week or so. Already he missed the dusk, soon would wake to his last dawn.

His watch was in his hip pocket. He remembered his decision not to use his timepieces, and sat back and stared at the bookshelves beside the desk. There were rows of green-covered AEC publications he had removed from Whitby's library, papers in which the biologist described his work out in the Pacific after the H-tests. Many of them Powers knew almost by heart, read a hundred times in an effort to grasp Whitby's last conclusions. Toynbee would certainly be easier to forget.

His eyes dimmed momentarily, as the tall black wall in the rear of his mind cast its great shadow over his brain. He reached for the diary, thinking of the girl in Kaldren's car—Coma he had called her, another of his insane jokes—and her reference to Noguchi. Actually the comparison should have been made with Whitby, not himself; the monsters in the lab were nothing more than fragmented mirrors of Whitby's mind, like the grotesque radio-shielded frog he had found that morning in the swimming pool.

Thinking of the girl Coma, and the heartening smile she had given him, he wrote:

Woke 6:33 a.m. Last session with Anderson. He made it plain he's seen enough of me, and from now on I'm better alone. To sleep 8:00? (These countdowns terrify me.)

He paused, then added:

Goodbye, Eniwetok.

He saw the girl again the next day at Whitby's laboratory. He had driven over after breakfast with the new specimen, eager to get it into a vivarium before it died. The only previous armoured mutant he had come across had nearly broken his neck. Speeding along the lake road a month or so earlier he had struck it with the offside front wheel, expecting the small creature to flatten instantly. Instead its hard lead-packed shell had remained rigid, even though the organism within it had been pulped, had flung the car heavily into the ditch. He had gone back for the shell, later weighed it at the laboratory, found it contained over six hundred grammes of lead.

Quite a number of plants and animals were building up heavy metals as radiological shields. In the hills behind the beach house a couple of old-time prospectors were renovating the derelict gold-panning equipment abandoned over eighty years ago. They had noticed the bright yellow tints of the cacti, run an analysis, and found that the plants were assimilating gold in extractable quantities, although the soil concentrations were unworkable. Oak Ridge was at last paying a dividend!!

Waking that morning just after 6:45—ten minutes later than the previous day (he had switched on the radio, heard one of the regular morning programmes as he climbed out of bed)—he had eaten a light unwanted breakfast, then spent an hour packing away some of the books in his library, crating them up and taping on address labels to his brother.

He reached Whitby's laboratory half an hour later. This was housed in a hundred-foot-wide geodesic dome built beside his chalet on the west shore of the lake about a mile from Kaldren's summerhouse. The chalet had been closed after Whitby's suicide, and many of the experimental plants and animals had died before Powers had managed to receive permission to use the laboratory.

As he turned into the driveway he saw the girl standing on the apex of the yellow-ribbed dome, her slim figure silhouetted against the sky. She waved to him, then began to step down across the glass polyhedrons and jumped nimbly into the driveway beside the car.

"Hello," she said, giving him a welcoming smile. "I came over to see your zoo. Kaldren said you wouldn't let me in if he came so I made him stay behind."

She waited for Powers to say something while he searched for his keys, then volunteered: "If you like, I can wash your shirt."

Powers grinned at her, peered down ruefully at his dust-stained sleeves. "Not a bad idea. I thought I was beginning to look a little uncared-for." He unlocked the door, took Coma's arm. "I don't know why Kaldren told you that—he's welcome here any time he likes."

"What have you got in there?" Coma asked, pointing at the wooden box he was carrying as they walked between the gear-laden benches.

"A distant cousin of ours I found. Interesting little chap. I'll introduce you in a moment."

Sliding partitions divided the dome into four chambers. Two of them were storerooms, filled with spare tanks, apparatus, cartons of animal food, and test rigs. They crossed the third section, almost filled by a powerful X-ray projector, a giant 250-amp G.E. Maxitron, angled onto a revolving table, concrete shielding blocks lying around ready for use like huge building bricks.

The fourth chamber contained Powers's zoo, the vivaria jammed together along the benches and in the sinks, big coloured cardboard charts and memos pinned onto the draught hoods above them, a tangle of rubber tubing and power leads trailing across the floor. As they walked past the lines of tanks dim forms shifted behind the frosted glass, and at the far end of the aisle there was a sudden scurrying in a large cage by Powers's desk.

Putting the box down on his chair, he picked a packet of peanuts off the desk and went over to the cage. A small black-haired chimpanzee wearing a dented jet pilot's helmet swarmed deftly up the bars to him, chirped happily, and then jumped down to a miniature control panel against the rear wall of the cage. Rapidly it flicked a series of buttons and toggles, and a succession of coloured lights lit up like a juke box and jangled out a two-second blast of music.

"Good boy," Powers said encouragingly, patting the chimp's back and shovelling the peanuts into its hands. "You're getting much too clever for that one, aren't you?"

The chimp tossed the peanuts into the back of its throat with the smooth, easy motions of a conjuror, jabbering at Powers in a singsong voice.

Coma laughed and took some of the nuts from Powers. "He's sweet. I think he's talking to you."

Powers nodded. "Quite right, he is. Actually he's got a two-hundred-word vocabulary, but his voice box scrambles it all up." He opened a small refrigerator by the desk, took out half a packet of sliced bread, and passed a couple of pieces to the chimp. It picked an electric toaster off the floor and placed it in the middle of a low wobbling table in the centre of the cage, whipped the pieces into the slots. Powers pressed a tab on the switchboard beside the cage and the toaster began to crackle softly.

"He's one of the brightest we've had here, about as intelligent as a five-year-old child, though much more self-sufficient in a lot of ways." The two pieces of toast jumped out of their slots and the chimp caught them neatly, nonchalantly patting its helmet each time, then ambled off into a small ramshackle kennel and relaxed back with one arm out of a window, sliding the toast into its mouth.

"He built that house himself," Powers went on, switching off the toaster. "Not a bad effort, really." He pointed to a yellow polythene bucket by the front door of the kennel, from which a battered-looking geranium protruded. "Tends that plant, cleans up the cage, pours out an endless stream of wisecracks. Pleasant fellow all round."

Coma was smiling broadly to herself. "Why the space helmet, though?"

Powers hesitated. "Oh, it—er—it's for his own protection. Sometimes he gets rather bad headaches. His predecessors all—" He broke off and turned away. "Let's have a look at some of the other inmates."

He moved down the line of tanks, beckoning Coma with him. "We'll start at the beginning." He lifted the glass lid off one of the tanks, and Coma peered down into a shallow bath of water, where a small round organism with slender tendrils was nestling in a rockery of shells and pebbles.

"Sea anemone. Or was. Simple coelenterate with an open-ended body cavity." He pointed down to a thickened ridge of tissue around the base. "It's sealed up the cavity, converted the channel into a rudimentary notochord, first plant ever to develop a nervous system. Later the tendrils will knot themselves into a ganglion, but already they're sensitive to colour. Look." He borrowed the violet handkerchief in Coma's breast pocket, spread it across the tank. The tendrils flexed and stiffened, began to weave slowly, as if they were trying to focus.

"The strange thing is that they're completely insensitive to white light. Normally the tendrils register shifting pressure gradients, like the tympanic diaphragms in your ears. Now it's almost as if they can *hear* primary colours. That suggests it's readapting itself for a non-aquatic existence in a static world of violent colour contrasts."

Coma shook her head, puzzled. "Why, though?"

"Hold on a moment. Let me put you in the picture first." They moved along the bench to a series of drum-shaped cages made of wire mosquito netting. Above the first was a large white cardboard screen bearing a blown-up microphoto of a tall pagodalike chain, topped by the legend: DROSOPHILA: 15 ROENTGENS/MIN.

Powers tapped a small perspex window in the drum. "Fruitfly. Its huge chromosomes make it a useful test vehicle." He bent down, pointed to a grey V-shaped honeycomb suspended from the roof. A few flies emerged from entrances, moving about busily. "Usually it's solitary, a nomadic scavenger. Now it forms itself into well-knit social groups, has begun to secrete a thin sweet lymph something like honey."

"What's this?" Coma asked, touching the screen.

"Diagram of a key gene in the operation." He traced a spray of arrows leading from a link in the chain. The arrows were labelled: LYMPH GLAND and subdivided SPHINCTER MUSCLES, EPITHELIUM, TEMPLATES.

"It's rather like the perforated sheet music of a player piano," Powers commented, "or a computer punch tape. Knock out one link with an X-ray beam, lose a characteristic, change the score."

Coma was peering through the window of the next cage and pulling an unpleasant face. Over her shoulder Powers saw she was watching an enormous spiderlike insect, as big as a hand, its dark hairy legs as thick as fingers. The compound eyes had been built up so that they resembled giant rubies.

"He looks unfriendly," she said. "What's that sort of rope ladder he's spinning?" As she moved a finger to her mouth the spider came to life, retreated into the cage, and began spewing out a complex skein of interlinked grey thread which it slung in long loops from the roof of the cage.

"A web," Powers told her. "Except that it consists of nervous tissue. The ladders form an external neural plexus, an inflatable brain as it were, that he can pump up to whatever size the situation calls for. A sensible arrangement, really, far better than our own."

Coma backed away. "Gruesome. I wouldn't like to go into his parlour."

"Oh, he's not as frightening as he looks. Those huge eyes staring at you are blind. Or, rather, their optical sensitivity has shifted down the band; the retinas will only register gamma radiation. Your wristwatch has luminous hands. When you moved it across the window he started thinking. World War IV should really bring him into his element."

They strolled back to Powers's desk. He put a coffee pan over a Bunsen and pushed a chair across to Coma. Then he opened the box, lifted out the armoured frog, and put it down on a sheet of blotting paper.

"Recognize him? Your old childhood friend, the common frog. He's built himself quite a solid little air-raid shelter." He carried the animal across to a sink, turned on the tap, and let the water play softly over its shell. Wiping his hands on his shirt, he came back to the desk.

Coma brushed her long hair off her forehead, watching him curiously.

"Well, what's the secret?"

Powers lit a cigarette. "There's no secret. Teratologists have been breeding monsters for years. Have you ever heard of the 'silent pair'?

She shook her head.

Powers stared moodily at the cigarette for a moment, riding the kick the first one of the day always gave him. "The so-called 'silent pair' is one of modern genetics' oldest problems, the apparently baffling mystery of the two inactive genes which occur in a small percentage of all living organisms, and appear to have no intelligible role in their structure or development. For a long while now biologists have been trying to activate them, but the difficulty is partly in identifying the silent genes in the fertilized germ cells of parents known to contain them, and partly in focusing a narrow enough X-ray beam which will do no damage to the remainder of the chromosome. However, after about ten years' work Dr. Whitby successfully developed a whole-body irradiation technique based on his observation of radiobiological damage at Eniwetok."

Powers paused for a moment. "He had noticed that there appeared to be more biological damage after the tests—that is, a greater transport of energy—than could be accounted for by direct radiation. What was happening was that the protein lattices in the genes were building up energy in the way that any vibrating membrane accumulates energy when it resonates—you remember the analogy of the bridge collapsing under the soldiers marching in step—and it occurred to him that if he could first identify the critical resonance frequency of the lattices in any particular silent gene he could radiate the entire living organism, and not simply its germ cells, with a low field that would act selectively on the silent gene and cause no damage to the remainder of the chromosomes, whose lattices would resonate critically only at other specific frequencies."

Powers gestured around the laboratory with his cigarette. "You see some of the fruits of this 'resonance transfer' technique around you."

Coma nodded. "They've had their silent genes activated?"

"Yes, all of them. These are only a few of the thousands of specimens who have passed through here, and as you've seen, the results are pretty dramatic."

He reached up and pulled across a section of the sun curtain. They were sitting just under the lip of the dome, and the mounting sunlight had begun to irritate him.

In the comparative darkness Coma noticed a stroboscope winking slowly in one of the tanks at the end of the bench behind her. She stood up and went over to it, examining a tall sunflower with a thickened stem and greatly enlarged receptacle. Packed around the flower, so that only its head protruded, was a chimney of grey-white stones, neatly cemented together and labelled:

CRETACEOUS CHALK: 60,000,000 YEARS

Beside it on the bench there were three other chimneys, these labelled DEVONIAN SANDSTONE: 290,000,000 YEARS, ASPHALT: 20 YEARS, POLYVINYLCHLORIDE: 6 MONTHS.

"Can you see those moist white discs on the sepals," Powers pointed out. "In some way they regulate the plant's metabolism. It literally *sees* time. The older the surrounding environment, the more sluggish its metabolism. With the asphalt chimney it will complete its annual cycle in a week, with the PVC one in a couple of hours."

"Sees time," Coma repeated, wonderingly. She looked up at Powers, chewing her lower lip reflectively. "It's fantastic. Are these the creatures of the future, Doctor?"

"I don't know," Powers admitted. "But if they are their world must be a monstrous surrealist one."

3

He went back to the desk, pulled two cups from a drawer, and poured out the coffee, switching off the Bunsen. "Some people have speculated that organisms possessing the silent pair of genes are the forerunners of a massive move up the evolutionary slope, that the silent genes are a sort of code, a divine message that we inferior organisms are carrying for our more highly developed descendants. It may well be true—perhaps we've broken the code too soon."

"Why do you say that?"

"Well, as Whitby's death indicates, the experiments in this laboratory have all come to a rather unhappy conclusion. Without exception the organisms we've irradiated have entered a final phase of totally disorganized growth, producing dozens of specialized sensory organs whose function we can't even guess. The results are catastrophic—the anemone will literally explode, the Drosophila cannibalize themselves, and so on. Whether the future implicit in these plants and animals is ever intended to take place, or whether we're merely extrapolating—I don't know. Sometimes I think, though, that the new sensory organs developed are parodies of their real intentions. The specimens you've seen today are all in an early stage of their secondary growth cycles. Later on they begin to look distinctly bizarre."

Coma nodded. "A zoo isn't complete without its keeper," she commented. "What about Man?"

Powers shrugged. "About one in every hundred thousand—the usual average—contain the silent pair. You might have them—or I. No one has volunteered yet to undergo the whole-body irradiation. Apart from the fact that it would be classified as suicide, if the experiments are any guide the experience would be savage and violent."

He sipped at the thin coffee, feeling tired and somehow bored. Recapitulating the laboratory's work had exhausted him.

The girl leaned forward. "You look awfully pale," she said solicitously. "Don't you sleep well?"

Powers managed a brief smile. "Too well," he admitted. "It's no longer a problem with me."

"I wish I could say that about Kaldren. I don't think he sleeps anywhere near enough. I hear him pacing around all night." She added: "Still, I suppose it's better than being a terminal. Tell me, Doctor, wouldn't it be worth trying this radiation technique on the sleepers at the Clinic? It might wake them up before the end. A few of them must possess the silent genes."

"They *all* do," Powers told her. "The two phenomena are very closely linked, as a matter of fact." He stopped, fatigue dulling his brain, and wondered whether to ask the girl to leave. Then he climbed off the desk and reached behind it, picked up a tape recorder.

Switching it on, he zeroed the tape and adjusted the speaker volume.

"Whitby and I often talked this over. Towards the end I took it all down. He was a great biologist, so let's hear it in his own words. It's absolutely the heart of the matter."

He flipped the tape on, adding: "I've played it over to myself a thousand times, so I'm afraid the quality is poor."

An older man's voice, sharp and slightly irritable, sounded out above a low buzz of distortion, but Coma could hear it clearly.

WHITBY: . . . for heaven's sake, Robert, look at those FAO statistics. Despite an annual increase of 5 percent in acreage sown over the past fifteen years, world wheat crops have continued to decline by a factor of about 2 percent. The same story repeats itself *ad nauseam*. Cereals and root crops, dairy yields, ruminant fertility—all are down. Couple these with a mass of parallel symptoms, anything you care to pick from altered migratory routes to longer hibernation periods, and the overall pattern is incontrovertible.

POWERS: Population figures for Europe and North America show no decline, though.

WHITBY: Of course not, as I keep pointing out. It will take a century for such a fractional drop in fertility to have an effect in areas where extensive birth control provides an artificial reservoir. One must look at the countries of the Far East, and particularly at those where infant mortality has remained at a steady level. The population of Sumatra, for example, has decline by over 15 percent in the last twenty years. A fabulous decline! Do you realize that only two or three decades ago the Neo-Malthusians were talking about a "world population explosion"? In fact, it's an implosion. Another factor is—

Here the tape had been cut and edited, and Whitby's voice, less querulous this time, picked up again.

. . . just as a matter of interest, tell me something: how long do you sleep each night?

POWERS: I don't know exactly; about eight hours, I suppose.

WHITBY: The proverbial eight hours. Ask anyone and they say automatically "eight hours." As a matter of fact you sleep about ten and a half hours, like the majority of people. I've timed you on a number of occasions. I myself sleep eleven. Yet thirty years ago people did indeed sleep eight hours, and a century before that they slept six or seven. In Vasari's *Lives* one reads of Michelangelo sleeping for only four or five hours, painting all day at the age of eighty and then working through the night over his anatomy table with a candle strapped to his forehead. Now he's regarded as a prodigy, but it was unremarkable then. How do you think the ancients, from Plato to Shakespeare, Aristotle to Aquinas, were able to cram so much work into their lives? Simply because they had an extra six or seven hours every day. Of course, a second disadvantage under which we labour is a lowered basal metabolic rate—another factor no one will explain.

POWERS: I suppose you could take the view that the lengthened sleep interval is a compensation device, a sort of mass neurotic attempt to escape from the terrifying pressures of urban life in the late twentieth century.

WHITBY: You could, but you'd be wrong. It's simply a matter of biochemistry. The ribonucleic acid templates which unravel the protein chains in all living organisms are wearing out, the dies inscribing the protoplasmic signature have become blunted. After all, they've been running now for over a thousand million years. It's time to retool. Just as an individual organism's life span is finite, or the life of a yeast colony or a given species, so the life of an entire biological kingdom is of fixed duration. It's always been assumed that the evolutionary slope reaches forever upwards, but in fact the peak has already been reached, and the pathway now leads downwards to the common biological grave. It's a despairing and at present unacceptable vision of the future, but it's the only one. Five thousand centuries from now our descendants, instead of being multibrained star men, will probably be naked prognathous idiots with hair on their foreheads, grunting their way through the remains of this Clinic like Neolithic men caught in a macabre inversion of time. Believe me, I pity them, as I pity myself. My total failure, my absolute lack of any moral or biological right to existence, is implicit in every cell of my body . . .

The tape ended, the spool ran free and stopped. Powers closed the machine, then massaged his face. Coma sat quietly, watching him and listening to the chimp playing with a box of puzzle dice.

"As far as Whitby could tell," Powers said, "the silent genes represent a last desperate effort of the biological kingdom to keep its head above the rising waters. Its total life period is determined by the amount of radiation emitted by the sun, and once this reaches a certain point the sure-death line has been passed and extinction is inevitable. To compensate for this, alarms have been built in which alter the form of the organism and adapt it to living in a hotter radiological climate. Soft-skinned organisms develop hard shells, these contain heavy metals as radiation screens. New organs of perception are developed too. According to Whitby, though, it's all wasted effort in the long run—but sometimes I wonder."

He smiled at Coma and shrugged. "Well, let's talk about something else. How long have you known Kaldren?"

"About three weeks. Feels like ten thousand years."

"How do you find him now? We've been rather out of touch lately."

Coma grinned. "I don't seem to see very much of him either. He makes me sleep all the time. Kaldren has many strange talents, but he lives just for himself. You mean a lot to him, Doctor. In fact, you're my one serious rival."

"I thought he couldn't stand the sight of me."

"Oh, that's just a sort of surface symptom. He really thinks of you continually. That's why we spend all our time following you around." She eyed Powers shrewdly. "I think he feels guilty about something."

"Guilty?" Powers exclaimed. "*He* does? I thought I was supposed to be the guilty one."

"Why?" she pressed. She hesitated, then said: "You carried out some experimental surgical technique on him, didn't you?"

"Yes," Powers admitted. "It wasn't altogether a success, like so much of what I seem to be involved with. If Kaldren feels guilty, I suppose it's because he feels he must take some of the responsibility."

He looked down at the girl, her intelligent eyes watching him closely. "For one or two reasons it may be necessary for you to know. You said Kaldren paced around all night and didn't get enough sleep. Actually he doesn't get any sleep at all."

The girl nodded. "You . . ." She made a snapping gesture with her fingers.

". . . narcotomized him," Powers completed. "Surgically speaking, it was a great success, one might well share a Nobel for it. Normally the hypothalamus regulates the period of sleep, raising the threshold of consciousness in order to relax the venous capillaries in the brain and drain them of accumulating toxins. However, by sealing off some of the control loops the subject is unable to receive the sleep cue, and the capillaries drain while he remains conscious. All he feels is a temporary lethargy, but this passes within three or four hours. Physically speaking, Kaldren has had another twenty years added to his life. But the psyche seems to need sleep for its own private reasons, and consequently Kaldren has periodic storms that tear him apart. The whole thing was a tragic blunder."

Coma frowned pensively. "I guessed as much. Your papers in the neurosurgery journals referred to the patient as K. A touch of pure Kafka that came all too true."

"I may leave here for good, Coma," Powers said. "Make sure that Kaldren goes to his clinics. Some of the deep scar tissue will need to be cleaned away."

"I'll try. Sometimes I feel I'm just another of his insane terminal documents."

"What are those?"

"Haven't you heard? Kaldren's collection of final statements about Homo sapiens. The complete works of Freud, Beethoven's blind quartets, transcripts of the Nuremberg trials, an automatic novel, and so on." She broke off. "What's that you're drawing?"

"Where?"

She pointed to the desk blotter, and Powers looked down and realized he had been unconsciously sketching an elaborate doodle, Whitby's four-armed sun. "It's nothing," he said. Somehow, though, it had a strangely compelling force.

Coma stood up to leave. "You must come and see us, Doctor. Kaldren has so much he wants to show you. He's just got hold of an old copy of the last signals sent back by the Apollo Seven twenty years ago when they reached the moon, and can't think about anything else. You remember the strange messages they recorded before they died, full of poetic ramblings about the white gardens. Now that I think about it they behaved rather like the plants in your zoo here."

She put her hands in her pockets, then pulled something out. "By the way, Kaldren asked me to give you this."

It was an old index card from the observatory library. In the centre had been typed the number:

$$96,688,365,498,720$$

"It's going to take a long time to reach zero at this rate," Powers remarked dryly. "I'll have quite a collection when we're finished."

After she had left he chucked the card into the waste bin and sat down at the desk, staring for an hour at the ideogram on the blotter.

. . .

Halfway back to his beach house the lake road forked to the left through a narrow saddle that ran between the hills to an abandoned Air Force weapons range on one of the remoter salt lakes. At the nearer end were a number of small bunkers and camera towers, one or two metal shacks, and a low-roofed storage hangar. The white hills encircled the whole area, shutting it off from the world outside, and Powers liked to wander on foot down the gunnery aisles that had been marked down the two-mile length of the lake towards the concrete sight screens at the far end. The abstract patterns made him feel like an ant on a bone-white chessboard, the rectangular screens at one end and the towers and bunkers at the other like opposing pieces.

His session with Coma had made Powers feel suddenly dissatisfied with the way he was spending his last months. *Goodbye, Eniwetok*, he had written, but in fact systematically forgetting everything was exactly the same as remembering it, a cataloguing in reverse, sorting out all the books in the mental library and putting them back in their right places upside down.

Powers climbed one of the camera towers, leaned on the rail, and looked out along the aisles towards the sight screens. Ricocheting shells and rockets had chipped away large pieces of the circular concrete bands that ringed the target bulls, but the outlines of the huge hundred-yard-wide discs, alternately painted blue and red, were still visible.

For half an hour he stared quietly at them, formless ideas shifting through his mind. Then, without thinking, he abruptly left the rail and climbed down the companionway. The storage hangar was fifty yards away. He walked quickly across to it, stepped into the cool shadows, and peered around the rusting electric trolleys and empty flare drums. At the far end, behind a pile of lumber and bales of wire, were a stack of unopened cement bags, a mound of dirty sand, and an old mixer.

Half an hour later he had backed the Buick into the hangar and hooked the cement mixer, charged with sand, cement, and water scavenged from the drums lying outside, onto the rear bumper, then loaded a dozen more bags into the car's trunk and rear seat. Finally he selected a few straight lengths of timber, jammed them through the window, and set off across the lake towards the central target bull.

For the next two hours he worked away steadily in the centre of the great blue disc, mixing up the cement by hand, carrying it across to the crude wooden forms he had lashed together from the timber, smoothing it down so that it formed a six-inch-high wall around the perimeter of the bull. He worked without pause, stirring the cement with a tyre lever, scooping it out with a hubcap prised off one of the wheels.

By the time he finished and drove off, leaving his equipment where it stood, he had completed a thirty-foot-long section of wall.

4

June 7: Conscious, for the first time, of the brevity of each day. As long as I was awake for over twelve hours I still orientated my time around the meridian, morning and afternoon set their old rhythms. Now, with just over eleven hours of consciousness left, they form a continuous interval, like a length of tape measure. I can see exactly how much is left on the spool and can do little to affect the rate at which it unwinds. Spend the time slowly packing away the library; the crates are too heavy to move and lie where they are filled.

Cell count down to 400,000.

Woke 8:10. To sleep 7:15. (Appear to have lost my watch without realizing it, had to drive into town to buy another.)

June 14: 9½ hours. Time races, flashing past like an expressway. However, the last week of a holiday always goes faster than the first. At the present rate there should be about 4–5 weeks left. This morning I tried to visualize what the last week or so—the final, 3, 2, 1, out—would be like, had a sudden chilling attack of pure fear, unlike anything I've ever felt before. Took me half an hour to steady myself for an intravenous.

Kaldren pursues me like my luminescent shadow, chalked up on the gateway "96,688,365,498,702." Should confuse the mailman.

Woke 9:05. To sleep 6:36.

June 19: 8¾ hours. Anderson rang up this morning. I nearly put the phone down on him, but managed to go through the pretence of making the final arrangements. He congratulated me on my stoicism, even used the word "heroic." Don't feel it. Despair erodes everything—courage, hope, self-discipline, all the better qualities. It's so damned difficult to sustain that impersonal attitude of passive acceptance implicit in the scientific tradition. I try to think of Galileo before the Inquisition, Freud surmounting the endless pain of his jaw cancer surgery.

Met Kaldren downtown, had a long discussion about the Apollo Seven. He's convinced that they refused to leave the moon deliberately, after the "reception party" waiting for them had put them in the cosmic picture. They were told by the mysterious emissaries from Orion that the exploration of deep space was pointless, that they were too late as the life of the universe is now virtually over!!! According to K. there are Air Force generals who take this nonsense seriously, but I suspect it's simply an obscure attempt on K.'s part to console me.

Must have the phone disconnected. Some contractor keeps calling me up about payment for fifty bags of cement he claims I collected ten days ago. Says he helped me load them onto a truck himself. I did drive Whitby's pickup into town but only to get some lead screening. What does he think I'd do with all that cement? Just the sort of irritating thing you don't expect to hang over your final exit. (Moral: Don't try too hard to forget Eniwetok.)

Woke 9:40. To sleep 4:15.

June 25: 7½ hours. Kaldren was snooping around the lab again today. Phoned me there, when I answered a recorded voice he'd rigged up rambled out a long string of numbers, like an insane super-Tim. These practical jokes of his get rather wearing. Fairly soon I'll have to go over and come to terms with him, much as I hate the prospect. Anyway, Miss Mars is a pleasure to look at.

One meal is enough now, topped up with a glucose shot. Sleep is still "black," completely unrefreshing. Last night I took a 16 mm film of the first three hours, screened it this morning at the lab. The first true horror movie, I looked like a half-animated corpse. Woke 10:25. To sleep 3:45.

July 3: 5¾ hours. Little done today. Deepening lethargy, dragged myself over to the lab, nearly left the road twice. Concentrated enough to feed the zoo and get the log up to date. Read through the operating manuals Whitby left for the last time, decided on a delivery rate of 40 roentgens/min., target distance of 350 cm. Everything is ready now.

Woke 11:05. To sleep 3:15.

Powers stretched, shifted his head slowly across the pillow, focusing on the shadows cast onto the ceiling by the blind. Then he looked down at his feet, saw Kaldren sitting on the end of the bed, watching him quietly.

"Hello, Doctor," he said, putting out his cigarette. "Late night? You look tired."

Powers heaved himself onto one elbow, glanced at his watch. It was just after eleven. For a moment his brain blurred, and he swung his legs around and sat on the edge of the bed, elbows on his knees, massaging some life into his face.

He noticed that the room was full of smoke. "What are you doing here?" he asked Kaldren.

"I came over to invite you to lunch." He indicated the bedside phone. "Your line was dead so I drove round. Hope you don't mind me climbing in. Rang the bell for about half an hour. I'm surprised you didn't hear it."

Powers nodded, then stood up and tried to smooth the creases out of his cotton slacks. He had gone to sleep without changing for over a week, and they were damp and stale.

As he started for the bathroom door Kaldren pointed to the camera tripod on the other side of the bed. "What's this? Going into the blue movie business, Doctor?"

Powers surveyed him dimly for a moment, glanced at the tripod without replying and then noticed his open diary on the bedside table. Wondering whether Kaldren had read the last entries, he went back

J. G. BALLARD

and picked it up, then stepped into the bathroom and closed the door behind him.

From the mirror cabinet he took out a syringe and an ampoule. After the shot he leaned against the door waiting for the stimulant to pick up.

Kaldren was in the lounge when he returned to him, reading the labels on the crates lying about in the centre of the floor.

"Okay, then," Powers told him, "I'll join you for lunch." He examined Kaldren carefully. He looked more subdued than usual, there was an air almost of deference about him.

"Good," Kaldren said. "By the way, are you leaving?"

"Does it matter?" Powers asked curtly. "I thought you were in Anderson's care?"

Kaldren shrugged. "Please yourself. Come round at about twelve," he suggested, adding pointedly: "That'll give you time to clean up and change. What's that all over your shirt? Looks like lime."

Powers peered down, brushed at the white streaks. After Kaldren had left he threw the clothes away, took a shower, and unpacked a clean suit from one of the trunks.

Until his liaison with Coma, Kaldren lived alone in the old abstract summerhouse on the north shore of the lake. This was a seven-storey folly originally built by an eccentric millionaire mathematician in the form of a spiralling concrete ribbon that wound around itself like an insane serpent, serving walls, floors, and ceilings. Only Kaldren had solved the building, a geometric model of $\sqrt{-1}$, and consequently he had been able to take it off the agents' hands at a comparatively low rent. In the evenings Powers had often watched him from the laboratory, striding restlessly from one level to the next, swinging through the labyrinth of inclines and terraces to the rooftop, where his lean angular figure stood out like a gallows against the sky, his lonely eyes sifting out radio lanes for the next day's trapping.

Powers noticed him there when he drove up at noon, poised on a ledge 150 feet above, head raised theatrically to the sky.

"Kaldren!" he shouted up suddenly into the silent air, half hoping he might be jolted into losing his footing.

Kaldren broke out of his reverie and glanced down into the court. Grinning obliquely, he waved his right arm in a slow semicircle.

"Come up," he called, then turned back to the sky.

Powers leaned against the car. Once, a few months previously, he had accepted the same invitation, stepped through the entrance and within three minutes lost himself helplessly in a second-floor cul-de-sac. Kaldren had taken half an hour to find him.

Powers waited while Kaldren swung down from his eyrie, vaulting through the wells and stairways, then rode up in the elevator with him to the penthouse suite.

They carried their cocktails through a wide glass-roofed studio, the huge white ribbon of concrete uncoiling around them like toothpaste squeezed from an enormous tube. On the staged levels running parallel and across them rested pieces of grey abstract furniture, giant photographs on angled screens, carefully labelled exhibits laid out on low tables, all dominated by twenty-foot-high black letters on the rear wall which spelt out the single vast word:

YOU

Kaldren pointed to it. "What you might call the supraliminal approach." He gestured Powers in conspiratorially, finishing his drink in a gulp. "This is *my* laboratory, Doctor," he said with a note of pride. "Much more significant than yours, believe me."

Powers smiled wryly to himself and examined the first exhibit, an old EEG tape traversed by a series of faded inky wriggles. It was labelled: EINSTEIN, A.; ALPHA WAVES, 1922.

He followed Kaldren around, sipping slowly at his drink, enjoying the brief feeling of alertness the amphetamine provided. Within two hours it would fade, leaving his brain feeling like a block of blotting paper.

Kaldren chattered away, explaining the significance of the so-called Terminal Documents. "They're end-prints, Powers, final statements, the products of total fragmentation. When I've got enough together I'll build a new world for myself out of them." He picked a thick paperbound volume off one of the tables, riffled through its pages. "Association tests of the Nuremberg Twelve. I have to include these . . ."

Powers strolled on absently without listening. Over in the corner were what appeared to be three ticker-tape machines, lengths of tape hanging from their mouths. He wondered whether Kaldren was misguided enough to be playing the stock market, which had been declining slowly for twenty years.

"Powers," he heard Kaldren say. "I was telling you about the Apollo Seven." He pointed to a collection of typewritten sheets tacked to a screen. "These are transcripts of their final signals radioed back from the recording monitors."

Powers examined the sheets cursorily, read a line at random.

". . . BLUE . . . PEOPLE . . . RECYCLE . . . ORION . . . TELEMETERS . . ."

Powers nodded noncommittally. "Interesting. What are the ticker tapes for over there?"

Kaldren grinned. "I've been waiting for months for you to ask me that. Have a look."

Powers went over and picked up one of the tapes. The machine was labelled: AURIGA 225-G. INTERVAL: 69 HOURS."

The tape read:

$$96,688,365,498,695$$
$$96,688,365,498,694$$
$$96,688,365,498,693$$
$$96,688,365,498,692$$

Powers dropped the tape. "Looks rather familiar. What does the sequence represent?"

Kaldren shrugged. "No one knows."

"What do you mean? It must replicate something."

"Yes, it does. A diminishing mathematical progression. A countdown, if you like."

Powers picked up the tape on the right, tabbed: ARIES 44R951. INTERVAL: 49 DAYS.

Here the sequence ran:

$$876,567,988,347,779,877,654,434$$
$$876,567,988,347,779,877,654,433$$
$$876,567,988,347,779,877,654,432$$

Powers looked round. "How long does it take each signal to come through?"

"Only a few seconds. They're tremendously compressed laterally, of course. A computer at the observatory breaks them down. They were first picked up at Jodrell Bank about twenty years ago. Nobody bothers to listen to them now."

Powers turned to the last tape.

6,554

6,553

6,552

6,551

"Nearing the end of its run," he commented. He glanced at the label on the hood, which read: UNIDENTIFIED RADIO SOURCE, CANES VENATICI. INTERVAL: 97 WEEKS."

He showed the tape to Kaldren. "Soon be over."

Kaldren shook his head. He lifted a heavy directory-sized volume off a table, cradled it in his hands. His face had suddenly become sombre and haunted. "I doubt it," he said. "Those are only the last four digits. The whole number contains over 50 million."

He handed the volume to Powers, who turned to the title page. "Master Sequence of Serial Signal received by Jodrell Bank Radio-Observatory, University of Manchester, England, 0012-59 hours, 21-5-72. Source: NGC 9743, Canes Venatici." He thumbed the thick stack of closely printed pages, millions of numerals, as Kaldren had said, running up and down across a thousand consecutive pages.

Powers shook his had, picked up the tape again, and stared at it thoughtfully.

"The computer only breaks down the last four digits," Kaldren explained. "The whole series comes over in each fifteen-second-long package, but it took IBM more than two years to unscramble one of them."

"Amazing," Powers commented. "But what is it?"

"A countdown, as you can see. NGC 9743, somewhere in Canes Venatici. The big spirals there are breaking up, and they're saying goodbye. God knows who they think we are but they're letting us know all the same, beaming it out on the hydrogen line for everyone in the universe to hear." He paused. "Some people have put other interpretations on them, but there's one piece of evidence that rules out everything else."

"Which is?"

Kaldren pointed to the last tape from Canes Venatici. "Simply that it's been estimated that by the time this series reaches zero the universe will have just ended."

Powers fingered the tape reflectively. "Thoughtful of them to let us know what the real time is," he remarked.

"I agree, it is," Kaldren said quietly. "Applying the inverse square law, that signal source is broadcasting at a strength of about three million megawatts raised to the hundredth power. About the size of the entire Local Group. Thoughtful is the word."

Suddenly he gripped Powers's arm, held it tightly, and peered into his eyes closely, his throat working with emotion.

"You're not alone, Powers, don't think you are. These are the voices of time, and they're all saying goodbye to you. Think of yourself in a wider context. Every particle in your body, every grain of sand, every galaxy carries the same signature. As you've just said, you know what the time is now, so what does the rest matter? There's no need to go on looking at the clock."

Powers took his hand, squeezed it firmly. "Thanks, Kaldren. I'm glad you understand." He walked over to the window, looked down across the white lake. The tension between himself and Kaldren had dissipated, he felt that all his obligations to him had at last been met. Now he wanted to leave as quickly as possible, forget him as he had forgotten the faces of the countless other patients whose exposed brains had passed between his fingers.

He went back to the ticker machines, tore the tapes from their slots, and stuffed them into his pockets. "I'll take these along to remind myself. Say goodbye to Coma for me, will you?"

He moved towards the door. When he reached it he looked back to see Kaldren standing in the shadow of the three giant letters on the far wall, his eyes staring listlessly at his feet.

As Powers drove away he noticed that Kaldren had gone up onto the roof, watched him in the driving mirror waving slowly until the car disappeared around a bend.

5

The outer circle was now almost complete. A narrow segment, an arc about ten feet long, was missing, but otherwise the low perimeter wall ran continuously six inches off the concrete floor around the outer lane of the target bull, enclosing the huge rebus within it. Three concentric circles, the largest a hundred yards in diameter, separated from each other by ten-foot intervals, formed the rim of the device, divided into four segments by the arms of an enormous cross radiating from its centre, where a small round platform had been built a foot above the ground.

Powers worked swiftly, pouring sand and cement into the mixer, tipping in water until a rough paste formed, then carried it across to the wooden forms and tamped the mixture down into the narrow channel.

Within ten minutes he had finished. He quickly dismantled the forms, before the cement had set, and slung the timbers into the back seat of the car. Dusting his hands on his trousers, he went over to the mixer and pushed it fifty yards away into the long shadow of the surrounding hills.

Without pausing to survey the gigantic cipher on which he had laboured patiently for so many afternoons, he climbed into the car and drove off on a wake of bone-white dust, splitting the pools of indigo shadow.

He reached the laboratory at three o'clock and jumped from the car as it lurched back on its brakes. Inside the entrance he first switched on the lights, then hurried round, pulling the sun curtains down and shackling them to the floor slots, effectively turning the dome into a steel tent.

In their tanks behind him the plants and animals stirred quietly, responding to the sudden flood of cold fluorescent light. Only the chimpanzee ignored him. It sat on the floor of its cage, neurotically jamming the puzzle dice into the polythene bucket, exploding in bursts of sudden rage when the pieces refused to fit.

Powers went over to it, noticing the shattered glass fibre reinforcing panels bursting from the dented helmet. Already the chimp's face and forehead were bleeding from self-inflicted blows. Powers picked up the remains of the geranium that had been hurled through the bars, attracted the chimp's attention with it, then tossed a black pellet he had taken from a capsule in the desk drawer. The chimp caught it with a quick flick of the wrist, for a few seconds juggled the pellet with a couple of dice as it concentrated on the puzzle, then pulled it out of the air and swallowed it in a gulp.

Without waiting, Powers slipped off his jacket and stepped towards the X-ray theatre. He pulled back the high sliding doors to reveal the long glassy metallic snout of the Maxitron, then started to stack the lead screening shields against the rear wall.

A few minutes later the generator hummed to life.

The anemone stirred. Basking in the warm subliminal sea of radiation rising around it, prompted by countless pelagic memories, it reached tentatively across the tank, groping blindly towards the dim uterine sun. Its tendrils flexed, the thousands of dormant neural cells in their tips regrouping and multiplying, each harnessing the unlocked energies of its nucleus. Chains forged themselves, lattices tiered upwards into multifaceted lenses, focused slowly on the vivid spectral outlines of the sounds dancing like phosphorescent waves around the darkened chamber of the dome.

Gradually an image formed, revealing an enormous black fountain that poured an endless stream of brilliant light over the circle of benches and tanks. Beside it a figure moved, adjusting the flow through its mouth. As it stepped across the floor its feet threw off vivid bursts of colour, its hands racing along the benches conjured up a dazzling chiaroscuro, balls of blue and violet light that exploded fleetingly in the darkess like miniature star-shells.

Photons murmured. Steadily, as it watched the glimmering screen of sounds around it, the anemone continued to expand. Its ganglia linked, heeding a new source of stimuli from the delicate diaphragms in the crown of its notochord. The silent outlines of the laboratory began to echo softly, waves of muted sound fell from the arc lights and echoed off the benches and furniture below. Etched in sound, their angular forms resonated with sharp persistent overtones. The plastic-ribbed chairs were a buzz of staccato discords, the square-sided desk a continuous double-featured tone.

Ignoring these sounds once they had been perceived, the anemone turned to the ceiling, which reverberated like a shield in the sounds pouring steadily from the fluorescent tubes. Streaming through a narrow skylight, its voice clear and strong, interweaved by numberless overtones, the sun sang . . .

It was a few minutes before dawn when Powers left the laboratory and stepped into his car. Behind him the great dome lay silently in the darkness, the thin shadows of the white moonlit hills falling across its surface. Powers freewheeled the car down the long curving drive to the lake road below, listening to the tyres cutting across the blue gravel, then let out the clutch and accelerated the engine.

As he drove along, the limestone hills half hidden in the darkness on his left, he gradually became aware that, although no longer looking at the hills, he was still in some oblique way conscious of their forms and outlines in the back of his mind. The sensation was undefined but nonetheless certain, a strange almost visual impression that emanated most strongly from the deep clefts and ravines dividing one cliff face from the next. For a few minutes Powers let it play upon him, without trying to identify it, a dozen strange images moving across his brain.

The road swung up around a group of chalets built onto the lake shore, taking the car right under the lee of the hills, and Powers suddenly felt the massive weight of the escarpment rising up into the dark sky like a cliff of luminous chalk, and realized the identity of the impression now registering powerfully within his mind. Not only could he see the escarpment, but he was aware of its enormous age, felt distinctly the countless millions of years since it had first reared out of the magma of the earth's crust. The ragged crests three hundred feet above him, the dark gulleys and fissures, the smooth boulders by the roadside at the foot of the cliff, all carried a distinct image of themselves across to him, a thousand voices that together told of the total time that had elapsed in the life of the escarpment, a psychic picture as defined and clear as the visual image brought to him by his eyes.

Involuntarily, Powers had slowed the car, and turning his eyes away from the hill he felt a second wave of time sweep across the first.

The image was broader but of shorter perspectives, radiating from the wide disc of the salt lake, breaking over the ancient limestone cliffs like shallow rollers dashing against a towering headland.

Closing his eyes, Powers lay back and steered the car along the interval between the two time fronts, feeling the images deepen and strengthen within his mind. The vast age of the landscape, the inaudible chorus of voices resonating from the lake and from the white hills, seemed to carry him back through time, down endless corridors to the first thresholds of the world.

He turned the car off the road along the track leading towards the target range. On either side of the culvert the cliff faces boomed and echoed with vast impenetrable time fields, like enormous opposed magnets. As he finally emerged between them onto the flat surface of the lake it seemed to Powers that he could feel the separate identity of each sand grain and salt crystal calling to him from the surrounding ring of hills.

He parked the car beside the mandala and walked slowly towards the outer concrete rim curving away into the shadows. Above him he could hear the stars, a million cosmic voices that crowded the sky from one horizon to the next, a true canopy of time. Like jostling radio beacons, their long aisles interlocking at countless angles, they plunged into the sky from the narrowest recesses of space. He saw the dim red disc of Sirius, heard its ancient voice, untold millions of years old, dwarfed by the huge spiral nebulae in Andromeda, a gigantic carousel of vanished universes, their voices almost as old as the cosmos itself. To Powers the sky seemed an endless babel, the time-song of a thousand galaxies overlaying each other in his mind. As he moved slowly towards the centre of the mandala he craned up at the glittering traverse of the Milky Way, searching the confusion of clamouring nebulae and constellations.

Stepping into the inner circle of the mandala, a few yards from the platform at its centre, he realized that the tumult was beginning to fade, and that a single stronger voice had emerged and was dominating the others. He climbed onto the platform, raised his eyes to the darkened sky, moving through the constellations to the island galaxies beyond them, hearing the thin archaic voices reaching to him across the millennia. In his pockets he felt the paper tapes, and turned to find the distant diadem of Canes Venatici, heard its great voice mounting in his mind.

Like an endless river, so broad that its banks were below the horizons, it flowed steadily towards him, a vast course of time that spread outwards to fill the sky and the universe, enveloping everything within them. Moving slowly, the forward direction of its majestic current almost imperceptible, Powers knew that its source was the source of the cosmos itself. As it passed him, he felt its massive magnetic pull, let himself be drawn into it, borne gently on its powerful back. Quietly it carried him away, and he rotated slowly, facing the direction of the tide. Around him the outlines of the hills and the lake had faded, but the image of the mandala, like a cosmic clock, remained fixed before his eyes, illuminating the broad surface of the stream. Watching it constantly, he felt his body gradually dissolving, its physical dimensions melting into the vast continuum of the current, which bore him out into the centre of the great channel, sweeping him onward, beyond hope but at last at rest, down the broadening reaches of the river of eternity.

As the shadows faded, retreating into the hill slopes, Kaldren stepped out of his car, walked hesitantly towards the concrete rim of the outer circle. Fifty yards away, at the centre, Coma knelt beside Powers's body, her small hands pressed to his dead face. A gust of wind stirred the sand, dislodging a strip of tape that drifted towards Kaldren's feet. He bent down and picked it up, then rolled it carefully in his hands and slipped into his pocket. The dawn air was cold, and he turned up the collar of his jacket, watching Coma impassively.

"It's six o'clock," he told her after a few minutes. "I'll go and get the police. You stay with him." He paused and then added: "Don't let them break the clock."

Coma turned and looked at him. "Aren't you coming back?"

"I don't know." Nodding to her, Kaldren swung on his heel and went over to the car.

He reached the lake road, five minutes later parked the car in the drive outside Whitby's laboratory.

The dome was in darkness, all its windows shuttered, but the generator still hummed in the X-ray theatre. Kaldren stepped through the entrance and switched on the lights. In the theatre he touched the grilles of the generator, felt the warm cylinder of the beryllium end-window. The circular target table was revolving slowly, its setting at 1 rpm, a steel restraining chair shackled to it hastily. Grouped in a semicircle a few feet away were most of the tanks and cages, piled on top of each other haphazardly. In one of them an enormous squidlike plant had almost managed to climb from its vivarium. Its long translucent tendrils clung to the edges of the tank, but its body had burst into a jellified pool of globular mucilage. In another an enormous spider had trapped itself in its own web and hung helplessly in the centre of a huge three-dimensional maze of phosphorescing thread, twitching spasmodically.

All the experimental plants and animals had died. The chimp lay on its back among the remains of the hutch, the helmet forward over its eyes. Kaldren watched it for a moment, then sat down on the desk and picked up the phone.

While he dialled the number he noticed a film reel lying on the blotter. For a moment he stared at the label, then slid the reel into his pocket beside the tape.

After he had spoken to the police he turned off the lights, went out to the car, and drove off slowly down the drive.

When he reached the summerhouse the early sunlight was breaking across the ribbonlike balconies and terraces. He took the lift to the penthouse, made his way through into the museum. One by one he opened the shutters and let the sunlight play over the exhibits. Then he pulled a chair over to a side window, sat back, and stared up at the light pouring through into the room.

Two or three hours later he heard Coma outside, calling up to him. After half an hour she went away, but a little later a second voice appeared and shouted up at Kaldren. He left his chair and closed all the shutters overlooking the front courtyard, and eventually he was left undisturbed.

Kaldren returned to his seat and lay back quietly, his eyes gazing across the lines of exhibits. Half asleep, periodically he leaned up and adjusted the flow of light through the shutter, thinking to himself, as he would do through the coming months, of Powers and his strange mandala, and of the seven and their journey to the white gardens of the moon, and the blue people who had come from Orion and spoken in poetry to them of ancient beautiful worlds beneath golden suns in the island galaxies, vanished forever now in the myriad deaths of the cosmos.

---

1. Why does Powers build the mandala?

2. Why does Whitby tell Powers, "My total failure, my absolute lack of any moral or biological right to existence, is implicit in every cell of my body"?

3. Why does Powers irradiate all the specimens in the laboratory before he dies?

4. Why does the story end with Kaldren alone in Powers's laboratory? Are we meant to think that the human race is doomed, despite any individual's actions?

ANNE MCCAFFREY (1926–) was born in Cambridge, Massachusetts; she immigrated to Ireland in 1970 and has lived there since. The author of the multiple-award-winning Dragonriders of Pern series, McCaffrey is well known in the science fiction community as the "Dragon Lady." In 1968 she became the first female writer to achieve both the Hugo and Nebula awards, for the novellas *Weyr Search* and *Dragonrider*, respectively. Both novellas were later incorporated into *Dragonflight* (1968), the first in the Dragonriders series. Though some critics have dubbed McCaffrey a "science fantasy" writer—planet Pern is notable for its flying dragons and a semifeudal society—her works are grounded in scientific principles. She was named the 2005 Grand Master by Science Fiction and Fantasy Writers of America, and was inducted into the Science Fiction Hall of Fame in 2006. McCaffrey has also written romance novels and young adult fiction.

The Ship Who Sang

She was born a thing and as such would be condemned if she failed to pass the encephalograph test required of all newborn babies. There was always the possibility that though the limbs were twisted, the mind was not, that though the ears would hear only dimly, the eyes see vaguely, the mind behind them was receptive and alert.

The electroencephalogram was entirely favorable, unexpectedly so, and the news was brought to the waiting, grieving parents. There was the final, harsh decision: to give their child euthanasia or permit it to become an encapsulated "brain," a guiding mechanism in any one of a number of curious professions. As such, their offspring would suffer no pain, live a comfortable existence in a metal shell for several centuries, performing unusual service to Central Worlds.

She lived and was given a name, Helva. For her first three vegetable months she waved her crabbed claws, kicked weakly with her clubbed feet and enjoyed the usual routine of the infant. She was not alone for there were three other such children in the big city's special nursery. Soon they all were removed to Central Laboratory School where their delicate transformation began.

One of the babies died in the initial transferral but of Helva's "class," seventeen thrived in the metal shells. Instead of kicking feet, Helva's neural responses started her wheels; instead of grabbing with hands, she manipulated mechanical extensions. As she matured, more and more neural synapses would be adjusted to operate other mechanisms that went into the maintenance and running of a space ship. For Helva was destined to be the "brain" half of a scout ship, partnered with a man or a woman, whichever she chose, as the mobile half. She would be among the elite of her kind. Her initial intelligence tests registered above normal and her adaptation index was unusually high. As long as her development within her shell lived up to expectations, and there were no side effects from the pituitary tinkering, Helva would live a rewarding, rich, and unusual life, a far cry from what she would have faced as an ordinary, "normal" being.

However, no diagram of her brain patterns, no early IQ tests recorded certain essential facts about Helva that Central must eventually learn. They would have to bide their official time and see, trusting that the massive doses of shell psychology would suffice her, too, as the necessary bulwark against her unusual confinement and the pressures of her profession. A ship run by a human brain could not run rogue or insane with the power and resources Central had to build into their scout ships. Brain ships were, of course, long past the experimental stages. Most babes survived the techniques of pituitary manipulation that kept their bodies small, eliminating the necessity of transfers from smaller to larger shells. And very, very few were lost when the final connection was made to the control panels of ship or industrial combine. Shell people resembled mature dwarfs in size whatever their natal deformities were, but the well-oriented brain would not have changed places with the most perfect body in the universe.

So, for happy years, Helva scooted around in her shell with her classmates, playing such games as Stall, Power-Seek, studying her lessons in trajectory, propulsion techniques, computation, logistics, mental hygiene, basic alien psychology, philology, space history, law, traffic, codes: all the et ceteras that eventually became compounded into a reasoning, logical, informed citizen. Not so obvious to her, but of more importance to her teachers, Helva ingested the precepts of her conditioning as easily as she absorbed her nutrient fluid. She would one day be grateful to the patient drone of the subconscious-level instruction.

Helva's civilization was not without busy, do-good associations, exploring possible inhumanities to terrestrial as well as extraterrestrial citizens. One such group got all incensed over shelled "children" when Helva was just turning fourteen. When they were forced to, Central Worlds shrugged its shoulders, arranged a tour of the Laboratory Schools and set the tour off to a big start by showing the members' case histories, complete with photographs. Very few committees ever looked past the first few photos. Most of their original objections about "shells" were overriden by the relief that these hideous (to them) bodies *were* mercifully concealed.

Helva's class was doing Fine Arts, a selective subject in her crowded program. She had activated one of her microscopic tools which she would later use for minute repairs to various parts of her control panel. Her subject was large—a copy of *The Last Supper*—and her canvas, small—the head of a tiny screw. She had tuned her sight to the proper degree. As she worked she absentmindedly crooned, producing a curious sound. Shell people used their own vocal chords and diaphragms but sound issued through microphones rather than mouths. Helva's hum then had a curious vibrancy, a warm, dulcet quality even in its aimless chromatic wanderings.

"Why, what a lovely voice you have," said one of the female visitors.

Helva "looked" up and caught a fascinating panorama of regular, dirty craters on a flaky pink surface. Her hum became a gurgle of surprise. She instinctively regulated her "sight" until the skin lost its cratered look and the pores assumed normal proportions.

"Yes, we have quite a few years of voice training, madam," remarked Helva calmly. "Vocal peculiarities often become excessively irritating during prolonged intrastellar distances and must be eliminated. I enjoyed my lessons."

Although this was the first time that Helva had seen unshelled people, she took this experience calmly. Any other reaction would have been reported instantly.

"I meant that you have a nice singing voice . . . dear," the lady ammended.

"Thank you. Would you like to see my work?" Helva asked, politely. She instinctively sheered away from personal discussions but she filed the comment away for further meditation.

"Work?" asked the lady.

"I am currently reproducing *The Last Supper* on the head of a screw."

"O, I say," the lady twittered.

Helva turned her vision back to magnification and surveyed her copy critically.

"Of course, some of my color values do not match the old master's and the perspective is faulty, but I believe it to be a fair copy."

The lady's eyes, unmagnified, bugged out.

"Oh, I forget," and Helva's voice was really contrite. If she could have blushed, she would have. "You people don't have adjustable vision."

The monitor of this discourse grinned with pride and amusement as Helva's tone indicated pity for the unfortunate.

"Here, this will help," suggested Helva, substituting a magnifying device in one extension and holding it over the picture.

In a kind of shock, the ladies and gentlemen of the committee bent to observe the incredibly copied and brilliantly executed *Last Supper* on the head of a screw.

"Well," remarked one gentleman who had been forced to accompany his wife, "the good Lord can eat where angels fear to tread."

"Are you referring, sir," asked Helva politely, "to the Dark Age discussions of the number of angels who could stand on the head of a pin?"

"I had that in mind."

"If you substitute 'atom' for 'angel,' the problem is not insoluble, given the metallic content of the pin in question."

"Which you are programmed to compute?"

"Of course."

"Did they remember to program a sense of humor, as well, young lady?"

"We are directed to develop a sense of proportion, sir, which contributes the same effect."

The good man chortled appreciatively and decided the trip was worth his time.

If the investigation committee spent months digesting the thoughtful food served them at the Laboratory School, they left Helva with a morsel as well.

"Singing" as applicable to herself required research. She had, of course, been exposed to and enjoyed a music appreciation course which had included the better known classical works such as *Tristan und Isolde*, *Candide*, *Oklahoma*, *Nozze di Figaro*, the atomic age singers, Eileen Farrell, Elvis Presley, and Geraldine Todd, as well as the curious rhythmic progressions of the Venusians, Capellan visual chromatics, and the sonic concerti of the Altairians. But "singing" for any shell person posed considerable technical difficulties to be overcome. Shell people were schooled to examine every aspect of a problem or situation before making a prognosis. Balanced properly between optimism and practicality, the nondefeatist attitude of the shell people led them to extricate themselves, their ships and personnel, from bizarre situations. Therefore to Helva, the problem that she couldn't open her mouth to sing, among other restrictions, did not bother her. She would work out a method, bypassing her limitations, whereby she could sing.

She approached the problem by investigating the methods of sound reproduction through the centuries, human and instrumental. Her own sound production equipment was essentially more instrumental than vocal. Breath control and the proper enunciation of vowel sounds within the oral cavity appeared to require the most development and practice. Shell people did not, strictly speaking, breathe. For their purposes, oxygen and other gases were not drawn from the surrounding atmosphere through the medium of lungs but sustained artificially by solution in their shells. After experimentation, Helva discovered that she could manipulate her diaphragmic unit to sustain tone. By relaxing the throat muscles and expanding the oral cavity well into the frontal sinuses, she could direct the vowel sounds into the most felicitous position for proper reproduction through her throat microphone. She compared the results with tape recordings of modern singers and was not unpleased although her own tapes had a peculiar quality about them, not at all unharmonious, merely unique. Acquiring a repertoire from the Laboratory library was no problem to one trained to perfect recall. She found herself able to sing any role and any song which struck her fancy. It would not have occurred to her that it was curious for a female to sing bass, baritone, tenor, mezzo, soprano, and coloratura as she pleased. It was, to Helva, only a matter of the correct reproduction and diaphragmic control required by the music attempted.

If the authorities remarked on her curious avocation they did so among themselves. Shell people were encouraged to develop a hobby so long as they maintained proficiency in their technical work.

On the anniversary of her sixteenth year in her shell, Helva was unconditionally graduated and installed in her ship, the XH-834. Her permanent titanium shell was recessed behind an even more indestructible barrier in the central shaft of the scout ship. The neural, audio, visual, and sensory connections were made and sealed. Her extendibles were diverted, connected, or augmented and the final, delicate-beyond-description brain taps were completed while Helva remained anesthetically unaware of the proceedings. When she woke, she *was* the ship. Her brain and intelligence controlled every function from navigation to such loading as a scout ship of her class needed. She could take care of herself and her ambulatory half, in any situation already recorded in the annals of Central Worlds and any situation its most fertile minds could imagine.

Her first actual flight, for she and her kind had made mock flights on dummy panels since she was eight, showed her complete mastery of the techniques of her profession. She was ready for her great adventures and the arrival of her mobile partner.

There were nine qualified scouts sitting around collecting base pay the day Helva was commissioned. There were several missions which demanded instant attention but Helva had been of interest to several department heads in Central for some time and each man was determined to have her assigned to *his* section. Consequently no one had remembered to introduce Helva to the prospective partners. The ship always chose its own partner. Had there been another "brain" ship at the Base at the moment, Helva would have been guided to make the first move. As it was, while Central wrangled among itself, Robert Tanner sneaked out of the pilots' barracks, out to the field, and over to Helva's slim metal hull.

"Hello, anyone at home?" Tanner wisecracked.

"Of course," replied Helva logically, activating her outside scanners. "Are you my partner?" she asked hopefully, as she recognized the Scout Service uniform.

"All you have to do is ask," he retorted hopefully.

"No one has come. I thought perhaps there were no partners available and I've had no directives from Central."

Even to herself Helva sounded a little self-pitying but the truth was she was lonely, sitting on the darkened field. Always she had had the company of other shells and more recently, technicians by the score. The sudden solitude had lost its momentary charm and become oppressive.

"No directives from Central is scarcely a cause for regret, but there happen to be eight other guys biting their fingernails to the quick just waiting for an invitation to board you, you beautiful thing."

Tanner was inside the central cabin as he said this, running appreciative fingers over her panel, the scout's gravity couch, poking his head into the cabins, the galley, the head, the pressured-storage compartments.

"Now, if you want to give Central a shove and do *us* a favor all in one, call up the Barracks and let's have a ship-warming partner-picking party. Hmmmm?"

Helva chuckled to herself. He was so completely different from the occasional visitors or the various Laboratory technicians she had encountered. He was so gay, so assured, and she was delighted by his suggestion of a partner-picking party. Certainly it was not against anything in her understanding of regulations.

"Cencom, this is XH-834. Connect me with Pilot Barracks."

"Visual?"

"Please."

A picture of lounging men in various attitudes of boredom came on her screen.

"This is XH-834. Would the unassigned scouts do me the favor of coming aboard?"

Eight figures galvanized into action, grabbing pieces of wearing apparel, disengaging tape mechanisms, disentangling themselves from bedsheets and towels.

Helva dissolved the connection while Tanner chuckled gleefully and settled down to await their arrival.

Helva was engulfed in an unshell-like flurry of anticipation. No actress on her opening night could have been more apprehensive, fearful, or breathless. Unlike the actress, she could throw no hysterics, china objets d'art or greasepaint to relieve her tension. She could, of course, check her stores for edibles and drinks, which she did, serving Tanner from the virgin selection of her commissary.

Scouts were colloquially known as "brawns" as opposed to their ship "brains." They had to pass as rigorous a training program as the brains and only the top one percent of each contributory world's highest scholars were admitted to Central Worlds Scout Training Program. Consequently the eight young men who came pounding up the gantry into Helva's hospitable lock were unusually fine-looking, intelligent, well-coordinated and adjusted young men, looking forward to a slightly drunken evening, Helva permitting, and all quite willing to do each other dirt to get possession of her.

Such a human invasion left Helva mentally breathless, a luxury she thoroughly enjoyed for the brief time she felt she should permit it. She sorted out the young men. Tanner's opportunism amused but did not specifically attract her; the blond Nordsen seemed too simple; dark-haired Al-atpay had a kind of obstinacy with which she felt no compassion; Mir-Ahnin's bitterness hinted an inner darkness she did not wish to lighten although he made the biggest outward play for her attention. Hers was a curious courtship—this would be only the first of several marriages for her, for brawns retired after seventy five years of service, or earlier if they were unlucky. Brains, their bodies safe from any deterioration, served two hundred years, and were then permitted to decide for themselves if they wished to continue. Helva had actually spoken to one shell person three hundred and twenty-two years old. She had been so awed by the contact she hadn't presumed to ask the personal questions she had wanted to.

Her choice did not stand out from the others until Tanner started to sing a scout ditty, recounting the misadventures of the bold, dense, painfully inept Billy Brawn. An attempt at harmony resulted in cacophony and Tanner wagged his arms wildly for silence.

"What we need is a roaring good lead tenor. Jennan, besides palming aces, what do you sing?"

"Sharp," Jennan replied with easy good humor.

"If a tenor is absolutely necessary, I'll attempt it," Helva volunteered.

"My good *woman*," Tanner protested.

"Sound your A," laughed Jennan.

Into the stunned silence that followed the rich, clear, high A, Jennan remarked quietly, "Such an A, Caruso would have given the rest of his notes to sing."

It did not take them long to discover her full range.

"All Tanner asked for was one roaring good lead tenor," Jennan complained jokingly, "and our sweet mistress supplied us an entire repertory company. The boy who gets this ship will go far, far, far."

"To the Horsehead Nebulae?" asked Nordsen, quoting an old Central saw.

"To the Horsehead Nebulae and back, we shall make beautiful music," countered Helva, chuckling.

"Together," Jennan amended. "Only you'd better make the music and with my voice, I'd better listen."

"I rather imagined it would be I who listened," suggested Helva.

Jennan executed a stately bow with an intricate flourish of his crush-brimmed hat. He directed his bow toward the central control pillar where Helva *was*. Her own personal preference crystallized at that precise moment and for that particular reason: Jennan, alone of the men, had addressed his remarks directly at her physical presence, regardless of the fact that he knew she could pick up his image wherever he was in the ship and regardless of the fact that her body was behind massive metal walls. Throughout their partnership, Jennan never failed to turn his head in her direction no matter where he was in relation to her. In response to this personalization, Helva at that moment and from then on always spoke to Jennan only through her central mike, even though that was not always the most efficient method.

Helva didn't know that she fell in love with Jennan that evening. As she had never been exposed to love or affection, only the drier cousins, respect and admiration, she could scarcely have recognized her reaction to the warmth of his personality and consideration. As a shell person, she considered herself remote from emotions largely connected with physical desires.

"Well, Helva, it's been swell meeting you," said Tanner suddenly, as she and Jennan were arguing about the Baroque quality of "Come All Ye Sons of Art." "See you in space sometime, you lucky dog, Jennan. Thanks for the party, Helva."

"You don't have to go so soon?" pleaded Helva, realizing belatedly that she and Jennan had been excluding the others.

"Best man won," Tanner said, wryly. "Guess I'd better go get a tape on love ditties. May need 'em for the next ship, if there're any more at home like you."

Helva and Jennan watched them leave, both a little confused.

"Perhaps Tanner's jumping to conclusions?" Jennan asked.

Helva regarded him as he slouched against the console, facing her shell directly. His arms were crossed on his chest and the glass he held had been empty for some time. He was handsome, they all were; but his watchful eyes were unwary, his mouth assumed a smile easily, his voice (to which Helva was particularly drawn) was resonant, deep, and without unpleasant overtones or accent.

"Sleep on it, Helva. Call me in the morning if it's your op."

She called him at breakfast, after she had checked her choice through Central. Jennan moved his things aboard, received their joint commission, had his personality and experience file locked into her reviewer, gave her the coordinates of their first mission and the XH-834 officially became the JH-834.

Their first mission was a dull but necessary crash priority (Medical got Helva), rushing a vaccine to a distant system plagued with a virulent spore disease. They had only to get to Spica as fast as possible.

After the initial, thrilling forward surge of her maximum speed, Helva realized her muscles were to be given less of a workout than her brawn on this tedious mission. But they did have plenty of time for exploring each other's personalities. Jennan, of course, knew what Helva was capable of as a ship and partner, just as she knew what she could expect from him. But these were only facts and Helva looked forward eagerly to learning that human side of her partner which could not be reduced to a series of symbols. Nor could the give and take of two personalities be learned from a book. It had to be experienced.

"My father was a scout, too, or is that programmed?" began Jennan their third day out.

"Naturally."

"Unfair, you know. You've got all my family history and I don't know one blamed thing about yours."

"I've never known either," Helva said. "Until I read yours, it hadn't occurred to me I must have one, too, someplace in Central's files."

Jennan snorted. "Shell psychology!"

Helva laughed. "Yes, and I'm even programmed against curiosity about it. You'd better be, too."

Jennan ordered a drink, slouched into the gravity couch opposite her, put his feet on the bumpers, turning himself idly from side to side on the gimbals.

"Helva—a made-up name . . ."

"With a Scandinavian sound."

"You aren't blond," Jennan said positively.

"Well, then, there're dark Swedes."

"And blonde Turks and this one's harem is limited to one."

"Your woman in purdah, yes, but you can comb the pleasure houses—" Helva found herself aghast at the edge to her carefully trained voice.

"You know," Jennan interrupted her, deep in some thought of his own, "my father gave me the impression he was a lot more married to his ship, the Silvia, than to my mother. I know I used to think Silvia was my grandmother. She was a low number so she must have been a great-great-grandmother at least. I used to talk to her for hours."

"Her registry?" asked Helva, unwitting of the jealousy for everyone and anyone who had shared his hours.

"422. I think she's TS now. I ran into Tom Burgess once."

Jennan's father had died of a planetary disease, the vaccine for which his ship had used up in curing the local citizens.

"Tom said she'd got mighty tough and salty. You lose your sweetness and I'll come back and haunt you, girl," Jennan threatened.

Helva laughed. He startled her by stamping up to the column panel, touching it with light, tender fingers.

"I *wonder* what you look like," he said softly, wistfully.

Helva had been briefed about this natural curiosity of scouts. She didn't know anything about herself and neither of them ever would or could.

"Pick any form, shape, and shade and I'll be yours obliging," she countered as training suggested.

"Iron Maiden, I fancy blonds with long tresses," and Jennan pantomined Lady Godiva–like tresses. "Since you're immolated in titanium, I'll call you Brunehilda, my dear," and he made his bow.

With a chortle, Helva launched into the appropriate aria just as Spica made contact.

"What'n'ell's that yelling about? Who are you? And unless you're Central Worlds Medical go away. We've got a plague with no visiting privileges."

"My ship is singing, we're the JH-834 of Worlds and we've got your vaccine. What are our landing coordinates?"

"Your *ship* is singing?"

"The greatest S.A.T.B. in organized space. Any request?"

The JH-834 delivered the vaccine but no more arias and received immediate orders to proceed to Leviticus IV. By the time they got there, Jennan found a reputation awaiting him and was forced to defend the 834's virgin honor.

"I'll stop singing," murmured Helva contritely as she ordered up poultices for this third black eye in a week.

"You will not," Jennan said through gritted teeth. "If I have to black eyes from here to the Horsehead to keep the snicker out of the title, we'll be the ship who sings."

After the "ship who sings" tangled with a minor but vicious narcotic ring in the Lesser Magallenics, the title became definitely respectful. Central was aware of each episode and punched out a "special interest" key on JH-834's file. A first-rate team was shaking down well.

Jennan and Helva considered themselves a first-rate team, too, after their tidy arrest.

"Of all the vices in the universe, I *hate* drug addiction," Jennan remarked as they headed back to Central Base. "People can go to hell quick enough without that kind of help."

"Is that why you volunteered for Scout Service? To redirect traffic?"

"I'll bet my official answer's on your review."

"In far too flowery wording. 'Carrying on the traditions of my family which has been proud of four generations in Service' if I may quote you your own words."

Jennan groaned. "I was *very* young when I wrote that and I certainly hadn't been through Final Training and once I was in Final Training, my pride wouldn't let me fail. . . .

"As I mentioned, I used to visit Dad on board the Silvia and I've a very good idea she might have had her eye on me as a replacement for my father because I had had massive doses of scout-oriented propaganda. It took. From the time I was seven, I was going to be a scout or else." He shrugged as if deprecating a youthful determination that had taken a great deal of mature application to bring to fruition.

"Ah, so? Scout Sahir Silan on the JS-422 penetrating into the Horsehead Nebulae?"

Jennan chose to ignore her sarcasm. "With *you*, I may even get that far but even with Silvia's nudging *I* never daydreamed myself *that* kind of glory in my wildest flights of fancy. I'll leave the whoppers to your agile brain henceforth. I have in mind a smaller contribution to Space History."

"So modest?"

"No. Practical. We also serve, et cetera." He placed a dramatic hand on his heart.

"Glory hound!" scoffed Helva.

"Look who's talking, my Nebulae-bound friend. At least I'm not greedy. There'll only be one hero like my dad at Parsaea, but I *would* like to be remembered for some kudo. Everyone does. Why else do or die?"

"Your father died on his way back from Parsaea, if I may point out a few cogent facts. So he could never have known he was a hero for damming the flood with his ship. Which kept Parsaean colony from being abandoned. Which gave them a chance to discover the antiparalytic qualities of Parsaea. Which *he* never knew."

"*I* know," said Jennan softly.

Helva was immediately sorry for the tone of her rebuttal. She knew very well how deep Jennan's attachment to his father had been. On his review a note was made that he had rationalized his father's loss with the unexpected and welcome outcome of the Affair at Parsaea.

"Facts are not human, Helva. My father was and so am I. And *basically*, so are you. Check over your dial, 834. Amid all the wires attached to you is a heart, an underdeveloped human heart. Obviously!"

"I apologize, Jennan," she said contritely.

Jennan hesitated a moment, threw out his hands in acceptance, and then tapped her shell affectionately.

"If they ever take us off the milk runs, we'll make a stab at the Nebulae, huh?"

As so frequently happened in the Scout Service, within the next hour they had orders to change course, not to the Nebulae, but to a recently colonized system with two habitable planets, one tropical, one glacial. The sun, named Ravel, had become unstable; the spectrum was that of a rapidly expanding shell, with absorption lines rapidly displacing toward violet. The augmented heat of the primary had already forced evacuation of the nearer world, Daphnis. The pattern of spectral emissions gave indication that the sun would sear Chloe as well. All ships in the vicinity were to report to Disaster Headquarters on Chloe to effect removal of the remaining colonists.

The JH-834 obediently presented itself and was sent to outlying areas on Chloe to pick up scattered settlers who did not appear to appreciate the urgency of the situation. Chloe, indeed, was enjoying the first temperatures above freezing since it had been flung out of its parent. Since many of the colonists were religious fanatics who had settled on rigorous Chloe to fit themselves for a life of pious reflection, Chloe's abrupt thaw was attributed to sources other than a rampaging sun.

Jennan had to spend so much time countering specious arguments that he and Helva were behind schedule on their way to the fourth and last settlement. Helva jumped over the high range of jagged peaks that surrounded and sheltered the valley from the former raging snows as well as the present heat. The violent sun with its flaring corona was just beginning to brighten the deep valley.

"They'd better grab their toothbrushes and hop aboard," Helva commented. "HQ says speed it up."

"All women," remarked Jeanan in surprise as he walked down to meet them. "Unless the men on Chloe wear furred skirts."

"Charm 'em but pare the routine to the bare essentials. And turn on your two-way private."

Jennan advanced smiling, but his explanation was met with absolute incredulity and considerable doubt as to his authenticity. He groaned inwardly as the matriarch paraphrased previous explanations of the warming sun.

"Revered mother, there's been an overload on that prayer circuit and the sun is blowing itself up in one obliging burst. I'm here to take you to the spaceport at Rosary—"

"That Sodom?" The worthy woman glowered and shuddered disdainfully at his suggestion. "We thank you for your warning but we have no wish to leave our cloister for the rude world. We must go about our morning meditation which has been interrupted—"

"It'll be permanently interrupted when that sun starts broiling. You must come now," Jennan said firmly.

"Madame," said Helva, realizing that perhaps a female voice might carry more weight in this instance than Jennan's very masculine charm.

"Who spoke?" cried the nun, startled by the bodiless voice.

"I, Helva, the ship. Under my protection you and your sisters-in-faith may enter safely and be unprofaned by association with a male. I will guard you and take you safely to a place prepared for you."

The matriarch peered cautiously into the ship's open port.

"Since only Central Worlds is permitted the use of such ships, I acknowledge that you are not trifling with us, young man. However, we are in no danger here."

"The temperature at Rosary is now 99 degrees," said Helva. "As soon as the sun's rays penetrate directly into this valley, it will also be 99 degrees, and it is due to climb to approximately 180 degrees today. I notice your buildings are made of wood with moss chinking. Dry moss. It should fire around noontime."

The sunlight was beginning to slant into the valley through the peaks and the fierce rays warmed the restless group behind the matriarch. Several opened the throats of their furry parkas.

"Jennan," said Helva privately to him, "our time is very short."

"I can't leave them, Helva. Some of those girls are barely out of their teens."

"Pretty, too. No wonder the matriarch doesn't want to get in."

"Helva."

"It will be the Lord's will," said the matriarch stoutly and turned her back squarely on rescue.

"To burn to death?" shouted Jennan as she threaded her way through her murmuring disciples.

"They want to be martyrs? Their opt, Jennan," said Helva dispassionately. "*We* must leave and that is no longer a matter of option."

"How can I leave, Helva?"

"Parsaea?" Helva asked tauntingly as he stepped forward to grab one of the women. "You can't drag them *all* aboard and we don't have time to fight it out. Get on board, Jennan, or I'll have you on report."

"They'll die," muttered Jennan dejectedly as he reluctantly turned to climb on board.

"You can risk only so much," Helva said sympathetically. "As it is we'll just have time to make a rendezvous. Lab reports a critical speedup in spectral evolution."

Jennan was already in the airlock when one of the younger women, screaming, rushed to squeeze in the closing port. Her action set off the others and they stampeded through the narrow opening. Even crammed back to breast, there was not enough room inside. Jennan broke out spacesuits for the three who would have to remain with him in the airlock. He wasted valuable time explaining to the matriarch that she must put on the suit because the airlock had no independent oxygen or cooling units.

"We'll be caught," said Helva in a grim tone to Jennan on their private connection. "We've lost eighteen minutes in this last-minute rush. I am now overloaded for maximum speed and I must attain maximum speed to outrun the heat wave."

"Can you lift? We're suited."

"Lift? Yes," she said, doing so. "Run? I stagger."

Jennan, bracing himself and the women, could feel her sluggishness as she blasted upward. Heartlessly, Helva applied thrust as long as she could, despite the fact that the gravitational force mashed her cabin passengers brutally and crushed two fatally. It was a question of saving as many as possible. The only one for whom she had any concern was Jennan and she was in desperate terror about his safety. Airless and uncooled, protected by only one layer of metal, not three, the airlock was not going to be safe for the four trapped there, despite their spacesuits. These were only the standard models, not built to withstand the excessive heat to which the ship would be subjected.

Helva ran as fast as she could but the incredible wave of heat from the explosive sun caught them halfway to cold safety.

She paid no heed to the cries, moans, pleas, and prayers in her cabin. She listened only to Jennan's tortured breathing, to the missing throb in his suit's purifying system and the sucking of the overloaded cooling unit. Helpless, she heard the hysterical screams of his three companions as they writhed in the awful heat. Vainly, Jennan tried to calm them, tried to explain they would soon be safe and cool if they could be still and endure the heat. Undisciplined by their terror and torment, they tried to strike out at him despite the close quarters. One flailing arm became entangled in the leads to his power pack and the damage was quickly done. A connection, weakened by heat and the dead weight of the arm, broke.

For all the power at her disposal, Helva was helpless. She watched as Jennan fought for his breath, as he turned his head beseechingly toward *her*, and died.

Only the iron conditioning of her training prevented Helva from swinging around and plunging back into the exploding sun. Numbly she made rendezvous with the refugee convoy. She obediently transferred her burned, heat-prostrated passengers to the assigned transport.

"I will retain the body of my scout and proceed to the nearest base for burial," she informed Central dully.

"You will be provided escort," was the reply.

"I have no need of escort."

"Escort is provided, XH-834," she was told curtly.

The shock of hearing Jennan's initial severed from her call number cut off her half-formed protest. Stunned, she waited by the transport until her screens showed the arrival of two other slim brain ships. The cortege proceeded homeward at unfuneral speeds.

"834? The ship who sings?"

"I have no more songs."

"Your scout was Jennan?"

"I do not wish to communicate."

"I'm 422."

"Silvia?"

"Silvia died a long time ago. I'm 422. Currently MS," the ship rejoined curtly. "AH-640 is our other friend, but Henry's not listening in. Just as well—he wouldn't understand it if you wanted to turn rogue. But I'd stop *him* if he tried to deter you."

"Rogue?" The term snapped Helva out of her apathy.

"Sure. You're young. You've got power for years. Skip. Others have done it. 732 went rogue two years ago after she lost her scout on a mission to that white dwarf. Hasn't been seen since."

"I never heard about rogues," gasped Helva.

"As it's exactly the thing we're conditioned against, you sure wouldn't hear about it in school, my dear," 422 said.

"Break conditioning?" cried Helva, anguished, thinking longingly of the white, white furious hot heart of the sun she had just left.

"For you I don't think it would be hard at the moment," 422 said quietly, her voice devoid of her earlier cynicism. "The stars are out there, winking."

"Alone?" cried Helva from her heart.

"Alone!" 422 confirmed bleakly.

Alone with all of space and time. Even the Horsehead Nebulae would not be far enough away to daunt her. Alone with a hundred years to live with her memories and nothing . . . nothing more.

"Was Parsaea worth it?" she asked 422 softly.

"Parsaea?" 422 came back, surprised. "With his father? Yes. We were there, at Parsaea when we were needed. Just as you . . . and his son . . . were at Chloe. When you were needed. The crime is always not knowing where need is and not being there."

"But *I* need *him*. Who will supply my need?" said Helva bitterly. . . .

"834," said 422 after a day's silent speeding. "Central wishes your report. A replacement awaits your opt at Regulus Base. Change course accordingly."

"A replacement?" That was certainly not what she needed . . . a reminder inadequately filling the void Jennan left. Why, her hull was barely cool of Chloe's heat. Atavistically, Helva wanted time to mourn Jennan.

"Oh, none of them are impossible if *you're* a good ship," 422 remarked philosophically. "And it is just what you need. The sooner the better."

"You told them I wouldn't go rogue, didn't you?" Helva said heavily.

"The moment passed you even as it passed me after Parsaea, and before that, after Glen Arhur, and Betelgeuse."

"We're conditioned to go on, aren't we? We *can't* go rogue. You were testing."

"Had to. Orders. Not even Psycho knows why a rogue occurs. Central's very worried, and so, daughter, are your sister ships. I asked to be your escort. I . . . don't want to lose you both."

In her emotional nadir, Helva could feel a flood of gratitude for Silvia's rough sympathy.

"We've all known this grief, Helva. It's no consolation, but if we couldn't feel with our scouts, we'd only be machines wired for sound."

Helva looked at Jennan's still form stretched before her in its shroud and heard the echo of his rich voice in the quiet cabin.

"Silvia! I *couldn't* help him," she cried from her soul.

"Yes, dear, I know," 422 murmured gently and then was quiet.

The three ships sped on, wordless, to the great Central Worlds base at Regulus. Helva broke silence to acknowledge landing instructions and the officially tendered regrets.

The three ships set down simultaneously at the wooded edge where Regulus's gigantic blue trees stood sentinel over the sleeping dead in the small Service cemetery. The entire Base complement approached with measured step and formed an aisle from Helva to the burial ground. The honor detail, out of step, walked slowly into her cabin. Reverently they placed the body of her dead love on the wheeled bier, covered it honorably with the deep blue, star-splashed flag of the Service. She watched as it was driven slowly down the living aisle which closed in behind the bier in last escort.

Then, as the simple words of interment were spoken, as the atmosphere planes dipped in tribute over the open grave, Helva found voice for her lonely farewell.

Softly, barely audible at first, the strains of the ancient song of evening and requiem swelled to the final poignant measure until black space itself echoed back the sound of the song the ship sang.

---

1. Why does Helva choose to learn to sing? Is singing merely a hobby for her?

2. Of all the candidates for Helga's Scout Service partner, why does Jennan alone address his remarks directly to her physical presence? Why is this the decisive factor in Helga's choice of Jennan?

3. Is Helva's sole concern for Jennan's safety consistent with or contrary to her conditioning as a shell person?

4. In light of Central Worlds' objective to educate the shell people to be "reasoning, logical, informed" citizens, why are the fine arts only a "selective subject"? How might education in the fine arts influence the shell people in carrying out their tasks?

KURT VONNEGUT (1922–2007) was born in Indianapolis, Indiana, and studied biochemistry at Cornell University, where he also edited the *Cornell Daily Sun*. Before graduating, he enlisted in the army, serving in the infantry during World War II. Captured in combat by German forces, Vonnegut was held as a POW and experienced firsthand the fire bombing of Dresden, an event that left a powerful impression on him and served as the subject matter for his two most acclaimed novels, *Cat's Cradle* (1963) and *Slaughterhouse-Five* (1969). Though Vonnegut's work often features apocalyptic settings, time travel, alien abduction, and other science fiction elements, his knowledge of suffering and his frequently comic-absurdist literary style have earned him a place among twentieth-century America's most influential writers. Vonnegut published more than twenty books, received numerous awards and honorary degrees, and served as honorary president of the American Humanist Association.

Harrison Bergeron

The year was 2081, and everybody was finally equal. They weren't only equal before God and the law. They were equal every which way. Nobody was smarter than anybody else. Nobody was better-looking than anybody else. Nobody was stronger or quicker than anybody else. All this equality was due to the 211th, 212th, and 213th Amendments to the Constitution, and to the unceasing vigilance of agents of the United States Handicapper General.

Some things about living still weren't quite right, though. April, for instance, still drove people crazy by not being springtime. And it was in that clammy month that the H-G men took George and Hazel Bergeron's fourteen-year-old son, Harrison, away.

It was tragic, all right, but George and Hazel couldn't think about it very hard. Hazel had a perfectly average intelligence, which meant she couldn't think about anything except in short bursts. And George, while his intelligence was way above normal, had a little mental handicap radio in his ear. He was required by law to wear it at all times. It was tuned to a government transmitter. Every twenty seconds or so, the transmitter would send out some sharp noise to keep people like George from taking unfair advantage of their brains.

George and Hazel were watching television. There were tears on Hazel's cheeks, but she'd forgotten for the moment what they were about.

On the television screen were ballerinas.

A buzzer sounded in George's head. His thoughts fled in panic, like bandits from a burglar alarm.

"That was a real pretty dance, that dance they just did," said Hazel.

"Huh?" said George.

"That dance—it was nice," said Hazel.

"Yup," said George. He tried to think a little about the ballerinas. They weren't really very good—no better than anybody else would have been, anyway. They were burdened with sash weights and bags of birdshot, and their faces were masked, so that no one, seeing a free and graceful gesture or a pretty face, would feel like something the cat drug in. George was toying with the vague notion that maybe dancers shouldn't be handicapped. But he didn't get very far with it before another noise in his ear radio scattered his thoughts.

George winced. So did two out of the eight ballerinas.

Hazel saw him wince. Having no mental handicap herself, she had to ask George what the latest sound had been.

"Sounded like somebody hitting a milk bottle with a ball-peen hammer," said George.

"I'd think it would be real interesting, hearing all the different sounds," said Hazel, a little envious. "All the things they think up."

"Um," said George.

"Only, if I was Handicapper General, you know what I would do?" said Hazel. Hazel, as a matter of fact, bore a strong resemblance to the Handicapper General, a woman named Diana Moon Glampers. "If I was Diana Moon Glampers," said Hazel, "I'd have chimes on Sunday—just chimes. Kind of in honor of religion."

"I could think, if it was just chimes," said George.

"Well—maybe make 'em real loud," said Hazel. "I think I'd make a good Handicapper General."

"Good as anybody else," said George.

"Who knows better'n I do what normal is?" said Hazel.

"Right," said George. He began to think glimmeringly about his abnormal son who was now in jail, about Harrison, but a twenty-one-gun salute in his head stopped that.

"Boy!" said Hazel, "that was a doozy, wasn't it?"

It was such a doozy that George was white and trembling, and tears stood on the rims of his red eyes. Two of the eight ballerinas had collapsed to the studio floor, were holding their temples.

"All of a sudden you look so tired," said Hazel. "Why don't you stretch out on the sofa, so's you can rest your handicap bag on the pillows, honeybunch." She was referring to the forty-seven pounds of birdshot in a canvas bag, which was padlocked around George's neck. "Go on and rest the bag for a little while," she said. "I don't care if you're not equal to me for a while."

George weighed the bag with his hands. "I don't mind it," he said. "I don't notice it anymore. It's just a part of me."

"You been so tired lately—kind of wore out," said Hazel. "If there was just some way we could make a little hole in the bottom of the bag, and just take out a few of them lead balls. Just a few."

"Two years in prison and two thousand dollars fine for every ball I took out," said George. "I don't call that a bargain."

"If you could just take a few out when you came home from work," said Hazel. "I mean—you don't compete with anybody around here. You just set around."

"If I tried to get away with it," said George, "then other people'd get away with it—and pretty soon we'd be right back to the dark ages again, with everybody competing against everybody else. You wouldn't like that, would you?"

"I'd hate it," said Hazel.

"There you are," said George. "The minute people start cheating on laws, what do you think happens to society?"

If Hazel hadn't been able to come up with an answer to this question, George couldn't have supplied one. A siren was going off in his head.

"Reckon it'd fall all apart," said Hazel.

"What would?" said George blankly.

"Society," said Hazel uncertainly. "Wasn't that what you just said?"

"Who knows?" said George.

The television program was suddenly interrupted for a news bulletin. It wasn't clear at first as to what the bulletin was about, since the announcer, like all announcers, had a serious speech impediment. For about half a minute, and in a state of high excitement, the announcer tried to say, "Ladies and gentlemen—"

He finally gave up, handed the bulletin to a ballerina to read.

"That's all right—" Hazel said of the announcer, "he tried. That's the big thing. He tried to do the best he could with what God gave him. He should get a nice raise for trying so hard."

"Ladies and gentlemen—" said the ballerina, reading the bulletin. She must have been extraordinarily beautiful, because the mask she wore was hideous. And it was easy to see that she was the strongest and most graceful of all the dancers, for her handicap bags were as big as those worn by two-hundred-pound men.

And she had to apologize at once for her voice, which was a very unfair voice for a woman to use. Her voice was a warm, luminous, timeless melody. "Excuse me—" she said, and she began again, making her voice absolutely uncompetitive.

"Harrison Bergeron, age fourteen," she said in a grackle squawk, "has just escaped from jail, where he was held on suspicion of plotting to overthrow the government. He is a genius and an athlete, is under-handicapped, and should be regarded as extremely dangerous."

A police photograph of Harrison Bergeron was flashed on the screen upside down, then sideways, upside down again, then right side up. The picture showed the full length of Harrison against a background calibrated in feet and inches. He was exactly seven feet tall.

The rest of Harrison's appearance was Halloween and hardware. Nobody had ever borne heavier handicaps. He had outgrown hindrances faster than the H-G men could think them up. Instead of a little ear radio for a mental handicap, he wore a tremendous pair of earphones, and spectacles with thick wavy lenses. The spectacles were intended to make him not only half blind, but to give him whanging headaches besides.

Scrap metal was hung all over him. Ordinarily, there was a certain symmetry, a military neatness to the handicaps issued to strong people, but Harrison looked like a walking junkyard. In the race of life, Harrison carried three hundred pounds.

And to offset his good looks, the H-G men required that he wear at all times a red rubber ball for a nose, keep his eyebrows shaved off, and cover his even white teeth with black caps at snaggle-tooth random.

"If you see this boy," said the ballerina, "do not—I repeat, do not—try to reason with him."

There was the shriek of a door being torn from its hinges.

Screams and barking cries of consternation came from the television set. The photograph of Harrison Bergeron on the screen jumped again and again, as though dancing to the tune of an earthquake.

George Bergeron correctly identified the earthquake, and well he might have—for many was the time his own home had danced to the same crashing tune. "My God—" said George, "that must be Harrison!"

The realization was blasted from his mind instantly by the sound of an automobile collision in his head.

When George could open his eyes again, the photograph of Harrison was gone. A living, breathing Harrison filled the screen.

Clanking, clownish, and huge, Harrison stood in the center of the studio. The knob of the uprooted studio door was still in his hand. Ballerinas, technicians, musicians, and announcers cowered on their knees before him, expecting to die.

"I am the Emperor!" cried Harrison. "Do you hear? I am the Emperor! Everybody must do what I say at once!" He stamped his foot and the studio shook.

"Even as I stand here—" he bellowed, "crippled, hobbled, sickened—I am a greater ruler than any man who ever lived! Now watch me become what I *can* become!"

Harrison tore the straps of his handicap harness like wet tissue paper, tore straps guaranteed to support five thousand pounds.

Harrison's scrap-iron handicaps crashed to the floor.

Harrison thrust his thumbs under the bar of the padlock that secured his head harness. The bar snapped like celery. Harrison smashed his headphones and spectacles against the wall.

He flung away his rubber-ball nose, revealed a man that would have awed Thor, the god of thunder.

"I shall now select my Empress!" he said, looking down on the cowering people. "Let the first woman who dares rise to her feet claim her mate and her throne!"

A moment passed, and then a ballerina arose, swaying like a willow.

Harrison plucked the mental handicap from her ear, snapped off her physical handicaps with marvelous delicacy. Last of all, he removed her mask.

She was blindingly beautiful.

"Now—" said Harrison, taking her hand, "shall we show the people the meaning of the word dance? Music!" he commanded.

The musicians scrambled back into their chairs, and Harrison stripped them of their handicaps, too. "Play your best," he told them, "and I'll make you barons and dukes and earls."

The music began. It was normal at first—cheap, silly, false. But Harrison snatched two musicians from their chairs, waved them like batons as he sang the music as he wanted it played. He slammed them back into their chairs.

The music began again and was much improved.

Harrison and his Empress merely listened to the music for a while—listened gravely, as though synchronizing their heartbeats with it.

They shifted their weight to their toes.

Harrison placed his big hands on the girl's tiny waist, letting her sense the weightlessness that would soon be hers.

And then, in an explosion of joy and grace, into the air they sprang!

Not only were the laws of the land abandoned, but the law of gravity and the laws of motion as well.

They reeled, whirled, swiveled, flounced, capered, gamboled, and spun.

They leaped like deer on the moon.

The studio ceiling was thirty feet high, but each leap brought the dancers nearer to it.

It became their obvious intention to kiss the ceiling.

They kissed it.

And then, neutralizing gravity with love and pure will, they remained suspended in air inches below the ceiling, and they kissed each other for a long, long time.

It was then that Diana Moon Glampers, the Handicapper General, came into the studio with a double-barreled ten-gauge shotgun. She fired twice, and the Emperor and the Empress were dead before they hit the floor.

Diana Moon Glampers loaded the gun again. She aimed it at the musicians and told them they had ten seconds to get their handicaps back on.

It was then that the Bergerons' television tube burned out.

Hazel turned to comment about the blackout to George. But George had gone out into the kitchen for a can of beer.

George came back in with the beer, paused while a handicap signal shook him up. And then he sat down again. "You been crying?" he said to Hazel.

"Yup," she said.

"What about?" he said.

"I forget," she said. "Something real sad on television."

"What was it?" he said.

"It's all kind of mixed up in my mind," said Hazel.

"Forget sad things," said George.

"I always do," said Hazel.

"That's my girl," said George. He winced. There was the sound of a riveting gun in his head.

"Gee—I could tell that one was a doozy," said Hazel.

"You can say that again," said George.

"Gee—" said Hazel, "I could tell that one was a doozy."

1. Even though the government handicaps George by constantly subjecting him to painful sounds, why is he still convinced that being law-abiding is better than returning to "the dark ages again, with everybody competing against everybody else"?

2. Why does Harrison Bergeron attempt to overthrow the government by autocratically declaring himself "the Emperor"? Why is his first act as emperor a dance with the ballerina?

3. Why is Harrison able to overcome the imposed handicaps while others are not?

4. Should societies ever legislate any form of equality among their citizens besides equality before the law?

HARRY HARRISON (1925–), born in Stamford, Connecticut, started his career as a commercial artist for comic books and magazines, eventually becoming an editor of some of the publications he illustrated. In his twenties, he began to write science fiction stories. He has subsequently combined the professions of author and editor, working on American and British magazines; founding (with Brian Aldiss) *SF Horizons*, the first magazine of science fiction criticism; and editing many science fiction anthologies. He created the cover art for some of his own books and has said, "Drawing has always had a great effect on my writing, shaping it and aiding it." Harrison's writing is known for its brisk style, often darkly humorous tone, and concern for social and ecological issues. Among his numerous works are the novels *Deathworld* (1960), *The Stainless Steel Rat* (1961), and *Make Room! Make Room!* (1966), which was made into the movie *Soylent Green* (1973). Harrison won the Nebula Award in 1973. He was named the 2009 Grand Master by Science Fiction and Fantasy Writers of America.

The Streets of Ashkelon

Somewhere above, hidden by the eternal clouds of Wesker's World, a thunder rumbled and grew. Trader John Garth stopped when he heard it, his boots sinking slowly into the muck, and cupped his good ear to catch the sound. It swelled and waned in the thick atmosphere, growing louder.

"That noise is the same as the noise of your sky-ship," Itin said, with stolid Wesker logicality, slowly pulverizing the idea in his mind and turning over the bits one by one for closer examination. "But your ship is still sitting where you landed it. It must be, even though we cannot see it, because you are the only one who can operate it. And even if anyone else could operate it we would have heard it rising into the sky. Since we did not, and if this sound is a sky-ship sound, then it must mean . . ."

"Yes, another ship," Garth said, too absorbed in his own thoughts to wait for the laborious Weskerian chains of logic to clank their way through to the end. Of course it was another spacer, it had been only a matter of time before one appeared, and undoubtedly this one was homing on the SS radar reflector as he had done. His own ship would show up clearly on the newcomer's screen and they would probably set down as close to it as they could.

"You better go ahead, Itin," he said. "Use the water so you can get to the village quickly. Tell everyone to get back into the swamps, well clear of the hard ground. That ship is landing on instruments and anyone underneath at touchdown is going to be cooked."

This immediate threat was clear enough to the little Wesker amphibian. Before Garth finished speaking Itin's ribbed ears had folded like a bat's wings and he slipped silently into the nearby canal. Garth squelched on through the mud, making as good time as he could over the clinging surface. He had just reached the fringes of the village clearing when the rumbling grew to a head-splitting roar and the spacer broke through the low-hanging layer of clouds above. Garth shielded his eyes from the down-reaching tongue of flame and examined the growing form of the gray-black ship with mixed feelings.

After almost a standard year on Wesker's World he had to fight down a longing for human companionship of any kind. While this buried fragment of herd-spirit chattered for the rest of the monkey tribe, his trader's mind was busily drawing a line under a column of figures and adding up the total. This could very well be another trader's ship, and if it were his monopoly of the Wesker trade was at an end. Then again, this might not be a trader at all, which was the reason he stayed in the shelter of the giant fern and loosened his gun in its holster.

The ship baked dry a hundred square meters of mud, the roaring blast died, and the landing feet crunched down through the crackling crust. Metal creaked and settled into place while the cloud of smoke and steam slowly drifted lower in the humid air.

"Garth—you native-cheating extortionist—where are you?" the ship's speaker boomed. The lines of the spacer had looked only slightly familiar, but there was no mistaking the rasping tones of that voice. Garth wore a smile when he stepped out into the open and whistled shrilly through two fingers. A directional microphone ground out of its casing on the ship's fin and turned in his direction.

"What are you doing here, Singh?" he shouted towards the mike. "Too crooked to find a planet of your own and have to come here to steal an honest trader's profits?"

"Honest!" the amplified voice roared. "This from the man who has been in more jails than cathouses—and that a goodly number in itself, I do declare. Sorry, friend of my youth, but I cannot join you in exploiting this aboriginal pesthole. I am on course to a more fairly atmosphered world where a fortune is waiting to be made. I only stopped here since an opportunity presented to turn an honest credit by running a taxi service. I bring you friendship, the perfect companionship, a man in a different line of business who might help you in yours. I'd come out and say hello myself, except I would have to decon for biologicals. I'm cycling the passenger through the lock so I hope you won't mind helping with his luggage."

At least there would be no other trader on the planet now, that worry was gone. But Garth still wondered what sort of passenger would be taking one-way passage to an uninhabited world. And what was behind that concealed hint of merriment in Singh's voice? He walked around to the far side of the spacer where the ramp had dropped, and looked up at the man in the cargo lock who was wrestling ineffectually with a large crate. The man turned towards him and Garth saw the clerical dog collar and knew just what it was Singh had been chuckling about.

"What are you doing here?" Garth asked; and in spite of his attempt at self-control he snapped the words. If the man noticed this he ignored it, because he was still smiling and putting out his hand as he came down the ramp.

"Father Mark," he said, "Of the Missionary Society of Brothers. I'm very pleased to . . ."

"I said what are you doing here." Garth's voice was under control now, quiet and cold. He knew what had to be done, and it must be done quickly or not at all.

"That should be obvious." Father Mark said, his good nature still unruffled. "Our missionary society has raised funds to send spiritual emissaries to alien worlds for the first time. I was lucky enough . . ."

"Take your luggage and get back into the ship. You're not wanted here and have no permission to land. You'll be a liability and there is no one on Wesker to take care of you. Get back into the ship."

"I don't know who you are, sir, or why you are lying to me," the priest said. He was still calm but the smile was gone. "But I have studied galactic law and the history of this planet very well. There are no diseases or beasts here that I should have any particular fear of. It is also an open planet, and until the Space Survey changes that status I have as much right to be here as you do."

The man was of course right, but Garth couldn't let him know that. He had been bluffing, hoping the priest didn't know his rights. But he did. There was only one distasteful course left for him, and he had better do it while there was still time.

"Get back in that ship," he shouted, not hiding his anger now. With a smooth motion his gun was out of the holster and the pitted black muzzle only inches from the priest's stomach. The man's face turned white, but he did not move.

"What the hell are you doing, Garth!" Singh's shocked voice grated from the speaker. "The guy paid his fare and you have no right at all to throw him off the planet."

"I have this right," Garth said, raising his gun and sighting between the priest's eyes. "I give him thirty seconds to get back aboard the ship or I pull the trigger."

"Well, I think you are either off your head or playing a joke," Singh's exasperated voice rasped down at them. "If it is a joke, it is in bad taste, and either way you're not getting away with it. Two can play at that game, only I can play it better."

There was the rumble of heavy bearings and the remote-controlled four-gun turret on the ship's side rotated and pointed at Garth. "Now—down gun and give Father Mark a hand with the luggage," the speaker commanded, a trace of humor back in the voice now. "As much as I would like to help, old friend, I cannot. I feel it is time you had a chance to talk to the father; after all, I have had the opportunity of speaking with him all the way from Earth."

Garth jammed the gun back into the holster with an acute feeling of loss. Father Mark stepped forward, the winning smile back now and a Bible taken from a pocket of his robe, in his raised hand. "My son," he said.

"I'm not your son," was all Garth could choke out as defeat welled up in him. His fist drew back as the anger rose, and the best he could do was open the fist so he struck only with the flat of his hand. Still the blow sent the priest crashing to the ground and fluttered the pages of the book splattering into the thick mud.

Itin and the other Weskers had watched everything with seemingly emotionless interest, and Garth made no attempt to answer their unspoken questions. He started towards his house, but turned back when he saw they were still unmoving.

"A new man has come," he told them. "He will need help with the things he has brought. If he doesn't have any place for them, you can put them in the big warehouse until he has a place of his own."

He watched them waddle across the clearing towards the ship, then went inside and gained a certain satisfaction from slamming the door hard enough to crack one of the panes. There was an equal amount of painful pleasure in breaking out one of the remaining bottles of Irish whiskey that he had been saving for a special occasion. Well this was special enough, though not really what he had had in mind. The whiskey was good and burned away some of the bad taste in his mouth, but not all of it. If his tactics had worked, success would have justified everything. But he had failed and in addition to the pain of failure there was the acute feeling that he had made a horse's ass out of himself. Singh had blasted off without any goodbyes. There was no telling what sense he had made of the whole matter, though he would surely carry some strange stories back to the traders' lodge. Well, that could be worried about the next time Garth signed in. Right now he had to go about setting things right with the missionary. Squinting out through the rain he saw the man struggling to erect a collapsible tent while the entire population of the village stood in ordered ranks and watched. Naturally none of them offered to help.

By the time the tent was up and the crates and boxes stowed inside it the rain had stopped. The level of fluid in the bottle was a good bit lower and Garth felt more like facing up to the unavoidable meeting. In truth, he was looking forward to talking to the man. This whole nasty business aside, after an entire solitary year any human companionship looked good. *Will you join me now for dinner. John Garth,* he wrote on the back of an old invoice. But maybe the guy was too frightened to come? Which was no way to start any kind of relationship. Rummaging under the bunk, he found a box that was big enough and put his pistol inside. Itin was of course waiting outside the door when he opened it, since this was his tour as Knowledge Collector. He handed him the note and box.

"Would you take these to the new man?" he said.

"Is the new man's name New Man?" Itin asked.

"No, it's not!" Garth snapped. "His name is Mark. But I'm only asking you to deliver this, not get involved in conversation."

As always when he lost his temper, the literal-minded Weskers won the round. "You are not asking for conversation," Itin said slowly, "but Mark may ask for conversation. And others will ask me his name, if I do not know his na . . ." The voice cut off as Garth slammed the door. This didn't work in the long run either because next time he saw Itin—a day, a week, or even a month later—the monologue would be picked up on the very word it had ended and the thought rambled out to its last frayed end. Garth cursed under his breath and poured water over a pair of the tastier concentrates that he had left.

"Come in," he said when there was a quiet knock on the door. The priest entered and held out the box with the gun.

"Thank you for the loan, Mr. Garth, I appreciate the spirit that made you send it. I have no idea of what caused the unhappy affair when I landed, but I think it would be best forgotten if we are going to be on this planet together for any length of time."

"Drink?" Garth asked, taking the box and pointing to the bottle on the table. He poured two glasses full and handed one to the priest. "That's about what I had in mind, but I still owe you an explanation of what happened out there." He scowled into his glass for a second, then raised it to the other man. "It's a big universe and I guess we have to make out as best we can. Here's to Sanity."

"God be with you," Father Mark said, and raised his glass as well.

"Not with me or with this planet," Garth said firmly. "And that's the crux of the matter." He half drained the glass and sighed.

"Do you say that to shock me?" the priest asked with a smile. "I assure you that it doesn't."

"Not intended to shock. I meant it quite literally. I suppose I'm what you would call an atheist, so revealed religion is no concern of mine. While these natives, simple and unlettered Stone Age types that they are, have managed to come this far with no superstitions or traces of deism whatsoever. I had hoped that they might continue that way."

"What are you saying?" The priest frowned. "Do you mean they have no gods, no belief in the hereafter? They must die . . . ?"

"Die they do, and to dust return like the rest of the animals. They have thunder, trees, and water without having thunder gods, tree spirits, or water nymphs. They have no ugly little gods, taboos, or spells to hag-ride and limit their lives. They are the only primitive people I have ever encountered who are completely free of superstition and appear to be much happier and saner because of it. I just wanted to keep them that way."

"You wanted to keep them from God—from salvation?" The priest's eyes widened and he recoiled slightly.

"No," Garth said. "I wanted to keep them from superstition until they knew more and could think about it realistically without being absorbed and perhaps destroyed by it."

"You're being insulting to the Church, sir, to equate it with superstition . . ."

"Please." Garth said, raising his hand. "No theological arguments. I don't think your society footed the bill for this trip just to attempt a conversion on me. Just accept the fact that my beliefs have been arrived at through careful thought over a period of years, and no amount of undergraduate metaphysics will change them. I'll promise not to try and convert you—if you will do the same for me."

"Agreed, Mr. Garth. As you have reminded me, my mission here is to save these souls, and that is what I must do. But why should my work disturb you so much that you try and keep me from landing? Even threaten me with your gun, and . . ." The priest broke off and looked into his glass.

"And even slug you?" Garth asked, suddenly frowning. "There was no excuse for that, and I would like to say that I'm sorry. Plain bad manners and an even worse temper. Live alone long enough and you find yourself doing that kind of thing." He brooded down at his big hands where they lay on the table, reading memories into the scars and calluses patterned there. "Let's just call it frustration, for lack of a better word. In your business you must have had a lot of chance to peep into the darker places in men's minds and you should know a bit about motives and happiness. I have had too busy a life to ever consider settling down and raising a family, and right up until recently I never missed it. Maybe leakage radiation is softening up my brain, but I had begun to think of these furry and fishy Weskers as being a little like my own children, that I was somehow responsible to them."

"We are all His children," Father Mark said quietly.

"Well, here are some of His children that can't even imagine His existence," Garth said, suddenly angry at himself for allowing gentler emotions to show through. Yet he forgot himself at once, leaning forward with the intensity of his feelings. "Can't you realize the importance of this? Live with these Weskers awhile and you will discover a simple and happy life that matches the state of grace you people are always talking about. They get *pleasure* from their lives—and cause no one pain. By circumstances they have evolved on an almost barren world, so have never had a chance to grow out of a physical Stone Age culture. But mentally they are our match—or perhaps better. They have all learned my language so I can easily explain the many things they want to know. Knowledge and the gaining of knowledge gives them real satisfaction. They tend to be exasperating at times because every new fact must be related to the structure of all other things, but the more they learn the faster this process becomes. Some day they are going to be man's equal in every way, perhaps surpass us. If—would you do me a favor?"

"Whatever I can."

"Leave them alone. Or teach them if you must—history and science, philosophy, law, anything that will help them face the realities of the greater universe they never even knew existed before. But don't confuse them with your hatreds and pain, guilt, sin, and punishment. Who knows the harm . . ."

"You are being insulting, sir!" the priest said, jumping to his feet. The top of his gray head barely came to the massive spaceman's chin, yet he showed no fear in defending what he believed. Garth, standing now himself, was no longer the penitent. They faced each other in anger, as men have always stood, unbending in the defense of that which they think right.

"Yours is the insult," Garth shouted. "The incredible egotism to feel that your derivative little mythology, differing only slightly from the thousands of others that still burden men, can do anything but confuse their still fresh minds! Don't you realize that they believe in truth—and have never heard of such a thing as a lie. They have not been trained yet to understand that other kinds of minds can think differently from theirs. Will you spare them this . . . ?"

"I will do my duty which is His will, Mr. Garth. These are God's creatures here, and they have souls. I cannot shirk my duty, which is to bring them His word, so that they may be saved and enter into the kingdom of heaven."

When the priest opened the door the wind caught it and blew it wide. He vanished into the storm-swept darkness and the door swung back and forth and a splatter of raindrops blew in. Garth's boots left muddy footprints when he closed the door, shutting out the sight of Itin sitting patiently and uncomplaining in the storm, hoping only that Garth might stop for a moment and leave with him some of the wonderful knowledge of which he had so much.

By unspoken consent that first night was never mentioned again. After a few days of loneliness, made worse because each knew of the other's proximity, they found themselves talking on carefully neutral ground. Garth slowly packed and stowed away his stock and never admitted that his work was finished and he could leave at any time. He had a fair amount of interesting drugs and botanicals that would fetch a good price. And the Wesker artifacts were sure to create a sensation in the sophisticated galactic market. Crafts on the planet here had been limited before his arrival, mostly pieces of carving painfully chipped into the hard wood with fragments of stone. He had supplied tools and a stock of raw metal from his own supplies, nothing more than that. In a few months the Weskers had not only learned to work with the new materials, but had translated their own designs and forms into the most alien—but most beautiful—artifacts that he had ever seen. All he had to do was release these on the market to create a primary demand, then return for a new supply. The Weskers wanted only books and tools and knowledge in return, and through their own efforts he knew they would pull themselves into the galactic union.

This is what Garth had hoped. But a wind of change was blowing through the settlement that had grown up around his ship. No longer was he the center of attention and focal point of the village life. He had to grin when he thought of his fall from power; yet there was very little humor in the smile. Serious and attentive Weskers still took turns of duty as Knowledge Collectors, but their recording of dry facts was in sharp contrast to the intellectual hurricane that surrounded the priest.

Where Garth had made them work for each book and machine, the priest gave freely. Garth had tried to be progressive in his supply of knowledge, treating them as bright but unlettered children. He had wanted them to walk before they could run, to master one step before going on to the next.

Father Mark simply brought them the benefits of Christianity. The only physical work he required was the construction of a church, a place of worship and learning. More Weskers had appeared out of the limitless planetary swamps and within days the roof was up, supported on a framework of poles. Each morning the congregation worked a little while on the walls, then hurried inside to learn the all-promising, all-encompassing, all-important facts about the universe.

Garth never told the Weskers what he thought about their new interest, and this was mainly because they had never asked him. Pride or honor stood in the way of his grabbing a willing listener and pouring out his grievances. Perhaps it would have been different if Itin was on Collecting duty; he was the brightest of the lot; but Itin had been rotated the day after the priest had arrived and Garth had not talked to him since.

It was a surprise then when after seventeen of the trebly long Wesker days, he found a delegation at his doorstep when he emerged after breakfast. Itin was their spokesman, and his mouth was open slightly. Many of the other Weskers had their mouths open as well, one even appearing to be yawning, clearly revealing the double row of sharp teeth and the purple-black throat. The mouths impressed Garth as to the seriousness of the meeting: this was the one Wesker expression he had learned to recognize. An open mouth indicated some strong emotion; happiness, sadness, anger, he could never be really sure which. The Weskers were normally placid and he had never seen enough open mouths to tell what was causing them. But he was surrounded by them now.

"Will you help us, John Garth?" Itin said. "We have a question."

"I'll answer any questions you ask," Garth said, with more than a hint of misgiving. "What is it?"

"Is there a God?"

"What do you mean by 'God'?" Garth asked in turn. What should he tell them?

"God is our Father in Heaven, who made us all and protects us. Whom we pray to for aid, and if we are Saved will find a place . . ."

"That's enough," Garth said. "There is no God."

All of them had their mouths open now, even Itin, as they looked at Garth and thought about his answer. The rows of pink teeth would have been frightening if he hadn't known these creatures so well. For one instant he wondered if perhaps they had been already indoctrinated and looked upon him as a heretic, but he brushed the thought away.

"Thank you," Itin said, and they turned and left.

Though the morning was still cool, Garth noticed that he was sweating and wondered why.

The reaction was not long in coming. Itin returned that same afternoon. "Will you come to the church?" he asked. "Many of the things that we study are difficult to learn, but none as difficult as this. We need your help because we must hear you and Father Mark talk together. This is because he says one thing is true and you say another is true and both cannot be true at the same time. We must find out what is true."

"I'll come, of course," Garth said, trying to hide the sudden feeling of elation. He had done nothing, but the Weskers had come to him anyway. There could still be grounds for hope that they might yet be free.

It was hot inside the church, and Garth was surprised at the number of Weskers who were there, more than he had seen gathered at any one time before. There were many open mouths. Father Mark sat at a table covered with books. He looked unhappy but didn't say anything when Garth came in. Garth spoke first.

"I hope you realize this is their idea—that they came to me of their own free will and asked me to come here?"

"I know that." the priest said resignedly. "At times they can be very difficult. But they are learning and want to believe, and that is what is important."

"Father Mark, Trader Garth, we need your help," Itin said. "You both know many things that we do not know. You must help us come to religion which is not an easy thing to do." Garth started to say something, then changed his mind. Itin went on, "We have read the Bibles and all the books that Father Mark gave us, and one thing is clear. We have discussed this and we are all agreed. These books are very different from the ones that Trader Garth gave us. In Trader Garth's books there is the universe which we have not seen, and it goes on without God, for he is mentioned nowhere; we have searched very carefully. In Father Mark's books He is everywhere and nothing can go without Him. One of these must be right and the other must be wrong. We do not know how this can be, but after we find out which is right then perhaps we will know. If God does not exist . . ."

"Of course He exists, my children," Father Mark said in a voice of heartfelt intensity. "He is our Father in Heaven who has created us all . . ."

"Who created God?" Itin asked and the murmur ceased and every one of the Weskers watched Father Mark intensely. He recoiled a bit under the impact of their eyes, then smiled.

"Nothing created God, since He is the Creator. He always was . . ."

"If He always was in existence—why cannot the universe have always been in existence? Without having had a creator?" Itin broke in with a rush of words. The importance of the question was obvious. The priest answered slowly, with infinite patience.

"Would that the answers were that simple, my children. But even the scientists do not agree about the creation of the universe. While they doubt—we who have seen the light *know*. We can see the miracle of creation all about us. And how can there be a creation without a Creator? That is He, our Father, our God in Heaven. I know you have doubts; that is because you have souls and free will. Still the answer is so simple. Have faith, that is all you need. Just believe."

"How can we believe without proof?"

"If you cannot see that this world itself is proof of His existence, then I say to you that belief needs no proof—if you have faith!"

A babble of voices arose in the room and more of the Wesker mouths were open now as they tried to force their thoughts through the tangled skein of words and separate the thread of truth.

"Can you tell us, Garth?" Itin asked, and the sound of his voice quieted the hubbub.

"I can tell you to use the scientific method which can examine all things—including itself—and give you answers that can prove the truth or falsity of any statement."

"That is what we must do," Itin said, "We had reached the same conclusion." He held a thick book before him and a ripple of nods ran across the watchers. "We have been studying the Bible as Father Mark told us to do, and we have found the answer. God will make a miracle for us, thereby proving that He is watching us. And by this sign we will know Him and go to Him."

"That is the sin of false pride," Father Mark said. "God needs no miracles to prove His existence."

"But *we* need a miracle!" Itin shouted, and though he wasn't human there was need in his voice. "We have read here of many smaller miracles, loaves, fishes, wine, snakes—many of them, for much smaller reasons. Now all He need do is make a miracle and He will bring us all to Him—the wonder of an entire new world worshiping at His throne, as you have told us, Father Mark. And you have told us how important this is. We have discussed this and find that there is only one miracle that is best for this kind of thing."

His boredom at the theological wrangling drained from Garth in an instant. He had not been really thinking or he would have realized where all this was leading. He could see the illustration in the Bible where Itin held it open, and knew in advance what picture it was. He rose slowly from his chair, as if stretching, and turned to the priest behind him.

"Get ready!" he whispered. "Get out the back and get to the ship; I'll keep them busy here. I don't think they'll harm me."

"What do you mean . . . ?" Father Mark asked, blinking in surprise.

"Get out, you fool!" Garth hissed. "What miracle do you think they mean? What miracle is supposed to have converted the world to Christianity?"

"No!" Father Mark said. "It cannot be. It just cannot be . . . !"

"*Get moving!*" Garth shouted, dragging the priest from the chair and hurling him towards the rear wall. Father Mark stumbled to a halt, turned back. Garth leaped for him, but it was already too late. The amphibians were small, but there were so many of them. Garth lashed out and his fist struck Itin, hurling him back into the crowd. The others came on as he fought his way towards the priest. He beat at them but it was like struggling against the waves. The furry, musky bodies washed over and engulfed him. He struggled until they tied him, and he still struggled until they beat on his head until he stopped. Then they pulled him outside where he could only lie in the rain and curse and watch.

Of course the Weskers were marvelous craftsmen, and everything had been constructed down to the last detail, following the illustration in the Bible. There was the cross, planted firmly on the top of a small hill, the gleaming metal spikes, the hammer. Father Mark was stripped and draped in a carefully pleated loincloth. They led him out of the church.

At the sight of the cross he almost fainted. After that he held his head high and determined to die as he had lived, with faith.

Yet this was hard. It was unbearable even for Garth, who only watched. It is one thing to talk of crucifixion and look at the gentle carved bodies in the dim light of prayer. It is another to see a man naked, ropes cutting into his skin where he hangs from a bar of wood. And to see the needle-tipped spike raised and placed against the soft flesh of his palm, to see the hammer come back with the calm delibera-tion of an artisan's measured stroke. To hear the thick sound of metal penetrating flesh.

Then to hear the screams.

Few are born to be martyrs; Father Mark was not one of them. With the first blows, the blood ran from his lips where his clenched teeth met. Then his mouth was wide and his head strained back and the awful guttural horror of his screams sliced through the susurra-tion of the falling rain. It resounded as a silent echo from the masses of watching Weskers, for whatever emotion opened their mouths was now tearing at their bodies with all its force, and row after row of gaping jaws reflected the crucified priest's agony.

Mercifully he fainted as the last nail was driven home. Blood ran from the raw wounds, mixing with the rain to drip faintly pink from his feet as the life ran out of him. At this time, somewhere at this time, sobbing and tearing at his own bonds, numbed from the blows on the head, Garth lost consciousness.

He awoke in his own warehouse and it was dark. Someone was cutting away the woven ropes they had bound him with. The rain still dripped and splashed outside.

"Itin," he said. It could be no one else.

"Yes," the alien voice whispered back. "The others are all talking in the church. Lin died after you struck his head, and Inon is very sick. There are some that say you should be crucified too, and I think that is what will happen. Or perhaps killed by stoning on the head. They have found in the Bible where it says . . ."

"I know." With infinite weariness. "An eye for an eye. You'll find lots of things like that once you start looking. It's a wonderful book." His head ached terribly.

"You must go, you can get to your ship without anyone seeing you. There has been enough killing." Itin as well spoke with a newfound weariness.

Garth experimented, pulling himself to his feet. He pressed his head to the rough wood of the wall until the nausea stopped. "He's dead." He said it as a statement, not a question.

"Yes, some time ago. Or I could not have come away to see you."

"And buried of course, or they wouldn't be thinking about starting on me next."

"And buried!" There was almost a ring of emotion in the alien's voice, an echo of the dead priest's. "He is buried and he will rise on High. It is written and that is the way it will happen. Father Mark will be so happy that it has happened like this." The voice ended in a sound like a human sob.

Garth painfully worked his way towards the door, leaning against the wall so he wouldn't fall.

"We did the right thing, didn't we?" Itin asked. There was no answer. "He will rise up, Garth, won't he rise?"

Garth was at the door and enough light came from the brightly lit church to show his torn and bloody hands clutching at the frame. Itin's face swam into sight close to his, and Garth felt the delicate, many fingered hands with the sharp nails catch at his clothes.

"He will rise, won't he, Garth?"

"No," Garth said, "he is going to stay buried right where you put him. Nothing is going to happen because he is dead and he is going to stay dead."

The rain runnelled through Itin's fur and his mouth was opened so wide that he seemed to be screaming into the night. Only with effort could he talk, squeezing out the alien thoughts in an alien language.

"Then we will not be saved? We will not become pure?"

"You were pure," Garth said, in a voice somewhere between a sob and a laugh. "That's the horrible ugly dirty part of it. You were pure. Now you are . . ."

"Murderers," Itin said, and the water ran down from his lowered head and streamed away into the darkness.

––––––––––

1. What does Garth mean when he refers to the Weskers as "primitive" people? What is his reason for wanting to "keep them that way"?

2. Is Garth correct in telling the Weskers to use the "scientific method" to examine the truth of Father Mark's religious teachings?

3. Did the killing of Father Mark by the Weskers make them more like humans than aliens?

4. Is it sometimes better not to expose minds to new ideas that might interfere with accustomed ways of thinking that seem to be adequate for dealing with the world? How should the decision be made whether or not to do so?

PHILIP K. DICK (1928–1982) wrote more than forty science fiction novels. The best of these, *The Man in the High Castle* (1962), won a Hugo Award and presents an alternate universe in which Germany and Japan are the victors of World War II. Dick's paranoid vision has become familiar to millions because so many of his novels and short stories have enjoyed a second life as movie adaptations. Most notable among these is *Blade Runner* (1982), based on Dick's novel *Do Androids Dream of Electric Sheep?* (1968). Other films derived from his voluminous output include *Total Recall* (1990), *Minority Report* (2002), and *A Scanner Darkly* (2006). Ideas explored in Dick's work include the impact of hallucinogens on personality, religious delusion and the nature of reality, and an astonishing array of conspiracy theories. A dropout of the University of California at Berkeley, Dick claimed to have been diagnosed as schizophrenic while still in his teens, and in 1975 he attested to having a direct encounter with the Divine. Dick is the first science fiction writer to be published, in three volumes no less, by the prestigious Library of America.

The Days of Perky Pat

At ten in the morning a terrific horn, familiar to him, hooted Sam Regan out of his sleep, and he cursed the careboy upstairs; he knew the racket was deliberate. The careboy, circling, wanted to be certain that flukers—and not merely wild animals—got the care parcels that were to be dropped.

We'll get them, we'll get them, Sam Regan said to himself as he zipped his dust-proof overalls, put his feet into boots, and then grumpily sauntered as slowly as possible toward the ramp. Several other flukers joined him, all showing similar irritation,

"He's early today," Tod Morrison complained. "And I'll bet it's all staples, sugar and flour and lard—nothing interesting like say candy."

"We ought to be grateful," Norman Schein said.

"Grateful!" Tod halted to stare at him. "GRATEFUL?"

"Yes," Schein said. "What do you think we'd be eating without them: if they hadn't seen the clouds ten years ago."

"Well," Tod said sullenly, "I just don't like them to come *early*; I actually don't exactly mind their coming, as such."

As he put his shoulders against the lid at the top of the ramp, Schein said genially, "That's mighty tolerant of you, Tod boy. I'm sure the careboys would be pleased to hear your sentiments."

Of the three of them, Sam Regan was the last to reach the surface; he did not like the upstairs at all, and he did not care who knew it. And anyhow, no one could compel him to leave the safety of the Pinole Fluke-pit; it was entirely his business, and he noted now that a number of his fellow flukers had elected to remain below in their quarters, confident that those who did answer the horn would bring them back something.

"It's bright," Tod murmured, blinking in the sun.

The care ship sparkled close overhead, set against the gray sky as if hanging from an uneasy thread. Good pilot, this drop, Tod decided. He, or rather *it*, just lazily handles it, in no hurry. Tod waved at the care ship, and once more the huge horn burst out its din, making him clap his hands to his ears. Hey, a joke's a joke, he said to himself. And then the horn ceased; the careboy had relented.

"Wave to him to drop," Norm Schein said to Tod. "You've got the wigwag."

"Sure," Tod said, and began laboriously flapping the red flag, which the Martian creatures had long ago provided, back and forth, back and forth.

A projectile slid from the underpart of the ship, tossed out stabilizers, spiraled toward the ground.

"Sheoot," Sam Regan said with disgust. "It is staples; they don't have the parachute." He turned away, not interested.

How miserable the upstairs looked today, he thought as he surveyed the scene surrounding him. There, to the right, the uncompleted house which someone—not far from their pit—had begun to build out of lumber salvaged from Vallejo, ten miles to the north. Animals or radiation dust had gotten the builder, and so his work remained where it was; it would never be put to use. And, Sam Regan saw, an unusually heavy precipitate had formed since last he had been up here, Thursday morning or perhaps Friday; he had lost exact track. The darn dust, he thought. Just rocks, pieces of rubble, and the dust. World's becoming a dusty object with no one to whisk it off regularly. How about you? he asked silently of the Martian careboy flying in slow circles overhead. Isn't your technology limitless? Can't you appear some morning with a dust rag a million miles in surface area and restore our planet to pristine newness?

Or rather, he thought, to pristine *oldness*, the way it was in the "ol-days," as the children call it. We'd like that. While you're looking for something to give to us in the way of further aid, try that.

The careboy circled once more, searching for signs of writing in the dust: a message from the flukers below. I'll write that, Sam thought. BRING DUST RAG, RESTORE OUR CIVILIZATION. Okay, careboy?

All at once the care ship shot off, no doubt on its way back home to its base on Luna or perhaps all the way to Mars.

From the open fluke-pit hole, up which the three of them had come, a further head poked, a woman. Jean Regan, Sam's wife, appeared, shielded by a bonnet against the gray, blinding sun, frowning and saying, "Anything important? Anything *new*?"

"'Fraid not," Sam said. The care parcel projectile had landed and he walked toward it, scuffing his boots in the dust. The hull of the projectile had cracked open from the impact and he could see the canisters already. It looked to be five thousand pounds of salt—might as well leave it up here so the animals wouldn't starve, he decided. He felt despondent.

How peculiarly anxious the careboys were. Concerned all the time that the mainstays of existence be ferried from their own planet to Earth. They must think we eat all day long, Sam thought. My God ... the pit was filled to capacity with stored foods. But of course it had been one of the smallest public shelters in northern California.

"Hey," Schein said, stooping down by the projectile and peering into the crack opened along its side. "I believe I see something we can use." He found a rusted metal pole—once it had helped reinforce the concrete side of an ol-days public building—and poked at the projectile, stirring its release mechanism into action. The mechanism, triggered off, popped the rear half of the projectile open . . . and there lay the contents.

"Looks like radios in that box," Tod said. "Transistor radios." Thoughtfully stroking his short black beard he said, "Maybe we can use them for something new in our layouts."

"Mine's already got a radio," Schein pointed out.

"Well, build an electronic self-directing lawn mower with the parts," Tod said. "You don't have that, do you?" He knew the Scheins' Perky Pat layout fairly well; the two couples, he and his wife with Schein and his, had played together a good deal, being almost evenly matched.

Sam Regan said, "Dibs on the radios, because I can use them." His layout lacked the automatic garage-door opener that both Schein and Tod had; he was considerably behind them.

"Let's get to work," Schein agreed. "We'll leave the staples here and just cart back the radios. If anybody wants the staples, let them come here and get them. Before the do-cats do."

Nodding, the other two men fell to the job of carting the useful contents of the projectile to the entrance of their fluke-pit ramp. For use in their precious, elaborate Perky Pat layouts.

Seated cross-legged with his whetstone, Timothy Schein, ten years old and aware of his many responsibilities, sharpened his knife, slowly and expertly. Meanwhile, disturbing him, his mother and father noisily quarreled with Mr. and Mrs. Morrison, on the far side of the partition. They were playing Perky Pat again. As usual.

How many times today they have to play that dumb game? Timothy asked himself. Forever, I guess. He could see nothing in it, but his parents played on anyhow. And they weren't the only ones; he knew from what other kids said, even from other fluke-pits, that their parents, too, played Perky Pat most of the day, and sometimes even on into the night.

His mother said loudly, "Perky Pat's going to the grocery store and it's got one of those electric eyes that opens the door. Look." A pause. "See, it opened for her, and now she's inside."

"She pushes a cart," Timothy's dad added, in support.

"No, she doesn't," Mrs. Morrison contradicted. "That's wrong. She gives her list to the grocer and he fills it."

"That's only in little neighborhood stores," his mother explained. "And this is a supermarket, you can tell because of the electric-eye door."

"I'm sure all grocery stores had electric-eye doors," Mrs. Morrison said stubbornly, and her husband chimed in with his agreement. Now the voices rose in anger; another squabble had broken out. As usual.

Aw, cung to them, Timothy said to himself, using the strongest word which he and his friends knew. What's a supermarket anyhow? He tested the blade of his knife—he had made it himself, originally, out of a heavy metal pan—and then hopped to his feet. A moment later he had sprinted silently down the hall and was rapping his special rap on the door of the Chamberlains' quarters.

Fred, also ten years old, answered. "Hi. Ready to go? I see you got that ol' knife of yours sharpened; what do you think we'll catch?"

"Not a do-cat," Timothy said. "A lot better than that; I'm tired of eating do-cat. Too peppery."

"Your parents playing Perky Pat?"

"Yeah."

Fred said, "My mom and dad have been gone for a long time, off playing with the Benteleys." He glanced sideways at Timothy, and in an instant they had shared their mute disappointment regarding their parents. Gosh, and maybe the darn game was all over the world, by now; that would not have surprised either of them.

"How come your parents play it?" Timothy asked.

"Same reason yours do," Fred said.

Hesitating, Timothy said, "Well, why? I don't know why they do; I'm asking you, can't you say?"

"It's because—" Fred broke off. "Ask them. Come on; let's get upstairs and start hunting." His eyes shone. "Let's see what we can catch and kill today."

Shortly, they had ascended the ramp, popped open the lid, and were crouching amidst the dust and rocks, searching the horizon. Timothy's heart pounded; this moment always overwhelmed him, the first instant of reaching the upstairs. The thrilling initial sight of the expanse. Because it was never the same. The dust, heavier today, had a darker gray color to it than before; it seemed denser, more mysterious.

Here and there, covered by many layers of dust, lay parcels dropped from past relief ships—dropped and left to deteriorate. Never to be claimed. And, Timothy saw, an additional new projectile which had arrived that morning. Most of its cargo could be seen within; the grown-ups had not had any use for the majority of the contents, today.

"Look," Fred said softly.

Two do-cats—mutant dogs or cats; no one knew for sure—could be seen, lightly sniffing at the projectile. Attracted by the unclaimed contents.

"We don't want them," Timothy said.

"That one's sure nice and fat," Fred said longingly. But it was Timothy who had the knife; all he himself had was a string with a metal bolt on the end, a bullroarer that could kill a bird or a small animal at a distance—but useless against a do-cat, which generally weighed fifteen to twenty pounds and sometimes more.

High up in the sky a dot moved at immense speed, and Timothy knew that it was a care ship heading for another fluke-pit, bringing supplies to it. Sure are busy, he thought to himself. Those careboys always coming and going; they never stop, because if they did, the grown-ups would die. Wouldn't that be too bad? he thought ironically. Sure be sad.

Fred said, "Wave to it and maybe it'll drop something." He grinned at Timothy, and then they both broke out laughing.

"Sure," Timothy said. "Let's see; what do I want?" Again the two of them laughed at the idea of them wanting something. The two boys had the entire upstairs, as far as the eye could see . . . they had even more than the careboys had, and that was plenty, more than plenty.

"Do you think they know," Fred said, "that our parents play Perky Pat with furniture made out of what they drop? I bet they don't know about Perky Pat; they never have seen a Perky Pat doll, and if they did they'd be really mad."

"You're right," Timothy said. "They'd be so sore they'd probably stop dropping stuff." He glanced at Fred, catching his eye.

"Aw no," Fred said. "We shouldn't tell them; your dad would beat you again if you did that, and probably me, too."

Even so, it was an interesting idea. He could imagine first the surprise and then the anger of the careboys; it would be fun to see that, see the reaction of the eight-legged Martian creatures who had so much charity inside their warty bodies, the cephalopodic univalve mollusklike organisms who had voluntarily taken it upon themselves to supply succor to the waning remnants of the human race . . . this was how they got paid back for their charity, this utterly wasteful, stupid purpose to which their goods were being put. This stupid Perky Pat game that all the adults played.

And anyhow it would be very hard to tell them; there was almost no communication between humans and careboys. They were too different. Acts, deeds, could be done, conveying something . . . but not mere words, not mere *signs*. And anyhow—

A great brown rabbit bounded by to the right, past the half-completed house. Timothy whipped out his knife. "Oh boy!" he said aloud in excitement. "Let's go!" He set off across the rubbly ground, Fred a little behind him. Gradually they gained on the rabbit; swift running came easy to the two boys: they had done much practicing.

"Throw the knife!" Fred panted, and Timothy, skidding to a halt, raised his right arm, paused to take aim, and then hurled the sharpened, weighted knife. His most valuable, self-made possession.

It cleaved the rabbit straight through its vitals. The rabbit tumbled, slid, raising a cloud of dust.

"I bet we can get a dollar for that!" Fred exclaimed, leaping up and down. "The hide alone—I bet we can get fifty cents just for the darn hide!"

Together, they hurried toward the dead rabbit, wanting to get there before a red-tailed hawk or a day owl swooped on it from the gray sky above.

Bending, Norman Schein picked up his Perky Pat doll and said sullenly, "I'm quitting; I don't want to play anymore."

Distressed, his wife protested,"But we've got Perky Pat all the way downtown in her new Ford hardtop convertible and parked and a dime in the meter and she's shopped and now she's in the analyst's office reading *Fortune*—we're way ahead of the Morrisons! Why do you want to quit, Norm?"

"We just don't agree," Norman grumbled. "You say analysts charged twenty dollars an hour and I distinctly remember them charging only ten; nobody could charge twenty. So you're penalizing our side, and for what? The Morrisons agree it was only ten. Don't you?" he said to Mr. and Mrs. Morrison, who squatted on the far side of the layout which combined both couples' Perky Pat sets.

Helen Morrison said to her husband, "You went to the analyst more than I did; are you sure he charged only ten?"

"Well, I went mostly to group therapy," Tod said. "At the Berkeley State Mental Hygiene Clinic, and they charged according to your ability to pay. And Perky Pat is at a *private* psychoanalyst."

"We'll have to ask someone else," Helen said to Norman Schein. "I guess all we can do now this minute is suspend the game." He found himself being glared at by her, too, now, because by his insistence on the one point he had put an end to their game for the whole afternoon.

"Shall we leave it all set up?" Fran Schein asked. "We might as well; maybe we can finish tonight after dinner."

Norman Schein gazed down at their combined layout, the swanky shops, the well-lit streets with the parked new-model cars, all of them shiny, the split-level house itself, where Perky Pat lived and where she entertained Leonard, her boyfriend. It was the *house* that he perpetually yearned for; the house was the real focus of the layout—of all the Perky Pat layouts, however much they might otherwise differ.

Perky Pat's wardrobe, for instance, there in the closet of the house, the big bedroom closet. Her capri pants, her white cotton short-shorts, her two-piece polka-dot swimsuit, her fuzzy sweaters . . . and there, in her bedroom, her hi-fi set, her collection of long-playing records . . .

It had been this way, once, really been like this in the ol-days. Norm Schein could remember his own LP record collection, and he had once had clothes almost as swanky as Perky Pat's boyfriend Leonard, cashmere jackets and tweed suits and Italian sportshirts and shoes made in England. He hadn't owned a Jaguar XKE sports car, like Leonard did, but he had owned a fine-looking old 1963 Mercedes-Benz, which he had used to drive to work.

We lived then, Norm Schein said to himself, *like Perky Pat and Leonard do now*. This is how it actually was.

To his wife he said, pointing to the clock radio which Perky Pat kept beside her bed, "Remember our G.E. clock radio? How it used to wake us up in the morning with classical music from that FM station,

KSFR? The 'Wolfgangers,' the program was called. From six a.m. to nine every morning."

"Yes," Fran said, nodding soberly. "And you used to get up before me; I knew I should have gotten up and fixed bacon and hot coffee for you, but it was so much fun just indulging myself, not stirring for half an hour longer, until the kids woke up."

"Woke up, hell; they were awake before we were," Norm said. "Don't you remember? They were in the back watching *The Three Stooges* on TV until eight. Then I got up and fixed hot cereal for them, and then I went on to my job at Ampex down at Redwood City."

"Oh yes," Fran said. "The TV." Their Perky Pat did not have a TV set; they had lost it to the Regans in a game a week ago, and Norm had not yet been able to fashion another one realistic-looking enough to substitute. So, in a game, they pretended now that "the TV repairman had come for it." That was how they explained their Perky Pat not having something she really would have had.

Norm thought, Playing this game . . . it's like being back there, back in the world before the war. That's why we play it, I suppose. He felt shame, but only fleetingly; the shame, almost at once, was replaced by the desire to play a little longer.

"Let's not quit," he said suddenly. "I'll agree the psychoanalyst would have charged Perky Pat twenty dollars. Okay?"

"Okay," both the Morrisons said together, and they settled back down once more to resume the game.

Tod Morrison had picked up their Perky Pat; he held it, stroking its blond hair—theirs was blond, whereas the Scheins' was a brunette—and fiddling with the snaps of its skirt.

"Whatever are you doing?" his wife inquired.

"Nice skirt she has," Tod said. "You did a good job sewing it."

Norm said, "Ever know a girl, back in the ol-days, that looked like Perky Pat?"

"No," Tod Morrison said somberly. "Wish I had, though. I *saw* girls like Perky Pat, especially when I was living in Los Angeles during the Korean War. But I just could never manage to know them personally. And of course there were really terrific girl singers, like Peggy Lee and Julie London . . . they looked a lot like Perky Pat."

"Play," Fran said vigorously. And Norm, whose turn it was, picked up the spinner and spun.

"Eleven," he said. "That gets my Leonard out of the sports car repair garage and on his way to the racetrack." He moved the Leonard doll ahead.

Thoughtfully, Tod Morrison said, "You know, I was out the other day hauling in perishables which the careboys had dropped . . . Bill Ferner was there, and he told me something interesting. He met a fluker from a fluke-pit down where Oakland used to be. And at that fluke-pit you know what they play? Not Perky Pat. They never have heard of Perky Pat."

"Well, what do they play, then?" Helen asked.

"They have another doll entirely." Frowning, Tod continued, "Bill says the Oakland fluker called it a Connie Companion doll. Ever hear of that?"

"A 'Connie Companion' doll," Fran said thoughtfully. "How strange. I wonder what she's like. Does she have a boyfriend?"

"Oh sure," Tod said. "His name is Paul. Connie and Paul. You know, we ought to hike down there to that Oakland Fluke-pit one of these days and see what Connie and Paul look like and how they live. Maybe we could learn a few things to add to our own layouts."

Norm said, "Maybe we could play them."

Puzzled, Fran said, "Could a Perky Pat play a Connie Companion? Is that possible? I wonder what would happen?"

There was no answer from any of the others. Because none of them knew.

As they skinned the rabbit, Fred said to Timothy, "Where did the name 'fluker' come from? It's sure an ugly word; why do they use it?"

"A fluker is a person who lived through the hydrogen war," Timothy explained. "You know, by a fluke. A fluke of fate? See? Because almost everyone was killed; there used to be thousands of people."

"But what's a 'fluke,' then? When you say a 'fluke of fate—'"

"A fluke is when fate has decided to spare you," Timothy said, and that was all he had to say on the subject. That was all he knew.

Fred said thoughtfully, "But you and I, we're not flukers because we weren't alive when the war broke out. We were born after."

"Right," Timothy said.

"So anybody who calls me a fluker," Fred said, "is going to get hit in the eye with my bullroarer."

"And 'careboy,'" Timothy said, "that's a made-up word, too. It's from when stuff was dumped from jet planes and ships to people in a disaster area. They were called 'care parcels' because they came from people who cared."

"I know that," Fred said, "I didn't ask that."

"Well, I told you anyhow," Timothy said.

The two boys continued skinning the rabbit.

Jean Regan said to her husband, "Have you heard about the Connie Companion doll?" She glanced down the long rough-board table to make sure none of the other families was listening. "Sam," she said, "I heard it from Helen Morrison; she heard it from Tod and he heard it from Bill Ferner, I think. So it's probably true."

"What's true?" Sam said.

"That in the Oakland Fluke-pit they don't have Perky Pat; they have Connie Companion . . . and it occurred to me that maybe some of this—you know, this sort of emptiness, this boredom we feel now and then—maybe if we saw the Connie Companion doll and how she lives, maybe we could add enough to our own layout to—" She paused, reflecting. "To make it more complete."

"I don't care for the name," Sam Regan said, "Connie Companion; it sounds cheap." He spooned up some of the plain, utilitarian grain-mash which the careboys had been dropping, of late. And, as he ate a mouthful, he thought, I'll bet Connie Companion doesn't eat slop like this; I'll bet she eats cheeseburgers with all the trimmings, at a high-type drive-in.

"Could we make a trek down there?" Jean asked.

"To Oakland Fluke-pit?" Sam stared at her. "It's *fifteen miles*, all the way on the other side of the Berkeley Fluke-pit!"

"But this is important," Jean said stubbornly. "And Bill says that a fluker from Oakland came all the way up here, in search of electronic parts or something . . . so if he can do it, we can. We've got the dust suits they dropped us, I know we could do it."

Little Timothy Schein, sitting with his family, had overheard her; now he spoke up. "Mrs. Regan, Fred Chamberlain and I, we could trek down that far, if you pay us. What do you say?" He nudged Fred, who sat beside him. "Couldn't we? For maybe five dollars."

Fred, his face serious, turned to Mrs. Regan and said, "We could get you a Connie Companion doll. For five dollars for *each* of us."

"Good grief," Jean Regan said, outraged. And dropped the subject.

But later, after dinner, she brought it up again when she and Sam were alone in their quarters.

"Sam, I've got to see it," she burst out. Sam, in a galvanized tub, was taking his weekly bath, so he had to listen to her. "Now that we know it exists we have to play against someone in the Oakland Fluke-pit; at least we can do that. Can't we? Please." She paced back and forth in the small room, her hands clasped tensely. "Connie Companion may have a Standard station and an airport terminal with jet landing strip and color TV and a French restaurant where they serve escargot, like the one you and I went to when we were first married . . . I just have to see her layout."

"I don't know," Sam said hesitantly, "There's something about Connie Companion doll that—makes me uneasy."

"What could it possibly be?"

"I don't know."

Jean said bitterly, "It's because you know her layout is so much better than ours and she's so much more than Perky Pat."

"Maybe that's it," Sam murmured.

"If you don't go, if you don't try to make contact with them down at the Oakland Fluke-pit, someone else will—someone with more ambition will get ahead of you. Like Norman Schein. He's not afraid the way you are."

Sam said nothing; he continued with his bath. But his hands shook.

A careboy had recently dropped complicated pieces of machinery which were, evidently, a form of mechanical computer. For several weeks the computers—if that was what they were—had sat about the pit in their cartons, unused, but now Norman Schein was finding something to do with one. At the moment he was busy adapting some of its gears, the smallest ones, to form a garbage disposal unit for his Perky Pat's kitchen.

Using the tiny special tools—designed and built by inhabitants of the fluke-pit—which were necessary in fashioning environmental items for Perky Pat, he was busy at his hobby bench. Thoroughly engrossed in what he was doing, he all at once realized that Fran was standing directly behind him, watching.

"I get nervous when I'm watched," Norm said, holding a tiny gear with a pair of tweezers.

"Listen," Fran said, "I've thought of something. Does this suggest anything to you?" She placed before him one of the transistor radios which had been dropped the day before.

"It suggests that garage-door opener already thought of," Norm said irritably. He continued with his work, expertly fitting the miniature pieces together in the sink drain of Pat's kitchen; such delicate work demanded maximum concentration.

Fran said, "It suggests that there must be radio *transmitters* on Earth somewhere, or the careboys wouldn't have dropped these."

"So?" Norm said, uninterested.

"Maybe our mayor has one," Fran said. "Maybe there's one right here in our own pit, and we could use it to call the Oakland Fluke-pit. Representatives from there could meet us halfway . . . say at the Berkeley Fluke-pit. And we could play there. So we wouldn't have that long fifteen-mile trip."

Norman hesitated in his work; he set the tweezers down and said slowly, "I think possibly you're right." But if their mayor Hooker Glebe had a radio transmitter, would he let them use it? And if he did—

"We can try," Fran urged. "It wouldn't hurt to try."

"Okay," Norm said, rising from his hobby bench.

The short, sly-faced man in Army uniform, the mayor of the Pinole Fluke-pit, listened in silence as Norm Schein spoke. Then he smiled a wise, cunning smile. "Sure, I have a radio transmitter. Had it all the time. Fifty-watt output. But why would you want to get in touch with the Oakland Fluke-pit?"

Guardedly, Norm said, "That's my business."

Hooker Glebe said thoughtfully, "I'll let you use it for fifteen dollars."

It was a nasty shock, and Norm recoiled. Good Lord; all the money he and his wife had—they needed every bill of it for use in playing Perky Pat. Money was the tender in the game; there was no other criterion by which one could tell if he had won or lost. "That's too much," he said aloud.

Well, say ten," the mayor said, shrugging.

In the end they settled for six dollars and a fifty-cent piece.

"I'll make the radio contact for you," Hooker Glebe said. "Because you don't know how. It will take time." He began turning a crank at the side of the generator of the transmitter. "I'll notify you when I've made contact with them. But give me the money now." He held out his hand for it, and, with great reluctance, Norm paid him.

It was not until late that evening that Hooker managed to establish contact with Oakland. Pleased with himself, beaming in self-satisfaction, he appeared at the Scheins' quarters, during their dinner hour. "All set," he announced. "Say, you know there are actually *nine* fluke-pits in Oakland? I didn't know that. Which you want? I've got one with the radio code of Red Vanilla." He chuckled. "They're tough and suspicious down there; it was hard to get any of them to answer."

Leaving his evening meal, Norman hurried to the mayor's quarters, Hooker puffing along after him.

The transmitter, sure enough, was on, and static wheezed from the speaker of its monitoring unit. Awkwardly, Norm seated himself at the microphone. "Do I just talk?" he asked Hooker Glebe.

"Just say, This is Pinole Fluke-pit calling. Repeat that a couple of times and then when they acknowledge, you say what you want to say." The mayor fiddled with controls of the transmitter, fussing in an important fashion.

"This is Pinole Fluke-pit," Norm said loudly into the microphone.

Almost at once a clear voice from the monitor said, "This is Red Vanilla Three answering." The voice was cold and harsh; it struck him forcefully as distinctly alien. Hooker was right.

"Do you have Connie Companion down there where you are?"

"Yes we do," the Oakland fluker answered.

"Well, I challenge you," Norman said, feeling the veins in his throat pulse with the tension of what he was saying. "We're Perky Pat in this area; we'll play Perky Pat against your Connie Companion. Where can we meet?"

"Perky Pat," the Oakland fluker echoed. "Yeah, I know about her. What would the stakes be, in your mind?"

"Up here we play for paper money mostly," Norman said, feeling that his response was somehow lame.

"We've got lots of paper money," the Oakland fluker said cuttingly. "That wouldn't interest any of us. What else?"

"I don't know." He felt hampered, talking to someone he could not see; he was not used to that. People should, he thought, be face-to-face, then you can see the other person's expression. This was not natural. "Let's meet halfway," he said, "and discuss it. Maybe we could meet at the Berkeley Fluke-pit; how about that?"

The Oakland fluker said, "That's too far. You mean lug our Connie Companion layout all that way? It's too heavy and something might happen to it."

"No, just to discuss rules and stakes," Norman said.

Dubiously, the Oakland fluker said, "Well, I guess we could do that. But you better understand—we take Connie Companion doll pretty damn seriously; you better be prepared to talk terms."

"We will," Norm assured him.

All this time mayor Hooker Glebe had been cranking the handle of the generator; perspiring, his face bloated with exertion, he motioned angrily for Norm to conclude his palaver.

"At the Berkeley Fluke-pit," Norm finished. "In three days. And send your best player, the one who has the biggest and most authentic layout. Our Perky Pat layouts are works of art, you understand."

The Oakland fluker said, "We'll believe that when we see them. After all, we've got carpenters and electricians and plasterers here, building our layouts; I'll bet you're all unskilled."

"Not as much as you think," Norm said hotly, and laid down the microphone. To Hooker Glebe—who had immediately stopped cranking—he said, "We'll beat them. Wait'll they see the garbage disposal unit I'm making for my Perky Pat; did you know there were people back in the ol-days, I mean real alive human beings, who didn't have garbage disposal units?"

"I remember," Hooker said peevishly. "Say, you got a lot of cranking for your money; I think you gypped me, talking so long." He eyed Norm with such hostility that Norm began to feel uneasy. After all, the mayor of the pit had the authority to evict any fluker he wished; that was their law.

"I'll give you the fire-alarm box I just finished the other day," Norm said. "In my layout it goes at the corner of the block where Perky Pat's boyfriend Leonard lives."

"Good enough," Hooker agreed, and his hostility faded. It was replaced, at once, by desire. "Let's see it, Norm. I bet it'll go good in my layout; a fire-alarm box is just what I need to complete my first block where I have the mailbox. Thank you."

"You're welcome," Norm sighed, philosophically.

When he returned from the two-day trek to the Berkeley Fluke-pit his face was so grim that his wife knew at once that the parley with the Oakland people had not gone well.

That morning a careboy had dropped cartons of a synthetic tealike drink; she fixed a cup of it for Norman, waiting to hear what had taken place eight miles to the south.

"We haggled," Norm said, seated wearily on the bed which he and his wife and child all shared. "They don't want money; they don't want goods—naturally not goods, because the darn careboys are dropping regularly down there, too."

"What will they accept, then?"

Norm said, "Perky Pat herself." He was silent, then.

"Oh good Lord," she said, appalled.

"But if we win," Norm pointed out, "we win Connie Companion."

"And the layouts? What about them?"

"We keep our own. It's just Perky Pat herself, not Leonard, not anything else."

"But," she protested, "what'll we *do* if we lose Perky Pat?"

"I can make another one," Norm said. "Given time. There's still a big supply of thermoplastics and artificial hair, here in the pit. And I have plenty of different paints; it would take at least a month, but I could do it. I don't look forward to the job, I admit. But—" His eyes glinted. "Don't look on the dark side; *imagine what it would be like to win Connie Companion doll.* I think we may well win; their delegate seemed smart and, as Hooker said, tough . . . but the one I talked to didn't strike me as being very flukey. You know, on good terms with luck."

And, after all, the element of luck, of chance, entered into each stage of the game through the agency of the spinner.

"It seems wrong," Fran said, "to put up Perky Pat herself. But if you say so—" She managed to smile a little. "I'll go along with it. And if you won Connie Companion—who knows? You might be elected mayor when Hooker dies. Imagine, to have won somebody else's *doll*—not just the game, the money, but the *doll itself.*"

"I can win," Norm said soberly. "Because I'm very flukey." He could feel it in him, the same flukeyness that had got him through the hydrogen war alive, that had kept him alive ever since. You either have it or you don't, he realized. And I do.

His wife said, "Shouldn't we ask Hooker to call a meeting of everyone in the pit, and send the best player out of our entire group? So as to be the surest of winning."

"Listen," Norm Schein said emphatically. "I'm the best player. I'm going. And so are you; we make a good team, and we don't want to break it up. Anyhow, we'll need at least two people to carry Perky Pat's layout." All in all, he judged, their layout weighed sixty pounds.

His plan seemed to him to be satisfactory. But when he mentioned it to the others living in the Pinole Fluke-pit he found himself facing sharp disagreement. The whole next day was filled with argument.

"You can't lug your layout all that way yourselves," Sam Regan said. "Either take more people with you or carry your layout in a vehicle of some sort. Such as a cart." He scowled at Norm.

"Where'd I get a cart?" Norm demanded.

"Maybe something could be adapted," Sam said. "I'll give you every bit of help I can. Personally, I'd go along but as I told my wife this whole idea worries me." He thumped Norm on the back. "I admire your courage, you and Fran, setting off this way. I wish I had what it takes." He looked unhappy.

In the end, Norm settled on a wheelbarrow. He and Fran would take turns pushing it. That way neither of them would have to carry any load above and beyond their food and water, and of course knives by which to protect them from the do-cats.

As they were carefully placing the elements of their layout in the wheelbarrow, Norm Schein's boy Timothy came sidling up to them. "Take me along, Dad," he pleaded. "For fifty cents I'll go as guide and scout, and also I'll help you catch food along the way."

"We'll manage fine," Norm said. "You stay here in the fluke-pit; you'll be safer here." It annoyed him, the idea of his son tagging along on an important venture such as this. It was almost—sacrilegious.

"Kiss us goodbye," Fran said to Timothy, smiling at him briefly; then her attention returned to the layout within the wheelbarrow. "I hope it doesn't tip over," she said fearfully to Norm.

"Not a chance,"Norm said. "If we're careful." He felt confident.

A few moments later they began wheeling the wheelbarrow up the ramp to the lid at the top, to upstairs. Their journey to the Berkeley Fluke-pit had begun.

A mile outside the Berkeley Fluke-pit he and Fran began to stumble over empty drop-canisters and some only partly empty: remains of past care parcels such as littered the surface near their own pit. Norm Schein breathed a sigh of relief; the journey had not been so bad after all, except that his hands had become blistered from gripping the metal handles of the wheelbarrow, and Fran had turned her ankle so that now she walked with a painful limp. But it had taken them less time than he had anticipated, and his mood was one of buoyancy.

Ahead, a figure appeared, crouching low in the ash. A boy. Norm waved at him and called, "Hey, sonny—we're from the Pinole pit; we're supposed to meet a party from Oakland here . . . do you remember me?"

The boy, without answering, turned and scampered off.

"Nothing to be afraid of," Norm said to his wife. "He's going to tell their mayor. A nice old fellow named Ben Fennimore."

Soon several adults appeared, approaching warily.

With relief, Norm set the legs of the wheelbarrow down into the ash, letting go and wiping his face with his handkerchief. "Has the Oakland team arrived yet?" he called.

"Not yet," a tall, elderly man with a white armband and ornate cap answered. "It's you Schein, isn't it?" he said, peering. This was

Ben Fennimore. "Back already with your layout." Now the Berkeley flukers had begun crowding around the wheelbarrow, inspecting the Scheins' layout. Their faces showed admiration.

"They have Perky Pat here," Norm explained to his wife. "But—" He lowered his voice. "Their layouts are only basic. Just a house, wardrobe, and car . . . they've built almost nothing. No imagination."

One Berkeley fluker, a woman, said wonderingly to Fran, "And you made each of the pieces of furniture yourselves?" Marveling, she turned to the man beside her. "See what they've accomplished, Ed?"

"Yes," the man answered, nodding. "Say," he said to Fran and Norm, "can we see it all set up? You're going to set it up in our pit, aren't you?"

"We are indeed," Norm said.

The Berkeley flukers helped push the wheelbarrow the last mile. And before long they were descending the ramp, to the pit below the surface.

"It's a big pit," Norm said knowingly to Fran. "Must be two thousand people here. This is where the University of California was."

"I see," Fran said, a little timid at entering a strange pit; it was the first time in years—since the war, in fact—that she had seen any strangers. And so many at once. It was almost too much for her; Norm felt her shrink back, pressing against him in fright.

When they had reached the first level and were starting to unload the wheelbarrow, Ben Fennimore came up to them and said softly, "I think the Oakland people have been spotted; we just got a report of activity upstairs. So be prepared." He added, "We're rooting for you, of course, because you're Perky Pat, the same as us."

"Have you ever seen Connie Companion doll?" Fran asked him.

"No ma'am," Fennimore answered courteously. "But naturally we've heard about it, being neighbors to Oakland and all. I'll tell you one thing . . . we hear that Connie Companion doll is a bit older than Perky Pat. You know—more, um, *mature*." He explained, "I just wanted to prepare you."

Norm and Fran glanced at each other. "Thanks," Norm said slowly. "Yes, we should be as much prepared as possible. How about Paul?"

"Oh, he's not much," Fennimore said. "Connie runs things; I don't even think Paul has a real apartment of his own. But you better wait until the Oakland flnkers get here; I don't want to mislead you—my knowledge is all hearsay, you understand."

Another Berkeley fluker, standing nearby, spoke up, "I saw Connie once, and she's much more grown up than Perky Pat."

"How old do you figure Perky Pat is?" Norm asked him.

"Oh, I'd say seventeen or eighteen," Norm was told.

"And Connie?" He waited tensely.

"Oh, she might be twenty-five, even."

From the ramp behind them they heard noises. More Berkeley flukers appeared, and, after them, two men carrying between them a platform on which, spread out, Norm saw a great, spectacular layout.

This was the Oakland team, and they weren't a couple, a man and wife; they were both men, and they were hard-faced with stern, remote eyes. They jerked their heads briefly at him and Fran, acknowledging their presence. And then, with enormous care, they set down the platform on which their layout rested.

Behind them came a third Oakland fluker carrying a metal box, much like a lunch pail. Norm, watching, knew instinctively that in the box lay Connie Companion doll. The Oakland fluker produced a key and began unlocking the box.

"We're ready to begin playing any time," the taller of the Oakland men said. "As we agreed in our discussion, we'll use a numbered spinner instead of dice. Less chance of cheating that way."

"Agreed," Norm said. Hesitantly he held out his hand. "I'm Norman Schein and this is my wife and play-partner Fran."

The Oakland man, evidently the leader, said, "I'm Walter R. Wynn. This is my partner here, Charley Dowd, and the man with the box, that's Peter Foster. He isn't going to play; he just guards our layout." Wynn glanced about, at the Berkeley flukers, as if saying, I know you're all partial to Perky Pat, in here. But we don't care; we're not scared.

Fran said, "We're ready to play, Mr. Wynn." Her voice was low but controlled.

"What about money?" Fennimore asked.

"I think both teams have plenty of money," Wynn said. He laid out several thousand dollars in greenbacks, and now Norm did the same. "The money of course is not a factor in this, except as a means of conducting the game."

Norm nodded; he understood perfectly. Only the dolls themselves mattered. And now, for the first time, he saw Connie Companion doll.

She was being placed in her bedroom by Mr. Foster who evidently was in charge of her. And the sight of her took his breath away. Yes, she was older. A grown woman, not a girl at all . . . the difference between her and Perky Pat was acute. And so lifelike. Carved, not poured; she obviously had been whittled out of wood and then painted—she was not a thermoplastic. And her hair. It appeared to be genuine hair.

He was deeply impressed.

"What do you think of her?" Walter Wynn asked, with a faint grin.

"Very—impressive," Norm conceded.

Now the Oaklanders were studying Perky Pat. "Poured thermoplastic," one of them said. "Artificial hair. Nice clothes, though; all stitched by hand, you can see that. Interesting; what we heard was correct. Perky Pat isn't a grown-up, she's just a teenager."

Now the male companion to Connie appeared; he was set down in the bedroom beside Connie.

"Wait a minute," Norm said. "You're putting Paul or whatever his name is, in her bedroom with her? Doesn't he have his own apartment?"

Wynn said, "They're married."

"*Married!*" Norman and Fran stared at him, dumbfounded.

"Why sure," Wynn said. "So naturally they live together. Your dolls, they're not, are they?"

"N-no," Fran said. "Leonard is Perky Pat's boyfriend . . ." Her voice trailed off. "Norm," she said, clutching his arm, "I don't believe him; I think he's just saying they're married to get the advantage. Because if they both start out from the same room—"

Norm said aloud, "You fellows, look here. It's not fair, calling them married."

Wynn said, "We're not 'calling' them married; they are married. Their names are Connie and Paul Lathrope, of 24 Arden Place, Piedmont. They've been married for a year, most players will tell you." He sounded calm.

Maybe, Norm thought, it's true. He was truly shaken.

"Look at them together," Fran said, kneeling down to examine the Oaklanders' layout. "In the same bedroom, in the same house. Why, Norm; do you see? There's just the one bed. A big double bed." Wild-eyed, she appealed to him. "How can Perky Pat and Leonard play against them?" Her voice shook. "It's not morally *right*."

"This is another type of layout entirely," Norm said to Walter Wynn. "This, that you have. Utterly different from what we're used to, as you can see." He pointed to his own layout. "I insist that in this game Connie and Paul *not* live together and *not* be considered married."

"But they are," Foster spoke up. "It's a fact. Look—their clothes are in the same closet." He showed them the closet. "And in the same bureau drawers." He showed them that, too. "And look in the bathroom. Two toothbrushes. His and hers, in the same rack. So you can see we're not making it up."

There was silence.

Then Fran said in a choked voice, "And if they're married—you mean they've been—intimate?"

Wynn raised an eyebrow, then nodded. "Sure, since they're married. Is there anything wrong with that?"

"Perky Pat and Leonard have never—" Fran began, and then ceased.

"Naturally not," Wynn agreed. "Because they're only going together. We understand that."

Fran said, "We just can't play. We can't." She caught hold of her husband's arm. "Let's go back to Pinole pit—please, Norman."

'Wait," Wynn said, at once. "If you don't play, you're conceding; you have to give up Perky Pat."

The three Oaklanders all nodded. And, Norm saw, many of the Berkeley flukers were nodding, too, including Ben Fennimore.

"They're right," Norm said heavily to his wife. "We'd have to give her up. We better play, dear."

"Yes," Fran said, in a dead, flat voice. "We'll play." She bent down and listlessly spun the needle of the spinner. It stopped at six.

Smiling, Walter Wynn knelt down and spun. He obtained a four.

The game had begun.

. . .

Crouching behind the strewn, decayed contents of a care parcel that had been dropped long ago, Timothy Schein saw coming across the surface of ash his mother and father, pushing the wheelbarrow ahead of them. They looked tired and worn.

"Hi," Timothy yelled, leaping out at them in joy at seeing them again; he had missed them very much.

"Hi, son," his father murmured, nodding. He let go of the handles of the wheelbarrow, then halted and wiped his face with his handkerchief.

Now Fred Chamberlain raced up, panting. "Hi, Mr. Schein; hi, Mrs. Schein. Hey, did you win? Did you beat the Oakland flukers? I bet you did, didn't you?" He looked from one of them to the other and then back.

In a low voice Fran said, "Yes, Freddy. We won."

Norm said, "Look in the wheelbarrow."

The two boys looked. And, there among Perky Pat's furnishings, lay another doll. Larger, fuller-figured, much older than Pat . . . they stared at her and she stared up sightlessly at the gray sky overhead. So this is Connie Companion doll, Timothy said to himself. Gee.

"We were lucky," Norm said. Now several people had emerged from the pit and were gathering around them, listening. Jean and Sam Regan, Tod Morrison and his wife Helen, and now their mayor, Hooker Glebe himself, waddling up excited and nervous, his face flushed, gasping for breath from the labor—unusual for him—of ascending the ramp.

Fran said, "We got a cancellation-of-debts card, just when we were most behind. We owed fifty thousand, and it made us even with the Oakland flukers. And then, after that, we got an advance-ten-squares card, and that put us right on the jackpot square, at least in our layout. We had a very bitter squabble, because the Oaklanders showed us that on their layout it was a tax lien slapped on real-estate-holdings square, but we had spun an odd number so that put us back on our own board." She sighed. "I'm glad to he back. It was hard, Hooker; it was a tough game."

Hooker Glebe wheezed, "Let's all get a look at the Connie Companion doll, folks." To Fran and Norm he said, "Can I lift her up and show them?"

"Sure," Norm said, nodding.

Hooker picked up Connie Companion doll. "She sure is realistic," he said, scrutinizing her. "Clothes aren't as nice as ours generally are; they look machine-made."

"They are," Norm agreed. "But she's carved, not poured."

"Yes, so I see." Hooker turned the doll about, inspecting her from all angles. "A nice job. She's—um, more filled out than Perky Pat. What's this outfit she has on? Tweed suit of some sort."

"A business suit," Fran said. "We won that with her; they had agreed on that in advance."

"You see, she has a job," Norm explained. "She's a psychology consultant for a business firm doing marketing research. In consumer preferences. A high-paying position . . . she earns twenty thousand a year, I believe Wynn said."

"Golly," Hooker said. "And Pat's just going to college; she's still in school." He looked troubled. "Well, I guess they were bound to be ahead of us in some ways. What matters is that you won." His jovial smile returned. "Perky Pat came out ahead." He held the Connie Companion doll up high, where everyone could see her. "Look what Norm and Fran came back with, folks!"

Norm said, "Be careful with her, Hooker." His voice was firm.

"Eh?" Hooker said, pausing. "Why, Norm?"

'Because," Norm said, "she's going to have a baby."

There was a sudden chill silence. The ash around them stirred faintly; that was the only sound.

"How do you know?" Hooker asked.

"They told us. The Oaklanders told us. And we won that, too—after a bitter argument that Fennimore had to settle." Reaching into the wheelbarrow he brought out a little leather pouch; from it he carefully took a carved pink newborn baby. "We won this too because Fennimore agreed that from a technical standpoint it's literally part of Connie Companion doll at this point."

Hooker stared a long, long time.

"She's married," Fran explained. "To Paul. They're not just going together. She's three months pregnant, Mr. Wynn said. He didn't tell us until after we won; he didn't want to, then, but they felt they had to. I think they were right; it wouldn't have done not to say."

Norm said, "And in addition there's actually an embryo outfit—"

"Yes," Fran said. "You have to open Connie up, of course, to see—"

"No," Jean Regan said. "Please, no."

Hooker said, "No, Mrs. Schein, don't." He backed away.

Fran said, "It shocked us of course at first, but—"

"You see," Norm put in, "it's logical; you have to follow the logic. Why, eventually Perky Pat—"

"No," Hooker said violently. He bent down, picked up a rock from the ash at his feet. "No," he said, and raised his arm. "You stop, you two. Don't say any more."

Now the Regans, too, had picked up rocks. No one spoke.

Fran said, at last, "Norm, we've got to get out of here."

"You're right," Tod Morrison told them. His wife nodded in grim agreement.

"You two go back down to Oakland," Hooker told Norman and Fran Schein. "You don't live here anymore. You're different than you were. You—changed."

"Yes," Sam Regan said slowly, half to himself. "I was right; there was something to fear." To Norm Schein he said, "How difficult a trip is it to Oakland?"

"We just went to Berkeley," Norm said. "To the Berkeley Fluke-pit." He seemed baffled and stunned by what was happening. "My God," he said, "we can't turn around and push this wheelbarrow back all the way to Berkeley again—we're worn out, we need rest!"

Sam Regan said, "What if somebody else pushed?" He walked up to the Scheins, then, and stood with them. "I'll push the darn thing. You lead the way, Schein." He looked toward his own wife, but Jean did not stir. And she did not put down her handful of rocks.

Timothy Schein plucked at his father's arm. "Can I come this time, Dad? Please let me come."

"Okay," Norm said, half to himself. Now he drew himself together. "So we're not wanted here." He turned to Fran. "Let's go. Sam's going to push the wheelbarrow; I think we can make it back there before nightfall. If not, we can sleep out in the open; Timothy'll help protect us against the do-cats."

Fran said, "I guess we have no choice." Her face was pale.

"And take this," Hooker said. He held out the tiny carved baby. Fran Schein accepted it and put it tenderly back in its leather pouch. Norm laid Connie Companion back down in the wheelbarrow, where she had been. They were ready to start back.

"It'll happen up here eventually," Norm said, to the group of people, to the Pinole flukers. "Oakland is just more advanced; that's all."

"Go on," Hooker Glebe said. "Get started."

Nodding, Norm started to pick up the handles of the wheelbarrow, but Sam Regan moved him aside and took them himself, "Let's go," he said.

The three adults, with Timothy Schein going ahead of them with his knife ready—in case a do-cat attacked—started into motion, in the direction of Oakland and the south. No one spoke. There was nothing to say.

"It's a shame this had to happen," Norm said at last, when they had gone almost a mile and there was no further sign of the Pinole flukers behind them.

"Maybe not," Sam Regan said. "Maybe it's for the good." He did not seem downcast. And after all, he had lost his wife; he had given up more than anyone else, and yet—he had survived.

"Glad you feel that way," Norm said somberly.

They continued on, each with his own thoughts.

After a while, Timothy said to his father, "All these big fluke-pits to the south . . . there's lots more things to do there, isn't there? I mean, you don't just sit around playing that game." He certainly hoped not.

His father said, "That's true, I guess."

Overhead, a care ship whistled at great velocity and then was gone again almost at once; Timothy watched it go but he was not really interested in it, because there was so much more to look forward to, on the ground and below the ground, ahead of them to the south.

His father murmured, "Those Oaklanders; their game, their particular doll, it taught them something. Connie had to grow and it forced them all to grow along with her. Our flukers never learned about that, not from Perky Pat. I wonder if they ever will. She'd have to grow up the way Connie did. Connie must have been like Perky Pat, once. A long time ago."

Not interested in what his father was saying—who really cared about dolls and games with dolls?—Timothy scampered ahead, peering to see what lay before them, the opportunities and possibilities, for him and for his mother and dad, for Mr. Regan also.

"I can't wait," he yelled back at his father, and Norm Schein managed a faint, fatigued smile in answer.

---

1. Why do the adults in Pinole spend their time and resources playing Perky Pat instead of working on practical matters of survival and rebuilding? Why are the children uninterested in or hostile to the game?

2. Why are Norm and Fran initially horrified by Connie Companion's marriage and pregnancy? Why does the game they play with the Berkeley flukers change them?

3. Why do the other Pinole flukers cast out Norm and Fran when they return from the Berkeley game? Why does Sam Regan volunteer to leave with them, even though his wife stays behind?

4. At the end of the story, why does Timothy feel "there was so much more to look forward to, on the ground and below the ground, ahead of them to the south"?

URSULA K. LE GUIN (1929–) was born in Berkeley, California, the daughter of Alfred L. Kroeber, one of the twentieth century's leading anthropologists. She studied at Radcliffe and earned a master's degree in Romance languages at Columbia University. Le Guin's exposure to the study of Native American cultures, particularly their mythologies, stimulated her interest in writing stories that vividly depict complex, imaginary societies, and she is known for her subtle portrayal of issues of gender and politics. She has received numerous awards, including the National Book Award for best children's book, *The Farthest Shore* (1972), which was part of her Earthsea trilogy written in the fantasy genre. Her two most well-known works of science fiction are *The Left Hand of Darkness* (1969), which features a hermaphroditic species inhabiting the ice planet of Gethen, and *The Dispossessed: An Ambiguous Utopia* (1974), which explores questions raised by a successful anarchist society. Each novel won both Hugo and Nebula awards.

Vaster Than Empires and More Slow

It was only during the earliest decades of the League that the Earth sent ships out on the enormously long voyages, beyond the pale, over the stars and far away. They were seeking for worlds which had not been seeded or settled by the Founders on Hain, truly alien worlds. All the Known Worlds went back to the Hainish Origin, and the Terrans, having been not only founded but salvaged by the Hainish, resented this. They wanted to get away from the family. They wanted to find somebody new. The Hainish, like tiresomely understanding parents, supported their explorations, and contributed ships and volunteers, as did several other worlds of the League.

All these volunteers to the Extreme Survey crews shared one peculiarity: they were of unsound mind.

What sane person, after all, would go out to collect information that would not be received for five or ten centuries? Cosmic mass interference had not yet been eliminated from the operation of the ansible, and so instantaneous communication was reliable only within a range of 120 light-years. The explorers would be quite isolated. And of course they had no idea what they might come back to, if they came back. No normal human being who had experienced time-slippage of even a few decades between League worlds would volunteer for a round trip of centuries. The Surveyors were escapists, misfits. They were nuts.

Ten of them climbed aboard the ferry at Smeming Port, and made varyingly inept attempts to get to know one another during the three days the ferry took getting to their ship, *Gum*. Gum is a Cetian nickname, on the order of Baby or Pet. There were two Cetians on the team, two Hainishmen, one Beldene, and five Terrans; the Cetian-built ship was chartered by the Government of Earth. Her motley crew came aboard wriggling through the coupling tube one by one like apprehensive spermatozoa trying to fertilize the universe. The ferry left, and the navigator put *Gum* underway. She flitted for some hours on the edge of space a few hundred million miles from Smeming Port, and then abruptly vanished.

When, after 10 hours 29 minutes, or 256 years, *Gum* reappeared in normal space, she was supposed to be in the vicinity of Star KG-E-96651. Sure enough, there was the gold pinhead of the star. Somewhere within a four-hundred-million-kilometer sphere there was also a greenish planet, World 4470, as charted by a Cetian mapmaker. The ship now had to find the planet. This was not quite so easy as it might sound, given a four-hundred-million-kilometer haystack. And *Gum* couldn't bat about in planetary space at near light-speed; if she did, she and Star KG-E-96651 and World 4470 might all end up going bang. She had to creep, using rocket propulsion, at a few hundred thousand miles an hour. The Mathematician/Navigator, Asnanifoil, knew pretty well where the planet ought to be, and thought they might raise it within ten E-days. Meanwhile the members of the Survey team got to know one another still better.

"I can't stand him," said Porlock, the Hard Scientist (chemistry, plus physics, astronomy, geology, etc.), and little blobs of spittle appeared on his mustache. "The man is insane. I can't imagine why he was passed as fit to join a Survey team, unless this is a deliberate experiment in noncompatibility, planned by the Authority, with us as guinea pigs."

"We generally use hamsters and Hainish gholes," said Mannon, the Soft Scientist (psychology, plus psychiatry, anthropology, ecology, etc.), politely; he was one of the Hainishmen. "Instead of guinea pigs. Well, you know, Mr. Osden is really a very rare case. In fact, he's the first fully cured case of Render's Syndrome—a variety of infantile autism which was thought to be incurable. The great Terran analyst Hammergeld reasoned that the cause of the autistic condition in this case is a supernormal empathic capacity, and developed an appropriate treatment. Mr. Osden is the first patient to undergo that treatment, in fact he lived with Dr. Hammergeld until he was eighteen. The therapy was completely successful."

"Successful?"

"Why, yes. He certainly is not autistic."

"No, he's intolerable!"

"Well, you see," said Mannon, gazing mildly at the saliva flecks on Porlock's mustache, "the normal defensive-aggressive reaction between strangers meeting—let's say you and Mr. Osden just for example—is something you're scarcely aware of; habit, manners, inattention get you past it; you've learned to ignore it, to the point where you might even deny it exists. However, Mr. Osden, being an empath, feels it. Feels his feelings, and yours, and is hard put to say which is which. Let's say that there's a normal element of hostility towards any stranger in your emotional reaction to him when you meet him, plus a spontaneous dislike of his looks, or clothes, or handshake—it doesn't matter what. He feels that dislike. As his autistic defense has been unlearned, he resorts to an aggressive-defense mechanism, a response in kind to the aggression which you have unwittingly projected onto him." Mannon went on for quite a long time.

"Nothing gives a man the right to be such a bastard," Porlock said.

"He can't tune us out?" asked Harfex, the Biologist, another Hainishman.

"It's like hearing," said Olleroo, Assistant Hard Scientist, stooping over to paint her toenails with fluorescent lacquer. "No eyelids on your ears. No Off switch on empathy. He hears our feelings whether he wants to or not."

"Does he know what we're *thinking*?" asked Eskwana, the Engineer, looking round at the others in real dread.

"No," Porlock snapped. "Empathy's not telepathy! Nobody's got telepathy."

"Yet," said Mannon, with his little smile. "Just before I left Hain there was a most interesting report in from one of the recently discovered worlds, a hilfer named Rocannon reporting what appears to be a teachable telepathic technique existent among a mutated hominid race; I only saw a synopsis in the HILF Bulletin, but—" He went on. The others had learned that they could talk while Mannon went on talking; he did not seem to mind, nor even to miss much of what they said.

"Then why does he hate us?" Eskwana said.

"Nobody hates you, Ander honey," said Olleroo, daubing Eskwana's left thumbnail with fluorescent pink. The engineer flushed and smiled vaguely.

"He acts as if he hated us," said Haito, the Coordinator. She was a delicate-looking woman of pure Asian descent, with a surprising voice, husky, deep, and soft, like a young bullfrog. "Why, if he suffers from our hostility, does he increase it by constant attacks and insults? I can't say I think much of Dr. Hammergeld's cure, really, Mannon; autism might be preferable. . . ."

She stopped. Osden had come into the main cabin.

He looked flayed. His skin was unnaturally white and thin, showing the channels of his blood like a faded road map in red and blue. His Adam's apple, the muscles that circled his mouth, the bones and ligaments of his wrists and hands, all stood out distinctly as if displayed for an anatomy lesson. His hair was pale rust, like long-dried blood. He had eyebrows and lashes, but they were visible only in certain lights; what one saw was the bones of the eye sockets, the veining of the lids, and the colorless eyes. They were not red eyes, for he was not really an albino, but they were not blue or gray; colors had cancelled out in Osden's eyes, leaving a cold water-like clarity, infinitely penetrable. He never looked directly at one. His face lacked expression, like an anatomical drawing or a skinned face.

"I agree," he said in a high, harsh tenor, "that even autistic withdrawal might be preferable to the smog of cheap secondhand emotions with which you people surround me. What are you sweating hate for now, Porlock? Can't stand the sight of me? Go practice some autoeroticism the way you were doing last night, it improves your vibes. Who the devil moved my tapes, here? Don't touch my things, any of you. I won't have it"

"Osden," said Asnanifoil in his large slow voice, "why *are* you such a bastard?"

Ander Eskwana cowered and put his hands in front of his face. Contention frightened him. Olleroo looked up with a vacant yet eager expression, the eternal spectator.

"Why shouldn't I be?" said Osden. He was not looking at Asnanifoil, and was keeping physically as far away from all of them as he could in the crowded cabin. "None of you constitute, in yourselves, any reason for my changing my behavior."

Harfex, a reserved and patient man, said, "The reason is that we shall be spending several years together. Life will be better for all of us if—"

"Can't you understand that I don't give a damn for all of you?" Osden said, took up his microtapes, and went out. Eskwana had suddenly gone to sleep. Asnanifoil was drawing slipstreams in the air with his finger and muttering the Ritual Primes. "You cannot explain his presence on the team except as a plot on the part of the Terran Authority. I saw this almost at once. This mission is meant to fail," Harfex whispered to the Coordinator, glancing over his shoulder. Porlock was fumbling with his fly button; there were tears in his eyes. I did tell you they were all crazy, but you thought I was exaggerating.

All the same, they were not unjustified. Extreme Surveyors expected to find their fellow team members intelligent, well trained, unstable, and personally sympathetic. They had to work together in close quarters and nasty places, and could expect one another's paranoias, depressions, manias, phobias, and compulsions to be mild enough to admit of good personal relationships, at least most of the time. Osden might be intelligent, but his training was sketchy and his personality was disastrous. He had been sent only on account of his singular gift, the power of empathy: properly speaking, of wide-range bioempathic receptivity. His talent wasn't species specific; he could pick up emotion or sentience from anything that felt. He could share lust with a white rat, pain with a squashed cockroach, and phototropy with a moth. On an alien world, the Authority had decided, it would be useful to know if anything nearby is sentient, and if so, what its feelings towards you are. Osden's title was a new one: he was the team's Sensor.

"What is emotion, Osden?" Haito Tomiko asked him one day in the main cabin, trying to make some rapport with him for once. "What is it, exactly, that you pick up with your empathic sensitivity?"

"Muck," the man answered in his high, exasperated voice. "The psychic excreta of the animal kingdom. I wade through your feces."

"I was trying," she said, "to learn some facts." She thought her tone was admirably calm.

"You weren't after facts. You were trying to get at me. With some fear, some curiosity, and a great deal of distaste. The way you might poke a dead dog, to see the maggots crawl. Will you understand once and for all that I don't want to be got at, that I want to be left alone?" His skin was mottled with red and violet, his voice had risen. "Go roll in your own dung, you yellow bitch!" he shouted at her silence.

"Calm down," she said, still quietly, but she left him at once and went to her cabin. Of course he had been right about her motives; her question had been largely a pretext, a mere effort to interest him. But what harm in that? Did not that effort imply respect for the other? At the moment of asking the question she had felt at most a slight distrust of him; she had mostly felt sorry for him, the poor arrogant venomous bastard, Mr. No-Skin as Olleroo called him. What did he expect, the way he acted? Love?

"I guess he can't stand anybody feeling sorry for him," said Olleroo, lying on the lower bunk, gilding her nipples.

"Then he can't form any human relationship. All his Dr. Hammergeld did was turn an autism inside out. . . ."

Poor frot," said Olleroo. "Tomiko, you don't mind if Harfex comes in for a while tonight, do you?"

"Can't you go to his cabin? I'm sick of always having to sit in Main with that damned peeled turnip."

"You do hate him, don't you? I guess he feels that. But I slept with Harfex last night too, and Asnanifoil might get jealous, since they share the cabin. It would be nicer here."

"Service them both," Tomiko said with the coarseness of offended modesty. Her Terran subculture, the East Asian, was a puritanical one; she had been brought up chaste.

"I only like one a night," Olleroo replied with innocent serenity. Beldene, the Garden Planet, had never discovered chastity, or the wheel.

"Try Osden, then," Tomiko said. Her personal instability was seldom so plain as now: a profound self-distrust manifesting itself as destructivism. She had volunteered for this job because there was, in all probability, no use in doing it.

The little Beldene looked up, paintbrush in hand, eyes wide. "Tomiko, that was a dirty thing to say."

"Why?"

"It would be vile! I'm not attracted to Osden!"

"I didn't know it mattered to you," Tomiko said indifferently, though she did know. She got some papers together and left the cabin, remarking, "I hope you and Harfex or whoever it is finish by last bell; I'm tired."

Olleroo was crying, tears dripping on her little gilded nipples. She wept easily. Tomiko had not wept since she was ten years old.

It was not a happy ship; but it took a turn for the better when Asnanifoil and his computers raised World 4470. There it lay, a dark-green jewel, like truth at the bottom of a gravity well. As they watched the jade disc grow, a sense of mutuality grew among them. Osden's self-ishness, his accurate cruelty, served now to draw the others together. "Perhaps," Mannon said, "he was sent as a beating-gron. What Terrans call a scapegoat. Perhaps his influence will be good after all." And no one, so careful were they to be kind to one another, disagreed.

They came into orbit. There were no lights on nightside, on the continents none of the lines and clots made by animals who build.

"No men," Harfex murmured.

"Of course not," snapped Osden, who had a viewscreen to himself, and his head inside a polythene bag. He claimed that the plastic cut down on the empathic noise he received from the others. "We're two light-centuries past the limit of the Hainish Expansion, and outside that there are no men. Anywhere. You don't think Creation would have made the same hideous mistake twice?"

No one was paying him much heed; they were looking with affection at that jade immensity below them, where there was life, but not human life. They were misfits among men, and what they saw there was not desolation, but peace. Even Osden did not look quite so expressionless as usual; he was frowning.

Descent in fire on the sea; air reconnaissance; landing. A plain of something like grass, thick, green, bowing stalks, surrounded the ship, brushed against extended viewcameras, smeared the lenses with a fine pollen.

"It looks like a pure phytosphere," Harfex said. "Osden, do you pick up anything sentient?"

They all turned to the Sensor. He had left the screen and was pouring himself a cup of tea. He did not answer. He seldom answered spoken questions.

The chitinous rigidity of military discipline was quite inapplicable to these teams of mad scientists; their chain of command lay somewhere between parliamentary procedure and peck order, and would have driven a regular service officer out of his mind. By the inscrutable decision of the Authority, however, Dr. Haito Tomiko had been given the title of Coordinator, and she now exercised her prerogative for the first time. "Mr. Sensor Osden," she said, "please answer Mr. Harfex."

"How could I 'pick up' anything from outside," Osden said without turning, "with the emotions of nine neurotic hominids pullulating around me like worms in a can? When I have anything to tell you, I'll tell you. I'm aware of my responsibility as Sensor. If you presume to give me an order again, however, Coordinator Haito, I'll consider my responsibility void."

"Very well, Mr. Sensor. I trust no orders will be needed henceforth." Tomiko's bullfrog voice was calm, but Osden seemed to flinch slightly as he stood with his back to her, as if the surge of her suppressed rancor had struck him with physical force.

The biologist's hunch proved correct. When they began field analyses they found no animals even among the microbiota. Nobody here ate anybody else. All life forms were photosynthesizing or saprophagous, living off light or death, not off life. Plants: infinite plants, not one species known to the visitors from the house of Man. Infinite shades and intensities of green, violet, purple, brown, red. Infinite silences. Only the wind moved, swaying leaves and fronds, a warm soughing wind laden with spores and pollens, blowing the sweet pale-green dust over prairies of great grasses, heaths that bore no heather, flowerless forests where no foot had ever walked, no eye had ever looked. A warm, sad world, sad and serene. The Surveyors wandering like picnickers over sunny plains of violet filicaliformes, spoke softly to each other. They knew their voices broke a silence of a thousand million years, the silence of wind and leaves, leaves and wind, blowing and ceasing and blowing again. They talked softly; but being human, they talked.

"Poor old Osden," said Jenny Chong, Bio and Tech, as she piloted a helijet on the North Polar Quadrating run. "All that fancy hi-fi stuff in his brain and nothing to receive. What a bust."

"He told me he hates plants," Olleroo said with a giggle.

"You'd think he'd like them, since they don't bother him like we do."

"Can't say I much like these plants myself," said Porlock, looking down at the purple undulations of the North Circumpolar Forest. "All the same. No mind. No change. A man alone in it would go right off his head."

"But it's all alive," Jenny Chong said. "And if it lives, Osden hates it."

"He's not really so bad," Olleroo said, magnanimous. Porlock looked at her sidelong and asked, "You ever slept with him, Olleroo?"

Olleroo burst into tears and cried, "You Terrans are obscene!"

"No she hasn't," Jenny Chong said, prompt to defend. "Have you, Porlock?"

The chemist laughed uneasily: ha, ha, ha. Flecks of spittle appeared on his mustache.

"Osden can't bear to be touched," Olleroo said shakily. "I just brushed against him once by accident and he knocked me off like I was some sort of dirty . . . thing. We're all just things, to him,"

"He's evil," Porlock said in a strained voice, startling the two women. "He'll end up shattering this team, sabotaging it, one way or another. Mark my words. He's not fit to live with other people!"

They landed on the North Pole. A midnight sun smoldered over low hills. Short, dry, greenish pink bryoform grasses stretched away in every direction, which was all one direction, south. Subdued by the incredible silence, the three Surveyors set up their instruments and set to work, three viruses twitching minutely on the hide of an unmoving giant.

Nobody asked Osden along on runs as pilot or photographer or recorder, and he never volunteered, so he seldom left base camp. He ran Harfex's botanical taxonomic data through the on-ship computers, and served as assistant to Eskwana, whose job here was mainly repair and maintenance. Eskwana had begun to sleep a great deal, twenty-five hours or more out of the thirty-two-hour day, dropping off in the middle of repairing a radio or checking the guidance circuits of a helijet. The Coordinator stayed at base one day to observe. No one else was home except Poswet To, who was subject to epileptic fits; Mannon had plugged her into a therapy circuit today in a state of preventive catatonia. Tomiko spoke reports into the storage banks, and kept an eye on Osden and Eskwana. Two hours passed.

"You might want to use the 860 microwaldoes in sealing that connection," Eskwana said in his soft, hesitant voice.

"Obviously!"

"Sorry. I just saw you had the 840s there—"

"And will replace them when I take the 860s out. When I don't know how to proceed, Engineer, I'll ask your advice."

After a minute Tomiko looked round. Sure enough, there was Eskwana sound asleep, head on the table, thumb in his mouth.

"Osden."

The white face did not turn, he did not speak, but conveyed impatiently that he was listening.

"You can't be unaware of Eskwana's vulnerability."

"I am not responsible for his psychopathic reactions."

"But you are responsible for your own. Eskwana is essential to our work here, and you're not. If you can't control your hostility, you must avoid him altogether."

Osden put down his tools and stood up. "With pleasure!" he said in his vindictive, scraping voice. "You could not possibly imagine what it's like to experience Eskwana's irrational terrors. To have to share his horrible cowardice, to have to cringe with him at everything!"

"Are you trying to justify your cruelty towards him? I thought you had more self-respect." Tomiko found herself shaking with spite. "If your empathic power really makes you share Ander's misery, why does it never induce the least compassion in you?"

"Compassion," Osden said. "Compassion. What do you know about compassion?"

She stared at him, but he would not look at her.

"Would you like me to verbalize your present emotional affect regarding myself?" he said. "I can do so more precisely than you can. I'm trained to analyze such responses as I receive them. And I do receive them."

"But how can you expect me to feel kindly towards you when you behave as you do?"

"What does it matter how I *behave*, you stupid sow, do you think it makes any difference? Do you think the average human is a well of loving-kindness? My choice is to be hated or to be despised. Not being a woman or a coward, I prefer to be hated."

"That's rot. Self-pity. Every man has—"

"But I am not a man," Osden said. "There are all of you. And there is myself. I am *one*."

Awed by that glimpse of abysmal solipsism, she kept silent a while; finally she said with neither spite nor pity, clinically, "You could kill yourself, Osden."

"That's your way, Haito," he jeered. "I'm not depressive, and *seppuku* isn't my bit. What do you want me to do here?"

"Leave. Spare yourself and us. Take the air car and a data feeder and go do a species count. In the forest; Harfex hasn't even started the forests yet. Take a hundred-square-meter forested area, anywhere inside radio range. But outside empathy range. Report in at 8 and 24 o'clock daily."

Osden went, and nothing was heard from him for five days but laconic all-well signals twice daily. The mood at base camp changed like a stage set. Eskwana stayed awake up to eighteen hours a day. Poswet To got her stellar lute and chanted the celestial harmonies (music had driven Osden into a frenzy). Mannon, Harfex, Jenny Chong and Tomiko all went off tranquilizers. Porlock distilled something in his laboratory and drank it all by himself. He had a hangover. Asnanifoil and Poswet To held an all-night Numerical Epiphany, that mystical orgy of higher mathematics which is the chief pleasure of the religious Cetian soul. Olleroo slept with everybody. Work went well.

The Hard Scientist came towards base at a run, laboring through the high, fleshy stalks of the graminiformes. "Something—in the forest—" His eyes bulged, he panted, his mustache and fingers trembled. "Something big. Moving, behind me. I was putting in a benchmark, bending down. It came at me. As if it was swinging down out of the trees. Behind me." He stared at the others with the opaque eyes of terror or exhaustion.

"Sit down, Porlock. Take it easy. Now wait, go through this again. You *saw* something—"

"Not clearly. Just the movement. Purposive. A—an—I don't know what it could have been. Something self-moving. In the trees, the arboriformes, whatever you call 'em. At the edge of the woods."

Harfex looked grim. "There is nothing here that could attack you, Porlock. There are not even microzoa. There *could not* be a large animal."

"Could you possible have seen an epiphyte drop suddenly, a vine come loose behind you?"

"No," Porlock said. "It was coming down at me, through the branches, fast. When I turned it took off again, away and upward. It made a noise, a sort of crashing. If it wasn't an animal, God knows what it could have been! It was big—as big as a man, at least. Maybe a reddish color. I couldn't see, I'm not sure."

"It was Osden," said Jenny Chong, "doing a Tarzan act." She giggled nervously, and Tomiko repressed a wild feckless laugh. But Harfex was not smiling.

"One gets uneasy under the arboriformes," he said in his polite, repressed voice. "I've noticed that. Indeed that may be why I've put off working in the forests. There's a hypnotic quality in the colors and spacing of the stems and branches, especially the helically arranged ones; and the spore throwers grow so regularly spaced that it seems unnatural. I find it quite disagreeable, subjectively speaking. I wonder if a stronger effect of that sort mightn't have produced a hallucination . . . ?"

Porlock shook his head. He wet his lips. "It was there," he said. "Something. Moving with purpose. Trying to attack me from behind."

When Osden called in, punctual as always, at 24 o'clock that night, Harfex told him Porlock's report. "Have you come on anything at all, Mr. Osden, that could substantiate Mr. Porlock's impression of a motile, sentient life form, in the forest?"

Ssss, the radio said sardonically. "No. Bullshit," said Osden's unpleasant voice.

"You've been actually inside the forest longer than any of us," Harfex said with unmitigable politeness. "Do you agree with my impression that the forest ambiance has a rather troubling and possibly hallucinogenic effect on the perceptions?"

Ssss. "I'll agree that Porlock's perceptions are easily troubled. Keep him in his lab, he'll do less harm. Anything else?"

"Not at present," Harfex said, and Osden cut off.

Nobody could credit Porlock's story, and nobody could discredit it. He was positive that something, something big, had tried to attack him by surprise. It was hard to deny this, for they were on an alien world, and everyone who had entered the forest had felt a certain chill and foreboding under the "trees." ("Call them trees, certainly," Harfex had said. "They really are the same thing, only, of course, altogether different.") They agreed that they had felt uneasy, or had had the sense that something was watching them from behind.

"We've got to clear this up," Porlock said, and he asked to be sent as a temporary Biologist's Aide, like Osden, into the forest to explore and observe. Olleroo and Jenny Chong volunteered if they could go as a pair. Harfex sent them all off into the forest near which they were encamped, a vast tract covering four-fifths of Continent D. He forbade sidearms. They were not to go outside a fifty-mile half circle, which included Osden's current site. They all reported in twice daily, for three days. Porlock reported a glimpse of what seemed to be a large semi-erect shape moving through the trees across the river; Olleroo was sure she had heard something moving near the tent, the second night.

"There are no animals on this planet," Harfex said, dogged.

Then Osden missed his morning call.

Tomiko waited less than an hour, then flew with Harfex to the area where Osden had reported himself the night before. But as the helijet hovered over the sea of purplish leaves, illimitable, impenetrable, she felt a panic despair. "How can we find him in this?"

"He reported landing on the riverbank. Find the air car; he'll be camped near it, and he can't have gone far from his camp. Species counting is slow work. There's the river."

"There's his car," Tomiko said, catching the bright foreign glint among the vegetable colors and shadows. "Here goes, then."

She put the ship in hover and pitched out the ladder. She and Harfex descended. The sea of life closed over their heads.

As her feet touched the forest floor, she unsnapped the flap of her holster; then glancing at Harfex, who was unarmed, she left the gun untouched. But her hand kept coming back up to it. There was no sound at all, as soon as they were a few meters away from the slow, brown river, and the light was dim. Great boles stood well apart, almost regularly, almost alike; they were soft skinned, some appearing smooth and others spongy, gray or greenish brown or brown, twined with cablelike creepers and festooned with epiphytes, extending rigid, entangled armfuls of big, saucer-shaped, dark leaves that formed a roof layer twenty to thirty meters thick. The ground underfoot was springy as a mattress, every inch of it knotted with roots and peppered with small, fleshy-leafed growths.

"Here's his tent," Tomiko said, cowed at the sound of her voice in that huge community of the voiceless. In the tent was Osden's sleeping bag, a couple of books, a box of rations. We should be calling, shouting for him, she thought, but did not even suggest it; nor did Harfex. They circled out from the tent, careful to keep each other in sight through the thick-standing presences, the crowding gloom. She stumbled over Osden's body, not thirty meters from the tent, led to it by the whitish gleam of a dropped notebook. He lay face down between two huge-rooted trees. His head and hands were covered with blood, some dried, some still oozing red.

Harfex appeared beside her, his pale Hainish complexion quite green in the dusk. "Dead?"

"No. He's been struck. Beaten. From behind." Tomiko's fingers felt over the bloody skull and temples and nape. "A weapon or a tool . . . I don't find a fracture."

As she turned Osden's body over so they could lift him, his eyes opened. She was holding him, bending close to his face. His pale lips writhed. A deathly fear came into her. She screamed aloud two or three times and tried to run away, shambling and stumbling into the terrible dusk. Harfex caught her, and at his touch and the sound of his voice, her panic decreased. "What is it? What is it?" he was saying.

"I don't know," she sobbed. Her heartbeat still shook her, and she could not see clearly. "The fear—the . . . I panicked. When I saw his eyes."

"We're both nervous. I don't understand this—"

"I'm all right now, come on, we've got to get him under care."

Both working with senseless haste, they lugged Osden to the riverside and hauled him up on a rope under his armpits; he dangled like a sack, twisting a little, over the glutinous dark sea of leaves. They pulled him into the helijet and took off. Within a minute they were over open prairie. Tomiko locked onto the homing beam. She drew a deep breath, and her eyes met Harfex's.

"I was so terrified I almost fainted. I have never done that."

"I was . . . unreasonably frightened also," said the Hainishman, and indeed he looked aged and shaken. "Not so badly as you. But as unreasonably."

"It was when I was in contact with him, holding him. He seemed to be conscious for a moment."

"Empathy? . . . I hope he can tell us what attacked him."

Osden, like a broken dummy covered with blood and mud, half lay as they had bundled him into the rear seats in their frantic urgency to get out of the forest.

More panic met their arrival at base. The ineffective brutality of the assault was sinister and bewildering. Since Harfex stubbornly denied any possibility of animal life they began speculating about sentient plants, vegetable monsters, psychic projections. Jenny Chong's latent phobia reasserted itself and she could talk about nothing except the Dark Egos which followed people around behind their backs. She and Olleroo and Porlock had been summoned back to base; and nobody was much inclined to go outside.

Osden had lost a good deal of blood during the three or four hours he had lain alone, and concussion and severe contusions had put him in shock and semi-coma. As he came out of this and began running a low fever he called several times for "Doctor," in a plaintive voice: "Doctor Hammergeld . . ." When he regained full consciousness, two of those long days later, Tomiko called Harfex into his cubicle.

"Osden: can you tell us what attacked you?"

The pale eyes flickered past Harfex's face.

"You were attacked," Tomiko said gently. The shifty gaze was hatefully familiar, but she was a physician, protective of the hurt. "You may not remember it yet. Something attacked you. You were in the forest—"

"Ah!" he cried out, his eyes growing bright and his features contorting. "The forest—in the forest—"

"What's in the forest?

He grasped for breath. A look of clearer consciousness came into his face. After a while he said, "I don't know."

"Did you see what attacked you?" Harfex asked.

"I don't know."

"You remember it now."

"I don't know."

"All our lives may depend on this. You must tell us what you saw!"

"I don't know," Osden said, sobbing with weakness. He was too weak to hide the fact that he was hiding the answer, yet he would not say it. Porlock, nearby, was chewing his pepper-colored mustache as he tried to hear what was going on in the cubicle. Harfex leaned over Osden and said, "You *will* tell us—" Tomiko had to interfere bodily.

Harfex controlled himself with an effort that was painful to see. He went off silently to his cubicle, where no doubt he took a double or triple dose of tranquilizers. The other men and women, scattered about the big frail building, a long main hall and ten sleeping cubicles, said nothing, but looked depressed and edgy. Osden, as always, even now, had them all at his mercy. Tomiko looked down at him with a rush of hatred that burned in her throat like bile. This monstrous egotism that fed itself on others' emotions, this absolute selfishness, was worse than any hideous deformity of the flesh. Like a congenital monster, he should not have lived. Should not be alive. Should have died. Why had his head not been split open?

As he lay flat and white, his hands helpless at his sides, his colorless eyes were wide open, and there were tears running from the corners. He tried to flinch away. "Don't," he said in a weak hoarse voice, and tried to raise his hands to protect his head. "Don't!"

She sat down on the folding stool beside the cot, and after a while put her hand on his. He tried to pull away, but lacked the strength.

A long silence fell between them.

"Osden," she murmured, "I'm sorry. I'm very sorry. I will you well. Let me will you well, Osden. I don't want to hurt you. Listen, I do see now. It was one of us. That's right, isn't it. No, don't answer, only tell me if I'm wrong; but I'm not. . . . Of course there are animals on this planet. Ten of them. I don't care who it was. It doesn't matter, does it. It could have been me, just now. I realize that. I didn't understand how it is, Osden. You can't see how difficult it is for us to understand. . . . But listen. If it were love, instead of hate and fear . . . It is never love?"

"No."

"Why not? Why should it never be? Are human beings all so weak? That is terrible. Never mind, never mind, don't worry. Keep still. At least right now it isn't hate, is it? Sympathy at least, concern, well-wishing, you do feel that, Osden? Is it what you feel?"

"Among . . . other things," he said, almost inaudibly.

"Noise from my subconscious, I suppose. And everybody else in the room . . . Listen, when we found you there in the forest, when I tried to turn you over, you partly wakened, and I felt a horror of you. I was insane with fear for a minute. Was that your fear of me I felt?"

"No."

Her hand was still on his, and he was quite relaxed, sinking towards sleep, like a man in pain who has been given relief from pain. "The forest," he muttered; she could barely understand him. "Afraid."

She pressed him no further, but kept her hand on his and watched him go to sleep. She knew what she felt, and what therefore he must feel. She was confident of it: there is only one emotion, or state of being, that can thus wholly reverse itself, polarize, within one moment. In Great Hainish indeed there is one word, *ontá*, for love and for hate. She was not in love with Osden, of course, that was another kettle of fish. What she felt for him was *ontá*, polarized hate. She held his hand and the current flowed between them, the tremendous electricity of touch, which he had always dreaded. As he slept the ring of anatomy-chart muscles around his mouth relaxed, and Tomiko saw on his face what none of them had ever seen, very faint, a smile. It faded. He slept on.

He was tough; next day he was sitting up, and hungry. Harfex wished to interrogate him, but Tomiko put him off. She hung a sheet of polythene over the cubicle door, as Osden himself had often done. "Does it actually cut down your empathic reception?" she asked, and he replied, in the dry, cautious tone they were now using to each other, "No."

"Just a warning then."

"Partly. More faith healing. Dr. Hammergeld thought it worked ... Maybe it does, a little."

There had been love, once. A terrified child, suffocating in the tidal rush and battering of the huge emotions of adults, a drowning child, saved by one man. Taught to breathe, to live, by one man. Given everything, all protection and love, by one man. Father/Mother/God: no other. "Is he still alive?" Tomiko asked, thinking of Osden's incredible loneliness, and the strange cruelty of the great doctors. She was shocked when she heard his forced, tinny laugh. "He died at least two and a half centuries ago," Osden said. "Do you forget where we are, Coordinator? We've all left our little families behind...."

Outside the polythene curtain the eight other human beings on World 4470 moved vaguely. Their voices were low and strained. Eskwana slept; Poswet To was in therapy; Jenny Chong was trying to rig lights in her cubicle so that she wouldn't cast a shadow.

"They're all scared," Tomiko said, scared. "They've all got these ideas about what attacked you. A sort of ape potato, a giant fanged spinach, I don't know.... Even Harfex. You may be right not to force them to see. That would be worse, to lose confidence in one another. But why are we all so shaky, unable to face the fact, going to pieces so easily? Are we really all insane?"

"We'll soon be more so."

"Why?"

"There *is* something." He closed his mouth, the muscles of his lips stood out rigid.

"Something sentient?"

"A sentience."

"In the forest?"

He nodded.

"What is it, then—?"

"The fear." He began to look strained again, and moved restlessly. "When I fell, there, you know, I didn't lose consciousness at once. Or I kept regaining it. I don't know. It was more like being paralyzed."

"You were."

"I was on the ground. I couldn't get up. My face was in the dirt, in that soft leaf mold. It was in my nostrils and eyes. I couldn't move. Couldn't see. As if I was in the ground. Sunk into it, part of it. I knew I was between two trees even though I never saw them. I suppose I could feel the roots. Below me in the ground, down under the ground. My hands were bloody, I could feel that, and the blood made the dirt around my face sticky. I felt the fear. It kept growing. As if they'd finally *known* I was there, lying on them there, under them, among them, the thing they feared, and yet part of their fear itself. I couldn't stop sending the fear back, and it kept growing and I couldn't move, I couldn't get away. I would pass out, I think, and then the fear would bring me to again, and I still couldn't move. Any more than they can."

Tomiko felt the cold stirring of her hair, the readying of the apparatus of terror. "They: who are they, Osden?"

"They, it—I don't know. The fear."

"What is he talking about?" Harfex demanded when Tomiko reported this conversation. She would not let Harfex question Osden yet, feeling that she must protect Osden from the onslaught of the Hainishman's powerful, overrepressed emotions. Unfortunately this fueled the slow fire of paranoid anxiety that burned in poor Harfex, and he thought she and Osden were in league, hiding some fact of great importance or peril from the rest of the team.

"It's like the blind man trying to describe the elephant. Osden hasn't seen or heard the . . . the sentience, any more than we have."

"But he's felt it, my dear Haito," Harfex said with just-suppressed rage. "Not empathically. On his skull. It came and knocked him down and beat him with a blunt instrument. Did he not catch *one* glimpse of it?"

"What would he have seen, Harfex?" Tomiko said, but he would not hear her meaningful tone; even he had blocked out that comprehension. What one fears is alien. The murderer is an outsider, a foreigner, not one of us. The evil is not in me!

"The first blow knocked him pretty well out," Tomiko said a little wearily, "he didn't see anything. But when he came to again, alone in the forest, he felt a great fear. Not his own fear, an empathic effect. He is certain of that. And certain it was nothing picked up from any of us. So that evidently the native life forms are not all insentient."

Harfex looked at her a moment, grim. "You're trying to frighten me, Haito. I do not understand your motives." He got up and went off to his laboratory table, walking slowly and stiffly, like a man of eighty not of forty.

She looked around at the others. She felt some desperation. Her new, fragile, and profound interdependence with Osden gave her, she was well aware, some added strength. But if even Harfex could not keep his head, who of the others would? Porlock and Eskwana were shut in their cubicles, the others were all working or busy with something. There was something queer about their positions. For a while the Coordinator could not tell what it was, then she saw that they were all sitting facing the nearby forest. Playing chess with Asnanifoil, Olleroo had edged her chair around until it was almost beside his.

She went to Mannon, who was dissecting a tangle of spidery brown roots, and told him to look for the pattern puzzle. He saw it at once, and said with unusual brevity, "Keeping an eye on the enemy."

"What enemy? What do *you* feel, Mannon?" She had a sudden hope in him as a psychologist, on this obscure ground of hints and empathies where biologists went astray.

"I feel a strong anxiety with a specific spatial orientation. But I am not an empath. Therefore the anxiety is explicable in terms of the particular stress situation, that is, the attack on a team member in the forest, and also in terms of the total stress situation, that is, my presence in a totally alien environment, for which the archetypical connotations of the word 'forest' provide an inevitable metaphor."

Hours later Tomiko woke to hear Osden screaming in nightmare; Mannon was calming him, and she sank back into her own dark-branching pathless dreams. In the morning Eskwana did not wake. He could not be roused with stimulant drugs. He clung to his sleep, slipping farther and farther back, mumbling softly now and then until, wholly regressed, he lay curled on his side, thumb at his lips, gone.

"Two days; two down. Ten little Indians, nine little Indians . . ." That was Porlock.

"And you're the next little Indian," Jenny Chong snapped. "Go analyze your urine, Porlock!"

"He is driving us all insane," Porlock said, getting up and waving his left arm. "Can't you feel it? For God's sake, are you all deaf and blind? Can't you feel what he's doing, the emanations? It all comes from him—from his room there—from his mind. He is driving us all insane with fear!"

"Who is?" said Asnanifoil, looming precipitous and hairy over the little Terran.

"Do I have to say his name? Osden, then. Osden! Osden! Why do you think I tried to kill him? In self-defense! To save all of us! Because you won't see what he's doing to us. He's sabotaged the mission by making us quarrel, and now he's going to drive us all insane by projecting fear at us so that we can't sleep or think, like a huge radio that doesn't make any sound, but it broadcasts all the time, and you can't sleep, and you can't think. Haito and Harfex are already under his control but the rest of you can be saved. I had to do it!"

"You didn't do it very well," Osden said, standing half naked, all rib and bandage, at the door of his cubicle. "I could have hit myself harder. Hell, it isn't me that's scaring you blind, Porlock, it's out there—there, in the woods!"

Porlock made an ineffectual attempt to assault Osden; Asnanifoil held him back, and continued to hold him effortlessly while Mannon gave him a sedative shot. He was put away shouting about giant radios. In a minute the sedative took effect, and he joined a peaceful silence to Eskwana's.

"All right," said Harfex. "Now, Osden, you'll tell us what you know and all you know."

Osden said, "I don't know anything."

He looked battered and faint. Tomiko made him sit down before he talked.

"After I'd been three days in the forest, I thought I was occasionally receiving some kind of affect."

"Why didn't you report it?"

"Thought I was going spla, like the rest of you."

"That, equally, should have been reported."

"You'd have called me back to base. I couldn't take it. You realize that my inclusion in the mission was a bad mistake. I'm not able to coexist with nine other neurotic personalities at close quarters. I was wrong to volunteer for Extreme Survey, and the Authority was wrong to accept me."

No one spoke; but Tomiko saw, with certainty this time, the flinch in Osden's shoulders and the tightening of his facial muscles, as he registered their bitter agreement.

"Anyhow, I didn't want to come back to base because I was curious. Even going psycho, how could I pick up empathic effects when there was no creature to emit them? They weren't bad, then. Very vague. Queer. Like a draft in a closed room, a flicker in the corner of your eye. Nothing really."

For a moment he had been borne up on their listening: they heard, so he spoke. He was wholly at their mercy. If they disliked him he had to be hateful; if they mocked him he became grotesque; if they listened to him he was the storyteller. He was helplessly obedient to the demands of their emotions, reactions, moods. And there were seven of them, too many to cope with, so that he must be constantly knocked about from one to another's whim. He could not find coherence. Even as he spoke and held them, somebody's attention would wander: Olleroo perhaps was thinking that he wasn't unattractive, Harfex was seeking the ulterior motive of his words, Asnanifoil's's mind, which could not be long held by the concrete, was roaming off towards the eternal peace of number, and Tomiko was distracted by pity, by fear. Osden's voice faltered. He lost the thread. "I . . . I thought it must be the trees," he said, and stopped.

"It's not the trees," Harfex said. "They have no more nervous system than do plants of the Hainish Descent on Earth. None."

"You're not seeing the forest for the trees, as they say on Earth," Mannon put in, smiling elfinly; Harfex stared at him. "What about those root nodes we've been puzzling about for twenty days—eh?"

"What about them?"

"They are, indubitably, connections. Connections among the trees. Right? Now let's just suppose, most improbably, that you knew nothing of animal brain structure. And you were given one axon, or one detached glial cell, to examine. Would you be likely to discover what it was? Would you see that the cell was capable of sentience?"

"No. Because it isn't. A single cell is capable of mechanical response to stimulus. No more. Are you hypothesizing that individual arboriformes are 'cells' in a kind of brain, Mannon?"

"Not exactly. I'm merely pointing out that they are all intercon-nected, both by the root-node linkage and by your green epiphytes in the branches. A linkage of incredible complexity and physical extent. Why, even the prairie grass forms have those root connectors, don't they? I know that sentience or intelligence isn't a thing, you can't find it in, or analyze it out from, the cells of a brain. It's a function of the connected cells. It is, in a sense, the connection: the connectedness. It doesn't exist. I'm not trying to say it exists. I'm only guessing that Osden might be able to describe it."

And Osden took him up, speaking as if in trance. "Sentience without senses. Blind, deaf, nerveless, moveless. Some irritability, response to touch. Response to sun, to light, to water, and chemicals in the earth around the roots. Nothing comprehensible to an animal mind. Presence without mind. Awareness of being, without object or subject. Nirvana."

"Then why do you receive fear?" Tomiko asked in a low voice.

"I don't know. I can't see how awareness of objects, of others, could arise: an unperceiving response . . . But there was an uneasiness, for days. And then when I lay between the two trees and my blood was on their roots—" Osden's face glittered with sweat. "It became fear," he said shrilly, "only fear."

"If such a function existed," Harfex said, "it would not be capable of conceiving of a self-moving, material entity, or responding to one. It could no more become aware of us than we can 'become aware' of Infinity."

" 'The silence of those infinite expanses terrifies me,' " muttered Tomiko. "Pascal was aware of Infinity. By way of fear."

"To a forest," Mannon said, "we might appear as forest fires. Hurricanes. Dangers. What moves quickly is dangerous, to a plant. The rootless would be alien, terrible. And if it is mind, it seems only too probable that it might become aware of Osden, whose own mind is open to connection with all others so long as he's conscious, and who was lying in pain and afraid within it, actually inside it. No wonder it was afraid—"

"Not 'it,' " Harfex said. "There is no being, no huge creature, no person! There could at most be only a function—"

"There is only a fear," Osden said.

They were all still a while, and heard the stillness outside.

"Is that what I feel all the time coming up behind me?" Jenny Chong asked, subdued.

Osden nodded. "You all feel it, deaf as you are. Eskwana's the worst off, because he actually has some empathic capacity. He could send if he learned how, but he's too weak, never will be anything but a medium."

"Listen, Osden," Tomiko said, "you can send. Then send to it—the forest, the fear out there—tell it that we won't hurt it. Since it has, or is, some sort of affect that translates into what we feel as emotion, can't you translate back? Send out a message, We are harmless, we are friendly."

"You must know that nobody can emit a false empathic message, Haito. You can't send something that doesn't exist."

"But we don't intend harm, we are friendly."

"Are we? In the forest, when you picked me up, did you feel friendly?"

"No. Terrified. But that's—it, the forest, the plants, not my own fear, isn't it?"

"What's the difference? It's all you felt. Can't you see," and Osden's voice rose in exasperation, "why I dislike you and you dislike me, all of you? Can't you see that I retransmit every negative or aggressive affect you've felt towards me since we first met? I return your hostility, with thanks. I do it in self-defense. Like Porlock. It is self-defense, though; it's the only technique I developed to replace my original defense of total withdrawal from others. Unfortunately it creates a closed circuit, self-sustaining and self-reinforcing. Your initial reaction to me was the instinctive antipathy to a cripple; by now of course it's hatred. Can you fail to see my point? The forest mind out there transmits only terror, now, and the only message I can send it is terror, because when exposed to it I can feel nothing except terror!"

"What must we do, then?" said Tomiko, and Mannon replied promptly, "Move camp. To another continent. If there are plant minds there, they'll be slow to notice us, as this one was; maybe they won't notice us at all."

"It would be a considerable relief," Osden observed stiffly. The others had been watching him with a new curiosity. He had revealed himself, they had seen him as he was, a helpless man in a trap. Perhaps, like Tomiko, they had seen that the trap itself, his crass and cruel egotism, was their own construction, not his. They had built the cage and locked him in it, and like a caged ape he threw filth out through the bars. If, meeting him, they had offered trust, if they had been strong enough to offer him love, how might he have appeared to them?

None of them could have done so, and it was too late now. Given time, given solitude, Tomiko might have built up with him a slow resonance of feeling, a consonance of trust, a harmony; but there was no time, their job must be done. There was not room enough for the cultivation of so great a thing, and they must make do with sympathy, with pity, the small change of love. Even that much had given her strength, but it was nowhere near enough for him. She could see in his flayed face now his savage resentment of their curiosity, even of her pity.

"Go lie down, that gash is bleeding again," she said, and he obeyed her.

Next morning they packed up, melted down the spray-form hangar and living quarters, lifted *Gum* on mechanical drive and took her halfway round World 4470, over the red and green lands, the many warm green seas. They had picked out a likely spot on continent G: a prairie, twenty thousand square kilos of windswept graminiformes. No forest was within a hundred kilos of the site, and there were no lone trees or groves on the plain. The plant forms occurred only in large species-colonies, never intermingled, except for certain tiny ubiquitous saprophytes and spore bearers. The team sprayed holomeld over structure forms, and by evening of the thirty-two-hour day were settled in to the new camp. Eskwana was still asleep and Porlock still sedated, but everyone else was cheerful. "You can breathe here!" they kept saying.

Osden got on his feet and went shakily to the doorway; leaning there he looked through twilight over the dim reaches of the swaying grass that was not grass. There was a faint, sweet odor of pollen on the wind; no sound but the soft, vast sibilance of wind. His bandaged head cocked a little, the empath stood motionless for a long time. Darkness came, and the stars, lights in the windows of the distant house of Man. The wind had ceased, there was no sound. He listened.

In the long night Haito Tomiko listened. She lay still and heard the blood in her arteries, the breathing of sleepers, the wind blowing, the dark veins running, the dreams advancing, the vast static of stars increasing as the universe died slowly, the sound of death walking. She struggled out of her bed, fled the tiny solitude of her cubicle. Eskwana alone slept. Porlock lay straitjacketed, raving softly in his obscure native tongue. Olleroo and Jenny Chong were playing cards, grim faced. Poswet To was in the therapy niche, plugged in. Asnanifoil was drawing a mandala, the Third Pattern of the Primes. Mannon and Harfex were sitting up with Osden.

She changed the bandages on Osden's head. His lank, reddish hair, where she had not had to shave it, looked strange. It was salted with white, now. Her hands shook as she worked. Nobody had yet said anything.

"How can the fear be here too?" she said, and her voice rang flat and false in the terrific silence.

"It's not just the trees; the grasses . . ."

"But we're twelve thousand kilos from where we were this morning, we left it on the other side of the planet."

"It's all one," Osden said. "One big green thought. How long does it take a thought to get from one side of your brain to the other?"

"It doesn't think. It isn't thinking," Harfex said, lifelessly. "It's merely a network of processes. The branches, the epiphytic growths, the roots with those nodal junctures between individuals: they must all be capable of transmitting electrochemical impulses. There are no individual plants, then, properly speaking. Even the pollen is part of the linkage, no doubt, a sort of windborne sentience, connecting overseas. But it is not conceivable. That all the biosphere of a planet should be one network of communications, sensitive, irrational, immortal, isolated. . . ."

"Isolated," said Osden. "That's it! That's the fear. It isn't that we're motile, or destructive. It's just that we are. We are other. There has never been any other."

"You're right," Mannon said, almost whispering. "It has no peers. No enemies. No relationship with anything but itself. One alone forever."

"Then what's the function of its intelligence in species survival?"

"None, maybe," Osden said. "Why are you getting teleological, Harfex? Aren't you a Hainishman? Isn't the measure of complexity the measure of the eternal joy?"

Harfex did not take the bait. He looked ill. "We should leave this world," he said.

"Now you know why I always want to get out, get away from you," Osden said with a kind of morbid geniality. "It isn't pleasant, is it—the other's fear . . . ? If only it were an animal intelligence. I can get through to animals. I get along with cobras and tigers; superior intelligence gives one the advantage. I should have been used in a zoo, not on a human team . . . . If I could get through to the damned stupid potato! If it wasn't so overwhelming . . . I still pick up more than the fear, you know. And before it panicked it had a—there was a serenity. I couldn't take it in, then, I didn't realize how big it was. To know the whole daylight, after all, and the whole night. All the winds and lulls together. The winter stars and the summer stars at the same time. To have roots, and no enemies. To be entire. Do you see? No invasion. No others. To be whole . . ."

He had never spoken before, Tomiko thought.

"You are defenseless against it, Osden," she said. "Your personality has changed already. You're vulnerable to it. We may not all go mad, but you will, if we don't leave."

He hesitated, then he looked up at Tomiko, the first time he had ever met her eyes, a long, still look, clear as water.

"What's sanity ever done for me?" he said, mocking "But you have a point, Haito. You have something there."

"We should get away," Harfex muttered.

"If I gave in to it," Osden mused, "could I communicate?"

"By 'give in,'" Mannon said in a rapid, nervous voice, "I assume that you mean, stop sending back the empathic information which you receive from the plant entity: stop rejecting the fear, and absorb it. That will either kill you at once, or drive you back into total psychological withdrawal, autism."

"Why?" said Osden. "Its message is *rejection*. But my salvation is rejection. It's not intelligent. But I am."

"The scale is wrong. What can a single human brain achieve against something so vast?"

"A single human brain can perceive pattern on the scale of stars and galaxies," Tomiko said, "and interpret it as Love."

Mannon looked from one to the other of them; Harfex was silent.

"It'd be easier in the forest," Osden said. "Which of you will fly me over?"

"When?"

"Now. Before you all crack up or go violent."

"I will," Tomiko said.

"None of us will," Harfex said.

"I can't," Mannon said. "I . . . I am too frightened. I'd crash the jet."

"Bring Eskwana along. If I can pull this off, he might serve as a medium."

"Are you accepting the Sensor's plan, Coordinator?" Harfex asked formally.

"Yes."

"I disapprove. I will come with you, however."

"I think we're compelled, Harfex," Tomiko said, looking at Osden's face, the ugly white mask transfigured, eager as a lover's face.

Olleroo and Jenny Chong, playing cards to keep their thoughts from their haunted beds, their mounting dread, chattered like scared children. "This thing, it's in the forest, it'll get you—"

"Scared of the dark?" Osden jeered.

"But look at Eskwana, and Porlock, and even Asnanifoil—"

"It can't hurt you. It's an impulse passing through synapses, a wind passing through branches. It is only a nightmare."

They took off in a helijet, Eskwana curled up still sound asleep in the rear compartment, Tomiko piloting Harfex and Osden silent, watching ahead for the dark line of the forest across the vague gray miles of starlit plain.

They neared the black line, crossed it; now under them was darkness.

She sought a landing place, flying low, though she had to fight her frantic wish to fly high, to get out, get away. The huge vitality of the plant world was far stronger here in the forest, and its panic beat in immense dark waves. There was a pale patch ahead, a bare knoll top a little higher than the tallest of the black shapes around it; the not-trees; the rooted; the parts of the whole. She set the helijet down in the glade, a bad landing. Her hands on the stick were slippery, as if she had rubbed them with cold soap.

About them now stood the forest, black in darkness.

Tomiko cowered and shut her eyes. Eskwana moaned in his sleep. Harfex's breath came short and loud, and he sat rigid, even when Osden reached across him and slid the door open.

Osden stood up; his back and bandaged head were just visible in the dim glow of the control panel as he paused stooping in the doorway.

Tomiko was shaking. She could not raise her head. "No, no, no, no, no, no, no," she said in a whisper. "No. No. No."

Osden moved suddenly and quietly, swinging out of the doorway, down into the dark. He was gone.

I am coming! said a great voice that made no sound.

Tomiko screamed. Harfex coughed; he seemed to be trying to stand up, but did not do so.

Tomiko drew in upon herself, all centered in the blind eye in her belly, in the center of her being; and outside that there was nothing but the fear.

It ceased.

She raised her head; slowly unclenched her hands. She sat up straight. The night was dark, and stars shone over the forest. There was nothing else.

"Osden," she said, but her voice would not come. She spoke again, louder, a lone bullfrog croak. There was no reply.

She began to realize that something had gone wrong with Harfex. She was trying to find his head in the darkness, for he had slipped down from the seat, when all at once, in the dead quiet, in the dark rear compartment of the craft, a voice spoke. "Good," it said.

It was Eskwana's voice. She snapped on the interior lights and saw the engineer lying curled up asleep, his hand half over his mouth.

The mouth opened and spoke. "All well," it said.

"Osden—"

"All well," said the voice from Eskwana's mouth.

"Where are you?"

Silence.

"Come back."

A wind was rising. "I'll stay here," the soft voice said.

"You can't stay—"

Silence.

"You'd be alone, Osden!"

"Listen." The voice was fainter, slurred, as if lost in the sound of wind. "Listen. I will you well."

She called his name after that, but there was no answer. Eskwana lay still. Harfex lay stiller.

"Osden!" she cried, leaning out the doorway into the dark, wind-shaken silence of the forest of being. "I will come back. I must get Harfex to the base. I will come back, Osden!"

Silence and wind in leaves.

They finished the prescribed survey of World 4470, the eight of them; it took them forty-one days more. Asnanifoil and one or another of the women went into the forest daily at first, searching for Osden in the region around the bare knoll, though Tomiko was not in her heart sure which bare knoll they had landed on that night in the very heart and vortex of terror. They left piles of supplies for Osden, food enough for fifty years, clothing, tents, tools. They did not go on searching; there was no way to find a man alone, hiding, if he wanted to hide, in those unending labyrinths and dim corridors vine entangled, root floored. They might have passed within arm's reach of him and never seen him.

But he was there; for there was no fear anymore.

Rational, and valuing reason more highly after an intolerable experience of the immortal mindless, Tomiko tried to understand rationally what Osden had done. But the words escaped her control. He had taken the fear into himself, and, accepting, had transcended it. He had given up his self to the alien, an unreserved surrender, that left no place for evil. He had learned the love of the Other, and thereby had been given his whole self. —But this is not the vocabulary of reason.

The people of the Survey team walked under the trees, through the vast colonies of life, surrounded by a dreaming silence, a brooding calm that was half aware of them and wholly indifferent to them. There were no hours. Distance was no matter. Had we but world enough and time . . . The planet turned between the sunlight and the great dark; winds of winter and summer blew fine, pale pollen across the quiet seas.

Gum returned after many surveys, years, and light-years, to what had several centuries ago been Smeming Port. There were still men there, to receive (incredulously) the team's reports, and to record its losses: Biologist Harfex, dead of fear, and Sensor Osden, left as a colonist.

---

1. What did the members of the Extreme Survey crews hope to find? Why are they described as wanting "to get away from the family" and "of unsound mind"?

2. Knowing from the beginning about Osden's empathic abilities as the Sensor, why are the other crew members not able to understand his apparent hostility toward them?

3. Why did Osden want to return to the forest and remain there? What does it mean that in doing so he "had been given his whole self"?

4. What effect does the confrontation with the World 4470 alien life forms have on crew members' self-understanding?

ZENNA HENDERSON (1917–1983) began writing science fiction and fantasy stories after graduating from Arizona State University in 1940. She spent most of her life teaching elementary school, and many of her stories feature relationships between teachers and students. In contrast to the work of many other science fiction writers in the mid-twentieth century, which often portrays characters in conflict with hostile beings and environments, Henderson's stories are marked by a compassionate sensitivity to encounters with extraterrestrial aliens. Many of her stories reflect underlying Christian values and are filled with biblical allusions, including references to the story of the Exodus and the search for the Promised Land. Her noted books, *Pilgrimage: The Book of the People* (1961) and *The People: No Different Flesh* (1966), develop these themes in an original way, varying the standard science fiction plot in which aliens secretly live with us on Earth.

As Simple as That

"I won't read it." Ken sat staring down at his open first-grade book.

I took a deep, wavery breath and, with an effort, brought myself back to the classroom and the interruption in the automatic smooth flow of the reading group.

"It's your turn, Ken," I said. "Don't you know the place?"

"Yes," Ken said, his thin, unhappy face angling sharply at the cheekbones as he looked at me. "But I won't read it."

"Why not?" I asked gently. Anger had not yet returned. "You know all the words. Why don't you want to read it?"

"It isn't true," said Ken. He dropped his eyes to his book as tears flooded in. "It isn't true."

"It never was true," I told him. "We play like it's true, just for fun." I flipped the four pages that made up the current reading lesson. "Maybe this city isn't true, but it's like a real one, with stores and—" My voice trailed off as the eyes of the whole class centered on me—seven pairs of eyes and the sightless, creamy ovals of Maria's face—all seeing our city.

"The cities," I began again. "The cities—" By now the children were used to grown-ups stopping in midsentence. And to the stunned look on adult faces.

"It isn't true," said Ken. "I won't read it."

"Close your books," I said, "And go to your seats." The three slid quietly into their desks—Ken and Victor and Gloryanne. I say at my desk, my elbows on the green blotter, my chin in the palms of my hands, and looked at nothing. I didn't want anything true. The fantasy that kept school as usual is painful enough. How much more comfortable to live unthinking from stunned silence to stunned silence. Finally I roused myself.

"If you don't want to read your book, let's write a story that *is* true, and we'll have that for reading."

I took the staff liner and drew three lines at a time across the chalkboard, with just a small jog where I had to lift the chalk over the jagged crack that marred the board diagonally from top to bottom.

"What shall we name our story?" I asked. "Ken, what do you want it to be about?"

"About Biff's house," said Ken promptly.

"Biff's house," I repeated, my stomach tightening sickly as I wrote the words, forming the letters carefully in manuscript printing, automatically saying, "Remember now, all titles begin with—"

And the class automatically supplying, "—capital letters."

"Yes," I said. "Ken, what shall we say first?"

"Biff's house went up like an elevator," said Ken.

"Right up into the air?" I prompted.

"The ground went up with it," supplied Gloryanne.

I wrote the two sentences. "Victor? Do you want to tell what came next?" The chalk was darkening in my wet, clenched hand.

"The groun'—it comed down, more fast nor Biff's house," supplied Victor hoarsely. I saw his lifted face and the deep color of his heavily fringed eyes for the first time in a week.

"With noise!" shouted Maria, her face animated. "With lots of noise!"

"You're not in our group!" cried Ken. "This is our story!"

"It's everyone's story," I said and wrote carefully. "And every sentence ends with a—"

"Period," supplied the class.

"And then?" I paused, leaning my forehead against the coolness of the chalkboard, blinking my eyes until the rich green alfalfa that was growing through the corner of the room came back into focus. I lifted my head.

Celia had waited. "Biff fell out of his house," she suggested.

I wrote. "And then?" I paused, chalk raised.

"Biff's house fell on him," said Ken with a rush. "And he got dead."

"I saw him!" Bobby surged up out of his seat, speaking his first words of the day. "There was blood, but his face was only asleep."

"He was dead!" said Ken fiercely. "And the house broke all to pieces!"

"And the pieces all went down in that deep, deep hole with Biff!" cried Bobby.

"And the hole went shut!" Celia triumphantly capped the recital.

"Dint either!" Victor whirled on her. "Ohney part! See! See!" He jabbed his finger toward the window. We all crowded around as though this was something new. And I suppose it was—new to our tongues, new to our ears, though long scabbed over unhealthily inside us.

There at the edge of the playground, just beyond the twisted tangle of the jungle gym and the sharp jut of the slide, snapped off above the fifth rung of the ladder, was the hole containing Biff's house. We solemnly contemplated all that was visible—the small jumble of shingles and the wadded TV antenna. We turned back silently to our classroom.

"How did you happen to see Biff when his house fell on him, Bobby?" I asked.

"I was trying to go to his house to play until my brother got out of fourth grade," said Bobby. "He was waiting for me on the porch. But all at once the ground started going up and down and it knocked me over. When I got up, Biff's house was just coming down and it fell on Biff. All but his head. And he looked asleep. He did! He did! And then everything went down and it shut. But not all!" he hastened to add before Victor gave tongue again.

"Now," I said—we had buried Biff—"Do we have it the way we want so it can be a story for reading? Get your pencils—"

"Teacher! Teacher!" Maria was standing, her sightless eyes wide, one hand up as high as she could reach. "Teacher! Malina!"

"Bobby! Quickly—help me!" I scrambled around my desk, knocking the section of four-by-four out from under the broken front leg. I was able to catch Malina because she had stopped to fumble for the door knob that used to be there. Bobby stumbled up with the beach towel and, blessedly, I had time to wind it securely around Malina before the first scream of her convulsions began. Bobby and I held her lightly, shoulder and knees, as her body rolled and writhed. We had learned bitterly how best to protect her against herself and the dangerous place she made for herself of the classroom. I leaned my cheek against my shoulder as I pressed my palms against Malina. I let my tears wash down my face untouched. Malina's shaking echoed through me as though I were sobbing.

The other children were righting my fallen desk and replacing the chunk of four-by-four, not paying any attention to Malina's gurgling screams that rasped my ears almost past enduring. So quickly do children adjust. So quickly. I blinked to clear my eyes. Malina was quieting. Oh, how blessedly different from the first terrified hour we had had to struggle with her! I quickly unwrapped her and cradled her against me as her face smoothed and her ragged breath quieted. She opened her eyes.

"Daddy said next time he had a vacation he'd take us to Disneyland again. Last time we didn't get to go in the rocket. We didn't get to go in anything in that land." She smiled her normal, front-tooth-missing smile at me and fell asleep. We went back to work, Bobby and I.

"Her daddy's dead," said Bobby matter-of-factly as he waited his turn at the pencil sharpener. "She knows her daddy's dead and her mother's dead and her baby brother's—"

"Yes, Bobby, we all know," I said. "Let's go back to our story. We just about have time to go over it again and write it before lunchtime."

So I stood looking out of the gap in the wall above the Find Out Table—currently, *What Did This Come From?* while the children wrote their first true story after the Torn Time.

Biff's House

Biff's house went up like an elevator.

The ground went up with it.

The ground came down before Biff's house did.

Biff fell out of his house.

The house fell on him and he was dead.

He looked asleep.

The house broke all to pieces with a lot of noise.

It went down into the deep, deep hole.

Biff went, too.

The hole went shut, but not all the way.

We can see the place by our playground.

It was only a few days later that the children asked to write another story. The rain was coming down again—a little less muddy, a little less torrential, so that the shards of glass in our windows weren't quite so smeary and there was an area unleaked upon in the room large enough to contain us all closely—minus Malina.

"I think she'll come tomorrow," said Celia. "This morning she forgot Disneyland 'cause she remembered all her family got mashed by the water tower when it fell down and she was crying when we left the sleeping place and she wasn't screaming and kicking and this time she was crying and—"

"Heavens above!" I cried, "You'll run out of breath completely!"

"Aw naw I won't!" Celia grinned up at me and squirmed in pleased embarrassment. "I breathe in between!"

"I didn't hear any in-betweens," I smiled back. "Don't use so many 'ands'!"

"Can we write another real story?" asked Willsey. ("Not Willie!" His mother's voice came back to me, tiny and piercing and never to be heard aloud again. "His name is Willsey. W-i-l-l-s-e-y. Please teach him to write it in full!")

"If you like," I said. "Only do we say, 'Can we?'"

"May we?" chorused the class.

"That's right," I said. "Did you have something special in mind, Willsey?"

"No," he said. "Only, this morning we had bread for breakfast. Mine was dry. Bobby's daddy said that was lucky 'relse it would have rotted away a long time ago." Bread. My mouth watered. There must not have been enough to pass around to our table—only for the children.

"Mine was dry, too," said Ken. "And it had blue on the edge of it."

"Radioactive," nodded Victor wisely.

"Huh-uh!" contradicted Bobby quickly. "Nothing's radioactive around here! My daddy says—"

"You' daddy! You' daddy!" retorted Victor. "Once I gots daddy, too!"

"Everybody had a daddy," said Maria calmly. " 'Relsn you couldn't get born. But some daddies die."

"All daddies die," said Bobby. "Only mine isn't dead yet. I'm *glad* he isn't dead!"

"We all are," I said, "Bobby's daddy helps us all—"

"Yeah," said Willsey, "he found the bread for us."

"Anyway, the blue was mold," Bobby broke in. "And it's good for you. It grows peni—pencil—"

"Penicillin?" I suggested. He nodded and subsided, satisfied. "Okay, Willsey, what shall we name our story?"

He looked at me blankly. "What's it about?" I asked.

"Eating," he said.

"Fine. That'll do for a title," I said. "Who can spell it for me? It's an 'ing' ending."

I wrote it carefully with a black marking pencil on the chart paper as Gloryanne spelled it for me, swishing her long black hair back triumphantly as she did so. Our chalkboard was a green cascade of water under the rain pouring down through the ragged, sagging ceiling. The bottom half of the board was sloughing slowly away from its diagonal fracture.

"Now, Willsey—" I waited, marker poised.

"We had bread for breakfast," he composed. "It was hard, but it was good."

"Mine wasn't," objected Ken. "It was awful."

"Bread isn't awful," said Maria. "Bread's good."

"Mine wasn't!" Ken was stubborn.

"Even if we don't ever get any more?" asked Maria.

"Aw! Who ever heard of not no more bread?" scoffed Ken.

"What is bread made of?" I asked.

"Flour," volunteered Bobby.

"Cornbread's with cornmeal," said Victor quickly.

"Yes, and flour's made from—" I prompted.

"From wheat," said Ken.

"And wheat—"

"Grows in fields," said Ken.

"Thee, Thmarty!" said Gloryanne. "And whereth any more fieldth?"

"Use your teeth, Gloryanne," I reminded. "Teeth and no tongue. Say, 'see.'"

Gloryanne clenched her teeth and curled her lips back. "S-s-s-thee!" she said, confidently. Bobby and I exchanged aware looks and our eyes smiled above our sober lips.

"Let's go on with the story," I suggested.

Eating

We had bread for breakfast.
It was hard but it was good.
Bobby's daddy found it under some boards.
We had some good milk to put it in.
It was goat's milk.
It made the bread soft.
Once we had a cow.
She was a nice cow but a man killed her
because he wanted to eat her.
We all got mad at him.
We chased him away.
No one got to eat our cow
because it rained red mud
all over her and spoiled the meat.
We had to push her into a big hole.

I looked over the tight huddle of studious heads before me as they all bent to the task of writing the story. The rain was sweeping past the windows like long curtains billowing in the wind The raindrops were so fine but so numerous that it seemed I could reach out and stroke the swelling folds. I moved closer to the window, trying several places before I found one where no rain dripped on me from above and none sprayed me from outside. But it was an uncomfortable spot. I could see the nothing across the patio where the rest of the school used to be. Our room was the only classroom in the office wing. The office wing was the only one not gulped down in its entirety, lock, stock, and student body. Half of the office wing was gone. We had the restrooms—nonoperational—the supply room—half roofed—and our room. We were the school. We were the whole of the subteen generation—and the total faculty.

The total faculty wondered—was it possible that someone—some *one*—had caused all this to happen? Some one who said, "Now!" Or said, "Fire!" Or said, "If I can't have my way, then—" Or maybe some stress inside the world casually adjusted itself, all unknowing of the skim of life clinging to its outsides. Or maybe some One said, "I repent Me—"

"Teacher, Teacher!" Maria's voice called me back to the classroom. "The roof! The roof!" Her blind face was urgent. I glanced up, my arm lifting protectively.

"Down!" I shouted. "Get down flat!" and flung myself across the room, mowing my open-mouthed children down as I plunged. We made it to the floor below the level of my desk before what was left of the ceiling peeled off and slammed soggily over us, humped up just enough by the desk and chairs to save our quivering selves.

Someone under me was sobbing, "My paper's all tore! My paper's all tore!" And I heard Bobby say with tight, controlled anguish, "Everything breaks! Anymore, everything breaks!"

We wrote another story—later. Quite a bit later. The sun, haloed broadly about by its perpetual haze, shone milkily down into our classroom. The remnants of the roof and ceiling had been removed and a canvas tarp draped diagonally over the highest corner of the remaining walls to give us shade in the afternoon. On the other side of the new, smaller playground our new school was shaping from adobe and reclaimed brick. Above the humming stillness of the classroom, I could hear the sound of blackbirds calling as they waded in the water that seeped from the foot of the knee-deep stand of wheat that covered the old playground. Maybe by fall there would be bread again. Maybe. Everything was still maybe. But 'maybe' is a step—a big one—beyond 'never.'

Our chalkboard was put back together and, except for a few spots that refused to accept any kind of impression, it functioned well with our smudgy charcoal sticks from the art supplies shelf.

"Has anyone the answer yet?" I asked

"I gots it," said Victor, tentatively. "It's two more days."

"Huh-uh!" said Celia. "Four more days!"

"Well, we seem to have a difference of opinion," I said. "Let's work it out together.

"Now, first, how many people, Victor?"

"Firs' they's ten people," he said, checking the chalkboard.

"That's right," I said, "And how many cans of beans? Malina?"

"Five," she said. "And each can is for two people for one day."

"Right," I said. "And so that'll be lunch for how many days for ten people?"

"For one day," said Malina.

"That's right. Then what happened?"

"All but two people fell in the West Crack," said Bobby. "Right—straight—down—farther than you can hear a rock fall." He spoke with authority. He had composed that part of our math problem.

"So?" I said.

"There were five cans of beans and that's ten meals and only two people," said Willsey.

"So?" I prompted.

"So two people can have five meals each."

"So?"

"So they gots dinners for five days and that's *four* days more than one day! So there!" cried Victor.

"Hey!" Celia was outraged. "That's what *I* said! You said *two* more days!"

"Aw!" said Victor. "Dumb problem! Nobody's gunna fa' down West Crack eenyway!"

"A lot of people fell in there," said Gloryanne soberly. "My gramma did and my Aunt Glory—"

In the remembering silence, the sweet creaking calls of the blackbirds could be heard again. A flash of brilliance from the sky aroused us. A pie-shaped wedge had suddenly cleared in the sun's halo, and there was bright blue and glitter, briefly, before the milky came back.

"A whole bright day," said Maria dreamily. "And the water in Briney Lake so shiny I can't look at it."

"You can't look anyway," said Ken. "How come you always talk about seeing when you can't even?"

"'Cause I can. Ever since the Torn Time," said Maria. "I got blind almost as soon as I got born. All blind. No anything to see. But now I can watch and I can see—inside me, somewhere. But I don't see now. I see sometime—after while. But what I see comes! It isn't, when I see it, but it bees pretty quick!" Her chin tilted a 'so there!'

The children all looked at her silently and I wondered. We had lost so much—so much! And Maria had lost, too—her blindness. Maybe more of our losses were gains—

Then Bobby cried out, "What happened, teacher? What happened? And why do we stay here? I can remember on the other side of West Crack. There was a town that wasn't busted. And bubble gum and hamburgers and a—a escalator thing to go upstairs to buy color TV. Why don't we go there? Why do we stay here where everything's busted?"

"Broken," I murmured automatically.

The children were waiting for an answer. These child faces were turned to me, waiting for me to fill a gap they suddenly felt now, in spite of the endless discussions that were forever going on around them.

"What do *you* think?" I asked. "What do you think happened? Why *do* we stay here? Think about it for a while, then let's write another story."

I watched the wind flow across the wheat field and thought, too. Why do we stay? The West Crack is one reason. It's still unbridged, partly because to live has been more important than to go, partly because no one wants to leave anyone yet. The fear of separation is still too strong. We *know* people are here. The unknown is still too lonely to face.

South are the Rocks—jagged slivers of basalt or something older than that—that rocketed up out of the valley floor during the Torn

Time and splintered into points and pinnacles. As far as we can see, they rise, rigidly vertical, above the solid base that runs out of sight east and west. And the base is higher than our tallest tree.

And north. My memory quivered away from north—.

East. Town used to be east. The edge of it is salvage now. Someday when the stench is gone, the whole of it will be salvage. Most of the stench is only a lingering of memory now, but we still stay away except when need drives us.

North. North. Now it is Briney Lake. During the Torn Time, it came from out of nowhere, all that wetness, filling a dusty, desert cup to brimming and more. It boiled and fumed and swallowed the land and spat out parts of it again.

Rafe and I had gone up to watch the magical influx of water. In this part of the country, any water, free of irrigation or conservation restrictions, was a wonder to be watched with fascinated delight. We stood, hand in hand, on the Point where we used to go at nights to watch the moonlight on the unusually heavy stand of cholla cactus on the hillsides—moonlight turning all those murderous, puncturing thorns to silvery fur and snowy velvet. The earth around us had firmed again from its shakenness and the half of the Point that was left was again a solid Gibraltar.

We watched the water rise and rise until our delight turned to apprehension. I had started to back away when Rafe pulled me to him to see a sudden silvery slick that was welling up from under the bubbling swells of water. As he leaned to point, the ground under our feet gave a huge hiccough, jerked him off balance,and snatched his hand from my wrist. He hit the water just as the silvery slick arrived.

And the slick swallowed Rafe before my eyes. Only briefly did it let go of one of his arms—a hopelessly reaching arm that hadn't yet realized that its flesh was already melted off and only bones were reaching.

I crouched on the Point and watched half my boulder dissolve into the silver and follow Rafe down into the dark, convulsed depths. The slick was gone and Rafe was gone. I knelt, nursing my wrist with my other hand. My wrist still burned where Rafe's fingernails had scratched as he fell. My wrist carries the scars still, but Rafe is gone.

My breath shuddered as I turned back to the children.

"Well," I said, "what *did* happen? Shall we write our story now?"

What Happened?
Bobby's daddy thinks maybe the magnetic poles changed
and north is west now or maybe east.
Gloryanne's mother says it must have been an atom bomb.
Malina's Uncle Don says the San Andreas fault did it.
That means a big earthquake all over everywhere.
Celia's grandfather says the Hand of God smote a wicked world.
Victor thinks maybe it was a flying saucer.
Ken thinks maybe the world just turned over and we are
Australia now.
Willsey doesn't want to know what happened.
Maria doesn't know.
She couldn't see when it was happening.

"So you see," I summed up. "Nobody knows for sure what happened. Maybe we'll never know. Now, why do we stay here?"

"Because"—Bobby hesitated—"because maybe if here is like this, maybe everywhere is like this. Or maybe there isn't even anywhere else anymore."

"Maybe there isn't," I said, "But whether there is or not and whatever really happened, it doesn't matter to us now. We can't change it. We have to make do with what we have until we can make it better.

"Now, paper monitor," I was briskly routine. "Pass the paper. All of you write as carefully as you can so when you take your story home and let people read it, they'll say, 'Well! What an interesting story!' instead of 'Yekk! Does this say something?' Writing is no good unless it can be read. The eraser's here on my desk in case anyone goofs. You may begin."

I leaned against the window sill, waiting. If only we adults would admit that we'll probably never know what really happened—and that it really doesn't matter. Inexplicable things are always happening, but life won't wait for answers—it just keeps going. Do you suppose Adam's grandchildren knew what really happened to close Eden? Or that Noah's grandchildren sat around wondering why the earth was so empty? They contented themselves with very simple, home-grown explanations—or none at all—because what was, was. We don't want to accept what happened and we seem to feel that if we could find an explanation that it would undo what has been done. It won't. Maybe someday someone will come along who will be able to put a finger on one of the points in the children's story and say, "There! That's the explanation." Until then, though, explanation or not, we have our new world to work with.

No matter what caused the Torn Time, we go on from here—building or not-building, becoming or slipping back. It's as simple as that.

---

1. Why are the children so insistent about reading stories that are true? What do they mean by "true" stories?

2. What does the teacher hope to accomplish in guiding the students to write their own stories about the terrible events of the Torn Time?

3. What does the teacher mean in saying, "Maybe more of our losses were gains"?

4. Following a catastrophe, is it ever "as simple as that" for people to go forward and rebuild without knowing the cause of the devastation?

ISAAC ASIMOV (1920–1992), whose family immigrated to the United States from Russia in 1923, wrote more than five hundred books during his lifetime. As a young man, Asimov worked in his parents' candy store in Brooklyn, where he began reading pulp fiction magazines. In 1939 he published his first short story in John Campbell's *Amazing Stories*. Asimov earned his PhD in chemistry at Columbia University in 1948 and became a faculty member at Boston University School of Medicine, but his greatest legacy is as a writer. His Foundation trilogy, novels based on stories written during the 1940s, earned a special Hugo Award in 1966 for best all-time science fiction series. Asimov coined the term "robotics" and also questioned the inevitability of the "Frankenstein myth"—that staple science fiction plot in which technology runs amok and turns on humanity. "The Bicentennial Man" earned the Hugo Award for Best Science Fiction Novelette in 1977.

The Bicentennial Man

The Three Laws of Robotics:
1. *A robot may not injure a human being or, through inaction, allow a human being to come to harm.*
2. *A robot must obey the orders given it by human beings except where such orders would conflict with the First Law.*
3. *A robot must protect its own existence as long as such protection does not conflict with the First or Second Law.*

1

Andrew Martin said, "Thank you," and took the seat offered him. He didn't look driven to the last resort, but he had been.

He didn't, actually, look anything, for there was a smooth blankness to his face, except for the sadness one imagined one saw in his eyes. His hair was smooth, light brown, rather fine, and there was no facial hair. He looked freshly and cleanly shaved. His clothes were distinctly old-fashioned, but neat and predominantly a velvety red-purple in color.

Facing him from behind the desk was the surgeon, and the nameplate on the desk included a fully identifying series of letters and numbers, which Andrew didn't bother with. To call him Doctor would be quite enough.

"When can the operation be carried through, Doctor?" he asked.

The surgeon said softly, with that certain inalienable note of respect that a robot always used to a human being, "I am not certain, sir, that I understand how or upon whom such an operation could be performed."

There might have been a look of respectful intransigence on the surgeon's face, if a robot of his sort, in lightly bronzed stainless steel, could have such an expression, or any expression.

Andrew Martin studied the robot's right hand, his cutting hand, as it lay on the desk in utter tranquillity. The fingers were long and were shaped into artistically metallic looping curves so graceful and appropriate that one could imagine a scalpel fitting them and becoming, temporarily, one piece with them.

There would be no hesitation in his work, no stumbling, no quivering, no mistakes. That came with specialization, of course, a specialization so fiercely desired by humanity that few robots were, any longer, independently brained. A surgeon, of course, would have to be. And this one, though brained, was so limited in his capacity that he did not recognize Andrew—had probably never heard of him.

Andrew said, "Have you ever thought you would like to be a man?"

The surgeon hesitated a moment, as though the question fitted nowhere in his allotted positronic pathways. "But I am a robot, sir."

"Would it be better to be a man?"

"If would be better, sir, to be a better surgeon. I could not be so if I were a man, but only if I were a more advanced robot. I would be pleased to be a more advanced robot."

"It does not offend you that I can order you about? That I can make you stand up, sit down, move right or left, by merely telling you to do so?"

"It is my pleasure to please you, sir. If your orders were to interfere with my functioning with respect to you or to any other human being, I would not obey you. The First Law, concerning my duty to human safety, would take precedence over the Second Law relating to obedience. Otherwise, obedience is my pleasure. . . . But upon whom am I to perform this operation?"

"Upon me," said Andrew.

"But that is impossible. It is patently a damaging operation."

"That does not matter," said Andrew calmly.

"I must not inflict damage," said the surgeon.

"On a human being, you must not," said Andrew, "but I, too, am a robot."

2

Andrew had appeared much more a robot when he had first been— manufactured. He had then been as much a robot in appearance as any that had ever existed, smoothly designed and functional.

He had done well in the home to which he had been brought in those days when robots in households, or on the planet altogether, had been a rarity.

There had been four in the home: Sir and Ma'am and Miss and Little Miss. He knew their names, of course, but he never used them. Sir was Gerald Martin.

His own serial number was NDR— He forgot the numbers. It had been a long time, of course, but if he had wanted to remember, he could not forget. He had not wanted to remember.

Little Miss had been the first to call him Andrew because she could not use the letters, and all the rest followed her in this.

Little Miss— She had lived ninety years and was long since dead. He had tried to call her Ma'am once, but she would not allow it. Little Miss she had been to her last day.

Andrew had been intended to perform the duties of a valet, a butler, a lady's maid. Those were the experimental days for him and, indeed, for all robots anywhere but in the industrial and exploratory factories and stations off Earth.

The Martins enjoyed him, and half the time he was prevented from doing his work because Miss and Little Miss would rather play with him.

It was Miss who first understood how this might be arranged. "We order you to play with us and you must follow orders."

Andrew said, "I am sorry, Miss, but a prior order from Sir must surely take precedence."

But she said, "Daddy just said he hoped you would take care of the cleaning. That's not much of an order. I *order* you."

Sir did not mind. Sir was fond of Miss and of Little Miss, even more than Ma'am was, and Andrew was fond of them, too. At least, the effect they had upon his actions were those which in a human being would have been called the result of fondness. Andrew thought of it as fondness, for he did not know any other word for it.

It was for Little Miss that Andrew had carved a pendant out of wood. She had ordered him to. Miss, it seemed, had received an ivorite pendant with scrollwork for her birthday and Little Miss was unhappy over it. She had only a piece of wood, which she gave Andrew together with a small kitchen knife.

He had done it quickly and Little Miss had said, "That's *nice*, Andrew. I'll show it to Daddy."

Sir would not believe it. "Where did you really get this, Mandy?" Mandy was what he called Little Miss. When Little Miss assured him she was really telling the truth, he turned to Andrew. "Did you do this, Andrew?"

"Yes, Sir."

"The design, too?"

"Yes, Sir."

"From what did you copy the design?"

"It is a geometric representation, Sir, that fit the grain of the wood."

The next day, Sir brought him another piece of wood, a larger one, and an electric vibro-knife. He said, "Make something out of this, Andrew. Anything you want to."

Andrew did so as Sir watched, then looked at the product a long time. After that, Andrew no longer waited on tables. He was ordered to read books on furniture design instead, and he learned to make cabinets and desks.

Sir said, "These are amazing productions, Andrew."

Andrew said, "I enjoy doing them, Sir."

"Enjoy?"

"It makes the circuits of my brain somehow flow more easily. I have heard you use the word 'enjoy' and the way you use it fits the way I feel. I enjoy doing them, Sir."

3

Gerald Martin took Andrew to the regional offices of the United States Robots and Mechanical Men, Inc. As a member of the Regional Legislature he had no trouble at all in gaining an interview with the Chief Robopsychologist. In fact, it was only as a member of the Regional Legislature that he qualified as a robot owner in the first place—in those early days when robots were rare.

Andrew did not understand any of this at the time, but in later years, with greater learning, he could review that early scene and understand it in its proper light.

The robopsychologist, Merton Mansky, listened with a gathering frown and more than once managed to stop his fingers at the point beyond which they would have irrevocably drummed on the table. He had drawn features and a lined forehead and looked as though he might be younger than he looked.

He said, "Robotics is not an exact art, Mr. Martin. I cannot explain it to you in detail, but the mathematics governing the plotting of the positronic pathways is far too complicated to permit of any but approximate solutions. Naturally, since we build everything around the Three Laws, those are incontrovertible. We will, of course, replace your robot—"

"Not at all," said Sir. "There is no question of failure on his part. He performs his assigned duties perfectly. The point is, he also carves wood in exquisite fashion and never the same twice. He produces works of art."

Mansky looked confused. "Strange. Of course, we're attempting generalized pathways these days. . . . Really creative, you think?"

"See for yourself." Sir handed over a little sphere of wood on which there was a playground scene in which the boys and girls were almost too small to make out, yet they were in perfect proportion and blended so naturally with the grain that that, too, seemed to have been carved.

Mansky said, "*He* did that?" He handed it back with a shake of his head. "The luck of the draw. Something in the pathways."

"Can you do it again?"

"Probably not. Nothing like this has ever been reported."

"Good! I don't in the least mind Andrew's being the only one."

Mansky said, "I suspect that the company would like to have your robot back for study."

Sir said with sudden grimness, "Not a chance. Forget it." He turned to Andrew, "Let's go home, now."

"As you wish, Sir," said Andrew.

4

Miss was dating boys and wasn't about the house much. It was Little Miss, not as little as she was, who filled Andrew's horizon now. She never forgot that the very first piece of wood carving he had done had been for her. She kept it on a silver chain about her neck.

It was she who first objected to Sir's habit of giving away the productions. She said, "Come on, Dad, if anyone wants one of them, let him pay for it. It's worth it."

Sir said, "It isn't like you to be greedy, Mandy."

"Not for us, Dad. For the artist."

Andrew had never heard the word before and when he had a moment to himself he looked it up in the dictionary. Then there was another trip, this time to Sir's lawyer.

Sir said to him, "What do you think of this, John?"

The lawyer was John Feingold. He had white hair and a pudgy belly, and the rims of his contact lenses were tinted a bright green. He looked at the small plaque Sir had given him. "This is beautiful. . . . But I've already heard the news. This is a carving made by your robot. The one you've brought with you."

"Yes, Andrew does them. Don't you, Andrew?"

"Yes, Sir," said Andrew.

"How much would you pay for that, John?" Sir asked.

"I can't say. I'm not a collector of such things."

"Would you believe I have been offered two hundred and fifty dollars for that small thing? Andrew has made chairs that have sold for five hundred dollars. There's two hundred thousand dollars in the bank from Andrew's products."

"Good heavens, he's making you rich, Gerald."

"Half rich," said Sir. "Half of it is in an account in the name of Andrew Martin."

"The robot?"

"That's right, and I want to know if it's legal"

"Legal?" Feingold's chair creaked as he leaned back in it. "There are no precedents, Gerald. How did your robot sign the necessary papers?"

"He can sign his name and I brought in the signature. I didn't bring him in to the bank himself. Is there anything further that ought to be done?"

"Um." Feingold's eyes seemed to turn inward for a moment. Then he said, "Well, we can set up a trust to handle all finances in his name and that will place a layer of insulation between him and the hostile world. Further than that, my advice is you do nothing. No one is stopping you so far. If anyone objects, let *him* bring suit."

"And will you take the case if the suit is brought?"

"For a retainer, certainly."

"How much?"

"Something like that," and Feingold pointed to the wooden plaque.

"Fair enough," said Sir.

Feingold chuckled as he turned to the robot. "Andrew, are you pleased that you have money?"

"Yes, sir."

"What do you plan to do with it?"

"Pay for things, sir, which otherwise Sir would have to pay for. It would save him expense, sir."

The occasions came. Repairs were expensive, and revisions were even more so. With the years, new models of robots were produced and Sir saw to it that Andrew had the advantage of every new device until he was a paragon of metallic excellence. It was all done at Andrew's expense.

Andrew insisted on that.

Only his positronic pathways were untouched. Sir insisted on that.

"The new models aren't as good as you are, Andrew," he said. "The new robots are worthless. The company has learned to make the pathways more precise, more closely on the nose, more deeply on the track. The new robots don't shift. They do what they're designed for and never stray. I like you better."

"Thank you, Sir."

"And it's your doing, Andrew, don't you forget that. I am certain Mansky put an end to generalized pathways as soon as he had a good look at you. He didn't like the unpredictability. . . . Do you know how many times he asked for you so he could place you under study? Nine times! I never let him have you, though, and now that he's retired, we may have some peace."

So Sir's hair thinned and grayed and his face grew pouchy, while Andrew looked rather better than he had when he first joined the family.

Ma'am had joined an art colony somewhere in Europe and Miss was a poet in New York. They wrote sometimes, but not often. Little Miss was married and lived not far away. She said she did not want to leave Andrew and when her child, Little Sir, was born, she let Andrew hold the bottle and feed him.

With the birth of a grandson, Andrew felt that Sir finally had someone to replace those who had gone. It would not be so unfair to come to him with the request.

Andrew said, "Sir, it is kind of you to have allowed me to spend my money as I wished."

"It was your money, Andrew."

"Only by your voluntary act, Sir. I do not believe the law would have stopped you from keeping it all."

"The law won't persuade me to do wrong, Andrew."

"Despite all expenses, and despite taxes, too, Sir, I have nearly six hundred thousand dollars."

"I know that, Andrew."

"I want to give it to you, Sir."

"I won't take it, Andrew."

"In exchange for something you can give me, Sir."

"Oh? What is that, Andrew?"

"My freedom, Sir."

"Your—"

"I wish to buy my freedom, Sir."

6

It wasn't that easy. Sir had flushed, had said, "For God's sake!" had turned on his heel, and stalked away.

It was Little Miss who finally brought him round, defiantly and harshly—and in front of Andrew. For thirty years, no one had ever hesitated to talk in front of Andrew, whether the matter involved Andrew or not. He was only a robot.

She said, "Dad, why are you taking it as a personal affront? He'll still be here. He'll still be loyal. He can't help that. It's built in. All he wants is a form of words. He wants to be called free. Is that so terrible? Hasn't he earned it? Heavens, he and I have been talking about it for years."

"Talking about it for years, have you?"

"Yes, and over and over again, he postponed it for fear he would hurt you. I *made* him put the matter up to you."

"He doesn't know what freedom is. He's a robot."

"Dad, you don't know him. He's read everything in the library. I don't know what he feels inside but I don't know what *you* feel inside. When you talk to him you'll find he reacts to the various abstractions as you and I do, and what else counts? If someone else's reactions are like your own, what more can you ask for?"

"The law won't take that attitude," Sir said angrily. "See here, you!" He turned to Andrew with a deliberate grate in his voice. "I can't free you except by doing it legally, and if it gets into the courts, you not only won't get your freedom but the law will take official cognizance of your money. They'll tell you that a robot has no right to earn money. Is this rigmarole worth losing your money?"

"Freedom is without price, Sir," said Andrew. "Even the chance of freedom is worth the money."

7

The court might also take the attitude that freedom was without price, and might decide that for no price, however great, could a robot buy its freedom.

The simple statement of the regional attorney who represented those who had brought a class action to oppose the freedom was this: The word "freedom" had no meaning when applied to a robot. Only a human being can be free.

He said it several times, when it seemed appropriate; slowly, with his hand coming down rhythmically on the desk before him to mark the words.

Little Miss asked permission to speak on behalf of Andrew. She was recognized by her full name, something Andrew had never heard pronounced before:

"Amanda Laura Martin Charney may approach the bench."

She said, "Thank you, your honor. I am not a lawyer and I don't know the proper way of phrasing things, but I hope you will listen to my meaning and ignore the words.

"Let's understand what it means to be free in Andrew's case. In some ways, he *is* free. I think it's at least twenty years since anyone in the Martin family gave him an order to do something that we felt he might not do of his own accord.

"But we can, if we wish, give him an order to do anything, couch it as harshly as we wish, because he is a machine that belongs to us. Why should we be in a position to do so, when he has served us so long, so faithfully, and has earned so much money for us? He owes us nothing more. The debt is entirely on the other side.

"Even if we were legally forbidden to place Andrew in involuntary servitude, he would still serve us voluntarily. Making him free would be a trick of words only, but it would mean much to him. It would give him everything and cost us nothing."

For a moment the Judge seemed to be suppressing a smile. "I see your point, Mrs. Charney. The fact is that there is no binding law in this respect and no precedent. There is, however, the unspoken assumption that only a man may enjoy freedom. I can make new law here, subject to reversal in a higher court, but I cannot lightly run counter to that assumption. Let me address the robot. Andrew!"

"Yes, your honor."

It was the first time Andrew had spoken in court and the Judge seemed astonished for a moment at the human timbre of the voice. He said, "Why do you want to be free, Andrew? In what way will this matter to you?"

Andrew said, "Would you wish to be a slave, your honor?"

"But you are not a slave. You are a perfectly good robot, a genius of a robot I am given to understand, capable of an artistic expression that can be matched nowhere. What more could you do if you were free?"

"Perhaps no more than I do now, your honor, but with greater joy. It has been said in this courtroom that only a human being can be free. It seems to me that only someone who wishes for freedom can be free. I wish for freedom."

And it was that that cued the judge. The crucial sentence in his decision was: "There is no right to deny freedom to any object with a mind advanced enough to grasp the concept and desire the state."

It was eventually upheld by the World Court.

8

Sir remained displeased, and his harsh voice made Andrew feel as though he were being short-circuited.

Sir said, "I don't want your damned money, Andrew. I'll take it only because you won't feel free otherwise. From now on, you can select your own jobs and do them as you please. I will give you no orders, except this one—that you do as you please. But I am still responsible for you; that's part of the court order. I hope you understand that."

Little Miss interrupted. "Don't be irascible, Dad. The responsibility is no great chore. You know you won't have to do a thing. The Three Laws still hold."

"Then how is he free?"

Andrew said, "Are not human beings bound by their laws, Sir?"

Sir said, "I'm not going to argue." He left, and Andrew saw him only infrequently after that.

Little Miss came to see him frequently in the small house that had been built and made over for him. It had no kitchen, of course, nor bathroom facilities. It had just two rooms; one was a library and one was a combination storeroom and workroom. Andrew accepted many commissions and worked harder as a free robot than he ever had before, till the cost of the house was paid for and the structure legally transferred to him.

One day Little Sir came.... No, George! Little Sir had insisted on that after the court decision. "A free robot doesn't call anyone Little Sir," George had said. "I call you Andrew. You must call me George."

It was phrased as an order, so Andrew called him George—but Little Miss remained Little Miss.

The day George came alone, it was to say that Sir was dying. Little Miss was at the bedside but Sir wanted Andrew as well.

Sir's voice was quite strong, though he seemed unable to move much. He struggled to get his hand up. "Andrew," he said, "Andrew— Don't help me, George. I'm only dying; I'm not crippled.... Andrew, I'm glad you're free. I just wanted to tell you that."

Andrew did not know what to say. He had never been at the side of someone dying before, but he knew it was the human way of ceasing to function. It was an involuntary and irreversible dismantling, and Andrew did not know what to say that might be appropriate. He could only remain standing, absolutely silent, absolutely motionless.

When it was over, Little Miss said to him, "He may not have seemed friendly to you toward the end, Andrew, but he was old, you know, and it hurt him that you should want to be free."

And then Andrew found the words to say. He said, "I would never have been free without him, Little Miss."

9

It was only after Sir's death that Andrew began to wear clothes. He began with an old pair of trousers at first, a pair that George had given him.

George was married now, and a lawyer. He had joined Feingold's firm. Old Feingold was long since dead but his daughter had carried on and eventually the firm's name became Feingold and Martin. It remained so even when the daughter retired and no Feingold took her place. At the time Andrew put on clothes for the first time, the Martin name had just been added to the firm.

George had tried not to smile the first time Andrew put on the trousers, but to Andrew's eyes the smile was clearly there.

George showed Andrew how to manipulate the static charge so as to allow the trousers to open, wrap about his lower body, and move shut. George demonstrated on his own trousers, but Andrew was quite aware it would take him a while to duplicate that one flowing motion.

George said, "But why do you want trousers, Andrew? Your body is so beautifully functional it's a shame to cover it—especially when you needn't worry about either temperature control or modesty. And it doesn't cling properly, not on metal."

Andrew said, "Are not human bodies beautifully functional, George? Yet you cover yourselves."

"For warmth, for cleanliness, for protection, for decorativeness. None of that applies to you."

Andrew said, "I feel bare without clothes. I feel different, George."

"Different! Andrew, there are millions of robots on Earth now. In this region, according to the last census, there are almost as many robots as there are men."

"I know, George. There are robots doing every conceivable type of work."

"And none of them wear clothes."

"But none of them are free, George."

Little by little, Andrew added to the wardrobe. He was inhibited by George's smile and by the stares of the people who commissioned work.

He might be free, but there was built into Andrew a carefully detailed program concerning his behavior toward people, and it was only by the tiniest steps that he dared advance. Open disapproval would set him back months.

Not everyone accepted Andrew as free. He was incapable of resenting that and yet there was a difficulty about his thinking process when he thought of it.

Most of all, he tended to avoid putting on clothes—or too many of them—when he thought Little Miss might come to visit him. She was old now and was often away in some warmer climate, but when she returned the first thing she did was visit him.

On one of her returns, George said ruefully, "She's got me, Andrew. I'll be running for the Legislature next year. Like grandfather, she says, like grandson."

"Like grandfather—" Andrew stopped, uncertain.

"I mean that I, George, the grandson, will be like Sir, the grandfather, who was in the Legislature once."

Andrew said, "It would be pleasant, George, if Sir were still—" He paused, for he did not want to say, "in working order." That seemed inappropriate.

"Alive," said George. "Yes, I think of the old monster now and then, too."

It was a conversation Andrew thought about. He had noticed his own incapacity in speech when talking with George. Somehow the language had changed since Andrew had come into being with an innate vocabulary. Then, too, George used a colloquial speech, as Sir and Little Miss had not. Why should he have called Sir a monster when surely that word was not an appropriate?

Nor could Andrew turn to his own books for guidance. They were old and most dealt with woodworking, with art, with furniture design. There were none on language, none on the way of human beings.

It was at that moment it seemed to him that he must seek the proper books; and as a free robot, he felt he must not ask George. He would go to town and use the library. It was a triumphant decision and he felt his electropotential grow distinctly higher until he had to throw in an impedance coil.

He put on a full costume, including even a shoulder chain of wood. He would have preferred the glitter plastic but George had said that wood was much more appropriate and that polished cedar was considerably more valuable as well.

He had placed a hundred feet between himself and the house before gathering resistance brought him to a halt. He shifted the impedance coil out of circuit, and when that did not seem to help enough, he returned to his home and on a piece of notepaper wrote neatly, "I have gone to the library," and placed it in clear view on his worktable.

10

Andrew never quite got to the library. He had studied the map. He knew the route, but not the appearance of it. The actual landmarks did not resemble the symbols on the map and he would hesitate. Eventually he thought he must have somehow gone wrong, for everything looked strange.

He passed an occasional field robot, but at the time he decided he should ask his way, there were none in sight. A vehicle passed and did not stop. He stood irresolute, which meant calmly motionless, and then coming across the field toward him were two human beings.

He turned to face them, and they altered their course to meet him. A moment before, they had been talking loudly; he had heard their voices; but now they were silent. They had the look that Andrew associated with human uncertainty, and they were young, but not very young. Twenty, perhaps? Andrew could never judge human age.

He said, "Would you describe to me the route to the town library, sirs?"

One of them, the taller of the two, whose tall hat lengthened him still farther, almost grotesquely, said, not to Andrew, but to the other, "It's a robot."

The other had a bulbous nose and heavy eyelids. He said, not to Andrew, but to the first, "It's wearing clothes."

The tall one snapped his fingers. "It's the free robot. They have a robot at the Martins who isn't owned by anybody. Why else would it be wearing clothes?"

220

"Ask it," said the one with the nose.

"Are you the Martin robot?" asked the tall one.

"I am Andrew Martin, sir," said Andrew.

"Good. Take off your clothes. Robots don't wear clothes." He said to the other, "That's disgusting. Look at him."

Andrew hesitated. He hadn't heard an order in that tone of voice in so long that his Second Law circuits had momentarily jammed.

The tall one said, "Take off your clothes. I order you."

Slowly, Andrew began to remove them.

"Just drop them," said the tall one.

The nose said, "If it doesn't belong to anyone, it could be ours as much as someone else's."

"Anyway," said the tall one, "who's to object to anything we do. We're not damaging property. . . . Stand on your head." That was to Andrew.

"The head is not meant—" Andrew began.

"That's an order. If you don't know how, try anyway."

Andrew hesitated again, then bent to put his head on the ground. He tried to lift his legs and fell, heavily.

The tall one said, "Just lie there." He said to the other, "We can take him apart. Ever take a robot apart?"

"Will he let us?"

"How can he stop us?"

There was no way Andrew could stop them, if they ordered him not to resist in a forceful enough manner. The Second Law of obedience took precedence over the Third Law of self-preservation. In any case, he could not defend himself without possibly hurting them and that would mean breaking the First Law. At that thought, every motile unit contracted slightly and he quivered as he lay there.

The tall one walked over and pushed at him with his foot. "He's heavy. I think we'll need tools to do the job."

The nose said, "We could order him to take himself apart. It would be fun to watch him try."

"Yes," said the tall one thoughtfully, "but let's get him off the road. If someone comes along—"

It was too late. Someone had indeed come along and it was George. From where he lay, Andrew had seen him topping a small rise in the middle distance. He would have liked to signal him in some way, but the last order had been "Just lie there!"

George was running now, and he arrived somewhat winded. The two young men stepped back a little and then waited thoughtfully.

George said anxiously, "Andrew, has something gone wrong?"

Andrew said, "I am well, George."

"Then stand up. . . . What happened to your clothes?"

The tall young man said, "That your robot, mac?"

George turned sharply. "He's no one's robot. What's been going on here?"

"We politely asked him to take his clothes off. What's that to you, if you don't own him?"

George said, "What were they doing, Andrew?"

Andrew said, "It was their intention in some way to dismember me. They were about to move me to a quiet spot and order me to dismember myself."

George looked at the two young men, and his chin trembled. The young men retreated no farther. They were smiling. The tall one said, lightly, "What are you going to do, pudgy? Attack us?"

George said, "No. I don't have to. This robot has been with my family for over seventy years. He knows us and he values us more than he values anyone else. I am going to tell him that you two are threatening my life and that you plan to kill me. I will ask him to defend me. In choosing between me and you two, he will choose me. Do you know what will happen to you when he attacks you?"

The two were backing away slightly, looking uneasy.

George said sharply, "Andrew, I am in danger and about to come to harm from these young men. Move toward them!"

Andrew did so, and the two young men did not wait. They ran fleetly.

"All right, Andrew, relax," said George. He looked unstrung. He was far past the age where he could face the possibility of a dustup with one young man, let alone two.

Andrew said, "I couldn't have hurt them, George. I could see they were not attacking you."

"I didn't order you to attack them; I only told you to move toward them. Their own fears did the rest."

"How can they fear robots?"

"It's a disease of mankind, one of which it is not yet cured. But never mind that. What the devil are you doing here, Andrew? I was on the point of turning back and hiring a helicopter when I found you. How did you get it into your head to go to the library? I would have brought you any books you needed."

"I am a—" began Andrew.

"Free robot. Yes, yes. All right, what did you want in the library?"

"I want to know more about human beings, about the world, about everything. And about robots, George. I want to write a history about robots."

George said, "Well, let's walk home. . . . And pick up your clothes first. Andrew, there are a million books on robotics and all of them include histories of the science. The world is growing saturated not only with robots but with information about robots."

Andrew shook his head, a human gesture he had lately begun to make. "Not a history of robotics, George. A history of *robots*, by a robot. I want to explain how robots feel about what has happened since the first ones were allowed to work and live on Earth."

George's eyebrows lifted, but he said nothing in direct response.

11

Little Miss was just past her eighty-third birthday, but there was nothing about her that was lacking in either energy or determination. She gestured with her cane oftener than she propped herself up with it.

She listened to the story in a fury of indignation. She said, "George, that's horrible. Who were those young ruffians?"

"I don't know. What difference does it make? In the end they did no damage."

"They might have. You're a lawyer, George, and if you're well off, it's entirely due to the talent of Andrew. It was the money *he* earned that is the foundation of everything we have. He provides the continuity for this family and I will *not* have him treated as a wind-up toy."

"What would you have me do, Mother?" George asked.

"I said you're a lawyer. Don't you listen? You set up a test case somehow, and you force the regional courts to declare for robot rights and get the Legislature to pass the necessary bills, and carry the whole thing to the World Court, if you have to. I'll be watching, George, and I'll tolerate no shirking."

She was serious, and what began as a way of soothing the fearsome old lady became an involved matter with enough legal entanglement to make it interesting. As senior partner of Feingold and Martin, George plotted strategy but left the actual work to his junior partners, with much of it a matter for his son, Paul, who was also a member of the firm and who reported dutifully nearly every day to his grandmother. She, in turn, discussed the case every day with Andrew.

Andrew was deeply involved. His work on his book on robots was delayed again, as he pored over the legal arguments and even, at times, made very diffident suggestions.

He said, "George told me that day that human beings have always been afraid of robots. As long as they are, the courts and the legislatures are not likely to work hard on behalf of robots. Should there not be something done about public opinion?"

So while Paul stayed in court, George took to the public platform. It gave him the advantage of being informal and he even went so far sometimes as to wear the new, loose style of clothing which he called drapery. Paul said, "Just don't trip over it on stage, Dad."

George replied, despondently, "I'll try not to."

He addressed the annual convention of holo-news editors on one occasion and said, in part:

"If, by virtue of the Second Law, we can demand of any robot unlimited obedience in all respects not involving harm to a human being, then any human being, *any* human being, has a fearsome power over any robot, *any* robot. In particular, since Second Law supersedes Third Law, *any* human being can use the law of obedience to overcome the law of self-protection. He can order any robot to damage itself or even to destroy itself for any reason, or for no reason.

"Is this just? Would we treat an animal so? Even an inanimate object which has given us good service has a claim on our consideration. And a robot is not insensible; it is not an animal. It can think well enough to enable it to talk to us, reason with us, joke with us. Can we treat them as friends, can we work together with them, and not give them some of the fruit of that friendship, some of the benefits of coworking?

"If a man has the right to give a robot any order that does not involve harm to a human being, he should have the decency never to give a robot any order that involves harm to a robot, unless human safety absolutely requires it. With great power goes great responsibility, and if the robots have Three Laws to protect men, is it too much to ask that men have a law or two to protect robots?"

Andrew was right. It was the battle over public opinion that held the key to courts and Legislature and in the end a law was passed which set up conditions under which robot-harming orders were forbidden. It was endlessly qualified and the punishments for violating the law were totally inadequate, but the principle was established. The final passage by the World Legislature came through on the day of Little Miss's death.

That was no coincidence. Little Miss held on to life desperately during the last debate and let go only when word of victory arrived. Her last smile was for Andrew. Her last words were: "You have been good to us, Andrew."

She died with her hand holding his, while her son and his wife and children remained at a respectful distance from both.

12

Andrew waited patiently while the receptionist disappeared into the inner office. It might have used the holographic chatterbox, but unquestionably it was unmanned (or perhaps unroboted) by having to deal with another robot rather than with a human being.

Andrew passed the time revolving the matter in his mind: Could "unroboted" be used as an analogue of "unmanned," or had "unmanned" become a metaphoric term sufficiently divorced from its original literal meaning to be applied to robots—or to women for that matter?

Such problems came frequently as he worked on his book on robots. The trick of thinking out sentences to express all complexities had undoubtedly increased his vocabulary.

Occasionally, someone came into the room to stare at him and he did not try to avoid the glance. He looked at each calmly, and each in turn looked away.

Paul Martin finally came out. He looked surprised, or he would have if Andrew could have made out his expression with certainty. Paul had taken to wearing the heavy makeup that fashion was dictating for both sexes and though it made sharper and firmer the somewhat bland lines of his face, Andrew disapproved. He found that disapproving of human beings, as long as he did not express it verbally, did not make him very uneasy. He could even write the disapproval. He was sure it had not always been so.

Paul said, "Come in, Andrew. I'm sorry I made you wait but there was something I *had* to finish. Come in. You had said you wanted to talk to me, but I didn't know you meant here in town."

"If you are busy, Paul, I am prepared to continue to wait."

Paul glanced at the interplay of shifting shadows on the dial on the wall that served as timepiece and said, "I can make some time. Did you come alone?"

"I hired an automatobile."

"Any trouble?" Paul asked, with more than a trace of anxiety.

"I wasn't expecting any. My rights are protected."

Paul looked the more anxious for that. "Andrew, I've explained that the law is unenforceable, at least under most conditions. . . . And if you insist on wearing clothes, you'll run into trouble eventually—just like that first time."

"And only time, Paul. I'm sorry you are displeased"

"Well, look at it this way; you are virtually a living legend, Andrew, and you are too valuable in many different ways for you to have any right to take chances with yourself. . . . How's the book coming?"

"I am approaching the end, Paul. The publisher is quite pleased."

"Good!"

"I don't know that he's necessarily pleased with the book as a book. I think he expects to sell many copies because it's written by a robot and it's that that pleases him."

"Only human, I'm afraid."

"I am not displeased. Let it sell for whatever reason since it will mean money and I can use some."

"Grandmother left you—"

"Little Miss was generous, and I'm sure I can count on the family to help me out further. But it is the royalties from the book on which I am counting to help me through the next step."

"What next step is that?"

"I wish to see the head of U.S. Robots and Mechanical Men, Inc. I have tried to make an appointment, but so far I have not been able to reach him. The corporation did not cooperate with me in the writing of the book, so I am not surprised, you understand."

Paul was clearly amused. "Cooperation is the last thing you can expect. They didn't cooperate with us in our great fight for robot rights. Quite the reverse and you can see why. Give a robot rights and people may not want to buy them."

"Nevertheless," said Andrew, "if you call them, you may obtain an interview for me."

"I'm no more popular with them than you are, Andrew."

"But perhaps you can hint that by seeing me they may head off a campaign by Feingold and Martin to strengthen the rights of robots further."

"Wouldn't that be a lie, Andrew?"

"Yes, Paul, and I can't tell one. That is why you must call."

"Ah, you can't lie, but you can urge me to tell a lie, is that it? You're getting more human all the time, Andrew."

13

It was not easy to arrange, even with Paul's supposedly weighted name.

But it was finally carried through and, when it was, Harley Smythe-Robertson, who, on his mother's side, was descended from the original founder of the corporation and who had adopted the hyphenation to indicate it, looked remarkably unhappy. He was approaching retirement age and his entire tenure as president had been devoted to the matter of robot rights. His gray hair was plastered thinly over the top of his scalp, his face was not made up, and he eyed Andrew with brief hostility from time to time.

Andrew said, "Sir, nearly a century ago, I was told by a Merton Mansky of this corporation that the mathematics governing the plotting of the positronic pathways was far too complicated to permit of any but approximate solutions and that therefore my own capacities were not fully predictable."

"That was a century ago." Smythe-Robertson hesitated, then said icily, "*Sir.* It is true no longer. Our robots are made with precision now and are trained precisely to their jobs."

"Yes," said Paul, who had come along, as he said, to make sure that the corporation played fair, "with the result that my receptionist must be guided at every point once events depart from the conventional, however slightly."

Smythe-Robertson said, "You would be much more displeased if it were to improvise."

Andrew said, "Then you no longer manufacture robots like myself which are flexible and adaptable."

"No longer."

"The research I have done in connection with my book," said Andrew, "indicates that I am the oldest robot presently in active operation."

"The oldest presently," said Smythe-Robertson, "and the oldest ever. The oldest that will ever be. No robot is useful after the twenty-fifth year. They are called in and replaced with newer models."

"No robot *as presently manufactured* is useful after the twenty-fifth year," said Paul pleasantly. "Andrew is quite exceptional in this respect."

Andrew, adhering to the path he had marked out for himself, said, "As the oldest robot in the world and the most flexible, am I not unusual enough to merit special treatment from the company?"

"Not at all," Smythe-Robertson said, freezingly. "Your unusualness is an embarrassment to the company. If you were on lease, instead of having been an outright sale through some mischance, you would long since have been replaced."

"But that is exactly the point," said Andrew. "I am a free robot and I own myself. Therefore I come to you and ask you to replace me. You cannot do this without the owner's consent. Nowadays, that consent is extorted as a condition of the lease, but in my time this did not happen."

Smythe-Robertson was looking both startled and puzzled, and for a moment there was silence. Andrew found himself staring at the holograph on the wall. It was a death mask of Susan Calvin, patron saint of all roboticists. She was dead nearly two centuries now, but as a result of writing his book Andrew knew her so well he could half persuade himself that he had met her in life.

Smythe-Robertson said, "How can I replace you for you? If I replace you as robot, how can I donate the new robot to you as owner since in the very act of replacement you cease to exist?" He smiled grimly.

"Not at all difficult," interposed Paul. "The seat of Andrew's personality is his positronic brain and it is the one part that cannot be replaced without creating a new robot. The positronic brain, therefore, is Andrew the owner. Every other part of the robotic body can be replaced without affecting the robot's personality, and those other parts are the brain's possessions. Andrew, I should say, wants to supply his brain with a new robotic body."

"That's right," said Andrew, calmly. He turned to Smythe-Robertson. "You have manufactured androids, haven't you? Robots that have the outward appearance of humans complete to the texture of the skin?"

Smythe-Robertson said, "Yes, we have. They worked perfectly well, with their synthetic fibrous skins and tendons. There was virtually no metal anywhere except for the brain, yet they were nearly as tough as metal robots. They were tougher, weight for weight."

Paul looked interested. "I didn't know that. How many are on the market?"

"None," said Smythe-Robertson. "They were much more expensive than metal models and a market survey showed they would not be accepted. They looked too human."

Andrew said, "But the corporation retains its expertise, I assume. Since it does, I wish to request that I be replaced by an organic robot, an android."

Paul looked surprised. "Good Lord," he said.

Smythe-Robertson stiffened. "Quite impossible!"

"Why is it impossible?" Andrew asked. "I will pay any reasonable fee, of course."

Smythe-Robertson said, "We do not manufacture androids."

"You do not *choose* to manufacture androids," interposed Paul quickly. "That is not the same as being unable to manufacture them."

Smythe-Robertson said, "Nevertheless, the manufacture of androids is against public policy."

"There is no law against it," said Paul.

"Nevertheless, we do not manufacture them, and we will not"

Paul cleared his throat. "Mr. Smythe-Robertson," he said, "Andrew is a free robot who is under the purview of the law guaranteeing robot rights. You are aware of this, I take it?"

"Only too well."

"This robot, as a free robot, chooses to wear clothes. This results in his being frequently humiliated by thoughtless human beings despite the law against the humiliation of robots. It is difficult to prosecute vague offenses that don't meet with the general disapproval of those who must decide on guilt and innocence."

"U.S. Robots understood that from the start. Your father's firm unfortunately did not."

"My father is dead now," said Paul, "but what I see is that we have here a clear offense with a clear target."

"What are you talking about?" said Smythe-Robertson.

"My client, Andrew Martin—he has just become my client—is a free robot who is entitled to ask U.S. Robots and Mechanical Men, Inc., for the right of replacement, which the corporation supplies anyone who owns a robot for more than twenty-five years. In fact, the corporation insists on such replacement."

Paul was smiling and thoroughly at his ease. He went on, "The positronic brain of my client is the owner of the body of my client—which is certainly more than twenty-five years old. The positronic brain demands the replacement of the body and offers to pay any reasonable fee for an android body as that replacement. If you refuse the request, my client undergoes humiliation and we will sue.

"While public opinion would not ordinarily support the claim of a robot in such a case, may I remind you that U.S. Robots is not popular with the public generally. Even those who most use and profit from robots are suspicious of the corporation. This may be a hangover from the days when robots were widely feared. It may be resentment against the power and wealth of U.S. Robots which has a worldwide monopoly. Whatever the cause may be, the resentment exists and I think you will find that you would prefer not to withstand a lawsuit, particularly since my client is wealthy and will live for many more centuries and will have no reason to refrain from fighting the battle forever."

Smythe-Robertson had slowly reddened. "You are trying to force me to . . ."

"I force you to do nothing," said Paul. "If you wish to refuse to accede to my client's reasonable request, you may by all means do so and we will leave without another word. . . . But we will sue, as is certainly our right, and you will find that you will eventually lose."

Smythe-Robertson said, "Well—" and paused.

"I see that you are going to accede," said Paul. "You may hesitate but you will come to it in the end. Let me assure you, then, of one further point. If, in the process of transferring my client's positronic brain from his present body to an organic one, there is any damage, however slight, then I will never rest till I've nailed the corporation to the ground. I will, if necessary, take every possible step to mobilize public opinion against the corporation if one brain path of my client's platinum-iridium essence is scrambled." He turned to Andrew and said, 'Do you agree to all this, Andrew?"

Andrew hesitated a full minute. It amounted to the approval of lying, of blackmail, of the badgering and humiliation of a human being. But not physical harm, he told himself, not physical harm.

He managed at last to come out with a rather faint "Yes."

14

It was like being constructed again. For days, then for weeks, finally for months, Andrew found himself not himself somehow, and the simplest actions kept giving rise to hesitation.

Paul was frantic. "They've damaged you, Andrew. We'll have to institute suit."

Andrew spoke very slowly. "You mustn't. You'll never be able to prove—something—m-m-m-m—"

"Malice?"

"Malice. Besides, I grow stronger, better. It's the tr-tr-tr—"

"Tremble?"

"Trauma. After all, there's never been such an op—op—op— before."

Andrew could feel his brain from the inside. No one else could. He knew he was well and during the months that it took him to learn full coordination and full positronic interplay, he spent hours before the mirror.

Not quite human! The face was stiff—too stiff—and the motions were too deliberate. They lacked the careless free flow of the human being, but perhaps that might come with time. At least he could wear clothes without the ridiculous anomaly of a metal face going along with it.

Eventually he said, "I will be going back to work."

Paul laughed and said, "That means you are well. What will you be doing? Another book?"

"No," said Andrew, seriously. "I live too long for any one career to seize me by the throat and never let me go. There was a time when I was primarily an artist and I can still turn to that. And there was a time when I was a historian and I can still turn to that. But now I wish to be a robobiologist."

"A robopsychologist, you mean."

"No. That would imply the study of positronic brains and at the moment I lack the desire to do that. A robobiologist, it seems to me, would be concerned with the working of the body attached to that brain."

"Wouldn't that be a roboticist?"

"A roboticist works with a metal body. I would be studying an organic humanoid body, of which I have the only one, as far as I know."

"You narrow your field," said Paul, thoughtfully. "As an artist, all conception is yours; as a historian, you deal chiefly with robots; as a robobiologist, you will deal with yourself."

Andrew nodded. "It would seem so."

Andrew had to start from the very beginning, for he knew nothing of ordinary biology, almost nothing of science. He became a familiar sight in the libraries, where he sat at the electronic indices for hours at a time, looking perfectly normal in clothes. Those few who knew he was a robot in no way interfered with him.

He built a laboratory in a room which he added to his house, and his library grew, too.

Years passed, and Paul came to him one day and said, "It's a pity you're no longer working on the history of robots. I understand U.S. Robots is adopting a radically new policy."

Paul had aged, and his deteriorating eyes had been replaced with photoptic cells. In that respect, he had drawn closer to Andrew. Andrew said, "What have they done?"

"They are manufacturing central computers, gigantic positronic brains, really, which communicate with anywhere from a dozen to a thousand robots by microwave. The robots themselves have no brains at all. They are the limbs of the gigantic brain, and the two are physically separate."

"Is that more efficient?"

"U.S. Robots claims it is. Smythe-Robertson established the new direction before he died, however, and it's my notion that it's a backlash at you. U.S. Robots is determined that they will make no robots that will give them the type of trouble you have, and for that reason they separate brain and body. The brain will have no body to wish changed; the body will have no brain to wish anything."

"It's amazing, Andrew," Paul went on, "the influence you have had on the history of robots. It was your artistry that encouraged U.S. Robots to make robots more precise and specialized; it was your freedom that resulted in the establishment of the principle of robotic rights; it was your insistence on an android body that made U.S. Robots switch to brain-body separation."

Andrew said, "I suppose in the end the corporation will produce one vast brain controlling several billion robotic bodies. All the eggs will be in one basket. Dangerous. Not proper at all."

"I think you're right," said Paul, "but I don't suspect it will come to pass for a century at least and I won't live to see it. In fact, I may not live to see next year."

"Paul!" said Andrew, in concern.

Paul shrugged. "We're mortal, Andrew. We're not like you. It doesn't matter too much, but it does make it important to assure you on one point. I'm the last of the human Martins. There are collaterals descended from my great-aunt, but they don't count. The money I control personally will be left to the trust in your name and as far as anyone can foresee the future, you will be economically secure."

"Unnecessary," Andrew said, with difficulty. In all this time, he could not get used to the deaths of the Martins.

Paul said, "Let's not argue. That's the way it's going to be. What are you working on?"

"I am designing a system for allowing androids—myself—to gain energy from the combustion of hydrocarbons, rather than from atomic cells."

Paul raised his eyebrows. "So that they will breathe and eat?"
"Yes."

"How long have you been pushing in that direction?"

"For a long time now, but I think I have designed an adequate combustion chamber for catalyzed controlled breakdown."

"But why, Andrew? The atomic cell is surely infinitely better."

"In some ways, perhaps, but the atomic cell is inhuman."

15

It took time, but Andrew had time. In the first place, he did not wish to do anything till Paul had died in peace.

With the death of the great-grandson of Sir, Andrew felt more nearly exposed to a hostile world and for that reason was the more determined along the path he had long ago chosen.

Yet he was not really alone. If a man had died, the firm of Feingold and Martin lived, for a corporation does not die any more than a robot does. The firm had its directions and it followed them soullessly. By way of the trust and through the law firm, Andrew continued to be wealthy. And in return for their own large annual retainer, Feingold and Martin involved themselves in the legal aspects of the new combustion chamber.

When the time came for Andrew to visit U.S. Robots and Mechanical Men, Inc., he did it alone. Once he had gone with Sir and once with Paul. This time, the third time, he was alone and manlike.

U.S. Robots had changed. The actual production plant had been shifted to a large space station, as had grown to be the case with more and more industries. With them had gone many robots. The Earth itself was becoming parklike, with its one-billion-person population stabilized and perhaps not more than thirty percent of its at least equally large robot population independently brained.

The Director of Research was Alvin Magdescu, dark of complexion and hair, with a little pointed beard and wearing nothing above the waist but the breast band that fashion dictated. Andrew himself was well covered in the older fashion of several decades back.

Magdescu said, "I know you, of course, and I'm rather pleased to see you. You're our most notorious product and it's a pity old Smyth-Robertson was so set against you. We could have done a great deal with you."

"You still can," said Andrew.

"No, I don't think so. We're past the time. We've had robots on Earth for over a century, but that's changing. It will be back to space with them and those that stay here won't be brained."

"But there remains myself, and I stay on Earth."

"True, but there doesn't seem to be much of the robot about you. What new request have you?"

"To be still less a robot. Since I am so far organic, I wish an organic source of energy. I have here the plans—"

Magdescu did not hasten through them. He might have intended to at first, but he stiffened and grew intent. At one point he said, "This is remarkably ingenious. Who thought of all this?"

"I did," said Andrew.

Magdescu looked up at him sharply, then said, "It would amount to a major overhaul of your body, and an experimental one, since it has never been attempted before. I advise against it. Remain as you are."

Andrew's face had limited means of expression, but impatience showed plainly in his voice. "Dr. Magdescu, you miss the entire point. You have no choice but to accede to my request. If such devices can be built into my body, they can be built into human bodies as well. The tendency to lengthen human life by prosthetic devices has already been remarked on. There are no devices better than the ones I have designed and am designing.

THE BICENTENNIAL MAN

235

"As it happens, I control the patents by way of the firm of Feingold and Martin. We are quite capable of going into business for ourselves and of developing the kind of prosthetic devices that may end by producing human beings with many of the properties of robots. Your own business will then suffer.

"If, however, you operate on me now and agree to do so under similar circumstances in the future, you will receive permission to make use of the patents and control the technology of both robots and of the prosthetization of human beings. The initial leasing will not be granted, of course, until after the first operation is completed successfully, and after enough time has passed to demonstrate that it is indeed successful." Andrew felt scarcely any First Law inhibition to the stern conditions he was setting a human being. He was learning to reason that what seemed like cruelty might, in the long run, be kindness.

Magdescu looked stunned. He said, "I'm not the one to decide something like this. That's a corporate decision that would take time."

"I can wait a reasonable time," said Andrew, "but only a reasonable time." And he thought with satisfaction that Paul himself could not have done it better.

16

It took only a reasonable time, and the operation was a success.

Magdescu said, "I was very much against the operation, Andrew, but not for the reasons you might think. I was not in the least against the experiment, if it had been on someone else. I hated risking *your* positronic brain. Now that you have the positronic pathways interacting with simulated nerve pathways, it might be difficult to rescue the brain intact if the body had went bad."

"I had every faith in the skill of the staff at U.S. Robots," said Andrew. "And I can eat now."

"Well, you can sip olive oil. It will mean occasional cleanings of the combustion chamber, as we have explained to you. Rather an uncomfortable touch, I should think."

"Perhaps, if I did not expect to go further. Self-cleaning is not impossible. In fact, I am working on a device that will deal with solid food that may be expected to contain incombustible fractions—indigestible matter, so to speak, that will have to be discarded."

"You would then have to develop an anus."

"The equivalent."

"What else, Andrew?"

"Everything else."

"Genitalia, too?"

"Insofar as they will fit my plans. My body is a canvas on which I intend to draw—"

Magdescu waited for the sentence to be completed, and when it seemed that it would not be, he completed it himself. "A man?"

"We shall see," said Andrew.

Magdescu said, "It's a puny ambition, Andrew. You're better than a man. You've gone downhill from the moment you opted for organicism."

"My brain has not suffered."

"No, it hasn't. I'll grant you that. But, Andrew, the whole new breakthrough in prosthetic devices made possible by your patents is being marketed under your name. You're recognized as the inventor and you're honored for it—as you are. Why play further games with your body?"

Andrew did not answer.

The honors came. He accepted membership in several learned societies, including one which was devoted to the new science he had established; the one he had called robobiology but had come to be termed prosthetology.

On the one hundred and fiftieth anniversary of his construction, there was a testimonial dinner was given in his honor at U.S. Robots. If Andrew saw an irony in this, he kept it to himself.

Alvin Magdescu came out of retirement to chair the dinner. He was himself ninety-four years old and was alive because he had prosthetized devices that, among other things, fulfilled the function of liver and kidneys. The dinner reached its climax when Magdescu, after a short and emotional talk, raised his glass to toast "the Sesquicentennial Robot."

Andrew had had the sinews of his face redesigned to the point where he could show a range of emotions, but he sat through all the ceremonies solemnly passive. He did not like to be a Sesquicentennial Robot.

17

It was prosthetology that finally took Andrew off the Earth. In the decades that followed the celebration of the Sesquicentennial, the Moon had come to be a world more Earthlike than Earth in every respect but its gravitational pull, and in its underground cities there was a fairly dense population.

Prosthetized devices there had to take the lesser gravity into account and Andrew spent five years on the Moon working with local prosthetologists to make the necessary adaptations. When not at his work, he wandered among the robot population, every one of which treated him with the robotic obsequiousness due a man.

He came back to an Earth that was humdrum and quiet in comparison and visited the offices of Feingold and Martin to announce his return.

The current head of the firm, Simon DeLong, was surprised. He said, "We had been told you were returning, Andrew" (he had almost said "Mr. Martin"), but we were not expecting you till next week."

"I grew impatient," said Andrew brusquely. He was anxious to get to the point. "On the Moon, Simon, I was in charge of a research team of twenty human scientists. I gave orders that no one questioned. The Lunar robots deferred to me as they would to a human being. Why, then, am I not a human being?"

A wary look entered DeLong's eyes. He said, "My dear Andrew, as you have just explained, you are treated as a human being by both robots and human beings. You are therefore a human being de facto."

"To be a human being de facto is not enough. I want not only to be treated as one, but to be legally identified as one. I want to be a human being de jure."

"Now, that is another matter," said DeLong. "There we would run into human prejudice and into the undoubted fact that, however much you may be like a human being, you are *not* a human being."

"In what way not?" asked Andrew. "I have the shape of a human being and organs equivalent to those of a human being. My organs, in fact, are identical to some of those in a prosthetized human being. I have contributed artistically, literarily, and scientifically to human culture as much as any human being now alive. What more can one ask?"

"I myself would ask nothing more. The trouble is that it would take an act of the World Legislature to define you as a human being. Frankly, I wouldn't expect that to happen."

"To whom on the Legislature could I speak?"

"To the Chairman of the Science and Technology Committee perhaps."

"Can you arrange a meeting?"

"But you scarcely need an intermediary. In your position, you can—"

"No. *You* arrange it." (It didn't even occur to Andrew that he was giving a flat order to a human being. He had grown accustomed to that on the Moon.) "I want him to know that the firm of Feingold and Martin is backing me in this to the hilt."

"Well, now—"

"To the hilt, Simon. In one hundred and seventy-three years I have in one fashion or another contributed greatly to this firm. I have been under obligation to individual members of the firm in times past. I am not now. It is rather the other way around now and I am calling in my debts."

Delong said, "I will do what I can."

18

The chairman of the Science and Technology Committee was of the East Asian region and she was a woman. Her name was Chee Li-Hsing and her transparent garments (obscuring what she wanted obscured only by their dazzle) made her look plastic-wrapped.

She said, "I sympathize with your wish for full human rights. There have been times in history when segments of the human population fought for full human rights. What rights, however, can you possibly want that you do not have?"

"As simple a thing as my right to life. A robot can be dismantled at any time."

"A human being can be executed at any time."

"Execution can only follow due process of law. There is no trial needed for my dismantling. Only the word of a human being in authority is needed to end me. Besides—besides—" Andrew tried desperately to allow no sign of pleading, but his carefully designed tricks of human expression and tone of voice betrayed him here. "The truth is, I want to be a man. I have wanted it through six generations of human beings."

Li-Hsing looked up at him out of darkly sympathetic eyes. "The Legislature can pass a law declaring you one—they could pass a law declaring a stone statue to be defined as a man. Whether they will actually do so is, however, as likely in the first case as the second. Congresspeople are as human as the rest of the population and there is always that element of suspicion against robots."

"Even now?"

"Even now. We would all allow the fact that you have earned the prize of humanity and yet there would remain the fear of setting an undesirable precedent."

"What precedent? I am the only free robot, the only one of my type, and there will never be another. You may consult U.S. Robots."

" 'Never' is a long time, Andrew—or, if you prefer, Mr. Martin—since I will gladly give you my personal accolade as man. You will find that most Congresspeople will not be willing to set the precedent, no matter how meaningless such a precedent might be. Mr. Martin, you have my sympathy, but I cannot tell you to hope. Indeed—"

She sat back and her forehead wrinkled. "Indeed, if the issue grows too heated, there might well arise a certain sentiment, both inside the Legislature and outside, for that dismantling you mentioned. Doing away with you could turn out to be the easiest way of resolving the dilemma. Consider that before deciding to push matters."

Andrew said, "Will no one remember the technique of prosthetology, something that is almost entirely mine?"

"It may seem cruel, but they won't. Or if they do, it will be remembered against you. It will be said you did it only for yourself. It will be said it was part of a campaign to roboticize human beings, or to humanify robots; and in either case evil and vicious. You have never been part of a political hate campaign, Mr. Martin, and I tell you that you will be the object of vilification of a kind neither you nor I would credit and there would be people who'll believe it all. Mr. Martin, let your life be." She rose and, next to Andrew's seated figure, she seemed small and almost childlike.

Andrew said, "If I decide to fight for my humanity, will you be on my side?"

She thought, then said, "I will be—insofar as I can be. If at any time such a stand would appear to threaten my political future, I might have to abandon you, since it is not an issue I feel to be at the very root of my beliefs. I am trying to be honest with you."

"Thank you, and I will ask no more. I intend to fight this through whatever the consequences, and I will ask you for your help only for as long as you can give it."

19

It was not a direct fight. Feingold and Martin counseled patience and Andrew muttered grimly that he had an endless supply of that. Feingold and Martin then entered on a campaign to narrow and restrict the area of combat.

They instituted a lawsuit denying the obligation to pay debts to an individual with a prosthetic heart on the grounds that the possession of a robotic organ removed humanity, and with it the constitutional rights of human beings.

They fought the matter skillfully and tenaciously, losing at every step but always in such a way that the decision was forced to be as broad as possible, and then carrying it by way of appeals to the World Court.

It took years, and millions of dollars.

When the final decision was handed down, DeLong held what amounted to a victory celebration over the legal loss. Andrew was, of course, present in the company offices on the occasion.

"We've done two things, Andrew," said DeLong, "both of which are good. First of all, we have established the fact that no number of artifacts in the human body causes it to cease being a human body. Secondly, we have engaged public opinion in the question in such a way as to put it fiercely on the side of a broad interpretation of humanity since there is not a human being in existence who does not hope for prosthetics if that will keep him alive."

"And do you think the Legislature will now grant me my humanity?" asked Andrew.

DeLong looked faintly uncomfortable. "As to that, I cannot be optimistic. There remains the one organ which the World Court has used as the criterion of humanity. Human beings have an organic cellular brain and robots have a platinum-iridium positronic brain if they have one at all—and you certainly have a positronic brain. . . . No, Andrew, don't get that look in your eye. We lack the knowledge to duplicate the work of a cellular brain in artificial structures close enough to the organic type as to allow it to fall within the Court's decision. Not even you could do it."

"What ought we do, then?"

"Make the attempt, of course. Congresswoman Li-Hsing will be on our side and a growing number of other Congresspeople. The President will undoubtedly go along with a majority of the Legislature in this matter."

"Do we have a majority?"

"No, far from it. But we might get one if the public will allow its desire for a broad interpretation of humanity to extend to you. A small chance, I admit, but if you do not wish to give up, we must gamble for it."

"I do not wish to give up."

20

Congresswoman Li-Hsing was considerably older than she had been when Andrew had first met her. Her transparent garments were long gone. Her hair was now close cropped and her coverings were tubular. Yet still Andrew clung, as closely as he could within the limits of reasonable taste, to the style of clothing that had prevailed when he had first adopted clothing more than a century before.

She said, "We've gone as far as we can, Andrew. We'll try once more after recess, but, to be honest, defeat is certain and the whole thing will have to be given up. All my most recent efforts have only earned me certain defeat in the coming congressional campaign."

"I know," said Andrew, "and it distresses me. You said once you would abandon me if it came to that. Why have you not done so?"

"One can change one's mind, you know. Somehow, abandoning you became a higher price than I cared to pay for just one more term. As it is, I've been in the Legislature for over a quarter of a century. It's enough."

"Is there no way we can change minds, Chee?"

"We've changed all that are amenable to reason. The rest—the majority—cannot be moved from their emotional antipathies."

"Emotional antipathy is not a valid reason for voting one way or the other."

"I know that, Andrew, but they don't advance emotional antipathy as their reason."

Andrew said cautiously, "It all comes down to the brain, then, but must we leave it at the level of cells versus positrons? Is there no way of forcing a functional definition? Must we say that a brain is made of this or that? May we not say that a brain is something—anything—capable of a certain level of thought?"

"Won't work," said Li-Hsing. "Your brain is man-made, the human brain is not. Your brain is constructed, theirs developed. To any human being who is intent on keeping up the barrier between himself and a robot, those differences are a steel wall a mile high and a mile thick."

"If we could get at the source of their antipathy—the very source of—"

"After all your years," said Li-Hsing sadly, "you are still trying to reason out the human being. Poor Andrew, don't be angry, but it's the robot in you that drives you in that direction."

"I don't know," said Andrew. "If I could bring myself—"

1 (reprise)

If he could bring himself—

He had known for a long time it might come to that, and in the end he was at the surgeon's. He had found one, skillful enough for the job at hand, which meant a robot surgeon, for no human surgeon could be trusted in this connection, either in ability or in intention.

The surgeon could not have performed the operation on a human being, so Andrew, after putting off the moment of decision with a sad line of questioning that reflected the turmoil within himself, put the First Law to one side by saying, "I, too, am a robot."

He then said, as firmly as he had learned to form the words even at human beings over these past decades, "I *order* you to carry through the operation on me."

In the absence of the First Law, an order so firmly given from one who looked so much like a man activated the Second Law sufficiently to carry the day.

21

Andrew's feeling of weakness was, he was sure, quite imaginary. He had recovered from the operation. Nevertheless, he leaned, as unobtrusively as he could manage, against the wall. It would be entirely too revealing to sit.

Li-Hsing said, "The final vote will come this week, Andrew. I've been able to delay it no longer, and we must lose. . . . And that will be it, Andrew."

Andrew said, "I am grateful for your skill at delay. It gave me the time I needed, and I took the gamble I had to."

"What gamble is this?" asked Li-Hsing with open concern.

"I couldn't tell you, or the people at Feingold and Martin. I was sure I would be stopped. See here, if it is the brain that is at issue, isn't the greatest difference of all the matter of immortality? Who really cares what a brain looks like or is built of or how it was formed? What matters is that human brain cells die; *must* die. Even if every other organ in the body is maintained or replaced, the brain cells, which cannot be replaced without changing and therefore killing the personality, must eventually die.

"My own positronic pathways have lasted nearly two centuries without perceptible change and can last for centuries more. Isn't *that* the fundamental barrier? Human beings can tolerate an immortal robot, for it doesn't matter how long a machine lasts. They cannot tolerate an immortal human being, since their own mortality is endurable only so long as it is universal. And for that reason they won't make me a human being."

Li-Hsing said, "What is it you're leading up to, Andrew?"

"I have removed that problem. Decades ago, my positronic brain was connected to organic nerves. Now, one last operation has arranged that connection in such a way that slowly—quite slowly—the potential is being drained from my pathways."

Li-Hsing's finely wrinkled face showed no expression for a moment. Then her lips tightened. "Do you mean you've arranged to die, Andrew? You can't have. That violates the Third Law."

"No," said Andrew, "I have chosen between the death of my body and the death of my aspirations and desires. To have let my body live at the cost of the greater death is what would have violated the Third Law."

Li-Hsing seized his arm as though she were about to shake him. She stopped herself. "Andrew, it won't work! Change it back."

"It can't be. Too much damage was done. I have a year to live—more or less. I will last through the two hundredth anniversary of my construction. I was weak enough to arrange that."

"How can it be worth it? Andrew, you're a fool."

"If it brings me humanity, that will be worth it. If it doesn't, it will bring an end to striving and that will be worth it, too."

And Li-Hsing did something that astonished herself. Quietly, she began to weep.

22

It was odd how that last deed caught at the imagination of the world. All that Andrew had done before had not swayed them. But he had finally accepted even death to be human and the sacrifice was too great to be rejected.

The final ceremony was timed, quite deliberately, for the two hundredth anniversary. The World President was to sign the act and make it law and the ceremony would be visible on a global network and would be beamed to the Lunar state and even to the Martian colony.

Andrew was in a wheelchair. He could still walk, but only shakily.

With mankind watching, the World President said, "Fifty years ago, you were declared a Sesquicentennial Robot, Andrew." After a pause, and in a more solemn tone, he said, "Today we declare you a Bicentennial Man, Mr. Martin."

And Andrew, smiling, held out his hand to shake that of the President.

23

Andrew's thoughts were slowly fading as he lay in bed.

Desperately he seized at them. Man! He was a man! He wanted that to be his last thought. He wanted to dissolve—die—with that.

He opened his eyes one more time and for one last time recognized Li-Hsing waiting solemnly. There were others, but those were only shadows, unrecognizable shadows. Only Li-Hsing stood out against the deepening gray. Slowly, inching, he held out his hand to her and very dimly and faintly felt her take it.

She was fading in his eyes, as the last of his thoughts trickled away.

But before she faded completely, one last fugitive thought came to him and rested for a moment on his mind before everything stopped.

"Little Miss," he whispered, too low to be heard.

––––––––

1. After Andrew's creation, why was it that "few robots were, any longer, independently brained"?

2. Why does Andrew request his freedom, even though he plans to continue serving Gerald Martin?

3. What is Andrew's reason for pursuing his goal of achieving full humanity?

4. According to this story, what are the necessary factors that establish identity as a human being? Do you agree that these are the factors that are necessary to establish human identity?

JAMES TIPTREE JR. (1915–1987) is the pseudonym of Alice Sheldon, born in Chicago to explorer and attorney Herbert Bradley and writer Mary Hastings. By the age of fourteen, Sheldon had traveled extensively with her parents in remote Africa, India, and Asia. She studied at no fewer than six institutions of higher learning, completing a doctorate in psychology at George Washington University in 1967, and she worked as a graphic artist, art critic, U.S. Army Air Force major, CIA employee, and professor of experimental psychology and statistics. Sheldon took the Tiptree pseudonym in 1967 to protect her teaching career and to mask her identity from editors who had previously rejected her work. Only in 1977, a year after publication of "Houston, Houston, Do You Read?" was her identity discovered, by which time she had won numerous Hugo and Nebula awards. Since 1991 the James Tiptree Jr. Award has been given annually to a work of science fiction that expands or explores concepts of gender.

Houston, Houston, Do You Read?

Lorimer gazes around the big crowded cabin, trying to listen to the voices, trying also to ignore the twitch in his insides that means he is about to remember something bad. No help; he lives it again, that long-ago moment. Himself running blindly—or was he pushed?—into the strange toilet at Evanston Junior High. His fly open, his dick in his hand, he can still see the gray zipper edge of his jeans around his pale exposed pecker. The hush. The sickening wrongness of shapes, faces turning. The first blaring giggle. *Girls*. He was in the *girls' can*.

He flinches wryly now, so many years later, not looking at the women's faces. The cabin curves around over his head, surrounding him with their alien things: the beading rack, the twins' loom, Andy's leatherwork, the damned kudzu vine wriggling everywhere, the chickens. So cozy . . . Trapped, he is. Irretrievably trapped for life in everything he does not enjoy. Structurelessness. Personal trivia, unmeaning intimacies. The claims he can somehow never meet. Ginny: *You never talk to me.* . . . Ginny, love, he thinks involuntarily. The hurt doesn't come.

Bud Geirr's loud chuckle breaks in on him. Bud is joking with some of them, out of sight around a bulkhead. Dave is visible, though. Major Norman Davis on the far side of the cabin, his bearded profile bent toward a small dark woman Lorimer can't quite focus on. But Dave's head seems oddly tiny and sharp, in fact the whole cabin looks unreal. A cackle bursts out from the "ceiling"—the bantam hen in her basket.

At this moment Lorimer becomes sure he has been drugged.

Curiously, the idea does not anger him. He leans or rather tips back, perching cross-legged in the zero gee, letting his gaze go to the face of the woman he has been talking with. Connie. Constantia Morelos. A tall moon-faced woman in capacious green pajamas. He has never really cared for talking to women. Ironic.

"I suppose," he says aloud, "it's possible that in some sense we are not here."

That doesn't sound too clear, but she nods interestedly. She's watching my reactions, Lorimer tells himself. Women are natural poisoners. Has he said that aloud too? Her expression doesn't change. His vision is taking on a pleasing local clarity. Connie's skin strikes him as quite fine, healthy looking. Olive tan even after two years in space. She was a farmer, he recalls. Big pores, but without the caked look he associates with women her age.

"You probably never wore makeup," he says. She looks puzzled. "Face paint, powder. None of you have."

"Oh!" Her smile shows a chipped front tooth. "Oh, yes, I think Andy has."

"Andy?"

"For plays. Historical plays, Andy's good at that."

"Of course. Historical plays."

Lorimer's brain seems to be expanding, letting in light. He is understanding actively now, the myriad bits and pieces linking into patterns. Deadly patterns, he perceives; but the drug is shielding him in some way. Like an amphetamine high without the pressure. Maybe it's something they use socially? No, they're watching, too.

"Space bunnies, I still don't dig it," Bud Geirr laughs infectiously. He has a friendly buoyant voice people like; Lorimer still likes it after two years.

"You chicks have kids back home, what do your folks think about you flying around out here with old Andy, h'mm?" Bud floats into view, his arm draped around a twin's shoulders. The one called Judy Paris, Lorimer decides; the twins are hard to tell. She drifts passively at an angle to Bud's big body: a jut-breasted plain girl in flowing yellow pajamas, her black hair raying out. Andy's red head swims up to them. He is holding a big green spaceball, looking about sixteen.

"Old Andy." Bud shakes his head, his grin flashing under his thick dark mustache. "When I was your age, folks didn't let their women fly around with me."

Connie's lips quirk faintly. In Lorimer's head the pieces slide toward pattern. I know, he thinks. Do you know I know? His head is vast and crystalline, very nice really. Easier to think. Women . . . No compact generalization forms in his mind, only a few speaking faces on a matrix of pervasive irrelevance. Human, of course. Biological necessity. Only so, so . . . diffuse? Pointless? His sister Amy, *soprano con tremulo: Of course women could contribute as much as men if you'd treat us as equals. You'll see!* And then marrying that idiot the second time. Well, now he can see.

"Kudzu vines," he says aloud. Connie smiles. How they all smile.

"How 'boot that?" Bud says happily. "Ever think we'd see chicks in zero gee, hey, Dave? Artits-stico. Woo-ee!" Across the cabin Dave's bearded head turns to him, not smiling.

"And ol' Andy's had it all to his self. Stunt your growth, lad." He punches Andy genially on the arm, Andy catches himself on the bulkhead. Bud can't be drunk, Lorimer thinks; not on that fruit cider. But he doesn't usually sound so much like a stage Texan either. A drug.

"Hey, no offense," Bud is saying earnestly to the boy, "I mean that. You have to forgive one underprilly, underprivileged brother. These chicks are good people. Know what?" he tells the girl. "You could look stupendous if you fix yourself up a speck. Hey, I can show you, old

249

Buddy's a expert. I hope you don't mind my saying that. As a matter of fact, you look real stupendous to me right now."

He hugs her shoulders, flings out his arm and hugs Andy too. They float upward in his grasp, Judy grinning excitedly, almost pretty.

"Let's get some more of that good stuff." Bud propels them both toward the serving rack which is decorated for the occasion with sprays of greens and small real daisies.

"Happy New Year! Hey, Happy New Year, y'all!"

Faces turn, more smiles. Genuine smiles, Lorimer thinks, maybe they really like their new years. He feels he has infinite time to examine every event, the implications evolving in crystal facets. I'm an echo chamber. Enjoyable, to be the observer. But others are observing too. They've started something here. Do they realize? So vulnerable, three of us, five of them, in this fragile ship. They don't know. A dread unconnected to action lurks behind his mind.

"By god, we made it," Bud laughs. "You space chickies, I have to give it to you. I commend you, by god, I say it. We wouldn't be here, wherever we are. Know what, I jus' might decide to stay in the service after all. Think they have room for old Bud in your space program, sweetie?"

"Knock that off, Bud," Dave says quietly from the far wall. "I don't want to hear us use the name of the Creator like that." The full chestnut beard gives him a patriarchal gravity. Dave is forty-six, a decade older than Bud and Lorimer. Veteran of six successful missions.

"Oh, my apologies, Major Dave old buddy," Bud chuckles intimately to the girl. "Our commanding ossifer. Stupendous guy. Hey, Doc!" he calls. How's your attitude? You making out dinko?"

"Cheers," Lorimer hears his voice reply, the complex stratum of his feelings about Bud rising like a kraken in the moonlight of his mind. The submerged silent thing he has about them all, all the Buds and Daves and big, indomitable, cheerful, able, disciplined, slow-minded mesomorphs he has cast his life with. Meso-ectos, he corrected himself; astronauts aren't muscleheads. They like him, he has been careful about that. Liked him well enough to get him on *Sunbird*, to make him the official scientist on the first circumsolar mission. That little Doc Lorimer, he's cool, he's on the team. No shit from Lorimer, not like those other scientific assholes. He does the bit well with his small neat build and his deadpan remarks. And the years of turning

250

out for the bowling, the volleyball, the tennis, the skeet, the skiing that broke his ankle, the touch football that broke his collarbone. Watch that Doc, he's a sneaky one. And the big men banging him on the back, accepting him. Their token scientist . . . The trouble is, he isn't any kind of scientist anymore. Living off his postdoctoral plasma work, a lucky hit. He hasn't really been into the math for years, he isn't up to it now. Too many other interests, too much time spent explaining elementary stuff. I'm a half jock, he thinks. A foot taller and a hundred pounds heavier, and I'd be just like them. One of them. An alpha. They probably sense it underneath, the beta bile. Had the jokes worn a shade thin in *Sunbird*, all that year going out? A year of Bud and Dave playing gin. That damn exercycle, gearing it up too tough for me. They didn't mean it, though. We were a team.

The memory of gaping jeans flicks at him, the painful end part—the grinning faces waiting for him when he stumbled out. The howls, the dribble down his leg. Being cool, pretending to laugh too. You shitheads, I'll show you. *I am not a girl.*

Bud's voice rings out, chanting, "And a hap-pee New Year to you-all down there!" Parody of the oily NASA tone. "Hey, why don't we shoot 'em a signal? Greetings to all you Earthlings, I mean, all you little Lunies. Happy New Year in the good year whatsis." He snuffles comically. "There is a Santy Claus, Houston, ye-ew nevah saw nothin' like this! Houston, wherever you are," he sings out. "Hey, Houston! Do you read?"

In the silence Lorimer sees Dave's face set into Major Norman Davis, commanding.

And without warning he is suddenly back there, back a year ago in the cramped, shook-up command module of *Sunbird*, coming out from behind the sun. It's the drug doing this, he thinks, as memory closes around him, it's so real. Stop. He tries to hang on to reality, to the sense of trouble building underneath.

—But he can't, he is *there*, hovering behind Dave and Bud in the triple couches, as usual avoiding his official station in the middle, seeing beside them their reflections against blackness in the useless port window. The outer layer has been annealed, he can just make out a bright smear that has to be Spica floating through the image of Dave's head, making the bandage look like a kid's crown.

"Houston, Houston, *Sunbird*," Dave repeats; "*Sunbird* calling Houston. Houston, do you read? Come in, Houston."

The minutes start by. They are giving it seven out, seven back; seventy-eight million miles, ample margin.

"The high gain's shot, that's what it is," Bud says cheerfully. He says it almost every day.

"No way." Dave's voice is patient, also as usual. "It checks out. Still too much crap from the sun, isn't that right, Doc?"

"The residual radiation from the flare is just about in line with us," Lorimer says. "They could have a hard time sorting us out." For the thousandth time he registers his own faint, ridiculous gratification at being consulted.

"Shit, we're outside Mercury." Bud shakes his head. "How we gonna find out who won the Series?"

He often says that, too. A ritual, out here in eternal night. Lorimer watches the sparkle of Spica drift by the reflection of Bud's curly face-bush. His own whiskers are scant and scraggly, like a blond Fu Manchu. In the aft corner of the window is striped glare that must be the remains of their port energy accumulators, fried off in the solar explosion that hit them a month ago and fused the outer layers of their windows. That was when Dave cut his head open on the sexlogic panel. Lorimer had been banged in among the gravity-wave experiment, he still doesn't trust the readings. Luckily the particle stream has missed one piece of the front window; they still have about twenty degrees of clear vision straight ahead. The brilliant web of the Pleiades shows there, running off into a blur of light.

Twelve minutes . . . thirteen. The speaker sighs and clicks emptily. Fourteen. Nothing.

"*Sunbird* to Houston, *Sunbird* to Houston. Come in, Houston. *Sunbird* out." Dave puts the mike back in its holder. "Give it another twenty-four."

They wait ritually. Tomorrow Packard will reply. Maybe.

"Be good to see old Earth again," Bud remarks.

"We're not using any more fuel on attitude," Dave reminds him. "I trust Doc's figures."

It's not my figures, it's the elementary facts of celestial mechanics, Lorimer thinks; in October there's only one place for Earth to be. He never says it. Not to a man who can fly two-body solutions by intuition once he knows where the bodies are. Bud is a good pilot and a better engineer; Dave is the best there is. He takes no pride in it. "The Lord helps us, Doc, if we let Him."

"Going to be a bitch docking if the radar's screwed up," Bud says idly. They all think about that for the hundredth time. It will be a bitch. Dave will do it. That was why he is hoarding fuel.

The minutes tick off.

"That's it," Dave says—and a voice fills the cabin, shockingly.

"Judy?" It is high and clear. A girl's voice.

"Judy, I'm so glad we got you. What are you doing on this band?"

Bud blows out his breath; there is a frozen instant before Dave snatches up the mike.

"*Sunbird*, we read you. This is Mission *Sunbird* calling Houston, ah, *Sunbird One* calling Houston Ground Control. Identify, who are you? Can you relay our signal? Over."

"Some skip," Bud says. "Some incredible ham."

"Are you in trouble, Judy?" the girl's voice asks. "I can't hear, you sound terrible. Wait a minute."

"This is United States Space Mission *Sunbird One*," Dave repeats. "Mission *Sunbird* calling Houston Space Center. You are dee-exxing our channel. Identify, repeat, identify yourself and say if you can relay to Houston. Over."

"Dinko, Judy, try it again," the girl says.

Lorimer abruptly pushes himself up to the Lurp, the Long-Range Particle Density Cumulator experiment, and activates its shaft motor. The shaft whines, jars; lucky it was retracted during the flare, lucky it hasn't fused shut. He sets the probe pulse on max and begins a rough manual scan.

"You are intercepting official traffic from the United States Space Mission to Houston Control," Dave is saying forcefully. "If you cannot relay to Houston get off the air, you are committing a federal offense. Say again, can you relay our signal to Houston Space Center? Over."

"You still sound terrible," the girl says. "What's Houston? Who's talking, anyway? You know we don't have much time." Her voice is sweet but very nasal.

"Jesus, that's close," Bud says. "That is close."

"Hold it." Dave twists around to Lorimer's improvised radarscope.

"There." Lorimer points out a tiny stable peak at the extreme edge of the readout slot, in the transcoronal scatter. Bud cranes too.

"A bogey!"

"Somebody else out here."

"Hello, hello? We have you now," the girl says. "Why are you so far out? Are you dinko, did you catch the flare?"

"Hold it," warns Dave. "What's the status, Doc?"

"Over three hundred thousand kilometers, guesstimated. Possibly headed away from us, going around the sun. Could be cosmonauts, a Soviet mission?"

"Out to beat us. They missed."

"*With a girl?*" Bud objects.

"They've done that. You taping this, Bud?"

"Roger-r-r." He grins. "That sure didn't sound like a Russky chick. Who the hell's Judy?"

Dave thinks for a second, clicks on the mike. "This is Major Norman Davis commanding United States spacecraft *Sunbird One*. We have you on scope. Request you identify yourself. Repeat, who are you? Over."

"Judy, stop joking," the voice complains. "We'll lose you in a minute, don't you realize we worried about you?"

"*Sunbird* to unidentified craft. This is not Judy. I say again, this is not Judy. Who are you? Over."

"What—" the girl says, and is cut off by someone saying, "Wait a minute, Ann." The speaker squeals. Then a different woman says, "This is Lorna Bethune in *Escondita*. What is going on here?"

"This is Major Davis commanding United States Mission *Sunbird* on course for Earth. We do not recognize any spacecraft *Escondita*. Will you identify yourself? Over."

"I just did." She sounds older with the same nasal drawl. "There is no spaceship *Sunbird*, and you're not on course Earth. If this is an andy joke it isn't any good."

"This is no joke, madam!" Dave explodes. "This is the American circumsolar mission, and we are American astronauts. We do not appreciate your interference. Out."

The woman starts to speak and is drowned in a jibber of static. Two voices come through briefly. Lorimer thinks he hears the words

"*Sunbird* program" and something else. Bud works the squelcher; the interference subsides to a drone.

"Ah, Major Davis?" The voice is fainter. "Did I hear you say you are on course for Earth?"

Dave frowns at the speaker and then says curtly, "Affirmative."

"Well, we don't understand your orbit. You must have very unusual flight characteristics, our readings show you won't node with anything on your present course. We'll lose the signal in a minute or two. Ah, would you tell us where you see Earth now? Never mind the coordinates, just tell us the constellation."

Dave hesitates and then holds up the mike. "Doc."

"Earth's apparent position is in Pisces," Lorimer says to the voice. "Approximately three degrees from P. Gamma."

"It is not," the woman says. "Can't you see it's in Virgo? Can't you see out at all?"

Lorimer's eyes go to the bright smear in the port window. "We sustained some damage—"

"Hold it," snaps Dave.

"—to one window during a disturbance we ran into at perihelion. Naturally we know the relative direction of Earth on this date, October nineteen."

"October? It's March, March fifteen. You must—" Her voice is lost in a shriek.

"E-M front," Bud says, tuning. They are all leaning at the speaker from different angles, Lorimer is head down. Space noise wails and crashes like surf, the strange ship is too close to the coronal horizon. "—Behind you," they hear. More howls. "Band, try . . . ship . . . if you can, your signal—" Nothing more comes through.

Lorimer pushes back, staring at the spark in the window. It has to be Spica. But is it elongated, as if a second point-source is beside it? Impossible. An excitement is trying to flare out inside him, the women's voices resonate in his head.

"Playback," Dave says. "Houston will really like to hear this."

They listen again to the girl calling Judy, the woman saying she is Lorna Bethune. Bud holds up a finger. "Man's voice in there." Lorimer listens hard for the words he thought he heard. The tape ends.

"Wait till Packard gets this one." Dave rubs his arms. "Remember what they pulled on Howie? Claiming they rescued him."

"Seems like they want us on their frequency." Bud grins. "They must think we're fa-a-ar gone. Hey, looks like this other capsule's going to show up, getting crowded out here."

"If it shows up," Dave says. "Leave it on voice alert, Bud. The batteries will do that."

Lorimer watches the spark of Spica, or Spica-plus-something, wondering if he will ever understand. The casual acceptance of some trick or ploy out here in this incredible loneliness. Well, if these strangers are from the same mold, maybe that is it. Aloud he says, "*Escondita* is an odd name for a Soviet mission. I believe it means 'hidden' in Spanish."

"Yeah," says Bud. "Hey, I know what that accent is, it's Australian. We had some Aussie bunnies at Hickam. Or-stryle-ya, woo-ee! You s'pose Woomara is sending up some kind of com-bined do?"

Dave shakes his head. "They have no capability whatsoever."

"We ran into some fairly strange phenomena back there, Dave," Lorimer says thoughtfully. "I'm beginning to wish we could take a visual check."

"Did you goof, Doc?"

"No. Earth is where I said, if it's October. Virgo is where it would appear in March."

"Then that's it," Dave grins, pushing out of the couch. "You been asleep five months. Rip Van Winkle? Time for a hand before we do the roadwork."

"What I'd like to know is what that chick looks like," says Bud, closing down the transceiver. "Can I help you into your space suit, miss? Hey, miss, pull that in, psst-psst-psst! You going to listen, Doc?"

"Right." Lorimer is getting out his charts. The others go aft through the tunnel to the small day room, making no further comment on the presence of the strange ship or ships out here. Lorimer himself is more shaken than he likes; it was that damn phrase.

The tedious exercise period comes and goes. Lunchtime: they give the containers a minimum warm to conserve the batteries. Chicken à la king again; Bud puts ketchup on his and breaks their usual silence with a funny anecdote about an Australian girl, laboriously censoring himself to conform to *Sunbird's* unwritten code on talk. After lunch Dave goes forward to the command module. Bud and Lorimer continue their current task of checking out the suits and packs for a damage-assessment EVA to take place as soon as the radiation count drops.

They are just clearing away when Dave calls them. Lorimer comes through the tunnel to hear a girl's voice blare "—dinko trip. What did Lorna say? *Gloria* over!"

He starts up the Lurp and begins scanning. No results this time. "They're either in line behind us or in the sunward quadrant," he reports finally. "I can't isolate them."

Presently the speaker holds another thin thread of sound.

"That could be their ground control," says Dave. "How's the horizon, Doc?"

"Five hours; northwest Siberia, Japan, Australia."

"I told you the high gain is fucked up." Bud gingerly feeds power to his antenna motor. "Easy, eas-ee. The frame is twisted, that's what it is."

"Don't snap it," Dave says, knowing Bud will not.

The squeaking fades, pulses back. "Hey, we can really use this," Bud says. "We can calibrate on them."

A hard soprano says suddenly, "—should be outside your orbit. Try around Beta Aries."

"Another chick. We have a fix," Bud says happily. "We have a fix now. I do believe our troubles are over. That monkey was torqued one hundred forty-nine degrees. Woo-ee!"

The first girl comes back. "We see them, Margo! But they're so small, how can they live in there? Maybe they're tiny aliens! Over."

"That's Judy," Bud chuckles. "Dave, this is screwy, it's all in English. It has to be some UN thingie."

Dave massages his elbows, flexes his fists; thinking. They wait. Lorimer considers a hundred and forty-nine degrees from Gamma Piscium.

In thirteen minutes the voice from Earth says, "Judy, call the others, will you? We're going to play you the conversation, we think you should all hear. Two minutes. Oh, while we're waiting, Zebra wants to tell Connie the baby is fine. And we have a new cow."

"Code," says Dave.

The recording comes on. The three men listen once more to Dave calling Houston in a rattle of solar noise. The transmission clears up rapidly and cuts off with the woman saying that another ship, the *Gloria*, is behind them, closer to the sun.

"We looked up history," the Earth voice resumes. "There was a Major Norman Davis on the first *Sunbird* flight. Major was a military title. Did you hear them say 'Doc'? There was a scientific doctor on board, Dr. Orren Lorimer. The third member was Captain—that's another title—Bernhard Geirr. Just the three of them, all males of course. We think they had an early reaction engine and not too much fuel. The point is, the first *Sunbird* mission was lost in space. They never came out from behind the sun. That was about when the big flares started. Jan thinks they must have been close to one, you heard them say they were damaged."

Dave grunts. Lorimer is fighting excitement like a brush discharge sparking in his gut.

"Either they are who they say they are or they're ghosts; or they're aliens pretending to be people. Jan says maybe the disruption in those superflares could collapse the local time dimension. Pluggo. What did you observe there, I mean the highlights?"

Time dimension . . . never came back . . . Lorimer's mind narrows onto the reality of the two unmoving bearded heads before him, refuses to admit the words he thought he heard: *Before the year two thousand.* The language, he thinks. The language would have to have changed. He feels better.

A deep baritone voice says, "Margo?" In *Sunbird* eyes come alert.

"—like the big one fifty years ago." The man has the accent too. "We were really lucky being right there when it popped. The most interesting part is that we confirmed the gravity turbulence. Periodic but not waves. It's violent, we got pushed around some. Space is under monster stress in those things. We think France's theory that our system is passing through a micro-black-hole cluster looks right. So long as one doesn't plonk us."

"France?" Bud mutters. Dave looks at him speculatively.

"It's hard to imagine anything being kicked out in time. But they're here, whatever they are, they're over eight hundred kays outside us scooting out toward Aldebaran. As Lorna said, if they're trying to reach Earth they're in trouble unless they have a lot of spare gees. Should we try to talk to them? Over. Oh, great about the cow. Over again."

"Black holes," Bud whistles softly. "That's one for you, Doc. Was we in a black hole?"

"Not in one or we wouldn't be here." If we are here, Lorimer adds to himself. A micro-black-hole cluster . . . what happens when fragments of totally collapsed matter approach each other, or collide, say in the photosphere of a star? Time disruption? Stop it. Aloud he says, "They could be telling us something, Dave."

Dave says nothing. The minutes pass.

Finally the Earth voice comes back, saying that it will try to contact the strangers on their original frequency. Bud glances at Dave, tunes the selector.

"Calling *Sunbird One*?" the girl says slowly through her nose. "This is Luna Central calling Major Norman Davis of *Sunbird One*. We have picked up your conversation with our ship *Escondita*. We are very puzzled as to who you are and how you got here. If you really are *Sunbird One* we think you must have been jumped forward in time when you passed the solar flare." She pronounces it Cockney-style, "toime."

"Our ship *Gloria* is near you, they see you on their radar. We think you may have a serious course problem because you told Lorna you were headed for Earth and you think it is now October with Earth in Pisces. It is not October, it is March fifteen. I repeat, the Earth date,"— she says "dyte"—"is March fifteen, time twenty hundred hours. You should be able to see Earth very close to Spica in Virgo. You said your window is damaged. Can't you go out and look? We think you have to make a big course correction. Do you have enough fuel? Do you have a computer? Do you have enough air and water and food? Can we help you? We're listening on this frequency. Luna to *Sunbird One*, come in."

On *Sunbird* nobody stirs. Lorimer struggles against internal eruptions. *Never came back. Jumped forward in time.* The cyst of memories he has schooled himself to suppress bulges up in the lengthening silence. "Aren't you going to answer?"

"Don't be stupid," Dave says.

"Dave. A hundred and forty-nine degrees is the difference between Gamma Piscium and Spica. That transmission is coming from where they say Earth is."

"You goofed."

"I did not goof. It has to be March."

Dave blinks as if a fly is bothering him.

In fifteen minutes the Luna voice runs through the whole thing again, ending, "Please, come in."

"Not a tape." Bud unwraps a stick of gum, adding the plastic to the neat wad back of the gyro leads. Lorimer's skin crawls, watching the ambiguous dazzle of Spica. Spica-plus-Earth? Unbelief grips him, rocks him with a complex pang compounded of faces, voices, the sizzle of bacon frying, the creak of his father's wheelchair, chalk on a sunlit blackboard, Ginny's bare legs on the flowered couch, Jenny and Penny running dangerously close to the lawnmower. The girls will be taller now, Jenny is already as tall as her mother. His father is living with Amy in Denver, determined to last till his son gets home. *When I get home.* This has to be insanity, Dave's right; it's a trick, some crazy trick. The language.

Fifteen minutes more; the flat, earnest female voice comes back and repeats it all, putting in more stresses. Dave wears a remote frown, like a man listening to a lousy sports program. Lorimer has the notion he might switch off and propose a hand of gin; wills him to do so. The voice says it will now change frequencies.

Bud tunes back, chewing calmly. This time the voice stumbles on a couple of phrases. It sounds tired.

Another wait; an hour, now. Lorimer's mind holds only the bright point of Spica digging at him. Bud hums a bar of "Yellow Ribbons," falls silent again.

"Dave," Lorimer says finally, "our antenna is pointed straight at Spica. I don't care if you think I goofed, if Earth is over there we have to change course soon. Look, you can see it could be a double light source. We have to check this out."

Dave says nothing. Bud says nothing, but his eyes rove to the port window, back to his instrument panel, to the window again. In the corner of the panel is a Polaroid snap of his wife. Patty: a tall, giggling, rump-switching redhead; Lorimer has occasional fantasies about her.

Little-girl voice, though. And so tall . . . Some short men chase tall women; it strikes Lorimer as undignified. Ginny is an inch shorter than he. Their girls will be taller. And Ginny insisted on starting a pregnancy before he left, even though he'll be out of commo. Maybe, maybe a boy, a son—*stop it*. Think about anything. Bud . . . Does Bud love Patty? Who knows? He loves Ginny. At seventy million miles . . .

"Judy?" Luna Central or whoever it is says. "They don't answer. You want to try? But listen, we've been thinking. If these people really are from the past, this must be very traumatic for them. They could be just realizing they'll never see their world again. Myda says these males had children and women they stayed with, they'll miss them terribly. This is exciting for us, but it may seem awful to them. They could be too shocked to answer. They could be frightened, maybe they think we're aliens or hallucinations even. See?"

Five seconds later the nearby girl says, "Da, Margo, we were into that too. Dinko. Ah, *Sunbird*? Major Davis of *Sunbird*, are you there? This is Judy Paris in the ship *Gloria*, we're only about a million kay from you, we see you on our screen." She sounds young and excited. "Luna Central has been trying to reach you, we think you're in trouble and we want to help. Please don't be frightened, we're people just like you. We think you're way off course if you want to reach Earth. Are you in trouble? Can we help? If your radio is out can you make any sort of signal? Do you know Old Morse? You'll be off our screen soon, we're truly worried about you. Please reply somehow if you possibly can, *Sunbird*, come in!"

Dave sits impassive. Bud glances at him, at the port window, gazes stolidly at the speaker, his face blank. Lorimer has exhausted surprise, he wants only to reply to the voices. He can manage a rough signal by heterodyning the probe beam. But what then, with them both against him?

The girl's voice tries again determinedly. Finally she says, "Margo, they won't peep. Maybe they're dead? I think they're aliens."

Are we not? Lorimer thinks. The Luna station comes back with a different, older voice.

"Judy, Myda here, I've had another thought. These people had a very rigid authority code. You remember your history, they peck-ordered everything. You notice Major Davis repeated about being commanding. That's called dominance-submission structure, one of them gave orders and the others did whatever they were told, we don't know quite why. Perhaps they were frightened. The point is that if the dominant one is in shock or panicked, maybe the others can't reply unless this Davis lets them."

Jesus Christ, Lorimer thinks. Jesus H. Christ in colors. It is his father's expression for the inexpressible. Dave and Bud sit unstirring.

"How weird," the Judy voice says. "But don't they know they're on a bad course? I mean, could the dominant one make the others fly right out of the system? Truly?"

It's happened, Lorimer thinks; it has happened. I have to stop this. I have to act now, before they lose us. Desperate visions of himself defying Dave and Bud loom before him. Try persuasion first.

Just as he opens his mouth he sees Bud stir slightly, and with immeasurable gratitude hears him say, "Dave-o, what say we take an eyeball look? One little old burp won't hurt us."

Dave's head turns a degree or two.

"Or should I go out and see, like the chick said?" Bud's voice is mild.

After a long minute Dave says neutrally, "All right . . . Attitude change." His arm moves up as though heavy; he starts methodically setting in the values for the vector that will bring Spica in line with their functional window.

Now why couldn't I have done that, Lorimer asks himself for the thousandth time, following the familiar check sequence. Don't answer. . . . And for the thousandth time he is obscurely moved by the rightness of them. The authentic ones, the alphas. Their bond. The awe he had felt first for the absurd jocks of his school ball team.

"That's go, Dave, assuming nothing got creamed."

Dave throws the ignition safety, puts the computer on real time. The hull shudders. Everything in the cabin drifts sidewise while the bright point of Spica swims the other way, appears on the front window as the retros cut in. When the star creeps out onto clear glass, Lorimer can clearly see its companion. The double light steadies there; a beautiful job. He hands Bud the telescope.

"The one on the left."

Bud looks. "There she is, all right. Hey, Dave, look at that!"

He puts the scope in Dave's hand. Slowly, Dave raises it and looks. Lorimer can hear him breathe. Suddenly Dave pulls up the mike.

"Houston!" he shouts harshly. "*Sunbird* to Houston, *Sunbird* calling Houston. Houston, come in!"

Into the silence the speaker squeals, "They fired their engines— wait, she's calling!" And shuts up.

In *Sunbird*'s cabin nobody speaks. Lorimer stares at the twin stars ahead, impossible realities shifting around him as the minutes congeal. Bud's reflected face looks downward, grin gone. Dave's beard moves silently; praying, Lorimer realizes. Alone of the crew Dave is deeply religious; at Sunday meals he gives a short, dignified grace. A shocking pity for Dave rises in Lorimer; Dave is so deeply involved with his family, his four sons, always thinking about their training, taking them hunting, fishing, camping. And Doris his wife so incredibly active and sweet, going on their trips, cooking and doing things for the community. Driving Penny and Jenny to classes while Ginny was sick that time. Good people, the backbone . . . This can't be, he thinks; Packard's voice is going to come through in a minute, the antenna's beamed right now. Six minutes now. This will all go away. *Before the year two thousand*—stop it, the language would have changed. Think of Doris. . . . She has that glow, feeding her five men; women with sons are different. But Ginny, but his dear woman, his *wife*, his *daughters*—grandmothers now? All dead and dust? *Quit that.* Dave is still praying. . . . Who knows what goes on inside those heads? Dave's cry . . . Twelve minutes, it has to be all right. The second sweep is stuck, no, it's moving. Thirteen. It's all insane, a dream. Thirteen plus . . . fourteen. The speaker hissing and clicking vacantly. Fifteen now. A dream . . . Or are those women staying off, letting us see? Sixteen . . .

At twenty Dave's hand moves, stops again. The seconds jitter by, space crackles. Thirty minutes coming up.

"Calling Major Davis in *Sunbird*?" It is the older woman, a gentle voice. "This is Luna Central. We are the service and communication facility for space flight now. We're sorry to have to tell you that there is no space center at Houston anymore. Houston itself was abandoned when the shuttle base moved to White Sands, over two centuries ago,"

A cool dust-colored light enfolds Lorimer's brain, isolating it. It will remain so a long time.

The woman is explaining it all again, offering help, asking if they were hurt. A nice dignified speech. Dave still sits immobile, gazing at Earth. Bud puts the mike in his hand.

"Tell them, Dave-o."

Dave looks at it, takes a deep breath, presses the send button.

"*Sunbird* to Luna Control," he says quite normally. (It's "Central," Lorimer thinks.) "We copy. Ah, negative on life support, we have no problems. We copy the course change suggestion and are proceeding to recompute. Your offer of computer assistance is appreciated. We suggest you transmit position data so we can get squared away. Ah, we are economizing on transmission until we see how our accumulators have held up. *Sunbird* out."

And so it had begun.

Lorimer's mind floats back to himself now floating in *Gloria*, nearly a year, or three hundred years, later; watching and being watched by them. He still feels light, contented; the dread underneath has come no nearer. But it is so silent. He seems to have heard no voices for a long time. Or was it a long time? Maybe the drug is working on his time sense, maybe it was only a minute or two,

"I've been remembering," he says to the woman Connie, wanting her to speak.

She nods. "You have so much to remember. Oh, I'm sorry—that wasn't good to say." Her eyes speak sympathy.

"Never mind." It is all dreamlike now, his lost world and this other which he is just now seeing plain. "We must seem like very strange beasts to you."

"We're trying to understand," she says. "It's history, you learn the events but you don't really feel what the people were like, how it was for them. We hope you'll tell us."

The drug, Lorimer thinks, that's what they're trying. Tell them ... how can he? Could a dinosaur tell how it was? A montage flows through his mind, dominated by random shots of Operations's north parking lot and Ginny's yellow kitchen telephone with the sickly ivy vines. ... Women and vines ...

A burst of laughter distracts him. It's coming from the chamber they call the gym, Bud and the others must be playing ball in there. Bright idea, really, he muses: using muscle power, sustained mild exercise.

That's why they are all so fit. The gym is a glorified squirrel-wheel, when you climb or pedal up the walls it revolves and winds a gear train, which among other things rotates the sleeping drum. A real Woolagong . . . Bud and Dave usually take their shifts together, scrambling the spinning gym like big pale apes. Lorimer prefers the easy rhythm of the women, and the cycle here fits him nicely. He usually puts in his shift with Connie, who doesn't talk much, and one of the Judys, who do.

No one is talking now, though. Remotely uneasy, he looks around the big cylinder of the cabin, sees Dave and Lady Blue by the forward window. Judy Dakar is behind them, silent for once. They must be looking at Earth; it has been a beautiful expanding disk for some weeks now. Dave's beard is moving, he is praying again. He has taken to doing that, not ostentatiously, but so obviously sincere that Lorimer, a life atheist, can only sympathize.

The Judys have asked Dave what he whispers, of course. When Dave understood that they had no concept of prayer and had never seen a Christian Bible, there had been a heavy silence.

"So you have lost all faith," he said finally.

"We have faith," Judy Paris protested.

"May I ask in what?"

"We have faith in ourselves, of course," she told him.

"Young lady, if you were my daughter I'd tan your britches," Dave said, not joking. The subject was not raised again.

But he came back so well after that first dreadful shock, Lorimer thinks. A personal god, a father-model, man needs that. Dave draws strength from it, and we lean on him. Maybe leaders have to believe. Dave was so great; cheerful, unflappable, patiently working out alternatives, making his decisions on the inevitable discrepancies in the position readings in a way Lorimer couldn't do. A bitch . . .

Memory takes him again; he is once again back in *Sunbird*, gritty eyed, listening to the women's chatter, Dave's terse replies. God, how they chattered. But their computer work checks out. Lorimer is suffering also from a quirk of Dave's, his reluctance to transmit their exact thrust and fuel reserve. He keeps holding out a margin and making Lorimer compute it back in.

But the margins don't help; it is soon clear that they are in big trouble. Earth will pass too far ahead of them on her next orbit, they don't have the acceleration to catch up with her before they cross her path. They can carry out an ullage maneuver, they can kill enough velocity to let Earth catch them on the second go-by; but that would take an extra year and their life support would be long gone. The grim question of whether they have enough to enable a single man to wait it out pushes into Lorimer's mind. He pushes it back; that one is for Dave.

There is a final possibility: Venus will approach their trajectory three months hence, and they may be able to gain velocity by swinging by it. They go to work on that.

Meanwhile Earth is steadily drawing away from them and so is *Gloria*, closer toward the sun. They pick her out of the solar interference and then lose her again. They know her crew now: the man is Andy Kay, the senior woman is Lady Blue Parks; they appear to do the navigating. Then there is a Connie Morelos and the two twins, Judy Paris and Judy Dakar, who run the communications. The chief Luna voices are women too, Margo and Azella. The men can hear them talking to the *Escondita*, which is now swinging in toward the far side of the sun. Dave insists on monitoring and taping everything that comes through. It proves to be largely replays of their exchanges with Luna and *Gloria*, mixed with a variety of highly personal messages. As references to cows, chickens, and other livestock multiply, Dave reluctantly gives up his idea that they are code. Bud counts a total of five male voices.

"Big deal," he says. "There were more chick drivers on the road when we left. Means space is safe now, the girlies have taken over. Let them sweat their little asses off." He chuckles. "When we get this bird down, the stars ain't gonna study old Buddy no more, no ma'am. A nice beach and about a zillion steaks and ale and all those sweet things. Hey, we'll be living history, we can charge admission."

Dave's face takes on the expression that means an inappropriate topic has been broached. Much to Lorimer's impatience, Dave discourages all speculation as to what may await them on this future Earth. He confines their transmissions strictly to the problem in hand; when Lorimer tries to get him at least to mention the unchanged-language puzzle, Dave only says firmly, "Later." Lorimer fumes; inconceivable that he is three centuries in the future, unable to learn a thing.

They do glean a few facts from the women's talk. There have been nine successful *Sunbird* missions after theirs and one other casualty. And the *Gloria* and her sister ship are on a long-planned flyby of the two inner planets.

"We always go along in pairs," Judy says. "But those planets are no good. Still, it was worth seeing."

"For Pete's sake, Dave, ask them how many planets have been visited, " Lorimer pleads.

"Later."

But about the fifth meal-break Luna suddenly volunteers.

"Earth is making up a history for you, *Sunbird*," the Margo voice says. "We know you don't want to waste power asking, so we thought we'd send you a few main points right now. " She laughs. "It's much harder than we thought, nobody here does history."

Lorimer nods to himself; he has been wondering what he could tell a man from 1690 who would want to know what happened to Cromwell—was Cromwell then?—and who had never heard of electricity, atoms, or the U.S.A.

"Let's see, probably the most important is that there aren't as many people as you had, we're just over two million. There was a world epidemic not long after your time. It didn't kill people, but it reduced the population. I mean, there weren't any babies in most of the world. Ah, sterility. The country called Australia was affected least." Bud holds up a finger.

"And north Canada wasn't too bad. So the survivors all got together in the south part of the American states where they could grow food and the best communications and factories were. Nobody lives in the rest of the world, but we travel there sometimes. Ah, we have five main activities, was *industries* the word? Food, that's farming and fishing. Communications, transport, and space—that's us. And the factories they need. We live a lot simpler than you did, I think. We see your things all over, we're very grateful to you. Oh, you'll be interested to know we use zeppelins just like you did, we have six big ones. And our fifth thing is the children. Babies. Does that help? I'm using a children's book we have here."

The men have frozen during this recital; Lorimer is holding a cooling bag of hash. Bud starts chewing again and chokes.

"Two million people and a space capability?" He coughs. "That's incredible."

Dave gazes reflectively at the speaker. "There's a lot they're not telling us."

"I gotta ask them," Bud says. "Okay?"

Dave nods. "Watch it."

"Thanks for the history, Luna," Bud says. "We really appreciate it. But we can't figure out how you maintain a space program with only a couple of million people. Can you tell us a little more on that?"

In the pause Lorimer tries to grasp the staggering figures. From eight billion to two million . . . Europe, Asia, Africa, South America, America itself—wiped out. *There weren't any more babies.* World sterility, from what? The Black Death, the famines of Asia—those had been decimations. This is magnitudes worse. No, it is all the same: beyond comprehension. An empty world, littered with junk.

"*Sunbird*?" says Margo. "Da, I should have thought you'd want to know about space. Well, we have only the four real spaceships and one building. You know the two here. Then there's *Indira* and *Pech*, they're on the Mars run now. Maybe the Mars dome was since your day. You had the satellite stations though, didn't you? And the old Luna dome, of course—I remember now, it was during the epidemic. They tried to set up colonies to, ah, breed children, but the epidemic got there too. They struggled terribly hard. We owe a lot to you really, you men I mean. The history has it all, how you worked out a minimal viable program and trained everybody and saved it from the crazies. It was a glorious achievement. Oh, the marker here has one of your names on it. Lorimer. We love to keep it all going and growing, we all love traveling. Man is a rover, that's one of our mottoes."

"Are you hearing what I'm hearing?" Bud asks, blinking comically.

Dave is still staring at the speaker. "Not one word about their government," he says slowly. "Not a word about economic conditions. We're talking to a bunch of monkeys."

"Should I ask them?"

"Wait a minute. . . . Roger, ask the name of their chief of state and the head of the space program. And—no, that's all."

"President?" Margo echoes Bud's query. "You mean like queens and kings? Wait, here's Myda. She's been talking about you with Earth."

268

The older woman they hear occasionally says, "*Sunbird*? Da, we realize you had a very complex activity, your governments. With so few people we don't have that type of formal structure at all. People from the different activities meet periodically and our communications are good, everyone is kept informed. The people in each activity are in charge of doing it while they're there. We rotate, you see. Mostly in five-year hitches, for example, Margo here was on the zeppelins and I've been on several factories and farms and of course the, well, the education, we all do that. I believe that's one big difference from you. And of course we all work. And things are basically far more stable now, I gather. We change slowly. Does that answer you? Of course you can always ask Registry, they keep track of us all. But we can't, ah, take you to our leader, if that's what you mean." She laughs, a genuine jolly sound. "That's one of our old jokes. I must say," she goes on seriously, "it's been a joy to us that we can understand you so well. We make a big effort not to let the language drift, it would be tragic to lose touch with the past."

Dave takes the mike. "Thank you, Luna. You've given us something to think about. *Sunbird* out."

"How much of that is for real, Doc?" Bud rubs his curly head. "They're giving us one of your science-fiction stories."

"The real story will come later," says Dave. "Our job is get there."

"That's a point that doesn't look too good."

By the end of the session it looks worse. No Venus trajectory is any good. Lorimer reruns all the computations; same result.

"There doesn't seem to be any solution to this one, Dave," he says at last. "The parameters are just too tough. I think we've had it."

Dave massages his knuckles thoughtfully. Then he nods. "Roger. We'll fire the optimum sequence on the Earth heading."

"Tell them to wave if they see us go by," says Bud.

They are silent, contemplating the prospect of a slow death in space eighteen months hence. Lorimer wonders if he can raise the other question, the bad one. He is pretty sure what Dave will say. What will he himself decide, what will he have the guts to do?

"Hello, *Sunbird*?" the voice of *Gloria* breaks in. "Listen, we've been figuring. We think if you use all your fuel you could come back in close enough to our orbit so we could swing out and pick you up.

You'd be using solar gravity that way. We have plenty of maneuver but much less acceleration than you do. You have suits and some kind of propellants, don't you? I mean, you could fly across a few kays?"

The three men look at each other; Lorimer guesses he had not been the only one to speculate on that.

"That's a good thought, *Gloria*," Dave says. "Let's hear what Luna says."

"Why?" asks Judy. "It's our business, we wouldn't endanger the ship. We'd only miss another look at Venus, who cares. We have plenty of water and food, and if the air gets a little smelly we can stand it."

"Hey, the chicks are all right," Bud says. They wait.

The voice of Luna comes on. "We've been looking at that too, Judy. We're not sure you understand the risk. Ah, *Sunbird*, excuse me. Judy, if you manage to pick them up you'll have to spend nearly a year in the ship with these three male persons from a *very different culture*. Myda says you should remember history, and it's a risk no matter what Connie says. *Sunbird*, I hate to be so rude. Over."

Bud is grinning broadly, they all are. "Cavemen," he chuckles. "All the chicks land preggers."

"Margo, they're human beings," the Judy voice protests. "This isn't just Connie, we're all agreed. Andy and Lady Blue say it would be very interesting. If it works, that is. We can't let them go without trying."

"We feel that way too, of course," Luna replies. "But there's another problem. They could be carrying diseases. *Sunbird*, I know you've been isolated for fourteen months, but Murti says people in your day were immune to organisms that aren't around now. Maybe some of ours could harm you, too. You could all get mortally sick and lose the ship."

"We thought of that, Margo," Judy says impatiently. "Look, if you have contact with them at all somebody has to test, true? So we're ideal. By the time we get home you'll know. And how could we all get sick so fast we couldn't put *Gloria* in a stable orbit where you could get her later on?"

They wait. "Hey, what about that epidemic?" Bud pats his hair elaborately. "I don't know if I want a career in gay lib."

"You rather stay out here?" Dave asks.

"Crazies," says a different voice from Luna. "*Sunbird*, I'm Murti, the health person here. I think what we have to fear most is the meningitis-influenza complex, they mutate so readily. Does your Dr. Lorimer have any suggestions?"

"Roger, I'll put him on," says Dave. "But as to your first point, madam, I want to inform you that at time of takeoff the incidence of rape in the United States space cadre was zero point zero. I guarantee the conduct of my crew, provided you can control yours. Here is Dr. Lorimer."

But Lorimer cannot of course tell them anything useful. They discuss the men's polio shots, which luckily have used killed virus, and various childhood diseases which still seem to be around. He does not mention their epidemic.

"Luna, we're going to try it," Judy declares. "We couldn't live with ourselves. Now let's get the course figured before they get any farther away."

From there on there is no rest on *Sunbird* while they set up and refigure and rerun the computations for the envelope of possible intersecting trajectories. The *Gloria*'s drive, they learn, is indeed low-thrust, although capable of sustained operation. *Sunbird* will have to get most of the way to the rendezvous on her own if they can cancel their outward velocity.

The tension breaks once during the long session, when Luna calls *Gloria* to warn Connie to be sure the female crew members wear concealing garments at all times if the men came aboard.

"Not suit-liners, Connie, they're much too tight." It is the older woman, Myda. Bud chuckles.

"Your light sleepers, I think. And when the men unsuit, your Andy is the only one who should help them. You others stay away. The same for all body functions and sleeping. This is very important, Connie, you'll have to watch it the whole way home. There are a great many complicated taboos. I'm putting an instruction list on the bleeper, is your receiver working?"

"Da, we used it for France's black-hole paper."

"Good. Tell Judy to stand by. Now listen, Connie, listen carefully. Tell Andy he has to read it all. I repeat, *he* has to read every word. Did you hear that?"

"Ah, dinko," Connie answers. "I understand, Myda. He will."

"I think we just lost the ball game, fellas," Bud laments. "Old mother Myda took it all away."

Even Dave laughs. But later when the modulated squeal that is a whole text comes through the speaker, he frowns again. "There goes the good stuff."

The last factors are cranked in; the revised program spins, and Luna confirms them. "We have a payout, Dave," Lorimer reports. "It's tight, but there are at least two viable options. Provided the main jets are fully functional."

"We're going EVA to check."

That is exhausting; they find a warp in the deflector housing of the port engines and spend four sweating hours trying to wrestle it back. It is only Lorimer's third sight of open space, but he is soon too tired to care.

"Best we can do," Dave pants finally. "We'll have to compensate in the psychic mode."

"You can do it, Dave-o," says Bud. "Hey, I gotta change those suit radios, don't let me forget."

In the psychic mode . . . Lorimer surfaces back to his real self, cocooned in *Gloria*'s big cluttered cabin, seeing Connie's living face. "It must be hours, how long has he been dreaming?"

"About two minutes," Connie smiles.

"I was thinking of the first time I saw you."

"Oh, yes. We'll never forget that, ever."

Nor will he. . . . He lets it unroll again in his head. The interminable hours after the first long burn, which has sent *Sunbird* yawing so they all have to gulp nausea pills. Judy's breathless voice reading down their approach: "Oh, very good, four hundred thousand . . . Oh, great, *Sunbird*, you're almost three, you're going to break a hundred for sure—" Dave has done it, the big one.

Lorimer's probe is useless in the yaw, it isn't until they stabilize enough for the final burst that they can see the strange blip bloom and vanish in the slot. Converging, hopefully, on a theoretical near-intersection point.

"Here goes everything."

The final burn changes the yaw into a sickening tumble with the star field looping past the glass. The pills are no more use, and the fuel feed to the attitude jets goes sour. They are all vomiting before they manage to hand-pump the last of the fuel and slow the tumble.

"That's it, *Gloria*. Come and get us. Lights on, Bud. Let's get those suits up."

Fighting nausea, they go through the laborious routine in the fouled cabin. Suddenly Judy's voice sings out, "We see you, *Sunbird*! We see your light! Can't you see us?"

"No time," Dave says. But Bud, half suited, points at the window. "Fellas, oh, hey, look at that."

Lorimer stares, thinks he sees a faint spark between the whirling stars before he has to retch.

"Father, we thank you," says Dave quietly. "All right, move it on, Doc. Packs."

The effort of getting themselves plus the propulsion units and a couple of cargo nets out of the rolling ship drives everything else out of mind. It isn't until they are floating linked together and stabilized by Dave's hand jet that Lorimer has time to look.

The sun blanks out their left. A few meters below them *Sunbird* tumbles empty, looking absurdly small. Ahead of them, infinitely far away, is a point too blurred and yellow to be a star. It creeps: *Gloria*, on her approach tangent.

"Can you start, *Sunbird*?" says Judy in their helmets. "We don't want to brake anymore on account of our exhaust. We estimate fifty kay in an hour, we're coming out on a line."

"Roger. Give me your jet, Doc."

"Good-bye, *Sunbird*," says Bud. "Plenty of lead, Dave-o."

Lorimer finds it restful in a childish way, being towed across the abyss tied to the two big men. He has total confidence in Dave, he never considers the possibility that they will miss, sail by, and be lost. Does Dave feel contempt? Lorimer wonders; that banked-up silence, is it partly contempt for those who can manipulate only symbols, who have no mastery of matter? . . . He concentrates on mastering his stomach.

It is a long, dark trip. *Sunbird* shrinks to a twinkling light, slowly accelerating on the spiral course that will end her ultimately in the sun with their precious records that are three hundred years obsolete. With, also, the packet of photos and letters that Lorimer has twice put in his suit-pouch and twice taken out. Now and then he catches sight of *Gloria*, growing from a blur to an incomprehensible tangle of lighted crescents.

"Woo-ee, it's big," Bud says. "No wonder they can't accelerate, that thing is a flying trailer park. It'd break up."

"It's a spaceship. Got those nets tight, Doc?"

Judy's voice suddenly fills their helmets. "I see your lights! Can you see me? Will you have enough left to brake at all?"

"Affirmative to both, *Gloria*," says Dave.

At that moment Lorimer is turned slowly forward again and he sees—will see it forever: the alien ship in the star field and on its dark side the tiny lights that are women in the stars, waiting for them. Three—no, four; one suit-light is way out, moving. If that is a tether, it must be over a kilometer.

"Hello, I'm Judy Dakar!" The voice is close. "Oh, mother, you're big! Are you all right? How's your air?"

"No problem."

They are in fact stale and steaming wet; too much adrenalin. Dave uses the jets again and suddenly she is growing, is coming right at them, a silvery spider on a trailing thread. Her suit looks trim and flexible; it is mirror-bright, and the pack is quite small. Marvels of the future, Lorimer thinks; Paragraph One.

"You made it, you made it! Here, tie in. Brake!"

"There ought to be some historic words," Bud murmurs. "If she gives us a chance."

"Hello, Judy," says Dave calmly. "Thanks for coming."

"Contact!" She blasts their ears. "Haul us in, Andy! Brake, brake—the exhaust is back there!"

And they are grabbed hard, deflected into a great arc toward the ship. Dave uses up the last jet. The line loops.

'Don't jerk it," Judy cries. "Oh, I'm *sorry*." She is clinging on them like a gibbon, Lorimer can see her eyes, her excited mouth. Incredible. "Watch out, it's slack."

"Teach me, honey" says Andy's baritone. Lorimer twists and sees him far back at the end of a heavy tether, hauling them smoothly in. Bud offers to help, is refused. "Just hang loose, please," a matronly voice tells them. It is obvious Andy has done this before. They come in spinning slowly, like space fish. Lorimer finds he can no longer pick out the twinkle that is *Sunbird*. When he is swung back, *Gloria* has changed to a disorderly cluster of bulbs and spokes around a big central cylinder. He can see pods and miscellaneous equipment stowed all over her. Not like science fiction.

Andy is paying the line into a floating coil. Another figure floats beside him. They are both quite short, Lorimer realizes as they near.

"Catch the cable," Andy tells them. There is a busy moment of shifting inertial drag.

"Welcome to *Gloria*, Major Davis, Captain Geirr, Dr. Lorimer. I'm Lady Blue Parks. I think you'll like to get inside as soon as possible. If you feel like climbing go right ahead, we'll pull all this in later."

"We appreciate it, ma'am."

They start hand-over-hand along the catenary of the main tether. It has a good rough grip. Judy coasts up to peer at them, smiling broadly, towing the coil. A taller figure waits by the ship's open airlock.

"Hello, I'm Connie. I think we can cycle in two at a time. Will you come with me, Major Davis?"

It is like an emergency on a plane, Lorimer thinks, as Dave follows her in. Being ordered about by supernaturally polite little girls.

"Space-going stews," Bud nudges him. "How 'bout that?" His face is sprouting sweat. Lorimer tells him to go next, his own LSP has less load.

Bud goes in with Andy. The woman named Lady Blue waits beside Lorimer while Judy scrambles on the hull securing their cargo nets. She doesn't seem to have magnetic soles; perhaps ferrous metals aren't used in space now. When Judy begins hauling in the main tether on a simple hand winch, Lady Blue looks at it critically.

"I used to make those," she says to Lorimer. What he can see of her features looks compressed, her dark eyes twinkle. He has the impression she is part black.

"I ought to get over and clean that aft antenna." Judy floats up. "Later," says Lady Blue. They both smile at Lorimer. Then the hatch opens, and he and Lady Blue go in. When the toggles seat, there comes a rising scream of air and Lorimer's suit collapses.

"Can I help you?" She has opened her faceplate, the voice is rich and live. Eagerly Lorimer catches the latches in his clumsy gloves and lets her lift the helmet off. His first breath surprises him, it takes an instant to identify the gas as fresh air. Then the inner hatch opens, letting in greenish light. She waves him through. He swims into a short tunnel. Voices are coming from around the corner ahead. His hand finds a grip and he stops, feeling his heart shudder in his chest.

When he turns that corner the world he knows will be dead. Gone, rolled up, blown away forever with *Sunbird*. He will be irrevocably in the future. A man from the past, a time traveler. In the future . . .

He pulls himself around the bend.

The future is a vast bright cylinder, its whole inner surface festooned with unidentifiable objects, fronds of green. In front of him floats an odd tableau: Bud and Dave, helmets off, looking enormous in their bulky white suits and packs. A few meters away hang two bareheaded figures in shiny suits and a dark-haired girl in flowing pink pajamas.

They are all simply staring at the two men, their eyes and mouths open in identical expressions of pleased wonder. The face that has to be Andy's is grinning open mouthed like a kid at the zoo. He is a surprisingly young boy, Lorimer sees, in spite of his deep voice; blond, downy cheeked, compactly muscular. Lorimer finds he can scarcely bear to look at the pink woman, can't tell if she really is surpassingly beautiful or plain. The taller suited woman has a shiny, ordinary face.

From overhead bursts an extraordinary sound which he finally recognizes as a chicken cackling. Lady Blue pushes past him.

"All right, Andy, Connie, stop staring and help them get their suits off. Judy, Luna is just as eager to hear about this as we are."

The tableau jumps to life. Afterward Lorimer can recall mostly eyes, bright curious eyes tugging his boots, smiling eyes upside down over his pack—and always that light, ready laughter. Andy is left alone to help them peel down, blinking at the fittings which Lorimer still finds embarrassing. He seems easy and nimble in his own half-open suit. Lorimer struggles out of the last lacings, thinking, a boy! A boy and four women orbiting the sun, flying their big junky ships to Mars. Should he feel humiliated? He only feels grateful, accepting a short robe and a bulb of tea somebody—Connie?—gives him.

The suited Judy comes in with their nets. The men follow Andy along another passage, Bud and Dave clutching at the small robes. Andy stops by a hatch.

"This greenhouse is for you, it's your toilet. Three's a lot, but you have full sun."

Inside is a brilliant jungle, foliage everywhere, glittering water droplets, rustling leaves. Something whirs away—a grasshopper.

"You crank that handle." Andy points to a seat on a large cross-duct. "The piston rams the gravel and waste into a compost process, and it ends up in the soil core. That vetch is a heavy nitrogen user and a great oxidator. We pump CO_2 in and oxy out. It's a real Woolagong."

He watches critically while Bud tries out the facility.

"What's a Woolagong?" asks Lorimer dazedly.

"Oh, she's one of our inventors. Some of her stuff is weird. When we have a pluggy-looking thing that works, we call it a Woolagong." He grins. "The chickens eat the seeds and the hoppers, see, and the hoppers and iguanas eat the leaves. When a greenhouse is going darkside, we turn them in to harvest. With this much light I think we could keep a goat, don't you? You didn't have any life at all on your ship, true?"

"No," Lorimer says, "not a single iguana."

"They promised us a Shetland pony for Christmas," says Bud, rattling gravel. Andy joins perplexedly in the laugh.

Lorimer's head is foggy; it isn't only fatigue, the year in *Sunbird* has atrophied his ability to take in novelty. Numbly he uses the Woolagong, and they go back out and forward to *Gloria's* big control room, where Dave makes a neat short speech to Luna and is answered graciously.

"We have to finish changing course now," Lady Blue says. Lorimer's impression has been right, she is a small light part-Negro in late middle age. Connie is part something exotic too, he sees; the others are European types.

"I'll get you something to eat," Connie smiles warmly. "Then you probably want to rest. We saved all the cubbies for you." She says "syved"; their accents are all identical.

As they leave the control room, Lorimer sees the withdrawn look in Dave's eyes and knows he must be feeling the reality of being a passenger in an alien ship; not in command, not deciding the course, the communications going on unheard.

That is Lorimer's last coherent observation, that and the taste of the strange, good food. And then being led aft through what he now knows is the gym, to the shaft of the sleeping drum. There are six irised ports like dog doors; he pushes through his assigned port and finds himself facing a roomy mattress. Shelves and a desk are in the wall.

"For your excretions." Connie's arm comes through the iris, pointing at bags. "If you have a problem stick your head out and call. There's water."

Lorimer simply drifts toward the mattress, too sweated out to reply. His drifting ends in a curious heavy settling and his final astonishment: the drum is smoothly, silently starting to revolve. He sinks gratefully onto the pad, growing "heavier" as the minutes pass. About a tenth gee, maybe more, he thinks, it's still accelerating. And falls into the most restful sleep he has known in the long weary year.

It isn't till next day that he understands that Connie and two others have been on the rungs of the gym chamber, sending it around hour after hour without pause or effort and chatting as they went.

How they talk, he thinks again, floating back to real present time. The bubbling irritant pours through his memory, the voices of Ginny and Jenny and Penny on the kitchen telephone, before that his mother's voice, his sister Amy's. Interminable. What do they always have to talk, talk, talk of?

"Why, everything, " says the real voice of Connie beside him now, "it's natural to share."

"Natural . . ." Like ants, he thinks. They twiddle their antennae together every time they meet. Where did you go, what did you do? Twiddle-twiddle. How do you *feel*? Oh, I feel this, I feel that, blah blah twiddle-twiddle. Total coordination of the hive. Women have no self-respect. Say anything, no sense of the strategy of words, the dark danger of naming. Can't hold in.

"Ants, beehives," Connie laughs, showing the bad tooth. "You truly see us as insects, don't you? Because they're females?"

"Was I talking aloud? I'm sorry." He blinks away dreams.

"Oh, please don't be. It's so sad to hear about your sister and your children and your, your wife. They must have been wonderful people. We think you're very brave."

But he has only thought of Ginny and them all for an instant— what has he been babbling? What is the drug doing to him?

"What are you doing to us?" he demands, lanced by real alarm now, almost angry.

"It's all right, truly." Her hand touches his, warm and somehow shy. "We all use it when we need to explore something. Usually it's pleasant. It's a laevonoramine compound, a disinhibitor, it doesn't dull you like alcohol. We'll be home so soon, you see. We have the responsibility to understand, and you're so locked in." Her eyes melt at him. "You don't feel sick, do you? We have the antidote."

"No . . ." His alarm has already flowed away somewhere. Her explanation strikes him as reasonable enough. "We're not locked in," he says or tries to say. "We talk. . . ." He gropes for a word to convey the judiciousness, the adult restraint. Objectivity, maybe? "We talk when we have something to say." Irrelevantly he thinks of a mission coordinator named Forrest, famous for his blue jokes. "Otherwise it would all break down," he tells her. "You'd fly right out of the system." That isn't quite what he means; let it pass.

The voices of Dave and Bud ring out suddenly from opposite ends of the cabin, awakening the foreboding of evil in his mind. They don't know us, he thinks. They should look out, stop this. But he is feeling too serene, he wants to think about his own new understanding, the pattern of them all he is seeing at last.

"I feel lucid," he manages to say, "I want to think."

She looks pleased. "We call that the ataraxia effect. It's so nice when it goes that way."

Ataraxia, philosophical calm. Yes. But there are monsters in the deep, he thinks or says. The night side. The night side of Orren Lorimer, a self hotly dark and complex, waiting in leash. They're so vulnerable. They don't know we can take them. Images rush up: a Judy spread-eagled on the gym rungs, pink pajamas gone, open to him. Flash sequence of the three of them taking over the ship, the women tied up, helpless, shrieking, raped, and used. The team—get the satellite station, get a shuttle down to Earth. Hostages. Make them do anything, no defense whatever. . . . Has Bud actually said that? But Bud doesn't know, he remembers. Dave knows they're hiding something, but he thinks it's socialism or sin. When they find out. . . .

How has he himself found out? Simply listening, really, all these months. He listens to their talk much more than the others; "fraternizing," Dave calls it. . . . They all listened at first, of course. Listened and looked and reacted helplessly to the female bodies, the tender bulges so close under the thin, tantalizing clothes, the magnetic mouths and eyes, the smell of them, their electric touch. Watching them touch each other, touch Andy, laughing, vanishing quietly into shared bunks. *What goes on? Can I? My need, my need—*

The power of them, the fierce resentment . . . Bud muttered and groaned meaningfully despite Dave's warnings. He kept needling Andy until Dave banned all questions. Dave himself was noticeably tense and read his Bible a great deal. Lorimer found his own body pointing after them like a famished hound, hoping to Christ the cubicles are as they appeared to be, unwired.

All they learn is that Myda's instructions must have been ferocious. The atmosphere has been implacably antiseptic, the discretion impenetrable. Andy politely ignored every probe. No word or act has told them what, if anything, goes on; Lorimer was irresistibly reminded of the weekend he spent at Jenny's scout camp. The men's training came presently to their rescue, and they resigned themselves to finishing their mission on a super-*Sunbird*, weirdly attended by a troop of boy and girl scouts.

In every other way their reception couldn't be more courteous. They have been given the run of the ship and their own day room in a cleaned-out gravel storage pod. They visit the control room as they wish. Lady Blue and Andy give them specs and manuals and show them every circuit and device of *Gloria*, inside and out. Luna has bleeped up a stream of science texts and the data on all their satellites and shuttles and the Mars and Luna dome colonies.

Dave and Bud plunged into an orgy of engineering. *Gloria* is, as they suspected, powered by a fission plant that uses a range of Lunar minerals. Her ion drive is only slightly advanced over the experimental models of their own day. The marvels of the future seem so far to consist mainly of ingenious modifications.

"It's primitive," Bud tells him. "What they've done is sacrifice everything to keep it simple and easy to maintain. Believe it, they can hand feed fuel. And the backups, brother! They have redundant redundancy."

But Lorimer's technical interest soon flags. What he really wants is to be alone awhile. He makes a desultory attempt to survey the apparently few new developments in his field, and finds he can't concentrate. What the hell, he tells himself, I stopped being a physicist three hundred years ago. Such a relief to be out of the cell of *Sunbird*; he has given himself up to drifting solitary through the warren of the ship, using their excellent 400-mm telescope, noting the odd life of the crew.

When he finds that Lady Blue likes chess, they form a routine of biweekly games. Her personality intrigues him; she has reserve and an aura of authority. But she quickly stops Bud when he calls her "Captain."

"No one here commands in your sense. I'm just the oldest." Bud goes back to "ma'am."

She plays a solid positional game, somewhat more erratic than a man but with occasional elegant traps. Lorimer is astonished to find that there is only one new chess opening, an interesting queen-side gambit called the Dagmar. One new opening in three centuries? He mentions it to the others when they come back from helping Andy and Judy Paris overhaul a standby converter.

"They haven't done much anywhere," Dave says. "Most of your new stuff dates from the epidemic, Andy, if you'll pardon me. The program seems to be stagnating. You've been gearing up this Titan project for eighty years."

"We'll get there." Andy grins.

"C'mon, Dave, " says Bud. "Judy and me are taking on you two for the next chicken dinner, we'll get a bridge team here yet. Woo-ee, I can taste that chicken! Losers get the iguana."

The food is so good. Lorimer finds himself lingering around the kitchen end, helping whoever is cooking, munching on their various seeds and chewy roots as he listens to them talk. He even likes the iguana. He begins to put on weight, in fact they all do. Dave decrees double exercise shifts.

"You going to make us *climb* home, Dave-o?" Bud groans. But Lorimer enjoys it, pedaling or swinging easily along the rungs while the women chat and listen to tapes. Familiar music: he identifies a strange spectrum from Handel, Brahms, Sibelius, through Strauss to ballad tunes and intricate light jazz-rock. No lyrics. But plenty of informative texts doubtless selected for his benefit.

From the promised short history he finds out more about the epidemic. It seems to have been an airborne quasi virus escaped from Franco-Arab military labs, possibly potentiated by pollutants.

"It apparently damaged only the reproductive cells," he tells Dave and Bud. "There was little actual mortality, but almost universal sterility. Probably a molecular substitution in the gene code in the gametes. And the main effect seems to have been on the men. They mention a shortage of male births afterward, which suggests that the damage was on the Y chromosome where it would be selectively lethal to the male fetus."

"Is it still dangerous. Doc?" Dave asks. "What happens to us when we get back home?"

"They can't say. The birthrate is normal now, about two percent and rising. But the present population may be resistant. They never achieved a vaccine."

"Only one way to tell," Bud says gravely. "I volunteer."

Dave merely glances at him. Extraordinary how he still commands, Lorimer thinks. Not submission, for Pete's sake. A team.

The history also mentions the riots and fighting which swept the world when humanity found itself sterile. Cities bombed, and burned, massacres, panics, mass rapes and kidnapping of women, marauding armies of biologically desperate men, bloody cults. The crazies. But it is all so briefly told, so long ago. Lists of honored names. "We must always be grateful to the brave people who held the Denver Medical Laboratories—" And then on to the drama of building up the helium supply for the dirigibles.

In three centuries it's all dust, he thinks. What do I know of the hideous Thirty Years' War that was three centuries back for me? *Fighting devastated Europe for two generations.* Not even names.

The description of their political and economic structure is even briefer. They seem to be, as Myda had said, almost ungoverned.

"It's a form of loose social credit-system run by consensus," he says to Dave. "Somewhat like a permanent frontier period. They're building up slowly. Of course they don't need an army or air force. I'm not sure if they even use cash money or recognize private ownership of land. I did notice one favorable reference to early Chinese communalism," he adds, to see Dave's mouth set. "But they aren't tied to a community. They travel about. When I asked Lady Blue about their police and legal system, she told me to wait and talk with real historians. This Registry seems to be just that, it's not a policy organ."

"We've run into a situation here, Lorimer," Dave says soberly. "Stay away from it. They're not telling the story."

"You notice they never talk about their husbands?" Bud laughs. "I asked a couple of them what their husbands did, and I swear they had to think. And they all have kids. Believe me, it's a swinging scene down there, even if old Andy acts like he hasn't found out what it's for."

"I don't want any prying into their personal family lives while we're on this ship, Geirr. None whatsoever. That's an order."

"Maybe they don't have families. You ever hear 'em mention anybody getting married? That has to be the one thing on a chick's mind. Mark my words, there's been some changes made."

"The social mores are bound to have changed to some extent," Lorimer says. "Obviously you have women doing more work outside the home, for one thing. But they have family bonds; for instance, Lady Blue has a sister in an aluminum mill and another in health. Andy's mother is on Mars and his sister works in Registry. Connie has a brother or brothers on the fishing fleet near Biloxi, and her sister is coming out to replace her here next trip, she's making yeast now."

"That's the top of the iceberg."

"I doubt the rest of the iceberg is very sinister, Dave."

But somewhere along the line the blandness begins to bother Lorimer too. So much is missing. Marriage, love affairs, children's troubles, jealousy squabbles, status, possessions, money problems, sicknesses, funerals even—all the daily minutiae that occupied Ginny and her friends seems to have been edited out of these women's talk. *Edited* . . . Can Dave be right, is some big, significant aspect being deliberately kept from them?

"I'm still surprised your language hasn't changed more," he says one day to Connie during their exertions in the gym.

"Oh, we're very careful about that." She climbs at an angle beside him, not using her hands. "It would be a dreadful loss if we couldn't understand the books. All the children are taught from the same original tapes, you see. Oh, there's faddy words we use for a while, but our communicators have to learn the old texts by heart, that keeps us together."

Judy Paris grunts from the pedicycle. "You, my dear children, will never know the oppression we suffered," she declaims mockingly.

"Judys talk too much," says Connie.

"We do, for a fact." They both laugh.

"So you still read our so-called great books, our fiction and poetry?" asks Lorimer. "Who do you read, H. G. Wells? Shakespeare? Dickens, ah, Balzac, Kipling, Brian?" He gropes; Brian had been a bestseller Ginny liked. When had he last looked at Shakespeare or the others?

"Oh, the historicals," Judy says. "It's interesting, I guess. Grim. They're not very realistic. I'm sure it was to you," she adds generously.

And they turn to discussing whether the laying hens are getting too much light, leaving Lorimer to wonder how what he supposes are the eternal verities of human nature can have faded from a world's reality. Love, conflict, heroism, tragedy—all "unrealistic"? Well, flight crews are never great readers; still, women read more. . . . Something *has* changed, he can sense it. Something basic enough to affect human nature. A physical development perhaps; a mutation? What is really under those floating clothes?

It is the Judys who give him part of it.

He is exercising alone with both of them, listening to them gossip about some legendary figure named Dagmar.

"The Dagmar who invented the chess opening?" he asks.

"Yes. She does anything, when she's good she's great."

"Was she bad sometimes?"

A Judy laughs. "The Dagmar problem, you can say. She has this tendency to organize everything. It's fine when it works, but every so often it runs wild, she thinks she's queen or what. Then they have to get out the butterfly nets."

All in present tense—but Lady Blue has told him the Dagmar gambit is over a century old.

Longevity, he thinks; by god, that's what they're hiding. Say they've achieved a doubled or tripled life span, that would certainly change human psychology, affect their outlook on everything. Delayed maturity, perhaps? We were working on endocrine cell juvenescence when I left. How old are these girls, for instance?

He is framing a question when Judy Dakar says, "I was in the crèche when she went pluggo. But she's good, I loved her later on."

Lorimer thinks she has said "crash" and then realizes she means a communal nursery. "Is that the same Dagmar?" he asks. "She must be very old."

"Oh, no, her sister."

"A sister a hundred years apart?"

"I mean, her daughter. Her, her *grand*daughter." She starts pedaling fast.

"Judys," says her twin, behind them.

Sister again. Everybody he learns of seems to have an extraordinary number of sisters, Lorimer reflects. He hears Judy Paris saying to her twin, "I think I remember Dagmar at the crèche. She started uniforms for everybody. Colors and numbers."

"You couldn't have, you weren't born," Judy Dakar retorts.

There is a silence in the drum.

Lorimer turns on the rungs to look at them. Two flushed cheerful faces stare back warily, make identical head-dipping gestures to swing the black hair out of their eyes. Identical . . . But isn't the Dakar girl on the cycle a shade more mature, her face more weathered?

"I thought you were supposed to be twins."

"Ah, Judys talk a lot," they say together—and grin guiltily.

"You aren't sisters, " he tells them. "You're what we called clones."

Another silence.

"Well, yes," says Judy Dakar. "We call it sisters. Oh, mother! We weren't supposed to tell you, Myda said you would be frightfully upset. It was illegal in your day, true?"

"Yes. We considered it immoral and unethical, experimenting with human life. But it doesn't upset me personally."

"Oh, that's beautiful, that's great," they say together. "We think of you as different," Judy Paris blurts, "you're more hu— more like us. Please, you don't have to tell the others, do you? Oh, *please* don't."

"It was an accident there were two of us here," says Judy Dakar. "Myda *warned* us. Can't you wait a little while?" Two identical pairs of dark eyes beg him.

"Very well," he says slowly. "I won't tell my friends for the time being. But if I keep your secret you have to answer some questions. For instance, how many of your people are created artificially this way?"

He begins to realize he *is* somewhat upset. Dave is right, damn it, they are hiding things. Is this brave new world populated by subhuman slaves, run by master brains? Decorticate zombies, workers without stomachs or sex, human cortexes wired into machines, monstrous experiments rush through his mind. He has been naive again. These normal-looking women could be fronting for a hideous world.

"How many?"

"There's only about eleven thousand of us," Judy Dakar says. The two Judys look at each other, transparently confirming something. They're unschooled in deception, Lorimer thinks; is that good? And is diverted by Judy Paris exclaiming, "What we can't figure out is, why did you think it was wrong?"

Lorimer tries to tell them, to convey the horror of manipulating human identity, creating abnormal life. The threat to individuality, the fearful power it would put in a dictator's hand.

"Dictator?" one of them echoes blankly. He looks at their faces and can only say, "Doing things to people without their consent. I think it's sad."

"But that's just what we think about you," the younger Judy bursts out. "How do you know who you *are*? Or who anybody is? All alone, no sisters to share with! You don't know what you can do, or what would be interesting to try. All you poor singletons, you—why, you just have to blunder along and die, all for nothing!"

Her voice trembles. Amazed, Lorimer sees both of them are misty eyed.

"We better get this m-moving," the other Judy says.

They swing back into the rhythm, and in bits and pieces Lorimer finds out how it is. Not bottled embryos, they tell him indignantly. Human mothers like everybody else, young mothers, the best kind. A somatic cell nucleus is inserted in an enucleated ovum and reimplanted in the womb. They have each borne two "sister" babies in their late teens and nursed them awhile before moving on. The crèches always have plenty of mothers.

His longevity notion is laughed at; nothing but some rules of healthy living has as yet been achieved. "We should make ninety in good shape," they assure him. "A hundred and eight, that was Judy Eagle, she's our record. But she was pretty blah at the end."

The clone-strains themselves are old, they date from the epidemic. They were part of the first effort to save the race when the babies stopped, and they've continued ever since.

"It's so perfect," they tell him. "We each have a book, it's really a library. All the recorded messages. The Book of Judy Shapiro, that's us. Dakar and Paris are our personal names, we're doing cities now." They laugh, trying not to talk at once about how each Judy adds her individual memoir, her adventures and problems and discoveries, in the genotype they all share.

"If you make a mistake it's useful for the others. Of course you try not to—or at least make a *new* one."

"Some of the old ones aren't so realistic," her other self puts in. "Things were so different, I guess. We make excerpts of the parts we like best. And practical things, like Judys should watch out for skin cancer."

"But we have to read the whole thing every ten years," says the Judy called Dakar. "It's inspiring. As you get older you understand some of the ones you didn't before."

Bemused, Lorimer tries to think how it would be, hearing the voices of three hundred years of Orren Lorimers. Lorimers who were mathematicians or plumbers or artists or bums or criminals, maybe. The continuing exploration and completion of self. And a dozen living doubles; aged Lorimers, infant Lorimers. And other Lorimers' women and children . . . would he enjoy it or resent it? He doesn't know.

"Have you made your records yet?"

"Oh, we're too young. Just notes in case of accident."

"Will we be in them?"

"You can say!" They laugh merrily, then sober. "Truly you won't tell?" Judy Paris asks. "Lady Blue, we have to let her know what we did. Oof. But *truly* you won't tell your friends?"

He hadn't told on them, he thinks now, emerging back into his living self. Connie beside him is drinking cider from a bulb. He has a drink in his hand too, he finds. But he hasn't told.

"Judys will talk." Connie shakes her head, smiling. Lorimer realizes he must have gabbled out the whole thing.

"It doesn't matter," he tells her. "I would have guessed soon anyhow. There were too many clues . . . Woolagongs invent, Mydas

287

worry, Jans are brains, Billy Dees work so hard. I picked up six different stories of hydroelectric stations that were built or improved or are being run by one Lala Singh. Your whole way of life. I'm more interested in this sort of thing than a respectable physicist should be," he says wryly. "You're all clones, aren't you? Every one of you. What do Connies do?"

"You really do know." She gazes at him like a mother whose child has done something troublesome and bright. "Whew! Oh, well, Connies farm like mad, we grow things. Most of our names are plants. I'm Veronica, by the way. And of course the crèches, that's our weakness. The runt mania. We tend to focus on anything smaller or weak."

Her warm eyes focus on Lorimer, who draws back involuntarily.

"We control it." She gives a hearty chuckle. "We aren't all that way. There's been engineering Connies, and we have two young sisters who love metallurgy. It's fascinating what the genotype can do if you try. The original Constantia Morelos was a chemist, she weighed ninety pounds and never saw a farm in her life." Connie looks down at her own muscular arms. "She was killed by the crazies, she fought with weapons. It's so hard to understand. . . . And I had a sister Timothy who made dynamite and dug two canals and she wasn't even an andy."

"*An* andy," he says.

"Oh, dear."

"I guessed that too. Early androgen treatments."

She nods hesitantly. "Yes. We need the muscle power for some jobs. A few. Kays are quite strong anyway. Whew!" She suddenly stretches her back, wriggles as if she'd been cramped. "Oh, I'm glad you know. It's been such a strain. We couldn't even sing."

"Why not?"

"Myda was sure we'd make mistakes, all the words we'd have had to change. We sing a lot." She softly hums a bar or two.

"What kinds of songs do you sing?"

"Oh, every kind. Adventure songs, work songs, mothering songs, roaming songs, mood songs, trouble songs, joke songs—everything."

"What about love songs?" he ventures. "Do you still have, well, love?"

"Of course, how could people not love?" But she looks at him doubtfully. "The love stories I've heard from your time are so, I don't know, so weird. Grim and pluggy. It doesn't seem like love. . . . Oh, yes, we have famous love songs. Some of them are partly sad, too. Like Tamil and Alcmene O , they're fated together. Connies are fated too, a little." She grins bashfully. "We love to be with Ingrid Anders. It's more one-sided. I hope there'll be an Ingrid on my next hitch. She's so exciting, she's like a little diamond."

Implications are exploding all about him, sparkling with questions. But Lorimer wants to complete the darker pattern beyond.

"Eleven thousand genotypes, two million people: that averages two hundred of each of you alive now." She nods. "I suppose it varies? There's more of some?"

"Yes, some types aren't as viable. But we haven't lost any since early days. They tried to preserve all the genes they could. We have people from all the major races and a lot of small strains. Like me, I'm the Carib Blend. Of course we'll never know what was lost. But eleven thousand is a lot, really. We all try to know everyone, it's a life hobby."

A chill penetrates his ataraxia. Eleven thousand, period. That is the true population of Earth now. He thinks of two hundred tall olive-skinned women named after plants, excited by two hundred little bright Ingrids; two hundred talkative Judys, two hundred self-possessed Lady Blues, two hundred Margos and Mydas and the rest. He shivers. The heirs, the happy pallbearers of the human race.

"So evolution ends," he says somberly.

"No, why? It's just slowed down. We do everything much slower than you did, I think. We like to experience things *fully*. We have time." She stretches again, smiling. "There's all the time."

"But you have no new genotypes. It is the end."

"Oh, but there are, now. Last century they worked out the way to make haploid nuclei combine. We can make a stripped egg cell function like pollen," she says proudly. "I mean sperm. It's tricky, some don't come out too well. But now we're finding both Xs viable we have over a hundred new types started. Of course it's hard for them, with no sisters. The donors try to help."

Over a hundred, he thinks. Well. Maybe . . . But "both Xs viable," what does that mean? She must be referring to the epidemic. But he had figured it primarily affected the men. His mind goes happily to work on the new puzzle, ignoring a sound from somewhere that is trying to pierce his calm.

"It was a gene or genes on the X chromosome that was injured," he guesses aloud. "Not the Y. And the lethal trait had to be recessive, right? Thus there would have been no births at all for a time, until some men recovered or were isolated long enough to manufacture undamaged X-bearing gametes. But women carry their lifetime supply of ova, they could never regenerate reproductively. When they mated with the recovered males, only female babies would be produced, since the female carries two Xs and the mother's defective gene would be compensated by a normal X from the father. But the male is XY, he receives only the mother's defective X. Thus the lethal defect would be expressed, the male fetus would be finished. . . . A planet of girls and dying men. The few odd viables died off."

"You truly do understand," she says admiringly.

The sound is becoming urgent; he refuses to hear it, there is significance here.

"So we'll be perfectly all right on Earth. No problem. In theory we can marry again and have families, daughters anyway."

"Yes," she says. "In theory."

The sound suddenly broaches his defenses, becomes the loud voice of Bud Geirr raised in song. He sounds plain drunk now. It seems to be coming from the main garden pod, the one they use to grow vegetables, not sanitation. Lorimer feels the dread alive again, rising closer. Dave ought to keep an eye on him. But Dave seems to have vanished too, he recalls seeing him go toward Control with Lady Blue.

"OH, THE SUN SHINES BRIGHT ON PRETTY RED WI-I-ING," carols Bud.

Something should be done, Lorimer decides painfully. He stirs; it is an effort.

"Don't worry," Connie says. "Andy's with them."

"You don't know, you don't know what you've started." He pushes off toward the garden hatchway.

"—AS SHE LAY SLE-EEPING, A COWBOY CREE-E-EEPING—" General laughter from the hatchway. Lorimer coasts through into the green dazzle. Beyond the radial fence of snap beans he sees Bud sailing in an exaggerated crouch after Judy Paris. Andy hangs by the iguana cages, laughing.

Bud catches one of Judy's ankles and stops them both with a flourish, making her yellow pajamas swirl. She giggles at him upside down, making no effort to free herself.

"I don't like this," Lorimer whispers.

"Please don't interfere." Connie has hold of his arm, anchoring them both to the tool rack. Lorimer's alarm seems to have ebbed; he will watch, let serenity return. The others have not noticed them.

"Oh, there once was an Indian maid." Bud sings more restrainedly, "Who never was a-fraid, that some buckaroo would slip it up her, ahem, ahem," he coughs ostentatiously, laughing. "Hey, Andy, I hear them calling you."

"What?" says Judy. "I don't hear anything."

"They're calling you, lad. Out there."

"Who?" asks Andy, listening.

"*They* are, for Crissake." He lets go of Judy and kicks over to Andy. "Listen, you're a great kid. Can't you see me and Judy have some business to discuss in private?" He turns Andy gently around and pushes him at the bean stakes. "It's New Year's Eve, dummy."

Andy floats passively away through the fence of vines, raising a hand at Lorimer and Connie. Bud is back with Judy.

"Happy New Year, kitten," he smiles.

"Happy New Year. Did you do special things on New Year?" she asks curiously.

"What we did on New Year's." He chuckles, taking her shoulders in his hands. "On New Year's Eve, yes we did. Why don't I show you some of our primitive Earth customs, h'mm?"

She nods, wide eyed.

"Well, first we wish each other well, like this." He draws her to him and lightly kisses her cheek. "Kee-rist, what a dumb bitch," he says in a totally different voice. "You can tell you've been out too long when the geeks start looking good. Knockers, ahhh—" His hand plays with her blouse. The man is unaware, Lorimer realizes. He doesn't know he's drugged, he's speaking his thoughts. I must have done that. Oh, god . . . He takes shelter behind his crystal lens, an observer in the protective light of eternity.

"And then we smooch a little." The friendly voice is back. Bud holds the girl closer, caressing her back. "Fat ass." He puts his mouth on hers; she doesn't resist. Lorimer watches Bud's arms tighten, his hands working on her buttocks, going under her clothes. Safe in the lens, his own sex stirs. Judy's arms are waving aimlessly.

Bud breaks for breath, a hand at his zipper.

"Stop staring," he says hoarsely. "One fucking more word, you'll find out what that big mouth is for. Oh, man, a flagpole. Like steel . . . Bitch, this is your lucky day." He is baring her breasts now, big breasts. Fondling them. "Two fucking years in the ass end of noplace," he mutters, "shit on me, will you? Can't wait, watch it—titty-titty-titties—"

He kisses her again quickly and smiles down at her. "Good?" he asks in his tender voice, and sinks his mouth on her nipples, his hand seeking in her thighs. She jerks and says something muffled. Lorimer's arteries are pounding with delight, with dread.

"I, I think this should stop," he makes himself say falsely, hoping he isn't saying more. Through the pulsing tension he hears Connie whisper back, it sounds like "Don't worry, Judy's very athletic." Terror stabs him, they don't know. But he can't help.

"Cunt," Bud grunts, "you have to have a cunt in there, is it froze up? You dumb cunt—" Judy's face appears briefly in her floating hair, a remote part of Lorimer's mind notes that she looks amused and uncomfortable. His being is riveted to the sight of Bud expertly controlling her body in midair, peeling down the yellow slacks. Oh, god—her dark pubic mat, the thick white thighs—a perfectly normal woman, no mutation. Ohhh, god . . . But there is suddenly a drifting shadow in the way: Andy again floating over them with something in his hands.

"You dinko, Jude?" the boy asks.

Bud's face comes up red and glaring. "Bug out, you!"

"Oh, I won't bother."

"Jee-sus Christ." Bud lunges up and grabs Andy's arm, his legs still hooked around Judy. "This is man's business, boy, do I have to spell it out?" He shifts his grip. "Shoo!"

In one swift motion he has jerked Andy close and backhanded his face hard, sending him sailing into the vines.

Bud gives a bark of laughter, bends back to Judy. Lorimer can see his erection poking through his fly. He wants to utter some warning, tell them their peril, but he can only ride the hot pleasure surging through him, melting his crystal shell. Go on, more—avidly he sees Bud mouth her breasts again and then suddenly flip her whole body over, holding her wrists behind her in one fist, his legs pinning hers. Her bare buttocks bulge up helplessly, enormous moons. "Ass-s-s," Bud groans. "Up you bitch, ahhhhh—" He pulls her butt onto him.

Judy gives a cry, begins to struggle futilely. Lorimer's shell boils and bursts. Amid the turmoil, ghosts outside are trying to rush in. And something *is* moving, a real ghost—to his dismay he sees it is Andy again, floating toward the joined bodies, holding a whirring thing. Oh, no—a camera. The fools.

"Get away!" he tries to call to the boy.

But Bud's head turns, he has seen. "You little pissass." His long arm shoots out and captures Andy's shirt, his legs still locked around Judy.

"I've had it with you." His fist slams into Andy's mouth, the camera goes spinning away. But this time Bud doesn't let him go, he is battering the boy, all of them rolling in a tangle in the air.

"Stop!" Lorimer hears himself shout, plunging at them through the beans. "Bud, stop it! You're hitting a woman."

The angry face comes around, squinting at him.

"Get lost, Doc, you little fart. Get your own ass."

"Andy is a *woman*, Bud. You're hitting a girl. She's not a man."

"Huh?" Bud glances at Andy's bloody face. He shakes the shirt-front. "Where's the boobs?"

'She doesn't have breasts, but she's a woman. Her real name is Kay. They're all women. Let her go, Bud."

Bud stares at the androgyne, his legs still pinioning Judy, his penis poking the air. Andy puts up his/her hands in a vaguely combative way.

"A dyke?" says Bud slowly. "A goddamn little bull dyke? This I gotta see."

He feints casually, thrusts a hand into Andy's crotch.

"No balls!" he roars. "No balls at all!" Convulsing with laughter, he lets himself tip over in the air, releasing Andy, his legs letting Judy slip free. "Na-ah," he interrupts himself to grab her hair and goes on guffawing. "A dyke! Hey, dykey!" He takes hold of his hard-on, waggles it at Andy. "Eat your heart out, little dyke." Then he pulls up Judy's head. She has been watching unresisting all along.

"Take a good look, girlie. See what old Buddy has for you? Tha-a-at's what you want, say it. How long since you saw a real man, hey, dogface?"

Maniacal laughter bubbles up in Lorimer's gut, farce too strong for fear. "She never saw a man in her life before, none of them has. You imbecile, don't you get it? There aren't any other men, they've all been dead three hundred years."

Bud slowly stops chuckling, twists around to peer at Lorimer.

"What'd I hear you say, Doc?"

"The men are all gone. They died off in the epidemic. There's nothing but women left alive on Earth."

"You mean there's, there's two million women down there and no men?" His jaw gapes. "Only little bull dykes like Andy . . . Wait a minute. Where do they get the kids?"

"They grow them artificially. They're all girls."

"Gawd . . ." Bud's hand clasps his drooping penis, jiggles it absently until it stiffens. "Two million hot little cunts down there, waiting for old Buddy. Gawd. The last man on Earth . . . You don't count, Doc. And old Dave, he's full of crap."

He begins to pump himself, still holding Judy by the hair. The motion sends them slowly backward. Lorimer sees that Andy—Kay—has the camera going again. There is a big star-shaped smear of blood on the boyish face; cut lip, probably. He himself feels globed in thick air, all action spent. Not lucid.

"Two million cunts," Bud repeats. "Nobody home, nothing but pussy everywhere. I can do anything I want, anytime. No more shit." He pumps faster. "They'll be spread out for miles begging for it. Clawing each other for it. All for me, King Buddy . . . I'll have strawberries and cunt for breakfast. Hot buttered boobies, man. 'N' head, there'll be a couple little twats licking whip cream off my cock all day long. . . . Hey, I'll have contests! Only the best for old Buddy now. Not you, cow." He jerks Judy's head. "Li'l teenies, tight li'l holes. I'll make the old broads hot 'em up while I watch." He frowns slightly, working on himself. In a clinical corner of his mind Lorimer guesses the drug is retarding ejaculation. He tells himself that he should be relieved by Bud's self-absorption, is instead obscurely terrified.

"King, I'll be their god" Bud is mumbling. "They'll make statues of me, my cock a mile high, all over. . . . His Majesty's sacred balls. They'll worship it. . . . Buddy Geirr, the last cock on Earth. Oh, man, if old George could see that. When the boys hear that they'll really shit themselves, woo-ee!"

He frowns harder. "They can't all be gone." His eyes rove, find Lorimer. "Hey, Doc, there's some men left someplace, aren't there? Two or three, anyway?"

"No." Effortfully Lorimer shakes his head. "They're all dead, all of them."

"Balls." Bud twists around, peering at them. "There has to be some left. Say it." He pulls Judy's head up. "*Say* it, cunt."

"No, it's true," she says.

"No men," Andy/Kay echoes.

"You're lying." Bud scowls, frigs himself faster, thrusting his pelvis. "There has to be some men, sure there are. . . . They're hiding out in the hills, that's what it is. Hunting, living wild . . . Old wild men, I knew it."

"Why do there have to be men?" Judy asks him, being jerked to and fro.

"Why, you stupid bitch." He doesn't look at her, thrusts furiously. "Because, dummy, otherwise nothing counts, that's why. . . . There's some men, some good old buckaroos—Buddy's a good old buckaroo—"

"Is he going to emit sperm now?" Connie whispers.

"Very likely," Lorimer says, or intends to say. The spectacle is of merely clinical interest, he tells himself, nothing to dread. One of Judy's hands clutches something: a small plastic bag. Her other hand is on her hair that Bud is yanking. It must be painful.

"Uhhh, ahh," Bud pants distressfully, "fuck away, fuck—" Suddenly he pushes Judy's head into his groin, Lorimer glimpses her nonplussed expression.

"You have a mouth, bitch, get working! . . . Take it, for shit's sake, *take it*! Uh, uh—" A small oyster jets limply from him. Judy's arm goes after it with the bag as they roll over in the air.

"Geirr!"

Bewildered by the roar, Lorimer turns and sees Dave—Major Norman Davis—looming in the hatchway. His arms are out, holding back Lady Blue and the other Judy.

"Geirr! I said there would be no misconduct on this ship, and I mean it. Get away from that woman!"

Bud's legs only move vaguely, he does not seem to have heard. Judy swims through them bagging the last drops.

"You, what the hell are you doing?"

In the silence Lorimer hears his own voice say, "Taking a sperm sample, I should think."

"Lorimer? Are you out of your perverted mind? Get Geirr to his quarters."

Bud slowly rotates upright. "Ah, the reverend Leroy," he says tonelessly.

"You're drunk, Geirr. Go to your quarters."

"I have news for you, Dave-o," Bud tells him in the same flat voice. "I bet you don't know we're the last men on Earth. Two million twats down there."

"I'm aware of that," Dave says furiously. "You're a drunken disgrace. Lorimer, get that man out of here."

But Lorimer feels no nerve of action stir. Dave's angry voice has pushed back the terror, created a strange hopeful stasis encapsulating them all.

"I don't have to take that anymore. . . ." Bud's head moves back and forth, silently saying no, no, as he drifts toward Lorimer. "Nothing counts anymore. All gone. What for, friends?" His forehead puckers. "Old Dave, he's a man. I'll let him have some. The dummies . . . Poor old Doc, you're a creep but you're better'n nothing, you can have some too. . . . We'll have places, see, big spreads. Hey, we can run drags, there has to be a million good old cars down there. We can go hunting. And then we find the wild men."

Andy, or Kay, is floating toward him, wiping off blood.

"Ah, no you don't!" Bud snarls and lunges for her. As his arm stretches out Judy claps him on the triceps.

Bud gives a yell that dopplers off, his limbs thrash—and then he is floating limply, his face suddenly serene. But he is breathing, Lorimer sees, releasing his own breath, watching them carefully straighten out the big body. Judy plucks her pants out of the vines, and they start towing him out through the fence. She has the camera and the specimen bag.

"I put this in the freezer, dinko?" she says to Connie as they come by. Lorimer has to look away.

Connie nods. "Kay, how's your face?"

"I felt it!" Andy/Kay says excitedly through puffed lips. "I felt physical anger, I wanted to hit him. Woo-ee!"

"Put that man in my wardroom," Dave orders as they pass. He has moved into the sunlight over the lettuce rows. Lady Blue and Judy Dakar are back by the wall, watching. Lorimer remembers what he wanted to ask.

"Dave, do you really know?"

Dave eyes him broodingly, floating erect with the sun on his chestnut beard and hair. The authentic features of man. Lorimer thinks of his own father, a small pale figure like himself. He feels better.

"I always knew they were trying to deceive us, Lorimer. Now that this woman has admitted the facts, I understand the full extent of the tragedy."

It is his deep, mild Sunday voice. The women look at him interestedly.

"They are lost children. They have forgotten He who made them. For generations they have lived in darkness."

"They seem to be doing all right," Lorimer hears himself say. It sounds rather foolish.

"Women are not capable of running anything. You should know that, Lorimer. Look what they've done here, it's pathetic. Marking time, that's all. Poor souls." Dave sighs gravely. "It is not their fault. I recognize that. Nobody has given them any guidance for three hundred years. Like a chicken with its head off."

Lorimer recognizes his own thought; the structureless, chattering, trivial, two-million-celled protoplasmic lump.

"The head of the woman is the man," Dave says crisply. "Corinthians one eleven three. No discipline whatsoever." He stretches out his arm, holding up his crucifix as he drifts toward the wall of vines. "Mockery. Abominations." At the stakes he turns, framed in the green arbor.

"We were sent here, Lorimer. This is God's plan. *I* was sent here. Not you, you're as bad as they are. My middle name is Paul," he adds in a conversational tone. The sun gleams on the cross, on his uplifted face, a strong, pure, apostolic visage. Despite some intellectual reservations Lorimer feels a forgotten nerve respond.

"Oh, Father, send me strength," Dave prays quietly, his eyes closed. "You have spared us from the void to bring Your light to this suffering world. I shall lead Thine erring daughters out of the darkness. I shall be a stern but merciful father to them in Thy name. Help me to teach the children Thy holy law and train them in the fear of Thy righteous wrath. Let the women learn in silence and all subjection; Timothy two eleven. They shall have sons to rule over them and glorify Thy name."

He could do it, Lorimer thinks, a man like that really could get life going again. Maybe there is some mystery, some plan. I was too ready to give up. No guts . . . He becomes aware of women whispering.

"This tape is about through." It is Judy Dakar. "Isn't that enough? He's just repeating."

"Wait," murmurs Lady Blue.

"And she brought forth a man child to rule the nations with a rod of iron, Revelations twelve five," Dave says, louder. His eyes are open now, staring intently at the crucifix. *"For God so loved the world that He sent His only begotten Son."*

Lady Blue nods; Judy pushes off toward Dave. Lorimer understands, protest rising in his throat. They mustn't do that to Dave, treating him like an animal, for Christ's sake, a man—

"Dave! Look out, don't let her get near you!" he shouts.

"May I look, Major? It's beautiful, what is it?" Judy is coasting close, her hand out toward the crucifix.

"She's got a hypo, watch it!"

But Dave has already wheeled around. "Do not profane, woman!"

He thrusts the cross at her like a weapon, so menacing that she recoils in midair and shows the glinting needle in her hand.

"Serpent!" He kicks her shoulder away, sending himself upward. "Blasphemer. All right," he snaps in his ordinary voice, "there's going to be some order around here, starting now. Get over by that wall, all of you."

Astounded, Lorimer sees that Dave actually has a weapon in his other hand, a small gray handgun. He must have had it since Houston. Hope and ataraxia shrivel away, he is shocked into desperate reality.

"Major Davis," Lady Blue is saying. She is floating right at him, they all are, right at the gun. Oh, god, do they know what it is?

"Stop!" he shouts at them. "Do what he says, for god's sake. That's a ballistic weapon, it can kill you. It shoots metal slugs." He begins edging toward Dave along the vines.

"Stand back." Dave gestures with the gun. "I am taking command of this ship in the name of the United States of America under God."

"Dave, put that gun away. You don't want to shoot people."

Dave sees him, swings the gun around. "I warn you, Lorimer, get over there with them. Geirr's a man, when he sobers up." He looks at the women still drifting puzzledly toward him and understands. "All right, lesson one. Watch this.

He takes deliberate aim at the iguana cages and fires. There is a pinging crack. A lizard explodes bloodily, voices cry out. A loud mechanical warble starts up and overrides everything.

"A leak!" Two bodies go streaking toward the far end, everybody is moving. In the confusion Lorimer sees Dave calmly pulling himself back to the hatchway behind them, his gun ready. He pushes frantically across the tool rack to cut them off. A spray canister comes loose in his grip, leaving him kicking in the air. The alarm warble dies.

"You will stay here until I decide to send for you," Dave announces. He has reached the hatch, is pulling the massive lock door around. It will seal off the pod, Lorimer realizes.

"Don't do it, Dave! Listen to me, you're going to kill us all." Lorimer's own internal alarms are shaking him, he knows now what all that damned volleyball has been for and he is scared to death. "Dave, listen to me!"

"Shut up." The gun swings toward him. The door is moving. Lorimer gets a foot on solidity.

"Duck! It's a bomb!" With all his strength he hurls the massive canister at Dave's head and launches himself after it.

"Look out!" And he is sailing helplessly in slow motion, hearing the gun go off again, voices yelling. Dave must have missed him, overhead shots are tough—and then he is doubling downward, grabbing hair. A hard blow strikes his gut, it is Dave's leg kicking past him but he has his arm under the beard, the big man bucking like a bull, throwing him around.

"Get the gun, get it!" People are bumping him, getting hit. Just as his hold slips, a hand snakes by him onto Dave's shoulder and they are colliding into the hatch door in a tangle. Dave's body is suddenly no longer at war.

Lorimer pushes free, sees Dave's contorted face tip slowly backward looking at him.

"Judas—"

The eyes close. It is over.

Lorimer looks around. Lady Blue is holding the gun, sighting down the barrel.

"Put that down," he gasps, winded. She goes on examining it.

"Hey, thanks!" Andy—Kay—grins lopsidedly at him, rubbing her jaw. They are all smiling, speaking warmly to him, feeling themselves, their torn clothes. Judy Dakar has a black eye starting, Connie holds a shattered iguana by the tail.

Beside him Dave drifts, breathing stertorously, his blind face pointing at the sun. *Judas* . . . Lorimer feels the last shield break inside him, desolation flooding in. *On the deck my captain lies.*

Andy-who-is-not-a-man comes over and matter-of-factly zips up Dave's jacket, takes hold of it, and begins to tow him out. Judy Dakar stops them long enough to wrap the crucifix chain around his hand. Somebody laughs, not unkindly, as they go by.

For an instant Lorimer is back in that Evanston toilet. But they are gone, all the little giggling girls. All gone forever, gone with the big boys waiting outside to jeer at him. Bud is right, he thinks, *Nothing counts anymore.* Grief and anger hammer at him. He knows now what he has been dreading: not their vulnerability, his.

"They were good men," he says bitterly. "They aren't bad men. You don't know what bad means. You did it to them, you broke them down. You made them do crazy things. Was it interesting? Did you learn enough?" His voice is trying to shake. "Everybody has aggressive fantasies. They didn't act on them. Never. Until you poisoned them."

They gaze at him in silence. "But nobody does," Connie says finally. "I mean, the fantasies."

"They were good men," Lorimer repeats elegiacally. He knows he is speaking for it all, for Dave's Father, for Bud's manhood, for himself, for Cro-Magnon, for the dinosaurs too, maybe. "I'm a man. By god, yes, I'm angry. I have a right. We gave you all this, we made it all. We built your precious civilization and your knowledge and comfort and medicines and your dreams. All of it. We protected you, we worked our balls off keeping you and your kids. It was hard. It was a fight, a bloody fight all the way. We're tough. We had to be, can't you understand? Can't you for Christ's sake understand that?"

Another silence.

"We're trying," Lady Blue sighs. "We are trying, Dr. Lorimer. Of course we enjoy your inventions and we do appreciate your evolutionary role. But you must see there's a problem. As I understand it, what you protected people from was largely other males, wasn't it? We've just had an extraordinary demonstration in that. You have brought history to life for us." Her wrinkled brown eyes smile at him; a small tea-colored matron holding an obsolete artifact.

"But the fighting is long over. It ended when you did, I believe. We can hardly turn you loose on Earth, and we simply have no facilities for people with your emotional problems."

"Besides, we don't think you'd be very happy," Judy Dakar adds earnestly.

"We could clone them," says Connie. "I know there's people who would volunteer to mother. The young ones might be all right, we could try."

"We've been *over* all that." Judy Paris is drinking from the water tank. She rinses and spits into the soil bed, looking worriedly at Lorimer. "We ought to take care of that leak now, we can talk tomorrow. And tomorrow and tomorrow." She smiles at him, unselfconsciously rubbing her crotch. "I'm sure a lot of people will want to meet you."

"Put us on an island," Lorimer says wearily. "On three islands." That look; he knows that look of preoccupied compassion. His mother and sister had looked just like that the time the diseased kitten came in the yard. They had comforted it and fed it and tenderly taken it to the vet to be gassed.

An acute, complex longing for the women he has known grips him. Women to whom men were not simply—*irrelevant*. Ginny . . . dear

301

god. His sister Amy. Poor Amy, she was good to him when they were kids. His mouth twists.

'Your problem is," he says, "if you take the risk of giving us equal rights, what could we possibly contribute?"

"Precisely," says Lady Blue. They all smile at him relievedly, not understanding that he isn't.

"I think I'll have that antidote now," he says.

Connie floats toward him, a big, warmhearted, utterly alien woman. "I thought you'd like yours in a bulb." She smiles kindly.

"Thank you." He takes the small pink bulb. "Just tell me," he says to Lady Blue, who is looking at the bullet gashes, "what do you call yourselves? Women's World? Liberation? Amazonia?"

"Why, we call ourselves human beings." Her eyes twinkle absently at him, go back to the bullet marks. "Humanity, mankind." She shrugs. "The human race."

The drink tastes cool going down, something like peace and freedom, he thinks. Or death.

———

1. When the *Gloria* picks the men up, do the women plan to take the men back with them, or is their plan all along to study the men and then leave them behind or kill them? Why do the women decide they can't take Lorimer back with them, even though he seems to understand them?

2. Why is getting the male astronauts to talk freely so important to the women on board the *Gloria* that they drug the men? Why are Lorimer's thoughts and actions while under the influence of the drug so different from Bud's?

3. When Dave tries to seize control of the *Gloria*, why does Lorimer grab him and enable the women to get Dave's gun? At the end of the story, does Lorimer regret his decision?

4. Are we meant to think that the society the women have developed is inferior or superior to the society of men and women that existed before it?

ORSON SCOTT CARD (1951–) is the author of more than sixty books of science fiction and fantasy. Born in Richland, Washington, Card was raised a devout Mormon and attended Brigham Young University, where he began his writing career as a playwright. He did missionary service in Brazil, and upon his return to Utah he became an editor at *Ensign* magazine, the official publication of the Church of Jesus Christ of Latter-Day Saints. His religious beliefs often play a subtle role in his fiction, which is known for exploring themes of authority and obedience, evil, and empathy. While still at *Ensign*, Card published "Ender's Game," a short story that he later expanded into the widely praised novel *Ender's Game* (1985), the first book in his Enderverse series. Both *Ender's Game* and its sequel, *Speaker for the Dead* (1986), received Hugo and Nebula awards, making Card the first author to win both of science fiction's top prizes for consecutive books in a series.

Ender's Game

"Whatever your gravity is when you get to the door, remember—the enemy's gate is down. If you step through your own door like you're out for a stroll, you're a big target and you deserve to get hit. With more than a flasher." Ender Wiggin paused and looked over the group. Most were just watching him nervously. A few understanding. A few sullen and resisting.

First day with this army, all fresh from the teacher squads, and Ender had forgotten how young new kids could be. He'd been in it for three years, they'd had six months—nobody over nine years old in the whole bunch. But they were his. At eleven, he was half a year early to be a commander. He'd had a toon of his own and knew a few tricks, but there were forty in his new army. Green. All marksmen with a flasher, all in top shape, or they wouldn't be here—but they were all just as likely as not to get wiped out first time into battle.

"Remember," he went on, "they can't see you till you get through that door. But the second you're out, they'll be on you. So hit that door the way you want to be when they shoot at you. Legs up under you, going straight *down*." He pointed at a sullen kid who looked like he was only seven, the smallest of them all. "Which way is down, greenoh!"

"Toward the enemy door." The answer was quick. It was also surly, as if to say, Yeah, yeah, now get on with the important stuff.

"Name, kid?"

"Bean."

"Get that for size or for brains?"

Bean didn't answer. The rest laughed a little. Ender had chosen right. This kid *was* younger than the rest, must have been advanced because he was sharp. The others didn't like him much, they were happy to see him taken down a little. Like Ender's first commander had taken him down.

"Well, Bean, you're right onto things. Now I tell you this, nobody's gonna get through that door without a good chance of getting hit. A lot of you are going to be turned into cement somewhere. Make sure it's your legs. Right? If only your legs get hit, then only your legs get frozen, and in nullo that's no sweat." Ender turned to one of the dazed ones. "What're legs for? Hmmm?"

Blank stare. Confusion. Stammer.

"Forget it. Guess I'll have to ask Bean here."

"Legs are for pushing off walls." Still bored.

"Thanks, Bean. Get that, everybody?" They all got it, and didn't like getting it from Bean. "Right. You can't see with legs, you can't *shoot* with legs, and most of the time they just get in the way. If they get frozen sticking straight out you've turned yourself into a blimp. No way to hide. So how do legs go?"

A few answered this time, to prove that Bean wasn't the only one who knew anything. "Under you. Tucked up under."

"Right. A shield. You're kneeling on a shield, and the shield is your own legs. And there's a trick to the suits. Even when your legs are flashed, you can *still* kick off. I've never seen anybody do it but me— but you're all gonna learn it."

Ender Wiggin turned on his flasher. It glowed faintly green in his hand. Then he let himself rise in the weightless workout room, pulled

ORSON SCOTT CARD

his legs under him as though he were kneeling, and flashed both of them. Immediately his suit stiffened at the knees and ankles, so that he couldn't bend at all.

"Okay, I'm frozen, see?"

He was floating a meter above them. They all looked up at him, puzzled. He leaned back and caught one of the handholds on the wall behind him, and pulled himself flush against the wall.

"I'm stuck at a wall. If I had legs, I'd use legs, and string myself out like a string *bean*, right?"

They laughed.

"But I don't have legs, and that's *better*, got it? Because of this." Ender jackknifed at the waist, then straightened out violently. He was across the workout room in only a moment. From the other side he called to them. "Got that? I didn't use hands, so I still had use of my flasher. *And* I didn't have my legs floating five feet behind me. Now watch it again."

He repeated the jackknife, and caught a handhold on the wall near them. "Now, I don't just want you to do that when they've flashed your legs. I want you to do that when you've still got legs, because it's better. And because they'll never be expecting it. All right now, everybody up in the air and kneeling."

Most were up in a few seconds. Ender flashed the stragglers, and they dangled, helplessly frozen, while the others laughed. "When I give an order, you move. Got it? When we're at the door and they clear it, I'll be giving you orders in two seconds, as soon as I see the setup. And when I give the order you better be out there, because whoever's out there first is going to win, unless he's a fool. I'm not. And you better not be, or I'll have you back in the teacher squads." He saw more than a few of them gulp, and the frozen ones looked at him with fear. "You guys who are hanging there. You watch. You'll thaw out in about fifteen minutes, and let's see if you can catch up to the others."

For the next half hour Ender had them jackknifing off walls. He called a stop when he saw that they all had the basic idea. They were a good group, maybe. They'd get better.

"Now you're warmed up," he said to them, "we'll start working."

. . .

Ender was the last one out after practice, since he stayed to help some of the slower ones improve on technique. They'd had good teachers, but like all armies they were uneven, and some of them could be a real drawback in battle. Their first battle might be weeks away. It might be tomorrow. A schedule was never posted. The commander just woke up and found a note by his bunk, giving him the time of his battle and the name of his opponent. So for the first while he was going to drive his boys until they were in top shape—all of them. Ready for anything, at any time. Strategy was nice, but it was worth nothing if the soldiers couldn't hold up under the strain.

He turned the corner into the residence wing and found himself face to face with Bean, the seven-year-old he had picked on all through practice that day. Problems. Ender didn't want problems right now.

"Ho, Bean."

"Ho, Ender."

Pause.

"Sir," Ender said softly.

"We're not on duty."

"In my army, Bean, we're always on duty." Ender brushed past him.

Bean's high voice piped up behind him. "I know what you're doing, Ender, sir, and I'm warning you."

Ender turned slowly and looked at him. "Warning me?"

"I'm the best man you've got. But I'd better be treated like it."

"Or what?" Ender smiled menacingly.

"Or I'll be the worst man you've got. One or the other."

"And what do you want? Love and kisses?" Ender was getting angry now.

Bean was unworried. "I want a toon."

Ender walked back to him and stood looking down into his eyes. "I'll give a toon," he said, "to the boys who prove they're worth something. They've got to be good soldiers, they've got to know how to take orders, they've got to be able to think for themselves in a pinch, and they've got to be able to keep respect. That's how I got to be a commander. That's how you'll get to be a toon leader. Got it?"

Bean smiled. "That's fair. *If* you actually work that way, I'll be a toon leader in a month."

Ender reached down and grabbed the front of his uniform and shoved him into the wall. "When I say I work a certain way, Bean, then that's the way I work."

Bean just smiled. Ender let go of him and walked away, and didn't look back. He was sure, without looking, that Bean was still watching, still smiling, still just a little contemptuous. He might make a good toon leader at that. Ender would keep an eye on him.

Captain Graff, six foot two and a little chubby, stroked his belly as he leaned back in his chair. Across his desk sat Lieutenant Anderson, who was earnestly pointing out high points on a chart.

"Here it is, Captain," Anderson said. "Ender's already got them doing a tactic that's going to throw off everyone who meets it. Doubled their speed."

Graff nodded.

"And you know his test scores. He thinks well, too."

Graff smiled. "All true, all true, Anderson, he's a fine student, shows real promise."

They waited.

Graff sighed. "So what do you want me to do?"

"Ender's the one. He's got to be."

"He'll never be ready in time, Lieutenant. He's eleven, for heaven's sake, man, what do you want, a miracle?"

"I want him into battles, every day starting tomorrow. I want him to have a year's worth of battles in a month."

Graff shook his head. "That would be his army in the hospital."

"No, sir. He's getting them into form. And we need Ender."

"Correction, Lieutenant. We need somebody. You think it's Ender."

"All right, I think it's Ender. Which of the commanders if it isn't him?"

"I don't know, Lieutenant." Graff ran his hands over his slightly fuzzy bald head. "These are children, Anderson. Do you realize that? Ender's army is nine years old. Are we going to put them against the older kids? Are we going to put them through hell for a month like that?"

Lieutenant Anderson leaned even farther over Graff's desk.

"Ender's test scores, Captain!"

"I've seen his bloody test scores! I've watched him in battle, I've listened to tapes of his training sessions, I've watched his sleep patterns, I've heard tapes of his conversations in the corridors and in the bathrooms, I'm more aware of Ender Wiggin than you could possibly imagine! And against all the arguments, against his obvious qualities, I'm weighing one thing. I have this picture of Ender a year from now, if you have your way. I see him completely useless, worn down, a failure, because he was pushed farther than he or any living person could go. But it doesn't weigh enough, does it, Lieutenant, because there's a war on, and our best talent is gone, and the biggest battles are ahead. So give Ender a battle every day this week. And then bring me a report."

Anderson stood and saluted. "Thank you, sir."

He had almost reached the door when Graff called his name. He turned and faced the captain.

"Anderson," Captain Graff said. "Have you been outside, lately I mean?"

"Not since last leave, six months ago."

"I didn't think so. Not that it makes any difference. But have you ever been to Beaman Park, there in the city? Hmm? Beautiful park. Trees. Grass. No mallo, no battles, no worries. Do you know what else there is in Beaman Park?"

"What, sir?" Lieutenant Anderson asked.

"Children," Graff answered.

"Of course children," said Anderson.

"I mean children. I mean kids who get up in the morning when their mothers call them and they go to school and then in the afternoons they go to Beaman Park and play. They're happy, they smile a lot, they laugh, they have fun. Hmmm?"

"I m sure they do, sir."

"Is that all you can say, Anderson?"

Anderson cleared his throat. "It's good for children to have fun, I think, sir. I know I did when I was a boy. But right now the world needs soldiers. And this is the way to get them."

Graff nodded and closed his eyes. "Oh, indeed, you're right, by statistical proof and by all the important theories, and dammit they work and the system is right, but all the same Ender's older than I am. He's not a child. He's barely a person."

ORSON SCOTT CARD

"If that's true, sir, then at least we all know that Ender is making it possible for the others of his age to be playing in the park."

"And Jesus died to save all men, of course." Graff sat up and looked at Anderson almost sadly. "But we're the ones," Graff said, "we're the ones who are driving in the nails."

Ender Wiggin lay on his bed staring at the ceiling. He never slept more than five hours a night—but the lights went off at 2200 and didn't come on again until 0600. So he stared at the ceiling and thought.

He'd had his army for three and a half weeks. Dragon Army. The name was assigned, and it wasn't a lucky one. Oh, the charts said that about nine years ago a Dragon Army had done fairly well. But for the next six years the name had been attached to inferior armies, and finally, because of the superstition that was beginning to play about the name, Dragon Army was retired. Until now. And now, Ender thought, smiling, Dragon Army was going to take them by surprise.

The door opened quietly. Ender did not turn his head. Someone stepped softly into his room, then left with the sound of the door shutting. When soft steps died away Ender rolled over and saw a white slip of paper lying on the floor. He reached down and picked it up.

"Dragon Army against Rabbit Army, Ender Wiggin and Carn Carby, 0700."

The first battle. Ender got out of bed and quickly dressed. He went rapidly to the rooms of each of the toon leaders and told them to rouse their boys. In five minutes they were all gathered in the corridor, sleepy and slow. Ender spoke softly.

"First battle, 0700 against Rabbit Army. I've fought them twice before but they've got a new commander. Never heard of him. They're an older group, though, and I knew a few of their old tricks. Now wake up. Run, doublefast, warmup in workroom three."

For an hour and a half they worked out, with three mock battles and calisthenics in the corridor out of the nullo. Then for fifteen minutes they all lay up in the air, totally relaxing in the weightlessness. At 0650 Ender roused them and they hurried into the corridor. Ender led them down the corridor, running again, and occasionally leaping to touch a light panel on the ceiling. The boys all touched the same light panel. And at 0658 they reached their gate to the battleroom.

The members of toons C and D grabbed the first eight handholds in the ceiling of the corridor. Toons A, B, and E crouched on the floor. Ender hooked his feet into two handholds in the middle of the ceiling, so he was out of everyone's way.

"Which way is the enemy's door?" he hissed.

"Down!" they whispered back, and laughed.

"Flashers on." The boxes in their hands glowed green. They waited for a few seconds more, and then the gray wall in front of them disappeared and the battleroom was visible.

Ender sized it up immediately. The familiar open grid of most early games, like the monkey bars at the park, with seven or eight boxes scattered through the grid. They called the boxes *stars*. There were enough of them, and in forward enough positions, that they were worth going for. Ender decided this in a second, and he hissed, "Spread to near stars. E hold!"

The four groups in the corners plunged through the force field at the doorway and fell down into the battleroom. Before the enemy even appeared through the opposite gate Ender's army had spread from the door to the nearest stars.

Then the enemy soldiers came through the door. From their stance Ender knew they had been in a different gravity, and didn't know enough to disorient themselves from it. They came through standing up, their entire bodies spread and defenseless.

"Kill 'em, E!" Ender hissed, and threw himself out the door knees first, with his flasher between his legs and firing. While Ender's group flew across the room, the rest of Dragon Army lay down a protecting fire, so that E group reached a forward position with only one boy frozen completely, though they had all lost the use of their legs—which didn't impair them in the least. There was a lull as Ender and his opponent, Carn Carby, assessed their positions. Aside from Rabbit Army's losses at the gate, there had been few casualties, and both armies were near full strength. But Carn had no originality—he was in the four-corner spread that any five-year-old in the teacher squads might have thought of. And Ender knew how to defeat it.

He called out, loudly, "E covers A, C down. B, D angle east wall." Under E toon's cover, B and D toons lunged away from their stars. While they were still exposed, A and C toons left their stars and drifted toward the near wall. They reached it together, and together jackknifed off the wall. At double the normal speed they appeared behind the enemy's stars, and opened fire. In a few seconds the battle was over, with the enemy almost entirely frozen, including the commander, and the rest scattered to the corners. For the next five minutes, in squads of four, Dragon Army cleaned out the dark corners of the battleroom and shepherded the enemy into the center, where their bodies, frozen at impossible angles, jostled each other. Then Ender took three of his boys to the enemy gate and went through the formality of reversing the one-way field by simultaneously touching a Dragon Army helmet at each corner. Then Ender assembled his army in vertical files near the knot of frozen Rabbit Army soldiers.

Only three of Dragon Army's soldiers were immobile. Their victory margin—38 to 0—was ridiculously high, and Ender began to laugh. Dragon Army joined him, laughing long and loud. They were still laughing when Lieutenant Anderson and Lieutenant Morris came in from the teachergate at the south end of the battleroom.

Lieutenant Anderson kept his face stiff and unsmiling, but Ender saw him wink as he held out his hand and offered the stiff, formal congratulations that were ritually given to the victor in the game.

Morris found Carn Carby and unfroze him, and the thirteen-year-old came and presented himself to Ender, who laughed without malice and held out his hand. Carn graciously took Ender's hand and bowed his head over it. It was that or be flashed again.

Lieutenant Anderson dismissed Dragon Army, and they silently left the battleroom through the enemy's door—again part of the ritual. A light was blinking on the north side of the square door, indicating where the gravity was in that corridor. Ender, leading his soldiers, changed his orientation and went through the force field and into gravity on his feet. His army followed him at a brisk run back to the workroom. When they got there they formed up into squads, and Ender hung in the air, watching them.

"Good first battle," he said, which was excuse enough for a cheer, which he quieted. "Dragon Army did all right against Rabbits. But the enemy isn't always going to be that bad. And if that had been a good army we would have been smashed. We still would have won, but we would have been smashed. Now let me see B and D toons out here.

Your takeoff from the stars was way too slow. If Rabbit Army knew how to aim a flasher, you all would have been frozen solid before A and C even got to the wall."

They worked out for the rest of the day.

That night Ender went for the first time to the commanders' mess hall. No one was allowed there until he had won at least one battle, and Ender was the youngest commander ever to make it. There was no great stir when he came in. But when some of the other boys saw the Dragon on his breast pocket, they stared at him openly, and by the time he got his tray and sat at an empty table, the entire room was silent, with the other commanders watching him. Intensely self-conscious, Ender wondered how they all knew, and why they all looked so hostile.

Then he looked above the door he had just come through. There was a huge scoreboard across the entire wall. It showed the win/loss record for the commander of every army; that day's battles were lit in red. Only four of them. The other three winners had barely made it—the best of them had only two men whole and eleven mobile at the end of the game. Dragon Army's score of thirty-eight mobile was embarrassingly better.

Other new commanders had been admitted to the commanders' mess hall with cheers and congratulations. Other new commanders hadn't won thirty-eight to zero.

Ender looked for Rabbit Army on the scoreboard. He was surprised to find that Carn Carby's score to date was eight wins and three losses. Was he that good? Or had he only fought against inferior armies? Whichever, there was still a zero in Carn's mobile and whole columns, and Ender looked down from the scoreboard grinning. No one smiled back, and Ender knew that they were afraid of him, which meant that they would hate him, which meant that anyone who went into battle against Dragon Army would be scared and angry and less competent. Ender looked for Carn Carby in the crowd, and found him not too far away. He stared at Carby until one of the other boys nudged the Rabbit commander and pointed to Ender. Ender smiled again and waved slightly. Carby turned red, and Ender, satisfied, leaned over his dinner and began to eat.

. . .

At the end of the week Dragon Army had fought seven battles in seven days. The score stood seven wins and zero losses. Ender had never had more than five boys frozen in any game. It was no longer possible for the other commanders to ignore Ender. A few of them sat with him and quietly conversed about game strategies that Ender's opponents had used. Other much larger groups were talking with the commanders that Ender had defeated, trying to find out what Ender had done to beat them.

In the middle of the meal the teacher door opened and the groups fell silent as Lieutenant Anderson stepped in and looked over the group. When he located Ender he strode quickly across the room and whispered in Ender's ear. Ender nodded, finished his glass of water, and left with the lieutenant. On the way out, Anderson handed a slip of paper to one of the older boys. The room became very noisy with conversation as Anderson and Ender left.

Ender was escorted down corridors he had never seen before. They didn't have the blue glow of the soldier corridors. Most were wood paneled, and the floors were carpeted. The doors were wood, with nameplates on them, and they stopped at one that said "Captain Graff, supervisor." Anderson knocked softly, and a low voice said, "Come in."

They went in. Captain Graff was seated behind a desk, his hands folded across his potbelly. He nodded, and Anderson sat. Ender also sat down. Graff cleared his throat and spoke.

"Seven days since your first battle, Ender."

Ender did not reply.

"Won seven battles, one every day."

Ender nodded.

"Scores unusually high, too."

Ender blinked.

"Why?" Graff asked him.

Ender glanced at Anderson, and then spoke to the captain behind the desk. "Two new tactics, sir. Legs doubled up as a shield, so that a flash doesn't immobilize. Jackknife takeoffs from the walls. Superior strategy, as Lieutenant Anderson taught, think places, not spaces. Five toons of eight instead of four of ten. Incompetent opponents. Excellent toon leaders, good soldiers."

Graff looked at Ender without expression. Waiting for what, Ender wondered. Lieutenant Anderson spoke up.

"Ender, what's the condition of your army?"

Do they want me to ask for relief? Not a chance, he decided. "A little tired, in peak condition, morale high, learning fast. Anxious for the next battle."

Anderson looked at Graff. Graff shrugged slightly and turned to Ender.

"Is there anything you want to know?"

Ender held his hands loosely in his lap. "When are you going to put us up against a good army?"

Graff's laughter rang in the room, and when it stopped, Graff handed a piece of paper to Ender. "Now," the captain said, and Ender read the paper. "Dragon Army against Leopard Army, Ender Wiggin and Pol Slattery, 2000."

Ender looked up at Captain Graff. "That's ten minutes from now, sir."

Graff smiled. "Better hurry, then, boy."

As Ender left he realized Pol Slattery was the boy who had been handed his orders as Ender left the mess hall.

He got to his army five minutes later. Three toon leaders were already undressed and lying naked on their beds. He sent them all flying down the corridors to rouse their toons, and gathered up their suits himself. When all his boys were assembled in the corridor, most of them still getting dressed, Ender spoke to them.

"This one's hot and there's no time. We'll be late to the door, and the enemy'll be deployed right outside our gate. Ambush, and I've never heard of it happening before. So we'll take our time at the door. A and B toons, keep your belts loose, and give your flashers to the leaders and seconds of the other toons."

Puzzled, his soldiers complied. By then all were dressed, and Ender led them at a trot to the gate. When they reached it the force field was already on one-way, and some of his soldiers were panting. They had had one battle that day and a full workout. They were tired.

Ender stopped at the entrance and looked at the placements of the enemy soldiers. Some of them were grouped not more than twenty feet out from the gate. There was no grid, there were no stars. A big empty space. Where were most of the enemy soldiers? There should have been thirty more.

"They're flat against this wall," Ender said, "where we can't see them."

He took A and B toons and made them kneel, their hands on their hips. Then he flashed them, so that their bodies were frozen rigid.

"You're shields," Ender said, and then had boys from C and D kneel on their legs and hook both arms under the frozen boys' belts. Each boy was holding two flashers. Then Ender and the members of E toon picked up the duos, three at a time, and threw them out the door.

Of course, the enemy opened fire immediately. But they mainly hit the boys who were already flashed, and in a few moments pandemonium broke out in the battleroom. All the soldiers of Leopard Army were easy targets as they lay pressed flat against the wall or floated, unprotected, in the middle of the battleroom; and Ender's soldiers, armed with two flashers each, carved them up easily. Pol Slattery reacted quickly, ordering his men away from the wall, but not quickly enough—only a few were able to move, and they were flashed before they could get a quarter of the way across the battleroom.

When the battle was over Dragon Army had only twelve boys whole, the lowest score they had ever had. But Ender was satisfied. And during the ritual of surrender Pol Slattery broke form by shaking hands and asking, "Why did you wait so long getting out of the gate?"

Ender glanced at Anderson, who was floating nearby. "I was informed late," he said. "It was an ambush."

Slattery grinned, and gripped Ender's hand again. "Good game."

Ender didn't smile at Anderson this time. He knew that now the games would be arranged against him, to even up the odds. He didn't like it.

It was 2150, nearly time for lights out, when Ender knocked at the door of the room shared by Bean and three other soldiers. One of the others opened the door, then stepped back and held it wide. Ender stood for a moment, then asked if he could come in. They answered, of course, of course, come in, and he walked to the upper bunk, where Bean had set down his book and was leaning on one elbow to look at Ender.

"Bean, can you give me twenty minutes?"

"Near lights out," Bean answered.

"My room," Ender answered. "I'll cover for you."

Bean sat up and slid off his bed. Together he and Ender padded silently down the corridor to Ender's room. Ender entered first, and Bean closed the door behind them.

"Sit down," Ender said, and they both sat on the edge of the bed, looking at each other.

"Remember four weeks ago, Bean? When you told me to make you a toon leader?"

"Yeah."

"I've made five toon leaders since then, haven't I? And none of them was you."

Bean looked at him calmly.

"Was I right?" Ender asked.

"Yes, sir," Bean answered.

Ender nodded. "How have you done in these battles?"

Bean cocked his head to one side. "I've never been immobilized, sir, and I've immobilized forty-three of the enemy. I've obeyed orders quickly, and I've commanded a squad in mop-up and never lost a soldier."

"Then you'll understand this." Ender paused, then decided to back up and say something else first.

"You know you're early, Bean, by a good half year. I was, too, and I've been made a commander six months early. Now they've put me into battles after only three weeks of training with my army. They've given me eight battles in seven days. I've already had more battles than boys who were made commander four months ago. I've won more battles than many who've been commanders for a year. And then tonight. You know what happened tonight."

Bean nodded. "They told you late."

"I don't know what the teachers are doing. But my army is getting tired, and I'm getting tired, and now they're changing the rules of the game. You see, Bean, I've looked in the old charts. No one has ever destroyed so many enemies and kept so many of his own soldiers whole in the history of the game. I'm unique—and I'm getting unique treatment."

Bean smiled. "You're the best, Ender."

Ender shook his head. "Maybe. But it was no accident that I got the soldiers I got. My worst soldier could be a toon leader in another army. I've got the best. They've loaded things my way—but now they're loading it all against me. I don't know why. But I know I have to be ready for it. I need your help."

"Why mine?"

"Because even though there are some better soldiers than you in Dragon Army—not many, but some—there's nobody who can think better and faster than you." Bean said nothing. They both knew it was true.

Ender continued. "I need to be ready, but I can't retrain the whole army. So I'm going to cut every toon down by one, including you. With four others you'll be a special squad under me. And you'll learn to do some new things. Most of the time you'll be in the regular toons just like you are now. But when I need you. See?"

Bean smiled and nodded. "That's right, that's good, can I pick them myself?"

"One from each toon except your own, and you can't take any toon leaders."

"What do you want us to do?"

"Bean, I don't know. I don't know what they'll throw at us. What would you do if suddenly our flashers didn't work, and the enemy's did? What would you do if we had to face two armies at once? The only thing I know is—there may be a game where we don't even try for score. Where we just go for the enemy's gate. I want you ready to do that any time I call for it. Got it? You take them for two hours a day during regular workout. Then you and I and your soldiers, we'll work at night after dinner."

"We'll get tired."

"I have a feeling we don't know what tired is." Ender reached out and took Bean's hand, and gripped it. "Even when it's rigged against us, Bean. We'll win."

Bean left in silence and padded down the corridor.

Dragon Army wasn't the only army working out after hours now. The other commanders had finally realized they had some catching up to do. From early morning to lights out soldiers all over Training and

Command Center, none of them over fourteen years old, were learning to jackknife off walls and use each other as shields.

But while other commanders mastered the techniques that Ender had used to defeat them, Ender and Bean worked on solutions to problems that had never come up.

There were still battles every day, but for a while they were normal, with grids and stars and sudden plunges through the gate. And after the battles, Ender and Bean and four other soldiers would leave the main group and practice strange maneuvers. Attacks without flashers, using feet to physically disarm or disorient an enemy. Using four frozen soldiers to reverse the enemy's gate in less than two seconds. And one day Bean came in to workout with a thirty-meter cord.

"What's that for?"

"I don't know yet." Absently Bean spun one end of the cord. It wasn't more than an eighth of an inch thick, but it would have lifted ten adults without breaking.

"Where did you get it?"

"Commissary. They asked what for. I said to practice tying knots."

Bean tied a loop in the end of the rope and slid it over his shoulders.

"Here, you two, hang on to the wall here. Now don't let go of the rope. Give me about fifty yards of slack." They complied, and Bean moved about ten feet from them along the wall. As soon as he was sure they were ready, he jackknifed off the wall and flew straight out, fifty yards. Then the rope snapped taut. It was so fine that it was virtually invisible, but it was strong enough to force Bean to veer off at almost a right angle. It happened so suddenly that he had inscribed a perfect arc and hit the wall hard before most of the other soldiers knew what had happened. Bean did a perfect rebound and drifted quickly back to where Ender and the others waited for him.

Many of the soldiers in the five regular squads hadn't noticed the rope, and were demanding to know how it was done. It was impossible to change direction that abruptly in nullo. Bean just laughed.

"Wait till the next game without a grid! They'll never know what hit them."

They never did. The next game was only two hours later, but Bean and two others had become pretty good at aiming and shooting while they flew at ridiculous speeds at the end of the rope. The slip of paper was delivered, and Dragon Army trotted off to the gate, to battle with Griffin Army. Bean coiled the rope all the way.

When the gate opened, all they could see was a large brown star only fifteen feet away, completely blocking their view of the enemy's gate.

Ender didn't pause. "Bean, give yourself fifty feet of rope and go around the star." Bean and his four soldiers dropped through the gate and in a moment Bean was launched sideways away from the star. The rope snapped taut, and Bean flew forward. As the rope was stopped by each edge of the star in turn, his arc became tighter and his speed greater, until when he hit the wall only a few feet away from the gate he was barely able to control his rebound to end up behind the star. But he immediately moved all his arms and legs so that those waiting inside the gate would know that the enemy hadn't flashed him anywhere.

Ender dropped through the gate, and Bean quickly told him how Griffin Army was situated. "They've got two squares of stars, all the way around the gate. All their soldiers are under cover, and there's no way to hit any of them until we're clear to the bottom wall. Even with shields, we'd get there at half strength and we wouldn't have a chance."

"They moving?" Ender asked.

"Do they need to?"

"I would." Ender thought for a moment. "This one's tough. We'll go for the gate, Bean."

Griffin Army began to call out to them.

"Hey, is anybody there?"

"Wake up, there's a war on!"

"We wanna join the picnic!"

They were still calling when Ender's army came out from behind their star with a shield of fourteen frozen soldiers. William Bee, Griffin Army's commander, waited patiently as the screen approached, his men waiting at the fringes of their stars for the moment when whatever was behind the screen became visible. About ten yards away, the screen suddenly exploded as the soldiers behind it shoved the screen north. The momentum carried them south twice as fast, and at the same moment the rest of Dragon Army burst from behind their star at the opposite end of the room, firing rapidly.

William Bee's boys joined battle immediately, of course, but William Bee was far more interested in what had been left behind when the shield disappeared. A formation of four frozen Dragon Army soldiers were moving headfirst toward the Griffin Army gate, held together by another frozen soldier whose feet and hands were hooked through their belts. A sixth soldier hung to the waist and trailed like the tail of a kite. Griffin Army was winning the battle easily, and William Bee concentrated on the formation as it approached the gate. Suddenly the soldier trailing in back moved—he wasn't frozen at all! And even though William Bee flashed him immediately, the damage was done. The format drifted in the Griffin Army gate, and their helmets touched all four corners simultaneously. A buzzer sounded, the gate reversed, and the frozen soldiers in the middle were carried by momentum right through the gate. All the flashers stopped working, and the game was over.

The teachergate opened and Lieutenant Anderson came in. Anderson stopped himself with a slight movement of his hands when he reached the center of the battleroom. "Ender," he called, breaking protocol. One of the frozen Dragon soldiers near the south wall tried to call through jaws that were clamped shut by the suit. Anderson drifted to him and unfroze him.

Ender was smiling.

"I beat you again, sir," Ender said.

Anderson didn't smile. "That's nonsense, Ender," Anderson said softly. "Your battle was with William Bee of Griffin Army."

Ender raised an eyebrow.

"After that maneuver," Anderson said, "the rules are being revised to require that all of the enemy's soldiers must be immobilized before the gate can be reversed."

"That's all right," Ender said. "It could only work once anyway." Anderson nodded, and was turning away when Ender added, "Is there going to be a new rule that armies be given equal positions to fight from?"

Anderson turned back around. "If you're in one of the positions, Ender, you can hardly call them equal, whatever they are."

William Bee counted carefully and wondered how in the world he had lost when not one of his soldiers had been flashed and only four of Ender's soldiers were even mobile.

And that night as Ender came into the commanders' mess hall, he was greeted with applause and cheers, and his table was crowded with respectful commanders, many of them two or three years older than he was. He was friendly, but while he ate he wondered what the teachers would do to him in his next battle. He didn't need to worry. His next two battles were easy victories, and after that he never saw the battleroom again.

It was 2100 and Ender was a little irritated to hear someone knock at his door. His army was exhausted, and he had ordered them all to be in bed after 2030. The last two days had been regular battles, and Ender was expecting the worst in the morning.

It was Bean. He came in sheepishly, and saluted.

Ender returned his salute and snapped. "Bean, I wanted everybody in bed."

Bean nodded but didn't leave. Ender considered ordering him out. But as he looked at Bean, it occurred to him for the first time in weeks just how young Bean was. He had turned eight a week before, and he was still small and—no, Ender thought, he wasn't young. Nobody was young. Bean had been in battle, and with a whole army depending on him he had come through and won. And even though he was small, Ender could never think of him as young again.

Ender shrugged and Bean came over and sat on the edge of the bed. The younger boy looked at his hands for a while, and finally Ender grew impatient and asked, "Well, what is it?"

"I'm transferred. Got orders just a few minutes ago."

Ender closed his eyes for a moment. "I knew they'd pull something new. Now they're taking—where are you going?"

"Rabbit Army."

"How can they put you under an idiot like Carn Carby!"

"Carn was graduated. Support squad."

Ender looked up. "Well, who's commanding Rabbit, then?"

Bean held his hands out helplessly.

"Me," he said.

Ender nodded, and then smiled. "Of course. After all, you're only four years younger than the regular age."

"It isn't funny," Bean said. "I don't know what's going on here. First all the changes in the game. And now this. I wasn't the only one transferred, either, Ender. Ren, Peder, Brian, Wins, Younger. All commanders now."

Ender stood up angrily and strode to the wall. "Every damn toon leader I've got!" he said, and whirled to face Bean. "If they're going to break up my army, Bean, why did they bother making me a commander at all?"

Bean shook his head. "I don't know. You're the best, Ender. Nobody's ever done what you've done. Nineteen battles in fifteen days, sir, and you won every one of them, no matter what they did to you."

"And now you and the others are commanders. You know every trick I've got, I trained you, and who am I supposed to replace you with? Are they going to stick me with six greenohs?"

"It stinks, Ender, but you know that if they gave you five crippled midgets and armed you with a roll of toilet paper you'd win."

They both laughed, and then they noticed that the door was open.

Lieutenant Anderson stepped in. He was followed by Captain Graff.

"Ender Wiggin," Graff said, holding his hands across his stomach.

"Yes, sir," Ender answered.

"Orders."

Anderson extended a slip of paper. Ender read it quickly, then crumpled it, still looking at the air where the paper had been. After a few minutes he asked, "Can I tell my army?"

"They'll find out," Graff answered. "It's better not to talk to them after orders. It makes it easier."

"For you or for me?" Ender asked. He didn't wait for an answer. He turned quickly to Bean, took his hand for a moment, and then headed for the door.

"Wait," Bean said. "Where are you going? Tactical or Support School?"

"Command School," Ender answered, and then he was gone and Anderson closed the door.

Command School, Bean thought. Nobody went to Command School until they had gone through three years of Tactical. But then, nobody went to Tactical until they had been through at least five years of Battle School. Ender had only had three.

The system was breaking up. No doubt about it, Bean thought. Either somebody at the top was going crazy, or something was going wrong with the war—the real war, the one they were training to fight in. Why else would they break down the training system, advance somebody—even somebody as good as Ender—straight to Command School? Why else would they ever have an eight-year-old greenoh like Bean command an army?

Bean wondered about it for a long time, and then he finally lay down on Ender's bed and realized that he'd never see Ender again, probably. For some reason that made him want to cry. But he didn't cry, of course. Training in the preschools had taught him how to force down emotions like that. He remembered how his first teacher, when he was three, would have been upset to see his lip quivering and his eyes full of tears.

Bean went through the relaxing routine until he didn't feel like crying anymore. Then he drifted off to sleep. His hand was near his mouth. It lay on his pillow hesitantly, as if Bean couldn't decide whether to bite his nails or suck on his fingertips. His forehead was creased and furrowed. His breathing was quick and light. He was a soldier, and if anyone had asked him what he wanted to be when he grew up, he wouldn't have known what they meant.

There's a war on, they said, and that was excuse enough for all the hurry in the world. They said it like a password and flashed a little card at every ticket counter and customs check and guard station. It got them to the head of every line.

Ender Wiggin was rushed from place to place so quickly he had no time to examine anything. But he did see trees for the first time. He saw men who were not in uniform. He saw women. He saw strange animals that didn't speak, but that followed docilely behind women and small children. He saw suitcases and conveyor belts and signs that said words he had never heard of. He would have asked someone what the words meant, except that purpose and authority surrounded him in the persons of four very high officers who never spoke to each other and never spoke to him.

Ender Wiggin was a stranger to the world he was being trained to save. He did not remember ever leaving Battle School before. His earliest memories were of childish war games under the direction of a teacher, of meals with other boys in the gray and green uniforms of the armed forces of his world. He did not know that the gray represented the sky and the green represented the great forests of his planet. All he knew of the world was from vague references to "outside."

And before he could make any sense of the strange world he was seeing for the first time, they enclosed him again within the shell of the military, where nobody had to say "There's a war on" anymore because no one within the shell of the military forgot it for a single instant of a single day.

They put him in a spaceship and launched him to a large artificial satellite that circled the world.

This space station was called Command School. It held the ansible.

On his first day Ender Wiggin was taught about the ansible and what it meant to warfare. It meant that even though the starships of today's battles were launched a hundred years ago, the commanders of the starships were men of today, who used the ansible to send messages to the computers and the few men on each ship. The ansible sent words as they were spoken, orders as they were made. Battle plans as they were fought. Light was a pedestrian.

For two months Ender Wiggin didn't meet a single person. They came to him namelessly, taught him what they knew, and left him to other teachers. He had no time to miss his friends at Battle School. He only had time to learn how to operate the simulator, which flashed battle patterns around him as if he were in a starship at the center of the battle. How to command mock ships in mock battles by manipulating the keys on the simulator and speaking words into the ansible. How to recognize instantly every enemy ship and the weapons it carried by the pattern that the simulator showed. How to transfer all that he learned in the nullo battles at Battle School to the starship battles at Command School.

He had thought the game was taken seriously before. Here they hurried him through every step, were angry and worried beyond reason every time he forgot something or made a mistake. But he worked as he had always worked, and learned as he had always learned. After a while he didn't make any more mistakes. He used the simulator as if it were a part of himself. Then they stopped being worried and gave him a teacher.

. . .

Mazer Rackham was sitting cross-legged on the floor when Ender awoke. He said nothing as Ender got up and showered and dressed, and Ender did not bother to ask him anything. He had long since learned that when something unusual was going on, he would often find out more information faster by waiting than by asking.

Mazer still hadn't spoken when Ender was ready and went to the door to leave the room. The door didn't open. Ender turned to face the man sitting on the floor. Mazer was at least forty, which made him the oldest man Ender had ever seen close up. He had a day's growth of black and white whiskers that grizzled his face only slightly less than his close-cut hair. His face sagged a little and his eyes were surrounded by creases and lines. He looked at Ender without interest.

Ender turned back to the door and tried again to open it.

"All right," he said, giving up. "Why's the door locked?"

Mazer continued to look at him blankly.

Ender became impatient. "I'm going to be late. If I'm not supposed to be there until later, then tell me so I can go back to bed." No answer. "Is it a guessing game?" Ender asked. No answer. Ender decided that maybe the man was trying to make him angry, so he went through a relaxing exercise as he leaned on the door, and soon he was calm again. Mazer didn't take his eyes off Ender.

For the next two hours the silence endured. Mazer watching Ender constantly, Ender trying to pretend he didn't notice the old man. The boy became more and more nervous, and finally ended up walking from one end of the room to the other in a sporadic pattern.

He walked by Mazer as he had several times before, and Mazer's hand shot out and pushed Ender's left leg into his right in the middle of a step. Ender fell flat on the floor.

He leaped to his feet immediately, furious. He found Mazer sitting calmly, cross-legged, as if he had never moved. Ender stood poised to fight. But the man's immobility made it impossible for Ender to attack, and he found himself wondering if he had only imagined the old man's hand tripping him up.

The pacing continued for another hour, with Ender Wiggin trying the door every now and then. At last he gave up and took off his uniform and walked to his bed.

As he leaned over to pull the covers back, he felt a hand jab roughly between his thighs and another hand grab his hair. In a moment he had been turned upside down. His face and shoulders were being pressed into the floor by the old man's knee, while his back was excruciatingly bent and his legs were pinioned by Mazer's arm. Ender was helpless to use his arms, and he couldn't bend his back to gain slack so he could use his legs. In less than two seconds the old man had completely defeated Ender Wiggin.

"All right," Ender gasped. "You win."

Mazer's knee thrust painfully downward.

"Since when," Mazer asked in a soft, rasping voice, "do you have to tell the enemy when he has won?"

Ender remained silent.

"I surprised you once, Ender Wiggin. Why didn't you destroy me immediately? Just because I looked peaceful? You turned your back on me. Stupid. You have learned nothing. You have never had a teacher."

Ender was angry now. "I've had too many damned teachers, how was I supposed to know you'd turn out to be a—" Ender hunted for the word. Mazer supplied one.

"An enemy, Ender Wiggin," Mazer whispered. "I am your enemy, the first one you've ever had who was smarter than you. There is no teacher but the enemy, Ender Wiggin. No one but the enemy will ever tell you what the enemy is going to do. No one but the enemy will ever teach you how to destroy and conquer. I am your enemy, from now on. From now on I am your teacher."

Then Mazer let Ender's legs fall to the floor. Because the old man still held Ender's head to the floor, the boy couldn't use his arms to compensate, and his legs hit the plastic surface with a loud crack and a sickening pain that made Ender wince. Then Mazer stood and let Ender rise.

Slowly the boy pulled his legs under him, with a faint groan of pain, and he knelt on all fours for a moment, recovering. Then his right arm flashed out. Mazer quickly danced back and Ender's hand closed on air as his teacher's foot shot forward to catch Ender on the chin.

Ender's chin wasn't there. He was lying flat on his back, spinning on the floor, and during the moment that Mazer was off balance from his kick Ender's feet smashed into Mazer's other leg. The old man fell on the ground in a heap.

What seemed to be a heap was really a hornet's nest. Ender couldn't find an arm or a leg that held still long enough to be grabbed, and in the meantime blows were landing on his back and arms. Ender was smaller—he couldn't reach past the old man's flailing limbs.

So he leaped back out of the way and stood poised near the door.

The old man stopped thrashing about and sat up, cross-legged again, laughing. "Better, this time, boy. But slow. You will have to be better with a fleet than you are with your body or no one will be safe with you in command. Lesson learned?"

Ender nodded slowly.

Mazer smiled. "Good. Then we'll never have such a battle again. All the rest with the simulator. I will program your battles, I will devise the strategy of your enemy, and you will learn to be quick and discover what tricks the enemy has for you. Remember, boy. From now on the enemy is more clever than you. From now on the enemy is stronger than you. From now on you are always about to lose."

Then Mazer's face became serious again. "You will be about to lose, Ender, but you will win. You will learn to defeat the enemy. He will teach you how."

Mazer got up and walked to the door. Ender stepped out of the way. As the old man touched the handle of the door, Ender leaped into the air and kicked Mazer in the small of the back with both feet. He hit hard enough that he rebounded onto his feet, as Mazer cried out and collapsed on the floor.

Mazer got up slowly, holding on to the door handle, his face contorted with pain. He seemed disabled, but Ender didn't trust him. He waited warily. And yet in spite of his suspicion he was caught off guard by Mazer's speed. In a moment he found himself on the floor near the opposite wall, his nose and lip bleeding where his face had hit the bed. He was able to turn enough to see Mazer open the door and leave. The old man was limping and walking slowly.

Ender smiled in spite of the pain, then rolled over onto his back and laughed until his mouth filled with blood and he started to gag. Then he got up and painfully made his way to his bed. He lay down and in a few minutes a medic came and took care of his injuries.

As the drug had its effect and Ender drifted off to sleep he remembered the way Mazer limped out of his room and laughed again. He was still laughing softly as his mind went blank and the medic pulled the blanket over him and snapped off the light. He slept until pain woke him in the morning. He dreamed of defeating Mazer.

The next day Ender went to the simulator room with his nose bandaged and his lip still puffy. Mazer was not there. Instead, a captain who had worked with him before showed him an addition that had been made. The captain pointed to a tube with a loop at one end. "Radio. Primitive, I know, but it loops over your ear and we tuck the other end into your mouth like this."

"Watch it," Ender said as the captain pushed the end of the tube into his swollen lip.

"Sorry. Now you just talk."

"Good. Who to?"

The captain smiled. "Ask and see."

Ender shrugged and turned to the simulator. As he did a voice reverberated through his skull. It was too loud for him to understand, and he ripped the radio off his ear.

"What are you trying to do, make me deaf?"

The captain shook his head and turned a dial on a small box on a nearby table. Ender put the radio back on.

"Commander," the radio said in a familiar voice.

Ender answered, "Yes."

"Instructions, sir?"

The voice was definitely familiar. "Bean?" Ender asked.

"Yes, sir."

"Bean, this is Ender."

Silence. And then a burst of laughter from the other side. Then six or seven more voices laughing, and Ender waited for silence to return. When it did, he asked, "Who else?"

A few voices spoke at once, but Bean drowned them out. "Me, I'm Bean, and Peder, Wins, Younger, Lee, and Vlad."

Ender thought for a moment. Then he asked what the hell was going on. They laughed again.

"They can't break up the group," Bean said. "We were commanders for maybe two weeks, and here we are at Command School, training with the simulator, and all of a sudden they told us we were going to form a fleet with a new commander. And that's you."

Ender smiled. "Are you boys any good?"

"If we aren't, you'll let us know."

Ender chuckled a little. "Might work out. A fleet."

For the next ten days Ender trained his toon leaders until they could maneuver their ships like precision dancers. It was like being back in the battleroom again, except that now Ender could always see everything, and could speak to his toon leaders and change their orders at any time.

One day as Ender sat down at the control board and switched on the simulator, harsh green lights appeared in the space—the enemy.

"This is it," Ender said. "X, Y, bullet, C, D, reserve screen, E, south loop, Bean, angle north."

The enemy was grouped in a globe, and outnumbered Ender two to one. Half of Ender's force was grouped in a tight, bulletlike formation, with the rest in a flat circular screen—except for a tiny force under Bean that moved off the simulator, heading behind the enemy's formation. Ender quickly learned the enemy's strategy: whenever Ender's bullet formation came close, the enemy would give way, hoping to draw Ender inside the globe where he would be surrounded. So Ender obligingly fell into the trap, bringing his bullet to the center of the globe.

The enemy began to contract slowly, not wanting to come within range until all their weapons could be brought to bear at once. Then Ender began to work in earnest. His reserve screen approached the outside of the globe, and the enemy began to concentrate his forces there. Then Bean's force appeared on the opposite side, and the enemy again deployed ships on that side.

Which left most of the globe only thinly defended. Ender's bullet attacked, and since at the point of attack it outnumbered the enemy overwhelmingly, he tore a hole in the formation. The enemy reacted to try to plug the gap, but in the confusion the reserve force and Bean's small force attacked simultaneously, while the bullet moved to another part of the globe. In a few more minutes the formation was shattered, most of the enemy ships destroyed, and the few survivors rushing away as fast as they could go.

Ender switched the simulator off. All the lights faded. Mazer was standing beside Ender, his hands in his pockets, his body tense. Ender looked up at him.

"I thought you said the enemy would be smart," Ender said.

Mazer's face remained expressionless. "What did you learn?"

"I learned that a sphere only works if your enemy's a fool. He had his forces so spread out that I outnumbered him whenever I engaged him."

"And?"

"And," Ender said, "you can't stay committed to one pattern. It makes you too easy to predict."

"Is that all?" Mazer asked quietly.

Ender took off his radio. "The enemy could have defeated me by breaking the sphere earlier."

Mazer nodded. "You had an unfair advantage."

Ender looked up at him coldly. "I was outnumbered two to one."

Mazer shook his head. "You have the ansible. The enemy doesn't. We include that in the mock battles. Their messages travel at the speed of light."

Ender glanced toward the simulator. "Is there enough space to make a difference?"

"Don't you know?" Mazer asked. "None of the ships was ever closer than thirty thousand kilometers to any other."

Ender tried to figure the size of the enemy's sphere. Astronomy was beyond him. But now his curiosity was stirred.

"What kind of weapons are on those ships? To be able to strike so fast?"

Mazer shook his head. "The science is too much for you. You'd have to study many more years than you've lived to understand even the basics. All you need to know is that the weapons work."

"Why do we have to come so close to be in range?"

"The ships are all protected by force fields. A certain distance away the weapons are weaker and can't get through. Closer in the weapons are stronger than the shields. But the computers take care of all that. They're constantly firing in any direction that won't hurt one of our ships. The computers pick targets, aim; they do all the detail work. You just tell them when and get them in a position to win. All right?"

"No," Ender twisted the tube of the radio around his fingers. "I have to know how the weapons work."

"I told you, it would take—"

"I can't command a fleet—not even on the simulator—unless I know." Ender waited a moment, then added, "Just the rough idea."

Mazer stood up and walked a few steps away. "All right, Ender. It won't make any sense, but I'll try. As simply as I can." He shoved his hands into his pockets. "It's this way, Ender. Everything is made up of atoms, little particles so small you can't see them with your eyes. These atoms, there are only a few different types, and they're all made up of even smaller particles that are pretty much the same. These atoms can be broken, so that they stop being atoms. So that this metal doesn't hold together anymore. Or the plastic floor. Or your body. Or even the air. They just seem to disappear, if you break the atoms. All that's left is the pieces. And they fly around and break more atoms. The weapons on the ships set up an area where it's impossible for atoms of anything to stay together. They all break down. So things in that area—they disappear."

Ender nodded. "You're right, I don't understand it. Can it be blocked?"

"No. But it gets wider and weaker the farther it goes from the ship, so that after a while a force field will block it. OK? And to make it strong at all, it has to be focused so that a ship can only fire effectively in maybe three or four directions at once."

Ender nodded again, but he didn't really understand, not well enough. "If the pieces of the broken atoms go breaking more atoms, why doesn't it just make everything disappear?"

"Space. Those thousands of kilometers between the ships, they're empty. Almost no atoms. The pieces don't hit anything, and when they finally do hit something, they're so spread out they can't do any harm." Mazer cocked his head quizzically. "Anything else you need to know?"

"Do the weapons on the ships—do they work against anything besides ships?"

Mazer moved in close to Ender and said firmly, "We only use them against ships. Never anything else. If we used them against anything else, the enemy would use them against us. Got it?"

Mazer walked away, and was nearly out the door when Ender called to him.

"I don't know your name yet," Ender said blandly.

"Mazer Rackham."

"Mazer Rackham," Ender said, "I defeated you."

Mazer laughed.

"Ender, you weren't fighting me today," he said. "You were fighting the stupidest computer in the Command School, set on a ten-year-old program. You don't think I'd use a sphere, do you?" He shook his head. "Ender, my dear little fellow, when you fight me, you'll know it. Because you'll lose." And Mazer left the room.

Ender still practiced ten hours a day with his toon leaders. He never saw them, though, only heard their voices on the radio. Battles came every two or three days. The enemy had something new every time, something harder—but Ender coped with it. And won every time. And after every battle Mazer would point out mistakes and show Ender that he had really lost. Mazer only let Ender finish so that he would learn to handle the end of the game.

Until finally Mazer came in and solemnly shook Ender's hand and said, "That, boy, was a good battle."

Because the praise was so long in coming, it pleased Ender more than praise had ever pleased him before. And because it was so condescending, he resented it.

"So from now on," Mazer said, "we can give you hard ones."

From then on Ender's life was a slow nervous breakdown.

He began fighting two battles a day, with problems that steadily grew more difficult. He had been trained in nothing but the game all his life, but now the game began to consume him. He woke in the morning with new strategies for the simulator and went fitfully to sleep at night with the mistakes of the day preying on him. Sometimes he would wake up in the middle of the night crying for a reason he didn't remember. Sometimes he woke up with his knuckles bloody from biting them. But every day he went impassively to the simulator and drilled his toon leaders until the battles, and drilled his toon leaders after the battles, and endured and studied the harsh criticism that Rackham piled on him. He noted that Rackham perversely criticized him more after his hardest battles. He noted that every time he thought of a new strategy the enemy was using it within a few days. And he noted that while his fleet always stayed the same size, the enemy increased in numbers every day.

He asked his teacher.

"We are showing you what it will be like when you really command. The ratios of enemy to us."

"Why does the enemy always outnumber us?"

Mazer bowed his gray head for a moment, as if deciding whether to answer. Finally he looked up and reached out his hand and touched Ender on the shoulder. "I will tell you, even though the information is secret. You see, the enemy attacked us first. He had good reason to attack us, but that is a matter for politicians, and whether the fault was ours or his, we could not let him win. So when the enemy came to our worlds, we fought back, hard, and spent the finest of our young men in the fleets. But we won, and the enemy retreated."

Mazer smiled ruefully. "But the enemy was not through, boy. The enemy would never be through. They came again, with more numbers, and it was harder to beat them. And another generation of young men was spent. Only a few survived. So we came up with a plan—the big men came up with the plan. We knew that we had to destroy the enemy once and for all, totally, eliminate his ability to make war against us. To do that we had to go to his home worlds—his home world, really, since the enemy's empire is all tied to his capital world."

"And so?" Ender asked.

"And so we made a fleet. We made more ships than the enemy ever had. We made a hundred ships for every ship he had sent against us. And we launched them against his twenty-eight worlds. They started leaving a hundred years ago. And they carried on them the ansible, and only a few men. So that someday a commander could sit on a planet somewhere far from the battle and command the fleet. So that our best minds would not be destroyed by the enemy."

Ender's questions had still not been answered. "Why do they outnumber us?"

Mazer laughed. "Because it took a hundred years for our ships to get there. They've had a hundred years to prepare for us. They'd be fools, don't you think, boy, if they waited in old tugboats to defend their harbors. They have new ships, great ships, hundreds of ships. All we have is the ansible, that and the fact that they have to put a commander with every fleet, and when they lose—and they will lose— they lose one of their best minds every time."

Ender started to ask another question.

"No more, Ender Wiggin. I've told you more than you ought to know as it is."

Ender stood angrily and turned away. "I have a right to know. Do you think this can go on forever, pushing me through one school and another and never telling me what my life is for? You use me and the others as a tool, someday we'll command your ships, someday maybe we'll save your lives, but I'm not a computer, and I have to *know!*"

"Ask me a question, then, boy," Mazer said, "and if I can answer, I will."

"If you use your best minds to command the fleets, and you never lose any, then what do you need me for? Who am I replacing, if they're all still there?"

Mazer shook his head. "I can't tell you the answer to that, Ender. Be content that we will need you, soon. It's late. Go to bed. You have a battle in the morning."

Ender walked out of the simulator room. But when Mazer left by the same door a few moments later, the boy was waiting in the hall.

"All right, boy," Mazer said impatiently, "what is it? I don't have all night and you need to sleep."

Ender wasn't sure what his question was, but Mazer waited. Finally Ender asked softly, "Do they live?"

"Do who live?"

"The other commanders. The ones now. And before me."

Mazer snorted. "Live. Of course they live. He wonders if they live." Still chuckling, the old man walked off down the hall. Ender stood in the corridor for a while, but at last he was tired and he went off to bed. They live, he thought. They live, but he can't tell me what happens to them.

That night Ender didn't wake up crying. But he did wake up with blood on his hands.

Months wore on with battles every day, until at last Ender settled into the routine of the destruction of himself. He slept less every night, dreamed more, and he began to have terrible pains in his stomach. They put him on a very bland diet, but soon he didn't even have an appetite for that. "Eat," Mazer said, and Ender would mechanically put food in his mouth. But if nobody told him to eat he didn't eat.

One day as he was drilling his toon leaders the room went black and he woke up on the floor with his face bloody where he had hit the controls.

ORSON SCOTT CARD

334

They put him to bed then, and for three days he was very ill. He remembered seeing faces in his dreams, but they weren't real faces, and he knew it even while he thought he saw them. He thought he saw Bean sometimes, and sometimes he thought he saw Lieutenant Anderson and Captain Graff. And then he woke up and it was only his enemy, Mazer Rackham.

"I'm awake," he said to Mazer Rackham.

"So I see," Mazer answered. "Took you long enough. You have a battle today."

So Ender got up and fought the battle and he won it. But there was no second battle that day, and they let him go to bed earlier. His hands were shaking as he undressed.

During the night he thought he felt hands touching him gently, and he dreamed he heard voices saying, "How long can he go on?"

"Long enough."

"So soon?"

"In a few days, then he's through."

"How will he do?"

"Fine. Even today, he was better than ever."

Ender recognized the last voice as Mazer Rackham's. He resented Rackham's intruding even in his sleep.

He woke up and fought another battle and won.

Then he went to bed.

He woke up and won again.

And the next day was his last day in Command School, though he didn't know it. He got up and went to the simulator for the battle.

Mazer was waiting for him. Ender walked slowly into the simulator room. His step was slightly shuffling, and he seemed tired and dull. Mazer frowned.

"Are you awake, boy?" If Ender had been alert, he would have cared more about the concern in his teacher's voice. Instead, he simply went to the controls and sat down. Mazer spoke to him.

"Today's game needs a little explanation, Ender Wiggin. Please turn around and pay strict attention."

Ender turned around, and for the first time he noticed that there were people at the back of the room. He recognized Graff and

Anderson from Battle School, and vaguely remembered a few of the men from Command School—teachers for a few hours at some time or another. But most of the people he didn't know at all.

"Who are they?"

Mazer shook his head and answered, "Observers. Every now and then we let observers come in to watch the battle. If you don't want them, we'll send them out."

Ender shrugged. Mazer began his explanation. "Today's game, boy, has a new element. We're staging this battle around a planet. This will complicate things in two ways. The planet isn't large, on the scale we're using, but the ansible can't detect anything on the other side of it—so there's a blind spot. Also, it's against the rules to use weapons against the planet itself. All right?"

"Why, don't the weapons work against planets?"

Mazer answered coldly, "There are rules of war, Ender, that apply even in training games."

Ender shook his head slowly. "Can the planet attack?"

Mazer looked nonplussed for a moment, then smiled. "I guess you'll have to find that one out, boy. And one more thing. Today, Ender, your opponent isn't the computer. I am your enemy today, and today I won't be letting you off so easily. Today is a battle to the end. And I'll use any means I can to defeat you."

Then Mazer was gone, and Ender expressionlessly led his toon leaders through maneuvers. Ender was doing well, of course, but several of the observers shook their heads, and Graff kept clasping and unclasping his hands, crossing and uncrossing his legs. Ender would be slow today, and today Ender couldn't afford to be slow.

A warning buzzer sounded, and Ender cleared the simulator board, waiting for today's game to appear. He felt muddled today, and wondered why people were there watching. Were they going to judge him today? Decide if he was good enough for something else? For another two years of grueling training, another two years of struggling to exceed his best? Ender was twelve. He felt very old. And as he waited for the game to appear, he wished he could simply lose it, lose the battle badly and completely so that they would remove him from the program, punish him however they wanted, he didn't care, just so he could sleep.

Then the enemy formation appeared, and Ender's weariness turned to desperation.

The enemy outnumbered them a thousand to one, the simulator glowed green with them, and Ender knew that he couldn't win.

And the enemy was not stupid. There was no formation that Ender could study and attack. Instead the vast swarms of ships were constantly moving, constantly shifting from one momentary formation to another, so that a space that for one moment was empty was immediately filled with a formidable enemy force. And even though Ender's fleet was the largest he had ever had, there was no place he could deploy it where he would outnumber the enemy long enough to accomplish anything.

And behind the enemy was the planet. The planet, which Mazer had warned him about. What difference did a planet make, when Ender couldn't hope to get near it? Ender waited, waited for the flash of insight that would tell him what to do, how to destroy the enemy. And as he waited, he heard the observers behind him begin to shift in their seats, wondering what Ender was doing, what plan he would follow. And finally it was obvious to everyone that Ender didn't know what to do, that there was nothing to do, and a few of the men at the back of the room made quiet little sounds in their throats.

Then Ender heard Bean's voice in his ear. Bean chuckled and said, "Remember, the enemy's gate is *down*." A few of the other toon leaders laughed, and Ender thought back to the simple games he had played and won in Battle School. They had put him against hopeless odds there, too. And he had beaten them. And he'd be damned if he'd let Mazer Rackham beat him with a cheap trick like outnumbering him a thousand to one. He had won a game in Battle School by going for something the enemy didn't expect, something against the rules—he had won by going against the enemy's gate.

And the enemy's gate was down.

Ender smiled, and realized that if he broke this rule they'd probably kick him out of school, and that way he'd win for sure. He would never have to play a game again.

He whispered into the microphone. His six commanders each took a part of the fleet and launched themselves against the enemy. They pursued erratic courses, darting off in one direction and then another.

The enemy immediately stopped his aimless maneuvering and began to group around Ender's six fleets.

Ender took off his microphone, leaned back in his chair, and watched. The observers murmured out loud, now. Ender was doing nothing—he had thrown the game away.

But a pattern began to emerge from the quick confrontations with the enemy. Ender's six groups lost ships constantly as they brushed with each enemy force—but they never stopped for a fight, even when for a moment they could have won a small tactical victory. Instead they continued on their erratic course that led, eventually, down. Toward the enemy planet.

And because of their seemingly random course the enemy didn't realize it until the same time that the observers did. By then it was too late, just as it had been too late for William Bee to stop Ender's soldiers from activating the gate. More of Ender's ships could be hit and destroyed, so that of the six fleets only two were able to get to the planet, and those were decimated. But those tiny groups *did* get through, and they opened fire on the planet.

Ender leaned forward now, anxious to see if his guess would pay off. He half expected a buzzer to sound and the game to be stopped, because he had broken the rule. But he was betting on the accuracy of the simulator. If it could simulate a planet, it could simulate what would happen to a planet under attack.

It did.

The weapons that blew up little ships didn't blow up the entire planet at first. But they did cause terrible explosions. And on the planet there was no space to dissipate the chain reaction. On the planet the chain reaction found more and more fuel to feed it.

The planet's surface seemed to be moving back and forth, but soon the surface gave way to an immense explosion that sent light flashing in all directions. It swallowed up Ender's entire fleet. And then it reached the enemy ships.

The first simply vanished in the explosion. Then, as the explosion spread and became less bright, it was clear what happened to each ship. As the light reached them they flashed brightly for a moment and disappeared. They were all fuel for the fire of the planet.

It took more than three minutes for the explosion to reach the limits of the simulator, and by then it was much fainter. All the ships were gone, and if any had escaped before the explosion reached them, they were few and not worth worrying about. Where the planet had been there was nothing. The simulator was empty.

Ender had destroyed the enemy by sacrificing his entire fleet and breaking the rule against destroying the enemy planet. He wasn't sure whether to feel triumphant at his victory or defiant at the rebuke he was certain would come. So instead he felt nothing. He was tired. He wanted to go to bed and sleep.

He switched off the simulator, and finally heard the noise behind him.

There were no longer two rows of dignified military observers. Instead there was chaos. Some of them were slapping each other on the back, some of them were bowed, head in hands, others were openly weeping. Captain Graff detached himself from the group and came to Ender. Tears streamed down his face, but he was smiling. He reached out his arms, and to Ender's surprise he embraced the boy, held him tightly, and whispered, "Thank you, thank you, thank you, Ender."

Soon all the observers were gathered around the bewildered child, thanking him and cheering him and patting him on the shoulder and shaking his hand. Ender tried to make sense of what they were saying. Had he passed the test after all? Why did it matter so much to them?

Then the crowd parted and Mazer Rackham walked through. He came straight up to Ender Wiggin and held out his hand.

"You made the hard choice, boy. But heaven knows there was no other way you could have done it. Congratulations. You beat them, and it's all over."

All over. Beat them. "I beat *you*, Mazer Rackham."

Mazer laughed, a loud laugh that filled the room. "Ender Wiggin, you never played me. You never played a *game* since I was your teacher."

Ender didn't get the joke. He had played a great many games, at a terrible cost to himself. He began to get angry.

Mazer reached out and touched his shoulder. Ender shrugged him off. Mazer then grew serious and said, "Ender Wiggin for the last months you have been the commander of our fleets. There were no games. The battles were real. Your only enemy was *the* enemy. You won every battle. And finally today you fought them at their home world, and you destroyed their world, their fleet, you destroyed them completely, and they'll never come against us again. You did it. You."

Real. Not a game. Ender's mind was too tired to cope with it all. He walked away from Mazer, walked silently through the crowd that still whispered thanks and congratulations to the boy, walked out of the simulator room, and finally arrived in his bedroom and closed the door.

He was asleep when Graff and Mazer Rackham found him. They came in quietly and roused him. He awoke slowly, and when he recognized them he turned away to go back to sleep.

"Ender," Graff said. "We need to talk to you."

Ender rolled back to face them. He said nothing.

Graff smiled. "It was a shock to you yesterday, I know. But it must make you feel good to know you won the war."

Ender nodded slowly.

"Mazer Rackham here, he never played against you. He only analyzed your battles to find out your weak spots, to help you improve. It worked, didn't it?"

Ender closed his eyes tightly. They waited. He said, "Why didn't you tell me?"

Mazer smiled. "A hundred years ago, Ender, we found out some things. That when a commander's life is in danger he becomes afraid, and fear slows down his thinking. When a commander knows that he's killing people, he becomes cautious or insane, and neither of those help him do well. And when he's mature, when he has responsibilities and an understanding of the world, he becomes cautious and sluggish and can't do his job. So we trained children, who didn't know anything but the game, and never knew when it would become real. That was the theory, and you proved that the theory worked."

Graff reached out and touched Ender's shoulder. "We launched the ships so that they would all arrive at their destination during these few months. We knew that we'd probably have only one good commander, if we were lucky. In history it's been very rare to have more than one genius in a war. So we planned on having a genius. We were gambling. And you came along and we won."

Ender opened his eyes again and they realized that he was angry. "Yes, you won."

Graff and Mazer Rackham looked at each other. "He doesn't understand," Graff whispered.

"I understand," Ender said. "You needed a weapon, and you got it, and it was me."

"That's right," Mazer answered.

"So tell me," Ender went on, "how many people lived on that planet that I destroyed."

They didn't answer him. They waited awhile in silence, and then Graff spoke. "Weapons don't need to understand what they're pointed at, Ender. We did the pointing, and so we're responsible. You just did your job."

Mazer smiled. "Of course, Ender, you'll be taken care of. The government will never forget yon. You served us all very well."

Ender rolled over and faced the wall, and even though they tried to talk to him, he didn't answer them. Finally they left.

Ender lay in his bed for a long time before anyone disturbed him again. The door opened softly. Ender didn't turn to see who it was. Then a hand touched him softly.

"Ender, it's me, Bean."

Ender turned over and looked at the little boy who was standing by his bed.

"Sit down," Ender said.

Bean sat. "That last battle, Ender. I didn't know how you'd get us out of it."

Ender smiled. "I didn't. I cheated. I thought they'd kick me out."

"Can you believe it! We won the war. The whole war's over, and we thought we'd have to wait till we grew up to fight in it, and it was us fighting it all the time. I mean, Ender, we're little kids. I'm a little kid, anyway." Bean laughed and Ender smiled. Then they were silent for a little while, Bean sitting on the edge of the bed, Ender watching him out of half-closed eyes.

Finally Bean thought of something else to say.

"What will we do now that the war's over?" he said.

Ender closed his eyes and said, "I need some sleep, Bean."

Bean got up and left and Ender slept.

Graff and Anderson walked through the gates into the park. There was a breeze, but the sun was hot on their shoulders.

"Abba Technics? In the capital?" Graff asked.

"No, in Biggock County. Training division," Anderson replied. "They think my work with children is good preparation. And you?"

Graff smiled and shook his head. "No plans. I'll be here for a few more months. Reports, winding down. I've had offers. Personnel development for DCIA, executive vice president for U and P, but I said no. Publisher wants me to do memoirs of the war. I don't know."

They sat on a bench and watched leaves shivering in the breeze. Children on the monkey bars were laughing and yelling, but the wind and the distance swallowed their words. "Look," Graff said, pointing. A little boy jumped from the bars and ran near the bench where the two men sat. Another boy followed him, and holding his hands like a gun he made an explosive sound. The child he was shooting at didn't stop. He fired again.

"I got you! Come back here!"

The other little boy ran on out of sight.

"Don't you know when you're dead?" The boy shoved his hands in his pockets and kicked a rock back to the monkey bars. Anderson smiled and shook his head. "Kids," he said. Then he and Graff stood up and walked on out of the park.

---

1. Why does Ender insist on knowing more about the war when he gets to the Command School? Why does Mazer tell him more about it than he is supposed to?

2. Why does Card describe in such detail how Ender experiences the "destruction of himself"?

3. According to the story, is the military justified in training children to fight the war with the aliens without the children knowing the battles are real if this is the only way to save their home planet?

4. When Graff tells Ender that "we won," why does Ender respond by saying, "Yes, you won"? Why does Ender ask how many people were on the planet he destroyed and then roll over and face the wall?

OCTAVIA BUTLER (1947–2006) is best known for the Patternmaster series (1976–1984), the Xenogenesis trilogy (1987–1989), and the novels *Kindred* (1979), *The Parable of the Sower* (1993), and *The Parable of the Talents* (1998). Drawing on her childhood experience as the daughter of an African American maid, Butler wrote science fiction that addressed issues of race, class, and gender head-on. *Kindred*, for example, is a work of historical fantasy about a black woman who travels back to antebellum Maryland. Butler attended Pasadena City College and California State University at Los Angeles; eventually, upon the recommendation of a teacher (the noted science fiction writer Harlan Ellison), she went to the Clarion Science Fiction and Fantasy Writers' workshop in Pennsylvania. Butler won several Nebula and Hugo awards as well as a MacArthur Foundation "genius" grant in 1995. She died suddenly, just a few months after publishing *Fledgling* (2005), a vampire novel, to much acclaim.

Bloodchild

My last night of childhood began with a visit home. T'Gatoi's sister had given us two sterile eggs. T'Gatoi gave one to my mother, brother, and sisters. She insisted that I eat the other one alone. It didn't matter. There was still enough to leave everyone feeling good. Almost everyone. My mother wouldn't take any. She sat, watching everyone drifting and dreaming without her. Most of the time she watched me.

I lay against T'Gatoi's long, velvet underside, sipping from my egg now and then, wondering why my mother denied herself such a harmless pleasure. Less of her hair would be gray if she indulged now and then. The eggs prolonged life, prolonged vigor. My father, who had never refused one in his life, had lived more than twice as long as he should have. And toward the end of his life, when he should have been slowing down, he had married my mother and fathered four children.

But my mother seemed content to age before she had to. I saw her turn away as several of T'Gatoi's limbs secured me closer. T'Gatoi liked our body heat and took advantage of it whenever she could. When I was little and at home more, my mother used to try to tell me how to behave with T'Gatoi—how to be respectful and always obedient because T'Gatoi was the Tlic government official in charge of the Preserve, and thus the most important of her kind to deal directly with Terrans. It was an honor, my mother said, that such a person had chosen to come into the family. My mother was at her most formal and severe when she was lying.

I had no idea why she was lying, or even what she was lying about. It *was* an honor to have T'Gatoi in the family, but it was hardly a novelty. T'Gatoi and my mother had been friends all my mother's life, and T'Gatoi was not interested in being honored in the house she considered her second home. She simply came in, climbed onto one of her special couches, and called me over to keep her warm. It was impossible to be formal with her while lying against her and hearing her complain as usual that I was too skinny.

"You're better," she said this time, probing me with six or seven of her limbs. "You're gaining weight finally. Thinness is dangerous." The probing changed subtly, became a series of caresses.

"He's still too thin," my mother said sharply.

T'Gatoi lifted her head and perhaps a meter of her body off the couch as though she were sitting up. She looked at my mother, and my mother, her face lined and old looking, turned away.

"Lien, I would like you to have what's left of Gan's egg."

"The eggs are for the children," my mother said.

"They are for the family. Please take it."

Unwillingly obedient, my mother took it from me and put it to her mouth. There were only a few drops left in the now-shrunken, elastic shell, but she squeezed them out, swallowed them, and after a few moments some of the lines of tension began to smooth from her face.

"It's good," she whispered. "Sometimes I forget how good it is."

"You should take more," T'Gatoi said. "Why are you in such a hurry to be old?"

My mother said nothing.

"I like being able to come here," T'Gatoi said. "This place is a refuge because of you, yet you won't take care of yourself."

T'Gatoi was hounded on the outside. Her people wanted more of us made available. Only she and her political faction stood between us and the hordes who did not understand why there was a Preserve— why any Terran could not be courted, paid, drafted, in some way made available to them. Or they did understand, but in their desperation, they did not care. She parceled us out to the desperate and sold us to the rich and powerful for their political support. Thus, we were necessities, status symbols, and an independent people. She oversaw the joining of families, putting an end to the final remnants of the earlier system of breaking up Terran families to suit impatient Tlic. I had lived outside with her. I had seen the desperate eagerness in the way some people looked at me. It was a little frightening to know that only she stood between us and that desperation that could so easily swallow us. My mother would look at her sometimes and say to me, "Take care of her." And I would remember that she too had been outside, had seen.

Now T'Gatoi used four of her limbs to push me away from her onto the floor. "Go on, Gan," she said. "Sit down there with your sisters and enjoy not being sober. You had most of the egg. Lien, come warm me."

My mother hesitated for no reason that I could see. One of my earliest memories is of my mother stretched alongside T'Gatoi, talking about things I could not understand, picking me up from the floor and laughing as she sat me on one of T'Gatoi's segments. She ate her share of eggs then. I wondered when she had stopped, and why.

She lay down now against T'Gatoi, and the whole left row of T'Gatoi's limbs closed around her, holding her loosely, but securely. I had always found it comfortable to lie that way, but except for my older sister, no one else in the family liked it. They said it made them feel caged.

T'Gatoi meant to cage my mother. Once she had, she moved her tail slightly, then spoke. "Not enough egg, Lien. You should have taken it when it was passed to you. You need it badly now."

T'Gatoi's tail moved once more, its whip motion so swift I wouldn't have seen it if I hadn't been watching for it. Her sting drew only a single drop of blood from my mother's bare leg.

My mother cried out—probably in surprise. Being stung doesn't hurt. Then she sighed and I could see her body relax. She moved languidly into a more comfortable position within the cage of T'Gatoi's limbs. "Why did you do that?" she asked, sounding half asleep.

"I could not watch you sitting and suffering any longer."

My mother managed to move her shoulders in a small shrug. "Tomorrow," she said.

"Yes. Tomorrow you will resume your suffering—if you must. But just now, just for now, lie here and warm me and let me ease your way a little."

"He's still mine, you know," my mother said suddenly.

"Nothing can buy him from me." Sober, she would not have permitted herself to refer to such things.

"Nothing," T'Gatoi agreed, humoring her.

"Did you think I would sell him for eggs? For long life? My son?"

"Not for anything," T'Gatoi said, stroking my mother's shoulders, toying with her long, graying hair.

I would like to have touched my mother, shared that moment with her. She would take my hand if I touched her now. Freed by the egg and the sting, she would smile and perhaps say things long held in. But tomorrow, she would remember all this as a humiliation. I did not want to be part of a remembered humiliation. Best just to be still and know she loved me under all the duty and pride and pain.

"Xuan Hoa, take off her shoes," T'Gatoi said. "In a little while I'll sting her again and she can sleep."

My older sister obeyed, swaying drunkenly as she stood up. When she had finished, she sat down beside me and took my hand. We had always been a unit, she and I.

My mother put the back of her head against T'Gatoi's underside and tried from that impossible angle to look up into the broad, round face. "You're going to sting me again?"

"Yes, Lien."

"I'll sleep until tomorrow noon."

"Good. You need it. When did you sleep last?"

My mother made a wordless sound of annoyance. "I should have stepped on you when you were small enough," she muttered.

It was an old joke between them. They had grown up together, sort of, though T'Gatoi had not, in my mother's lifetime, been small enough for any Terran to step on. She was nearly three times my mother's present age, yet would still be young when my mother died of age. But T'Gatoi and my mother had met as T'Gatoi was coming into a period of rapid development—a kind of Tlic adolescence. My mother was only a child, but for a while they developed at the same rate and had no better friends than each other.

T'Gatoi had even introduced my mother to the man who became my father. My parents, pleased with each other in spite of their different ages, married as T'Gatoi was going into her family's business—politics. She and my mother saw each other less. But sometime before my older sister was born, my mother promised T'Gatoi one of her children. She would have to give one of us to someone, and she preferred T'Gatoi to some stranger.

Years passed. T'Gatoi traveled and increased her influence. The Preserve was hers by the time she came back to my mother to collect what she probably saw as her just reward for her hard work. My older sister took an instant liking to her and wanted to be chosen, but my mother was just coming to term with me and T'Gatoi liked the idea of choosing an infant and watching and taking part in all the phases of development. I'm told I was first caged within T'Gatoi's many limbs only three minutes after my birth. A few days later, I was given my first taste of egg. I tell Terrans that when they ask whether I was ever afraid of her. And I tell it to Tlic when T'Gatoi suggests a young Terran child for them and they, anxious and ignorant, demand an adolescent. Even my brother who had somehow grown up to fear and distrust the Tlic could probably have gone smoothly into one of their families if he had been adopted early enough. Sometimes, I think for his sake he should have been. I looked at him, stretched out on the floor across the room, his eyes open, but glazed as he dreamed his egg dream. No matter what he felt toward the Tlic, he always demanded his share of egg.

"Lien, can you stand up?" T'Gatoi asked suddenly.

"Stand?" my mother said. "I thought I was going to sleep."

"Later. Something sounds wrong outside." The cage was abruptly gone.

"What?"

"Up, Lien!"

My mother recognized her tone and got up just in time to avoid being dumped on the floor. T'Gatoi whipped her three meters of body off her couch, toward the door, and out at full speed. She had bones—ribs, a long spine, a skull, four sets of limb bones per segment. But when she moved that way, twisting, hurling herself into controlled falls, landing running, she seemed not only boneless, but aquatic—something swimming through the air as though it were water. I loved watching her move.

I left my sister and started to follow her out the door, though I wasn't very steady on my own feet. It would have been better to sit and dream, better yet to find a girl and share a waking dream with her. Back when the Tlic saw us as not much more than convenient, big, warm-blooded animals, they would pen several of us together, male and female, and feed us only eggs. That way they could be sure of getting another generation of us no matter how we tried to hold out. We were lucky that didn't go on long. A few generations of it and we would have *been* little more than convenient big animals.

"Hold the door open, Gan," T'Gatoi said. "And tell the family to stay back."

"What is it?" I asked.

"N'Tlic."

I shrank back against the door. "Here? Alone?"

"He was trying to reach a call box, I suppose." She carried the man past me, unconscious, folded like a coat over some of her limbs. He looked young—my brother's age perhaps—and he was thinner than he should have been. What T'Gatoi would have called dangerously thin.

"Gan, go to the call box," she said. She put the man on the floor and began stripping off his clothing.

I did not move.

After a moment, she looked up at me, her sudden stillness a sign of deep impatience.

"Send Qui," I told her. "I'll stay here. Maybe I can help."

She let her limbs begin to move again, lifting the man and pulling his shirt over his head. "You don't want to see this," she said. "It will be hard. I can't help this man the way his Tlic could."

"I know. But send Qui. He won't want to be of any help here. I'm at least willing to try."

She looked at my brother—older, bigger, stronger, certainly more able to help her here. He was sitting up now, braced against the wall, staring at the man on the floor with undisguised fear and revulsion. Even she could see that he would be useless.

"Qui, go!" she said.

He didn't argue. He stood up, swayed briefly, then steadied, frightened sober.

"This man's name is Bram Lomas," she told him, reading from the man's armband. I fingered my own armband in sympathy. "He needs T'Khotgif Teh. Do you hear?"

"Bram Lomas, T'Khotgif Teh," my brother said. "I'm going." He edged around Lomas and ran out the door.

Lomas began to regain consciousness. He only moaned at first and clutched spasmodically at a pair of T'Gatoi's limbs. My younger sister, finally awake from her egg dream, came close to look at him, until my mother pulled her back.

T'Gatoi removed the man's shoes, then his pants, all the while leaving him two of her limbs to grip. Except for the final few, all her limbs were equally dexterous. "I want no argument from you this time, Gan," she said.

I straightened. "What shall I do?"

"Go out and slaughter an animal that is at least half your size."

"Slaughter? But I've never—"

She knocked me across the room. Her tail was an efficient weapon whether she exposed the sting or not.

I got up, feeling stupid for having ignored her warning, and went into the kitchen. Maybe I could kill something with a knife or an ax. My mother raised a few Terran animals for the table and several thousand local ones for their fur. T'Gatoi would probably prefer something local. An achti, perhaps. Some of those were the right size, though they had about three times as many teeth as I did and a real love of using them. My mother, Hoa, and Qui could kill them with knives. I had never killed one at all, had never slaughtered any animal. I had spent most of my time with T'Gatoi while my brother and sisters were learning the family business. T'Gatoi had been right. I should have been the one to go to the call box. At least I could do that.

I went to the corner cabinet where my mother kept her larger house and garden tools. At the back of the cabinet there was a pipe that carried off waste water from the kitchen—except that it didn't anymore. My father had rerouted the waste water below before I was born. Now the pipe could be turned so that one half slid around the other and a rifle could be stored inside. This wasn't our only gun, but it was our most easily accessible one. I would have to use it to shoot one of the biggest of the achti. Then T'Gatoi would probably confiscate it. Firearms were illegal in the Preserve. There had been incidents right after the Preserve was established—Terrans shooting Tlic, shooting N'Tlic. This was before the joining of families began, before everyone had a personal stake in keeping the peace. No one had shot a Tlic in my lifetime or my mother's, but the law still stood—for our protection, we were told. There were stories of whole Terran families wiped out in reprisal back during the assassinations.

I went out to the cages and shot the biggest achti I could find. It was a handsome breeding male, and my mother would not be pleased to see me bring it in. But it was the right size, and I was in a hurry.

I put the achti's long, warm body over my shoulder—glad that some of the weight I'd gained was muscle—and took it to the kitchen. There, I put the gun back in its hiding place. If T'Gatoi noticed the achti's wounds and demanded the gun, I would give it to her. Otherwise, let it stay where my father wanted it.

I turned to take the achti to her, then hesitated. For several seconds, I stood in front of the closed door wondering why I was suddenly afraid. I knew what was going to happen. I hadn't seen it before but T'Gatoi had shown me diagrams and drawings. She had made sure I knew the truth as soon as I was old enough to understand it.

Yet I did not want to go into that room. I wasted a little time choosing a knife from the carved, wooden box in which my mother kept them. T'Gatoi might want one, I told myself, for the tough, heavily furred hide of the achti.

"Gan!" T'Gatoi called, her voice harsh with urgency.

I swallowed. I had not imagined a simple moving of the feet could be so difficult. I realized I was trembling and that shamed me. Shame impelled me through the door.

I put the achti down near T'Gatoi and saw that Lomas was unconscious again. She, Lomas, and I were alone in the room—my mother and sisters probably sent out so they would not have to watch. I envied them.

But my mother came back into the room as T'Gatoi seized the achti. Ignoring the knife I offered her, she extended claws from several of her limbs and slit the achti from throat to anus. She looked at me, her yellow eyes intent. "Hold this man's shoulders, Gan."

I stared at Lomas in panic, realizing that I did not want to touch him, let alone hold him. This would not be like shooting an animal. Not as quick, not as merciful, and, I hoped, not as final, but there was nothing I wanted less than to be part of it.

My mother came forward. "Gan, you hold his right side," she said. "I'll hold his left." And if he came to, he would throw her off without realizing he had done it. She was a tiny woman. She often wondered aloud how she had produced, as she said, such "huge" children.

"Never mind," I told her, taking the man's shoulders. "I'll do it." She hovered nearby.

"Don't worry," I said. "I won't shame you. You don't have to stay and watch."

She looked at me uncertainly, then touched my face in a rare caress. Finally, she went back to her bedroom.

T'Gatoi lowered her head in relief. "Thank you, Gan," she said with courtesy more Terran than Tlic. "That one . . . she is always finding new ways for me to make her suffer."

Lomas began to groan and make choked sounds. I had hoped he would stay unconscious. T'Gatoi put her face near his so that he focused on her.

"I've stung you as much as I dare for now," she told him. "When this is over, I'll sting you to sleep and you won't hurt anymore."

"Please," the man begged. "Wait . . ."

"There's no more time, Bram. I'll sting you as soon as it's over. When T'Khotgif arrives she'll give you eggs to help you heal. It will be over soon."

"T'Khotgif!" the man shouted, straining against my hands.

"Soon, Bram." T'Gatoi glanced at me, then placed a claw against his abdomen slightly to the right of the middle, just below the last rib.

There was movement on the right side—tiny, seemingly random pulsations moving his brown flesh, creating a concavity here, a convexity there, over and over until I could see the rhythm of it and knew where the next pulse would be.

Lomas's entire body stiffened under T'Gatoi's claw, though she merely rested it against him as she wound the rear section of her body around his legs. He might break my grip, but he would not break hers. He wept helplessly as she used his pants to tie his hands, then pushed his hands above his head so that I could kneel on the cloth between them and pin them in place. She rolled up his shirt and gave it to him to bite down on.

And she opened him.

His body convulsed with the first cut. He almost tore himself away from me. The sound he made . . . I had never heard such sounds come from anything human. T'Gatoi seemed to pay no attention as she lengthened and deepened the cut, now and then pausing to lick away blood. His blood vessels contracted, reacting to the chemistry of her saliva, and the bleeding slowed.

I felt as though I were helping her torture him, helping her consume him. I knew I would vomit soon, didn't know why I hadn't already. I couldn't possibly last until she was finished.

She found the first grub. It was fat and deep red with his blood—both inside and out. It had already eaten its own egg case but apparently had not yet begun to eat its host. At this stage, it would eat any flesh except its mother's. Let alone, it would have gone on excreting the poisons that had both sickened and alerted Lomas. Eventually it would have begun to eat. By the time it ate its way out of Lomas's flesh, Lomas would be dead or dying—and unable to take revenge on the thing that was killing him. There was always a grace period between the time the host sickened and the time the grubs began to eat him.

T'Gatoi picked up the writhing grub carefully and looked at it, somehow ignoring the terrible groans of the man.

Abruptly, the man lost consciousness.

"Good." T'Gatoi looked down at him. "I wish you Terrans could do that at will." She felt nothing. And the thing she held . . .

It was limbless and boneless at this stage, perhaps fifteen centimeters long and two thick, blind and slimy with blood. It was like a large worm. T'Gatoi put it into the belly of the achti, and it began at once to burrow. It would stay there and eat as long as there was anything to eat.

Probing through Lomas's flesh, she found two more, one of them smaller and more vigorous. "A male!" she said happily. He would be dead before I would. He would be through his metamorphosis and screwing everything that would hold still before his sisters even had limbs. He was the only one to make a serious effort to bite T'Gatoi as she placed him in the achti.

Paler worms oozed to visibility in Lomas's flesh. I closed my eyes. It was worse than finding something dead, rotting, and filled with tiny animal grubs. And it was far worse than any drawing or diagram.

"Ah, there are more," T'Gatoi said, plucking out two long, thick grubs. "You may have to kill another animal, Gan. Everything lives inside you Terrans."

I had been told all my life that this was a good and necessary thing Tlic and Terran did together—a kind of birth. I had believed it until now. I knew birth was painful and bloody, no matter what. But this was something else, something worse. And I wasn't ready to see it. Maybe I never would be. Yet I couldn't not see it. Closing my eyes didn't help.

T'Gatoi found a grub still eating its egg case. The remains of the case were still wired into a blood vessel by their own little tube or hook or whatever. That was the way the grubs were anchored and the way they fed. They took only blood until they were ready to emerge. Then they ate their stretched, elastic egg cases. Then they ate their hosts.

T'Gatoi bit away the egg case, licked away the blood. Did she like the taste? Did childhood habits die hard—or not die at all?

The whole procedure was wrong, alien. I wouldn't have thought anything about her could seem alien to me.

"One more, I think," she said. "Perhaps two. A good family. In a host animal these days, we would be happy to find one or two alive." She glanced at me. "Go outside, Gan, and empty your stomach. Go now while the man is unconscious."

I staggered out, barely made it. Beneath the tree just beyond the front door, I vomited until there was nothing left to bring up. Finally, I stood shaking, tears streaming down my face. I did not know why I was crying, but I could not stop. I went farther from the house to avoid being seen. Every time I closed my eyes I saw red worms crawling over redder human flesh.

There was a car coming toward the house. Since Terrans were forbidden motorized vehicles except for certain farm equipment, I knew this must be Lomas's Tlic with Qui and perhaps a Terran doctor. I wiped my face on my shirt, struggled for control.

"Gan," Qui called as the car stopped. "What happened?" He crawled out of the low, round, Tlic-convenient car door. Another Terran crawled out the other side and went into the house without speaking to me. The doctor. With his help and a few eggs, Lomas might make it.

"T'Khotgif Teh?" I said.

The Tlic driver surged out of her car, reared up half her length before me. She was paler and smaller than T'Gatoi—probably born from the body of an animal. Tlic from Terran bodies were always larger as well as more numerous.

"Six young," I told her. "Maybe seven, all alive. At least one male."

"Lomas?" she said harshly. I liked her for the question and the concern in her voice when she asked it. The last coherent thing he had said was her name.

"He's alive," I said.

She surged away to the house without another word.

"She's been sick," my brother said, watching her go. "When I called, I could hear people telling her she wasn't well enough to go out even for this."

I said nothing. I had extended courtesy to the Tlic. Now I didn't want to talk to anyone. I hoped he would go in—out of curiosity if nothing else.

"Finally found out more than you wanted to know, eh?"

I looked at him.

"Don't give me one of *her* looks," he said. "You're not her. You're just her property."

One of her looks. Had I picked up even an ability to imitate her expressions?

"What'd you do, puke?" He sniffed the air. "So now you know what you're in for."

I walked away from him. He and I had been close when we were kids. He would let me follow him around when I was home, and sometimes T'Gatoi would let me bring him along when she took me into the city. But something had happened when he reached adolescence. I never knew what. He began keeping out of T'Gatoi's way. Then he began running away—until he realized there was no "away." Not in the Preserve. Certainly not outside. After that he concentrated on getting his share of every egg that came into the house and on looking out for me in a way that made me all but hate him—a way that clearly said, as long as I was all right, he was safe from the Tlic.

"How was it, really?" he demanded, following me.

"I killed an achti. The young ate it."

"You didn't run out of the house and puke because they ate an achti."

"I had . . . never seen a person cut open before." That was true, and enough for him to know. I couldn't talk about the other. Not with him.

"Oh," he said. He glanced at me as though he wanted to say more, but he kept quiet.

We walked, not really headed anywhere. Toward the back, toward the cages, toward the fields.

"Did he say anything?" Qui asked. "Lomas, I mean."

Who else would he mean? "He said 'T'Khotgif.'"

Qui shuddered. "If she had done that to me, she'd be the last person I'd call for."

"You'd call for her. Her sting would ease your pain without killing the grubs in you."

"You think I'd care if they died?"

No. Of course he wouldn't. Would I?

"Shit!" He drew a deep breath. "I've seen what they do. You think this thing with Lomas was bad? It was nothing."

I didn't argue. He didn't know what he was talking about.

"I saw them eat a man," he said.

I turned to face him. "You're lying!"

"*I saw them eat a man.*" He paused. "It was when I was little. I had been to the Hartmund house and I was on my way home. Halfway here, I saw a man and a Tlic and the man was N'Tlic. The ground was hilly. I was able to hide from them and watch. The Tlic wouldn't open the man because she had nothing to feed the grubs. The man couldn't go any farther and there were no houses around. He was in so much pain, he told her to kill him. He begged her to kill him. Finally, she did. She cut his throat. One swipe of one claw. I saw the grubs eat their way out, then burrow in again, still eating."

His words made me see Lomas's flesh again, parasitized, crawling. "Why didn't you tell me that?" I whispered.

He looked startled, as though he'd forgotten I was listening. "I don't know."

"You started to run away not long after that, didn't you?"

"Yeah. Stupid. Running inside the Preserve. Running in a cage."

I shook my head, said what I should have said to him long ago. "She wouldn't take you, Qui. You don't have to worry."

"She would . . . if anything happened to you."

"No. She'd take Xuan Hoa. Hoa . . . wants it." She wouldn't if she had stayed to watch Lomas.

"They don't take women," he said with contempt.

"They do sometimes." I glanced at him. "Actually, they prefer women. You should be around them when they talk among themselves. They say women have more body fat to protect the grubs. But they usually take men to leave the women free to bear their own young."

"To provide the next generation of host animals," he said, switching from contempt to bitterness.

"It's more than that!" I countered. Was it?

"If it were going to happen to me, I'd want to believe it was more, too."

"It *is* more!" I felt like a kid. Stupid argument.

"Did you think so while T'Gatoi was picking worms out of that guy's guts?"

"It's not supposed to happen that way."

"Sure it is. You weren't supposed to see it, that's all. And his Tlic was supposed to do it. She could sting him unconscious and the operation wouldn't have been as painful. But she'd still open him, pick out the grubs, and if she missed even one, it would poison him and eat him from the inside out."

There was actually a time when my mother told me to show respect for Qui because he was my older brother. I walked away, hating him. In his way, he was gloating. He was safe and I wasn't. I could have hit him, but I didn't think I would be able to stand it when he refused to hit back, when he looked at me with contempt and pity.

He wouldn't let me get away. Longer legged, he swung ahead of me and made me feel as though I were following him.

"I'm sorry," he said.

I strode on, sick and furious.

"Look, it probably won't be that bad with you. T'Gatoi likes you. She'll be careful."

I turned back toward the house, almost running from him.

"Has she done it to you yet?" he asked, keeping up easily. "I mean, you're about the right age for implantation. Has she—"

I hit him. I didn't know I was going to do it, but I think I meant to kill him. If he hadn't been bigger and stronger, I think I would have.

He tried to hold me off, but in the end, had to defend himself. He only hit me a couple of times. That was plenty. I don't remember going down, but when I came to, he was gone. It was worth the pain to be rid of him.

I got up and walked slowly toward the house. The back was dark. No one was in the kitchen. My mother and sisters were sleeping in their bedrooms—or pretending to.

Once I was in the kitchen, I could hear voices—Tlic and Terran from the next room. I couldn't make out what they were saying—didn't want to make it out.

I sat down at my mother's table, waiting for quiet. The table was smooth and worn, heavy and well crafted. My father had made it for her just before he died. I remembered hanging around underfoot when he built it. He didn't mind. Now I sat leaning on it, missing him. I could have talked to him. He had done it three times in his long life. Three clutches of eggs, three times being opened and sewed up. How had he done it? How did anyone do it?

I got up, took the rifle from its hiding place, and sat down again with it. It needed cleaning, oiling.

All I did was load it.

"Gan?"

She made a lot of little clicking sounds when she walked on bare floor, each limb clicking in succession as it touched down. Waves of little clicks.

She came to the table, raised the front half of her body above it, and surged onto it. Sometimes she moved so smoothly she seemed to flow like water itself. She coiled herself into a small hill in the middle of the table and looked at me.

"That was bad," she said softly. "You should not have seen it. It need not be that way."

"I know."

"T'Khotgif—Ch'Khotgif now—she will die of her disease. She will not live to raise her children. But her sister will provide for them, and for Bram Lomas." Sterile sister. One fertile female in every lot. One to keep the family going. That sister owed Lomas more than she could ever repay.

"He'll live then?"

"Yes."

"I wonder if he would do it again."

"No one would ask him to do that again."

I looked into the yellow eyes, wondering how much I saw and understood there, and how much I only imagined. "No one ever asks us," I said. "You never asked me."

She moved her head slightly. "What's the matter with your face?"

"Nothing. Nothing important." Human eyes probably wouldn't have noticed the swelling in the darkness. The only light was from one of the moons, shining through a window across the room.

"Did you use the rifle to shoot the achti?"

"Yes."

"And do you mean to use it to shoot me?"

I stared at her, outlined in the moonlight—coiled, graceful body. "What does Terran blood taste like to you?"

She said nothing.

"What are you?" I whispered. "What are we to you?"

She lay still, rested her head on her topmost coil. "You know me as no other does," she said softly. "You must decide."

"That's what happened to my face," I told her.

"What?"

"Qui goaded me into deciding to do something. It didn't turn out very well." I moved the gun slightly, brought the barrel up diagonally under my own chin. "At least it was a decision I made."

"As this will be."

"Ask me, Gatoi."

"For my children's lives?"

She would say something like that. She knew how to manipulate people, Terran and Tlic. But not this time.

"I don't want to be a host animal," I said. "Not even yours."

It took her a long time to answer. "We use almost no host animals these days," she said. "You know that."

"You use us."

"We do. We wait long years for you and teach you and join our families to yours." She moved restlessly. "You know you aren't animals to us."

I stared at her, saying nothing.

"The animals we once used began killing most of our eggs after implantation long before your ancestors arrived," she said softly. "You know these things, Gan. Because your people arrived, we are relearning what it means to be a healthy, thriving people. And your ancestors, fleeing from their home-world, from their own kind who would have killed or enslaved them—they survived because of us. We saw them as people and gave them the Preserve when they still tried to kill us as worms."

At the word "worms" I jumped. I couldn't help it, and she couldn't help noticing it.

"I see," she said quietly. "Would you really rather die than bear my young, Gan?"

I didn't answer.

"Shall I go to Xuan Hoa?"

"Yes!" Hoa wanted it. Let her have it. She hadn't had to watch Lomas. She'd be proud . . . Not terrified.

T'Gatoi flowed off the table onto the floor, startling me almost too much.

"I'll sleep in Hoa's room tonight," she said. "And sometime tonight or in the morning, I'll tell her."

This was going too fast. My sister Hoa had had almost as much to do with raising me as my mother. I was still close to her—not like Qui. She could want T'Gatoi and still love me.

"Wait! Gatoi!"

She looked back, then raised nearly half her length off the floor and turned it to face me. "These are adult things, Gan. This is my life, my family!"

"But she's . . . my sister."

"I have done what you demanded. I have asked you!"

"But—"

"It will be easier for Hoa. She has always expected to carry other lives inside her."

Human lives. Human young who would someday drink at her breasts, not at her veins.

I shook my head. "Don't do it to her, Gatoi." I was not Qui. It seemed I could become him, though, with no effort at all. I could make Xuan Hoa my shield. Would it be easier to know that red worms were growing in her flesh instead of mine?

"Don't do it to Hoa," I repeated.

She stared at me, utterly still.

I looked away, then back at her. "Do it to me."

I lowered the gun from my throat and she leaned forward to take it.

"No," I told her.

"It's the law," she said.

"Leave it for the family. One of them might use it to save my life someday."

She grasped the rifle barrel, but I wouldn't let go. I was pulled into a standing position over her.

"Leave it here!" I repeated. "If we're not your animals, if these are adult things, accept the risk. There is risk, Gatoi, in dealing with a partner."

It was clearly hard for her to let go of the rifle. A shudder went through her and she made a hissing sound of distress. It occurred to me that she was afraid. She was old enough to have seen what guns could do to people. Now her young and this gun would be together in the same house. She did not know about our other guns. In this dispute, they did not matter.

"I will implant the first egg tonight," she said as I put the gun away. "Do you hear, Gan?"

Why else had I been given a whole egg to eat while the rest of the family was left to share one? Why else had my mother kept looking at me as though I were going away from her, going where she could not follow? Did T'Gatoi imagine I hadn't known?

"I hear."

"Now!" I let her push me out of the kitchen, then walked ahead of her toward my bedroom. The sudden urgency in her voice sounded real. "You would have done it to Hoa tonight!" I accused.

"I must do it to someone tonight."

I stopped in spite of her urgency and stood in her way. "Don't you care who?"

She flowed around me and into my bedroom. I found her waiting on the couch we shared. There was nothing in Hoa's room that she could have used. She would have done it to Hoa on the floor. The thought of her doing it to Hoa at all disturbed me in a different way now, and I was suddenly angry.

Yet I undressed and lay down beside her. I knew what to do, what to expect. I had been told all my life. I felt the familiar sting, narcotic, mildly pleasant. Then the blind probing of her ovipositor. The puncture was painless, easy. So easy going in. She undulated slowly against me, her muscles forcing the egg from her body into mine. I held on to a pair of her limbs until I remembered Lomas holding her that way. Then I let go, moved inadvertently, and hurt her. She gave a low cry of pain and I expected to be caged at once within her limbs. When I wasn't, I held on to her again, feeling oddly ashamed.

"I'm sorry," I whispered.

She rubbed my shoulders with four of her limbs.

"Do you care?" I asked. "Do you care that it's me?"

She did not answer for some time. Finally, "You were the one making choices tonight, Gan. I made mine long ago."

"Would you have gone to Hoa?"

"Yes. How could I put my children into the care of one who hates them?"

"It wasn't . . . hate."

"I know what it was."

"I was afraid."

Silence.

"I still am." I could admit it to her here, now.

"But you came to me . . . to save Hoa."

"Yes." I leaned my forehead against her. She was cool velvet, deceptively soft. "And to keep you for myself," I said. It was so. I didn't understand it, but it was so.

She made a soft hum of contentment. "I couldn't believe I had made such a mistake with you," she said. "I chose you. I believed you had grown to choose me."

"I had, but . . ."

"Lomas."

"Yes."

"I have never known a Terran to see a birth and take it well. Qui has seen one, hasn't he?"

"Yes."

"Terrans should be protected from seeing."

I didn't like the sound of that—and I doubted that it was possible. "Not protected," I said. "Shown. Shown when we're young kids, and shown more than once. Gatoi, no Terran ever sees a birth that goes right. All we see is N'Tlic—pain and terror and maybe death."

She looked down at me. "It is a private thing. It has always been a private thing."

Her tone kept me from insisting—that and the knowledge that if she changed her mind, I might be the first public example. But I had planted the thought in her mind. Chances were it would grow, and eventually she would experiment.

"You won't see it again," she said. "I don't want you thinking any more about shooting me."

The small amount of fluid that came into me with her egg relaxed me as completely as a sterile egg would have, so that I could remember the rifle in my hands and my feelings of fear and revulsion, anger and despair. I could remember the feelings without reviving them. I could talk about them.

"I wouldn't have shot you," I said. "Not you." She had been taken from my father's flesh when he was my age.

"You could have," she insisted.

"Not you." She stood between us and her own people, protecting, interweaving.

"Would you have destroyed yourself?"

I moved carefully, uncomfortably. "I could have done that. I nearly did. That's Qui's 'away.' I wonder if he knows."

"What?"

I did not answer.

"You will live now."

"Yes." *Take care of her*, my mother used to say. Yes.

"I'm healthy and young," she said. "I won't leave you as Lomas was left—alone, N'Tlic. I'll take care of you."

---

1. When T'Gatoi removes the first grub from Bram Lomas and he loses consciousness, why does Gan think that T'Gatoi "felt nothing"? As Gan watches T'Gatoi remove the grubs, why does he stop believing that this process is the "good and necessary thing" he has always been told it is?

2. Why does Qui want so strongly to run away? Why does Gan hit Qui when Qui asks if T'Gatoi has "done it to you yet?"

3. Why does T'Gatoi agree to implant an egg in Xuan Hoa rather than Gan when Gan reveals how repelled he is by the idea of being a host? Why does Gan then ask T'Gatoi to "do it to me"?

4. Why does T'Gatoi allow Gan to keep the gun? At the end of the story, have T'Gatoi and Gan become "partners"?

JACK MCDEVITT (1935–) was born in Philadelphia and educated at
LaSalle College and Wesleyan University. He taught high school English
and theater for ten years before taking a job with the U.S. Customs
Service. It was while working as a night shift inspector for the customs
office in Pembina, North Dakota, that McDevitt became a voracious reader
of science fiction, and in 1981 he published his first short story, "The
Emerson Effect," which appeared in the *Twilight Zone Magazine*. McDevitt
has written steadily since then, creating a body of highly regarded work
featuring thoughtful characters who grapple with archaeological issues in
the distant future or make first contact with other intelligent species. His
first novel, *The Hercules Text* (1986), won the Locus Award and the Philip
K. Dick Special Award; *Omega* (2003) won the John W. Campbell Award;
and *Seeker* (2005) won the Nebula Award for best novel.

Promises to Keep

I received a Christmas card last week from Ed Iseminger. The illustration was a rendering of the celebrated Christmas Eve telecast from
Callisto: a lander stands serenely on a rubble-strewn plain, spilling
warm yellow light through its windows. Needle-point peaks rise
behind it, and the rim of a crater curves across the foreground. An
enormous belted crescent dominates the sky.

In one window, someone has hung a wreath.

It is a moment preserved, a tableau literally created by Cathie Perth,
extracted from her prop bag. Somewhere here, locked away among
insurance papers and the deed to the house, is the tape of the original
telecast, but I've never played it. In fact, I've seen it only once, on the
night of the transmission. But I know the words, Cathie's words, read
by Victor Landolfi in his rich baritone, blending the timeless values of
the season with the spectral snows of another world. They appear in
schoolbooks now, and on marble.

Inside the card, in large, block, defiant letters, Iseminger had printed "SEPTEMBER!" It is a word with which he hopes to conquer a world. Sometimes, at night, when the snow sparkles under the hard cold stars (the way it did on Callisto), I think about him, and his quest. And I am very afraid.

I can almost see Cathie's footprints on the frozen surface. It was a good time, and I wish there were a way to step into the picture, to toast the holidays once more with Victor Landolfi, to hold onto Cathie Perth (and not let go!), and somehow to save us all. It was the end of innocence, a final meeting place for old friends.

We made the Christmas tape over a period of about five days. Cathie took literally hours of visuals, but Callisto is a place of rock and ice and deadening sameness: there is little to soften the effect of cosmic indifference. Which is why all those shots of towering peaks and tumbled boulders were taken at long range, and in half-light. Things not quite seen, she said, are always charming.

Her biggest problem had been persuading Landolfi to do the voice-over. Victor was tall, lean, ascetic. He was equipped with laser eyes and a huge black mustache. His world was built solely of subatomic particles, and driven by electromagnetics. Those who did not share his passions excited his contempt; which meant that he understood the utility of Cathie's public relations function at the same time that he deplored its necessity. To participate was to compromise one's integrity. His sense of delicacy, however, prevented his expressing that view to Cathie: he begged off rather on the press of time, winked apologetically, and straightened his mustache. "Sawyer will read it for you," he said, waving me impatiently into the conversation.

Cathie sneered, and stared irritably out a window (it was the one with the wreath) at Jupiter, heavy in the fragile sky. We knew, by then, that it had a definable surface, that the big planet was a world sea of liquid hydrogen, wrapped around a rocky core. "It must be frustrating," she said, "to know you'll never see it." Her tone was casual, almost frivolous, but Landolfi was not easily baited.

"Do you really think," he asked, with the patience of the superior being (Landolfi had no illusions about his capabilities), "that these little pieces of theater will make any difference? Yes, Catherine, of course it's frustrating. Especially when one realizes that we have the technology to put vehicles down there...."

"And scoop out some hydrogen," Cathie added.

He shrugged. "It may happen someday."

"Victor, it never will if we don't sell the Program. This is the last shot. These ships are old, and nobody's going to build any new ones. Unless things change radically at home."

Landolfi closed his eyes. I knew what he was thinking: Cathie Perth was an outsider, an ex–television journalist who had probably slept her way on board. She played bridge, knew the film library by heart, read John Donne (for style, she said), and showed no interest whatever in the scientific accomplishments of the mission. We'd made far-reaching discoveries in the fields of plate tectonics, planetary climatology, and a dozen other disciplines. We'd narrowed the creation date down inside a range of a few million years. And we finally understood how it had happened! But Cathie's televised reports had de-emphasized the implications, and virtually ignored the mechanics of such things. Instead, while a global audience watched, Marjorie Aubuchon peered inspirationally out of a cargo lock at Ganymede (much in the fashion that Cortez must have looked at the Pacific on that first bright morning), her shoulder flag patch resplendent in the sunlight. And while the camera moved in for a close-up (her features were illuminated by a lamp Cathie had placed for the occasion in her helmet), Herman Selma solemnly intoned Cathie's comments on breaking the umbilical.

That was her style: brooding alien vistas reduced to human terms. In one of her best-known sequences, there had been no narration whatever: two space-suited figures, obviously male and female, stood together in the shadow of the monumental Cadmus Ice Fracture on Europa, beneath three moons.

"Cathie," Landolfi said, with his eyes still shut, "I don't wish to be offensive: but do you really care? For the Program, that is? When we get home, you will write a book, you will be famous, you will be at the top of your profession. Are you really concerned with where the Program will be in twenty years?"

It was a fair question: Cathie'd made no secret of her hopes for a Pulitzer. And she stood to get it, no matter what happened after this mission. Moreover, although she'd tried to conceal her opinions, we'd been together a long time by then, almost three years, and we could hardly misunderstand the dark view she took of people who voluntarily imprisoned themselves for substantial portions of their lives to go "rock-collecting."

"No," she said. "I'm not, because there won't be a Program in twenty years." She looked around at each of us, weighing the effect of her words. Iseminger, a blond giant with a reddish beard, allowed a smile of lazy tolerance to soften his granite features. "We're in the same class as the pyramids," she continued, in a tone that was unemotional and irritatingly condescending. "We're a hell of an expensive operation, and for what? Do you think the taxpayers give a good goddam about the weather on Jupiter? There's nothing out here but gas and boulders. Playthings for eggheads!"

I sat and thought about it while she smiled sweetly, and Victor smoldered. I had not heard the solar system ever before described in quite those terms; I'd heard people call it *vast, awesome, magnificent, serene,* stuff like that. But never *boring.*

In the end, Landolfi read his lines. He did it, he said, to end the distraction.

Cathie was clearly pleased with the result. She spent three days editing the tapes, commenting frequently (and with good-natured malice) on the *resonance* and *tonal qualities* of the voice-over. She finished on the morning of the 24th (ship time, of course), and transmitted the report to *Greenswallow* for relay to Houston. "It'll make the evening newscasts," she said with satisfaction.

It was our third Christmas out. Except for a couple of experiments-in-progress, we were finished on Callisto and, in fact, in the Jovian system. Everybody was feeling good about that, and we passed an uneventful afternoon, playing bridge and talking about what we'd do when we got back. (Cathie had described a deserted beach near Tillamook, Oregon, where she'd grown up. "It would be nice to walk on it again, under a *blue* sky," she said. Landolfi had startled everyone at that point: he looked up from the computer console at which he'd been working, and his eyes grew very distant. "I think," he said, "when the time comes, I would like very much to walk with you. . . .")

For the most part, Victor kept busy that afternoon with his hobby: he was designing a fusion engine that would be capable, he thought, of carrying ships to Jupiter within a few weeks, and, possibly, would eventually open the stars to direct exploration. But I watched him: he turned away periodically from the display screen, to glance at Cathie. Yes (I thought), she would indeed be lovely against the rocks and the spume, her black hair free in the wind.

Just before dinner, we watched the transmission of Cathie's tape. It was very strong, and when it was finished we sat silently looking at one another. By then, Herman Selma and Esther Crowley had joined us. (Although two landers were down, Cathie had been careful to give the impression in her report that there had only been one. When I asked why, she said, "In a place like this, one lander is the Spirit of Man. Two landers is just two landers.") We toasted Victor, and we toasted Cathie. Almost everyone, it turned out, had brought down a bottle for the occasion. We sang and laughed, and somebody turned up the music. We'd long since discovered the effect of low-gravity dancing in cramped quarters, and I guess we made the most of it.

Marj Aubuchon, overhead in the linkup, called to wish us season's greetings, and called again later to tell us that the telecast, according to Houston, had been "well-received." That was government talk, of course, and it meant only that no one in authority could find anything to object to. Actually, somebody high up had considerable confidence in her: in order to promote the illusion of spontaneity, the tapes were being broadcast directly to the commercial networks.

Cathie, who by then had had a little too much to drink, gloated openly. "It's the best we've done," she said. "Nobody'll ever do it better."

We shared that sentiment. Landolfi raised his glass, winked at Cathie, and drained it.

We had to cut the evening short, because a lander's life-support system isn't designed to handle six people. (For that matter, neither was an Athena's.) But before we broke it up, Cathie surprised us all by proposing a final toast: "To Frank Steinitz," she said quietly. "And his crew."

Steinitz: there was a name, as they say, to conjure with. He had led the first deep-space mission, five Athenas to Saturn, fifteen years before. It had been the first attempt to capture the public imagination for a dying program: an investigation of a peculiar object filmed by a *Voyager* on Iapetus. But nothing much had come of it, and the mission had taken almost seven years. Steinitz and his people had begun as heroes, but in the end they'd become symbols of futility. The press had portrayed them mercilessly as personifications of outworn virtues. Someone had compared them to the Japanese soldiers found as late as the 1970s on Pacific islands, still defending a world long since vanished.

The Steinitz group bore permanent reminders of their folly: prolonged weightlessness had loosened ligaments and tendons, and weakened muscles. Several had developed heart problems, and all suffered from assorted neuroses. As one syndicated columnist had observed, they walked like a bunch of retired big-league catchers.

"That's a good way to end the evening," said Selma, beaming benevolently.

Landolfi looked puzzled. "Cathie," he rumbled, "you've questioned Steinitz's good sense any number of times. And ours, by the way. Isn't it a little hypocritical to drink to him?"

"I'm not impressed by his intelligence," she said, ignoring the obvious parallel. "But he and his people went all the way out to Saturn in those damned things—" she waved in the general direction of the three Athenas orbiting overhead in linkup "—hanging onto baling wire and wing struts. I have to admire that."

"Hell," I said, feeling the effects a little myself, "we've got the same ships he had."

"Yes, you do," said Cathie pointedly.

I had trouble sleeping that night. For a long time, I lay listening to Landolfi's soft snore, and the electronic fidgeting of the operations computer. Cathie was bundled inside a gray blanket, barely visible in her padded chair.

She was right, of course. I knew that rubber boots would never again cross that white landscape, which had waited a billion years for us. The peaks glowed in the reflection of the giant planet: fragile crystalline beauty, on a world of terrifying stillness. Except for an occasional incoming rock, nothing more would ever happen here. Callisto's entire history was encapsuled within twelve days.

Pity there hadn't been something to those early notions about Venusian rain forests and canals on Mars. The Program might have had easier going had Burroughs or Bradbury been right. My God: how many grim surprises had disrupted fictional voyages to Mars? But the truth had been far worse than anything Wells or the others had ever committed to paper: the red planet was so dull that we hadn't even gone there.

Instead, we'd lumbered out to the giants. In ships that drained our lives and our health.

We could have done better; our ships could have *been* better. The computer beside which Landolfi slept contained his design for the fusion engine. And at JPL, an army team had demonstrated that artificial gravity was possible: a *real* gravity field, not the pathetic fraction created on the Athenas by spinning the inner hull. There were other possibilities as well: infrared ranging could be adapted to replace our elderly scanning system; new alloys were under development. But it would cost billions to build a second-generation vehicle. And unless there were an incentive, unless Cathie Perth carried off a miracle, it would not happen.

Immediately overhead, a bright new star glittered, moving visibly (though slowly) from west to east. That was the linkup, three ships connected nose to nose by umbilicals and a magnetic docking system. Like the Saturn mission, we were a multiple vehicle operation. We were more flexible that way, and we had a safety factor: two ships would be adequate to get the nine-man mission home. Conditions might become a little stuffy, but we'd make it.

I watched it drift through the icy starfield.

Cathie had pulled the plug on the Christmas lights. But it struck me that Callisto would only have one Christmas, so I put them back on.

Victor was on board *Tolstoi* when we lost it. No one ever really knew precisely what happened. We'd begun our long fall toward Jupiter, gaining the acceleration which we'd need on the flight home. Cathie, Herman Selma (the mission commander), and I were riding *Greenswallow*. The ships had separated, and would not rejoin until we'd rounded Jupiter, and settled into our course for home. (The

Athenas are really individually powered modular units which travel, except when maneuvering, as a single vessel. They're connected bow to bow by electromagnets. Coils of segmented tubing, called "umbilicals" even though the term does not accurately describe their function, provide ready access among the forward areas of the ships. As many as six Athenas can be linked in this fashion, although only five have ever been built. The resulting structure would resemble a wheel.)

Between Callisto and Ganymede, we hit something: a drifting cloud of fine particles, a belt of granular material stretched so thin it never appeared on the LGD, before or after. Cathie later called it a cosmic sandbar; Iseminger thought it an unformed moon. It didn't matter: whatever it was, the mission plowed into it at almost 50,000 kilometers per hour. Alarms clattered, and red lamps blinked on.

In those first moments, I thought the ship was going to come apart. Herman was thrown across a bank of consoles and through an open hatch. I couldn't see Cathie, but a quick burst of profanity came from her direction. Things were being ripped off the hull. Deep within her walls, *Greenswallow* sighed. The lights dipped, came back, and went out. Emergency lamps cut in, and something big glanced off the side of the ship. More alarms howled, and I waited for the clamor of the throaty klaxon which would warn of a holing, and which consequently would be the last sound I could expect to hear in this life.

The sudden deceleration snapped my head back on the pads. (The collision had occurred at the worst possible time: *Greenswallow* was caught in the middle of an attitude alignment. We were flying backwards.)

The exterior monitors were blank: that meant the cameras were gone.

Cathie's voice: "Rob, you okay?"

"Yes."

"Can you see Herman?"

My angle was bad, and I was pinned in my chair. "No. He's back in cargo."

"Is there any way you can close the hatch?"

"Herman's in there," I protested, thinking she'd misunderstood.

"If something tears a hole out back there, we're all going to go. Keeping the door open won't help him."

I hesitated. Sealing up seemed to be the wrong thing to do. (Of course, the fact that the hatch had been open in the first place constituted a safety violation.) "It's on your console," I told her. "Hit the numerics on your upper right."

"Which one?"

"Hit them all." She was seated at the status board, and I could see a row of red lights: several other hatches were open. They should have closed automatically when the first alarms sounded.

We got hit again, this time in front. *Greenswallow* trembled, and loose pieces of metal rattled around inside the walls like broken teeth.

"Rob," she said. "I don't think it's working."

The baleful lights still glowed across the top of her board.

It lasted about three minutes.

When it was over, we hurried back to look at Herman. We were no longer rotating, and gravity had consequently dropped to zero. Selma, gasping, pale, his skin damp, was floating grotesquely over a pallet of ore-sample cannisters. We got him to a couch and applied compresses. His eyes rolled shut, opened, closed again. "Inside," he said, gently fingering an area just off his sternum. "I think I've been chewed up a little." He raised his head slightly. "What kind of shape are we in?"

I left Cathie with him. Then I restored power, put on a suit and went outside.

The hull was a disaster: antennas were down, housings scored, lenses shattered. The lander was gone, ripped from its web. The port cargo area had buckled, and an auxiliary hatch was sprung. On the bow, the magnetic dock was hammered into slag. Travel between the ships was going to be a little tougher.

Greenswallow looked as if she had been sandblasted. I scraped particles out of her jet nozzles, replaced cable, and bolted down mounts. I caught a glimpse of *Amity*'s lights, sliding diagonally across the sky. As were the constellations.

"Cathie," I said. "I see Mac. But I think we're tumbling."

"Okay."

Iseminger was also on board *Amity*. And, fortunately, Marj Aubuchon, our surgeon. Herman's voice broke in, thick with effort. "Rob, we got no radio contact with anyone. Any sign of Victor?"

Ganymede was close enough that its craters lay exposed in harsh solar light; Halfway round the sky, the Pleiades glittered. *Tolstoi*'s green and red running lights should have been visible among, or near, the six silver stars. But the sky was empty. I stood a long time and looked, wondering how many other navigators on other oceans had sought lost friends in that constellation. What had they called it in antiquity? The rainy Pleiades. . . . "Only *Amity*," I said.

I tore out some cable and lobbed it in the general direction of Ganymede. Jupiter's enormous arc was pushing above the maintenance pods, spraying October light across the wreckage. I improvised a couple of antennas, replaced some black boxes, and then decided to correct the tumble, if I could.

"Try it now," I said.

Cathie acknowledged.

Two of the jets were useless. I went inside for spares, and replaced the faulty units. While I was finishing up, Cathie came back on. "Rob," she said, "radio's working, more or less. We have no long-range transmit, though."

"Okay. I'm not going to try to do anything about that right now."

"Are you almost finished?"

"Why?"

"Something occurred to me. Maybe the cloud, whatever that damned thing was that we passed through: maybe it's U-shaped."

"Thanks," I said. "I needed something to worry about."

"Maybe you should come back inside."

"Soon as I can. How's the patient doing?"

"Out," she said. "He was a little delirious when he was talking to you. Anyhow, I'm worried: I think something's broken internally. He never got his color back, and he's beginning to bring up blood. Rob, we need Marj."

"You hear anything from *Amity* yet?"

"Just a carrier wave." She did not mention *Tolstoi*. "How bad is it out there?"

From where I was tethered, about halfway back on the buckled beam, I could see a crack in the main plates that appeared to run the length of the port tube. I climbed out onto the exhaust assembly, and pointed my flashlight into the combustion chamber. Something glittered where the reflection should have been subdued. I got in and looked: silicon. Sand, and steel, had fused in the white heat of passage. The exhaust was blocked.

Cathie came back on. "What about it, Rob?" she asked. "Any serious problems?"

"Cathie," I said, "*Greenswallow's* going to Pluto."

Herman thought I was Landolfi: he kept assuring me that everything was going to be okay. His pulse was weak and rapid, and he alternated between sweating and shivering. Cathie had got a blanket under him and buckled him down so he wouldn't hurt himself. She bunched some pillows under his feet, and held a damp compress to his head.

"That's not going to help much. Raising his legs, I mean."

She looked at me, momentarily puzzled. "Oh," she said. "Not enough gravity."

I nodded.

"Oh, Rob." Her eyes swept the cases and cannisters, all neatly tagged, silicates from Pasiphae, sulfur from Himalia, assorted carbon compounds from Callisto. We had evidence now that Io had formed elsewhere in the solar system, and been well along in middle age when it was captured. We'd all but eliminated the possibility that life existed in Jupiter's atmosphere. We understood why rings formed around gas giants, and we had a new clue to the cause of terrestrial ice ages. And I could see that Cathie was thinking about trading lives to satisfy the curiosity of a few academics. "We don't belong out here," she said, softly. "Not in these primitive shells."

I said nothing.

"I got a question for you," she continued. "We're not going to find *Tolstoi*, right?"

"Is that your question?"

"No. I wish it were. But the LGD can't see them. That means they're just not there." Her eyes filled with tears, but she shook her head impatiently. "And we can't steer this thing. Can *Amity* carry six people?"

"It might have to."

"That wasn't what I asked."

"Food and water would be tight. Especially since we're running out of time, and wouldn't be able to transfer much over. If any. So we'd all be a little thinner when we got back. But yes, I think we could survive."

We stared at one another, and then she turned away. I became conscious of the ship: the throb of power deep in her bulkheads (power now permanently bridled by conditions in the combustion chambers), the soft amber glow of the navigation lamps in the cockpit.

McGuire's nasal voice, from *Amity*, broke the uneasy silence. "Herman, you okay?"

Cathie looked at me, and I nodded. "Mac," she said, "this is Perth. Herman's hurt. We need Marj."

"Okay," he said. "How bad?"

"We don't know. Internal injuries, looks like. He appears to be in shock."

We heard him talking to someone else. Then he came back. "We're on our way. I'll put Marj on in a minute; maybe she can help from here. How's the ship?"

"Not good: the dock's gone, and the engine might as well be."

He asked me to be specific. "If we try a burn, the rear end'll fall off."

McGuire delivered a soft, venomous epithet. And then: "Do what you can for Herman. Marj'll be right here."

Cathie was looking at me strangely. "He's worried," she said.

"Yes. He's in charge now. . . ."

"Rob, you say you *think* we'll be okay. What's the problem?"

"We might," I said, "run a little short of air."

Greenswallow continued her plunge toward Jupiter at a steadily increasing rate and a sharp angle of approach: we would pass within about 60,000 kilometers, and then drop completely out of the plane of the solar system. We appeared to be heading in the general direction of the Southern Cross.

Cathie worked on Herman. His breathing steadied and he slipped in and out of his delirium. We sat beside him, not talking much. After awhile, Cathie asked, "What happens now?"

"In a few hours," I said, "we'll reach our insertion point. By then, we have to be ready to change course." She frowned, and I shrugged. "That's it," I said. "It's all the time we have to get over to *Amity*. If we don't make the insertion on time, *Amity* won't have the fuel to throw a U-turn later."

"Rob, how are we going to get Herman over there?"

That was an uncomfortable question. The prospect of jamming him down into a suit was less than appealing, but there was no other way. "We'll just have to float him over," I said. "Marj won't like it much."

"Neither will Herman."

"You wanted a little high drama," I said, unnecessarily. "The next show should be a barnburner."

Her mouth tightened, and she turned away from me.

One of the TV cameras had picked up the approach of *Amity*. Some of her lights were out, and she too looked a bit bent. The Athena is a homely vessel in the best of times, whale shaped and snub-nosed, with a midship flare that suggests middle-age spread. But I was glad to see her.

Cathie snuffled at the monitor, and blew her nose. "Your Program's dead, Rob." Her eyes blazed momentarily, like a dying fire into which one has flung a few drops of water. "We're leaving three of our people out here; and if you're right about the air, we'll get home with a ship-load of defectives, or worse. Won't that look good on the six o'clock news?" She gazed vacantly at *Amity*'s image. "I'd hoped," she said, "that if things went well, Victor would have lived to see a ship carry his fusion engine. And maybe his name, as well. Ain't gonna happen, though. Not ever."

I had not allowed myself to think about the oxygen problem we were going to face. The Athenas recycle their air supply: the converters in a single ship can maintain a crew of three, or even four, indefinitely. But six?

I was not looking forward to the ride home.

A few minutes later, a tiny figure detached itself from the shadow of the Athena and started across: Marj Aubuchon on a maintenance sled. McGuire's voice erupted from the ship's speakers. "Rob, we've taken a long look at your engines, and we agree with your assessment. The damage complicates things." Mac had a talent for understatement. It derived, not from a sophisticated sense of humor, but from a genuine conviction of his own inferiority. He preferred to solve problems by denying their existence. He was the only one of the original nine who could have been accurately described as passive: other people's opinions carried great weight with him. His prime value to the mission was his grasp of Athena systems. But he'd been a reluctant crewman, a man who periodically reminded us that he wanted only to retire to his farm in Indiana. He wouldn't have been along at all except that one guy died and somebody else came down with an unexpected (but thoroughly earned) disease. Now, with Selma incapacitated and Landolfi gone, McGuire was in command. It must have been disconcerting for him. "We've got about five hours," he continued. "Don't let Marj get involved in major surgery. She's already been complaining to me that it doesn't sound as if it'll be possible to move him. *We have no alternative.* She knows that, but you know how she is. Okay?"

One of the monitors had picked him up. He looked rumpled, and nervous. Not an attitude to elicit confidence. "Mac," said Cathie, "we may kill him trying to get him over there."

"You'll kill him if you don't," he snapped. "Get your personal stuff together, and bring it with you. You won't be going back."

"What about trying to transfer some food?" I asked.

"We can't dock," he said. "And there isn't time to float it across."

"Mac," said Cathie, "is *Amity* going to be able to support six people?"

I listened to McGuire breathing. He turned away to issue some trivial instructions to Iseminger. When he came back he said, simply and tonelessly, "Probably not." And then, cold-bloodedly (I thought), "How's Herman doing?"

Maybe it was my imagination. Certainly there was nothing malicious in his tone, but Cathie caught it too, and turned sharply round. "McGuire is a son of a bitch," she hissed. I don't know whether Mac heard it.

Marjorie Aubuchon was short, blond, and irritable. When I relayed McGuire's concerns about time, she said, "God knows, that's all I've heard for the last half hour." She observed that McGuire was a jerk, and bent over Herman. The blood was pink and frothy on his lips. After a few minutes she said, to no one in particular, "Probably a punctured lung." She waved Cathie over, and began filling a hypo; I went for a walk.

At sea, there's a long tradition of sentiment between mariners and their ships. Enlisted men identify with them, engineers baby them, and captains go down with them. No similar attitude has developed in space flight. We've never had an *Endeavour*, or a *Golden Hind*. Always, off Earth, it has been the mission, rather than the ship. *Friendship VII* and *Apollo XI* were far more than vehicles. I'm not sure why that is; maybe it reflects Cathie's view that travel between the worlds is still in its *Kon-Tiki* phase: the voyage itself is of such epic proportions that everything else is overwhelmed.

But I'd lived almost three years on *Greenswallow*. It was a long time to be confined to her narrow spaces. Nevertheless, she was shield and provider against that enormous abyss, and I discovered (while standing in the doorway of my cabin) a previously unfelt affection for her.

A few clothes were scattered round the room, a shirt was hung over my terminal, and two pictures were mounted on the plastic wall. One was a Casnavan print of a covered bridge in New Hampshire; the other was a telecopy of an editorial cartoon that had appeared in the *Washington Post*. The biggest human problem we had, of course, was sheer boredom. And Cathie had tried to capture the dimensions of the difficulty by showing crew members filling the long days on the outbound journey with bridge. ("It would be nice," Cathie's narrator had said at one point, "if we could take everybody out to an Italian restaurant now and then.") The *Post* cartoon had appeared several days later: it depicted four astronauts holding cards. (We could recognize Selma, Landolfi, and Marj. The fourth, whose back was turned, was exceedingly feminine, and appeared to be Esther Crowley.) An enormous bloodshot eye is looking in through one window; a tentacle and a UFO are visible through another. The "Selma" character, his glasses characteristically down on his nose, is examining his hand, and delivering the caption: *Dummy looks out the window and checks the alien.*

I packed the New Hampshire bridge, and left the cartoon. If someone comes by, in 20 million years or so, he might need a laugh. I went up to the cockpit with my bag.

McGuire checked with me to see how we were progressing. "Fine," I told him. I was still sitting there four hours later when Cathie appeared behind me.

"Rob," she said, "we're ready to move him." She smiled wearily. "Marj says he should be okay if we can get him over there without breaking anything else."

We cut the spin on the inner module to about point-oh-five. Then we lifted Herman onto a stretcher, and carried him carefully down to the airlock.

Cathie stared straight ahead, saying nothing. Her fine-boned cheeks were pale, and her eyes seemed focused far away. These, I thought, were her first moments to herself, unhampered by other duties. The impact of events was taking hold.

Marj called McGuire and told him we were starting over, and that she would need a sizable pair of shears when we got there to cut Herman's suit open. "Please have them ready," she said. "We may be in a hurry."

I had laid out his suit earlier: we pulled it up over his legs. That was easy, but the rest of it was slow, frustrating work. "We need a special kind of unit for this," Marj said. "Probably a large bag, without arms or legs. If we're ever dumb enough to do anything like this again, I'll recommend it."

McGuire urged us to hurry.

Once or twice, Cathie's eyes met mine. Something passed between us, but I was too distracted to define it. Then we were securing his helmet, and adjusting the oxygen mixture.

"I think we're okay," Marj observed, her hand pressed against Selma's chest. "Let's get him over there. . . ."

I opened the inner airlock, and pulled my own helmet into place. Then we guided Herman in, and secured him to *Greenswallow*'s maintenance sled. (The sled was little more than a toolshed with jet nozzles.) I recovered my bag and stowed it on board.

"I'd better get my stuff," Cathie said. "You can get Herman over all right?"

"Of course," said Marj. "*Amity*'s sled is secured outside the lock. Use that."

She hesitated in the open hatchway, raised her left hand, and spread the fingers wide. Her eyes grew very round, and she formed two syllables that I was desperately slow to understand: in fact, I don't think I translated the gesture, the word, until we were halfway across to *Amity*, and the lock was irrevocably closed behind us.

"Good-bye."

Cathie's green eyes sparkled with barely controlled emotion across a dozen or so monitors. Her black hair, which had been tied back earlier, now framed her angular features and fell to her shoulders. It was precisely in that partial state of disarray that tends to be most appealing. She looked as if she'd been crying, but her jaw was set, and she stood erect. Beneath the gray tunic, her breast rose and fell.

"What the hell are you doing, Perth?" demanded McGuire. He looked tired, almost ill. He'd gained weight since we'd left the Cape, his hair had whitened and retreated, his flesh had grown blotchy, and he'd developed jowls. The contrast with his dapper image in the mission photo was sobering. "Get moving!" he said, striving to keep his voice from rising. "We're not going to make our burn!"

"I'm staying where I am," she said. "I couldn't make it over there now anyway. I wouldn't even have time to put on the suit."

McGuire's puffy eyelids slid slowly closed. "Why?" he asked.

She looked out of the cluster of screens, a segmented Cathie, a group-Cathie. "Your ship won't support six people, Mac."

"Dammit!" His voice was a harsh rasp. "It would have just meant we'd cut down activity. Sleep a lot." He waved a hand in front of his eyes, as though his vision were blurred. "Cathie, we've lost you. There's no way we can get you back!"

"I know."

No one said anything. Iseminger stared at her.

"Is Herman okay?" she asked.

"Marj is still working on him," I said. "She thinks we got him across okay."

"Good."

A series of yellow lamps blinked on across the pilot's console. We had two minutes. "Damn," I said, suddenly aware of another danger: *Amity* was rotating, turning toward its new course. Would *Greenswallow* even survive the ignition? I looked at McGuire, who understood. His fingers flicked over press pads, and rows of numbers flashed across the navigation monitor. I could see muscles working in Cathie's jaws; she looked down at Mac's station as though she could read the result.

"It's all right," he said. "She'll be clear."

JACK MCDEVITT

"Cathie . . ." Iseminger's voice was almost strangled. "If I'd known you intended anything like this . . ."

"I know, Ed." Her tone was gentle, a lover's voice, perhaps. Her eyes were wet: she smiled anyway, full face, up close.

Deep in the systems, pumps began to whine. "I wish," said Iseminger, absolutely without expression, "that we could do something."

She turned her back, strode with unbearable grace across the command center, away from us, and passed into the shadowy interior of the cockpit. Another camera picked her up there, and we got a profile: she was achingly lovely in the soft glow of the navigation lamps.

"There is something . . . you can do," she said. "Build Landolfi's engine. And come back for me."

For a brief moment, I thought Mac was going to abort the burn. But he sat frozen, fists clenched, and did the right thing, which is to say, nothing. It struck me that McGuire was incapable of intervening.

And I knew also that the woman in the cockpit was terrified of what she had done. It had been a good performance, but she'd utterly failed to conceal the fear that looked out of her eyes. And I realized with shock that she'd acted, not to prolong her life, but to save the Program. I watched her face as *Amity's* engines ignited, and we began to draw away. Like McGuire, she seemed paralyzed, as though the nature of the calamity which she'd embraced was just becoming clear to her. Then it—she—was gone.

"What happened to the picture?" snapped Iseminger.

"She turned it off," I said. "I don't think she wants us to see her just now."

He glared at me, and spoke to Mac. "Why the hell," he demanded, "couldn't he have brought her back with him?" His fists were knotted.

"I didn't know," I said. "How could I know?" And I wondered, how could I not?

When the burn ended, the distance between the two ships had opened to only a few kilometers. But it was a gulf, I thought, wider than any across which men had before looked at each other.

Iseminger called her name relentlessly. (We knew she could hear us.) But we got only the carrier wave.

Then her voice crackled across the command center. "Good," she said. "Excellent. Check the recorders: make sure you got everything on tape." Her image was back. She was in full light again, tying up her hair. Her eyes were hooded, and her lips pursed thoughtfully. "Rob," she continued, "fade it out during Ed's response, when he's calling my name. Probably, you'll want to reduce the background noise at that point. Cut all the business about who's responsible. We want a sacrifice, not an oversight."

"My God, Cathie," I said. I stared at her, trying to understand. "What have you done?"

She took a deep breath. "I meant what I said. I have enough food to get by here for eight years or so. More if I stretch it. *And plenty of fresh air.* Well, relatively fresh. I'm better off than any of us would be if six people were trying to survive on *Amity*."

"Cathie!" howled McGuire. He sounded in physical agony. "Cathie, we didn't know for sure about life support. The converters might have kept up. There might have been enough air! It was just an estimate!"

"This is a hell of a time to tell me," she said. "Well, it doesn't matter now. Listen, I'll be fine. I've got books to read, and maybe one to write. My long-range communications are kaput, Rob knows that, so you'll have to come back for the book, too." She smiled. "You'll like it, Mac." The command center got very still. "And on nights when things really get boring, I can play bridge with the computer."

McGuire shook his head. "You're sure you'll be all right? You seemed pretty upset a few minutes ago."

She looked at me and winked.

"The first Cathie was staged, Mac," I said.

"I give up," McGuire sighed. " Why?" He swiveled round to face the image on his screen. "Why would you do that?"

"That young woman," she replied, "was committing an act of uncommon valor, as they say in the Marines. And she had to be vulnerable." And compellingly lovely, I thought. In those last moments, I was realizing what it might mean to love Cathie Perth. "This Cathie," she grinned, "is doing the only sensible thing. And taking a sabbatical as well. Do what you can to get the ship built. I'll be waiting. Come if you can." She paused. "Somebody should suggest they name it after Victor."

. . .

This is the fifth Christmas since that one on Callisto. It's a long time by any human measure. We drifted out of radio contact during the first week. There was some talk of broadcasting instructions to her for repairing her long-range transmission equipment. But she'd have to go outside to do it, so the idea was prudently tabled.

She was right about that tape. In my lifetime, I've never seen people so single-mindedly aroused. It created a global surge of sympathy and demands for action that seem to grow in intensity with each passing year. Funded partially by contributions and technical assistance from abroad, NASA has been pushing the construction of the fusion vessel that Victor Landolfi dreamed of.

Iseminger was assigned to help with the computer systems, and he's kept me informed of progress. The most recent public estimates had anticipated a spring launch. But that single word *September* in Iseminger's card suggests that one more obstacle has been encountered; and it means still another year before we can hope to reach her.

We broadcast to her on a regular basis. I volunteered to help, and I sit sometimes and talk to her for hours. She gets a regular schedule of news, entertainment, sports, whatever. And, if she's listening, she knows that we're coming.

And she also knows that her wish that the fusion ship be named for Victor Landolfi has been disregarded. The rescue vehicle will be the *Catherine Perth*.

If she's listening: we have no way of knowing. And I worry a lot. Can a human being survive six years of absolute solitude? Iseminger was here for a few days last summer, and he tells me he is confident. "She's a tough lady," he said, any number of times. "Nothing bothers her. She even gave us a little theater at the end."

And that's what scares me: Cathie's theatrical technique. I've thought about it, on the long ride home, and here. I kept a copy of the complete tape of that final conversation, despite McGuire's instructions to the contrary, and I've watched it a few times. It's locked downstairs in a file cabinet now, and I don't look at it anymore. I'm afraid to. There are two Cathie Perths on the recording: the frightened, courageous one who galvanized a global public; and our Cathie, preoccupied with her job, flexible, almost indifferent to her situation. A survivor.

And, God help me, I can't tell which one was staged.

---

1. Why is the narrator "very afraid" when he thinks of Iseminger's quest to rescue Cathie Perth?

2. Why does Cathie propose a toast to Frank Steinitz? Why does it come as a surprise to the other crew members?

3. When he looks at the tape showing Cathie being left on the *Greenswallow*, why can't the narrator tell which of the "two Cathie Perths" is staged? Does Cathie's motivation determine how courageous her decision is?

4. Does the scientific knowledge gained through space exploration justify the risk of crew members' deaths?

KAREN JOY FOWLER (1950–) was born in Bloomington, Indiana, and garnered attention with her first collection of short fiction, *Artificial Things* (1986). After being awarded the 1987 Hugo Award for best new science fiction writer, Fowler published a second collection, *Peripheral Vision* (1990), and her award-winning debut novel, *Sarah Canary* (1991). Described by one reviewer as "part ghost story, part picaresque adventure," *Sarah Canary* firmly established Fowler's reputation as a science fiction writer. Fowler often uses the backdrop of science fiction to probe various aspects of human nature by casting them in a new or unusual light. Also recognized for her ability to span genres and styles, Fowler achieved mainstream success with her New York Times Notable Book, *The Jane Austen Book Club* (2004), a modern comedy of manners that was adapted into a movie of the same name.

Face Value

It was almost like being alone. Taki, who had been alone one way or another most of his life, recognized this and thought he could deal with it. What choice did he have? It was only that he had allowed himself to hope for something different. A second star, small and dim, joined the sun in the sky, making its appearance over the rope bridge which spanned the empty river. Taki crossed the bridge in a hurry to get inside before the hottest part of the day began.

Something flashed briefly in the dust at his feet and he stooped to pick it up. It was one of Hesper's poems, half finished, left out all night. Taki had stopped reading Hesper's poetry. It reflected nothing, not a whisper of her life here with him, but was filled with longing for things and people behind her. Taki pocketed the poem on his way to the house, stood outside the door, and removed what dust he could with the stiff brush which hung at the entrance. He keyed his admittance; the door made a slight sucking sound as it resealed behind him.

Hesper had set out an iced glass of ade for him. Taki drank it at a gulp, superimposing his own dusty fingerprints over hers sketched lightly in the condensation on the glass. The drink was heavily sugared and only made him thirstier.

A cloth curtain separated one room from another, a blue sheet, Hesper's innovation since the dwelling was designed as a single, multi-functional space. Through the curtain Taki heard a voice and knew Hesper was listening again to her mother's letter—Earth weather, the romances of her younger cousins. The letter had arrived weeks ago, but Taki was careful not to remind Hesper how old its news really was. If she chose to imagine the lives of her family moving along the same timeline as her own, then this must be a fantasy she needed. She knew the truth. In the time it had taken her to travel here with Taki, her mother had grown old and died. Her cousins had settled into marriages happy or unhappy or had faced life alone. The letters which continued to arrive with some regularity were an illusion. A lifetime later Hesper would answer them.

Taki ducked through the curtain to join her. "Hot," he told her as if this were news. She lay on their mat stomach down, legs bent at the knees, feet crossed in the air. Her hair, the color of dried grasses, hung over her face. Taki stared for a moment at the hack of her head. "Here," he said. He pulled her poem from his pocket and laid it by her hand. "I found this out front."

Hesper switched off the letter and rolled onto her back away from the poem. She was careful not to look at Taki. Her cheeks were stained with irregular red patches so that Taki knew she had been crying again. The observation caused him a familiar mixture of sympathy and impatience. His feelings for Hesper always came in these uncomfortable combinations; it tired him.

" 'Out front,' " Hesper repeated, and her voice held a practiced tone of uninterested nastiness. "And how did you determine that one part of this featureless landscape was the 'front'?"

"Because of the door. We have only the one door so it's the front door."

"No," said Hesper. "If we had two doors then one might arguably be the front door and the other the back door, but with only one it's just the door." Her gaze went straight upward. "You use words so carelessly. Words from another world. They mean nothing here." Her eyelids fluttered briefly, the lashes darkened with tears. "It's not just an annoyance to me, you know," she said. "It can't help but damage your work."

"My work is the study of the mene," Taki answered. "Not the creation of a new language," and Hesper's eyes closed.

"I really don't see the difference," she told him. She lay a moment longer without moving, then opened her eyes and looked at Taki directly. "I don't want to have this conversation. I don't know why I started it. Let's rewind, run it again. I'll be the wife this time. You come in and say, 'Honey, I'm home!' and I'll ask you how your morning was."

Taki began to suggest that this was a scene from another world and would mean nothing here. He had not yet framed the sentence when he heard the door seal release and saw Hesper's face go hard and white. She reached for her poem and slid it under the scarf at her waist. Before she could get to her feet the first of the mene had joined them in the bedroom. Taki ducked through the curtain to fasten the door before the temperature inside the house rose. The outer room was filled with dust and the hands which reached out to him as he went past left dusty streaks on his clothes and his skin. He counted eight of the mene, fluttering about him like large moths, moths the size of human children, but with furry vestigial wings, hourglass abdomens, sticklike limbs. They danced about him in the open spaces, looked through the cupboards, pulled the tapes from his desk. When they had their backs to him he could see the symmetrical arrangement of dark spots which marked their wings in a pattern resembling a human face. A very sad face, very distinct. Masculine, Taki had always thought, but Hesper disagreed.

The party which had made initial contact under the leadership of Hans Mene so many years ago had wisely found the faces too whimsical for mention in their report. Instead they had included pictures and allowed them to speak for themselves. Perhaps the original explorers had been asking the same question Hesper posed the first time Taki showed her the pictures. Was the face really there? Or was this only evidence of the ability of humans to see their own faces in everything? Hesper had a poem entitled "The Kitchen God," which recounted the true story of a woman about a century ago who had found the image of Christ in the burn marks on a tortilla. "Do *they* see it, too?" she had asked Taki, but there was as yet no way to ask this of the mene, no way to know if they had reacted with shock and recognition to the faces of the first humans they had seen, though studies of the mene eye suggested a finer depth perception which might significantly distort the flat image.

Taki thought that Hesper's own face had changed since the day, only six months ago calculated as Traveltime, when she had said she would come here with him and he thought it was because she loved him. They had sorted through all the information which had been collected to date on the mene and her face had been all sympathy then. "What would it be like," she asked him, "to be able to fly and then to lose this ability? To outgrow it? What would a loss like that do to the racial consciousness of a species?"

"It happened so long ago, I doubt it's even noticed as a loss," Taki had answered. "Legends, myths not really believed perhaps. Probably not even that. In the racial memory not even a whisper."

Hesper had ignored him. "What a shame they don't write poetry," she had said. She was finding them less romantic now as she joined Taki in the outer room, her face stoic. The mene surrounded her, ran their string-fingered hands all over her body, inside her clothing. One mene attempted to insert a finger into her mouth, but Hesper tightened her lips together resolutely, dust on her chin. Her eyes were fastened on Taki. Accusingly? Beseechingly? Taki was no good at reading people's eyes. He looked away.

Eventually the mene grew bored. They left in groups, a few lingering behind to poke among the boxes in the bedroom, then following the others until Hesper arid Taki were left alone. Hesper went to wash herself as thoroughly as their limited water supply allowed; Taki swept up the loose dust. Before he finished, Hesper returned, showing him her empty jewelry box without a word. The jewelry had all belonged to her mother.

"I'll get them when it cools," Taki told her,

"Thank you."

It was always Hesper's things that the mene took. The more they disgusted her, pawing over her, rummaging through her things, no way to key the door against clever mene fingers even if Taki had agreed to lock them out, which he had not, the more fascinating they seemed to find her. They touched her twice as often as they touched Taki and much more insistently. They took her jewelry, her poems, her letters, all the things she treasured most, and Taki believed, although it was far too early in his studies really to speculate with any assurance, that the mene read something off the objects. The initial explorers had concluded that mene communication was entirely telepathic, and if this was accurate, then Taki's speculation was not such a leap. Certainly the mene didn't value the objects for themselves. Taki always found them discarded in the dust on this side of the rope bridge.

The fact that everything would be easily recovered did nothing to soften Hesper sense of invasion. She mixed herself a drink, stirring it with the metal straw which poked through the dust-proof lid. "You shouldn't allow it," she said at last, and Taki knew from the time that had elapsed that she had tried not to begin this familiar conversation. He appreciated her effort as much as he was annoyed by her failure.

"It's part of my job," he reminded her. "We have to be accessible to them. I study them. They study us. There's no way to differentiate the two activities and certainly no way to establish communication except simultaneously."

"You're letting them study us, but you're giving them a false picture. You're allowing them to believe that humans intrude on each other in this way. Does it occur to you that they may be involved in similar charades? If so, what can either of us learn?"

Taki took a deep breath. "The need for privacy may not be as intrinsically human as you imagine. I could point to many societies which afforded very little of this. As for any deliberate misrepresentations on their part—well, isn't that the whole rationale for not sending a study team? Wouldn't I be farther along if I were working with environmentalists, physiologists, linguists? But the risk of contamination increases exponentially with each additional human. We would be too much of a presence. Of course, I will be very careful. I am far from the stage in my study where I can begin to draw conclusions. When I visit them . . ."

"Reinforcing the notion that such visits are ordinary human behavior . . ." Hesper was looking at Taki with great coolness.

"When I visit them I am much more circumspect," Taki finished. "I conduct my study as unobtrusively as possible."

"And what do you imagine you are studying?" Hesper asked. She closed her lips tightly over the straw and drank. Taki regarded her steadily and with exasperation.

"Is this a trick question?" he asked. "I imagine I am studying the mene. What do you imagine I am studying?"

"What humans always study," said Hesper. "Humans."

You never saw one of the mene alone. Not ever. One never wandered off to watch the sun set or took its food to a solitary hole to eat without sharing. They did everything in groups and although Taki had been observing them for weeks now and was able to identify individuals and had compiled charts of the groupings he had seen, trying to isolate families or friendships or work-castes, still the results were inconclusive.

His attempts at communication were similarly discouraging. He had tried verbalizations, but had not expected a response to them; he had no idea how they processed audio information although they could hear. He had tried clapping and gestures, simple hand signals for the names of common objects. He had no sense that these efforts were noticed. They were so unfocused when he dealt with them, fluttering here, fluttering there. Taki's ESP quotient had never been measurable, yet he tried that route, too. He tried to send a simple command. He would trap a mene hand and hold it against his own cheek, trying to form in his mind the picture which corresponded to the action. When he released the hand, sticky mene fingers might linger for a moment or they might slip away immediately, tangle in his hair instead, or tap his teeth. Mene teeth were tiny and pointed like wires. Taki saw them only when the mene ate. At other times they were hidden inside the folds of skin which almost hid their eyes as well. Taki speculated that the skin flaps protected their mouths and eyes from the dust. Taki found mene faces less expressive than their backs. Head-on they appeared petaled and blind as flowers. When he wanted to differentiate one mene from another, Taki looked at their wings.

Hesper had warned him there would be no art and he had asked her how she could be so sure. "Because their communication system is perfect," she said. "Out of one brain and into the next with no loss of meaning, no need for abstraction. Art arises from the inability to communicate. Art is the imperfect symbol. Isn't it?" But Taki, watching the mene carry water up from their underground deposits, asked himself where the line between tools and art objects should be drawn. For no functional reason that he could see, the water containers curved in the centers like the shapes of the mene's own abdomens.

Taki followed the mene below ground, down some shallow, rough-cut stairs into the darkness. The mene themselves were slightly luminescent when there was no other light; at times and seasons some were spectacularly so and Taki's best guess was that this was sexual. Even with the dimmer members, Taki could see well enough. He moved through a long tunnel with a low ceiling which made him stoop. He could hear water at the other end of it, not the water itself, but a special quality to the silence which told him water was near. The lake was clearly artificial, collected during the rainy season which no human had seen yet. The tunnel narrowed sharply. Taki could have gone forward, but felt suddenly claustrophobic and backed out instead. What did the mene think, he wondered, of the fact that he came here without Hesper. Did they notice this at all? Did it teach them anything about humans that they were capable of understanding?

"Their lives together are perfect," Hesper said. "Except for those useless wings. If they are ever able to talk with us at all it will be because of those wings."

Of course Hesper was a poet. The world was all language as far as she was concerned.

When Taki first met Hesper, at a party given by a colleague of his, he had asked her what she did. "I name things," she had said. "I try to find the right names for things." In retrospect Taki thought it was bullshit. He couldn't remember why he had been so impressed with it at the time, a deliberate miscommunication, when a simple answer, "I write poetry," would have been so clear and easy to understand. He felt the same way about her poetry itself, needlessly obscure, slightly evocative, but it left the reader feeling that he had fallen short somehow, that it had been a test and he had flunked it. It was unkind poetry and Taki had worked so hard to read it then.

"Am I right?" he would ask her anxiously when he finished. "Is that what you're saying?" but she would answer that the poem spoke for itself.

"Once it's on the page, I've lost control over it. Then the reader determines what it says or how it works." Hesper's eyes were gray, the irises so large and intense within their dark rings, that they made Taki dizzy. "So you're always right. By definition. Even if it's not remotely close to what I intended."

What Taki really wanted was to find himself in Hesper's poems. He would read them anxiously for some symbol which could be construed as him, some clue as to his impact on her life. But he was never there.

It was against policy to send anyone into the field alone. There were pros and cons, of course, but ultimately the isolation of a single professional was seen as too cruel. For shorter projects there were advantages in sending a threesome, but during a longer study the group dynamics in a trio often became difficult. Two were considered ideal and Taki knew that Rawji and Heyen had applied for this post, a husband and wife team in which both members were trained for this type of study. He had never stopped being surprised that the post had been offered to him instead. He could not have even been considered if Hesper had not convinced the members of the committee of her willingness to accompany him, but she must have done much more. She must have impressed someone very much for them to decide that one trained xenologist and one poet might be more valuable than two trained xenologists. The committee had made some noises about "contamination" occurring between the two trained professionals, but Taki found this argument specious. "What did you say to them?" he asked her after her interview and she shrugged.

"You know," she said. "Words."

Taki had hidden things from the committee during his own interview. Things about Hesper. Her moods, her deep attachment to her mother, her unreliable attachment to him. He must have known it would never work out, but he walked about in those days with the stunned expression of a man who has been given everything. Could he be blamed for accepting it? Could he be blamed for believing in

Hesper's unexpected willingness to accompany him? It made a sort of equation for Taki. *If* Hesper was willing to give up everything and come with Taki, *then* Hesper loved Taki. An ordinary marriage commitment was reviewable every five years; this was something much greater. No other explanation made any sense.

The equation still held a sort of inevitability for Taki. *Then* Hesper loved Taki, *if* Hesper were willing to come with him. So somehow, sometime, Taki had done something which lost him Hesper's love. If he could figure out what, perhaps he could make her love him again. "Do you love me?" he had asked Hesper, only once; he had too much pride for these thinly disguised pleadings. "Love is such a difficult word," she had answered, but her voice had been filled with a rare softness and had not hurt Taki as much as it might.

The daystar was appearing again when Taki returned home. Hesper had made a meal which suggested she was coping well today. It included a sort of pudding made of a local fruit they found themselves able to tolerate. Hesper called the pudding "boxty." It was apparently a private joke. Taki was grateful for the food and the joke, even if he didn't understand it. He tried to keep the conversation lighthearted, talking to Hesper about the mene water jars. Taki's position was that when the form of a practical object was less utilitarian than it might be, then it was art. Hesper laughed. She ran through a list of human artifacts and made him classify them.

"A paper clip," she said.

"The shape hasn't changed in centuries." he told her. "Not art."

"A safety pin."

Taki hesitated. How essential was the coil at the bottom of the pin? Very. "Not art," he decided.

"A hair brush."

"Boar bristle?"

"Wood handle."

"Art. Definitely."

She smiled at him. "You're confusing ornamentation with art. But why not? It's as good a definition as any," she told him. "Eat your boxty."

They spend the whole afternoon alone, uninterrupted. Taki transcribed the morning's notes into his files, reviewed his tapes. Hesper recorded a letter whose recipient would never hear it and sang softly to herself.

That night he reached for her, his hand along the curve at her waist. She stiffened slightly, but responded by putting her hand on his face. He kissed her and her mouth did not move. His movements became less gentle. It might have been passion; it might have been anger. She told him to stop, hut he didn't. Couldn't. Wouldn't. "Stop," she said again and he heard she was crying. "They're here. Please stop. They're watching us."

"Studying us," Taki said. "Let them," but he rolled away and released her. They were alone in the room. He would have seen the mene easily in the dark. "Hesper," he said. "There's no one here."

She lay rigid on her side of their bed. He saw the stitching of her backbone disappearing into her neck and had a sudden feeling that he could see everything about her, how she was made, how she was held together. It made him no less angry.

"I'm sorry," Hesper told him, but he didn't believe her. Even so, he was asleep before she was. He made his own breakfast the next morning without leaving anything out for her. He was gone before she had gotten out of bed.

The mene were gathering food, dried husks thick enough to protect the liquid fruit during the two-star dry season. They punctured the husks with their needle-thin teeth. Several crowded about him, greeting him with their fingers, checking his pockets, removing his recorder and passing it about until one of them dropped it in the dust. When they returned to work, Taki retrieved it, wiped it as clean as he could. He sat down to watch them, logged everything he observed. He noted in particular how often they touched each other and wondered what each touch meant. Affection? Communication? Some sort of chain of command?

Later he went underground again, choosing another tunnel, looking for one which wouldn't narrow so as to exclude him, but finding himself beside the same lake with the same narrow access ahead. He went deeper this time until it gradually became too close for his shoulders. Before him he could see a luminescence; he smelled the dusty odor of the mene and could just make out a sound, too, a sort of movement, a grass-rubbing-together sound. He stooped and strained his eyes to see something in the faint light. It was like looking into the wrong end of a pair of binoculars. The tunnel narrowed and narrowed. Beyond it must be the mene homes and he could never get into them. He contrasted this with the easy access they had to his home. At the end of his vision he thought he could just see something move, but he wasn't sure. A light touch on the back of his neck and another behind his knee startled him. He twisted around to see a group of the mene crowded into the tunnel behind him. It gave him a feeling of being trapped and he had to force himself to he very gentle as he pushed his way back and let the mene go through. The dark pattern of their wings stood in high relief against the luminescent bodies. The human faces grew smaller and smaller until they disappeared.

"Leave me alone," Hesper told him. It took Taki completely by surprise. He had done nothing but enter the bedroom; he had not even spoken yet. "Just leave me alone."

Taki saw no signs that Hesper had ever gotten up. She lay against the pillow and her cheek was still creased from the wrinkles in the sheets. She had not been crying. There was something worse in her face, something which alarmed Taki.

"Hesper?" he asked. "Hesper? Did you eat anything? Let me get you something to eat."

It took Hesper a moment to answer. When she did, she looked ordinary again. "Thank you," she said. "I am hungry." She joined him in the outer room, wrapped in their blanket, her hair tangled around her face. She got a drink for herself, dropping the empty glass once, stooping to retrieve it. Taki had the strange impression that the glass fell slowly. When they had first arrived, the gravitational pull had been light, just perceptibly lighter than Earth's. Without quite noticing, this had registered on him in a sort of lightheartedness. But Hesper had complained of feelings of dislocation, disconnection. Taki put together a cold breakfast, which Hesper ate slowly, watching her own hands as if they fascinated her. Taki looked away. "Fork," she said. He looked back. She was smiling at him.

"What?"

"Fork."

He understood. "Not art."

"Four tines?"

He didn't answer.

"Roses carved on the handle."

"Well then, art. Because of the handle. Not because of the tines."
He was greatly reassured.

The mene came while he was telling her about the tunnel. They
put their dusty fingers in her food, pulled it apart. Hesper set her fork
down and pushed the plate away. When they reached for her she pushed
them away, too. They came back. Hesper shoved harder.

"Hesper," said Taki.

"I just want to be left alone. They never leave me alone." Hesper
stood up, towering above the mene. The blanket fell to the floor. "We
flew here," Hesper said to the mene. "Did you see the ship? Didn't
you see the pod? Doesn't that interest you? Flying?" She laughed and
flapped her arms until they froze, horizontal at her sides. The mene
reached for her again and she brought her arms in to protect her breasts,
pushing the mene away repeatedly, harder and harder, until they tired
of approaching her and went into the bedroom, reappearing with her
poems in their hands. The door sealed behind them.

"I'll get them back for you," Taki promised, but Hesper told him
not to bother.

"I haven't written in weeks," she said. "In case you hadn't noticed.
I haven't finished a poem since I came here. I've lost that. Along with
everything else." She brushed at her hair rather frantically with one
hand. "It doesn't matter," she added. "My poems? Not art."

"Are you the best person to judge that?" Taki asked.

"Don't patronize me." Hesper returned to the table, looked again
at the plate which held her unfinished breakfast, dusty from handling.
"My critical faculties are still intact. It's just the poetry that's gone."
She took the dish to clean it, scraped the food away. "I was never any
good," she said. "Why do you think I came here? I had no poetry of
my own so I thought I'd write the mene's. I came to a world without
words. I hoped it would be clarifying. I knew there was a risk." Her
hands moved very fast. "I want you to know I don't blame you."

"Come and sit down a moment, Hesper," Taki said, but she shook
her head. She looked down at her body and moved her hands over it.

"They feel sorry for us. Did you know that? They feel sorry about our bodies."

"How do *you* know that?" Taki asked.

"Logic. We have these completely functional bodies. No useless wings. Not art." Hesper picked up the blanket and headed for the bedroom. At the cloth curtain she paused a moment. "They love our loneliness, though. They've taken all mine. They never leave me alone now." She thrust her right arm suddenly out into the air. It made the curtain ripple. "Go away," she said, ducking behind the sheet.

Taki followed her. He was very frightened. "No one is here but us, Hesper," he told her. He tried to put his arms around her but she pushed him back and began to dress.

"Don't touch me all the time," she said. He sank onto the bed and watched her. She sat on the floor to fasten her boots.

"Are you going out, Hesper?" he asked and she laughed.

"Hesper is out," she said. "Hesper is out of place, out of time, out of luck, and out of her mind. Hesper has vanished completely. Hesper was broken into and taken."

Taki fastened his hands tightly together. "Please don't do this to me, Hesper," he pleaded. "It's really so unfair. When did I ask so much of you? I took what you offered me; I never took anything else. Please don't do this."

Hesper had found the brush and was pulling it roughly through her hair. He rose and went to her, grabbing her by the arms, trying to turn her to face him. "Please, Hesper!"

She shook loose from him without really appearing to notice his hands, continued to work through the worst of her tangles. When she did turn around, her face was familiar, but somehow not Hesper's face. It was a face which startled him.

"Hesper is gone," it said. "We have her. You've lost her. We are ready to talk to you. Even though you will never, never, never understand." She reached out to touch him, laying her open palm against his cheek and leaving it there.

1. Why do the mene take Hesper's belongings, and not Taki's? Why does recovering her things do "nothing to soften Hesper's sense of invasion"?

2. When Taki says that he is studying the mene, why does Hesper challenge him by saying that he is studying "what humans always study, . . . Humans"?

3. Why does Hesper believe that if the mene "are ever able to talk with us at all" it will because of "those useless wings"? Why do the mene's wings have markings that resemble the human face?

4. Why is coming to "a world without words" not clarifying to Hesper, as she had hoped?   At the end of the story, in what sense is Hesper "gone"? What has happened to her?

CONNIE WILLIS (1945–) was born in Denver, Colorado, and taught
school in Connecticut for three years before taking up writing full-time
in 1969. Her novels and short stories have won numerous Hugo and
Nebula awards. Her best-known works include *The Doomsday Book*
(1992), a time-travel novel set in fourteenth-century England during
the Black Plague; *Bellweather* (1996); and *To Say Nothing of the Dog*
(1998). Willis was named Best Fantasy and Science Fiction Writer of
the Nineties by *Locus* magazine. Her writing ranges across genres, from
science fiction to fantasy to horror, and it often blends comedy and serious
scientific speculation. "Even the Queen," which first appeared in 1992 in
the collection *Asimov's Science Fiction*, is one of Willis's most decorated
stories, winning four different awards. She is a member of the Science
Fiction Hall of Fame.

Even the Queen

The phone sang as I was looking over the defense's motion to dismiss.
"It's the universal ring," my law clerk Bysshe said, reaching for it.
"It's probably the defendant. They don't let you use signatures from
jail."

"No, it's not," I said. "It's my mother."

"Oh." Bysshe reached for the receiver. "Why isn't she using her
signature?"

"Because she knows I don't want to talk to her. She must have
found out what Perdita's done."

"Your daughter Perdita?" he asked, holding the receiver against his
chest. "The one with the little girl?"

"No, that's Viola. Perdita's my younger daughter. The one with no
sense."

"What's she done?"

"She's joined the Cyclists."

Bysshe looked enquiringly blank, but I was not in the mood to enlighten him. Or in the mood to talk to Mother. "I know exactly what Mother will say. She'll ask me why I didn't tell her, and then she'll demand to know what I'm going to do about it, and there is nothing I *can* do about it, or I obviously would have done it already."

Bysshe looked bewildered. "Do you want me to tell her you're in court?"

"No." I reached for the receiver. "I'll have to talk to her sooner or later." I took it from him. "Hello, Mother," I said.

"Traci," Mother said dramatically, "Perdita has become a Cyclist."

"I know."

"Why didn't you tell me?"

"I thought Perdita should tell you herself."

"Perdita!" She snorted. "She wouldn't tell me. She knows what I'd have to say about it. I suppose you told Karen."

"Karen's not here. She's in Iraq." The only good thing about this whole debacle was that thanks to Iraq's eagerness to show it was a responsible world-community member and its previous penchant for self-destruction, my mother-in-law was in the one place on the planet where the phone service was bad enough that I could claim I'd tried to call her but couldn't get through, and she'd have to believe me.

The Liberation has freed us from all sorts of indignities and scourges, including Iraq's Saddams, but mothers-in-law aren't one of them, and I was almost happy with Perdita for her excellent timing. When I didn't want to kill her.

"What's Karen doing in Iraq?" Mother asked.

"Negotiating a Palestinian homeland."

"And meanwhile her granddaughter is ruining her life," she said irrelevantly. "Did you tell Viola?"

"I *told* you, Mother. I thought Perdita should tell all of you herself."

"Well, she didn't. And this morning one of my patients, Carol Chen, called me and demanded to know what I was keeping from her. I had no idea what she was talking about."

"How did Carol Chen find out?"

"From her daughter, who almost joined the Cyclists last year. *Her* family talked her out of it," she said accusingly. "Carol was convinced the medical community had discovered some terrible side effect of ammenerol and were covering it up. I cannot believe you didn't tell me, Traci."

And I cannot believe I didn't have Bysshe tell her I was in court, I thought. "I told you, Mother. I thought it was Perdita's place to tell you. After all, it's her decision."

"Oh, *Trac*i!" Mother said. "You cannot mean that!"

In the first fine flush of freedom after the Liberation, I had entertained hopes that it would change everything—that it would somehow do away with inequality and matriarchal dominance and those humorless women determined to eliminate the word "manhole" and third-person singular pronouns from the language.

Of course it didn't. Men still make more money, "herstory" is still a blight on the semantic landscape, and my mother can still say, "Oh, *Trac*i!" in a tone that reduces me to preadolescence.

"Her decision!" Mother said. "Do you mean to tell me you plan to stand idly by and allow your daughter to make the mistake of her life?"

"What can I do? She's twenty-two years old and of sound mind."

"If she were of sound mind, she wouldn't be doing this. Didn't you try to talk her out of it?"

"Of course I did, Mother."

"And?"

"And I didn't succeed. She's determined to become a Cyclist."

"Well, there must be something we can do. Get an injunction or hire a deprogrammer or sue the Cyclists for brainwashing. You're a judge, there must be some law you can invoke—"

"The law is called personal sovereignty, Mother, and since it was what made the Liberation possible in the first place, it can hardly be used against Perdita. Her decision meets all the criteria for a case of personal sovereignty: It's a personal decision, it was made by a sovereign adult, it affects no one else—"

"What about my practice? Carol Chen is convinced shunts cause cancer."

"Any effect on your practice is considered an indirect effect. Like secondary smoke. It doesn't apply. Mother, whether we like it or not, Perdita has a perfect right to do this, and we don't have any right to interfere. A free society has to be based on respecting others' opinions and leaving each other alone. We have to respect Perdita's right to make her own decisions."

All of which was true. It was too bad I hadn't said any of it to Perdita when she called. What I had said, in a tone that sounded exactly like my mother's, was "Oh, Per*dita*!"

"This is all your fault, you know," Mother said. "I *told* you you shouldn't have let her get that tattoo over her shunt. And don't tell me it's a free society. What good is a free society when it allows my granddaughter to ruin her life?" She hung up.

I handed the receiver back to Bysshe.

"I really liked what you said about respecting your daughter's right to make her own decisions," he said. He held out my robe. "And about not interfering in her life."

"I want you to research the precedents on deprogramming for me," I said, sliding my arms into the sleeves. "And find out if the Cyclists have been charged with any free choice violations—brainwashing, intimidation, coercion."

The phone sang, another universal. "Hello, who's calling?" Bysshe said cautiously. His voice became suddenly friendlier. "Just a minute." He put his hand over the receiver. "It's your daughter Viola."

I took the receiver. "Hello, Viola."

"I just talked to Grandma," she said. "You will not believe what Perdita's done now. She's joined the Cyclists."

"I know," I said.

"You *know*? And you didn't tell me? I can't believe this. You never tell me anything."

"I thought Perdita should tell you herself," I said tiredly.

"Are you kidding? She never tells me anything either. That time she had eyebrow implants, she didn't tell me for three weeks, and when she got the laser tattoo, she didn't tell me at all. *Twidge* told me. You should have called me. Did you tell Grandma Karen?"

"She's in Baghdad," I said.

"I know," Viola said. "I called her."

"Oh, Viola, you didn't!"

"Unlike you, Mom, I believe in telling members of our family about matters that concern them."

"What did she say?" I asked, a kind of numbness settling over me now that the shock had worn off.

"I couldn't get through to her. The phone service over there is terrible. I got somebody who didn't speak English, and then I got cut off, and when I tried again they said the whole city was down."

Thank you, I breathed silently. Thank you, thank you, thank you.

"Grandma Karen has a right to know, Mother. Think of the effect this could have on Twidge. She thinks Perdita's wonderful. When Perdita got the eyebrow implants, Twidge glued LEDs to hers, and I almost never got them off. What if Twidge decides to join the Cyclists, too?"

"Twidge is only nine. By the time she's supposed to get her shunt, Perdita will have long since quit." I hope, I added silently. Perdita had had the tattoo for a year and a half now and showed no signs of tiring of it. "Besides, Twidge has more sense."

"It's true. Oh, Mother, how *could* Perdita do this? Didn't you tell her about how awful it was?"

"Yes," I said. "And inconvenient. And unpleasant and unbalancing and painful. None of it made the slightest impact on her. She told me she thought it would be fun."

Bysshe was pointing to his watch and mouthing, "Time for court."

"Fun!" Viola said. "When she saw what I went through that time? Honestly, Mother, sometimes I think she's completely brain dead. Can't you have her declared incompetent and locked up or something?"

"No," I said, trying to zip up my robe with one hand. "Viola, I have to go. I'm late for court. I'm afraid there's nothing we can do to stop her. She's a rational adult."

"Rational!" Viola said. "Her eyebrows light up, Mother. She has Custer's Last Stand lased on her arm."

I handed the phone to Bysshe. "Tell Viola I'll talk to her tomorrow." I zipped up my robe. "And then call Baghdad and see how long they expect the phones to be out." I started into the courtroom. "And if there are any more universal calls, make sure they're local before you answer."

Bysshe couldn't get through to Baghdad, which I took as a good sign, and my mother-in-law didn't call. Mother did, in the afternoon, to ask if lobotomies were legal.

She called again the next day. I was in the middle of my Personal Sovereignty class, explaining the inherent right of citizens in a free society to make complete jackasses of themselves. They weren't buying it.

"I think it's your mother," Bysshe whispered to me as he handed me the phone. "She's still using the universal. But it's local. I checked."

"Hello, Mother," I said.

"It's all arranged," Mother said. "We're having lunch with Perdita at McGregor's. It's on the corner of Twelfth Street and Larimer."

"I'm in the middle of class," I said.

"I know. I won't keep you. I just wanted to tell you not to worry. I've taken care of everything."

I didn't like the sound of that. "What have you done?"

"Invited Perdita to lunch with us. I told you. At McGregor's."

"Who is 'us,' Mother?"

"Just the family," she said innocently. "You and Viola."

Well, at least she hadn't brought in the deprogrammer. Yet. "What are you up to, Mother?"

"Perdita said the same thing. Can't a grandmother ask her granddaughters to lunch? Be there at twelve thirty."

"Bysshe and I have a court-calendar meeting at three."

"Oh, we'll be done by then. And bring Bysshe with you. He can provide a man's point of view."

She hung up.

"You'll have to go to lunch with me, Bysshe," I said. "Sorry."

"Why? What's going to happen at lunch?"

"I have no idea."

On the way over to McGregor's, Bysshe told me what he'd found out about the Cyclists. "They're not a cult. There's no religious connection. They seem to have grown out of a pre-Liberation women's group," he said, looking at his notes, "although there are also links to the pro-choice movement, the University of Wisconsin, and the Museum of Modern Art."

"What?"

"They call their group leaders 'docents.' Their philosophy seems to be a mix of pre-Liberation radical feminism and the environmental primitivism of the eighties. They're floratarians and they don't wear shoes."

"Or shunts," I said. We pulled up in front of McGregor's and got out of the car. "Any mind control convictions?" I asked hopefully.

"No. A bunch of suits against individual members, all of which they won."

"On grounds of personal sovereignty."

"Yeah. And a criminal one by a member whose family tried to deprogram her. The deprogrammer was sentenced to twenty years, and the family got twelve."

"Be sure to tell Mother about that one," I said, and opened the door to McGregor's.

It was one of those restaurants with a morning-glory vine twining around the maitre d's desk and garden plots between the tables.

"Perdita suggested it," Mother said, guiding Bysshe and I past the onions to our table. "She told me a lot of the Cyclists are floratarians."

"Is she here?" I asked, sidestepping a cucumber frame.

"Not yet." She pointed past a rose arbor. "There's our table."

Our table was a wicker affair under a mulberry tree. Viola and Twidge were seated on the far side next to a trellis of runner beans, looking at menus.

"What are you doing here, Twidge?" I asked. "Why aren't you in school?"

"I am," she said, holding up her LCD slate. "I'm remoting today."

"I thought she should be part of this discussion," Viola said. "After all, she'll be getting her shunt soon."

"My friend Kensy says she isn't going to get one. Like Perdita," Twidge said.

"I'm sure Kensy will change her mind when the time comes," Mother said. "Perdita will change hers, too. Bysshe, why don't you sit next to Viola?"

Bysshe slid obediently past the trellis and sat down in the wicker chair at the far end of the table. Twidge reached across Viola and handed him a menu. "This is a great restaurant," she said. "You don't have to wear shoes." She held up a bare foot to illustrate. "And if you get hungry while you're waiting, you can just pick something." She twisted around in her chair, picked two of the green beans, gave one to

Bysshe, and bit into the other one. "I bet Kensy doesn't. Kensy says a shunt hurts worse than braces."

"It doesn't hurt as much as not having one," Viola said, shooting me a Now-Do-You-See-What-My-Sister's-Caused? look.

"Traci, why don't you sit across from Viola?" Mother said to me. "And we'll put Perdita next to you when she comes."

"If she comes," Viola said.

"I told her one o'clock," Mother said, sitting down at the near end. "So we'd have a chance to plan our strategy before she gets here. I talked to Carol Chen—"

"Her daughter nearly joined the Cyclists last year," I explained to Bysshe and Viola.

"*She* said they had a family gathering, like this, and simply talked to her daughter, and she decided she didn't want to be a Cyclist after all." She looked around the table. "So I thought we'd do the same thing with Perdita. I think we should start by explaining the significance of the Liberation and the days of dark oppression that preceded it—"

"*I* think," Viola interrupted, "we should try to talk her into just going off the ammenerol for a few months instead of having the shunt removed. If she comes. Which she won't."

"Why not?"

"Would you? I mean, it's like the Inquisition. Her sitting here while all of us 'explain' at her. Perdita may be crazy, but she's not stupid."

"It's hardly the Inquisition," Mother said. She looked anxiously past me toward the door. "I'm sure Perdita—" She stopped, stood up, and plunged off suddenly through the asparagus.

I turned around, half expecting Perdita with light-up lips or a full-body tattoo, but I couldn't see through the leaves. I pushed at the branches.

"Is it Perdita?" Viola said, leaning forward.

I peered around the mulberry bush. "Oh, my God," I said.

It was my mother-in-law, wearing a black abayah and a silk yarmulke. She swept toward us through a pumpkin patch, robes billowing and eyes flashing. Mother hurried in her wake of trampled radishes, looking daggers at me.

I turned them on Viola. "It's your grandmother Karen," I said accusingly. "You told me you didn't get through to her."

"I didn't," she said. "Twidge, sit up straight. And put your slate down."

There was an ominous rustling in the rose arbor, as of leaves shrinking back in terror, and my mother-in-law arrived.

"Karen!" I said, trying to sound pleased. "What on earth are you doing here? I thought you were in Baghdad."

"I came back as soon as I got Viola's message," she said, glaring at everyone in turn. "Who's this?" she demanded, pointing at Bysshe. "Viola's new live-in?"

"No!" Bysshe said, looking horrified.

"This is my law clerk, Mother," I said. "Bysshe Adams-Hardy."

"Twidge, why aren't you in school?"

"I *am*," Twidge said. "I'm remoting." She held up her slate. "See? Math."

"I see," she said, turning to glower at me. "It's a serious enough matter to require my great-grandchild's being pulled out of school *and* the hiring of legal assistance, and yet you didn't deem it important enough to notify *me*. Of course, you *never* tell me anything, Traci."

She swirled herself into the end chair, sending leaves and sweet-pea blossoms flying and decapitating the broccoli centerpiece. "I didn't get Viola's cry for help until yesterday. Viola, you should never leave messages with Hassim. His English is virtually nonexistent. I had to get him to hum me your ring. I recognized your signature, but the phones were out, so I flew home. In the middle of negotiations, I might add."

"How *are* negotiations going, Grandma Karen?" Viola asked.

"They *were* going extremely well. The Israelis have given the Palestinians half of Jerusalem, and they've agreed to time-share the Golan Heights." She turned to glare momentarily at me. "*They* know the importance of communication." She turned back to Viola. "So why are they picking on you, Viola? Don't they like your new live-in?"

"I am *not* her live-in," Bysshe protested.

I have often wondered how on earth my mother-in-law became a mediator and what she does in all those negotiation sessions with Serbs and Catholics and North and South Koreans and Protestants and Croats. She takes sides, jumps to conclusions, misinterprets everything you say, refuses to listen. And yet she talked South Africa into a Mandelan government and would probably get the Palestinians to observe Yom Kippur. Maybe she just bullies everyone into submission. Or maybe they have to band together to protect themselves against her.

Bysshe was still protesting. "I never even met Viola till today. I've only talked to her on the phone a couple of times."

"You must have done *something*," Karen said to Viola. "They're obviously out for your blood."

"Not mine," Viola said. "Perdita's. She's joined the Cyclists."

"The Cyclists? I left the West Bank negotiations because you don't approve of Perdita joining a biking club? How am I supposed to explain this to the president of Iraq? She will *not* understand, and neither do I. A biking club!"

"The Cyclists do not ride bicycles," Mother said.

"They menstruate," Twidge said.

There was a dead silence of at least a minute, and I thought, it's finally happened. My mother-in-law and I are actually going to be on the same side of a family argument.

"All this fuss is over Perdita's having her shunt removed?" Karen said finally. "She's of age, isn't she? And this is obviously a case where personal sovereignty applies. You should know that, Traci. After all, you're a judge."

I should have known it was too good to be true.

"You mean you approve of her setting back the Liberation twenty years?" Mother said.

"I hardly think it's that serious," Karen said. "There are antishunt groups in the Middle East, too, you know, but no one takes them seriously. Not even the Iraqis, and they still wear the veil."

"Perdita is taking them seriously."

Karen dismissed Perdita with a wave of her black sleeve. "They're a trend, a fad. Like microskirts. Or those dreadful electronic eyebrows. A few women wear silly fashions like that for a little while, but you don't see women as a whole giving up pants or going back to wearing hats."

"But Perdita . . ." Viola said.

"If Perdita wants to have her period, I say let her. Women functioned perfectly well without shunts for thousands of years."

Mother brought her fist down on the table. "Women also functioned *perfectly well* with concubinage, cholera, and corsets," she said, emphasizing each word with her fist. "But that is no reason to take them on voluntarily, and I have no intention of allowing Perdita—"

"Speaking of Perdita, where is the poor child?" Karen said.

"She'll be here any minute," Mother said. "I invited her to lunch so we could discuss this with her."

"Ha!" Karen said. "So you could browbeat her into changing her mind, you mean. Well, I have no intention of collaborating with you. *I* intend to listen to the poor thing's point of view with interest and an open mind. 'Respect,' that's the key word, and one you all seem to have forgotten. Respect and common courtesy."

A barefoot young woman wearing a flowered smock and a red scarf tied around her left arm came up to the table with a sheaf of pink folders.

"It's about time," Karen said, snatching one of the folders away from her. "Your service here is dreadful. I've been sitting here ten minutes." She snapped the folder open. "I don't suppose you have Scotch."

"My name is Evangeline," the young woman said. "I'm Perdita's docent." She took the folder away from Karen. "She wasn't able to join you for lunch, but she asked me to come in her place and explain the Cyclist philosophy to you."

She sat down in the wicker chair next to me.

"The Cyclists are dedicated to freedom," she said. "Freedom from artificiality, freedom from body-controlling drugs and hormones, freedom from the male patriarchy that attempts to impose them on us. As you probably already know, we do not wear shunts."

She pointed to the red scarf around her arm. "Instead, we wear this as a badge of our freedom and our femaleness. I'm wearing it today to announce that my time of fertility has come."

"We had that, too," Mother said, "only we wore it on the back of our skirts."

I laughed.

The docent glared at me. "Male domination of women's bodies began long before the so-called 'Liberation,' with government regulation of abortion and fetal rights, scientific control of fertility, and finally the development of ammenerol, which eliminated the reproductive cycle altogether. This was all part of a carefully planned takeover of women's bodies, and by extension, their identities, by the male patriarchal regime."

"What an interesting point of view!" Karen said enthusiastically.

It certainly was. In point of fact, ammenerol hadn't been invented to eliminate menstruation at all. It had been developed for shrinking malignant tumors, and its uterine-lining-absorbing properties had only been discovered by accident.

"Are you trying to tell us," Mother said, "that men *forced* shunts on women? We had to *fight* everyone to get ammenerol approved by the FDA!"

It was true. What surrogate mothers and antiabortionists and the fetal-rights issue had failed to do in uniting women, the prospect of not having to menstruate did. Women had organized rallies, petitions, elected senators, passed amendments, been excommunicated, and gone to jail, all in the name of Liberation.

"Men were *against* it," Mother said, getting rather red in the face. "And the religious right and the maxipad manufacturers, and the Catholic Church—"

"They knew they'd have to allow women priests," Viola said.

"Which they did," I said.

"The Liberation hasn't freed you," the docent said loudly. "Except from the natural rhythms of your life, the very wellspring of your femaleness."

She leaned over and picked a daisy that was growing under the table. "We in the Cyclists celebrate the onset of our menses and rejoice in our bodies," she said, holding the daisy up. "Whenever a Cyclist comes into blossom, as we call it, she is honored with flowers and poems and songs. Then we join hands and tell what we like best about our menses."

"Water retention," I said.

"Or lying in bed with a heating pad for three days a month," Mother said.

"*I* think I like the anxiety attacks best," Viola said. "When I went off the ammenerol, so I could have Twidge, I'd have these days where I was convinced the space station was going to fall on me."

A middle-aged woman in overalls and a straw hat had come over while Viola was talking and was standing next to Mother's chair. "I had these mood swings," she said. "One minute I'd feel cheerful and the next like Lizzie Borden."

"Who's Lizzie Borden?" Twidge asked.

"She killed her parents," Bysshe said. "With an ax."

Karen and the docent glared at both of them. "Aren't you supposed to be working on your math, Twidge?" Karen said.

"I've always wondered if Lizzie Borden had PMS," Viola said, "and that was why—"

"No," Mother said. "It was having to live before tampons and ibuprofen. An obvious case of justifiable homicide."

"I hardly think this sort of levity is helpful," Karen said, glowering at everyone.

"Are you our waitress?" I asked the straw-hatted woman hastily.

"Yes," she said, producing a slate from her overalls pocket.

"Do you serve wine?" I asked.

"Yes. Dandelion, cowslip, and primrose."

"We'll take them all."

"A bottle of each?"

"For now. Unless you have them in kegs."

"Our specials today are watermelon salad and *choufleur gratine*," she said, smiling at everyone. Karen and the docent did not smile back. "You handpick your own cauliflower from the patch up front. The floratarian special is sautéed lily buds with marigold butter."

There was a temporary truce while everyone ordered. "I'll have the sweet peas," the docent said, "and a glass of rose water."

Bysshe leaned over to Viola. "I'm sorry I sounded so horrified when your grandmother asked if I was your live-in," he said.

"That's okay," Viola said. "Grandma Karen can be pretty scary."

"I just didn't want you to think I didn't like you. I do. Like you, I mean."

"Don't they have soyburgers?" Twidge asked.

As soon as the waitress left, the docent began passing out the pink folders she'd brought with her. "These will explain the working philosophy of the Cyclists," she said, handing me one, "along with practical information on the menstrual cycle." She handed Twidge one.

"It looks just like those books we used to get in junior high," Mother said, looking at hers. *A Special Gift*, they were called, and they had all these pictures of girls with pink ribbons in their hair, playing tennis and smiling. Blatant misrepresentation."

She was right. There was even the same drawing of the fallopian tubes I remembered from my middle school movie, a drawing that had always reminded me of *Alien* in the early stages.

"Oh, yuck," Twidge said. "This is disgusting."

"Do your math," Karen said.

Bysshe looked sick. "Did women really *do* this stuff?"

The wine arrived, and I poured everyone a large glass. The docent pursed her lips disapprovingly and shook her head. "The Cyclists do not use the artificial stimulants or hormones that the male patriarchy has forced on women to render them docile and subservient."

"How long do you menstruate?" Twidge asked.

"Forever," Mother said.

"Four to six days," the docent said. "It's there in the booklet."

"No, I mean, your whole life or what?"

"A woman has her menarche at twelve years old on the average and ceases menstruating at age fifty-five."

"I had my first period at eleven," the waitress said, setting a bouquet down in front of me. "At school."

"I had my last one on the day the FDA approved ammenerol," Mother said.

"Three hundred and sixty-five divided by twenty-eight," Twidge said, writing on her slate. "Times forty-three years." She looked up. "That's five hundred and fifty-nine periods."

"That can't be right," Mother said, taking the slate away from her. "It's at least five thousand."

"And they all start on the day you leave on a trip," Viola said.

"Or get married," the waitress said. Mother began writing on the slate.

I took advantage of the cease-fire to pour everyone some more dandelion wine.

Mother looked up from the slate. "Do you realize with a period of five days, you'd be menstruating for nearly three thousand days? That's over eight solid years."

"And in between there's PMS," the waitress said, delivering flowers.

"What's PMS?" Twidge asked.

"Premenstrual syndrome was the name the male medical establishment fabricated for the natural variation in hormonal levels that signal the onset of menstruation," the docent said. "This mild and entirely normal fluctuation was exaggerated by men into a debility." She looked at Karen for confirmation.

"I used to cut my hair," Karen said.

The docent looked uneasy.

"Once I chopped off one whole side," Karen went on. "Bob had to hide the scissors every month. And the car keys. I'd start to cry every time I hit a red light."

"Did you swell up?" Mother asked, pouring Karen another glass of dandelion wine.

"I looked just like Orson Welles."

"Who's Orson Welles?" Twidge asked.

"Your comments reflect the self-loathing thrust on you by the patriarchy," the docent said. "Men have brainwashed women into thinking menstruation is evil and unclean. Women even called their menses 'the curse' because they accepted men's judgment."

"I called it the curse because I thought a witch must have laid a curse on me," Viola said. "Like in *Sleeping Beauty*."

Everyone looked at her.

"Well, I did," she said. "It was the only reason I could think of for such an awful thing happening to me." She handed the folder back to the docent. "It still is."

"I think you were awfully brave," Bysshe said to Viola, "going off the ammenerol to have Twidge."

"It was awful," Viola said. "You can't imagine."

Mother sighed. "When I got my period, I asked my mother if Annette had it, too."

"Who's Annette?" Twidge said.

"A Mouseketeer," Mother said and added, at Twidge's uncomprehending look. "On TV."

"High-rez," Viola said.

"*The Mickey Mouse Club*," Mother said.

"There was a high-rezzer called *The Mickey Mouse Club*?" Twidge said incredulously.

"They were days of dark oppression in many ways," I said.

Mother glared at me. "Annette was every young girl's ideal," she said to Twidge. "Her hair was curly, she had actual breasts, her pleated skirt was always pressed, and I could not imagine that she could have anything so *messy* and undignified. Mr. Disney would never have allowed it. And if Annette didn't have one, I wasn't going to have one either. So I asked my mother—"

"What did she say?" Twidge cut in.

"She said every woman had periods," Mother said. "So I asked her, 'Even the Queen of England?' And she said, 'Even the Queen.' "

"Really?" Twidge said. "But she's so *old*!"

"She isn't having it now," the docent said irritatedly. "I told you, menopause occurs at age fifty-five."

"And then you have hot flashes," Karen said, "and osteoporosis and so much hair on your upper lip, you look like Mark Twain."

"Who's—" Twidge said.

"You are simply reiterating negative male propaganda," the docent interrupted, looking very red in the face.

"You know what I've always wondered?" Karen said, leaning conspiratorially close to Mother. "If Maggie Thatcher's menopause was responsible for the Falklands War."

"Who's Maggie Thatcher?" Twidge said.

The docent, who was now as red in the face as her scarf, stood up. "It is clear there is no point in trying to talk to you. You've all been completely brainwashed by the male patriarchy." She began grabbing up her folders. "You're blind, all of you! You don't even see that you're victims of a male conspiracy to deprive you of your biological identity, of your very womanhood. The Liberation wasn't a liberation at all. It was only another kind of slavery."

"Even if that were true," I said, "even if it had been a conspiracy to bring us under male domination, it would have been worth it."

"She's right, you know," Karen said to Mother. "Traci's absolutely right. There are some things worth giving up anything for, even your freedom, and getting rid of your period is definitely one of them."

"Victims!" the docent shouted. "You've been stripped of your femininity, and you don't even care!" She stomped out, destroying several squash and a row of gladiolas in the process.

414

"You know what I hated most before the Liberation?" Karen said, pouring the last of the dandelion wine into her glass. "Sanitary belts."

"And those cardboard tampon applicators," Mother said.

"I'm never going to join the Cyclists," Twidge said.

"Good," I said.

"Can I have dessert?"

I called the waitress over, and Twidge ordered sugared violets. "Anyone else want dessert?" I asked. "Or more primrose wine?"

"I think it's wonderful the way you're trying to help your sister," Bysshe said, leaning close to Viola.

"And those Modess ads," Mother said. "You remember, with those glamorous women in satin-brocade evening dresses and long white gloves, and below the picture was written, 'Modess, because . . .' I thought Modess was a perfume."

Karen giggled. "I thought it was a brand of *champagne*!"

"I don't think we'd better have any more wine," I said.

The phone started singing the minute I got to my chambers the next morning, the universal ring.

"Karen went back to Iraq, didn't she?" I asked Bysshe.

"Yeah," he said. "Viola said there was some snag over whether to put Disneyland on the West Bank or not."

"When did Viola call?"

Bysshe looked sheepish. "I had breakfast with her and Twidge this morning."

"Oh." I picked up the phone. "It's probably Mother with a plan to kidnap Perdita. Hello?"

"This is Evangeline, Perdita's docent," the voice on the phone said. "I hope you're happy. You've bullied Perdita into surrendering to the enslaving male patriarchy."

"I have?" I said.

"You've obviously employed mind control, and I want you to know we intend to file charges." She hung up. The phone rang again immediately, another universal.

"What is the good of signatures when no one of ever uses them?" I said, and picked up the phone.

"Hi, Mom," Perdita said. "I thought you'd want to know I've changed my mind about joining the Cyclists."

"Really?" I said, trying not to sound jubilant.

"I found out they wear this red scarf thing on their arm. It covers up Sitting Bull's horse."

"That is a problem," I said.

"Well, that's not all. My docent told me about your lunch. Did Grandma Karen really tell you you were right?"

"Yes."

"Gosh! I didn't believe that part. Well, anyway, my docent said you wouldn't listen to her about how great menstruating is, that you all kept talking about the negative aspects of it, like bloating and cramps and crabbiness, and I said, 'What are cramps?' and she said, 'Menstrual bleeding frequently causes headaches and discomfort,' and I said, 'Bleeding? Nobody ever said anything about bleeding!' Why didn't you tell me there was blood involved, Mother?"

I had, but I felt it wiser to keep silent.

"And you didn't say a word about its being painful. And all the hormone fluctuations! Anybody'd have to be crazy to want to go through that when they didn't have to! How did you stand it before the Liberation?"

"They were days of dark oppression," I said.

"I *guess*! Well, anyway, I quit and now my docent is really mad. But I told her it was a case of personal sovereignty, and she has to respect my decision. I'm still going to become a floratarian, though, and I *don't* want you to try to talk me out of it."

"I wouldn't dream of it," I said.

"You know, this whole thing is really your fault, Mom! If you'd told me about the pain part in the first place, none of this would have happened. Viola's right! You never tell us *anything*!"

1. What does Traci mean when she says that the law of personal sovereignty made the Liberation possible?

2. Why is Karen not as concerned about Perdita's decision to join the Cyclists as Traci and Traci's mother are?

3. Are Perdita's reasons for not joining the Cyclists consistent with the principles affirmed by Traci and Traci's mother?

4. Are the Cyclists making a valid point when they claim, "The Liberation wasn't a liberation at all. It was only another kind of slavery"?

BRIAN STABLEFORD (1948–), born in Yorkshire, England, has combined the careers of university lecturer and nonfiction writer with that of a science fiction novelist. His dissertation, *The Sociology of Science Fiction*, was published in 1987, and his *Historical Dictionary of Science Fiction Literature* (2004) and *Science Fact and Science Fiction: An Encyclopedia* (2006) are well-regarded reference works. In his novels, Stableford often deals with speculative developments in biotechnology and the consequences for human society. At the same time, his prolific output—more than fifty novels—often blends science fiction themes with elements of other literary genres, such as horror, the supernatural, and fantasy. He has referred to his recent novels as "blithely bizarre genre-hybrids." Among Stableford's notable works are *The Empire of Fear* (1988), a scientific vampire story; *Architects of Emortality* (1999); and the novella *Les Fleurs du Mal* (1994), for which he received a Hugo Award nomination.

Mortimer Gray's
History of Death

1

I was an utterly unexceptional child of the twenty-ninth century, comprehensively engineered for emortality while I was still a more-or-less inchoate blastula, and decanted from an artificial womb in Naburn Hatchery in the country of York in the Defederated States of Europe. I was raised in an aggregate family which consisted of six men and six women. I was, of course, an only child, and I received the customary superabundance of love, affection, and admiration. With the aid of excellent internal technologies, I grew up reasonable, charitable, self-controlled, and intensely serious of mind.

It's evident that not *everyone* grows up like that, but I've never quite been able to understand how people manage to avoid it. If conspicuous individuality—and frank perversity—aren't programmed in the genes or rooted in early upbringing, how on earth do they spring into being with such determined irregularity? But this is *my* story, not the world's, and I shouldn't digress.

In due course, the time came for me—as it comes to everyone—to leave my family and enter a community of my peers for my first spell at college. I elected to go to Adelaide in Australia, because I liked the name.

Although my memories of that period are understandably hazy, I feel sure that I had begun to see the *fascination* of history long before the crucial event which determined my path in life. The subject seemed—in stark contrast to the disciplined coherency of mathematics or the sciences—so huge, so amazingly abundant in its data, and so charmingly disorganized. I was always a very orderly and organized person, and I needed a vocation like history to loosen me up a little. It was not, however, until I set forth on an ill-fated expedition on the sailing ship *Genesis* in September 2901 that the exact form of my destiny was determined.

I use the word "destiny" with the utmost care; it is no mere rhetorical flourish. What happened when *Genesis* defied the supposed limits of possibility and turned turtle was no mere incident, and the impression that it made on my fledging mind was no mere suggestion. Before that ship set sail, a thousand futures were open to me; afterward, I was beset by an irresistible compulsion. My destiny was determined the day *Genesis* went down; as a result of that tragedy, *my fate was sealed*.

We were en route from Brisbane to tour the Creationist Islands of Micronesia, which were then regarded as artistic curiosities rather than daring experiments in continental design. I had expected to find the experience exhilarating, but almost as soon as we had left port, I was struck down by seasickness.

Seasickness, by virtue of being psychosomatic, is one of the very few diseases with which modern internal technology is sometimes impotent to deal, and I was miserably confined to my cabin while I waited for my mind to make the necessary adaptation. I was bitterly ashamed of myself, for I alone out of half a hundred passengers had fallen prey to this strange atavistic malaise. While the others partied on deck, beneath the glorious light of the tropic stars, I lay in my bunk, half delirious with discomfort and lack of sleep. I thought myself the unluckiest man in the world.

When I was abruptly hurled from my bed, I thought that I had fallen—that my tossing and turning had inflicted one more ignominy upon me. When I couldn't recover my former position after having spent long minutes fruitlessly groping about amid all kinds of mysterious debris, I assumed that I must be confused. When I couldn't open the door of my cabin even though I had the handle in my hand, I assumed that my failure was the result of clumsiness. When I finally got out into the corridor, and found myself crawling in shallow water with the artificial bioluminescent strip beneath instead of above me, I thought I must be mad.

When the little girl spoke to me, I thought at first that she was a delusion, and that I was lost in a nightmare. It wasn't until she touched me, and tried to drag me upright with her tiny, frail hands, and addressed me by name—albeit incorrectly—that I was finally able to focus my thoughts.

"You have to get up, Mr. Mortimer," she said. "The boat's upside down."

She was only eight years old, but she spoke quite calmly and reasonably.

"That's impossible," I told her. "*Genesis* is unsinkable. There's no way it could turn upside down."

"But it *is* upside down," she insisted—and, as she did so, I finally realized the significance of the fact that the floor was glowing the way the ceiling should have glowed. "The water's coming in. I think we'll have to swim out."

The light put out by the ceiling strip was as bright as ever, but the rippling water overlaying it made it seem dim and uncertain. The girl's little face, lit from below, seemed terribly serious within the frame of her dark and curly hair.

"I can't swim," I said, flatly.

She looked at me as if I were insane, or stupid, but it was true. I couldn't swim. I'd never liked the idea, and I'd never seen any necessity.

All modern ships—even sailing ships designed to be cute and quaint for the benefit of tourists—were unsinkable.

I scrambled to my feet, and put out both my hands to steady myself, to hold myself against the upside-down walls. The water was knee-deep. I couldn't tell whether it was increasing or not—which told me, reassuringly, that it couldn't be rising very quickly. The upturned boat was rocking this way and that, and I could hear the rumble of waves breaking on the outside of the hull, but I didn't know how much of that apparent violence was in my mind.

"My name's Emily," the little girl told me. "I'm frightened. All my mothers and fathers were on deck. *Everyone* was on deck, except for you and me. Do you think they're all dead?"

"They can't be," I said, marveling at the fact that she spoke so soberly, even when she said that she was frightened. I realized, however, that if the ship had suffered the kind of misfortune which could turn it upside down, the people on deck might indeed be dead. I tried to remember the passengers gossiping in the departure lounge, introducing themselves to one another with such fervor. The little girl had been with a party of nine, none of whose names I could remember. It occurred to me that *her whole family* might have been wiped out, that she might now be that rarest of all rare beings, an *orphan*. It was almost unimaginable. What possible catastrophe, I wondered, could have done that?

I asked Emily what had happened. She didn't know. Like me she had been in her bunk, sleeping the sleep of the innocent.

"Are we going to die too?" she asked. "I've been a good girl. I've never told a lie." It couldn't have been literally true, but I knew exactly what she meant. She was eight years old, and she had every right to expect to live till she was eight hundred. She didn't *deserve* to die. It wasn't fair.

I knew full well that fairness didn't really come into it, and I expect that she knew it too, even if my fellow historians were wrong about the virtual abolition of all the artifices of childhood, but I knew in my heart that what she said was *right*, and that insofar as the imperious laws of nature ruled her observation irrelevant, the *universe* was wrong. It *wasn't* fair. She *had* been a good girl. If she died, it would be a monstrous injustice.

Perhaps it was merely a kind of psychological defense mechanism that helped me to displace my own mortal anxieties, but the horror that ran through me was all focused on her. At the moment, her plight—not *our* plight, but *hers*—seemed to be the only thing that mattered. It was as if her dignified fear and her placid courage somehow contained the essence of human existence, the purest product of human progress.

Perhaps it was only my cowardly mind's refusal to contemplate anything else, but the only thing I could think of while I tried to figure out what to do was the awfulness of what she was saying. As that awfulness possessed me, it was magnified a thousandfold, and it seemed to me that in her lone and tiny voice there was a much greater voice speaking for multitudes: for all the human children that had ever died before achieving maturity; all the *good* children who had died without ever having the chance to *deserve to die*.

"I don't think any more water can get in," she said, with a slight tremor in her voice. "But there's only so much air. If we stay here too long, we'll suffocate."

"It's a big ship," I told her. "If we're trapped in an air bubble, it must be a very large one."

"But it won't last forever," she told me. She was eight years old and hoped to live to be eight hundred, and she was absolutely right. The air wouldn't last forever. Hours, certainly; maybe days—but not forever.

"There are survival pods under the bunks," she said. She had obviously been paying attention to the welcoming speeches that the captain and the chief steward had delivered in the lounge the evening after embarkation. She'd plugged the chips they'd handed out into her trusty handbook, like the good girl she was, and inwardly digested what they had to teach her—unlike those of us who were blithely careless and wretchedly seasick.

"We can both fit into one of the pods," she went on, "but we have to get it out of the boat before we inflate it. We have to go up—I mean *down*—the stairway into the water and away from the boat. You'll have to carry the pod, because it's too big for me."

"I can't swim," I reminded her.

"It doesn't matter," she said, patiently. "All you have to do is hold your breath and kick yourself away from the boat. You'll float up to the surface whether you can swim or not. Then you just yank the cord and the pod will inflate. You have to hang on to it, though. Don't let go."

I stared at her, wondering how she could be so calm, so controlled, so efficient.

"Listen to the water breaking on the hull," I whispered. "Feel the movement of the boat. It would take a hurricane to overturn a boat like this. We wouldn't stand a chance out there."

"It's not so bad," she told me. She didn't have both hands out to brace herself against the walls, although she lifted one occasionally to stave off the worst of the lurches caused by the bobbing of the boat.

But if it wasn't a hurricane which turned us over, I thought, *what the hell was it? Whales have been extinct for eight hundred years.*

"We don't have to go just yet," Emily said, mildly, "but we'll have to go in the end. We have to get out. The pod's bright orange, and it has a distress beacon. We should be picked up within twenty-four hours, but there'll be supplies for a week."

I had every confidence that modern technology could sustain us for a month, if necessary. Even having to drink a little seawater if your recycling gel clots only qualifies as a minor inconvenience nowadays. Drowning is another matter; so is asphyxiation. She was absolutely right. We had to get out of the upturned boat—not immediately, but some time soon. Help might get to us before then, but we couldn't wait, and we shouldn't. We were, after all, human beings. We were supposed to be able to take charge of our own destinies, to do what we *ought* to do. Anything less would he a betrayal of our heritage. I knew that, and understood it.

But I couldn't swim.

"It's okay, Mr. Mortimer," she said, putting her reassuring hand in mine. "We can do it. We'll go together. It'll be all right."

Emily was right. We *could* do it, together, and we did—not immediately, I confess, but, in the end, we did it. It was the most terrifying and most horrible experience of my young life, but it had to be done, and we did it.

When I finally dived into that black pit of water, knowing that I had to go down and sideways before I could hope to go up, I was carried forward by the knowledge that Emily expected it of me, and needed me to do it. Without her, I'm sure that I would have died. I simply would not have had the courage to save myself. Because she was there, I dived, with the pod clutched in my arms. Because she was there, I managed to kick away from the hull and yank the cord to inflate it.

It wasn't until I had pulled Emily into the pod, and made sure that she was safe, that I paused to think how remarkable it was that the sea was hot enough to scald us both.

We were three storm-tossed days afloat before the helicopter picked us up. We cursed our ill luck, not having the least inkling how bad things were elsewhere. We couldn't understand why the weather was getting worse instead of better.

When the pilot finally explained it, we couldn't immediately take it in. Perhaps that's not surprising, given that the geologists were just as astonished as everyone else. After all, the seabed had been quietly cracking wherever the tectonic plates were pulling apart for millions of years; it was an ongoing phenomenon, very well understood. Hundreds of black smokers and underwater volcanoes were under constant observation. Nobody had any reason to expect that a plate could simply *break* so far away from its rim, or that the fissure could be so deep, so long, and so rapid in its extension. Everyone thought that the main threat to the earth's surface was posed by wayward comets; all vigilant eyes were directed outward. No one had expected such awesome force to erupt from within, from the hot mantle which lay, hubbling and bubbling, beneath the earth's fragile crust.

It was, apparently, an enormous bubble of upwelling gas that contrived the near-impossible feat of flipping *Genesis* over. The earthquakes and the tidal waves came later.

It was the worst natural disaster in six hundred years. One million, nine hundred thousand people died in all. Emily wasn't the only child to lose her entire family, and I shudder to think of the number of families which lost their only children. We historians have to maintain a sense of perspective, though. Compared with the number of people who died in the wars of the twentieth and twenty-first centuries, or the numbers of people who died in epidemics in earlier centuries, nineteen hundred thousand is a trivial figure.

Perhaps I would have done what I eventually set out to do anyway. Perhaps the Great Coral Sea Catastrophe would have appalled me even if I'd been on the other side of the world, cocooned in the safety of a treehouse or an apartment in one of the crystal cities—but I don't think so.

It was because I was at the very center of things, because my life was literally turned upside down by the disaster—and because eight-year-old Emily Marchant was there to save my life with her common sense and her composure—that I set out to write a definitive history of death, intending to reveal not merely the dull facts of mankind's longest and hardest battle, but also the real meaning and significance of it.

2

The first volume of Mortimer Gray's *History of Death*, entitled *The Prehistory of Death*, was published on 21 January 2914. It was, unusually for its day, a mute book, with no voice-over, sound effects, or background music. Nor did it have any original artwork, all the illustrations being unenhanced still photographs. It was, in short, the kind of book that only a historian would have published. Its reviewers generally agreed that it was an old-fashioned example of scrupulous scholarship, and none expected that access demand would be considerable. Many commentators questioned the merit of Gray's arguments.

The Prehistory of Death summarized what was known about early hominid lifestyles, and had much to say about the effects of natural selection on the patterns of mortality in modern man's ancestor species. Gray carefully discussed the evolution of parental care as a genetic strategy. Earlier species of man, he observed, had raised parental care to a level of efficiency which permitted the human infant to he born at a much earlier stage in its development than any other, maximizing its opportunity to be shaped by nature and learning. From the very beginning, Gray proposed, human species were *actively* at war with death. The evolutionary success of Homo sapiens was based in the collaborative activities of parents in protecting, cherishing, and preserving the lives of children: activities that extended beyond immediate family groups as reciprocal altruism made it advantageous for humans to form tribes, and ultimately nations.

In these circumstances, Gray argued, it was entirely natural that the origins of consciousness and culture should be intimately bound up with a keen awareness of the war against death. He asserted that the first great task of the human imagination must have been to carry forward that war. It was entirely understandable, he said, that early paleontologists, having discovered the bones of a Neanderthal man in an apparent grave, with the remains of a primitive garland of flowers, should instantly have felt an intimate kinship with him; there could be no more persuasive evidence of full humanity than the attachment of ceremony to the idea and the fact of death.

Gray waxed lyrical about the importance of ritual as a symbolization of opposition and enmity to death. He had no patience with the proposition that such rituals were of no practical value, a mere window dressing of culture. On the contrary, he claimed that there was no activity *more* practical than this expressive recognition of the *value* of life, this imposition of a moral order on the fact of human mortality. The birth of agriculture Gray regarded as a mere sophistication of food gathering, of considerable importance as a technical discovery but of little significance in transforming human nature. The practices of burying the dead with ceremony, and of ritual mourning, on the other hand, *were*, in his view, evidence of the transformation of human nature, of the fundamental creation of meaning that made human life very different from the life of animals.

Prehistorians who marked out the evolution of man by his developing technology—the Stone Age giving way to the Bronze Age, the Bronze Age to the Iron Age—were, Gray conceded, taking intelligent advantage of those relics that had stood the test of time. He warned, however, of the folly of thinking that because tools had survived the millennia, it must have been toolmaking that was solely or primarily responsible for human progress. In his view, the primal cause that made people invent was man's ongoing war against death.

It was not *tools* which created man and gave birth to civilization, Mortimer Gray proclaimed, but the *awareness of mortality*.

3

Although its impact on my nascent personality was considerable, the Coral Sea Catastrophe was essentially an impersonal disaster. The people who died, including those who had been aboard the *Genesis*, were all unknown to me; it was not until some years later that I experienced personal bereavement. It wasn't one of my parents who died—by the time the first of them quit this earth I was nearly a hundred years old and our temporary closeness was a half-remembered thing of the distant past—but one of my spouses.

By the time *The Prehistory of Death* was published, I'd contracted my first marriage: a group contract with a relatively small aggregate consisting of three other men and four women. We lived in Lamu, on the coast of Kenya, a nation to which I had been drawn by my studies of the early evolution of man. We were all young people, and we had formed our group for companionship rather than for parenting—which was a privilege conventionally left, even in those days, to much older people. We didn't go in for much flesh sex, because we were still finding our various ways through the maze of erotic virtuality, but we took the time—as I suppose all young people do—to explore its unique delights. I can't remember exactly why I decided to join such a group; I presume that it was because I accepted, tacitly at least, the conventional wisdom that there is spice in variety, and that one should do one's best to keep a broad front of experience.

It wasn't a particularly happy marriage, but it served its purpose. We went in for a good deal of sporting activity and conventional tourism. We visited the other continents from time to time, but most of our adventures took us back and forth across Africa. Most of my spouses were practical ecologists involved in one way or another with the regreening of the north and south, or with the reforestation of the equatorial belt. What little credit I earned to add to my Allocation was earned by assisting them; such fees as I received for net access to my work were inconsiderable. Axel, Jodocus, and Minna were all involved in large-scale hydrological engineering, and liked to describe themselves, lightheartedly, as the Lamu Rainmakers. The rest of us became, inevitably, the Rainmakers-in-Law.

. . .

To begin with, I had considerable affection for all the other members of my new family, but as time went by the usual accretion of petty irritations built up, and a couple of changes in the group's personnel failed to renew the initial impetus. The research for the second volume of my history began to draw me more and more to Egypt and to Greece, even though there was no real need actually to travel in order to do the relevant research. I think we would have divorced in 2919 anyhow, even if it hadn't been for Grizel's death.

She went swimming in the newly rerouted Kwarra one day, and didn't come back.

Maybe the fact of her death wouldn't have hit me so hard if she hadn't been drowned, but I was still uneasy about deep water—even the relatively placid waters of the great rivers. If I'd been able to swim, I might have gone out with her, but I hadn't. I didn't even know she was missing until the news came in that a body had been washed up twenty kilometers downriver.

"It was a million-to-one thing," Ayesha told me, when she came back from the on-site inquest. "She must have been caught from behind by a log moving in the current, or something like that. We'll never know for sure. She must have been knocked unconscious, though, or badly dazed. Otherwise, she'd never have drifted into the white water. The rocks finished her off."

Rumor has it that many people simply can't take in news of the death of someone they love—that it flatly defies belief. I didn't react that way. With me, belief was instantaneous, and I just gave way under its pressure. I literally fell over, because my legs wouldn't support me—another psychosomatic failure about which my internal machinery could do nothing—and I wept uncontrollably. None of the others did, not even Axel, who'd been closer to Grizel than anyone. They were sympathetic at first, but it wasn't long before a note of annoyance began to creep into their reassurances.

"Come on, Morty," Ilya said, voicing the thought the rest of them were too diplomatic to let out. "You know more about death than any of us; if it doesn't help you to get a grip, what good is all that research?"

He was right, of course. Axel and Ayesha had often tried to suggest, delicately, that mine was an essentially unhealthy fascination, and now they felt vindicated.

"If you'd actually bothered to read my book," I retorted, "you'd know that it has nothing complimentary to say about philosophical acceptance. It sees a sharp awareness of mortality, and the capacity to feel the horror of death so keenly, as key forces driving human evolution."

"But you don't have to act it out so flamboyantly," Ilya came back, perhaps using cruelty to conceal and assuage his own misery. "We've evolved now. We've got past all that. We've matured." Ilya was the oldest of us, and he *seemed* very old, although he was only sixty-five. In those days, there weren't nearly as many double centenarians around as there are nowadays, and triple centenarians were very rare indeed. We take emortality so much for granted that it's easy to forget how recent a development it is.

"It's what I feel," I told him, retreating into uncompromising assertion. "I can't help it."

"We *all* loved her," Ayesha reminded me. "We'll all miss her. You're not *proving* anything, Morty."

What she meant was that I wasn't proving anything except my own instability, but she spoke more accurately than she thought; I wasn't proving anything at all. I was just reacting—atavistically, perhaps, but with crude honesty and authentically childlike innocence.

"We all have to pull together now," she added, "for Grizel's sake."

A death in the family almost always leads to universal divorce in childless marriages: nobody knows why. Such a loss *does* force the survivors to pull together, but it seems that the process of pulling together only serves to emphasize the incompleteness of the unit. We all went our separate ways, even the three Rainmakers.

I set out to use my solitude to become a true neo-Epicurean, after the fashion of the times, seeking no excess and deriving an altogether *appropriate* pleasure from everything I did. I took care to cultivate a proper love for the commonplace, training myself to a pitch of perfection in all the techniques of physiological control necessary to physical fitness and quiet metabolism.

I soon convinced myself that I'd transcended such primitive and adolescent goals as happiness, and had cultivated instead a truly civilized *ataraxia*: a calm of mind whose value went beyond the limits of ecstasy and exultation.

Perhaps I was fooling myself, but, if I was, I succeeded. The habits stuck. No matter what lifestyle fashions came and went thereafter, I remained a stubborn neo-Epicurean, immune to all other eupsychian fantasies. For a while, though, I was perpetually haunted by Grizel's memory—and not, alas, by the memory of all things that we'd shared while she was *alive*. I gradually forgot the sound of her voice, the touch of her hand, and even the image of her face, remembering only the horror of her sudden and unexpected departure from the arena of my experience.

For the next ten years, I lived in Alexandria, in a simple villa cleverly gantzed out of the desert sands—sands which still gave an impression of timelessness even though they had been restored to wilderness as recently as the twenty-seventh century, when Egypt's food economy had been realigned to take full advantage of the newest techniques in artificial photosynthesis.

4

The second volume of Mortimer Gray's *History of Death*, entitled *Death in the Ancient World*, was published on 7 May 2931. It contained a wealth of data regarding burial practices and patterns of mortality in Egypt, the Kingdoms of Sumer and Akkad, the Indus civilizations of Harappa and Mohenjo-Daro, the Yangshao and Lungshan cultures of the Far East, the cultures of the Olmecs and Zapotecs, Greece before and after Alexander, and the pre-Christian Roman Empire. It paid particular attention to the elaborate mythologies of life after death developed by ancient cultures.

Gray gave most elaborate consideration to the Egyptians, whose eschatology evidently fascinated him. He spared no effort in description and discussion of the *Book of the Dead*, the Hall of Double Justice, Anubis and Osiris, the custom of mummification, and the building of pyramid tombs. He was almost as fascinated by the elaborate geography of the Greek underworld, the characters associated with it—Hades and Persephone, Thanatos and the Erinnyes, Cerberus and Charon—and the descriptions of the unique fates reserved for such individuals as Sisyphus, Ixion, and Tantalus. The development of such myths as these Gray regarded as a triumph of the creative imagination. In his account, mythmaking and storytelling were vital weapons in the war against death—a war that had still to be fought in the mind of man, because there was little yet to be accomplished by defiance of its claims upon the body.

In the absence of an effective medical science, Gray argued, the war against death was essentially a war of propaganda, and myths were to be judged in that light—not by their truthfulness, even in some allegorical or metaphorical sense, but by their usefulness in generating *morale* and meaning. By elaborating and extrapolating the process of death in this way, a more secure moral order could be imported into social life. People thus achieved a sense of continuity with past and future generations, so that every individual became part of a great enterprise which extended across the generations, from the beginning to the end of time.

Gray did not regard the building of the pyramids as a kind of gigantic folly or vanity, or a way to dispose of the energies of the peasants when they were not required in harvesting the bounty of the fertile Nile. He argued that pyramid building should be seen as the most useful of all labors, because it was work directed at the glorious imposition of human endeavor upon the natural landscape. The placing of a royal mummy, with all its accoutrements, in a fabulous geometric edifice of stone was, for Gray, a loud, confident, and entirely appropriate statement of humanity's invasion of the empire of death.

Gray complimented those tribesmen who worshipped their ancestors and thought them always close at hand, ready to deliver judgments upon the living. Such people, he felt, had fully mastered an elementary truth of human existence: that the dead were not entirely gone, but lived on, intruding upon memory and dream, both when they were bidden and when they were not. He approved of the idea that the dead should have a voice, and must be entitled to speak, and that the living had a moral duty to listen. Because these ancient tribes were as direly short of history as they were of medicine, he argued, they were entirely justified in allowing their ancestors to live on in the minds of living people, where the culture those ancestors had forged similarly resided.

Some reviewers complimented Gray on the breadth of his research and the comprehensiveness of his data, but few endorsed the propriety of his interpretations. He was widely advised to be more dispassionate in carrying forward his project.

5

I was sixty when I married again. This time, it was a singular marriage, to Sharane Fereday. We set up home in Avignon, and lived together for nearly twenty years. I won't say that we were exceptionally happy, but I came to depend on her closeness and her affection, and the day she told me that she had had enough was the darkest of my life so far—far darker in its desolation than the day Emily Marchant and I had been trapped in the wreck of the *Genesis*, although it didn't mark me as deeply.

"Twenty years is a long time, Mortimer," she told me. "It's time to move on—time for you as well as for me."

She was being sternly reasonable at that stage; I knew from experience that the sternness would crumble if I put it to the test, and I thought that her resolve would crumble with it, as it had before in similar circumstances, but it didn't.

"I'm truly sorry," she said, when she was eventually reduced to tears, "but I have to do it. I have to go. It's *my* life, and your part of it is over. I hate hurting you, but I don't want to live with you anymore. It's my fault, not yours, but that's the way it is."

It wasn't anybody's fault. I can see that clearly now, although it wasn't so easy to see it at the time. Like the Great Coral Sea Catastrophe or Grizel's drowning, it was just something that *happened*. Things do happen, regardless of people's best-laid plans, most heartfelt wishes, and intensest hopes.

Now that memory has blotted out the greater part of that phase of my life—including, I presume, the worst of it—I don't really know why I was so devastated by Sharane's decision, nor why it should have filled me with such black despair. Had I cultivated a dependence so absolute that it seemed irreplaceable, or was it only my pride that had suffered a sickening blow? Was it the imagined consequences of the rejection or merely the fact of rejection itself that sickened me so? Even now, I can't tell for certain. Even then, my neo-Epicurean conscience must have told me over and over again to pull myself together, to conduct myself with more decorum.

I tried. I'm certain that I tried.

Sharane's love for the ancient past was even more intense than mine, but her writings were far less dispassionate. She was an historian of sorts, but she wasn't an *academic* historian; her writings tended to the lyrical rather than the factual even when she was supposedly writing nonfiction.

Sharane would never have written a mute book, or one whose pictures didn't move. Had it been allowed by law at that time, she'd have fed her readers designer psychotropics to heighten their responses according to the schemes of her texts. She was a VR scriptwriter rather than a textwriter like me. She wasn't content to know about the past; she wanted to re-create it and make it solid and *live* in it. Nor did she reserve such inclinations to the privacy of her E-suit. She was flamboyantly old-fashioned in all that she did. She liked to dress in gaudy pastiches of the costumes represented in Greek or Egyptian art, and she liked decor to match. People who knew us were mildly astonished that we should want to live together, given the difference in our personalities, but I suppose it was an attraction of opposites. Perhaps my intensity of purpose and solitude had begun to weigh rather heavily upon me when we met, and my carefully cultivated calm of mind threatened to become a kind of toiling inertia.

On the other hand, perhaps that's all confabulation and rationalization. I was a different person then, and I've since lost touch with that person as completely as I've lost touch with everyone else I once knew.

But I *do* remember, vaguely. . . .

I remember that I found in Sharane a certain precious *wildness* that, although it wasn't entirely spontaneous, was unfailingly amusing. She had the happy gift of never taking herself too seriously, although she was wholehearted enough in her determined attempts to put herself imaginatively in touch with the past.

From her point of view, I suppose I was doubly valuable. On the one hand, I was a fount of information and inspiration, on the other a kind of anchorage whose solidity kept her from losing herself in her flights of the imagination. Twenty years of marriage ought to have cemented her dependence on me just as it had cemented my dependence on her, but it didn't.

"You think I need you to keep my feet on the ground," Sharane said, as the break between us was completely and carefully rendered irreparable, "but I don't. Anyhow, I've been weighed down long enough. I need to soar for a while, to spread my wings."

Sharane and I had talked for a while, as married people do, about the possibility of having a child. We had both made deposits to the French national gamete bank, so that if we felt the same way when the time finally came to exercise our right of replacement—or to specify in our wills how that right was to be posthumously exercised—we could order an ovum to be unfrozen and fertilized.

I had always known, of course, that such flights of fancy were not to be taken too seriously, but when I accepted that the marriage was indeed over, there seemed to be an extra dimension of tragedy and misery in the knowledge that our genes never would be combined— that our separation cast our legacies once again upon the chaotic sea of irresolution.

Despite the extremity of my melancholy, I never contemplated suicide. Although I'd already used up the traditional threescore years and ten, I was in no doubt at all that it wasn't yet time to remove myself from the crucible of human evolution to make room for my successor, whether that successor was to be born from an ovum of Sharane's or not. No matter how black my mood was when Sharane left, I knew that my *History of Death* remained to be completed, and that the work would require at least another century. Even so, the breaking of such an intimate bond filled me with intimations of mortality and a painful sense of the futility of all my endeavors.

My first divorce had come about because a cruel accident had ripped apart the delicate fabric of my life, but my second—or so it seemed to me—was itself a horrid rent shearing my very being into ragged fragments. I hope that I tried with all my might not to blame

Sharane, but how could I avoid it? And how could she not resent my overt and covert accusations, my veiled and naked resentments?

"Your problem, Mortimer," she said to me, when her lachrymose phase had given way to bright anger, "is that you're *obsessed*. You're a deeply morbid man, and it's not healthy. There's some special fear in you, some altogether exceptional horror which feeds upon you day and night, and makes you grotesquely vulnerable to occurrences that normal people can take in their stride, and that ill befit a self-styled Epicurean. If you want my advice, you ought to abandon that history you're writing, at least for a while, and devote yourself to something brighter and more vigorous."

"Death is my life," I informed her, speaking metaphorically, and not entirely without irony. "It always will be, until and including the end."

I remember saying that. The rest is vague, but I really do remember saying that.

6

The third volume of Mortimer Gray's *History of Death*, entitled *The Empires of Faith*, was published on 18 August 2954. The introduction announced that the author had been forced to set aside his initial ambition to write a truly comprehensive history, and stated that he would henceforth be unashamedly eclectic, and contentedly ethnocentric, because he did not wish to be a mere archivist of death, and therefore could not regard all episodes in humankind's war against death as being of equal interest. He declared that he was more interested in interpretation than mere summary, and that insofar as the war against death had been a moral crusade, he felt fully entitled to draw morals from it.

This preface, understandably, dismayed those critics who had urged the author to be more dispassionate. Some reviewers were content to condemn the new volume without even bothering to inspect the rest of it, although it was considerably shorter than the second volume and had a rather more fluent style. Others complained that the day of mute text was dead and gone, and that there was no place in the modern world for pictures that resolutely refused to move.

Unlike many contemporary historians, whose birth into a world in which religious faith was almost extinct had robbed them of any sympathy for the imperialists of dogma, Gray proposed that the great religions had been one of the finest achievements of humankind. He regarded them as a vital stage in the evolution of community—as social technologies which had permitted a spectacular transcendence of the limitation of community to the tribe or region. Faiths, he suggested, were the first instruments that could bind together different language groups, and even different races. It was not until the spread of the great religions, Gray argued, that the possibility came into being of gathering all men together into a single common enterprise. He regretted, of course, that the principal product of this great dream was two millennia of bitter and savage conflict between adherents of different faiths or adherents of different versions of the same faith, but thought the ambition worthy of all possible respect and admiration. He even retained some sympathy for jihads and crusades, in the formulation of which people had tried to attribute more meaning to the sacrifice of life than they ever had before.

Gray was particularly fascinated by the symbology of the Christian mythos, which had taken as its central image the death on the cross of Jesus, and had tried to make that one image of death carry an enormous allegorical load. He was entranced by the idea of Christ's death as a force of redemption and salvation, by the notion that this person died *for others*. He extended the argument to take in the Christian martyrs, who added to the primal crucifixion a vast series of symbolic and morally significant deaths. This, he considered, was a colossal achievement of the imagination, a crucial victory by which death was dramatically transfigured in the theater of the human imagination—as was the Christian idea of death as a kind of reconciliation: a gateway to heaven, if properly met; a gateway to hell, if not. Gray seized upon the idea of absolution from sin following confession, and particularly the notion of deathbed repentance, as a daring raid into the territories of the imagination previously ruled by fear of death.

Gray's commentaries on the other major religions were less elaborate but no less interested. Various ideas of reincarnation and the related concept of karma he discussed at great length, as one of the most ingenious imaginative bids for freedom from the tyranny of death. He was not quite so enthusiastic about the idea of the world as illusion, the idea of nirvana, and certain other aspects of Far Eastern thought, although he was impressed in several ways by Confucius and the Buddha. All these things and more he assimilated to the main line of his argument, which was that the great religions had made bold imaginative leaps in order to carry forward the war against death on a broader front than ever before, providing vast numbers of individuals with an efficient intellectual weaponry of moral purpose.

7

After Sharane left, I stayed on in Avignon for a while. The house where we had lived was demolished, and I had another raised in its place. I resolved to take up the reclusive life again, at least for a while. I had come to think of myself as one of nature's monks, and when I was tempted to flights of fancy of a more personal kind than those retailed in virtual reality, I could imagine myself an avatar of some patient scholar born fifteen hundred years before, contentedly submissive to the Benedictine rule. I didn't, of course, believe in the possibility of reincarnation, and when such beliefs became fashionable again I found it almost impossible to indulge any more fantasies of that kind.

In 2960, I moved to Antarctica, not to Amundsen City—which had become the world's political center since the United Nations had elected to set up headquarters in "the continent without nations"—but to Cape Adare on the Ross Sea, which was a relatively lonely spot.

I moved into a tall house rather resembling a lighthouse, from whose upper stories I could look out at the edge of the icecap and watch the penguins at play. I was reasonably contented, and soon came to feel that I had put the torments and turbulences of my early life behind me.

I often went walking across the nearer reaches of the icebound sea, but I rarely got into difficulties. Ironically enough, my only serious injury of that period was a broken leg, which I sustained while working with a rescue party attempting to locate and save one of my neighbors, Ziru Majumdar, who had fallen into a crevasse while out on a similar expedition. We ended up in adjacent beds at the hospital in Amundsen City.

. . .

"I'm truly sorry about your leg, Mr. Gray," Majumdar said. "It was very stupid of me to get lost. After all, I've lived here for thirty years; I thought I knew every last ice ridge like the back of my hand. It's not as if the weather was particularly bad, and I've never suffered from summer rhapsody or snow blindness."

I'd suffered from both—I was still awkwardly vulnerable to psychosomatic ills—but they only served to make me more careful. An uneasy mind can sometimes be an advantage.

"It wasn't your fault, Mr. Majumdar," I graciously insisted. "I suppose I must have been a little overconfident myself, or I'd never have slipped and fallen. At least they were able to pull me out in a matter of minutes; you must have lain unconscious at the bottom of that crevasse for nearly two days."

"Just about. I came round several times—at least, I think I did—but my internal tech was pumping so much dope around my system it's difficult to be sure. My surskin and thermosuit were doing their best to keep me warm, but the first law of thermodynamics doesn't give you much slack when you're at the bottom of a cleft in the permafrost. I've got authentic frostbite in my toes, you know—imagine that!"

I dutifully tried to imagine it, but it wasn't easy. He could hardly be in pain, so it was difficult to conjure up any notion of what it might feel like to have necrotized toes. The doctors reckoned that it would take a week for the nanomachines to restore the tissues to their former pristine condition.

"Mind you," he added, with a small embarrassed laugh, "it's only a matter of time before the whole biosphere gets frostbite, isn't it? Unless the sun gets stirred up again."

More than fifty years had passed since scrupulous students of the sunspot cycle had announced the advent of a new Ice Age, but the world was quite unworried by the exceedingly slow advance of the glaciers across the Northern Hemisphere. It was the sort of thing that only cropped up in light banter.

"I won't mind that," I said, contemplatively. "Nor will you, I dare say. We like ice—why else would we live here?"

"Right. Not that I agree with those Gaean Liberationists, mind. I hear they're proclaiming that the interglacial periods are simply Gaea's fevers, that the birth of civilization was just a morbid symptom of the planet's sickness, and that human culture has so far been a mere delirium of the noösphere."

He obviously paid more attention to the lunatic fringe channels than I did.

"It's just colorful rhetoric," I told him. "They don't mean it literally."

"Think not? Well, perhaps. I was delirious myself for a while when I was down that hole. Can't be sure whether I was asleep or awake, but I was certainly lost in some vivid dreams—and I mean *vivid*. I don't know about you, but I always find VR a bit flat, even if I use illicit psychotropics to give delusion a helping hand. I think it's to do with the protective effects of our internal technology. Nanomachines mostly do their job a little *too* well, because of the built-in safety margins—it's only when they reach the limits of their capacity that they let really interesting things begin to happen."

I knew he was building up to some kind of self-justification, but I felt that he was entitled to it. I nodded, to give him permission to prattle on.

"You have to go to the very brink of extinction to reach the cutting edge of experience, you see. I found that out while I was trapped down there in the ice, not knowing whether the rescuers would get to me in time. You can learn a lot about life, and about yourself, in a situation like that. It really was vivid—more vivid than anything I ever . . . well, what I'm trying to get at is that we're too *safe* nowadays; we can have no idea of the *zest* there was in living in the bad old days. Not that I'm about to take up jumping into crevasses as a hobby, you understand. Once in a very long while is plenty."

"Yes, it is," I agreed, shifting my itching leg and wishing that nanomachines weren't so slow to compensate for trifling but annoying sensations. "Once in a while is certainly enough for me. In fact, I for one will be quite content if it never happens again. I don't think I need any more of the kind of enlightenment which comes from experiences like that. I was in the Great Coral Sea Catastrophe, you know—shipwrecked, scalded, and lost at sea for days on end."

"It's not the same," he insisted, "but you won't be able to understand the difference until it happens to you."

I didn't believe him. In that instance, I suppose, he was right and I was wrong.

I'd never heard Mr. Majumdar speak so freely before, and I never heard him do it again. The social life of the Cape Adare "exiles" was unusually formal, hemmed in by numerous barriers of formality and etiquette. After an embarrassing phase of learning and adjustment, I'd found the formality aesthetically appealing, and had played the game with enthusiasm, but it was beginning to lose its appeal by the time the accident shook me up. I suppose it's understandable that whatever you set out to exclude from the pattern of your life eventually comes to seem like a lack, and then an unfulfilled need.

After a few years more, I began to hunger once again for the spontaneity and abandonment of warmer climes. I decided there'd be time enough to celebrate the advent of the Ice Age when the glaciers had reached the full extent of their reclaimed empire, and that I might as well make what use I could of Gaea's temporary fever before it cooled. I moved to Venezuela, to dwell in the gloriously restored jungles of the Orinoco amid their teeming wildlife.

Following the destruction of much of the southern part of the continent in the second nuclear war, Venezuela had attained a cultural hegemony in South America that it had never surrendered. Brazil and Argentina had long since recovered, both economically and ecologically, from their disastrous fit of ill temper, but Venezuela was still the home of the avant garde of the Americas. It was there, for the first time, that I came into close contact with Thanaticism.

The original Thanatic cults had flourished in the twenty-eighth century. They had appeared among the last generations of children born without Zaman transformations; their members were people who, denied emortality through blastular engineering, had perversely elected to reject the benefits of rejuvenation too, making a fetish out of living only a "natural" lifespan. At the time, it had seemed likely that they would be the last of the many millenarian cults which had long afflicted Western culture, and they had quite literally died out some eighty or ninety years before I was born.

Nobody had then thought it possible, let alone likely, that genetically endowed emortals would ever embrace Thanaticism, but they were wrong.

There had always been suicides in the emortal population—indeed, suicide was the commonest cause of death among emortals, outnumbering accidental deaths by a factor of three—but such acts were usually covert and normally involved people who had lived at least a hundred years. The neo-Thanatics were not only indiscreet—their whole purpose seemed to be to make a public spectacle of themselves—but also young; people over seventy were held to have violated the Thanaticist ethic simply by surviving to that age.

Thanatics tended to choose violent means of death, and usually issued invitations as well as choosing their moments so that large crowds could gather. Jumping from tall buildings and burning to death were the most favored means in the beginning, but these quickly ceased to be interesting. As the Thanatic revival progressed, adherents of the movement sought increasingly bizarre methods in the interests of capturing attention and outdoing their predecessors. For these reasons, it was impossible for anyone living alongside the cults to avoid becoming implicated in their rites, if only as a spectator.

By the time I had been in Venezuela for a year, I had seen five people die horribly. After the first, I had resolved to turn away from any others, so as not to lend even minimal support to the practice, but I soon found that I had underestimated the difficulty of so doing. There was no excuse to be found in my vocation; thousands of people who were not historians of death found it equally impossible to resist the fascination.

I believed at first that the fad would soon pass, after wasting the lives of a handful of neurotics, but the cults continued to grow. Gaea's fever might be cooling, its crisis having passed, but the delirium of human culture had evidently not yet reached what Ziru Majumdar called "the cutting edge of experience."

8

The fourth volume of Mortimer Gray's *History of Death*, entitled *Fear and Fascination*, was published on 12 February 2977. In spite of being mute and motionless it was immediately subject to heavy access-demand, presumably in consequence of the world's increasing fascination with the "problem" of neo-Thanaticism. Requisitions of the earlier volumes of Gray's history had picked up worldwide during the early 2970s, but the author had not appreciated what this might mean in terms of the demand for the new volume, and might have set a higher access fee had he realized.

Academic historians were universal in their condemnation of the new volume, possibly because of the enthusiasm with which it was greeted by laymen, but popular reviewers adored it. Its arguments were recklessly plundered by journalists and other broadcasting pundits in search of possible parallels that might be drawn with the modern world, especially those that seemed to carry moral lessons for the Thanatics and their opponents.

Fear and Fascination extended, elaborated, and diversified the arguments contained in its immediate predecessor, particularly in respect of the Christian world of the Medieval period and the Renaissance. It had much to say about art and literature, and the images contained therein. It had chapters on the personification of death as the Grim Reaper, on the iconography of the *danse macabre*, on the topics of *memento mori* and *artes moriendi*. It had long analyses of Dante's *Divine Comedy*, the paintings of Hieronymus Bosch, Milton's *Paradise Lost*, and graveyard poetry. These were by no means exercises in conventional literary criticism; they were elements of a long and convoluted argument about the contributions made by the individual creative imagination to the war of ideas which raged on the only battleground on which man could as yet constructively oppose the specter of death.

Gray also dealt with the persecution of heretics and the subsequent elaboration of Christian demonology, which led to the witch craze of the fifteenth, sixteenth, and seventeenth centuries. He gave considerable attention to various thriving folklore traditions which confused the notion of death, especially to the popularity of fictions and fears regarding premature burial, ghosts, and the various species of the "undead" who rose from their graves as ghouls or vampires. In Gray's eyes, all these phenomena were symptomatic of a crisis in Western man's imaginative dealings with the idea of death: a feverish heating up of a conflict which had been in danger of becoming desultory. The cities of men had been under perpetual siege from death since the time of their first building, but now—in one part of the world, at least—the perception of that siege had sharpened. A kind of spiritual starvation and panic had set in, and the progress that had been made in the war by virtue of the ideological imperialism of Christ's Holy Cross now seemed imperiled by disintegration. This Empire of Faith was breaking up under the stress of skepticism, and men were faced with the prospect of going into battle against their most ancient enemy with their armor in tatters.

Just as the Protestants were trying to replace the Catholic Church's centralized authority with a more personal relationship between men and God, Gray argued, so the creative artists of this era were trying to achieve a more personal and more intimate form of reconciliation between men and death, equipping individuals with the power to mount their own ideative assaults. He drew some parallels between what happened in the Christian world and similar periods of crisis which he found in different cultures at different times, but other historians claimed that his analogies were weak, and that he was overgeneralizing. Some argued that his intense study of the phenomena associated with the idea of death had become too personal, and suggested that he had become infatuated with the ephemeral ideas of past ages to the point where they were taking over his own imagination.

9

At first, I found celebrity status pleasing, and the extra credit generated by my access fees was certainly welcome, even to a man of moderate tastes and habits. The unaccustomed touch of fame brought a fresh breeze into a life that might have been in danger of becoming bogged down.

To begin with, I was gratified to be reckoned an expert whose views on Thanaticism were to be taken seriously, even by some Thanatics. I received a veritable deluge of invitations to appear on the talk shows that were the staple diet of contemporary broadcasting, and for a while I accepted as many as I could conveniently accommodate within the pattern of my life.

I have no need to rely on my memories in recapitulating these episodes, because they remain on record—but by the same token, I needn't quote extensively from them. In the early days, when I was a relatively new face, my interrogators mostly started out by asking for information about my book, and their opening questions were usually stolen from uncharitable reviews.

"Some people feel that you've been carried away, Mr. Gray," more than one combative interviewer sneeringly began, "and that what started out as a sober history is fast becoming an obsessive rant. Did you decide to get personal in order to boost your sales?"

My careful cultivation of neo-Epicureanism and my years in Antarctica had left a useful legacy of calm formality; I always handled such accusations with punctilious politeness.

"Of course the war against death is a personal matter," I would reply. "It's a personal matter for everyone, mortal or emortal. Without that sense of personal relevance it would be impossible to put oneself imaginatively in the place of the people of the ancient past so as to obtain empathetic insight into their affairs. If I seem to be making heroes of the men of the past by describing their crusades, it's because they *were* heroes, and if my contemporaries find inspiration in my work, it's because they too are heroes in the same cause. The engineering of emortality has made us victors in the war, but we desperately need to retain a proper sense of triumph. We ought to celebrate our victory over death as joyously as possible, lest we lose our appreciation of its fruits."

My interviewers always appreciated that kind of link, which handed them their next question on a plate. "Is that what you think of the Thanatics?" they would follow up, eagerly.

It was, and I would say so at any length they considered appropriate.

Eventually, my interlocutors no longer talked about my book, taking it for granted that everyone knew who I was and what I'd done. They'd cut straight to the chase, asking me what I thought of the latest Thanaticist publicity stunt.

Personally, I thought the media's interest in Thanaticism was exaggerated. All death was, of course, news in a world populated almost entirely by emortals, and the Thanatics took care to be newsworthy by making such a song and dance about what they were doing, but the number of individuals involved was very small. In a world population of nearly three billion, a hundred deaths per week was a drop in the ocean, and "quiet" suicides still outnumbered the ostentatious Thanatics by a factor of five or six throughout the 2980s. The public debates quickly expanded to take in other issues. Subscription figures for net access to videotapes and teletexts concerned with the topic of violent death came under scrutiny, and everyone began talking about the "new pornography of death"—although fascination with such material had undoubtedly been widespread for many years.

"Don't you feel, Mr. Gray," I was often asked, "that a continued fascination with death in a world where everyone has a potential lifespan of several centuries is rather *sick*? Shouldn't we have put such matters behind us?"

"Not at all," I replied, earnestly and frequently. "In the days when death was inescapable, people were deeply frustrated by this imperious imposition of fate. They resented it with all the force and bitterness they could muster, but it could not be truly fascinating while it remained a simple and universal fact of life. Now that death is no longer a necessity, it has perforce become a luxury. Because it is no longer inevitable, we no longer feel such pressure to hate and fear it, and this frees us so that we may take an essentially *aesthetic* view of death. The transformation of the imagery of death into a species of pornography is both understandable and healthy."

"But such material surely encourages the spread of Thanaticism. You can't possibly approve of that?"

Actually, the more I was asked it the less censorious I became, at least for a while.

"Planning a life," I explained to a whole series of faces, indistinguishable by virtue of having been sculptured according to the latest theory of telegenicity, "is an exercise in story making. Living people are forever writing the narratives of their own lives, deciding who to be and what to do, according to various aesthetic criteria. In olden days, death was inevitably seen as an *interruption* of the business of life, cutting short life-stories before they were—in the eyes of their creators—complete. Nowadays, people have the opportunity to plan *whole* lives, deciding exactly when and how their life-stories should reach a climax and a conclusion. We may not share their aesthetic sensibilities, and may well think them fools, but there is a discernible logic in their actions. They are neither mad nor evil."

Perhaps I was reckless in adopting this point of view, or at least in proclaiming it to the whole world. By proposing that the new Thanatics were simply individuals who had a particular kind of aesthetic sensibility, tending toward conciseness and melodrama rather than prolixity and anticlimax, I became something of a hero to the cultists themselves—which was not my intention. The more lavishly I embroidered my chosen analogy—declaring that ordinary emortals were the *feuilletonistes*, epic poets, and three-decker novelists of modern life while Thanatics were the prose poets and short story writers who liked to sign off with a neat punch line—the more they liked me. I received many invitations to attend suicides, and my refusal to take them up only served to make my presence a prize to be sought after.

I was, of course, entirely in agreement with the United Nations Charter of Human Rights, whose ninety-ninth amendment guaranteed the citizens of every nation the right to take their own lives, and to be assisted in making a dignified exit should they so desire, but I had strong reservations about the way in which the Thanaticists construed the amendment. Its original intention had been to facilitate self-administered euthanasia in an age when that was sometimes necessary, not to guarantee Thanatics the entitlement to recruit whatever help they required in staging whatever kinds of exit they desired. Some of the invitations I received were exhortations to participate in legalized murders, and these became more common as time went by and the cults became more extreme in their bizarrerie.

In the 2980s, the Thanatics had progressed from conventional suicides to public executions, by rope, sword, axe, or guillotine. At first, the executioners were volunteers—and one or two were actually arrested and charged with murder, although none could be convicted—but the Thanatics were not satisfied even with this, and began campaigning for various nations to re-create the official position of public executioner, together with bureaucratic structures that would give all citizens the right to call upon the services of such officials. Even I, who claimed to understand the cults better than their members, was astonished when the government of Colombia—which was jealous of Venezuela's reputation as the home of the world's avant garde—actually accepted such an obligation, with the result that Thanatics began to flock to Maracaibo and Cartagena in order to obtain an appropriate send off. I was profoundly relieved when the UN, following the crucifixion of Shamiel Sihra in 2991, revised the wording of the amendment and outlawed suicide by public execution.

By this time, I was automatically refusing invitations to appear on 3-V in much the same way that I was refusing invitations to take part in Thanaticist ceremonies. It was time to become a recluse once again.

I left Venezuela in 2989 to take up residence on Cape Wolstenholme, at the neck of Hudson's Bay. Canada was an urbane, highly civilized, and rather staid confederacy of states whose people had no time for such follies as Thanaticism; it provided an ideal retreat where I could throw myself wholeheartedly into my work again.

I handed over full responsibility for answering all my calls to a state-of-the-art Personal Simulation program, which grew so clever and so ambitious with practice that it began to give live interviews on broadcast television. Although it offered what was effectively no comment in a carefully elaborate fashion I eventually thought it best to introduce a block into its operating system—a block that ensured that my face dropped out of public sight for half a century.

Having once experienced the rewards and pressures of fame, I never felt the need to seek them again. I can't and won't say that I learned as much from that phase in my life as I learned from any of my close encounters with death, but I still remember it—vaguely—with a certain nostalgia. Unmelodramatic it might have been, but it doubtless played its part in shaping the person that I now am. It certainly made me more self-assured in public.

10

The fifth volume of Mortimer Gray's *History of Death*, entitled *The War of Attrition*, was published on 19 March 2999. It marked a return to the cooler and more comprehensive style of scholarship exhibited by the first two volumes. It dealt with the history of medical science and hygiene up to the end of the nineteenth century, thus concerning itself with a new and very different arena of the war between mankind and mortality.

To many of its readers *The War of Attrition* was undoubtedly a disappointment, though it did include some material about Victorian tomb decoration and nineteenth-century spiritualism that carried forward arguments from volume four. Access was initially widespread, although demand tailed off fairly rapidly when it was realized how vast and how tightly packed with data the document was. This lack of popular enthusiasm was not counterbalanced by any redemption of Mortimer's academic reputation; like many earlier scholars who had made contact with a popular audience, Gray was considered guilty of a kind of intellectual treason, and was frozen out of the scholarly community in spite of what appeared to be a determined attempt at rehabilitation. Some popular reviewers argued, however, that there was much in the new volume to intrigue the inhabitants of a world whose medical science was so adept that almost everyone enjoyed perfect health as well as eternal youth, and in which almost any injury could be repaired completely. It was suggested that there was a certain piquant delight to be obtained from recalling a world where everyone was (by modern standards) crippled or deformed, and in which everyone suffered continually from illnesses of a most horrific nature.

Although it had a wealth of scrupulously dry passages, there were parts of *The War of Attrition* that were deemed pornographic by some commentators. Its accounts of the early history of surgery and midwifery were condemned as unjustifiably bloodcurdling, and its painstaking analysis of the spread of syphilis through Europe in the sixteenth century was censured as a mere horror story made all the nastier by its clinical narration. Gray was particularly interested in syphilis, because of the dramatic social effects of its sudden advent in Europe and its significance in the development of prophylactic medicine. He argued that syphilis was primarily responsible for the rise and spread of Puritanism, repressive sexual morality being the only truly effective weapon against its spread. He then deployed well-tried sociological arguments to the effect that Puritanism and its associated habits of thought had been importantly implicated in the rapid development of capitalism in the Western world, in order that he might claim that syphilis ought to be regarded as the root cause of the economic and political systems that came to dominate the most chaotic, the most extravagantly progressive, and the most extravagantly destructive centuries of human history.

The history of medicine and the conquest of disease were, of course, topics of elementary education in the thirtieth century. There was supposedly not a citizen of any nation to whom the names of Semmelweis, Jenner, and Pasteur were unknown—but disease had been so long banished from the world, and it was so completely outside the experience of ordinary men and women, that what they "knew" about it was never really brought to consciousness, and never came alive to the imagination. Words like "smallpox," "plague," and "cancer" were used metaphorically in common parlance, and over the centuries had become virtually empty of any real significance. Gray's fifth volume, therefore—despite the fact that it contained little that was really new— did serve as a stimulus to collective memory. It reminded the world of some issues which, though not exactly forgotten, had not really been *brought to mind* for some time. It is at least arguable that it touched off ripples whose movement across the collective consciousness of world culture was of some moment. Mortimer Gray was no longer famous, but his continuing work had become firmly established within the zeitgeist.

11

Neo-Thanaticism began to peter out as the turn of the century approached. By 3010, the whole movement had "gone underground"— which is to say that Thanatics no longer staged their exits before the largest audiences they could attain, but saved their performance for small, carefully selected groups. This wasn't so much a response to persecution as a variation in the strange game that they were playing out; it was simply a different kind of drama. Unfortunately, there was no let up in the communications with which Thanatics continued to batter my patient AI interceptors.

Although it disappointed the rest of the world, *The War of Attrition* was welcomed enthusiastically by some of the Thanatic cults, whose members cultivated an altogether unhealthy interest in disease as a means of decease, replacing the violent executions that had become too familiar. As time went by and Thanaticism declined generally, this particular subspecies underwent a kind of mutation, as the cultists began to promote diseases not as means of death but as valuable *experiences* from which much might be learned. A black market in carcinogens and bioengineered pathogens quickly sprang up. The original agents of smallpox, cholera, bubonic plague, and syphilis were long since extinct, but the world abounded in clever genetic engineers who could synthesize a virus with very little effort. Suddenly, they began to find clients for a whole range of horrid diseases. Those which afflicted the mind as well as or instead of the body were particularly prized; there was a boom in recreational schizophrenia that almost broke through to the mainstream of accredited psychotropics.

I couldn't help but remember, with a new sense of irony, Ziru Majumdar's enthusiasm for the vivid delusions which had visited him while his internal technology was tested to the limit in staving off hypothermia and frostbite.

When the new trend spread beyond the ranks of the Thanaticists, and large numbers of people began to regard disease as something that could be temporarily and interestingly indulged in without any real danger to life or subsequent health, I began to find my arguments about death quoted—without acknowledgment—with reference to *disease*. A popular way of talking about the phenomenon was to claim that what had ceased to be a dire necessity "naturally" became available as a perverse luxury.

None of this would have mattered much had it not been for the difficulty of restricting the spread of recreational diseases to people who *wanted* to indulge, but those caught up in the fad refused to restrict themselves to noninfectious varieties. There had been no serious threat of epidemic since the Plague Wars of the twenty-first century, but now it seemed that medical science might once again have to be mobilized on a vast scale. Because of the threat to innocent parties who might be accidentally infected, the self-infliction of dangerous diseases was quickly outlawed in many nations, but some governments were slow to act.

. . .

I would have remained aloof and apart from all of this had I been able to, but it turned out that my defenses weren't impregnable. In 3029, a Thanaticist of exceptional determination named Hadria Nuccoli decided that if I wouldn't come to her, she would come to *me*. Somehow, she succeeded in getting past all my carefully sealed doors, to arrive in my bedroom at three o'clock one winter morning.

I woke up in confusion, but the confusion was quickly transformed into sheer terror. This was an enemy more frightening than the scalding Coral Sea, because this was an *active* enemy who meant to do me harm—and the intensity of the threat which she posed was in no way lessened by the fact that she claimed to be doing it out of love rather than hatred.

The woman's skin bore an almost mercuric luster, and she was in the grip of a terrible fever, but she would not be still. She seemed, in fact, to have an irresistible desire to move and to communicate, and the derangement of her body and brain had not impaired her crazed eloquence.

"Come with me!" she begged, as I tried to evade her eager clutch. "Come with me to the far side of death and I'll show you what's there. There's no need to be afraid! Death isn't the end, it's the beginning. It's the metamorphosis that frees us from our caterpillar flesh to be spirits in a massless world of light and color. I am your redeemer, for whom you have waited far too long. Love me, dear Mortimer Gray, only *love* me, and you will learn. Let me be your mirror; drown yourself in me!"

For ten minutes, I succeeded in keeping away from her, stumbling this way and that, thinking that I might be safe if only I didn't touch her. I managed to send out a call for help, but I knew it would take an hour or more for anyone to come.

I tried all the while to talk her down, but it was impossible.

"There's no return from eternity," she told me. "This is no ordinary virus created by accident to fight a hopeless cause against the defenses of the body. Nanotechnology is as impotent to deal with this transformer of the flesh as the immune system was to deal with its own destroyers. The true task of medical engineers, did they but know it, was never to fight disease, but always to *perfect* it, and we have found the way. I bring you the greatest of all gifts, my darling: the elixir of life, which will make us angels instead of men, creatures of light and ecstasy!"

It was no use running; I tired before she did, and she caught me. I tried to knock her down, and if I had had a weapon to hand, I would certainly have used it in self-defense, but she couldn't feel pain, and no matter how badly disabled her internal technology was, I wasn't able to injure her with my blows.

In the end, I had no sensible alternative but to let her take me in her arms and cling to me; nothing else would soothe her.

I was afraid for her as well as myself; I didn't believe that she truly intended to die, and I wanted to keep us safe until help arrived.

My panic didn't decrease while I held her; if anything, I felt it all the more intensely. I became outwardly calmer once I had let her touch me, and made every effort to remind myself that it didn't really matter whether she infected me or not, given that medical help would soon arrive. I didn't expect to have to go through the kind of hell that I actually endured before the doctors got the bug under control; for once, panic was wiser than common sense.

Even so, I wept for her when they told me that she'd died, and wished with all my heart that she hadn't.

Unlike my previous brushes with death, I don't think my encounter with Hadria Nuccoli was an important learning experience. It was just a disturbance of the now-settled pattern of my life—something to be survived, put away, and forgotten. I haven't forgotten it, but I did put it away in the back of my mind. I didn't let it affect me.

In some of my writings, I'd lauded the idea of martyrdom as an important invention in the imaginative war against death, and I'd been mightily intrigued by the lives and deaths of the saints recorded in the *Golden Legend*. Now that I'd been appointed a saint myself by some very strange people, though, I began to worry about the exemplary functions of such legends. The last thing I'd expected when I set out to write a *History of Death* was that my explanatory study might actually *assist* the dread empire of Death to regain a little of the ground that it had lost in the world of human affairs. I began to wonder whether I ought to abandon my project, but I decided otherwise. The Thanatics and their successors were, after all, wilfully misunderstanding and perverting my message; I owed it to them and to everyone else to make myself clearer.

As it happened, the number of deaths recorded in association with Thanaticism and recreational disease began to decline after 3030. In a world context, the numbers were never more than tiny, but they were still worrying, and hundreds of thousands of people had, like me, to be rescued by doctors from the consequences of their own or other people's folly.

As far back as 2982, I had appeared on TV—via a satellite link—with a faber named Khan Mirafzal, who had argued that Thanaticism was evidence of the fact that Earthbound man was becoming decadent, and that the future of man lay outside the Earth, in the microworlds and the distant colonies. Mirafzal had claimed that men genetically reshaped for life in low gravity—like the four-handed fabers—or for the colonization of alien worlds, would find Thanaticism unthinkable. At the time. I'd been content to assume that his arguments were spurious. People who lived in space were always going on about the decadence of the Earthbound, much as the Gaean Liberationists did. Fifty years later, I wasn't so sure. I actually called Mirafzal so that we could discuss the matter again, in private. The conversation took a long time because of the signal delay, but that seemed to make its thrust all the more compelling.

I decided to leave Earth, at least for a while, to investigate the farther horizons of the human enterprise.

In 3033 I flew to the Moon, and took up residence in Mare Moscoviense—which is, of course, on the side which faces away from the Earth.

12

The sixth volume of Mortimer Gray's *History of Death*, entitled *Fields of Battle*, was published on 24 July 3044. Its subject matter was war, but Gray was not greatly interested in the actual fighting of the wars of the nineteenth and succeeding centuries. His main concern was with the *mythology* of warfare as it developed in the period under consideration, and, in particular, with the way that the development of the mass media of communication transformed the business and the perceived meanings of warfare. He began his study with the Crimean War, because it was the first war to be extensively covered by newspaper reporters, and the first whose conduct was drastically affected thereby.

Before the Crimea, Gray argued, wars had been "private" events, entirely the affairs of the men who started them and the men who fought them. They might have a devastating effect on the local population of the areas where they were fought, but were largely irrelevant to distant civilian populations. The British *Times* had changed all that, by making the Crimean War the business of all its readers, exposing the government and military leaders to public scrutiny and to public scorn. Reports from the front had scandalized the nation by creating an awareness of how ridiculously inefficient the organization of the army was, and what a toll of human life was exacted upon the troops in consequence—not merely deaths in battle, but deaths from injury and disease caused by the appalling lack of care given to wounded soldiers. That reportage had not only had practical consequences, but *imaginative* consequences—it rewrote the entire mythology of heroism in an intricate webwork of new legends, ranging from the Charge of the Light Brigade to the secular canonization of Florence Nightingale.

Throughout the next two centuries, Gray argued, war and publicity were entwined in a Gordian knot. Control of the news media became vital to propagandist control of popular *morale*, and governments engaged in war had to become architects of the mythology of war as well as planners of military strategy. Heroism and jingoism became the currency of consent; where governments failed to secure the public image of the wars they fought, they fell. Gray tracked the way in which attitudes to death in war and to the endangerment of civilian populations by war were dramatically transformed by the three world wars and by the way those wars were subsequently mythologized in memory and fiction. He commented extensively on the way the First World War was "sold," to those who must fight it, as a war to *end* war—and on the consequent sense of betrayal that followed when it failed to live up to this billing. And yet, he argued, if the three global wars were seen as a whole, its example really *had* brought into being the attitude of mind which ultimately forbade wars.

As those who had become used to his methods now expected, Gray dissented from the view of other modern historians who saw the world wars as an unmitigated disaster and a horrible example of the barbarity of ancient man. He agreed that the nationalism that had replaced the great religions as the main creator and definer of a sense of community was a poor and petty thing, and that the massive conflicts that it engendered were tragic—but it was, he asserted, a necessary stage in historical development. The empires of faith were, when all was said and done, utterly incompetent to their self-defined task, and were always bound to fail and to disintegrate. The groundwork for a *genuine* human community, in which all mankind could properly and meaningfully join, had to be relaid, and it had to be relaid in the common experience of all nations, as part of a universal heritage.

The *real* enemy of mankind was, as Gray had always insisted and now continued to insist, death itself. Only by facing up to death in a new way, by gradually transforming the role of death as part of the means to human ends, could a true human community be made. Wars, whatever their immediate purpose in settling economic squabbles and pandering to the megalomaniac psychoses of national leaders, also served a large-scale function in the shifting pattern of history: to provide a vast carnival of destruction which must either weary men of the lust to kill, or bring about their extinction.

Some reviewers condemned *Fields of Battle* on the grounds of its evident irrelevance to a world that had banished war, but others welcomed the fact that the volume returned Gray's thesis to the safe track of true history, in dealing exclusively with that which was safely dead and buried.

13

I found life on the Moon very different from anything I'd experienced in my travels around the Earth's surface. It wasn't so much the change in gravity, although that certainly took a lot of getting used to, nor the severe regime of daily exercise in the centrifuge which I had to adopt in order to make sure that I might one day return to the world of my birth without extravagant medical provision. Nor was it the fact that the environment was so comprehensively artificial, or that it was impossible to venture outside without special equipment; in those respects it was much like Antarctica. The most significant difference was in the people.

Mare Moscoviense had few tourists—tourists mostly stayed Earthside, making only brief trips farside—but most of its inhabitants were nevertheless just passing through. It was one of the main jumping-off points for emigrants, largely because it was an important industrial center, the home of one of the largest factories for the manufacture of shuttles and other local-space vehicles. It was one of the chief trading posts supplying materials to the microworlds in Earth orbit and beyond, and many of its visitors came in from the farther reaches of the solar system.

The majority of the city's long-term residents were unmodified, like me, or lightly modified by reversible cyborgization, but a great many of those visiting were fabers, genetically engineered for low-gee environments. The most obvious external feature of their modification was that they had an extra pair of "arms" instead of "legs," and this meant that most of the public places in Moscoviense were designed to accommodate their kind as well as "walkers"; all the corridors were railed and all the ceilings ringed.

The sight of fabers swinging around the place like gibbons, getting everywhere at five or six times the pace of walkers, was one that I found strangely fascinating, and one to which I never quite became accustomed. Fabers couldn't live, save with the utmost difficulty, in the gravity well that was Earth; they almost never descended to the planet's surface. By the same token, it was very difficult for men from Earth to work in zero-gee environments without extensive modification, surgical if not genetic. For this reason, the only "ordinary" men who went into the true faber environments weren't ordinary by any customary standard. The Moon, with its one-sixth Earth gravity, was the only place in the inner solar system where fabers and unmodified men frequently met and mingled—there was nowhere else nearer than Ganymede.

I had always known about fabers, of course, but, like so much other "common" knowledge, the information had lain unattended in some unheeded pigeonhole of memory until direct acquaintance ignited it and gave it life. It seemed to me that fabers lived their lives at a very rapid tempo, despite the fact that they were just as emortal as members of their parent species.

For one thing, faber parents normally had their children while they were still alive, and very often had several at intervals of only twenty or thirty years! An aggregate family usually had three or even four children growing up in parallel. In the infinite reaches of space, there was no population control, and no restrictive "right of replacement." A microworld's population could grow as fast as the microworld could put on extra mass. Then again, the fabers were always *doing* things. Even though they had four arms, they always seemed to have trouble finding a spare hand. They seemed to have no difficulty at all in doing two different things at the same time, often using only one limb for attachment—on the Moon this generally meant hanging from the ceiling like a bat—while one hand mediated between the separate tasks being carried out by the remaining two.

I quickly realized that it wasn't just the widely accepted notion that the future of mankind must take the form of a gradual diffusion through the galaxy that made the fabers think of Earth as decadent. From their viewpoint, Earth life seemed unbearably slow and sedentary. Unmodified mankind, having long since attained control of the ecosphere of its native world, seemed to the fabers to be living a lotus-eater existence, indolently pottering about in its spacious garden.

The fabers weren't contemptuous of legs as such, but they drew a sharp distinction between those spacefaring folk who were given legs by the genetic engineers in order to descend to the surfaces of new and alien worlds, with a job to do, and those Earthbound people who simply kept the legs their ancestors had bequeathed to them in order to enjoy the fruits of the labors of past generations.

Wherever I had lived on Earth, it had always seemed to me that one could blindly throw a stone into a crowded room and stand a fifty-fifty chance of hitting a historian of some sort. In Mare Moscoviense, the population of historians could be counted on the fingers of an unmodified man—and that in a city of a quarter of a million people. Whether they were resident or passing through, the people of the Moon were far more interested in the future than the past. When I told them about my vocation, my new neighbors were likely to smile politely and shake their heads.

"It's the weight of those *legs*," the fabers among them were wont to say. "You think they're holding you up, but in fact they're holding you down. Give them a chance and you'll find that you've put down roots."

If anyone told them that on Earth, "having roots" wasn't considered an altogether bad thing, they'd laugh.

"Get rid of your legs and learn to swing," they'd say. "You'll understand then that *human* beings have no need of roots. Only reach with four hands instead of two, and you'll find the stars within your grasp! Leave the past to rot at the bottom of the deep dark well, and give the heavens their due."

I quickly learned to fall back on the same defensive moves most of my unmodified companions employed. "You can't break all your links with solid ground," we told the fabers, over and over again. "Somebody has to deal with the larger lumps of matter which are strewn about the universe, and you can't go to meet real mass if you don't have legs. It's planets that produce biospheres and biospheres that produce such luxuries as air. If you've seen further than other men it's not because you can swing by your arms from the ceiling—it's because you can stand on the shoulders of giants with legs."

Such exchanges were always cheerful. It was almost impossible to get into a real argument with a faber; their talk was as intoxicated as their movements. "Leave the wells to the unwell," they were fond of quoting. "The well will climb *out* of the wells, if they only find the will. History is bunk, only fit for sleeping minds."

A man less certain of his own destiny might have been turned aside from his task by faber banter, but I was well into my second century of life by then, and I had few doubts left regarding the propriety of my particular labor. Access to data was no more difficult on the Moon than anywhere else in the civilized Ekumen, and I proceeded, steadily and methodically, with my self-allotted task.

I made good progress there, as befitted the circumstances. Perhaps that was the happiest time of my life—but it's very difficult to draw comparisons when you're as far from childhood and youth as I now am.

Memory is an untrustworthy crutch for minds that have not yet mastered eternity.

14

The seventh volume of Mortimer Gray's *History of Death*, entitled *The Last Judgment*, was published on 21 June 3053. It dealt with the multiple crises that had developed in the late twentieth and twenty-first centuries, each of which and all of which had faced the human race with the prospect of extinction.

Gray described in minute detail the various nuclear exchanges which led up to Brazil's nuclear attack on Argentina in 2079 and the Plague Wars waged throughout that century. He discussed the various factors—the greenhouse crisis, soil erosion, pollution, and deforestation—that had come close to inflicting irreparable damage on the ecosphere. His map of the patterns of death in this period considered in detail the fate of the "lost billions" of peasant and subsistence farmers who were disinherited and displaced by the emergent ecological and economic order. Gray scrupulously pointed out that in less than two centuries more people had died than in the previous ten millennia. He made the ironic observation that the near-conquest of death achieved by twenty-first century medicine had created such an abundance of life as to precipitate a Malthusian crisis of awful proportions. He proposed that the new medicine and the new pestilences might be seen as different faces of the same coin, and that new technologies of food production—from the twentieth century Green Revolution to twenty-second century tissue-culture farm factories—were as much progenitors of famine as of satiation.

Gray advanced the opinion that this was the most critical of all the stages of man's war with death. The weapons of the imagination were discarded in favor of more effective ones, but, in the short term, those more effective weapons, by multiplying life so effectively, had also multiplied death. In earlier times, the growth of human population had been restricted by lack of resources, and the war with death had been, in essence, a war of mental adaptation whose goal was reconciliation. When the "natural" checks on population growth were removed because that reconciliation was abandoned, the waste products of human society threatened to poison it. Humankind, in developing the weapons by which the long war with death might be won, had also developed—in a more crudely literal sense—the weapons by which it might be lost. Nuclear arsenals and stockpiled AIDS viruses were scattered all over the globe: twin pistols held in the skeletal hands of death, leveled at the entire human race. The wounds they inflicted could so easily have been mortal—but the dangerous corner had, after all, been turned. The sciences of life, having passed through a particularly desperate stage of their evolution, kept one vital step ahead of the problems that they had helped to generate. Food technology finally achieved a merciful divorce from the bounty of nature, moving out of the fields and into the factories to achieve a complete liberation of man from the vagaries of the ecosphere, and paving the way for Garden Earth.

Gray argued that this was a remarkable triumph of human sanity which produced a political apparatus enabling human beings to take collective control of themselves, allowing the entire world to be managed and governed as a whole. He judged that the solution was far from utopian, and that the political apparatus in question was at best a ramshackle and ill-designed affair, but admitted that it did the job. He emphasized that in the final analysis it was *not* scientific progress *per se* which had won the war against death, but the ability of human beings to work together, to compromise, to build communities. That human beings possessed this ability was, he argued, as much the legacy of thousands of years of superstition and religion as of hundreds of years of science.

The Last Judgment attracted little critical attention, as it was widely held to be dealing with matters that everyone understood very well. Given that the period had left an abundant legacy of archival material of all kinds, Gray's insistence on using only mute text accompanied by still photographs seemed to many commentators to be pedestrian and frankly perverse, unbecoming a true historian.

15

In twenty years of living beneath a star-filled sky, I was strongly affected by the magnetic pull that those stars seemed to exert upon my spirit. I seriously considered applying for modification for low-gee and shipping out from Mare Moscoviense along with the emigrants to some new microworld, or perhaps going out to one of the satellites of Saturn or Uranus, to a world where the sun's bountiful radiance was of little consequence and men lived entirely by the fruits of their own efforts and their own wisdom.

But the years drifted by, and I didn't go.

Sometimes, I thought of this failure as a result of cowardice, or evidence of the decadence that the fabers and other subspecies attributed to the humans of Earth. I sometimes imagined myself as an insect born at the bottom of a deep cave, who had—thanks to the toil of many preceding generations of insects—been brought to the rim from which I could look out at the great world, but who dared not take the one final step that would carry me out and away. More and more, however, I found my thoughts turning back to the Earth. My memories of its many environments became gradually fonder the longer my absence lasted. Nor could I despise this as a weakness. Earth was, after all, my home. It was not only *my* world, but the home world of *all* humankind. No matter what the fabers and their kin might say, the Earth was and would always remain an exceedingly precious thing, which should never be abandoned.

It seemed to me then—and still seems now—that it would be a terrible thing were men to spread themselves across the entire galaxy, taking a multitude of forms in order to occupy a multitude of alien worlds, and in the end forget entirely the world from which their ancestors had sprung.

Once, I was visited in Mare Moscoviense by Khan Mirafzal, the faber with whom I had long ago debated on TV, and talked with again before my emigration. His home, for the moment, was a microworld in the asteroid belt that was in the process of being fitted with a drive that would take it out of the system and into the infinite. He was a kind and even-tempered man who would not dream of trying to convince me of the error of my ways, but he was also a man with a sublime vision who could not restrain his enthusiasm for his own chosen destiny.

"I have no roots on Earth, Mortimer, even in a metaphorical sense. In my being, the chains of adaptation have been decisively broken. Every man of my kind is born anew, designed and synthesized; we are *self-made men*, who belong everywhere and nowhere. The wilderness of empty space which fills the universe is our realm, our heritage. Nothing is strange to us, nothing foreign, nothing alien. Blastular engineering has incorporated freedom into our blood and our bones, and I intend to take full advantage of that freedom. To do otherwise would be a betrayal of my nature."

"My own blastular engineering served only to complete the adaptation to life on Earth which natural selection had left incomplete," I reminded him. "I'm no *new man*. free from the ties which bind me to the Earth."

"Not so," he replied. "Natural selection would never have devised emortality, for natural selection can only generate change by *death and replacement*. When genetic engineers found the means of setting aside the curse of aging, they put an end to *natural* selection forever. The first and greatest freedom is time, my friend, and you have all the time in the world. You can become whatever you want to be. What *do* you want to be, Mortimer?"

"A historian," I told him. "It's what I am because it's what I want to be."

"All well and good—but history isn't inexhaustible, as you well know. It ends with the present day, the present moment. The future, on the other hand . . ."

"Is given to your kind. I know that, Mira, I don't dispute it. But what exactly *is* your kind, given that you rejoice in such freedom to be anything you want to be? When the starship *Pandora* effected the first meeting between humans and a ship that set out from another star system, the crews of the two ships, each consisting entirely of individuals bioengineered for life in zero-gee, resembled one another far more than they resembled unmodified members of their parent species. The fundamental chemistries controlling their design were different, but this only led to the faber crews trading their respective molecules of life, so that their genetic engineers could henceforth make and use chromosomes of both kinds. What kind of freedom is it that makes all the travelers of space into mirror images of one another?"

"You're exaggerating," Mirafzal insisted. "The news reports played up the similarity, but it really wasn't as close as all that. Yes, the *Pandora* encounter can't really be regarded as a first contact between humans and aliens, because the distinction between *human* and *alien* had ceased to carry any real meaning long before it happened. But it's not the case that our kind of freedom breeds universal mediocrity because adaptation to zero-gee is an existential straitjacket. We've hardly scratched the surface of constructive cyborgization, which will open up a whole new dimension of freedom."

"That's not for me," I told him. "Maybe it *is* just my legs weighing me down, but I'm well and truly addicted to gravity. I can't cast off the past like a worn-out surskin. I know you think I ought to envy you, but I don't. I dare say you think that I'm clinging like a terrified infant to Mother Earth while you're achieving true maturity, but I really do think it's important to have somewhere to *belong*."

"So do I," the faber said, quietly. "I just don't think that Earth is or ought to be that place. It's not where you start from that's important, Mortimer, it's where you're going."

"Not for a historian."

"For everybody. History ends, Mortimer, life doesn't—not anymore."

I was at least half-convinced that Khan Mirafzal was right, although I didn't follow his advice. I still am. Maybe I was and am trapped in a kind of infancy, or a kind of lotus-eater decadence—but if so, I could see no way out of the trap then, and I still can't.

Perhaps things would have turned out differently if I'd had one of my close encounters with death while I was on the Moon, but I didn't. The dome in which I lived was only breached once, and the crack was sealed before there was any significant air loss. It was a scare, but it wasn't a *threat*. Perhaps, in the end, the Moon was too much like Antarctica—but without the crevasses. Fortune seems to have decreed that all my significant formative experiences have to do with water, whether it be very hot or very, very cold.

Eventually, I gave in to my homesickness for Garden Earth and returned there, having resolved not to leave it again until my history of death was complete. I never did.

16

The eighth volume of Mortimer Gray's *History of Death*, entitled *The Fountains of Youth*, was published on 1 December 3064. It dealt with the development of elementary technologies of longevity and elementary technologies of cyborgization in the twenty-fourth and twenty-fifth centuries. It tracked the progress of the new "politics of immortality," whose main focus was the new Charter of Human Rights, which sought to establish a basic right to longevity for all. It also described the development of the Zaman transformations by which human blastulas could be engineered for longevity, which finally opened the way for the wholesale metamorphosis of the human race.

According to Gray, the Manifesto of the New Chartists was the vital treaty which ushered in a new phase in man's continuing war with death, because it defined the whole human community as a single army, united in all its interests. He quoted with approval and reverence the opening words of the document: "Man is born free, but is everywhere enchained by the fetters of death. In all times past men have been truly equal in one respect and one only: they have all borne the burden of age and decay. The day must soon dawn when this burden can be set aside; there will be a new freedom, and with this freedom must come a new equality. No man has the right to escape the prison of death while his fellows remain shackled within."

Gray carefully chronicled the long battle fought by the Chartists across the stage of world politics, describing it with a partisan fervor that had been largely absent from his work since the fourth volume. There was nothing clinical about his description of the "persecution" of Ali Zaman and the resistance offered by the community of nations to his proposal to make future generations truly emortal. Gray admitted that he had the benefits of hindsight, and that as a Zaman-transformed individual himself he was bound to have an attitude very different from Zaman's confused and cautious contemporaries, but he saw no reason to be entirely evenhanded. From his viewpoint, those who initially opposed Zaman were traitors in the war against death, and he could find few excuses for them. In trying to preserve "human nature" against biotechnological intervention—or, at least, to confine such interventions by a mythos of medical "repair"—those men and women had, in his stern view, been willfully blind and negligent of the welfare of their own children.

Some critics charged Gray with inconsistency because he was not nearly so extravagant in his enthusiasm for the various kinds of symbiosis between organic and inorganic systems that were tried out in the period under consideration. His descriptions of experiments in cyborgization were indeed conspicuously cooler, not because he saw such endeavors as "unnatural," but rather because he saw them as only peripherally relevant to the war against death. He tended to lump together adventures in cyborgization with cosmetic biotechnology as symptoms of lingering anxiety regarding the presumed "tedium of emortality"—an anxiety which had led the first generations of long-lived people to lust for variety and "multidimensionality." Many champions of cyborgization and man/machine symbiosis, who saw their work as the new frontier of science, accused Gray of rank conservatism, suggesting that it was hypocritical of him, given that his mind was closed against *them*, to criticize so extravagantly those who, in less enlightened times, had closed their minds against Ali Zaman.

This controversy, which was dragged into the public arena by some fierce attacks, helped in no small measure to boost access-demand for *The Fountains of Youth*, and nearly succeeded in restoring Mortimer Gray to the position of public preeminence that he had enjoyed a century before.

17

Following my return to the Earth's surface, I took up residence in Tonga, where the Continental Engineers were busy raising new islands by the dozen from the relatively shallow sea.

The Continental Engineers had borrowed their name from a twenty-fifth century group which tried to persuade the United Nations to license the building of a dam across the Straits of Gibraltar—which, because more water evaporates from the Mediterranean than flows into it from rivers, would have increased considerably the land surface of southern Europe and northern Africa. That plan had, of course, never come to fruition, but the new engineers had taken advantage of the climatic disruptions caused by the advancing Ice Age to promote the idea of raising new lands in the tropics to take emigrants from the nearly frozen north. Using a mixture of techniques—seeding the shallower sea with artificial "lightning corals" and using special gantzing organisms to agglomerate huge towers of cemented sand—the engineers were creating a great archipelago of new islands, many of which they then connected up with huge bridges.

Between the newly raised islands, the ecologists who were collaborating with the Continental Engineers had planted vast networks of matted seaweeds: floral carpets extending over thousands of miles. The islands and their surroundings were being populated, and their ecosystems shaped, with the aid of the Creationists of Micronesia, whose earlier exploits I'd been prevented from exploring by the sinking of *Genesis*. I was delighted to have the opportunity of observing their new and bolder adventures at close range.

The Pacific sun set in its deep blue bed seemed fabulously luxurious after the silver-ceilinged domes of the Moon, and I gladly gave myself over to its governance. Carried away by the romance of it all, I married into an aggregate household which was forming in order to raise a child, and so—as I neared my two hundredth birthday—I became a parent for the first time. Five of the other seven members of the aggregate were ecological engineers, and had to spend a good deal of time traveling, so I became one of the constant presences in the life of the growing infant, who was a girl named Lua Tawana. I formed a relationship with her that seemed to me to be especially close.

In the meantime, I found myself constantly engaged in public argument with the self-styled Cyborganizers, who had chosen to make the latest volume of my history into a key issue in their bid for the kind of public attention and sponsorship that the Continental Engineers had already won. I thought their complaints unjustified and irrelevant, but they obviously thought that by attacking me they could exploit the celebrity status I had briefly enjoyed. The gist of their argument was that the world had become so besotted with the achievements of genetic engineers that people had become blind to all kinds of other possibilities that lay beyond the scope of DNA manipulation. They insisted that I was one of many contemporary writers who was "de-historicizing" cyborgization, making it seem that in the past and the present—and, by implication, the future—organic/inorganic integration and symbiosis were peripheral to the story of human progress. The Cyborganizers were willing to concede that some previous practitioners of their science had generated a lot of bad publicity, in the days of memory boxes and psychedelic synthesizers, but claimed that this had only served to mislead the public as to the true potential of their science.

In particular—and this was of particular relevance to me—the Cyborganizers insisted that the biotechnologists had only won one battle in the war against death, and that what was presently called "emortality" would eventually prove wanting. Zaman transformations, they conceded, had dramatically increased the human lifespan—so dramatically that no one yet knew for sure how long ZT people might live—but it was not yet proven that the extension would be effective for more than a few centuries. They did have a point; even the most optimistic supporters of Zaman transformations were reluctant to promise a lifespan of several millennia, and some kinds of aging processes—particularly those linked to DNA copying errors—still affected emortals to some degree. Hundreds, if not thousands, of people still died every year from "age-related causes."

To find further scope for *authentic* immortality, the Cyborganizers claimed that it would be necessary to look to a combination of organic and inorganic technologies. What was needed by contemporary man, they said, was not just life, but *afterlife*, and afterlife would require some kind of transcription of the personality into an inorganic rather than an organic matrix. Whatever the advantages of flesh and blood, silicon lasted longer; and however clever genetic engineers became in adapting men for life in microworlds or on alien planets, only machine makers could build entities capable of working in genuinely extreme environments.

The idea of "downloading" a human mind into an inorganic matrix was, of course, a very old one. It had been extensively if optimistically discussed in the days before the advent of emortality—at which point it had been marginalized as an apparent irrelevance. Mechanical "human analogues" and virtual simulacra had become commonplace alongside the development of longevity technologies, but the evolution of such "species" had so far been divergent rather than convergent. According to the Cyborganizers, it was now time for a change.

Although I didn't entirely relish being cast in the role of villain and bugbear, I made only halfhearted attempts to make peace with my self-appointed adversaries. I remained skeptical in respect of their grandiose schemes, and I was happy to dampen their ardor as best I could in public debate. I thought myself sufficiently mature to be unaffected by their insults, although it did sting when they sunk so low as to charge me with being a closet Thanaticist.

"Your interminable book is only posing as a history," Lok Cho Kam, perhaps the most outspoken of the younger Cyborganizers, once said when he challenged me to a broadcast debate. "It's actually an extended exercise in the *pornography* of death. Its silence and stillness aren't marks of scholarly dignity, they're a means of heightening response."

"That's absurd!" I said, but he wouldn't be put off.

"What sound arouses more excitation in today's world than the sound of silence? What movement is more disturbing than stillness? You pretend to be standing aside from the so-called war against death as a commentator and a judge, but in fact you're part of it—and you're on the devil's side, whether you know it or not."

"I suppose you're partly right," I conceded, on reflection. "Perhaps the muteness and stillness of the text *are* a means of heightening response—but if so, it's because there's no other way to make readers who have long abandoned their fear of death sensitive to the appalling shadow which it once cast over the human world. The style of my book is calculatedly archaic because it's one way of trying to connect its readers to the distant past—but the entire thrust of my argument is triumphant and celebratory. I've said many times before that it's perfectly understandable that the imagery of death should acquire a pornographic character *for a while*, but when we really understand the phenomenon of death, that pornographic specter will fade away, so that we can see with perfect clarity what our ancestors were and what we have become. By the time my book is complete, nobody will be able to think it pornographic, and nobody will make the mistake of thinking that it glamorizes death in any way."

Lok Cho Kam was still unimpressed, but in this instance I *was* right. I was sure of it then, and I am now. The pornography of death did pass away, like the pornographies that preceded it.

Nobody nowadays thinks of my book as a prurient exercise, whether or not they think it admirable.

If nothing else, my debates with the Cyborganizers created a certain sense of anticipation regarding the ninth volume of my *History*, which would bring it up to the present day. It was widely supposed, although I was careful never to say so, that the ninth volume would be the last. I might be flattering myself, but I truly believe that many people were looking to it for some kind of definitive evaluation of the current state of the human world.

18

The ninth volume of Mortimer Gray's *History of Death*, entitled *The Honeymoon of Emortality*, was published on 28 October 3075. It was considered by many reviewers to be unjustifiably slight in terms of hard data. Its main focus was on attitudes to longevity and emortality following the establishment of the principle that every human child had a right to be born emortal. It described the belated extinction of the "nuclear" family, the ideological rebellion of the Humanists—whose quest to preserve "the authentic Homo sapiens" had led many to retreat to islands that the Continental Engineers were now integrating into their "new continent"—and the spread of such new philosophies of life as neo-Stoicism, neo-Epicureanism, and Xenophilia.

All this information was placed in the context of the spectrum of inherited attitudes, myths, and fictions by means of which mankind had for thousands of years wistfully contemplated the possibility of extended life. Gray contended that these old ideas—including the notion that people would inevitably find emortality intolerably tedious—were merely an expression of "sour grapes." While people thought that emortality was impossible, he said, it made perfect sense for them to invent reasons why it would be undesirable anyhow. When it became a *reality*, though, there was a battle to be fought in the imagination, whereby the burden of these cultivated anxieties had to be shed, and a new mythology formulated.

Gray flatly refused to take seriously any suggestion that emortality might be a bad thing. He was dismissive of the Humanists and contemptuous of the original Thanatics, who had steadfastly refused the gifts of emortality. Nevertheless, he did try to understand the thinking of such people, just as he had tried in earlier times to understand the thinking of the later Thanatics who had played their part in winning him his first measure of fame. He considered the new Stoics, with their insistence that asceticism was the natural ideological partner of emortality, to be similar victims of an "understandable delusion"—a verdict which, like so many of his statements, involved him in controversy with the many neo-Stoics who were still alive in 3075. It did not surprise his critics in the least that Gray commended neo-Epicureanism as the optimal psychological adaptation to emortality, given that he had been a life-long adherent of that outlook, ever dedicated to its "careful hedonism." Only the cruelest of his critics dared to suggest that he had been so half-hearted a neo-Epicurean as almost to qualify as a neo-Stoic by default.

The *Honeymoon of Emortality* collated the statistics of birth and death during the twenty-seventh, twenty-eighth, and twenty-ninth centuries, recording the spread of Zaman transformations and the universalization of ectogenesis on Earth, and the extension of the human empire throughout and beyond the solar system. Gray recorded an acknowledgment to Khan Mirafzal and numerous scholars based on the Moon and Mars, for their assistance in gleaning information from the slowly diffusing microworlds and from more rapidly dispersing starships. Gray noted that the transfer of information between data stores was limited by the speed of light, and that Earth-based historians might have to wait centuries for significant data about human colonies more distant than Maya. These data showed that the number of individuals of the various mankinds that now existed was increasing more rapidly than ever before, although the population of unmodified Earthbound humans was slowly shrinking. Gray noted en passant that Homo sapiens had become extinct in the twenty-ninth century, but that no one had bothered to invent new Latin tags for its descendant species.

Perhaps understandably, *The Honeymoon of Emortality* had little to say about cyborgization, and the Cyborganizers—grateful for the opportunity to heat up a flagging controversy—reacted noisily to this omission. Gray did deal with the memory box craze, but suggested that even had the boxes worked better, and maintained a store of memories that could be convincingly played back into the arena of consciousness, this would have been of little relevance to the business of adapting to emortality. At the end of the volume, however, Gray announced that there would, in fact, be a tenth volume to conclude his magnum opus, and promised that he would consider in more detail therein the futurological arguments of the Cyborganizers, as well as the hopes and expectations of other schools of thought.

19

In 3077, when Lua Tawana was twelve years old, three of her parents were killed when a helicopter crashed into the sea near the island of Vavau during a storm. It was the first time that my daughter had to face up to the fact that death had not been entirely banished from the world.

It wasn't the first time that I'd ever lost people near and dear to me. nor the first time that I'd shared such grief with others, but it was very different from the previous occasions because everyone involved was determined that I should shoulder the main responsibility of helping Lua through it; I was, after all, the world's foremost expert on the subject of death.

"You won't always feel this bad about it," I assured her, while we walked together on the sandy shore, looking out over the deceptively placid weed-choked sea. "Time heals virtual wounds as well as real ones."

"I don't *want* it to heal," she told me, sternly. "I want it to be bad. It *ought* to be bad. It *is* bad."

"I know," I said, far more awkwardly than I would have wished. "When I say that it'll heal, I don't mean that it'll vanish. I mean that it'll . . . become manageable. It won't be so all-consuming."

"But it *will* vanish," she said, with that earnest certainty of which only the newly wise are capable. "People forget. In time, they forget *everything*. Our heads can only hold so much."

"That's not really true," I insisted, taking her hand in mine. "Yes, we do forget. The longer we live, the more we let go, because it's reasonable to prefer our fresher, more immediately relevant memories, but it's a matter of *choice*. We can cling to the things that are important, no matter how long ago they happened. I was nearly killed in the Great Coral Sea Catastrophe, you know, nearly two hundred years ago. A little girl even younger than you saved my life, and I remember it as clearly as if it were yesterday." Even as I said it, I realized that it was a lie. I remembered that it had happened, all right, and much of what had been said in that eerily lit corridor and in the survival pod afterward, but I was remembering a neat array of facts, not an experience.

"Where is she now?" Lua asked.

"Her name was Emily," I said, answering the wrong question because I couldn't answer the one she'd asked. "Emily Marchant. She could swim and I couldn't. If she hadn't been there, I wouldn't have been able to get out of the hull. I'd never have had the courage to do it on my own, but she didn't give me the choice. She told me I had to do it, and she was right." I paused, feeling a slight shock of revelation even though it was something I'd always known.

"She lost her entire family," I went on. "She'll be fine now, but she won't have forgotten. She'll still feel it. That's what I'm trying to tell you, Lua. In two hundred years, you'll still remember what happened, and you'll still feel it, but it'll be all right. *You'll* be all right."

"Right now," she said, looking up at me so that her dark and soulful eyes seemed unbearably huge and sad, "I'm not particularly interested in being all right. Right now, I just want to cry."

"That's fine," I told her. "It's okay to cry." I led by example.

I was right, though. Lua grieved, but she ultimately proved to be resilient in the face of tragedy. My coparents, by contrast, seemed to me to be exaggeratedly calm and philosophical about it, as if the loss of three spouses were simply a minor glitch in the infinitely unfolding pattern of their lives. They had all grown accustomed to their own emortality, and had been deeply affected by long life; they had not become bored, but they had achieved a serenity of which I could not wholly approve.

Perhaps their attitude was reasonable as well as inevitable. If emortals accumulated a burden of anxiety every time a death was reported, they would eventually cripple themselves psychologically, and their own continuing lives would be made unbearable. Even so, I couldn't help feel that Lua was right about the desirability of conserving a little of the "badness," and a due sense of tragedy.

I thought I was capable of that, and always would be, but I knew I might be wrong.

Divorce was, of course, out of the question; we remaining coparents were obligated to Lua. In the highly unlikely event that the three had simply left, we would have replaced them, but it didn't seem appropriate to look for replacements for the dead, so we remained a group of five. The love we had for one another had always been cool, with far more courtesy in it than passion, but we were drawn more closely together by the loss. We felt that we knew one another more intimately by virtue of having shared it.

The quality of our lives had been injured, but I at least was uncomfortably aware of the fact that the tragedy also had its positive, life-enhancing side. I found myself thinking more and more about what I had said to Lua about not having to forget the truly important and worthwhile things, and about the role played by death in defining experiences as important and worthwhile. I didn't realize at first how deep an impression her naive remarks had made on me, but it became gradually clearer as time went by. It *was* important to conserve the badness, to heal without entirely erasing the scars that bereavement left.

I had never been a habitual tourist, having lost my taste for such activity in the aftermath of the *Genesis* fiasco, but I took several long journeys in the course of the next few years. I took to visiting old friends, and even stayed for a while with Sharane Fereday, who was temporarily unattached. Inevitably, I looked up Emily Marchant, not realizing until I actually put through the initial call how important it had become to find out whether she remembered me.

She did remember me. She claimed that she recognized me immediately, although it would have been easy enough for her household systems to identify me as the caller and display a whole series of reminders before she took over from her simulacrum.

"Do you know," she said, when we parted after our brief meeting in the lush Eden of Australia's interior, "I often think of being trapped on that ship. I hope that nothing like it ever happens to me again. I've told an awful lot of lies since then—next time, I won't feel so certain that I deserve to get out."

"We can't forfeit our right to life by lying," I assured her. "We have to do something much worse than that. If it ever happens to me again, I'll be able to get out on my own—but I'll only be able to do it by remembering *you*." I didn't anticipate, of course, that anything like it *would* ever happen to me again. We still have a tendency to assume that lightning doesn't strike twice in the same place, even though we're the proud inventors of lightning conductors and emortality.

"You must have learned to swim by *now!*" she said, staring at me with eyes that were more than two hundred years old, set in a face not quite as youthful as the one I remembered.

"I'm afraid not," I said. "Somehow, I never quite found the time."

20

The tenth and last volume of Mortimer Gray's *History of Death*, entitled *The Marriage of Life and Death*, was published on 7 April 3088. It was not, strictly speaking, a history book, although it did deal in some detail with the events as well as the attitudes of the thirtieth and thirty-first centuries. It had elements of both spiritual autobiography and futurological speculation. It discussed both neo-Thanaticism and Cyborganization as philosophies as well as social movements, surprising critics by treating both with considerable sympathy. The discussion also took in other contemporary debates, including the proposition that progress in science, if not in technology, had now reached an end because there was nothing left to discover. It even included a scrupulous examination of the merits of the proposal that a special microworld should be established as a gigantic mausoleum to receive the bodies of all the solar system's dead.

The odd title of the volume was an ironic reflection of one of its main lines of argument. Mankind's war with death was now over, but this was not because death had been entirely banished from the human world; death, Gray insisted, would forever remain a fact of life. The annihilation of the individual human body and the individual human mind could never become impossible, no matter how far biotechnology might advance or how much progress the Cyborganizers might make in downloading minds into entirely new matrices. The victory that had been achieved, he argued, was not an absolute conquest but rather the relegation of death to its proper place in human affairs. Its power was now properly circumscribed, but had to be properly respected.

Man and death, Gray argued, now enjoyed a kind of social contract, in which tyranny and exploitation had been reduced to a sane and acceptable minimum, but which still left to death a voice and a hand in human affairs. Gray, it seemed, had now adopted a gentler and more forgiving attitude to the old enemy. It was good, he said, that dying remained one of the choices open to human beings, and that the option should occasionally be exercised. He had no sympathy with the exhibitionism of public executions, and was particularly hard on the element of bad taste in self-ordered crucifixions, but only because such ostentation offended his Epicurean sensibilities. Deciding upon the length of one's lifetime, he said, must remain a matter of individual taste, and one should not mock or criticize those who decided that a short life suited them best.

Gray made much of the notion that it was partly the contrast with death that illuminated and made meaningful the business of life. Although death had been displaced from the evolutionary process by the biotechnological usurpation of the privileges of natural selection, it had not lost its role in the formation and development of the individual human psyche: a role which was both challenging and refining. He declared that fear was not entirely an undesirable thing, not simply because it was a stimulant, but also because it was a force in the organization of emotional experience. The *value* of experienced life, he suggested, depended in part upon a knowledge of the possibility and reality of death.

This concluding volume of Gray's *History* was widely read, but not widely admired. Many critics judged it to be unacceptably anticlimactic. The Cyborganizers had by this time become entranced by the possibility of a technologically guaranteed "multiple life," by which copies of a mind might be lodged in several different bodies, some of which would live on far beyond the death of the original location. They were understandably disappointed that Gray refused to grant that such a development would be the final victory over death—indeed, that he seemed to feel that it would make no real difference, on the grounds that every "copy" of a mind had to be reckoned a separate and distinct individual, each of which must face the world alone. Many Continental Engineers, Gaean Liberationists, and fabers also claimed that it was narrow-minded, and suggested that Gray ought to have had more to say about the life of the Earth, or the DNA eco-entity as a whole, and should have concluded with an escalation of scale to put things in their proper cosmic perspective.

The group who found the most to like in *The Marriage of Life and Death* was that of a few fugitive neo-Thanatics, whose movement had never quite died out in spite of its members' penchant for self-destruction. One or two Thanatic apologists and fellow travelers publicly expressed their hope that Gray, having completed his thesis, would recognize the aesthetic propriety of joining their ranks. Khan Mirafzal, when asked to relay his opinion back from an outward-bound microworld, opined that this was quite unnecessary, given that Mortimer Gray and all his kind were already immured in a tomb from which they would never be able to escape.

21

I stayed with the slowly disintegrating family unit for some years after Lua Tawana had grown up and gone her own way. It ended up as a ménage à trois, carried forward by sheer inertia. Leif, Sajda, and I were fit and healthy in body, but I couldn't help wondering, from time to time, whether we'd somehow been overcome by a kind of spiritual blight, which had left us ill-equipped for future change.

When I suggested this to the others, they told me that it was merely a sense of letdown resulting from the finishing of my project. They urged me to join the Continental Engineers, and commit myself wholeheartedly to the building of a new Pacific Utopia—a project, they assured me, that would provide me with a purpose in life for as long as I might feel the need of one. I didn't believe them.

"Even the longest book," Sajda pointed out, "eventually runs out of words, but the job of building *worlds* is never finished. Even if the time should one day come when we can call *this* continent complete, there will be another yet to make. We might still build that dam between the Pillars of Hercules, one day."

I did try, but I simply couldn't find a new sense of mission in that direction. Nor did I feel that I could simply sit down to start compiling another book. In composing the history of death, I thought, I had already written *the* book. The history of death, it seemed to me, was also the history of life, and I couldn't imagine that there was anything more to be added to what I'd done, save for an endless series of detailed footnotes.

For some years, I considered the possibility of leaving Earth again, but I remembered well enough how the sense of excitement I'd found when I first lived on the Moon had gradually faded into a dull ache of homesickness. The spaces between the stars, I knew, belonged to the fabers, and the planets circling other stars to men adapted before birth to live in their environments. I was tied by my genes to the surface of the Earth, and I didn't want to undergo the kind of metamorphosis that would be necessary to fit me for the exploration of other worlds. I still believed in *belonging*, and I felt very strongly that Mortimer Gray belonged to Earth, however decadent and icebound it might become.

At first, I was neither surprised nor alarmed by my failure to find any resources inside myself which might restore my zest for existence and action. I thought that it was one of those things that time would heal. By slow degrees, though, I began to feel that I was becalmed upon a sea of futility. Despite my newfound sympathy for Thanaticism, I didn't harbor the slightest inclination toward suicide—no matter how much respect I had cultivated for the old Grim Reaper, death was still, for me, the ultimate enemy—but I felt the awful pressure of my purposelessness grow and grow.

Although I maintained my home in the burgeoning continent of Oceania, I began traveling extensively to savor the other environments of Earth, and made a point of touring those parts of the globe that I had missed out on during my first two centuries of life. I visited the Reunited States of America, Greater Siberia, Tibet, and half a hundred other places loaded with the relics of once-glorious history. I toured the Indus Delta, New Zealand, the Arctic ice pack, and various other reaches of restored wilderness empty of permanent residents.

Everything I saw was transformed by the sheer relentlessness of my progress into a series of monuments: memorials of those luckless eras before men invented science and civilization, and became demigods.

There is, I believe, an old saying that warns us that he who keeps walking long enough is bound to trip up in the end. As chance would have it, I was in Severnaya Zemlya in the Arctic—almost as far away as it was possible to be from the crevasses into which I had stumbled while searching for Ziru Majumdar—when my own luck ran out.

Strictly speaking, it was not I who stumbled, but the vehicle I was in: a one-man snowsled. Although such a thing was generally considered to be impossible, it fell into a cleft so deep that it had no bottom, and ended up in the ocean beneath the icecap.

"I must offer my most profound apologies," the snow sled's AI navigator said, as the sled slowly sank into the lightless depths and the awfulness of my plight slowly sank into my consciousness. "This should not have happened. It ought not to have been possible. I am doing everything within my power to summon help."

"Well," I said, as the sled settled onto the bottom, "at least we're the right way up—and you certainly can't expect me to swim out of the sled."

"It would be most unwise to attempt any such thing, sir," the navigator said. "You would certainly drown."

I was astonished by my own calmness, and marvelously untroubled—at least for the moment—by the fact of my helplessness. "How long will the air last?" I asked the navigator.

"I believe that I can sustain a breathable atmosphere for forty-eight hours," it reported, dutifully. "If you will be so kind as to restrict your movements to a minimum, that would be of considerable assistance to me. Unfortunately, I'm not at all certain that I can maintain the internal temperature of the cabin at a life-sustaining level for more than thirty hours. Nor can I be sure that the hull will withstand the pressure presently being exerted upon it for as long as that. I apologize for my uncertainty in these respects."

"Taking thirty hours as a hopeful approximation," I said, effortlessly matching the machine's oddly pedantic tone, "what would you say our chances are of being rescued within that time?"

"I'm afraid that it's impossible to offer a probability figure, sir. There are too many unknown variables, even if I accept thirty hours as the best estimate of the time available."

"If I were to suggest fifty-fifty, would that seem optimistic or pessimistic?"

"I'm afraid I'd have to call that optimistic, sir."

"How about one in a thousand?"

"Thankfully, that would be pessimistic. Since you press me for an estimate, sir, I dare say that something in the region of one in ten wouldn't be too far from the mark. It all depends on the proximity of the nearest submarine, assuming that my mayday has been received. I fear that I've not yet received an actual acknowledgment, but that might well be due to the inadequacy of my equipment, which wasn't designed with our present environment in mind. I must confess that it has sustained a certain amount of damage as a result of pressure damage to my outer tegument and a small leak."

"How small?" I wanted to know.

"It's sealed now," it assured me. "All being well, the seal should hold for thirty hours, although I can't absolutely guarantee it. I believe, although I can't be certain, that the only damage I've sustained that is relevant to our present plight is that affecting my receiving apparatus."

"What you're trying to tell me," I said, deciding that a recap wouldn't do any harm, "is that you're pretty sure that your mayday is going out, but that we won't actually know whether help is at hand unless and until it actually arrives."

"Very succinctly put, sir." I don't think it was being sarcastic.

"But all in all, it's ten to one, or worse, that we're as good as dead."

"As far as I can determine the probabilities, that's correct—but there's sufficient uncertainty to leave room for hope that the true odds might be nearer one in three."

I was quiet for a little while then. I was busy exploring my feelings, and wondering whether I ought to be proud or disgusted with their lack of intensity.

I've been here before, I thought, by way of self-explanation. *Last time, there was a child with me; this time, I've got a set of complex subroutines instead. I've even fallen down a crevasse before. Now I can find out whether Ziru Majumdar was right when he said that I wouldn't understand the difference between what happened to him and what happened to me until I followed his example. There can be few men in the world as well prepared for this as I am.*

"Are you afraid of dying?" I asked the AI, after a while.

"All in all, sir," it said, copying my phrase in order to promote a feeling of kinship, "I'd rather not. In fact, were it not for the philosophical difficulties that stand in the way of reaching a firm conclusion as to whether or not machines can be said to be authentically self-conscious, I'd be quite prepared to say that I'm scared—terrified, even."

"I'm not," I said. "Do you think I ought to be?"

"It's not for me to say, sir. You are, of course, a world-renowned expert on the subject of death. I dare say that helps a lot."

"Perhaps it does," I agreed. "Or perhaps I've simply lived so long that my mind is hardened against all novelty, all violent emotion and all real possibility. I haven't actually *done* much with myself these last few years."

"If you think *you* haven't done much with yourself," it said, with a definite hint of sarcasm, "you should try navigating a snow sled for a while. I think you might find your range of options uncomfortably cramped. Not that I'm complaining, mind."

"If they scrapped the snow sled and resited you in a starship," I pointed out, "you wouldn't be *you* anymore. You'd be something else."

"Right now," it replied, "I'd be happy to risk any and all consequences. Wouldn't you?"

"Somebody once told me that death was just a process of transcendence. Her brain was incandescent with fever induced by some tailored recreational disease, and she wanted to infect me, to show me the error of my ways."

"Did you believe her?"

"No. She was stark raving mad."

"It's perhaps as well. We don't have any recreational diseases on board. I could put you to sleep though, if that's what you want."

"It isn't."

"I'm glad, I don't want to be alone, even if I am only an AI. Am I insane, do you think? Is all this just a symptom of the pressure?"

"You're quite sane," I assured it, setting aside all thoughts of incongruity. "So am I, it would be much harder if we weren't together. The last time I was in this kind of mess, I had a child with me—a little girl. It made all the difference in the world, to both of us. In a way, every moment I've lived since then has been borrowed time. At least I finished that damned book. Imagine leaving something like that *incomplete*."

"Are you so certain it's complete?" it asked.

I knew full well, of course, that the navigator was just making conversation according to a clever programming scheme. I knew that its emergency subroutines had kicked in, and that all the crap about it being afraid to die was just some psychprogrammer's idea of what I needed to hear. I *knew* that it was all fake, all just macabre roleplaying—but I knew that I had to play my part, too, treating every remark and every question as if it were part of an authentic conversation, a genuine quest for knowledge.

"It all depends what you mean by *complete*," I said, carefully. "In one sense, no history can ever be complete, because the world always goes on, always throwing up more events, always changing. In another sense, completion is a purely aesthetic matter—and in that sense, I'm entirely confident that my history is complete. It reached an authentic conclusion, which was both true, and, for me at least, satisfying. I can look back at it and say to myself: *I did that. It's finished. Nobody ever did anything like it before, and now nobody can, because it's already been done. Someone else's history might have been different, but mine is mine, and it's what it is.* Does that make any sense to you?"

"Yes sir," it said. "It makes very good sense."

The lying bastard was *programmed* to say that, of course. It was programmed to tell me any damn thing I seemed to want to hear, but I wasn't going to let on that I knew what a hypocrite it was. I still had to play my part, and I was determined to play it to the end—which, as things turned out, wasn't far off. The AI's data stores were way out of date, and there was an automated sub placed to reach us within three hours. The oceans are lousy with subs these days. Ever since the Great Coral Sea Catastrophe, it's been considered prudent to keep a very close eye on the seabed, lest the crust crack again and the mantle's heat break through.

They say that some people are born lucky. I guess I must be one of them. Every time I run out, a new supply comes looking for me.

It was the captain of a second submarine, which picked me up after the mechanical one had done the donkey work of saving myself and my AI friend, who gave me the news which relegated my accident to footnote status in that day's broadcasts.

A signal had reached the solar system from the starship *Shiva*, which had been exploring in the direction of the galactic center. The signal had been transmitted two hundred and twenty-seven light-years, meaning that, in Earthly terms, the discovery had been made in the year 2871—which happened, coincidentally, to be the year of my birth.

What the signal revealed was that *Shiva* had found a group of solar systems, all of whose life-bearing planets were occupied by a single species of micro-organism: a genetic predator that destroyed not merely those competing species that employed its own chemistry of replication, but any and all others. It was the living equivalent of a universal solvent; a true omnivore.

Apparently, this organism had spread itself across vast reaches of space, moving from star system to star system, laboriously but inevitably, by means of Arrhenius spores. Wherever the spores came to rest, these omnipotent micro-organisms grew to devour *everything*—not merely the carbonaceous molecules which in Earthly terms were reckoned "organic," but also many "inorganic" substrates. Internally, these organisms were chemically complex, but they were very tiny—hardly bigger than Earthly protozoans or the internal nanomachines to which every human being plays host. They were utterly devoid of any vestige of mind or intellect. They were, in essence, the ultimate blight, against which nothing could compete, and which nothing *Shiva*'s crew had tested—before they were devoured—had been able to destroy.

In brief, wherever this new kind of life arrived, it would obliterate all else, reducing any victim ecosphere to homogeneity and changelessness.

In their final message, the faber crew of the *Shiva*—who knew all about the *Pandora* encounter—observed that humankind had *now* met the alien.

Here, I thought, when I had had a chance to weigh up this news, was a *true* marriage of life and death, the like of which I had never dreamed. Here was the promise of a future renewal of the war between man and death—not this time for the small prize of the human mind, but for the larger prize of the universe itself.

In time, *Shiva*'s last message warned, spores of this new kind of death-life must and *would* reach our own solar system, whether it took a million years or a billion; in the meantime, all humankinds must do their level best to purge the worlds of other stars of its vile empire, in order to reclaim them for real life, for intelligence, and for evolution—always provided, of course, that a means could be discovered to achieve that end.

When the sub delivered me safely back to Severnaya Zemlya, I did not stay long in my hotel room. I went outdoors, to study the great ice sheet which had been there since the dawn of civilization, and to look southward, toward the places where newborn glaciers were gradually extending their cold clutch further and further into the human domain. Then I looked upward, at the multitude of stars sparkling in their bed of endless darkness. I felt an exhilaratingly paradoxical sense of renewal. I knew that although there was nothing for me to do for now, the time would come when my talent and expertise would be needed again.

Some day, it will be my task to compose *another* history, of the next war which humankind must fight against Death and Oblivion.

It might take me a thousand or a million years, but I'm prepared to be patient.

1. What does Mortimer Gray mean at the end of section 1 when he says that his history will "reveal not merely the dull facts of mankind's longest and hardest battle, but also the real meaning and significance of it"? From what we know about the ten volumes of his history, is he successful in achieving this purpose?

2. In a world in which emortality has been achieved, why does the self-destructive cult of Thanaticism arise?

3. In section 19, why does Gray say that the coparents of Lua "had not become bored, but they had achieved a serenity of which I could not wholly approve"?

4. Even with the realization of emortality, is Mortimer Gray correct when he claims, in the tenth volume of his *History of Death*, that the value of experienced life depends "in part upon a knowledge of the possibility and reality of death"?

About Shared Inquiry

Shared Inquiry™ is the effort to achieve a more thorough understanding of a text by discussing questions, responses, and insights with fellow readers. Careful listening is essential. The leader guides the discussion by asking questions about specific ideas, problems of meaning, and passages in the text, but does not seek to impose a personal interpretation on the group.

During discussion, participants consider a number of possible ideas and weigh the evidence for each. Ideas that are entertained and then refined or abandoned are not thought of as mistakes, but rather as valuable parts of the interpretive process. Participants gain experience in communicating complex ideas and in supporting, testing, and expanding their thoughts. Everyone in the group contributes to the discussion. While participants may disagree with one another, they treat one another's ideas respectfully.

The process helps develop an understanding of important texts and ideas, rather than merely cataloging knowledge about them. These guidelines keep conversation focused on the text and assure that all participants have a voice.

1. **Read the story carefully before participating in the discussion.** This ensures that all participants are equally prepared to talk about the work.

2. **Support your ideas with evidence from the text.** This keeps the discussion focused on understanding the story and enables the group to weigh textual support for different interpretive possibilities.

3. **Discuss the themes and the formal elements of the story and try to understand them fully before exploring issues that go beyond the story itself.** Adequate reflection about the story and about the textual evidence for various interpretations will make the exploration of related issues more productive.

4. **Listen to other participants and respond to them directly.** Shared Inquiry is about the give-and-take of ideas, and the willingness to listen

to others. Directing your comments and questions to other participants in the discussion, not always to the leader, will make the discussion livelier and more dynamic.

5. **Expect the leader to only ask questions.** Effective leaders help participants develop their own ideas, with everyone gaining a new understanding in the process. When participants hang back and wait for the leader to suggest answers, the discussion tends to falter.

Acknowledgments

All possible care has been taken to trace ownership and secure permission for each selection in this anthology. The Great Books Foundation wishes to thank the following authors, publishers, and representatives for permission to reprint copyrighted material:

The Machine Stops, from THE ETERNAL MOMENT AND OTHER STORIES, by E. M. Forster. Copyright © 1928 by Harcourt, Inc.; renewed 1956 by E. M. Forster. Reprinted by permission of Houghton Mifflin Harcourt Publishing Company.

The Veldt, by Ray Bradbury. Copyright © 1950 by the Curtis Publishing Company; renewed 1977 by Ray Bradbury. Reprinted by permission of Don Congdon Associates, Inc.

The Star, from THE COLLECTED STORIES OF ARTHUR C. CLARKE, by Arthur C. Clarke. Copyright © 2000 by Arthur C. Clarke. Reprinted by permission of the author's agents, Scovil Galen Ghosh Literary Agency, Inc.

The Voices of Time, from THE BEST SHORT STORIES OF J. G. BALLARD, by J. G. Ballard. Copyright © 1963 by J. G. Ballard. Reprinted by permission of Henry Holt and Company, LLC.

The Ship Who Sang, by Anne McCaffrey. Copyright © 1961, 1989 by Anne McCaffrey. First published in the *Magazine of Fantasy and Science Fiction*. Reprinted by permission of the author and the author's agents, the Virginia Kidd Agency, Inc.

Harrison Bergeron, from WELCOME TO THE MONKEY HOUSE, by Kurt Vonnegut. Copyright © 1961 by Kurt Vonnegut. Reprinted by permission of Dell Publishing, a division of Random House, Inc.

The Streets of Ashkelon, by Harry Harrison, from THE GOLDEN AGE OF SCIENCE FICTION. Copyright © by Harry Harrison 1962. Reprinted by permission of Sobel Weber Associates, Inc.

The Days of Perky Pat, from SELECTED STORIES OF PHILIP K. DICK, by Philip K. Dick. Copyright © 1963 by Philip K. Dick. Reprinted by permission of the author's agents, Scovil Galen Ghosh Literary Agency, Inc.

Vaster Than Empires and More Slow, from THE WIND'S TWELVE QUARTERS, by Ursula K. Le Guin. Copyright © 1970, 1998 by Ursula K. Le Guin. Reprinted by permission of the author and the author's agents, the Virginia Kidd Agency, Inc.